SEAL BROTHERHOOD: LEGACY BUNDLE

Books 5–9

SHARON HAMILTON

SHARON HAMILTON'S BOOK LIST

SEAL BROTHERHOOD BOOKS

SEAL BROTHERHOOD SERIES
Accidental SEAL Book 1
Fallen SEAL Legacy Book 2
SEAL Under Covers Book 3
SEAL The Deal Book 4
Cruisin' For A SEAL Book 5
SEAL My Destiny Book 6
SEAL of My Heart Book 7
Fredo's Dream Book 8
SEAL My Love Book 9
SEAL Encounter Prequel to Book 1
SEAL Endeavor Prequel to Book 2
Ultimate SEAL Collection Vol. 1 Books 1-4 / 2 Prequels
Ultimate SEAL Collection Vol. 2 Books 5-9

SEAL BROTHERHOOD LEGACY SERIES
Watery Grave Book 1
Honor The Fallen Book 2
Grave Injustice Book 3
Deal With The Devil Book 4
Cruisin' For Love Book 5
Destiny of Love Book 6
Heart of Gold Book 7
Father's Dream Book 8
Second Time Love Book 9
Little Miracles Novella

BAD BOYS OF SEAL TEAM 3 SERIES
SEAL's Promise Book 1
SEAL My Home Book 2
SEAL's Code Book 3
Big Bad Boys Bundle Books 1-3

BAND OF BACHELORS SERIES
Lucas Book 1
Alex Book 2
Jake Book 3
Jake 2 Book 4
Big Band of Bachelors Bundle

BONE FROG BROTHERHOOD SERIES
New Year's SEAL Dream Book 1
SEALed At The Altar Book 2
SEALed Forever Book 3
SEAL's Rescue Book 4
SEALed Protection Book 5
Bone Frog Brotherhood Superbundle

BONE FROG BACHELOR SERIES
Bone Frog Bachelor Book 0.5
Unleashed Book 1
Restored Book 2
Revenge Book 3
Legacy Book 4

SUNSET SEALS SERIES
SEALed at Sunset Book 1
Second Chance SEAL Book 2
Treasure Island SEAL Book 3
Escape to Sunset Book 4
The House at Sunset Beach Book 5
Second Chance Reunion Book 6
Love's Treasure Book 7
Finding Home Book 8
Sunset SEALs Duet #1
Sunset SEALs Duet #2

LOVE VIXEN
Bone Frog Love

SHADOW SEALS
Shadow of the Heart
Shadow Warrior

SILVER SEALS SERIES
SEAL Love's Legacy

SLEEPER SEALS SERIES
Bachelor SEAL

STAND ALONE BOOKS & SERIES
SEAL's Goal: The Beautiful Game
Nashville SEAL: Jameson
True Blue SEALS: Zak
Paradise: In Search of Love
Love Me Tender, Love You Hard

NOVELLAS
SEAL You In My Dreams Magnolias and Moonshine

PARANORMALS

FREE TO LOVE SERIES
Free As A Bird Book 1
Romance Book 2
Science Of The Heart Book 3
The Promise Directive Book 4
New Beginnings Book 5

GOLDEN VAMPIRES OF TUSCANY SERIES
Honeymoon Bite Book 1
Mortal Bite Book 2
Christmas Bite Book 3
Midnight Bite Book 4

THE GUARDIANS
Heavenly Lover Book 1
Underworld Lover Book 2
Underworld Queen Book 3
Redemption Book 4

FALL FROM GRACE SERIES
Gideon: Heavenly Fall

SUNSET BEACH SERIES
I'll Always Love You
Back To You

NOVELLAS
SEAL Of Time: Trident Legacy

All of Sharon's books are available on Audible, narrated by the talented J.D. Hart.

ABOUT THE BUNDLE

Cruisin' For Love

Mark Beale and his wife, Sophia, plan to celebrate ten years of marriage by going on a trans-Atlantic cruise from Italy to the Caribbean at Christmas with their three daughters. Hoping to erase the memories of past cruises, which turned out to be complete disasters, they plan to renew their wedding vows, enjoy a relaxing family vacation, and visit Sophia's mother in Italy.

But for this Navy SEAL and his family, will the third time be the charm, or will they be unlucky again? Why does danger threaten to not only ruin their cruise but their family?

Enjoy appearances by Captain Teseo Dominichello and other characters from SEAL Team 3.

Readers should enjoy reading Cruisin' For A SEAL first, the story of how Mark and Sophia met years ago. This book is a continuation of their relationship and the growth of their family after ten years have passed.

Destiny of Love

The heart has no limits. Love grows from tragedy.

Luke and Julie adopt his sister's and her brother's three children after their parents are killed in a traffic accident. Suddenly, their finances take center stage as they embrace their new blended family just at the point where Luke had been planning to leave the Teams and Julie was in line for a big promotion.

But being a man of action with a somewhat fragile ego, will assuming the role of stay-at-home dad, changing diapers and wearing an apron fill the billet while Julie becomes the sole breadwinner?

And what happens when an investigation into the car accident reveals perhaps it wasn't? As danger lurks all around them, Luke discovers his new unexpected role of family protector is one he's been rehearsing for a decade.

And he was made for this!

Heart of Gold

Tyler has been a Navy SEAL for nearly ten years and he's wearing out. The prospect of doing another re-up has him worried that his body, banged up, shot, stabbed and multiple bones broken, can't take any more. After performing over a thousand HALO jumps in hostile territory and five times that in practice jumps, he thinks perhaps he's run out of time and is concerned he'll suffer permanent disabilities if he pushes the envelope too far.

But, like a professional athlete, giving up the life he loves, working out and doing missions with his best buds from SEAL Team 3, something he knew he was made for, he can't see himself doing anything else. Certainly not anything as exciting.

He has choices, especially if he wants to keep his wife happy, even if he gives up some of the glory and glamor of being a member the elite warrior class. And he would like to be able to chase his three kids around in something other than a wheelchair.

But an enemy from the past has appeared in the shadows, forcing Tyler to make a decision that might ruin his marriage, and cost him his cherished family.

Which is more important, his promise or the safety of the ones he loves?

Father's Dream

Navy SEAL Fredo Chavez and his wife, Mia, learn how far their love will stretch to include an unloved orphan, abandoned and abused. They open their hearts to this little one, only to find the whole world bloom in unexpected ways.

Balancing work and being a family, Fredo must make the difficult distinction which is more important. He considers the heartbreaking decision of retirement, detaching from his brotherhood of warriors, until this little addition teaches him the value of being a true blue dad in all ways possible.

Once again, love comes to this elite operator's rescue.

Second Time Love

On the eve of his stepdaughter's wedding, Navy SEAL Trace Bennett receives an urgent cry for help from an unexpected source—the bride's father, Tony, his wife's ex-husband who is about to be released from prison.

As the celebration ends, Trace rushes to Portland to aid Tony, a former NBA star who has fallen from grace.

Weeks later, while Gretchen and the girls remain in San Diego, Trace deploys with SEAL Team 3 to the Canary Islands and North Africa. From across the globe, Trace's contacts uncover a sinister group known as "The Organization," which operates a dark network involved in gambling, child prostitution, and human trafficking. This group targets Tony to settle old gambling debts, but now they also threaten to harm Trace's family while he's overseas.

As the situation intensifies, Trace must find a way to safeguard his loved ones and take down this vile organization, all without compromising his principles or his SEAL integrity. Racing against time, he battles to protect his family and eradicate the evil that preys on those he cherishes.

This captivating novel is a tale of second-time love, even sweeter than before. It continues the gripping saga from "SEAL My Love," Book 9 of the original SEAL Brotherhood Series, which narrates the heartwarming journey of how Trace and Gretchen found each other, leading to him becoming the loving father and husband that they truly deserved.

AUTHOR'S NOTE

I always dedicate my SEAL Brotherhood books to the brave men and women who defend our shores and keep us safe. Without their sacrifice and that of their families—because a warrior's fight always includes his or her family—I wouldn't have the freedom and opportunity to make a living writing these stories. They sometimes pay the ultimate price so we can debate, argue, go have coffee with friends, raise our children, and see them have children of their own.

One of my favorite tributes to warriors resides on many memorials, including one I saw honoring the fallen of WWII on an island in the Pacific:

> "When you go home
> Tell them of us, and say,
> For your tomorrow,
> We gave our today."

These are my stories created out of my own imagination. Anything that is inaccurately portrayed is either my mistake or done intentionally to disguise something I might have overheard over a beer or in the corner of one of the hangouts along the Coronado Strand.

I support two main charities. Navy SEAL/UDT Museum operates in Ft. Pierce, Florida. Please learn about this wonderful museum, all run by active and former SEALs and their friends and families, and who rely on public support, not that of the United States Government. www.navysealmuseum.org

I also support Wounded Warriors, who tirelessly bring together the warrior as well as the family members who are just learning to deal with their soldier's condition and have nowhere to turn. It is a long path to becoming well, but I've seen first-hand what this organization does for its warriors and the families who love them. Please give what your heart tells you is right. If you cannot give, volunteer at one of the many service centers all over the United States. Get involved. Do something meaningful for someone who gave so much of themselves, to families who have paid the price for your freedom. You'll find a family there unlike any other on the planet. www.woundedwarriorproject.org

TABLE OF CONTENTS

Cruisin' For Love   1

Destiny of Love   141

Heart of Gold   283

Father's Dream   427

Second Time Love   569

CRUISIN' FOR LOVE

SEAL Brotherhood: Legacy Series
Book 5

SHARON HAMILTON

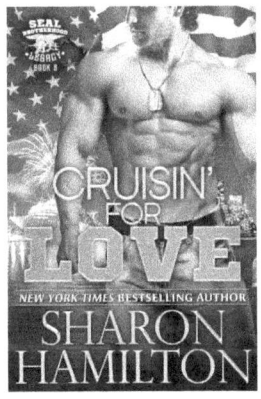

CHAPTER 1

MARK BEALE ENTERED his small galley kitchen, cartoons playing in the background. The girls had awakened him again, just like they did every Saturday morning, no matter if he was just returning from a deployment the night before or not.

He was wearing a pair of shorts, but no T-shirt, and was barefoot. His wife, Sophia, was reading a newspaper and had her hair flopped on top of her head, secured with a big clip, dark curly strands running all down the back of her neck and shoulders. Her peach-colored nightie gaped in the front. The nightie was well used, slightly frayed, and hopelessly stained where she had spilled coffee in previous days.

Mark remembered giving it to Sophia on their anniversary nearly ten years ago.

How things change.

But then he looked down at himself with his bare feet, wrinkled boxers, and sleep crust clinging to both eyes. He could have said something but chose to just reach for the coffee and overlook that part.

Sophia didn't say a word and didn't look up at him, just like his girls had done as he passed them on his trek to the kitchen for his cup of Joe.

He moved aside the pickles, the lime yogurts, and almond milk to find his coveted heavy whipping cream, which was as important to his morning routine as the coffee.

"Well, would you look at us, honey?" he said to his wife.

That's when Sophia did manage to get a good look at him. "Whatever do you mean?"

"Aren't we a pair? Did you ever think when we got married some ten years ago that we would be spending Saturday morning looking like this?"

He demonstrated on himself first and then motioned to her with a stylish gesture.

"I did not."

She was rather blunt. Okay, he could have expected that.

"And instead of elevator music or Italian romantic songs playing in the promenades and hallways of the cruise ships, we'd be listening to Sesame Street and Mr. Buck on the TV? Not to mention the dog channel or the Cockapoo station."

"You're complaining now? Is that what's going on now?"

He should have answered he discovered too late.

"Mark, maybe it's just as simple as not getting laid enough?"

God help him for her frankness, the way she just skewered him with the look of her eyes, the little flippant comments she made in Italian—sometimes under her breath, her haughty attitude, and her vivacious-ness. She exuded confidence over the table, even when she was in her nightie, her *stained* nightie, and had been up half the night with their youngest, Domenica.

"So it was a tough night for you?" he asked her. "Sorry about that, but thanks for letting me sleep a little at least."

"My fault then?"

"Don't start with me. I woke up to the sound of the TV blaring, and you know I got in last night at two o'clock. I like to sleep in on Satur-days. It's always been like this, at least since the children came. With babies, even without babies. Before I got married and all ten years since we got married. It was even like this on the cruise ship. Remember?"

"How could I forget? The mysterious man coming back from mis-sions all hours of the night, his need for sex so strong we could fuck for six hours afterwards. But no, now you come home and sleep for a day and a half. And what about the sex? You know, Mark, I have needs as well."

Mark knew it wouldn't be very smart to mention something about her appearance, especially as his own appearance looked far from sexy or masculine or warrior-type. Yes, he had tattoos, he had some scars, and he certainly had muscles, including six pack abs and biceps. He knew that even though she was shorter and weighed half what he did, he would pay dearly for that comment. He kept it to himself and decided to finish his coffee.

"You're just gonna leave it like that?" she asked him.

"I am." It was Mark's turn to be smug.

"What are you saying exactly?"

"Nothing, just that your nightie reminded me of the fact that there are anniversaries, and there are people who celebrate them. I just thought that since we're going to have a ten-year one coming up here soon we could do something special for it. Maybe take the kids to Disneyland or some other thing? How about camping?"

Sophia stared over the newspaper like he was wearing the contents of Domenica's dirty diaper.

"I'm open to suggestions. This is me being flexible, being awake, and asking you what you would like to do for your anniversary?"

Sophia sighed heavily, looking down at the paper rattling between her hands, letting her feet tap on the floor, which was something Mark had discovered was common amongst dancers, and impatiently returned an answer he didn't expect.

"I'd like you to surprise me. Do something spontaneous, dangerous!"

"Can you give me a hint?"

"Then that wouldn't be spontaneous." Sophia shook her head from side to side. "No."

Mark knew better than to walk on thin ice, and the kitchen certainly had lots of thin ice. "What do you think the kids would like to do?"

"I thought you said this is for our anniversary?"

"Dammit, Sophia, this *is* for our anniversary. But are you thinking about leaving them somewhere?"

"I guess that's out of the question then. My mistake." She was getting frostier by the minute.

He knew that, in very short order, she was going to be suggesting that perhaps they could spend their anniversary apart, and since it was Christmas, she might make an exit to Italy to visit her mother, who had been failing health-wise. He didn't like the idea of it, and if he could stop her from doing this, he certainly would try his darndest.

He poured himself another cup of coffee, adding more cream, asking her if she'd like a refill, which she declined. Grabbing his mug, he sat at a forty-five-degree angle to her at the table. Putting his chin in his left palm, his elbow on the table, in his best masculine, sexy voice, he said, "Sophia, the love of my life, the mother of my insanely beautiful daughters, who are the most spectacular little girls in the whole world, I want to do something that is *special* for you. I'd like to do something that would excite you, and I'd like to do something the kids would like as well. I don't even care if it's something like going to ballet camp because I'll do anything. I just want to do something that doesn't cost too much money, but that we can do together to celebrate our family after ten years. It's gone by so fast and I'm gone so much of the time that it would be really a good idea if we could try to do a family vacation. All of us together!"

At first, he waited for her answer. Her eyes studied him, moving from his right eye to his left eye and back to his right, examining the stubble on his chin then following the trail of chest hair down lower, making him swallow with a parched mouth. He was hoping that was a good sign. He certainly *needed* a good sign right about now.

And then she folded the paper up in front of her, lacing her fingers together, and waited again.

"Sophia? Well?"

"I think we should take a trip to Italy. Take the girls to see their grandma. What about that?"

"Well, it's Christmas time, and the flights to Italy are going to be outrageously expensive. It's November. No deals this time of year. I just am not sure whether we can afford to do that right now with your studio closing. I mean, we could max out our credit cards, but is that smart? It's Christmas."

"Exactly, it's Christmas. We can go as a family for our family Christmas present."

He thought about this for a while and knew that Mrs. Negri lived in a very tiny apartment over the meat market. He also knew that there was no way all five of them could fit there, so it would involve renting a hotel room, a car, and other things. As he started to add up the numbers, his stomach began to tumble a bit, not just from the coffee, but from the understanding that he was looking at a vacation that was easily going to cost him about ten grand. And he didn't have it in his bank account.

But giving up was not an option.

"I'll tell you what, I'll go to the bank today, and I'll see if they'll give me a small loan for the vacation. Maybe then we could pay for it on an installment-type basis, not use the expensive credit cards. How about that?"

"Okay."

Little Ophelia, their middle daughter who was seven years old, entered the kitchen, asking for some breakfast.

"Would you like cereal this morning or would you like some eggs?"

"Pancakes," she blurted out stubbornly.

"Okay, but your daddy's gonna go to the store to get a few things that I'm missing. Why don't we have cereal today, and then tomorrow we can have the pancakes?"

Mark watched as Ophelia protruded her lower lip as she so often did on just about every occasion when she wasn't going to be getting her way. He fully saw in his young daughter his wife's spirit and personality. He imagined Sophia probably was just like her when she was young.

It was no wonder Mark felt trapped. He was surrounded by his women.

And he loved them all to the ends of the earth.

BY MONDAY MORNING, Sophia had arranged their trip through the cruise ship she used to work for, which had several unblocked bookings that were bargains at nearly seventy-five percent of the original price. She even signed up to be a tour director and part-time dance instructor, requesting a paid position for Mark to be her co-instructor as well. The arrangement would nearly pay their expenses in full. The airfare was included in the price, and there were slots available for the cruise over Christmas, so the girls wouldn't miss more than a few days of school. The cruise would originate in Naples and, after a stop in the Caribbean, would arrive in Miami.

The girls were delighted with the plans, calling their grandmother in Italy to spread the good news. Mark double-checked the schedule and was given some leeway to return a few days late.

So, on a windy, light rain day in San Diego, all five of them boarded their flight to Italy for their anniversary vacation. Sophia outfitted all three of the girls in red dresses and, for the first time in weeks, allowed a smile to creep into her expression.

Mark knew the two other cruises he'd been on were just unlucky happenstances, and the odds were in their favor for a smooth, relaxing family trip well out of harm's way. He wasn't going to let his teammates spook him, either.

Earlier, when he'd announced their plans and the reason for his absence, he withstood the catcalls from the Team during their meetings and workouts, where Fredo and Cooper especially rubbed in everything they could throw at him.

"Terrorists, they got terrorists in North Africa, and you'll be going right around the bulge, Mark. You remember the Canaries? The Azores? Morocco?" Fredo teased. "You want to show your girls cobras and have your wife kidnapped to become someone's third wife?"

"Shut up, you asshole. That's not going to happen."

"Yeah, but you got to admit, SEAL Team 3 has bad luck when it comes to ocean voyages," added Cooper. "Somehow, if there's something going on, we seem to get right in the middle of it."

"Now, God wouldn't do that to me. After the first one and then the redo to bury Gunny, he wouldn't put me in that boat," insisted Mark. "Besides, I *earned* a nice vacation with my lovely wife. She's so grateful she's going to get to see her mother she might stop making me clean up the dishes. I'm earning brownie points, gents. Not to worry there. My future looks bright, and I can't wait to have it all!"

"Well," Cooper said with his quiet drawl and tall-drink-of-water-stance, "let's hope the God of Navy SEALs has a heart. All that rocking and rolling. You guys might as well try for number four!"

"Hey, don't push it, Coop. I'm not sure that's luck. Three is a good number, and I'm never complaining about that again."

"Ah, you're probably right, Mark. Besides, you two would have to be bent over the railing and keeping it quiet with all those girls, and you know they'll be watching you guys. Just make sure you don't fall overboard. Those ships don't turn on a dime."

Mark brushed it off. No way in Hell was he going to be bobbing up and down in the Atlantic Ocean by himself.

Just no fuckin' way.

CHAPTER 2

SOPHIA'S MOTHER LIVED on a tiny, winding street above an Italian meat market, several blocks off the city square. A little sub-shopping center of the town of Naples, the district was known as the Artesian District. Something about an artesian well that had probably dried up during Roman times, but that was what it was called. The village was known for its charm and quaint architecture with small archways over windows and doors, front stoops made of a solid block of granite or marble, well-worn into a U pattern, as if it was a soft pillow that had been stepped on. The wear was to be expected with buildings constructed nearly four hundred years ago.

The smells of the city were welcoming to her, not bested by the smells of the neighborhood, where some of the best butchers and pastry makers in Italy lived. There was a huge training center for hotel chefs in an extravagant 15th century villa, surrounded by vineyards and fresh herb and flower gardens. The whole area in this district was magical, appearing with its apricot-orange glow to the land. The burnt umber reflection of the buildings on the sidewalk also reflected in the faces of the people as they hurried past.

It was a rainy day, and Sophia did her best to keep the girls holding hands single file, with the other end being manned by Mark. Of course, little Domenica couldn't walk for more than ten or fifteen minutes before she needed to be carried, and that was Mark's job. He also carried Sophia's computer case, his computer case, and a carry-on for the girls. Each of the older two had a small fuzzy animal backpack holding all their activity projects while on the plane, plus a change of clothes.

As they wandered through the cobblestone walkway approaching her mother's apartment, Mark turned to her and gave her a sexy smile.

"Now it all comes back to me, Sophia." He bent over to explain to Ophelia and Carrie Ann with loving patience. "Your mother and I met on a little street just like this. That day, she was having lunch with her mother in the piazza. You remember that, sweetheart?"

"Where did you have that lunch?" asked Ophelia. "I want to see it."

"It wasn't here. It was in Genoa. But a very similar village. Mother moved here to Naples to be closer to her specialist. And she has several close friends in the area as well."

In fact, one of the things Sophia was going to check on was what kind of a job her brother and sister-in-law were doing taking care of their mother, since the sole responsibility for doing so was on their shoulders, not on Sophia's. But Mark and Sophia contributed to the fund where they could, which kept her mother playing bingo, practicing bocce ball, and hiring an occasional aid to accompany her to the markets. But more and more, she was confined to the apartment and seldom left unless it was for a special occasion.

She had not seen her mother's new apartment but had seen pictures that her brother, Paolo, had sent, and he gave her a FaceTime video of all the shops nearby where she could hop downstairs and make a quick purchase if she felt so inclined. She was now letting others do the errands for her.

"I think this is it, Mark," she spoke. The window of the meat market in front of them had several hanging plucked birds, sausages, and salamis of every size and color, with a healthy customer line feeding out onto the roadway.

"Yes, it looks like it's the green door to the right of the glass front. Did I get the number?"

"I think so. Ring the doorbell."

That got the two older girls' attention. "I want to do it!" shouted Carrie Ann. She soon was arguing with her sister.

Mark knelt and whispered to both his girls, "Let's push the button at the same time, okay? And you both can greet Grandma when she answers. How about that?"

"Okay."

As they pressed the smooth black button, a scratchy crackling sound came over the radio. "Hello?" said a very faint and raspy older woman's voice.

"Hi, Grandma!" Both girls said exuberantly.

"Ah, belle bambini! I am most pleased you have come to visit. You are early, no? I will buzz and you will enter, girls."

"Hi, Mom," inserted Sophia. "Yes, we're all here. Do you need anything first before we come up?"

"No, dear, I'm all prepared. I've baked you some light dinner. Just prepared a little something, not much."

Sophia stepped back and rolled her eyes creasing her forehead. It was her signal that Mark picked up on immediately. Her mother had probably stayed up very late for two nights in a row making homemade pasta and anything else she could muster, since it was a sacrilege for anyone to leave her home without being totally stuffed to the gills.

The buzzer sounded, and Mark quickly turned the handle and carried the little one upstairs, rehoisting the computer cases over his shoulder again, bringing the handled bag as well. The girls noisily clop-clopped up the stairs like young horses. Sophia made sure that the door downstairs was closed and locked behind her. At the top of the landing, she began to smell that glorious olive oil, tomato, and basil combination that was almost like apple pie to an American. That familiar scent of good home cooking. Regardless of what else was going on in the outside world, everything that was going to happen in the kitchen would be ample, warm, extremely tasty, and filling.

She found her mother's appearance quite changed. Sophia was taken aback at the arc of her mother's upper spine, causing her to bend down and strain to look up to anything taller than about five feet. She had thinned out quite a bit, and her fingers contained swollen joints of arthritis. Her movements were shaky and not graceful, and her voice was cut to half the decibels it usually was, very raspy and almost like she had a chronic smoker's cough. She was not a smoker, but her body was suffering from several ailments, including a mild case of emphysema and high blood pressure. But she had aged probably twenty years in the last five years since Sophia and Mark last visited her.

Even with her bowed and frail body, she relished the hugs from her grandchildren, especially the little one, Domenica, coming up and grabbing Granny's knees with both her arms nearly to the point of causing her to lose her balance. Mark helped his mother-in-law and maneuvered the group into her tiny living room overlooking the cobblestone street, a small blue sliver of the Mediterranean visible beyond the town.

"Mm-mm, I have been dreaming of this kind of aroma for weeks and weeks. Mom, I think you outdid yourself again," Mark said.

"Well, son, this is a very special day. I have not met this little one here, Domenica, named after me, I understand. Is that correct?"

She was holding the baby, who reached out and tried to grab her glasses but got a clump of graying hair instead. That wasn't going to stop the baby, who continued to poke at and pinch all sorts of things from the buttonhole on her sweater to the edge of her collar where she had tiny flowers embroidered along the edge, the safety pins she wore in her hair, and the gold-rimmed spectacles she wore that flashed in the sunshine and was just pure eye candy to Domenica. She was desperately looking to get into trouble.

"Here, Mom, I'm going to take her. She's a real handful. I'll wait till you're seated, and then we can perhaps have her sit on your lap. That's probably safer."

Her mother didn't argue.

"Well, you come here and have a seat, girls. We have a nice table set for you, and I put out all the crystal and the silver. I have your little cups here; I don't know if you remember I bought them when each of you were born. This is yours, Ophelia, and this is yours, Carrie Ann, and I even have a small stainless-steel cup for Domenica." She held up the tiny cup, and Domenica, understanding that it probably belonged to her, reached out and was able to grab it before anyone could stop her.

Mrs. Negri chuckled, pressing her palms together as if in prayer. "She is so willful, just like her mother. I'm sure you've noticed, Mark."

"Actually, Mom, they all have her spirit. They are little hurricanes in progress, tornadoes. Every room they go through is destroyed. We are a very active family, and it's hard to keep up with them sometimes. I think I get more exhausted playing with the girls than I do working."

Sophia knew it was an exaggeration, but she didn't mind. She was basking in the glow of her aging mother's countenance, the kind woman who had raised her, cared for her under very difficult circumstances when her American pilot father was killed, and never remarried. She lived a very simple life, taking on several jobs at once and allowing Sophia to go to dance and music school, which worked very well as a glorified daycare setup for her and her jobs. Sophia was filled with pride at how her mother had bore her simple life and had never complained or been angry at anyone, except for her children.

Just as she'd expected, the dinner was huge. She made cannelloni, chicken cacciatore, and Sophia's favorite lobster raviolis with the scallop cream sauce. She had put together a pear currant and fresh lettuce salad with lots of grated Parmesan cheese and a thin oil and vinegar dressing that Sophia had not been able to recreate, even though the ingredients were so simple. They drank two bottles of wine, her mother nearly finishing off one all by herself. This surprised Sophia, as it was a new occurrence.

"Are you being well taken care of? Is there anything you need?" she asked her mother.

"I'm fine. I don't get out to see my friends as much anymore, and I have a young girl that comes to wash and cut my hair every other week. She is learning to be a hair stylist, but she's not passed her exams yet. She also helps me do some house cleaning when I feel up to it."

"Do you see Raphael and Julia?"

"No, my dear, I have not. Your cousins are very busy. I only see Paolo on certain occasions, but he telephones me. And we have a good chat now and then."

"How often do you see the doctor?"

"I go every three months for a checkup, I have a monitor that I wear that reports directly to my doctor. It gives him all sorts of information including my pulse, so in case I am in a danger zone, they can send an ambulance. It's quite a handy thing. But I think the worst part of living alone and being this age is not having friends. The television has never been something I enjoy, and I can't figure out how to work my computer or my cell phone. Some of my friends do, but I don't. I prefer to read."

"I actually think that's better for you, Mom," Mark added. "They say reading and playing games, as well as walking and a little exercise, is what keeps you young. I think you're doing all the right things. And if you eat well and take your medications, I think you could go quite a while without any serious complications. Don't strain yourself, don't stand on ladders, and don't try to go down those stairs by yourself. Those are awfully steep and tiny."

"But I am a size four shoe, Mark. The stairs are no problem for me with the handrails on both sides. I glide down those stairs almost like a fire pole at a station." She gave Mark one of those loving smiles that Sophia imagined the Virgin Mary might have worn in one of the frescoes in several of the churches they attended as she was growing up. Her mother was the picture of peace.

"That's good to hear, Mom," said Sophia.

"Why don't the girls go sit in the living room? I can bring out some cards," she said without asking permission. "How about playing cards, the two of you?"

The girls agreed, and Mrs. Negri went to the cabinet and brought out a deck of cards with kittens on the backside. The girls were more interested in pictures of the kittens than they were setting up their card game.

Mrs. Negri returned to the table and sat down with a grunt. "Sophia, I am slowing down. And I really don't know how long I will be here. I do not want to be a burden. They do have state facilities here in Italy, but I don't want to be housed in one of those places. I would prefer to live with Paolo and his wife, but they have no room. Do you suppose, if I could pay for the plane fare, that someday when the time comes, I could live with you in California?"

Mark's eyes got as big as saucers. Sophia knew he was wondering where the heck her mom would stay. More than likely he was making a private joke to himself that she might have to sleep in the Land Rover since there would be no room in their tiny house.

He spoke up immediately. "Our place is not much bigger than this apartment, Mom. We have two bedrooms. All three of the girls stay together in one, and Sophia and I have the other."

"Oh, I don't mind, I can sleep just fine on a couch."

Mark leaned into the table, putting his right hand on top of Mrs. Negri's gnarled fingers, maintaining a knot on the tablecloth beneath.

"Mom, if you want to come live with us in California, we'll make it work. Somehow, we'll make it work. I'm not sure whether this house would work, but perhaps we can find something that would be bigger. We live a very simple life, but I would be honored if you'd come live with us, and the girls would get to know their grandmother. I think it would be wonderful. In fact, I'm going to consider it my anniversary present. *Please* come. You are more than welcome."

Sophia's eyes filled with tears. She had never seen or heard anything so beautiful coming from Mark's mouth before. She held her mother's hand with Mark's on her left side and reached out for Mark's other hand with her right.

The three of them formed a perfect circle.

CHAPTER 3

THE SHIP TERMINAL in Napoli was a complete zoo. They had spent two relaxing days with Sophia's mother, taking her shopping, getting her ready for Christmas, and exchanging little gifts, mostly for the girls. But transitioning from the little sleepy village she lived in to the boat terminal with the masses of international population was quite an adjustment.

There were four cruise ships docked, and each terminal had a staged embarkation setup to try to mitigate traffic. But this being Italy, Mark was extremely familiar with how delivery vehicles, tour operators, and the general European public did things, so he knew it would be a complete clusterfuck.

He didn't mind large crowds when he was doing surveillance for an upcoming op. He could blend into the audience and watch certain people, because he was generally targeting specific individuals rather than the crowd. That was an unmanageable thing to do. He would never do well trying to run a massive exodus of tourists from all over the world, no matter how patient or skilled he was in communication.

But it was different when his natural training as a SEAL made him suspicious of absolutely every person in the terminal. He was uncomfortable because he was not allowed to be near a doorway or a window for a speedy exit in case of an emergency event. He was smack in the center, waiting in line. Even if he wanted to bolt, it would be impossible without climbing over old ladies, children, dogs, and porters with huge carts piled high with luggage.

It was claustrophobic, hot and sweaty. The tour operators were trying to keep their buses of passengers together, holding signs above their heads and screaming in their language of choice. Since this cruise was going to stop in several countries that bordered the Mediterranean, including France and Spain, there were passengers arriving on board who would be leaving the next day or two. It was more like a ferry terminal than an actual cruise ship embarkation.

By the time they made their way through the line and up to the final immigration desk, Mark's neck was sore from whipping around, watching every loud shout or event, a dropped bag or something that would resemble in any way a gunshot. He was packing, which was allowed if he went through proper channels and showed his credentials. That was one thing Sophia managed to verify before she even placed the reservation, because cruise ship rules had changed significantly since the onset of COVID, as well as the increase in international piracy at sea.

On top of the noise, the congestion, and the sheer abundance of humanity, half the passengers were wearing masks and half were not. Identification was nearly impossible, and he knew that people who had nefarious reputations were using that to the highest effectiveness.

They were asked several questions. The handsome Italian gentleman in his uniform even had medals adorning his outfit, including a ten-year pin and a bunch of brassy epaulets made with spun golden braid on both shoulders. He was trim with a neatly trimmed mustache, and his warm brown eyes lovingly caressed every single beautiful woman he encountered, as well as the children. And when he perused Mark, he gave a distracted, utterly bored, and very cool stare.

"Everything is in order, sir. I bid you good day, and I hope you enjoy your cruise," The gentleman said, handing Mark the stack of passports. Sophia had Dominica's picture with her passport, but both older girls, Ophelia and Carrie Ann, had their own passports.

They walked up the gangway way behind the two girls, who were hopping like bunnies, holding up the entire line of people anxious to get to their cabins. He moved aside to allow others to go around him, which earned him a couple slaps in the thigh with luggage, computer cases, and, in one case, a barking Lhasa Apso in a pink, sequined hard case.

They approached a landing before entering the ship where the obligatory photo was to be taken with two clown characters. The first clown had bright red hair with a fully painted up Edgar Gacy-style. Next to him stood a female ship's captain with disheveled uniform and wrinkled tie lopping off over her shoulder. She had smudge marks on her face and dressed up in caricature as a drunken officer of the ship.

Mark thought it was an odd way to help people feel comfortable about their crews. He hated clowns and knew Sophia did as well.

But the girls didn't care, and even though Mark heard Sophia groan, they ran to the clowns and stood in front of them beaming wide for the camera.

The photographer, a big man with a squeaky voice addressed them both. "Come, come. Mom, Dad? Come, we can't have you out of the photo. You must come." The photographer barked like a huckster.

"But you have the pictures of the girls. That's all we want," said Sophia.

"No, no, no. You do not have to buy, but it is a rule we must take your whole picture as a family."

Resigned to it, Mark put his aviators back on, which served as an ample disguise, and stood with his hand on his wife's shoulder. His other hand rested on Carrie Ann's shoulder in front of him as he smiled, showing his freshly cleaned teeth.

There was a flurry of Italian spoken by both clowns and the photographer fussing about straightening the girls' dresses and smoothing down their hair, and for Mark's taste, they got a little too close to Sophia.

Sophia was right on it.

"Excuse me? I didn't give you permission to touch me or my children. And besides, I am staff." Sophia dug in her day bag finding her badge for the two of them and held them up not more than two inches from the photographer's eyeballs. "Understand?"

"Si. Si, si, signora. We are almost finished. One more picture. Please." He had his hands together. His head bowed slightly as if he was truly begging for forgiveness.

She grabbed the girls by their arms and whispered, "Goddammit, next time we just walk right past it, okay? It'll be like this at every single port of call. They'll make you go in front of the dancers or the musicians, the handcrafts, or whatever. No more pictures, Mark. Okay? Can you help me with that?"

"Absolutely, sweetheart."

Next, they picked up their packet from the information desk. Taking turns, Sophia and Mark entered the employee only area, leaving the other to watch the girls, picking up their informational packet and checking their medical records and their contracts. Sophia had set it up so that their remuneration came directly into their bank account, which Mark appreciated. They were told of an informational staff meeting in approximately four hours once the ship left port, which would delay their evening seating, so they were temporarily given the late seating for dinner.

"I'm hungry," said Ophelia.

"Oh, just wait until you see the promenade, sweetheart. There are all kinds of things there. There's a pastry store. They have a cappuccino place where you can get custom hot chocolates and chocolate-covered jellybeans. They also have an ice cream shop and a candy store," Sophia said.

"Candy? Can we have some candy now?" Ophelia asked.

"Not until after dinner. We can pick some out, but only a sample for right now. We must find our rooms. I think maybe you should take a little nap…"

The groans from the girls were loud and unforgiving.

"If you want candy," Mark started, "you're going to have to play by the rules here. Now if you get candy before dinner, it's an exception, because this is a special trip. But I don't want any guff, and I don't want you giving your mother a hard time about anything she asks you to do. There are a lot of people here, and it's very difficult to keep track of everything that's going on, so make it easy on us and do what you're told and stay close to us. If something should happen and you get separated, you want to find out where the information desk is, and it's usually on… what is it, Sophia?"

"It's on floor three."

"It's the information desk on three." He held up three fingers. "You walk up, and you tell them you are lost, and they will contact us. They might make a loudspeaker announcement, but that's what you do if you get lost. Under no circumstances do you leave each other alone. You go together, and I'd prefer that you hold hands everywhere except in the dining room. Okay?"

"Okay. Do they have a kids' area?" Carrie Ann asked.

"Of course, they do. They have a climbing wall; they have a kids' kitchen where you can do some baking and other projects. And…"

Carrie interrupted her. "Will I be stuck with the babies? Or can I go with the older kids?"

"Well, honey, you're not quite old enough to go with the teenagers, so you will be with the children's group, but I'm sure they keep the babies like your sister here separate. They require different attention. But you and Ophelia will probably be together when you're there the whole time. And if you like, you can hang out with us. No problem. But once you go to the room, you must stay there for at least an hour. Okay?"

"I think it would be a good idea if we take a tour of the place too," Mark said.

"Yeah, let's do that!" said Ophelia.

They walked through the well-lit three-story promenade with stores to the right and left of them, most closed until they pulled out to sea. But several of the pizza markets, cappuccino shops, pastry, and candy stores were open. There was a children's welcome center, which presented all three girls with a little backpack with the ship's logo on it. Each of the girls had a small white teddy bear inside.

They bought waters, and Sophia and Mark each got a cappuccino and then entered a candy shop that was adorned wall to wall with huge clear tubes of brightly colored candies from all over. They had vintage candies, gum, chocolate, licorice, all kinds of things. They even had the wax red lips and mustaches Mark remembered wearing as a child and candy cigarettes that Ophelia wanted to buy, but her parents wouldn't let her.

After each girl picked out her bag, they made their way farther until they came to the ice cream shop. Mark was squinting his eyes together hoping Sophia would allow them to have a small cone, and she did.

They heard the announcement that the cabins were available, and that the luggage would be delivered during their dinner. They were due to leave port in roughly an hour and thirty minutes.

They showed the girls the play center, which was two stories, with a small fenced off area for the younger children. A climbing wall was rigged with harnesses so that even the younger kids could attempt to use it with supervision. There was an adequately staffed group of counselors there, looking young but well-trained and very friendly. The girls were enamored with the climbing wall. One of the passenger's boys was already approaching the top and rang the bell when he got there.

They walked through the library, and Sophia showed the girls the children's section with small tables and chairs separated from the adult books. They perused up and down the rows of the big stage in the theater for evening shows and walked through the gym with the Jacuzzis, the sauna, and then back out onto the deck to look at the swimming pool.

This ship also had a corkscrew slide, and Mark knew exactly what the girls were going to be doing before dinner if they could arrange it. There was a private adult pool in the aft, where children under 12 were not admitted. There were hammocks and little tents for kids, plus large round wicker chairs suitable for the whole gang of five of them. Music was operatic. All the waiters wore black vests and bow ties and started passing out trays of champagne, getting ready for the launch. The girls were brought orange juice.

At last, their drinks in hand and standing around the pool, it was announced that the ship would be leaving port. With three long pulls of the horn, the ship was so loud that both girls covered their ears. They toasted to a successful trip. Mark said a little prayer and then led them up to the 12th floor to their rooms.

Sophia had been able to upgrade since she was a former full-time employee, and they managed to have a suite at no extra cost, because this booking was so empty. It had a large balcony off the living room, which contained the red leather couch that converted to a hideabed for the girls.

Mark and Sophia's bedroom also had a sliding door to the balcony and not quite a queen-sized bed. Mark knew it would have to do.

As the ship's engines rumbled and began pushing away from the pier, they all went outside, sitting on patio chairs. Mark, holding Domenica, went to the railing, and together, they watched as Napoli was left behind them, the town appearing smaller and smaller as they headed out into the deep blue waters of the Mediterranean.

The rain had stopped temporarily, but the clouds were dark gray, so they were expecting more rain this evening. The sea was calm. White and gray shorebirds made a huge ruckus whenever the ships horns blasted.

Several vendors and tour guides and staff waved at the ship as it pulled away, Ophelia and Carrie Ann waving back. Even the baby waved.

Carrie Ann looked up at Mark. "This is fun. I can tell we are going to have a blast!"

"Absolutely, sweetheart."

As the ship moved faster, it began to feel chilly. Sophia instructed the girls to come inside and lay down for a short nap.

"We can leave the curtains open so you can be all fresh and rested for dinner tonight. Okay?"

"Mom and I have a meeting we must go to. When the time comes, we're going to take you all to the play area for a trial run."

"Okay, Daddy," Ophelia said.

With the girls safely resting, Sophia took the baby in with them into their bedroom, kicked off their shoes, and laid back on the pillows, watching as the sun began to hang lower and lower in the sky.

"If you'll indulge me, Mrs. Beale, I'd like to go get us some champagne or a beer or something? What would you like?"

"I don't know. Surprise me."

"Okay. Alcoholic or non-alcoholic or caffeine?" he asked her.

"You decide. I don't want to think about a single thing. I just want to sit here with her and relax for a couple of minutes. Then I'll start making decisions."

"You got it."

He headed to the door, but before he could open it, she called out to him.

"Hey, Mark?"

"What is it?"

"I love you. And thanks for doing this. I have a feeling you and I are going to need a little bit of alone time after we get back to San Diego, but thank you for putting up with all of this and for being such a good dad. I think this was a perfect way to celebrate ten years of marriage."

"It's nothing but smooth sailing from here on out. If you can last ten years, sweetheart, we can last them all. And I can't think of anybody I'd rather share my life with than you and all our girls here. The best is yet to come. I promise."

CHAPTER 4

T HE STAFF MEETING was held in one of the cocktail lounges large enough to hold roughly a hundred people. Only the information and tour staff, medical bay/EMT services, dance and fitness instructors, and special translators were there. Most of these individuals had private cabins. The bulk of the 1,500 crew members on board this ship were downstairs in the crew quarters, where they were packed four to a room and, on some of the cruise lines, had to alternate sharing beds depending on their shift.

Sophia knew it was a long grueling trip, and she had done those jobs before she earned her way up to dance instructor, but ever since she had become one of the popular staff members on the cruise, she was always given a private room or shared with another instructor.

She didn't know most of the team present since it had been nearly a decade when she last worked this line, but several of the officers, she recognized.

Mark sat next to her patiently while they waited for the tour director to show up. Old friends greeted each other. There was a little bit of smack talk about some of the officers and other staff members. There had been a generous raise given over the past year to encourage a return to work. Everyone in the industry was having trouble filling their staffing quotas. The raise was a big hit, and several noted it enthusiastically.

Sophia's salary was double what she'd received ten years prior, a pleasant surprise. It almost covered the cost of the entire vacation.

Over in the corner stood the ship's clergy, a Catholic priest dressed in a black frock and reverse collar. He was young with sharp, angular model features. Sophia pointed him out to Mark.

"You should speak to him about redoing our vows. They usually designate one afternoon or evening and do everyone at once. But you'll have to get on the list because it fills quickly."

"Got it." Mark rose, making his way across the plum-colored thick movie theater carpet, greeting the priest with a smile and handshake.

"Sophia? Is that really you?" she heard from behind her.

Twisting in her chair, she recognized Thiago, who had been a teenage bus boy working on the cruise where she met Mark. He was fully grown now and had turned into an attractive young man.

"Thiago!"

"Ah, I can't believe you remember me!"

"But of course. My goodness, you grew up so handsome, look at you. And your uniform, what is your job here?"

Thiago pointed to his badge where Sophia read, *Assistant Cruise Director.*

"Very good. Wow, that didn't take long, did it?"

Thiago shook his head, showing some disagreement. "Well, ten years. I guess that's not long. Sure seemed like it to me. So how is everybody in your life?"

"Well, Mark is here. He's over there talking to the priest."

"Oh, that's Father Santiago. He's very nice. You are getting married?"

"No, we've been married for ten years, but we are going to renew our vows."

Thiago's eyes sparkled, his white teeth an attractive underscore to his dark and neatly trimmed mustache.

"I remember your romance. It was quite the talk of the staff quarters and became a problem when we got to Brazil. And all that adventure in between? My goodness. Let's hope we don't have that again!"

"No. Lightning doesn't strike twice, er, I mean, a third time." She answered his puzzled expression with further explanation. "We have been on another cruise that also had issues, but not a terrorist takeover of the ship."

Her words floated across the room, and too late, Sophia realized she'd been speaking too loudly. Several of the staff members turned, frowning in her direction. She placed her hand over her mouth. "Excuse me. It was a long time ago. Much safer now," she said, stopping to check for further reaction, this time finding only two.

She brought her forehead close to Thiago, whispering, "I hope I'm not causing a problem. I shouldn't have said that, Thiago. I'm going to have to apologize."

"No, don't. They've heard the stories. You remember the captain who beached his ship?"

"Oh, yes, we were on that boat. One of the other passengers told us about it. Horrible."

"You were? I didn't know that."

"*After* they repaired it. But it had a forty-foot gash repaired along the water line."

"Yes, well, luckily they don't allow that anymore. The captains no longer have that kind of authority. He went to jail."

"I know he did. Poor man. He was just trying to save someone's life. He thought one of his American tourists was having a heart attack."

"Sophia, it was a little more than that. It was determined he had a drinking problem, as well. They are extremely strict these days. So many of the old captains retired during COVID. We have a lot of fresh new former military captains, and they're excellent. I mean they're just excellent. And we have a lot more protocols for ship safety these days. The tracking and electronics are much better. It was really the Wild West when you guys went before. I'm sure other cruise lines are the same, but we've never had an incident like that since."

"Good to know. I will make sure to tell people that if it comes up."

As Mark headed back over to their seat, a rather rotund cruise director in a white uniform, also sporting epaulets and medals, came in through the back door, accompanied by a tall extremely handsome captain with a black dress uniform.

Mark stiffened. "Holy shit, it's Teseo. Teseo Dominichello, you remember him?"

"Oh, you're right. He's the captain?"

"Yes. Notice his sleeves. We're lucky. He's good."

Thiago leaned forward and extended his hand. "Sir, my name is

Thiago, and I was barely legal when I last saw you. I was a bus boy in the dining room for your group. What a fun group. First time I'd met a bunch of Navy SEALs and their families. I was so impressed. Still am."

"Thank you, son."

"I haven't seen Sophia in ten years. It's nice to make your acquaintance again."

Mark continued to shake Thiago's hand.

"Did you get your ceremony arranged?" Sophia asked him.

"Tuesday night. That's when they'll do it. They'll announce it tonight at dinner."

The tour director began to address the crowd with a microphone.

"Ladies and gentlemen, if I could have your attention, please. We are pleased to welcome you to the Fantastico Nautica, our largest and most exclusive ship. Our captain is Captain Teseo Dominichello, and he has been at the helm ever since its original launch nearly one year ago."

The tall Captain waved to the crowd as they clapped for him, several standing.

The tour director continued, stepping in front of the captain. "I am Rodrigo Choppa, and I am your tour director for this cruise. I have arranged office hours from 9:00 to 10:00 in the morning, and 9:00 to 10:00 in the evening if you should need me. The ship's operator can also put you through to my state room. We are not quite full and have a very international group. Most of our passengers, as you know, come from Italy, Spain, or France. However, we do have a contingent from Denmark. We also have a large contingent from Brazil who are going to be stopping off in the States on their way back home. They have sailed with us prior, and now are sailing with us for the return."

"Wow, we've got some big travelers here," whispered Mark.

"You do know that some people retire and just go from cruise to cruise to cruise. They find it's cheaper to cruise than to stay in a retirement village. It's the new thing now."

"Yeah, I'd heard that somewhere."

The microphone crackled. "I would like to have all of you who are new to this ship please raise your hand and introduce yourselves, introduce your job, and what your nationality is or what your country of residence is please." He pointed to a young blonde woman on his right.

As the group introduced themselves and finally came to Mark and Sophia, Mark waved to Teseo as he spoke. "My name is Mark Beale. I'm an American, and I live in California with my wife, Sophia, who is Italian by birth, but she is my wife, so she is an American citizen now. We met on one of these cruises, and I am fortunate enough to make the acquaintance previously of Captain Dominichello. It will guarantee that we are all in very good hands," Mark finished.

Captain Teseo shouted across the room, "And we are also in very good hands, as this gentleman here is an elite warrior."

The room was suddenly silent.

"Now, that's not a skill we're going to need on this cruise, I hope," the captain said to scores of twitters in the audience. "But I also want to put you at ease to let you know that we have one of the Navy's finest in our midst, and he is going to assist his wife as a dance instructor. We're going to see if he can walk and chew gum at the same time. He's not Italian or Brazilian, so you are going to have to forgive him if he has American feet."

The audience laughed. Mark delivered Teseo a lopsided grin. Sophia wasn't sure he was comfortable with the remarks, but he took it well.

Sophia introduced herself again and explained her background in dance and what she hoped to do and mentioned that they were traveling with their three girls. "If anyone would like to earn a little bit of extra money doing babysitting, we might be interested. There may be times when the children's center is closed, but I know we have sitters on board, and if you would introduce yourselves to me, I would be happy to discuss working out something. Not too much."

The meeting was short, and the later meeting, supposed to be by department, was postponed until the next morning. As they broke, Mark headed over to talk to Teseo with Sophia in tow.

Teseo addressed him with a warm smile. "Mark Beale. I never thought I would see you again."

"And I thought you were getting out?"

"Ah yes, well, you know I was in the process of a divorce last time we saw each other, and now I've fallen in love again and we are happy to celebrate the birth of our son. He's already two. So now I must work again, and this job pays well. We need to pay for his college education.

She sometimes comes with me, although it's frowned upon, but she is good at the information desk and in the office, so we try to include them as much as possible, so I won't be gone for so long. Life goes on, right?"

Teseo studied Mark's eyes deeply. Sophia knew they shared something that she would ask Mark about later.

"And forgive me, I've forgotten my manners. Nice to meet you, Sophia, is it?"

"Ah! Quick recovery. You are right. I do remember that you were very quick thinking, and Mark has told me also about the other thing."

She didn't want to say what she knew from that previous mission that took Zak's eye and nearly ended in disaster.

"Oh, you mean the ambassador?" he whispered.

"Well, I wasn't going to say it. But good thinking on your part."

Teseo agreed. "It was a lucky day for everybody. Luckily, that has never happened again either."

Mark laughed. "You mean the part about dressing him up with lipstick and a wig in a woman's dress and putting him in the freezer or the part about having to transport an important United States official back home as excess vegetables?"

Mark's grin told Sophia everything she needed to know about how he felt about Teseo's comment. It was a get-even trick.

"Well, yes, both. And you know, what doesn't kill you makes you stronger, right?"

"On that, we agree." Mark added, "So is there anything about this particular group, anybody special who's traveling here?"

"No, I don't really recognize people even though there are several regulars, I understand. But I will tell you this, and it's always this way, we are an Italian line, so we usually don't have many American tourists. I believe we have less than two dozen. We have 3,400 passengers, and yes, I think about 24 Americans. Believe it or not, we have about 50 Canadians. So you'll find most everybody speaks English, but you're going to be hearing lots of Italian, Spanish, and some French. There are the customary provincial attitudes of those passengers, and we give the Italians the toga night, where we run around with tablecloths and swing napkins over our heads. You remember, don't you?"

"Oh yes, I remember that. What an event that was."

"Here's a little secret. Your tour director, as it happens, is a former operatic star, so he will surprise you at the dinner. Italian night is Thursday; don't miss it. It's a spectacle beyond your wildest dreams."

"One of the things I like about cruising with you guys is that the food is excellent."

Teseo bowed and agreed. "Italian, of course."

"The entertainment spectacular."

"Cirque du Soleil, yes, we have excellent Russian gymnasts."

"But the ship itself is just gorgeous. I mean marble and the Murano glass, everything about this is so Italian and so beautiful—statues, waterfalls, romantic and colorful clubs, and restaurants. Even the carpet is different than other cruise ships."

"And the music, of course, is mostly Italian pop. Yes, that's the nice thing when you come from America and you cruise with a different country's line. You get a little bit of their culture. It's a little extra bonus for you not being Italian. I've heard it said this way."

"Your cruise director said that you are not even 90% full. Is that right?" Sophia asked.

"That is correct. We had a very large block cancel. They were following with a musical group on a special European tour. Apparently, several of the members of the band, part of our entertainment as well, came down with COVID, so the whole thing's been postponed for a few months. Perhaps till next year. But that was a cancellation of some three hundred rooms."

"Wow." Sophia was shocked.

"We try to honor repeat and loyal customers requests for refunds, especially if the band can't perform, but it's taken its toll. I'm glad we could accommodate you at the last minute. How fortunate for all of us."

"It's been a while since I've done this. We have the three girls, which we'll try to introduce you to later," Mark added.

"I would like that. Are they as beautiful as your wife?" Captain Dominichello said bowing once again.

"Absolutely. Although their mother is quite the stunner."

Teseo checked his watch. "I must get back to the bridge. Will you join me tonight at my table in the Captain's Dining Room? The girls are, of course, invited to join you."

"They switched us to late seating tonight," said Sophia.

"Makes no difference. I don't eat much anyway, and I'm served both times. So I'll see you at 8:30 then?"

"Absolutely. Maybe we can discuss further some of my other questions."

"Mark, you're not going to be a worry wort, are you? With all your training and experience?"

"No, sir. But I've learned to ask lots of questions. Is there anything different that I need to pay attention to? I just want to keep my wife and children safe. Where do you have your biggest problems?"

Teseo thought about that for a minute, putting his forefinger up to his lips, and then spoke, "I would say we have something pop up every cruise. I have not piloted a ship where we didn't. Sometimes it's one of the waiters or the cooks or the bus boys who are fugitives. It could be that they take the job and leave port so they can escape going to jail. Occasionally, we must have them arrested and take them off the ship. We have the obvious drinking issues, which is always a problem. Now we have fentanyl. We have drugs. We have people selling drugs. And those distress me a great deal. It's very difficult to control."

"Any human trafficking?" asked Mark.

"Well, I think we did before it got so easy to just walk across your border, yes, sure. But this is a rather expensive and long way to do it. And there are more than ten days where they must be hidden. That's a long time. I don't think it's recommended or the desired way to do this. And that's a good thing. We have good cooperation with our ports of call, and I think the policing is much better than it used to be. I just think every cruise is different. There's always something that I wasn't paying attention to. And that's what I try to remember—to expect the unexpected. Because, let's face it, Mark, evil exists, right?"

Sophia felt her hand close reflexively in Mark's.

Teseo added, "You know this. They never go away. The bad guys never go on vacation."

CHAPTER 5

M ARK AND SOPHIA prepared for a more formal dinner than they had planned. On the way, they took in the show in the Grand Theater. The girls enjoyed the snappy dance routines.

The water was calm, and Mark had seen dancers do lifts and twirls and leaps when the seas were choppy, but tonight, the Mediterranean was nearly like glass, the full moon sweeping its light over the still water, beaconing like a huge lighthouse. He knew just under the surface the sea was filled with unknown secrets and abundant aquatic life.

Mark had done a good deal of scuba diving both professionally and for recreation. He knew it was one of the richest resources on the planet. The bed was littered with wrecked ships and odd rock formations, giving rise to stories of lost civil civilizations buried by tons of water. Marine life was very abundant and varied.

Tonight's program was a snappy 1950s type of review, with dancers dressed in saddle shoes, full skirts, and petticoats—a takeoff on Grease or Happy Days or one of those shows. Ophelia and Carrie Ann loved it. Dominica slept in her mother's arms nearly the whole time.

Mark knew the girls had watched their mother practice, and she had taken them to the dance studio, even attempted to teach them some ballet, so watching the dancers with their brightly colored costumes, whooping and hollering, was extra fascinating to them. He was anxious to hear their reaction afterwards. Their eyes were relentlessly searching every movement, noise, and flash of color.

Sophia seemed to enjoy it as well.

"They're good, aren't they?" he whispered in his wife's ear.

"They usually are. They do a lot of practicing and a lot of dancing on these cruises. It's quite a rigorous routine. But the company does pick up some of the best in the business. And it's a short commitment for the performers, a four-month contract usually, so it's something a young dancer can do when they don't have a family. It's kind of the ideal job if you're single. Great way to meet people."

Ophelia turned to her mother and put her finger in front of her lips. "Shh, Mom. People are watching the show."

Mark shared a chuckle with Sophia and turned his attention back to the program.

Afterwards, as the house lights came on, they took the girls down to the stage to introduce them to some of the dancers, who teased them. One of them brought the girls up on the stage itself and pretended to polka with them very gently. Several of the other dancers chimed in, and before long, the two girls were the center of attention and loving the action, the colors, the makeup, and everything about it.

"I think we have ourselves a couple of exhibitionists here. Perhaps they have some streak of entertainer in their psyche?" he asked her.

"I think you're right. I was not attuned to this. But they really do appear to have great interest now."

"Just remember, they have to work pretty darn hard, and of course, we want to impress upon them that it's not okay to just leave and join the circus when they're fifteen, right?" Mark whispered.

"Yup. I'm sure if they took their ballet shoes off and the girls could get a good look at the knuckles on their toes, their bent and sore, bruised and cut skin and bones, they'd be horrified. But they make it look easy, and fun. And that's what entertainers do. They make you think anybody could do it."

Mark was watching the lights dance in her eyes, the way she almost reverently gazed up at the stage, took in all the colors and the characters zipping past, hearing the squeals of laughter from her girls, and knew if there was a heaven, to Sophia, it would look very much like this tonight.

Later, at the captain's table, they were seated next to a couple from California who owned a winery in Sonoma County. Sophia wasn't familiar with it but stated that new wineries were popping up all the time, and it wasn't very uncommon.

The girls sat to Sophia's left and got rather fidgety with the many courses of the dinner. Once they discovered that they could order anything they wanted off the menu, the evening was saved. From then on, it was all ice cream, hot dogs, and macaroni and cheese served one after the other and never refused.

Sophia leaned in and whispered to Carrie, "If you eat too much of that stuff, you're going to be sick tomorrow. And don't you want to have a nice day in the pool?"

"I eat like this all the time when I'm over at my friend's house. There we have pizza too."

The waiter overheard her comment. "Pizza? You would like pizza? We have pepperoni or we have cheese, Miss. Which would be your preference?"

"Cheese," Carrie Ann said.

"Pepperoni," barked Ophelia.

"Very well, I shall bring you a half and half. I will be right back."

Mark spoke to the couple on his right. "I think we've just spoiled them forever. They're going to be ordering us around the kitchen, learning how to dial up takeout. It's going to be no vegetables for us, or at least for them, when we get home."

Everybody laughed.

Teseo raised his wine glass to Mark, and they toasted silently together across the table.

"I understand you are a Navy SEAL? Was I right in assuming that?" Mr. Brandon asked Mark.

"Yes, I am. I'm not accustomed to running around shouting about it, so feel free to keep it between us. But yes, I've been a SEAL for twelve years now. I went in right out of high school."

"Ah," Mrs. Brandon added. "How did you come to that decision?"

"Well, there was this little event called 9/11. I just felt like doing something other than watching the TV show people dying and buildings collapse in ruin. It was an easy decision for me. I wasn't enjoying college very much, and my chosen field was hopelessly boring. Accounting."

"Oh my! I can't see you being an accountant, not with what you do."

"Well, actually, there are a lot of SEALs who do a lot of things. We have buddies back home that also have a winery. Frog Haven Vineyards.

Have you heard of it?"

The couple shook their heads.

"You are an investor in this winery?" Mr. Brandon inquired.

"No, didn't get in on that one in time. But my other former team-mate buddy runs the Lavender Farm out in Bennett Valley. He's very good at what he does, and he and his wife run an event center, a wedding center."

"Oh, I've been there. A delightful little place," Mrs. Brandon answered. "Used to be a nursery, and I went there all the time."

Mark chose not to elaborate further on the history of the farm. "They work very hard at it. Sophia and I have spent many weekends up there working big parties. It's fun. Someday, perhaps we'll help them out."

"And leave San Diego?" she asked.

"I don't know. San Diego's nice, but man, there's so many beautiful places we could live in the United States. We're just biding our time. Some day."

"You won't make this a long-term career then?" Mr. Brandon asked.

"Well, I've put in twelve years. That's quite a bit for me. We'll see. It all depends on what the family wants. It's not all about me."

While Sophia headed back to the room with all three girls, Mark stayed up in the dining room hoping to have a short conversation with Teseo, who had disappeared. The American couple offered to buy him a cocktail, so they sat at the lounge, people-watching and chatting. He was impatient to join Sophia and turn in early if he could.

The couple explained the development of the winery, how they had put together investors, and had turned a relatively unprofitable piece of land into perfect soil to raise premium grapes that they were able to sell at the highest prices.

"You don't bottle it or ferment it there on site? You just raise the grapes to sell?"

"We sell the grapes to a conglomerate," Mr. Brandon corrected. "And then we purchase bulk wine from the same conglomerate, which has some of our wine in it as well. That way we get some of the best varietals from other wineries, which is a more expensive mixture than if we just relied on our own grapes by themselves. All the new wineries are doing this now since tastes for the wine-drinking public are changing year by year."

Mark thought it sounded like a good strategy but soon found himself becoming bored with the conversation. He remained polite, and the couple finally took their leave, allowing him to get back to the cabin.

All the girls were sleeping soundly. Sophia had moved Domenica to a small portable crib at the side of their bed and donned her favorite black silky nightgown. She was propped up in bed reading a book with her tiny nightlight.

Mark took one needy look at her, and then climbed up on the bed. "Mrs. Beale, you have good instincts. I love you in black," he said as he kissed her.

"Well, hurry up and get down to your American flag boxers, then. I've got plans for those instincts."

"Your will is my command," he whispered back and immediately disrobed.

True to his nature, Sophia had guessed his choice of boxers. He always wore the stars and stripes or some combination of the flag colors in his boxers. It was just something he'd adopted doing when he once saw a Senior Master Chief undress on an op and never forgot it. The man was crusty as Hell, but he insisted on wearing red, white, and blue with some form of stars on his shorts, and several of the other senior officers did the same. What was good for them was certainly good enough for Mark.

He pulled Sophia up off the bed, holding her close to him while he maneuvered the two of them to the balcony. The warm, balmy night was exciting, and as he absorbed the love in her soft brown eyes, which reflected the deep yellow moon, he felt like the luckiest man alive.

She had already brought out a chilled bottle of champagne and two flutes. He liked the way she did her advanced planning, and her recon was spot-on as well.

Smart and stubborn at the same time, what Mark really loved about her was her spontaneity and zest for life.

And the way she trembled in his arms every time he held her. She never held back showing him how she felt about him.

CHAPTER 6

THE SHIP WAS scheduled for a sea day, so Sophia and Mark had their first ballroom dance clinic. She knew, even though he had been practicing incessantly before they left for the cruise, that he was nervous. His hands were sweaty; his arms were stiff.

As they took to the center of the floor and the music was turned on, Mark had an expression of worry, pursing his lips together and biting a side of his tongue. He had a funny habit of doing that whenever he was unsure or headed into unfamiliar territory.

He had the same reaction for speaking in front of crowds. But Sophia mused that he never was nervous going overseas, getting into a firefight, competing on the shooting range, repelling from helicopters, or doing a HALO jump at midnight in enemy territory. That was the easy stuff, he'd told her on more than one occasion.

But ballroom dancing in front of a group of nearly seventy passengers of all ages, nationalities, and skill levels, most of whom had English as a second language, was out of his comfort zone. She loved that he was so honest about giving it a good try, however. And she knew he would do his best.

He always did. It was his *only* option.

"Relax, Mark," she whispered as the music began to play. She pressed on his arms a little bit to show him how rigid his shoulders and elbows were. "Be flexible and fluid. We're going to glide, not work at it."

With one hand positioned between her shoulder blades on her back and the other clutched in hers out to the side, he was ready when she whispered, "On my mark. Count of three. One Mississippi, two Mississippi, three, and we begin."

He began on the wrong foot, but she quickly skipped and matched sides with him. She had told him many times that the woman's job was to always follow the man's lead in ballroom dancing, so it was incumbent on him to make the moves to direct her. He made a lot of jokes about all the things he'd like to do to direct her, but it had nothing to do with ballroom dancing.

"I—I'm sorry."

"No problem, my love. Remember, you're right, and I follow. Even if you're out of step, your cadence is wrong, or the timing's wrong, you're always right." She gave him a wide grin and nodded her head as he led her into a turn while they twirled in the center of the floor.

She scanned the faces of all the onlookers and saw nothing registered in their expressions that indicated they even understood he started on the wrong foot. All except one person.

Tall and handsome, Captain Teseo Dominichello stood in the shadows just outside a secret doorway in the corner. His arms crossed his chest, his head hung to the left, and his grin completely went the other way. He was in rapt attention, watching the two of them, and she saw him make eye contact each time Mark twirled her so that she was facing his direction.

On certain occasions, she continued to count in a gentle purr when Mark was overly working his arms and the direction his hand gave the middle of her back. But in doing so, they stayed in step with the beat of the music. It was a beautiful waltz. They demonstrated a twirl, a turn to the right, and a graceful dip and turn to the left. At the end of the two-minute clip, they stopped, greeted each other one more time with a bow, and then released their hands to their sides.

As the audience clapped, Sophia looked up to him and smiled. "Mark, that was perfect."

But he wasn't buying any of it. She could see he was upset with himself, always obsessed with doing things 100% correctly down to the smallest detail. He was ashamed that the very first step of the dance was wrong, even though he improved. He was rigid, still nervous, and hadn't yet learned to relax and just try to enjoy himself.

Sophia took the microphone and thanked everyone for their applause.

"You can see, it's a very simple step, a box step, but you can alter it by doing various turns and twirls. You can even change it up to do double time if you're doing a jig or a faster waltz. It begins to look like a cakewalk instead of a smooth lilting waltz. But the music and the dance steps were truly made for waltz, and if you master this, you can just about dance to any kind of music."

She demonstrated as they put on a 1940's Andrews Sisters' number, and with the syncopation in their steps, doing a move to the right, a move to the left, and then a quick step together at the end, they were essentially doing the waltz except putting emphasis on different measures in the beat.

"You can also do cha-chas and salsas with the same step. It's just a matter of whether or not you're in box formation with your partner, or you walk it up and down the line like this."

She showed a syncopated cha-cha, which basically used the same steps, and by adding some hand signals, expressions, and kicks, the whole dance resembled something else, certainly not a waltz. But it was still using the same basic steps.

The crowd was ecstatic, clapping at every movement, and even when they could see Mark struggled occasionally, the laughing was all in good fun. Afterwards, they received a rousing applause for the third time.

Sophia asked everyone to pair up in whatever combination they wished. There were several women who chose to dance together and even a couple of men who danced in a foursome, switching out partners occasionally. Out of the corner of her eye, she saw Captain Dominichello approach the circle, take a female partner, and stand to attention like she had instructed.

"We have a celebrity in our midst today, ladies and gentlemen. Please welcome Captain Dominichello."

She motioned with both her hands in his direction, and he took a bow, grinning.

From past dance classes, Sophia knew that all the ladies in the room, especially the single ones, were going to be cutting in on Captain Dominichello, which was as it should be. The captain was always Prince Charming at the Cinderella ball.

Mark observed as she walked around the circle and helped everybody position their arms properly. When she came to Captain Dominichello, his partner was a young buxom woman. She decided to address this head-on.

"Now in this instance, Captain, you have to judge what's a safe space for *her*, not what you might desire," she said, not making eye contact. "There are some women that are girthy, and you need to leave room for that. Other women are well-endowed, unlike me."

The woman spoke up quickly.

"Oh, please, Sophia. It's no problem for me. He can squeeze me as tight as he wants to," she said in an attractive southern drawl.

"Ah, one of our two dozen Americans then, is that correct?"

"Yes, ma'am. I'm Noreen, and I am from Georgia. Yes, ma'am."

Captain Dominichello firmly splayed his fingers against her back and did not force her to come closer to him. However, Noreen took the opportunity to sneak in a step closer and made sure her front side happened to brush up against his, which caused a slight ripple amongst the others in the class.

After Sophia completed correcting all the body positions, adjusting fingers and the way the male partner held the female partner, she demonstrated with Mark, showing how he held his hand out like a cup and how she placed her two middle fingers in the center of that cup and used it as a gauge. In this way, they demonstrated how she could twirl and not lose her bearing, be aware of how close or far away her partner was.

"Sometimes, it gets quite busy. You're avoiding other couples, and it's very helpful that you don't have to look at his hand to know exactly where you are. And remember, ladies, the man is *always* right." Before she returned to Mark, she noted that Captain Dominichello was beaming. It concerned her a little, but she was used to Italian men being rather loose and forward, and though she was Italian by birth, she was now an American, and American women were always fair game for Italian men.

"Okay, ladies and gentlemen, we're going to try to twirl while stepping in time to the music. So we are going to count one-two-three-four, one-two-three-four repeatedly. You are to make your turn in the count of four."

A few of the elderly couples who were normally used to using canes or walkers struggled a bit with this, so Sophia helped them with the modification. Instead of twirling, they could move gently and gracefully from side to side. "One-two-three-four to the right. One-two-three-four to the left."

After a few more demonstrations, she asked Mark to join her in the center again, and they demonstrated the box step of the waltz about ten times before she cut the music.

"Now what I'm going to do is dance with all the opposing partners, males or females, whichever you have, and I'm going to have Mark dance with the women partners or opposing partners man or woman. Now remember, Mark is the person who is always right. And, ladies, your job is to do whatever he does. Now if he goes one-two-three, one-two-three-four, that's what you do. If he goes one-two and stops and tries to do it all over again, you match his steps. On the dance floor, if the woman matches what the man does, nobody is ever going to notice whether he is doing the steps correctly or if he keeps time with the music. If you two are in sync, the dance looks good. Are we clear about that?"

The group was excited to get moving, and Sophia played a long piece that repeated itself. She followed around and danced with all thirty men in the audience. She was surprised that many of them were quite good dancers and had good balance on their feet. Most were even more relaxed than Mark was.

Mark struggled a bit with the women, having difficulty taking charge. So Sophia decided to stop the music and make it a teaching moment.

"I want to ask you, ladies, what did you learn dancing with Mark?"

"He's a good dancer," somebody said.

"Thank you," Mark replied.

"I found it hard to follow him. But I think we got in sync." Someone else nodded, and Mark acknowledged it, agreeing.

"Anything else?"

"Actually, it really didn't matter whether he stayed with the music or whether he used his right or his left foot or gave me the instruction to turn, I just tried to match his every movement but on the reverse side. It actually was quite easy."

Delighted with the answer, Sophia clapped for the student.

"Bingo, we have a winner. That's the right answer. Dancing is easy. When you stress about it, when you get tense, when you worry about how you look, you don't dance well. You need to relax and just dance as if you know how. Remember, the more you dance the better you get."

Sophia got another ovation.

"I remember hearing an interview with Ginger Rogers and Fred Astaire. She was his all-time favorite partner, and the comment was made that Fred Astaire and Ginger Rogers always made it look so easy. Somebody asked her, 'How did that happen? Did you just spend every waking moment practicing?'"

Several people knew the story and started to nod.

"Fred Astaire said, 'It's actually very easy for me. Because the man is always right. What she must do is follow my lead. The man never makes a mistake, right, Ginger?' he said to her." A few of the men chuckled, and Sophia continued. "The questioner then asked Ginger the same question. Her answer was this, 'Sure, it's very easy to just follow Fred's steps, except I get to do it in high heels and backwards.'" She waited for the laughs to stop, smiling softly.

"But even Ginger Rogers made it look easy, and it will be easy the more you do it. So have fun. Practice all you can. There are numerous little clubs and bistros all over the ship. You can even practice by the pool, if you want, in your bathing suit. There's no right or wrong way to master your ballroom dancing skills. You can get together with three or four or five couples and practice all your dance steps, even choreograph a few things where you switch partners. All that is simply a function of enjoying what you're doing."

Sophia had finished the hour lesson with moving about the dance floor and demonstrating some individual turns that she had perfected, certain movements that sent her off in the distance and then they reconnected in the middle of the floor later, indicating that if they advanced, they would be learning some of these steps as well.

"I hope you have enjoyed our lesson today; it was a pleasure. Mark and I had a great time. And I'm going to leave the music running for another half hour, so you can practice, but this is the end for today. And thank you."

Again, the audience gave both she and Mark hearty applause.

One of the older ladies grabbed Mark's arm and sashayed with him across the dance floor, obviously not listening to anything Sophia had said, because she was guiding Mark, leading him instead of vice versa. Sophia found it funny and enjoyed watching the battle of the sexes in front of her.

From behind her, she heard a deep voice. "May I have this dance please, Instructor Beale?"

She didn't have to turn around to know it was the gravelly voice of the handsome Captain Dominichello. She curtsied and said, "With pleasure."

Captain Dominichello was quite good at ballroom dancing and probably had taken lessons so that he could play his part well.

"You're a good dancer, Captain."

"My mother forced me to take ballroom dance lessons when I was in early school. It was not the sort of masculine activity I liked, but I'm grateful to her now that she insisted."

Sophia recognized the scent of his cologne, guessed it was Italian, a little on the flowery side with a bit of spice mixed in. Italian men seemed to enjoy using citrus, bergamot, and honeysuckle, along with a healthy dose of all-spice mixture. On a woman, the scent would be delicious. On a man, it was absolutely devastating. She was going to have to buy some for Mark.

"May I ask you a question?"

"Absolutely. Fire away."

"What is that scent?"

"Ah, it's a private mixture blended for me. I buy it on the Island of Capri. I can send you a bottle if you like. I don't have any extras with me, but I can have a bottle sent to you if you like."

"Oh, just the name. You don't have to buy me a bottle. I'm sure it's expensive."

"But so well worth it. I shall smile every time I think of it. The lovely Sophia buys it for her husband. I think that's romantic, don't you?"

"It is." She toyed with the idea of laying some ground rules and decided it was time to do so. "I have to tell you that Mark and I are happily married. I am very happy to be dancing with you, but I don't want you to misunderstand me."

"But nothing like that is intended, Sophia. I just enjoy the company of beautiful women, intelligent, cultured, beautiful women. I guess I haven't been fully domesticated."

"Well, I think you probably are a smart gentleman, as well, and you wouldn't do anything that would jeopardize my comfort on this cruise. Mark is good at a lot of amazing things. He probably would've had a hard time if he lived during Queen Victoria's time and was a man at court. I think he would find it too restrictive and not at all fun. But I give him kudos for always trying and always willing to support me. He gives me a long leash."

"Indeed, he does," the captain whispered.

"And that's because he knows he can trust me."

CHAPTER 7

MARK WAS HEADED with Ophelia and Carrie Ann to the pool, expecting to ride with them down the corkscrew-tunneled tube splashing into the deep end. They ran smack dab into the second seating crowd for lunch, coming in the opposite direction, and for a moment he lost sight of the girls ahead of him. But as they waited for the elevator, he caught up to them, and they took it up to the 12th floor where the pool deck was.

Ophelia had brought her bag stuffed with a book, her teddy bear, and some of her candy. They found three chaises next to each other and then located a big wicker daybed with a canvas cover to block the sun. They laid out their towels and stashed their bags, heading for the ladder leading up to the tubes.

Mark was impressed with the speed of the slide and how fast they dropped. The girls, who followed behind him one at a time, were visibly shaken when they got to the bottom. He caught them mid-air as they came shooting out about ten feet from the spout.

"Should we do it again?" he posed.

Ophelia immediately shook her head. "I don't think so. Unless I ride with you? Like sit on your lap?"

"Sure." He looked over at Carrie Ann. "Kiddo, are you okay?"

"That was really fast, Daddy, but I want to do it again. I'm not scared."

"Okay then. Let's hop on up there."

The second time down was much better, and although Ophelia was screaming the whole way, it was nothing but good fun. They took turns riding with him for the next half hour, and finally, Ophelia admitted that she was tired.

They had skipped the seated lunch, so Mark ordered hot dogs and sodas, and they sat in the little tented chaise, almost like a camping experience in their own backyard. The food tasted excellent. The girls ate their chips and hot dogs and asked for more.

Mark wanted to sample some of Ophelia's candy. "Can I have something from your bag?"

"Sure, Daddy." She pulled the pink plastic bag out of her beach carryall and handed it to him.

Without looking too closely, Mark dug in, swarming around and then looking to see if he could find anything made of chocolate. But his eyes landed on a cellophane bag holding what appeared to be a tiny bag of colored cereal loops. He knew from the work they'd been doing down in Mexico and other places, that this was not candy, not cereal, but drugs. His daughter had drugs in her candy bag!

"Ophelia? Where did you get this?" He held up the bag.

"There were some kids running down the hallway last night, and one of them dropped it. I asked him if he wanted it back, and he didn't hear me. So I just kept it."

"Have you taken any of these?"

"No."

"Well, these are not cereal or candies. These are very harmful. Who were the kids that you saw with these bags, and did you see if they had any more?"

Ophelia got pensive and then added, "The boy who dropped it has red hair. But they didn't speak English and I don't know where they are."

"How many of them were there?"

"Five or six of them—all boys. But the one who dropped it, he had really curly red hair."

"So would you recognize him if you saw him again?"

"I think so. But I don't want to get him in trouble. What if it wasn't his? What if I made a mistake?"

"Did you steal it?"

"No, Daddy, I wouldn't do that."

Carrie Ann inserted herself into the conversation. "I saw what happened, and Ophelia's right. They dropped it. I don't remember the red-haired boy, but I've seen the boys around. They hang out in the video rooms, and they were at the teen dance, I think. We walked past it last night if you remember."

"Yes, I remember that. They go to the teen parties. They're not young men but teenagers?"

"They look like high school to me. I don't know. But I'll tell you if I see them again." Carrie Ann was satisfied, but Mark knew he had to alert the medical director, as well as Teseo about this new development. And he needed to find Sophia to let her know as well.

"Carrie Ann, do you have anything like this in your bag?"

She looked down at her lap. "I finished mine."

Mark's stomach lurched. "But you didn't eat anything like this, did you?"

"No, I don't like those anyway."

"Just so you know, these are not candy. You wouldn't like them. And they can kill you. And if those boys are carrying this on the ship, there are kids who are in danger here. We have to do something about it."

Ophelia began to cry.

Mark grabbed her and gave her a hug, smoothing her hair and whispering to the top of her head. "It's okay, sweetheart. You didn't do anything wrong. I'm just glad I found this. God, I would not forgive myself if something like this happened to you. This is very, very dangerous."

"I'm scared. Do you think those boys would hurt me if they found out I told on them?"

Mark thought about it and decided to lie. "Oh no, they aren't going to know it was you and your sister. They don't even know that you picked it up. I wouldn't worry about it. But if we don't tell somebody, if someone else picks it up and eats it, it could be very bad. And we're going to stop that from happening."

"MARK, I'M GLAD you brought this to my attention," said Teseo. "We've received warnings, but you're the first person who found these."

"Just a lucky break she didn't ingest any of these."

"Indeed. I'll call the office. We'll have to find these kids. It's good that your girls will be able to recognize them. The fact that they're not English speakers doesn't do us much good, but the red hair? That will help us out."

"Do you think these kids are selling this stuff or using it?" Mark asked.

"Doesn't matter, Mark. It's illegal as hell. And depending on what port of call we come into, different countries have a very different way of handling this. Like, you don't want to have any kind of drugs on you in Morocco, even though they openly smoke hashish. Any kind of pills or other drugs? It can be a prison sentence for kids who are way underage. They have a big problem with that. I'm going to have to find their parents and figure out what circle they're traveling in. But we're going to isolate them and get them off the ship."

"Thank you. Sorry about this, but just thought you should know."

"Oh, absolutely. This is just like what I told you the other night. We never used to have things like this happen, and now, it's hard to separate the good people from the bad people, if you know what I mean. Sometimes the kids on these cruises are left to run around on their own in packs, and they do get into trouble. On one of the ships, one of my captains caught them setting fire to one of the lifeboats on deck seven. I can't imagine kids who would think it's okay to be that destructive or violent. Melted the whole thing, ruining it. And it was a black mark against the company."

"Well, you let me know if we need to do anything else."

They were due to come to port that evening, docking at a private cruise ship island off the coast of Italy, and the next day there were several shore excursions people had signed up for. Sophia and Mark hadn't decided to do that and were going to rent a car or just stay at the beach all day. They weren't interested in taking a tour of anything.

As the sun was setting, he headed back towards his cabin. Behind him, he heard laughter and spotted a group of teens laughing, kicking a beer bottle around the deck as if playing soccer, until it finally broke, and then the kids chucked it overboard.

"Hey! You guys stop that," Mark shouted. "That's glass. People walk around here barefoot all the time. Are you idiots?"

Two of the boys mounted a very lackluster "I'm sorry" chorus. They were not interested in receiving any of Mark's correction. He halfway expected to see the red-haired boy in the middle of them. They spoke English, but their native tongue was Italian.

The boys drifted off around the corner while Mark was looking for a waiter to get something to clean up the glass.

Dinner was seated, and Mark was starved. They were sharing a table with four other people, two couples. Since it was the habit of the cruise line to place people at tables who shared a common language, he thought that he'd probably be seated with Americans.

As Mark's family sat down, the couple from California joined them, as well as another couple from New York. Introductions were made, and Mr. Brandon made a pitch to Mark about investing in his winery.

"You know, I've been thinking about what you said about the wineries, the ones your friends have?"

"Frog Haven, you mean?"

"Yes. You know, we do investment pools with our winery where you can buy a share, and then you get a percentage of the vintage for the year. We sell off the others to our distributors, and you get a share of the profits in that. It's actually a very nice arrangement, because you get good quality wine for a decent price, and you're encouraged to share the wine with other people because it can make you additional money as well if they also buy in. I'm not sure what kind of discretionary funds you have, but we even take small denominations as investors. You should think about that," Brandon said.

Mark wasn't interested in the slightest, keeping what little cash they had left over for the possible move to a larger house someday soon and for the girls' education. But he thanked the gentleman. The missus was adorned with expensive jewelry, large diamond rings, and gold dangle bracelets banded several inches up from her wrist toward her elbow. She was heavyset but, with her rosy complexion and extra makeup, was far more attractive than he had noticed her the night before.

The dinner came as usual, in seven courses and the girls got fidgety. Mark and Sophia dismissed themselves early, so the rest of the group could enjoy their meal. Dominica was fussy and running a small fever.

While Sophia put her to bed, Mark read a story to Carrie Ann and Ophelia until they both fell asleep.

"Are they all done?" Sophia whispered.

"Yes, ma'am."

"What is Captain Dominichello going to do about this? Have you heard anything more?"

"No. But I was thinking of walking around and seeing if I could maybe locate these kids on my own. I studied the dining hall tonight to see if I could find anybody but didn't see anyone that matched their description."

"Oh, so you did that too, huh? So did I."

"You know it's going to fester until we find them. I'm just surprised that they're so blatant about bringing drugs onboard. And where the hell are their parents? I didn't realize this type of thing could even happen on a ship like this. I mean I think they checked the bags for weapons and things. But I'm not sure how they got these drugs on board."

"Well, maybe it was a staff person who brought it on board, or maybe they brought it on their person instead of in the luggage. You know kids who want to do drugs, they'll find it anywhere. And if they have money and their parents are off doing whatever else they're doing, they'll get in trouble. I feel sorry for them, though. Very dangerous."

"You know, I think I will walk around and see if I can find a couple of the hangouts and just look into it a bit. You okay with that?"

"Absolutely. You go do that. I'm going to turn in early. I know tomorrow we're going to have a busy day, so I'll just get the rest. Don't be late, though. No gambling, Mark. And stay away from the Brandons."

"No way am I going to involve them."

Mark changed his clothes, donning a pair of khakis, flip-flops, and a long-sleeved T-shirt. He wore a baseball cap and his aviators, even though it was nearly dark, but he thought it would make a good disguise in case he was spotted. He didn't want to trigger anybody's attention.

He walked down the promenade, poking his head into the different stores, especially the candy store and a couple of the shops that catered to people buying electronic devices, movies, and music.

Sounds of the ship slowing down were followed by the motors complete shut off. One quick glance outside, and he determined that they were already in port, tied up for the next day's excursions.

Several of the bars were going to close early, and there was a two-story brightly colored dance and party room for teens that had a billiard table, mirrored dance floor, and brightly painted murals on the walls. There were roughly twenty kids in there, boys and girls, but again, Mark didn't see any teenagers who looked like they were from the group he saw or the boys Ophelia saw.

He turned a corner and almost ran into a freckle-faced kid with bright red hair who was about a foot shorter than he was. There was no question in Mark's mind that this was the kid who dropped the drugs.

"Hey, I want to talk to you."

The boy, with several others behind him, pushed Mark so hard that he fell on his rear while they took off running, eventually breaking through double doors to the outside balcony. Mark scrambled to get back on his feet and followed the series of noises he heard at the end of the hallway. A door opened, music blared, and then it stopped when the door slammed shut. They had run down the outside balcony and returned to the interior of the ship, somewhere near the theater. He ran after them, hoping to catch glimpse of exactly where they wound up. But he had no luck. There were no teens to be found anywhere in this vicinity.

He walked back out through the double doors, scanning both directions of the balcony, traveling down the line of bright orange rescue boats tethered to the sides on this floor. He even peered inside several of the windows to see if the kids might be hiding inside the boats. But he found nothing.

One by one, he examined underneath the boats inside and down toward the railing which faced the sea, not the port side. He was leaning over the balcony after hearing sounds of voices, trying to get a glimpse, when suddenly someone came up behind him and pushed him over the edge into the water.

He took a hard fall in the water, not expecting to be tossed, and shouted for help. He wasn't worried about being able to tread water, but he was concerned with the equipment on the ship and the temperature of the water at nighttime. A large doorway was slid open as several of the crew who were washing windows on the lower two decks noticed his fall and quickly came to his aid, tossing him a lifebuoy and dragging him up into the hull of the ship.

"What happened?" asked an older gentleman in a white painter's overalls. He spoke broken English with a heavy Russian accent.

"Somebody pushed me over the railing. I think some kids did it."

"Kids?" the man asked.

"I was following some teenagers. Perhaps you know, the captain has found drugs on board ship. I'm not sure the word has got out yet, but there are some kids apparently who have drugs."

"Here, you take this, and you should get back to your cabin, but are you okay? Do you want to be seen by the doctor?"

He handed him a warm blanket that had just come out of the dryer. It felt heavenly.

"Is your ship's physician here right now?" Mark asked.

"He is. Why don't you come this way?"

The man and two of his helpers accompanied Mark as two others closed the door and wiped up the excess water from Mark's re-entry. He knew he was going to have to report this as well to Captain Dominichello. He remembered the comment one of his teammates had made before he left, and he remembered vowing there was going to be no way he'd be bobbing in the water.

Well, cross that one off the bucket list, he thought.

The ship's doctor and medic approached him and did a cursory check of his vitals.

"Did you hit the side of the ship on the way down? Does anything feel bruised or cut?"

"No. I'm fine. Really."

"You know, the sides of these ships are loaded with chains and hooks and all kinds of things. I have seen some awful cuts, and we have crew that fall all the time. When you get back to your cabin, if you notice something, please let us know."

The doctor looked up at the overalled gentleman who helped Mark. "Damien? You will make an incident report of this?"

Damien nodded agreement. "Si si, I will make sure it's done within the hour."

"You bring it to me, and I'm going to take it to Teseo."

"Okay, fine, Doctor."

Damien left the group, and Mark asked if he could bring the blanket with him to his cabin.

"Oh, sure. Give it to your porter tonight or tomorrow when you're done. Now let me ask you this, did you see whoever pushed you?" the doctor questioned.

"I did not. I didn't hear a thing. I was chasing the boys, so perhaps it was somebody from their group. There were four of them. But no, I didn't see or hear anybody."

"Well, son, you're very lucky. You go back. I'll make sure Captain Dominichello knows about this, and here…" The doctor handed him an injury form in triplicate. "I want you to fill this out and have it ready for the captain. Can you do that?"

"I will. What about these kids?" Mark asked.

"Let's get the incident registered first, and then we'll see what the captain wants to do about searching the ship for them. It sounds like we have a problem. In my experience, it's never a good idea to sleep on a problem. There's going to be a few of us working all night long to try to figure this out. Thank you for bringing it to our attention. And I am so sorry this occurred."

CHAPTER 8

S OPHIA HEARD MARK'S voice outside the cabin door, engaging in heated conversation with their cabin steward. She was sitting in bed, exhausted from the last hour and a half. Domenica had woken up screaming with a higher fever than she'd had earlier in the day and her gargantuan diaper filled to overflowing all over the cradle and bedsheets, including her blanket. After a full change and bath, she was safely asleep again, but not before she woke up her two older sisters. As soon as Domenica had dozed off, Sophia jumped in the shower and changed her nightie as well.

Mark was back later than he told her he would be.

The cabin door opened. Sophia was shocked to find her husband standing in front of her with a blanket draped around him, a dripping wet blanket. She examined the growing puddle at his feet. He had an unpleasant expression on his face.

"Whatever the hell—"

Mark interrupted her. "Let's just say it's been a bad evening." He strained to step out of his khaki pants, which stubbornly clung to him. He was barefoot. Next, he slipped off his shirt and reached to take off his baseball cap and glasses, but then swore.

"Goddammit, I left them."

"You left them? What do you mean?"

"It's a long story, but let me get clean and dry first, okay?"

Naked, he carefully opened the cabin door and tossed the blanket into the hallway where it was retrieved by their steward. After further conversation, Mark using the door as a privacy shield, she realized that her husband had arranged for their steward to stand by to take the blanket away.

"Did you get thrown in the pool, Mark?"

"No, I got thrown in the sea." He gave her that blank stare, waiting for her to get the significance of what he just told her. "Somebody threw me overboard."

At first, she'd thought it was a joke, but then realized he wasn't kidding. "Overboard? As in over the railing? Where?"

"Deck 12, at least that's where I started from. I wound up coming in through one of the cargo bays down at level one. I had some help getting out."

"Did you get in a fight?"

Exasperated, he threw his hands down at his naked sides, looking every bit the drowned rat. Whispering, he grumbled, "Sophia, for Christ's sakes. No, I didn't get in a fight. I don't do that anymore. Somebody just threw me overboard."

"But why? What did you do?"

"You think because I got thrown overboard that I must have done something to cause this? Are you fucking kidding me?"

His voice had carried, and the timbre was urgent, soaring into higher decibels, which caused Carrie Ann to stir.

"Please, don't wake the kids," she whispered, adding a glare.

Mark shrugged his shoulders, kicked his khakis and shirt into the bathroom, and pulled the shower door closed behind him.

Sophia carefully got up, confronting him as he turned on the water. "So where are your Aviators and your Team 3 cap? I thought you were going incognito tonight?"

"Apparently it didn't work, Sophia. Somebody must have seen through the disguise."

"I just don't understand this, I mean, people have to have a reason to throw someone overboard—"

"Well, maybe it has to do with the drugs I discovered, or I don't know maybe somebody just got drunk and felt like it," Mark sputtered through the water.

"Where are your flip-flops then? You walked all the way down the hallway and through the promenade dressed like that? In a wet blanket?

Barefoot?"

"Last I saw, my flip-flops were headed to North Africa in the current. Thank God we had already docked or, who knows, you might still be looking for your husband."

"Well, I can see you're in no mood—"

"You think?" Mark again stared at her, shampoo running down his forehead into his eyes. He brushed the soap clear and spat.

Something about the whole situation was becoming comical, but Sophia didn't dare show it. She'd let him have the next say.

"I'm just as surprised as you are. And no, I didn't see who did it. I wish the hell I did, but I have some ideas. Now if you don't mind, I'd like to take my shower and get myself right, and if you could bring me my pajama bottoms, I promise when I get dry and get clean, I will come out and sit and talk to you in the bedroom, okay?"

"Fair enough."

She searched through the small dresser next to Mark's side of the bed and retrieved his red, white, and blue drawstring cotton pajama bottoms. She hesitated but decided not to bring him his T-shirt. That was for her own benefit. Perhaps she would be able to find some way to sweeten him up a bit. But he was extremely angry and probably felt ridiculous.

She folded the pajama bottoms and left them on the toilet seat. She also added an extra towel from the bedroom and retrieved his wet clothes after wringing them in the sink.

Tiptoeing through the living room, she exited the sliding glass door from their room and placed his khakis and T-shirt over the railing. They weren't supposed to do this, but she thought under the circumstances she might be forgiven.

Sounds of the little village where they would be spending some time tomorrow drifted across the dark water on the wings of a gentle breeze. She heard music, drums, and laughter. All along the Mediterranean coast, it was a continual party, starting at the eastern coast of Italy around the boot and winding up on the coast of Spain at Mallorca. Things changed drastically once the landscape turned to North Africa. But the whole Mediterranean coast was filled with yachts and jetsetters staying in all the countries in between—socializing, gambling, and living the life of the rich and famous. It was the Europeans' playground par excellence.

The door opened behind her, and Mark, smelling wonderful, stepped out onto the balcony, placing his towel over the railing and then sitting next to her on the plastic deck chair.

"At last. I've never had this happen to me before. If some of the team guys were on board, I'd accuse them. But no way was this a prank. I think it was those damn kids."

"So you found them?"

"Yup. Ran right into the carrot top. And he's one ugly little kid. Mean too. He took off as soon as we connected, and I tried to keep up, but the deck was wet, and there were people out there, a lot of chairs and kids and stuff to avoid. I didn't quite make it. He disappeared into the interior. I searched the theater and several other places, including a couple of hangouts, but no luck. I decided to wait outside and considered that maybe he'd show his face again. He was with a group of several other kids. They're about 13, 15, something like that."

"Do you think one of his buddies came to get him or went after you to defend him?"

"I have no idea. I wouldn't have thought that a kid could do that to me because I hung on. But I twisted around to see if I could make heads or tails of who was there, and I didn't see a thing. No shouts, no language, no nothing. They just picked me up by the shins and tossed me right over like yesterday's meal. Fucking idiot. I'm just lucky I didn't scrape my back or arms or legs on some of those God-awful hooks that are embedded in the hull. You know, the ones they use for tying things off and hoisting?"

"Yeah, it's a regular workstation there by the cargo door. On both sides. They winch a lot of things through there, depending on the port they're at. You were lucky somebody saw you."

"Well, the ship had stopped. I heard the engines stop before I got tossed. It was still moving very slightly until it hit the edge. That kind of threw off my balance, and then boom I was gone."

"Lucky thing they didn't get you on the port side. That might have proved to be fatal."

"You can say that again. Ouch. Well, I wasn't on that side, so I guess if I had, it would be a different story, wouldn't it?"

"Did you report this to Teseo?"

"No, I've got a goddamn form I have to fill out and submit to him. He said they were going to be doing an investigation all night long to see if they could locate the kids. They won't get away with it."

"You said he? One of the engineers or crew hands?"

"Yes. A Russian guy helps in the engine room—he's an engineer. I've got the paperwork; I'll fill it out and then have our steward take it up to the bridge."

Sophia was concerned at the obvious attack on her husband. She was grateful he hadn't been with the girls, and she was also grateful that she wasn't the one targeted.

The cruise, only being two days now, was already turning into quite an adventure, on the negative side.

"So how was your evening?" Mark asked, finally.

"You don't want to know. Domenica woke up with a fever, screaming her head off, wet all the way through every layer she had, almost soaking the mattress. I had to rip everything off and dump it in the hallway while Corky gave us some cleaning wipes and two extra sets of linens for her crib. I gave her a small bath in our bathroom, and she was happy. After that, her temperature reduced slightly, and I gave her cough syrup so she could sleep and reduce the fever. She went right to bed. Out like a light. But then Carrie Ann and Ophelia, they were moaning, awake and rather upset with their little sister. I let them watch about a half an hour TV, and then Ophelia had already fallen asleep. Carrie Ann had to be convinced, but they went down. No big deal. I do it all the time at home, but we have a larger house."

"Yep, much easier in a small place to keep everybody controlled. I guess I should thank our lucky stars for such a tiny house."

"Mark, it'll change. You'll see. Maybe this is a signal that we should be searching our other options. I have lots of help with the wives, but three kids when you're gone for weeks at a time, I'm not happy with that. But we'll talk about it when we get home. Right now, I'm exhausted and glad to have you back. I need to get some sleep."

"Well, that dashes the second plan I had for this evening," he said.

Sophia smiled. "Hold on there, sailor, not entirely. I can be convinced. Don't give up on me yet."

Mark leaned over and planted a deep kiss on her lips. She still tasted the salt water from the sea and the scent of shampoo, which still over-powered the nice cologne she'd bought him today.

Mark kissed her again. "I've only just begun, sweetheart."

CHAPTER 9

MARK GRABBED SOME fruit, a bagel, and cream cheese then packed up some bananas and apples and several yogurts for the girls, who weren't hungry yet. He gathered his little brood together, and they were one of the first groups to line up going through the crew bypass of the metal detector and down the gangway to the pier.

"One of the things you got to remember on these cruises is you want to be one of the first ones off the ship," Sophia said.

"Why is that?"

"The vendors and hucksters aren't quite ready yet, still drinking their coffee and chewing the fat with their colleagues. They get kind of geared up after a few minutes when the bulk of the population exits. That's when it's like threading a gauntlet. They're going to leave us alone. Besides, we're wearing our badges, and they don't treat the staff the same as they do the guests."

One of the perks of being a staff member was that they got to use the staff exit, which was much faster than waiting in the long lines for the tourists to line up and be called by grouping. They were staged all over the boat. A line of five buses waited for the offloading passengers.

"You've been on this tour before?" Mark asked.

"No, this is a new island for them. But I'd rather go to a real place, not a company-owned island, if I was doing a tour. This is a beach party today in the Mediterranean, but not a shopping tour especially. They will take them all over the mountain, which is an extinct volcano. It's like the Canaries here. Except it's a little warmer even."

"So you *have* been here."

"No, I read about it. I had no interest in doing any of the bus groups. Besides I think the girls would get carsick."

Mark was carrying Domenica in the baby pack on his front side, her legs bouncing as she pointed and giggled and had a good time looking at all the colors of the island. Mark discovered she liked music as well. The older girls encouraged her and had taught her to dance, which was cute as hell.

"Well, Domenica's liking it. That's a good thing. She doesn't feel warm to me now."

"I think she just had to sweat it off. When she's happy, you know she's not sick."

Mark used his long strides to get past the small contingent of greeters and tour guides trying to sell tickets to unfilled buses. He waved them off carefully and then turned around, realizing that he had forgotten the rest of his family, who were hanging back looking at embroidered tablecloths, something Sophia had been hoping to purchase on this trip. Mark waved to her, and she took the girls by their hands, and all three of them ran to his side.

"Did you get a car?"

"I did even better. I got a driver."

Sophia put her hand up to her forehead to block the sun. "You did not do that. Really?"

"I did."

"In light of everything that's been going on, and you certainly don't know this fellow. I mean, is this wise?" Sophia asked him.

"I think so. Besides, my fanny pack has more than just my wallet in there. I dare the son of a bitch who tries to interfere with our little tour group."

"But Italy's pretty strict on gun control, Mark."

"Listen, we do this for a living, right? I know what I can get away with and what I can't. I have a special badge. You, on the other hand if you carry one, you'll get in trouble. The only difference between you and me, sweetheart, love of my life, mother of my girls—"

He kissed her gently.

"Only difference is I don't care what the fuck they do to me. And you do."

"Somebody has to take care of the kids."

Pierre, their driver, had a handlebar mustache and wore white pants with a striped navy-and-white long sleeve T-shirt, and a beret. Mark was sickened with his attire when he announced himself and asked him rather forcefully if he could please remove his beret.

First order of business was replacing the hat that Mark lost in the water. This involved the girls, and they had a delightful time showing him tie-dye reggae hats with dreadlocks sprouting from the brim or hats with naked women or dumb sayings like 'life is just a beach' on them. Finally, with Sophia's help, they chose a navy-blue hat with an anchor on the front, and that was damn close to something he would have bought for himself.

Next, he had to get a new pair of Aviators but, when he discovered the prices, chose a cheap pair instead. He could get one when they had one of the sales on board the ship later; he wasn't going to pay two hundred dollars plus for a knockoff.

They had burned up the first forty-five minutes of Pierre's time, so Mark asked him if he could take them to a nice, secluded beach area where they could just lay out their towels and wade in the water if it wasn't too choppy.

"Oui, oui. There are many such places. Do you want to snorkel?"

Mark almost didn't answer him, because it suddenly occurred to him that being dressed as a Frenchman, with a name like Pierre but working in Italy was such a mismatch. He wondered why he didn't notice it before. He had to ask him.

"No snorkel today. But say, Pierre, I assume you're French?"

"Mais oui. I live here now. My wife is an Italian citizen, so we live here close to her family."

"Oh, I see. That completely explains it. You live on the island?"

"No, it is not that type of an island, resources are very limited. I live in Capri. You've heard of it, the place for lovers?"

"Oh, yes, we've both been there," Sophia said. "Lovely place. I'd like to do that too, but I'm not sure how much time we're going to have."

"I don't believe your ship has more than three or four hours there. I could meet you at port and drive you up over the mountain and back again. But that's about it. No shopping, just a sight-seeing trip, and it's long and windy."

"Yes, I know. I think you'll have to save it for another time. But if we manage to get a sitter, maybe Mark and I will do that." She wiggled her eyebrows at her husband, who matched the expression.

"Well then, my dear, take my card. You can call me from your cell phone tonight and let me know if it would work out. I'm sure they have someone who could babysit for a few hours for you. I know lots of cute little restaurants and bars that you would just love. Things have changed quite a bit since COVID. We have new people here. We have a lot of the old places shut down and rebuilt. And we had several Mediterranean storms about two years ago that damaged a lot of the coastline. But all the favorite places are still there, and of course, the scenery, the drive, is beautiful."

"Absolutely. The most beautiful scenery I've ever seen in my life," said Sophia.

She saw that Mark had made a note of it, and before she could take Pierre's card, he grabbed it from his fingers and placed it in his pocket.

"We'll see if we can do something about that later on. Thanks, Pierre. Now, where are we going to?"

"On the other side, on the shoreside of the island, you can look across the inlet and see the mainland of Italy. It's a most beautiful location, and they have a resort there that caters to American tourists and other celebrities, and they've imported a sand beach. The best beaches, of course, are on this side, but you have no view."

Mark pointed to the bright blue sky and the turquoise horizon of the Mediterranean. "I'd say that's a pretty damn good view, wouldn't you?"

"Indeed. But if you want that view, you can go to Florida. You can go to Brazil, you can go to a beach in Southern California or New Jersey. This beach has beautiful sugar white sand just like what you Americans have in Florida, and you can see all the terracotta villages that are stair-stepped on the mainland. You can see the vineyards in this very famous agricultural region."

As promised, the views were outstanding, and several times, Sophia asked him to slow down so that the girls, who were seated lower than she and Mark were, wouldn't begin getting carsick. At the very top of the extinct volcano, there was a coffee shop, and they ate their apples and yogurt and picked up sandwiches in the shop overlooking the beautiful blue waters of the Mediterranean as well as the villages beyond. Their ship, of course, was a striking pure white crystal shard floating on that blue pond. A sight that Sophia would never grow tired of viewing.

"I can't believe we actually did this, Mark. And it's not going to break the bank," she said, leaning against him.

"Ten years, my dear. Can you believe it? Ten years and look at these little angels. I think I'm the luckiest man alive."

Sophia surveyed the expansive view from on high. "Odds are, now that we've gotten all the excitement out of the way, all we'll have to do is just sit back and enjoy our Christmas cruise. I think we should let Teseo and the others go after those kids. We've got a family to entertain, and that's way more important. After all, Christmas is for children. If I could, I'd love all of them all over the world, and I'd forgive the bad ones."

Mark was impressed with her huge heart.

Sophia continued. "I just want to get back to our cabin, take a nice long shower in the bigger bathroom, wash my hair, and get ready for a wonderful dinner in the dining room with my Prince Charming and my three little angels. I'm ready for a perfect night. How about you?"

"We'll eat ice cream for dessert," Mark whispered in her ear, careful not to let the girls know. "Drink hot chocolate and watch the stars show up. Then we'll go to the theater for the fairy dust show. After, my love, we're going to dream all night about what the next ten years is going to be about."

She kissed him as they headed back to the car.

"All the other stuff is just crap, anyway," she ended.

CHAPTER 10

SOPHIA AND THE girls came early to the dinner table, as Mark was having a short meeting with Teseo and some of his senior staff at the bridge. The Cloptons, the couple from New York, were the next to arrive, followed by the Brandons about ten minutes later.

Mrs. Brandon gushed over how nice the girls looked tonight. "Is it a special occasion of some kind?"

"Well, this whole cruise is special for us since it's coming up on our ten-year anniversary. We are going to be redoing our marriage vows while we're here, but I don't know. Today, I just felt like dressing up extra fancy. And the girls are going to love the show tonight at the theater."

"Oh? You know, Kevin and I did not see the first show. Was it good?"

"Yes, they have a very talented group. We enjoyed the first one. It was a rock and roll, fifties type of dance, and the girls were glued to it, even went up on stage afterwards. Usually, they hire very good talent here."

Mr. and Mrs. Clopton vowed that they'd try to take in a show at least once. "But we kind of enjoy the casino. When we're at sea, that's pretty much where you'll find us," Mrs. Brandon laughed.

"And the drinks are free," Mr. Brandon added.

"I've got the girls, and they can't go in the casino, so we do other things. But not to worry, I'm not a gambler. Neither is Mark."

They were asked for their orders, the girls ordering everything off the children's menu, plus desserts from the adult list. They'd caught on very early that, if they didn't like something, they just didn't have to eat it and could order something else. It was an arrangement Sophia thought was going to greatly impact their dinners at home.

"Did you hear the news?"

Mrs. Clopton was eager to spill something. Sophia was guarded, hoping there wasn't anything about Mark that was going to be discussed.

"No, I'm not sure. What are you talking about?"

"Well, it seems someone has hacked into some of the passengers' accounts here onboard, and all kinds of people are finding charges to their accounts that they didn't authorize. If you ask me, it's those darn teenagers. And I think next time we take a cruise, I'm going to request that it be either a full family cruise or adults only," her tablemate said.

Sophia knew that Mrs. Clopton's radar was correct.

"Do you know who's doing it? I understand there are a bunch of rowdy kids on here, not being looked after," Sophia offered.

Mr. Clopton scrunched up his nose. "They're awful. Practically knocked us over last night. They were running all around the outside of the ship. They came barreling into the theater, I was told, and nearly interrupted the show. I just don't understand what parent would let their child do crazy things. It's dangerous. It's dangerous for the rest of us."

"Well, the good news is the captain of the ship is a friend of ours, from past cruises and from the time when I used to work for this company full time. That's how Mark and I met. But he's aware of certain individuals who are causing some problems, so I don't think it'll be very long before they'll find out who these kids are, but I don't understand how they would get credit card information and room charge information."

Mr. and Mrs. Brandon were frowning but didn't have much to say. Finally, Mr. Brandon asked his wife if perhaps she should check their balance.

Sophia agreed. "Yeah, I'm going to have Mark do the same thing. When did you hear about this?"

"Everybody was talking about it in the library. And on the buses when we took the tour of the island! Oh my gosh, I think out of the thirty or so on that bus, there must have been ten couples who had unauthorized charges on their account. They had to wait a long time before they could get somebody in customer service to help them, and they promised it would get straightened out in the next day or so."

Mr. Clopton began, "What kind of an operation is this that allows these types of things to happen?"

"The only problem I've ever had with this cruise is—years ago on one of my trips—I used a brand-new credit card. I hadn't called and told the credit card company that I was going to be traveling overseas, but I had a huge balance that was available to use, and I planned on maximizing it during the voyage. Well, I used it one time, and then the next time my card was shut down. I had a difficult time getting through to anybody in the US to get it straightened out, and I wound up having to borrow from the ship. It was most embarrassing. Now I understand to let them know in advance."

"You wonder if even that is safe," added Mrs. Brandon.

"Well, friends of ours back in New Jersey said that this is one of the safest cruise lines you could be on. And they have a very good track record as far as illnesses and cleanliness. The food's great." Mrs. Clopton shrugged. "I guess they can't monitor everything. Life is just so complicated these days," she added.

"I agree, the staff and food and service, it's first rate," said Mrs. Brandon.

Just then, Sophia saw Mark sashaying attractively through the dining room, stopping conversations wherever he walked past a table. He smiled and nodded to those who acknowledged him for being one of the dance instructors. He gave Sophia a peck on the cheek before he sat down next to her.

"Everything okay?" she was curious to know.

Mark surveyed the table. He lowered his voice to make it difficult to hear. "Maybe we could talk about it later, but we got problems. Don't say anything yet."

Sophia's dream of a quiet evening of shows, fun, good food, and better conversation were in jeopardy.

"Should we leave?" she asked him, alerted to what might be happening.

"No, no. We're good for now. Not here, sweetheart. But here, we're fine."

Mrs. Clopton addressed him. "Mark, we were just talking about how some of the passengers seem to have been charged fraudulently on their cabin tab."

"It could just be an inexperienced clerk at the desk," Mrs. Brandon disagreed. "We don't want to spread rumors, do we?" Then she peered at Mark. "You don't think the captain suspects anything like that, do you? Weren't you just talking to him?"

Mark studied her, searched the group again, glanced over the tops of the girls, who were drawing on the menus provided them, and then gave a worried look to Sophia.

"Whoa, well, I wasn't sure that information was going around. Captain Teseo is a friend of ours. As a friend, if I see something I think is wrong, I'm going to tell him. I think I need to keep our conversation private, ladies."

Sophia was confused, but Mrs. Clopton wasn't giving up.

"But you will mention this to the captain, won't you? Or I will."

Her attitude was huffy. Sophia figured she didn't like having her gossip skills curtailed.

"No worries there."

"They think it's a bunch of teens," added Mrs. Brandon.

"Yes, I understand," Mark answered. "I did talk to him about them. He's doing everything he can. Captain Teseo must maneuver his way around the different police jurisdictions as we go from port to port. But he is looking into a couple of things I mentioned. Others have as well. No need to panic or go spreading rumors, like Mrs. Brandon said. Let's get the facts first."

Sophia felt a bit frosty with the coverup Mark was using but gave him the benefit of the doubt. She would be peppering him with questions when they returned to their cabin after the shows unless that was now put on hold. She didn't like that they didn't have their own table to themselves.

Mark staved off her questions, which drew Sophia's ire even further. Soon, however, she got lost in the performances and how the girls reacted to them. Even little Domenica, in her father's arms, was fascinated with the show and bounced her upper body in rhythm to the beat of the music.

They headed down the glass elevators to the Promenade for some ice cream and to peruse the shops. Sophia spotted a group of teen boys. Included in that group was a red-haired boy who matched the description of the one both Mark and her girls had seen.

"Is that him?" she asked Mark, pointing.

"I believe so. You stay near the candy store. I'll try to be right back."

When the elevator stopped, Mark took off after the boy and was soon lost in the crowd.

Sophia purchased peppermint hot chocolate since both the girls were done with candy since so much was made of the drugs in Ophelia's bag.

"I don't think I even like candy anymore," she mumbled, glumly.

"Where has Daddy gone?" asked Carrie Ann.

"You know he's trying to find that red-haired boy, sweetheart. Come on, let's get you seated, and we'll wait for him to return."

After over a half hour waiting, Sophia's nerves were beginning to fray. Crowds of laughing party-going passengers, mostly without children, passed her by. Couples dressed in their eveningwear held hands. On an evening where she'd intended to have an easy-going time, her insides were feeling stretched and sad. Even morose.

Come on, Mark.

She knew she was going to have to have that talk. Of course, he was always there to protect the innocent, but this was becoming ridiculous. The burden of most of the entertainment for the girls was left with her while he was chasing kids like a Boy Scout. She wanted to be positive and knew his good and honorable spirit would always win out, that commitment had to also include his own family. It was not okay that they should be abandoned.

Maybe for Mark, putting himself at risk was something he wasn't afraid of and would do anytime. But for Sophia and the family, who were here to celebrate, not right the wrongs of the world, him risking his life or theirs seemed like an ill-conceived mission. Was he going to be like this the rest of their marriage together as they tried to do the right thing for the girls? Was it right risking their safety as well?

As the girls began to stir, it was difficult to contain them. Sophia was tiring and felt exposed, vulnerable without Mark around to watch over and help. She made the decision to return to the cabin. She knew Mark would understand if he returned and found they weren't still at the shop.

She didn't want to spook the two older girls, so she kept the conversation light and tried to get them interested in tee shirts, trinkets, and toys, which Domenica was hard to extract from, and the movie store where passengers could rent DVDs.

Domenica was getting heavy and needed a change. She ushered her brood into a lavatory and let the girls use two of the stalls for privacy. The toddler's dress was wet. Her tights were smeared with diaper detritus, which she attempted to wipe clean. The girls were babbling on in the stalls, sharing toilet paper and talking about the show.

With Domenica cleaned, she hoisted her up onto her hip to take everyone back to the room. But instead of two locked bathroom stall doors, both were open, ajar, and there was no sign of the girls anywhere.

In panic, she called out. "Carrie Ann? Ophelia? Where are you?"

There was no answer.

"Girls! Come on, don't hide on me. Where are you?"

Still, there was no answer.

She checked the two other stalls. The girls were no longer in the bathroom!

Sophia darted out into the lobby area at the end of the Promenade, searching right and left.

"Carrie Ann, Ophelia? Where are you girls?" She tried it again, this time so loud, half the lobby area turned.

Several clerks behind the information desk looked in her direction.

"Please! Help me find my girls!"

Immediately, one of the Korean crew members ran over to her.

"You have a problem, madam?"

"Yes, yes. My girls. They were in the bathroom with me, and now they're missing. Oh my God! Help me find them! Please, please help me!"

Several passengers approached, suggesting they could help, and she tried to describe the girls but hadn't brought her regular purse with all her photos in them.

"My husband. Can you put out an announcement, have him paged?"

"Yes, yes," the clerk answered. "Let me contact the Assistant Tour Director. I'll be just one moment." She ran, disappearing into a door behind the long counter.

The crowd started to surround her, several people asking questions all at once. Domenica became concerned and then started to wail, screaming at the top of her lungs, and was inconsolable. Sophia couldn't hear any of the comments.

As Domenica's tears began to flow, Sophia's did as well. She'd been searching every face she could see, looking for someone who might help, who might know, who might be talking to her girls. Did they wander off or were they—?

"Sophia!"

The sound of Mark's voice instantly brought a combination of relief and anger. She turned on her heels, doing an about-face, and beheld her husband's worried expression.

"Mark, they're gone!" she shouted as he ran toward her.

She'd barely noticed Ophelia and Carrie Ann holding hands with their dad, trying to keep up with him. Again, anger flared. Not knowing who to blame for all the terrible things she'd thought about, she chose to unload on Mark.

"Where have you been? Why didn't you tell me you took the girls? I've been worried sick about this. This is so not okay."

But Domenica was still crying then reaching for her dad. Sophia realized she was scaring the baby. Pushing Domenica into his arms, she grabbed her girls, knelt, and hugged them.

"Mommy loves you so much! But don't do this ever again. This was very, very bad."

"But we were just waiting outside the bathroom, and we saw Daddy!" Carrie Ann protested.

"Do you know what I thought had happened? I thought you'd been kidnapped!"

"I'm sorry, Mommy," Ophelia said, her lower lip protruding, a single tear running down her cheek. Her breathing was labored, and Sophia saw she was building up to a big cry.

"I'm sorry too. Mommy's sorry." She hugged the girls again and then stood.

Mark was having a hard time calming Domenica down. He didn't look back at her. But he whispered just loud enough so she could hear.

"Come on. We need to get out of here. You're scaring the girls."

Sophia stopped following him to the elevator.

After a deep, cleansing breath and some courage self-talk, she blurted out, "*I'm* the one scaring the girls. Where the hell were you?"

"Trying not to get arrested."

CHAPTER 11

S OPHIA DIDN'T LOOK at him the whole trek back to their cabin. She stripped the girls down and put nighties on them, rechanged Domenica and put her into a onesie. She brought the crib in from the bedroom and set it next to Ophelia and Carrie Ann. The girls sat in their beds, looking back and forth between Mark and Sophia, understanding that everything was on tenterhooks, Mom was mad, and they would eventually get free of all this stuff, but they knew they needed to just wait and behave. Which is exactly what they did.

While Sophia finished putting the girls down, Mark changed into his pajama bottoms. He grabbed a beer from the refrigerator, walked through the sliding glass door, and sat on the balcony outside overlooking the ocean. It had been another tough day, and things weren't the way they should be when he was turning in to bed. So much had to be resolved, he halfway wished that he could just stay up all night and drink. But that had been years and years since that kind of behavior had consumed him. He wished he could forget.

He knew she'd come out and talk to him eventually. He needed to just let her stay busy and take care of her babies.

Sophia wore one of his oversized cotton t-shirts with the Bone Frog logo on it that hit her about the mid-thigh. She silently joined him on the deck, drinking a bottle of mineral water.

"I'm ready to talk whenever you want to," he offered.

"Let me catch my breath. In a couple of minutes."

They sat listening to the waves lap and crash against the sides of the hull. The moist warm air, even at nightfall, was refreshing, not to mention the calm he needed. He so didn't want to have this conversation, but he was going to have it anyhow.

He waited, and then she examined the side of his face. "I'm ready. Go for it."

"I didn't want to make a scene, Sophia, but whatever you're thinking, you need to know that I'm very sorry, and this was beyond my control."

"You're telling me, Mark, that I have to just put up with this? I had all three girls for over an hour waiting for you in the candy shop, which is where you told me to wait. I didn't receive a message from you. You said it'd be just a few minutes and you'd be back. You should have come back and told us or sent somebody to tell us. I was worried sick. And then this whole thing about the girls in the bathroom, I honest to God thought we'd lost them. I thought you took off to go be a Boy Scout and I was stuck trying to do something I couldn't control. That's the long and the short of it. And I am, yes, I am pissed."

"I don't fault you for that, sweetheart. But just hear me out."

"This must be one whopper of an explanation. It is unbelievable."

"It is. I went after the kid—his name is Samuel, by the way. His parents are very well respected and VIP passengers on this cruise. Not that any of his behavior is forgiven, but it's a very delicate situation for Captain Dominichello."

"What you're telling me is it's so important that it was worth risking the lives of your wife and your three daughters? Is that really what you're saying to me? You're right. It is unbelievable."

"Hear me out."

"Mark, come on; give me a break. You're not thinking, sailor."

He felt the anger welling inside of him, but of course, that wasn't really directed at Sophia. It was directed at the situation he found himself in.

"Let me tell you something first that might shed a whole new light on things. There is a possibility tomorrow on Capri I will be arrested and taken to jail. They have lodged a formal complaint."

"Who?"

"His parents. You see, I caught up to that kid. I grabbed him by the collar, and I pressed him against the wall as his friends tried to beat me down. I kicked a couple of them. I asked for help. Of course, everyone went running in all different directions—even his friends took off—and I dragged his ass into the lobby and took him to the information booth. I asked if they could page the captain, but he was unavailable, I was told. I held onto him there. I couldn't let him go, and nobody else wanted to take him. I took him downstairs to the medical bay and left word that the captain could meet me down there."

Mark rubbed his hands together and then took another long sip of his beer.

"Fuck it all. The next thing I know, security is down there. They put handcuffs on me, Sophia. I was constrained in a tiny holding cell just outside the medical bay where the security office is. And they demanded that I released the kid. Next thing I know, the captain and his parents are barreling through the doorway, the missus screaming at the top of her lungs and saying she's going to press charges."

"Charges? For what? He was a suspect in drug selling."

"He did get a little bit of a bloody nose when I forced him up next to the wall, and unfortunately, drawing blood is considered assault. They can press charges. The cruise line will not come to my aid. Captain Dominichello has to wash his hands of it because we're friends, and I have to fall on the mercy of a magistrate on Capri."

"Goddammit, Mark, didn't you see any of this coming?"

"I admit, I acted hastily, and you know he's sixteen. He's doing things, like with the pills, and I explained to the parents. I explained to them that my daughter found the drugs in the hallway after they passed by. They accused *me* of getting my nine-year-old daughter to sell drugs for me, can you believe that?"

She pondered before she answered. Mark had hope she'd understand.

"Certainly, the fact that you are a Navy SEAL, that's going to hold some weight," she answered.

"It certainly will. It also might get me tossed. I might lose my Trident."

She sat back, and from the expression on her face, Mark knew she finally understood what was at stake.

"They are allowed to press charges against you even though you told them about being tossed overboard?"

"They said I got into a bar fight, or I was drunk and fell over. I have no proof, and I don't know who did it, but I did push the kid up against the wall and I did bloody his nose. That little asshole stood there smirking while I was getting reamed by this ridiculous woman."

"Who you're going to have to be very nice to, Mark. So we go see the consulate in Capri. There must be a US consulate on the island."

"There isn't. We'd have to go to the mainland for that. But I can maybe get somebody from the Navy to come in and help get a JAG officer or something. Teseo has the drugs, but I'm not sure he's going to release them. He just wants the whole thing to go away, and he's pretty disgusted with me."

"I can understand that. In a way, you jeopardized his captainship. Or am I getting this wrong?" she asked.

Mark didn't have an answer for that, merely shrugged his shoulders, repeating the you-stupid-son-of-a-bitch self-talk in his head. He realized that he'd allowed his emotions to get the better of him. Because it involved his daughter, because it involved drugs, because he'd been tossed overboard which made him feel ashamed and could have caused him some serious medical issues, because the teenagers were riding roughshod on all the other passengers, picking on the innocents, he felt he was battling in a situation with both hands tied behind his back.

"Mark, they released you, and that's a good thing. What did Dominichello say?"

"He told me to go and stay in my cabin, that we are not to join the group tour of Capri until further notice. I'm under cabin arrest for a while unless I want to spend the night in their jail. I'll stay here with you and the girls, thank you. And then he said we'd have to sort it out in the morning."

Mark was going to elaborate further but thought better of it. Sophia caught onto this and asked him.

"What is it that's going on? I don't understand how you, a Navy SEAL, could be questioned and doubted going up against the parents of a teenager who obviously has been acting up this whole cruise so far. You are a decorated war veteran, still an active-duty SEAL, and you'll never raise children who will behave so despicably like their son. You didn't start this. I don't see why that won't hold credibility for you tomorrow. I just have a hard time thinking that they would let the word of two strangers override your reputation and what you do for a living. And the fact that it put your daughters in danger. Well, what father wouldn't react like that?"

Mark decided it was going to be no use. He was going to have to tell her the rest.

"Well, the complication, Sophia, is Samuel's mother is the daughter of the Secretary of Defense. The *Italian* Secretary of Defense. And her husband is the new ambassador to England. They were headed from Italy to England to start his new post, and taking the cruise was their way to celebrate his new appointment. It's the very beginning of his new career, but she's so well connected there isn't anybody who's going to touch my defense, not from Italy anyway. They're saying the whole family has diplomatic immunity. I'm just hoping Uncle Sam decides I'm good enough to defend me. And frankly, it was a dumb ass move on my part. This whole thing has been horrible. And we haven't even started finding out how the drugs got here and whether they really belonged to this ambassador's kid. But my money says yes."

"I agree with you."

He was encouraged when she took his hand and placed it up to her face, pressing it against her cheek.

"Somehow, sweetheart, we'll get through this. This isn't supposed to happen to us. Something's come off track. We'll find it."

He was relieved yet disappointed he'd let everyone down.

"Sophia, I love you even more now than I did this morning. Thank you for putting aside your anger and listening to me. I'm going to need your support. Thank you so much. I'm going to fight this every way I know how."

"No, Mark. There you're wrong. We're going to fight it. All of us. We're going to do it together."

CHAPTER 12

T HE KNOCK CAME on their cabin door at 7:00 a.m., and two uni-formed officers from Capri stood in the hallway to greet Mark when he answered.

"I'm afraid you're going to have to come with us."

Sophia stood next to him. They had discussed what might happen and was certainly happening right now.

"I'll just get my clothes on, and can I bring some things?" he asked the officers.

"You can bring some toiletries and a change of clothes if you like, sir. However, you will probably not be returning to the ship."

Mark turned to look at Sophia, and she could see he hadn't antici-pated this.

"We are traveling with our three daughters, gentlemen, and I am also employed by the ship. So is Mark, as a dance instructor. We've signed a contract."

"Which is null and void if he's found guilty of manhandling a mi-nor. We have put in an inquiry to your U.S. Navy, and once we are assigned someone, we will let you know. But you have two choices, ma'am. You can stay on the ship with your daughters by yourself, or you can come to Capri with us. He will be housed in the local jail downtown in the city center. You will have to arrange accommodations."

Sophia swallowed hard. She knew Mark was going to suggest that she call Kyle as soon as she was out of earshot of the local security officers, and she couldn't wait to do so.

"Gentlemen, just give us five or ten minutes to get the girls dressed and for us to get dressed as well, and we'll accompany you. I do have luggage—"

"If you want to come with him, you need to leave your luggage behind."

"But—"

"I'm sure the captain will make sure that all your things are collected. Just bring something you can put together in the next five or ten minutes, and then you must come with us. We have a police skiff waiting to take you all to the island. Your arrangements with the cruise line as far as any reimbursement or remuneration is not of our concern. He needs to be held until a determination is made as to whether or not charges are going to be filed."

They woke the girls up gently and got them to put on pants and T-shirts. Sophia packed their day bags and cleaned out the little refrigerator, tossing in all the yogurts, fruits, and healthy snacks that were stored there. Then she packed her own bag and added it to Mark's.

"Make sure you bring some reading material. We're probably going to wait long hours until we get answers," Mark said.

"Once we get you situated, I'm going to give Kyle a call, or is there someone else you need me to call instead?" she asked him.

"No. Tell him I'm going to call him as well, and I'm assuming we'll get the name of an officer in charge here. Kyle's going to have to give that to the Navy. It sounds like they haven't pressed charges yet, but it's imminent."

With several hundred passengers watching the police vehicle leave the crew bay, heading for the island, their family among the four other uniformed officers, Sophia was glad she couldn't recognize anybody or see their expressions.

"HEY, SOPHIA, HOW'S it going?" Kyle asked her.

"Well, this is a phone call you never thought you would ever get from us, but Mark's been arrested, being held for roughing up a minor on the cruise ship."

"Geez, that doesn't sound like Mark at all. What happened?"

Sophia explained to him the drugs that they found, the accusations about certain things like how the boys had been basically getting into trouble since the first day on board and explained who his parents were.

"I see, I really do. That's not a very enviable position. You are not staying on board, is that correct?"

"I'm not leaving Mark. We can always stay nearby, and that's the next thing I'm going to do after you hang up. But I need to know what kind of representation we're going to get here, if the Navy can help out, or if I have to get an attorney myself to help represent Mark."

"I don't know how that works; I just know the command will probably send someone over to look at the case file and help him strategize a defense. You can probably start by making a list of all the sympathetic viewers on that cruise. We want somebody who can vouch for what you guys were doing there, and I'm real disappointed to hear about Captain Teseo's decision. But I'm understanding that perhaps he has no choice in the matter. Not if he wants to stay employed."

"Do you think he will find a way to help us?" she asked.

"I'd bet on it. But he won't do it publically. He's a good guy."

"That makes me feel a little better. What should I do next?"

"Honestly, Sophia, I'd start looking for an attorney. I'll see if I can do some research for you over here, but see if you can get someone good in Italy. I'm afraid you'll need one. At least temporarily."

Kyle promised to get back to Sophia with some contact information, and he also mentioned that he would be having their team liaison reach out to her.

"If you want to bring the girls back to San Diego, maybe that would be better. I'm sure we can take care of them here, so you can focus on helping Mark. I'm not so sure having all of you over there is a good idea."

Sophia had not thought about that and, frankly, thought it was a good idea.

"Do they have State Department representation on Capri? Are they familiar with how these proceedings go? And one other thing Mark was wondering, if the parents have diplomatic immunity, does the kid have that too? What if he's the one supplying the drugs?"

"That's all above my paygrade, sweetheart. Just tell Mark not to worry. Is it okay if I tell the team, or do you need to check with Mark about that first?"

"Yes, go ahead tell them. Who knows, maybe that group will know somebody."

"Sure thing. You take care of those beautiful ladies in your care, and we'll fill the holes where we can. Now I've got some calls and work to do."

"Thanks, Kyle, and I'll think about your offer with the girls. It might help us all concentrate if I had less distractions."

The Old Savona Hotel had been one of their stays during their honeymoon. From the hand-painted china to the "smoking room" that now allowed women and cigars to the finely feathered beds and silky sheets, it transported her to happier times, when her whole future was in front of her.

She put it all out of her mind and tried to remember how it felt to be newly married to her Prince Charming, when the whole world was not big enough to express her love for Mark.

Her evening prayer at starlight was that she could feel that way again, but this time do it as a whole family of five.

"God, we don't ever leave anyone behind. He never does it. I'm certainly not going to do it either. Like the SEAL motto, Only Easy Day was Yesterday, yesterday was indeed easier. But tomorrow we're going to start to fix it."

CHAPTER 13

MARK WAS TOLD he'd be transferred to another facility. His guard told him he'd be kept out of the general criminal population, and he was told confidentially by one of the senior officers transporting him that it was being done for his own safety and out of respect for the fact that he was a United States citizen.

"I've not been able to telephone anybody. My wife thinks I'm at your port station. How are they going to find me?"

He knew things happened when an individual member of any of their teams was transported to somewhere and where the police were not being forthcoming with where and why and what was the timeline he was facing. While he didn't suspect he was the victim of foul play, the longer this went on, the less confident he was that his own government, the Navy, or even Kyle or Sophia could intervene on his behalf. It would be useless to fight, and yet it was not like him to just sit and wait until he'd been victimized.

"You are not to worry, my friend. We are a law-abiding country here, and our police force is the finest anywhere. I am just doing my duty. And if you do not resist, I am sure you will find the new accommodations much better for your interests."

"I want to know who ordered this? I didn't ask for it. Did my attorneys or the consulate or the Navy request this?"

"I am not privy to all that information, sir. It will be revealed in time. I am just given the duty of getting you safely to the regional holding center. It is not a facility that is large, nor will you be placed into a large population of ordinary criminals. First, you are a US citizen, and you have certain rights. Second, you are a member of the armed forces of our allies, and we treat our friends as we would want to be treated in your country."

It didn't make any difference to Mark; he was still worried.

"Can I just have a phone call then?"

"Not until I am directed that it is okay."

He had made the comment to Sophia to bring some reading material. However, it looked like he was going to be the one needing the reading material since there was nothing he could physically do about his situation. They told him he could bring an extra set of clothes and personal items for toiletries, but that bag never made it into the car, which scared the shit out of him. Was he just going to be taken somewhere to be done away with? And the new ambassador to Great Britain, even though his son was an asshole, surely, he would have some say over what would happen to him, and no matter what, there would be repercussions. It was hardly the type of action that warranted an international incident. But Mark knew very well that that didn't always make a difference.

He was thinking about this whole situation. It was his fault that he'd reacted so strongly with the kid. He regretted that. In hindsight, his normal patient self should have jumped in, and he could have restrained the boy, who was not his match in physical strength, without causing any harm and certainly without causing bloodshed. But once blood was spilled, it seemed to set in a whole new set of rules, and what might have been considered a harmless encounter or misunderstanding suddenly became a full-blown assault and battery.

He was concerned about Sophia. She was stuck in Italy with all three girls, their cruise was ruined, and their anniversary was trashed. And it was entirely possible that Mark's career was wrecked as well. Of all those things, he knew whatever he needed to do to make it right, even if it cost him his career, he would apologize and do just that. But he needed to know Sophia would be safe, that they could get back to the States, regardless of what happened to him.

He wished he could talk to her. He wished he could let her know that at least he was not rotting in a rat-infested cell with a bunch of low-level criminals or, worse, drug dealers or murderers. He had no idea how the criminal justice system worked in Italy, although he had nothing to necessarily think negatively about it. He really didn't like the fact that he didn't seem to have any rights as a detainee, almost as if they were treating him like his country did a terrorist. Now he knew exactly how they felt.

When he asked Sophia to marry him, this was not at all what he envisioned. He knew there would be dark days, there would be difficult times, married to a Navy SEAL, and he thought he'd prepared her well for all the possibilities that could occur. But never in his wildest dreams did he ever guess that something like this would happen. And wouldn't it just be his luck to be the one to expose some new danger. It seemed like every day their team members had to be more and more careful about what they said, what they did, their public persona, and the media attention. Some had written books; some had gone on speaking tours and been outspoken about all sorts of things, including politics. None of that was anything Mark ever wanted to do. He was just trying to protect his family. And he knew that somebody on that cruise was dealing drugs. He wanted to stop it before somebody died unnecessarily.

There was no crime in that.

It was the source of his frustration. His actions were taken for the good of everyone. Not for his own personal benefit, although he did allow his anger to take over.

That he regretted most of all.

On a normal day, he could have looked out the window and appreciated the beautiful little tiled villages, the switchback streets and cobblestones, the happy commerce of vendors and marketplaces they passed. He loved the culture and the countryside in Italy. That's why they'd chosen to be there for their honeymoon. And Sophia, being raised here with an American father but an Italian mother, loved her country as well. She became an American citizen because she wanted to for Mark. She could have held onto her dual citizenship forever if she'd wanted to.

But Sophia now was going to experience a second tragedy in her young years. Her father had been killed in the military, and her mother moved them back to Italy, back to her family, upon his death. So she'd been uprooted twice, and now she was having to spend her time with three children, worrying about Mark's welfare.

He hoped she had it in her to stick with him. But if she decided she'd had enough, if she blamed him for all of this and couldn't forgive him, whatever it is she wanted to do, whether she wanted to go back to live in Italy and not have anything to do with the SEAL Teams or the military or the United States, he would let her do it. He loved her that much. If she honestly thought it was better for the girls, he would go along with it. He'd try to fight, but he'd go along with it.

The hardest thing in the world was sitting and waiting. He had told her this repeatedly. He'd said it to his LPO Kyle. No, he didn't do wait at all.

The town of Montepulciano was atop a hill, sort of an artist community, with many large villas, olive trees, and vineyards. He remembered this little village when they were on their honeymoon and had spent several afternoons there walking through the shops. They had stayed at a villa in Imprunetta and walked the olive orchards in the evening at sunset.

Today, it looked dark and foreboding. A solid rain had started, and unlike the coastal area, since they were inland quite a way now, it was dreary. The rain-washed cobblestones glistened and steamed in the afternoon sun. Every person he saw on the street, every driver that passed them on the road, was a stranger. There was not one friendly face the whole trip.

They had handcuffed his wrists but uncuffed his ankles. But when he got there, no doubt he would be doing a perp walk for whoever's benefit it was that he was transferred. Or if they drove into some tunnel somewhere and there was no daylight, well, Mark knew what that might mean. Maybe they were just going to stash him away somewhere and lose him. Claim nobody knew what happened to him.

The wait and the trip were killing him.

"So am I going to be charged please? I adhere to a very strong code of conduct. It's very likely that this whole situation is going to end my career as a Navy SEAL. My wife is in the country, and she's Italian by birth, with our three daughters, not knowing where I am. If anyone is trying to get a hold of me to help me, they aren't going to find me unless you give me information or allow a phone call."

His driver, the medaled officer in full dress black uniform, stopped at a stop sign. Mark could see a large prison-type structure up ahead.

"We are almost here. This is a special facility for very high value assets, some military, some political, and yes, some spies. Very famous prison. But you will not be registered in the general population, as I have told you several times. You simply must wait. And once we process you and put you in your room—"

"Is it a room or a cell?"

"I am not supposed to promise, but I believe that it is like a dormitory. It is the facility where some of our ministers and high-profile businessmen are held while they serve time. It's not like your vision of what a full-on prison would be. But it is fortified, because through the years, there have been attempts at certain people's lives. It's quite safe. You just need to be patient. And I will make sure that the authorities here know what your desire is and that you need to speak to your wife or your commanding officer. So I can help you, who is your commanding officer?"

"His name is Master Chief Kyle Lansdowne. I'm with SEAL Team 3 based out of Coronado, California. I have been a Navy SEAL for twelve years, and I have never had a blemish on my record."

Mark decided not to reveal to him several of the ops where there were certain questions asked about his performance, but that had been straightened out, and as far as he knew, nothing was negative on his record.

"This Officer Lansdowne is the person you wish to speak to or your wife?"

"Both of them. And he's Master Chief Kyle Lansdowne. I need to speak to both. Sophia, my wife, doesn't know what to do because she is not an attorney. But she needs to help me find somebody to represent me. Kyle Lansdowne is the person in charge of the entire team, and he's going to be grilled by the Navy as to what happened to me. They aren't going to just stand by and allow this to happen. And I don't understand why it even is."

"Navy SEAL Mark Beale, I sympathize with your situation, but again, I must tell you, you have to be patient and let things work out as they do. I am not your enemy here. I am only the person who is driving you from point A to point B. It was determined that this would be a safer place to put you. I must trust that decision. I'm sure you will be one of the first to know if anything else develops."

They had stopped at the sentry gate just ahead of the two-story archway leading inside the prison. Rather than having building upon building of cells, the central area was a courtyard, complete with a garden, including an herb and vegetable bed. This surprised him.

The perimeter of the facility looked like office buildings, and in one wing, which was about four stories tall, there were bars on the windows. It did look like it was a holding facility, but he didn't see any prison yard, and gardeners working on the garden were dressed in white, looking more like chefs than gardeners. There were heavily armed men at the sentry gate, and opposite the courtyard was a second exit with large steel doors that could roll back to accommodate a large truck or equipment of some kind. Those were locked, and a guard posted in two barrack houses on either side.

The driver stopped at a wide stairway. There was an intricate metal and glass overhang which shielded anybody from rain who exited their vehicle to walk inside.

The driver uncuffed him.

"No shackles?" Mark asked.

"No, sir, if you will please walk behind me, cooperate, there will be no need for that. I want you to just follow me please, and we will deal with the desk duty officer."

Mark rubbed his wrists, which had become raw from the handcuffs, and slowly walked up the steps to the double doors into a rather ornate lobby area that could have been the inside of any of the nicer Italian hotels. The floor was exquisitely patterned with tiled inlay work; wrought iron balconies overlooked the lobby area from the second and third floors. Statues of various military figures, angels, and busts of several favored Italian patriots decorated the room. Mark recognized a few, like the busts of Garibaldi and several other military conquerors he had studied in his classes.

The day desk was up another two steps. Nearly twenty feet long, it was made of white Carrara marble. The woman behind a glass shield sitting at the desk lowered her glasses and greeted the driver.

"He is to be placed in the conference room first. You may leave as soon as our liaison takes charge."

She was an attractive woman in her forties, with hair spun up into a French bun, her uniform tight, and she looked like she was all business.

"Ma'am—"

His driver tried to interrupt him.

"It's okay. Let him speak please," she said.

"Ma'am, my wife is half-Italian, half-American. We were on a cruise—"

"Yes, Mr. Beale, I'm aware of your circumstance."

"She doesn't know I'm here, and I need to speak to her. I have not been permitted one phone call yet."

"We are aware of this. All in due time. I believe the arrangements are being made now. If you please follow your driver down the hallway, he will show you to a pleasant interview room, and we will get you some water. Are you hungry as well?"

Mark was famished, more from nervousness than anything else.

"Maybe some fruit, some bread? But mostly I need water. Thank you."

"Do you need to use the facilities?"

Mark looked over at his driver and frowned.

The man nodded. "Yes, I have to accompany you. I have to watch everything."

That pissed Mark off big time. "Yes, I will need to use the facilities. And if I may ask one more thing? I brought a change of clothes and some personal items—toothbrush and deodorant, that sort of thing. I don't believe they came with me in the vehicle. Will I be given a chance to wash up?"

"Once you get to your permanent room, you will be provided with prison-approved attire and your personal items. Ricardo, would you please show Mr. Beale the restroom please?"

Mark took it as a good sign that they were going to allow him to use the regular lavatory off the lobby area, which might mean that they didn't consider him a dangerous criminal. He walked behind Ricardo, entered the men's room, and took a long pee. He washed his hands and whispered to his observant driver, "This is fucking insane. I've never had anybody watch me do this. You would think I could get a little bit of privacy."

"Not until you've been searched. But they're going to speak to you first, it sounds like."

As he washed his hands and dried them, Mark added, "Ricardo, huh? Where I come from, we have a famous actor Ricky Ricardo from Cuba."

"My father was Cuban."

Score one for intuition. "So how did your Cuban father get to Italy?"

"He was protesting. Arrested, did his time, and was released. That's when he met my mother."

Mark was stunned, not knowing what to say.

"You see, Mr. Beale, you are not the only one with a checkered past. We sometimes don't always choose the path we get here, but if we follow the rules, life turns out. I think I'm an example of that. I've had good fortune. And I have it because I play by the rules."

CHAPTER 14

SOPHIA HAD WAITED all morning for a call from Kyle or the Navy or even Mark himself. Without getting through to anyone, she had taken the girls downstairs to have breakfast, trying to soak up the time, while she devised her plans.

She needed to find an Italian attorney and was hoping that Kyle or somebody from the Navy could point her in the right direction. She didn't want to just pick somebody or ask the hotel manager for a recommendation, since this could be a criminal manner, and it involved immigration and political issues. The longer she didn't hear from Mark, the more she worried.

She was trying to stay calm, trying to stay present with the girls. How did women in war-torn areas hold it all together? She wondered about this. Now she knew how it felt. Nobody around her to help her, all the men in her life she normally counted on for protection were gone, and the roles were reversed. She was supposed to do something to help Mark, whereas normally it was the other way around.

Sophia knew that if she could just concentrate and think, she'd be able to sort out what was the right path forward. Just like she'd seen Mark do in the past, she got out her notebook and started making a list of all her questions.

Number one was what were the rules for detaining a non-Italian citizen? Were there circumstances where a US serviceman was arrested in a foreign country, what were his rights, and what would the military do to help him? She figured that it probably depended on the country.

Getting her computer out, she Googled several topics and didn't find anything but advertisements for attorneys for people trying to stay in the country. But nothing mentioned international or immigration convictions for battery or assault. She knew it was an advantage that she spoke fluent Italian, because of her heritage, so she could make those calls, but she didn't trust that information would be helpful.

"Where are you, Kyle? Mark? Why haven't I heard from you?" she asked herself.

Finally, she packed the girls up and hired a driver to take her over to the detention center in Naples.

Domenica was being stubborn today, and she fidgeted in her arms, so she set the toddler down and gave strict instructions for Ophelia and Carrie Ann to both keep an eye on her if they were all in the same room. Domenica caught onto this little game quickly and began running back and forth, screaming and giggling, which annoyed the officers who were working the front desk. She barely got three words out before she'd have to turn and reprimand her kids.

She looked into the eyes of one of the officers who appeared to take pity on her and begged him.

"I'm looking for my husband, Mark Beale. He was brought in here early this morning. It's noon, and I have not received a call from him nor a call from his superior officer, or anybody in the Navy. Can you please tell me what's going on? And is there any chance I could see him?"

In Italian, the police officer explained to Sophia that Mark was no longer in the facility.

"Excuse me? Where has he gone? And how come we were never told this? I'm staying at the Savona Hotel just a few miles away. Why wasn't I told that he'd been moved?"

"I believe someone is in the process of getting in touch with you, but it was decided that he would need to be moved to a more secure facility."

"A more secure facility? You mean like a regular prison instead of a holding area?"

"Yes, it is a prison. It is about two and a half hours away, in Montepulciano. You know this town?"

"Yes. Again, I do not have a car. We've been offloaded from a cruise ship, and all my luggage has not arrived yet, and nobody has called me to help me find an attorney to represent him. Surely there must be protocol here. May I speak to your commanding officer?"

The gentleman she'd been speaking to had an immediate change of expression. His warmth evaporated, and a cold blue icy stare substituted it. Sophia became worried that there was something planned for Mark that they didn't want to reveal to her. She began to get hysterical. Her lower lip quivered as she felt her will crumbling.

Two women officers came out into the lobby and helped to occupy the girls so the entire front office could think straight. Sophia was about to have a meltdown of major proportions, but she knew she had to keep it together for the girls. On tenterhooks, she shouted out a command at the girls several times, which was not like her normally. But the stress level was driving her nuts. The uncertainty of Mark's position also felt like she was trying to climb out of a pit of quicksand, making no headway and with nobody in sight to rescue her.

"What is the address of this facility? Can you name it for me?"

The officer in charge handed her a piece of paper with driving instructions to the prison and suggested, if she wanted to save money, she could take a bus.

"I'm not going to take a bus with my three girls and no luggage. I'm supposed to be getting return calls. This is ridiculous. I'd be better off to stay in the hotel. At least there, I'll have food and a place to sleep and change diapers. I just can't pick up and travel, and I have no one to watch the girls."

"Do you have relatives nearby?" he asked her.

Sophia thought about her mother, but that was going to be out of the question, as well as her brother. If she could reach the ship and get permission to come back on board, at least there would be facilities there to entertain them, but at this juncture that was going to be impossible.

She took the directions given her, thanked the ladies for helping with the girls, and asked for a taxi to take her back to the hotel. One of the women officers offered to take her back in a police vehicle, which she accepted.

Exhausted, hungry, and tired, she leaned against the door to their room and broke down crying. She slid down the back of the door until she sat in a ball on the floor, tucking her knees up, pulling her arms over, and sinking her head low.

Little Ophelia came over to her and gave her a hug.

"Mommy? Where's Daddy? He needs to help you," she said.

"Daddy is in a meeting, and I'm trying to find out how to reach him. I'm not having any luck, and I'm very upset. And I'm so sorry. I need to get some help, but I'm striking out as far as finding the right person."

"Why don't you call him?"

"Because he doesn't have his phone, sweetheart. He's not allowed to take calls in his meeting." She smoothed over Ophelia's sweet cheeks and gave her a kiss.

"Thank you, sweetheart, for caring about Mommy. I promise this will all be over soon."

Domenica ran over to her and gave her a hug as well. Carrie Ann was a little more cautious approaching her mother.

"When are we going to go back on the boat?" she asked.

"Well, plans have changed, and I'm afraid we are not going to be going back there. This important meeting Daddy has meant that we all had to leave. I will know more as soon as I can reach someone. Until then, we can stay here, or we can go downstairs to the pool, whatever you like."

"I don't have my swimsuit," said Carrie Ann.

"Neither do I," said Ophelia.

That's when she decided to give the police a call again, complaining about the lack of luggage.

The hotel front desk knew they were expecting a delivery to be brought to her from the ship but noted that they had not received a call and were not expecting that delivery today.

"I need a favor, if you might. Since our luggage isn't here, is there some place I can find some cheap swimming suits for us? A second-hand store nearby? I'm not prepared to spend the money at your hotel store, if you understand what I mean."

"We have a lost and found, and at the end of the year, we donate these clothes to charity. Let me see if I can find some suits in there. People are always leaving them behind. Not worth contacting the guests to try to mail them. You're welcome if that meets your approval."

"That would be lovely. Thanks so much. Do I—?"

"Give me a few minutes, and I'll bring what I have up to your room."

"You are very kind."

"Will you be staying one or two more days, or longer?" the desk clerk asked her.

"I'm not sure yet. I will know more in the next twenty-four hours. If you get any indication that the luggage or our personal effects are arriving, would you please call me or text me on my cell?"

"Absolutely."

The clerk paused then added, "You know that tomorrow is Christmas Eve. We have a special dinner here at the hotel, in two seatings so that guests can attend the candlelight children's choir. It's a tradition here in Naples. Can I put down a reservation for you?"

"I'm afraid I'll have to do something less expensive. But thank you for thinking of us. Is the church very far? Can we walk, and is it safe?"

"Very safe, and only four blocks away. You'll find lots of other parishioners going as well."

"That sounds lovely. The girls will love it, I'm sure."

"And about the dinner, let me see if my manager can approve the four of you being our guest tomorrow. I understand your Christmas has been impacted. I don't want you to think all of Italy is unfriendly. I'm sorry you are going through this, and I'm praying for you."

Sophia called Kyle's number again and got a recording. Then she kicked herself for not having called Christy before but did so now.

"Oh, Sophia, I heard all about it from Kyle. You must be beside yourself. I can't imagine going through all that." Christy said.

"Well, I'm hearing nothing, and I feel like I should be interviewing attorneys or getting instructions from our State Department or someplace. I don't know what to do, and now I'm told that Mark has been moved. He's in a facility that's about two and a half hours away, up in the mountains. I don't understand this. Is he being taken away for some solitary confinement? Has he been charged with anything? What do I do? We don't have any luggage. I'm using credit cards for this hotel, but if I don't need to stay here, if I could go to a cheaper place—Oh my gosh, Christy, I'm beside myself and feel so powerless. I want to do the right thing, but I need something I can accomplish. Do you understand?"

"Yes, I do. I really do. And I'm going to get all over Kyle for not getting back to you. Have you tried calling Teseo, the captain of the ship?"

"I don't have his number. Can you get that for me? I'd be happy to call him. I need a referral for an attorney. I could be meeting with attorneys. I could be strategizing. I could be helping get petitions going so we could try to intervene here and get him released. But I just don't know the first thing about this."

"Let me see what I can do, and either I or Kyle will call you back. Have you heard from the Navy at all?"

"No, I have not. Wouldn't they reach out to me? Isn't that standard procedure?"

"It usually is. My worry is that they may not be tuned into everything that's gone on. Perhaps it's just a question of them getting up to speed."

"But meanwhile, Mark is farther away from me. I have no contact with him. They're not allowing him to call me, and he could be in great danger, and there's nobody on his side to help. I just feel like a fifth wheel here, and then I've got all three girls."

"Well, if you were here in California or could get on a plane back to California, we can help you with that. But I'm not sure you want to do that. It's going to feel like abandoning Mark. I must tell you, Sophia, if this is a long, protracted situation, you probably are best to come back home, get them into a routine they're used to, and the wives will help. There's no problem there. It could be very expensive if you wind up having to stay there the whole time. And I'm sure they'll allow you to come home."

Sophia hadn't even considered that perhaps Mark's family would not be allowed to return to the United States.

"What kind of a world is this?"

"I think it's an unusual situation. From what Kyle has said, and I know he is looking into this, because of the involvement of the new ambassador to England, things must go through channels. Until the right people get together and start talking, nobody in the rank and file in Italy is going to touch this. I'm sure once we figure out what's going on, there will be a solution presented. But try to keep calm, and I know that sounds flippant, but your best asset is if you stay calm and you stay clearheaded. In your shoes, I don't think I'd be as coherent as you are. We're tough, but there is a limit to what we can live with, isn't there?"

"I never expected this. I didn't even know all the ins and outs of what happened. But we'll get to the bottom of it. Please have Kyle call me."

Sophia thought about calling her mother but knew it would just upset her. She decided to call Devon Brandenburg, who had married Mark's best friend, Nicholas Dunn. It was approximately eight hours ahead in Italy, so it would be early in California, but this was important enough that she hoped Nicholas and Devon would forgive her for calling before sunrise.

Nick picked up on the first ring.

"This better be good, or I'm going to ram this phone down your throat. Who's calling at four o'clock in the morning?"

"Nick, it's me, Sophia. Mark's been arrested in Italy. I am beside myself. I'm stuck in a hotel in Naples. We've been taken off the ship for our ten-year anniversary cruise, and I have all three girls with me. I'm trying to get through to somebody at the Navy. Kyle's working on something, but I just wanted to call somebody and brainstorm a little bit. Do you know anybody in the Navy or the State Department who could maybe give me a hand?"

"Geez, Sophia. Why was he arrested?"

"It's a long story, Nicholas, but the long and short of it is he caught some kids he thinks were dealing drugs, and it turns out one of the kids' parents are headed to England, his father recently appointed the new ambassador to England from Italy. I guess the complaint was made because Mark confronted the son, who is a minor, and gave him a bloody nose while he was restraining him, and the guy's mother just completely freaked out. They pressed charges or are going to press charges, and I need to get an Italian attorney or somebody from the State Department or the Navy to intervene."

"I understand. Is Mark innocent of this?"

"No, he did get angry with the kid, but it happened because he was trying to restrain him and the kid was struggling. He was trying to take him to the authorities, so that he wouldn't be selling drugs to other kids or adults on the cruise ship. He tried to protect the passengers. But unfortunately, it's being portrayed that he beat up a minor."

"Yep, that sounds like a clusterfuck all right. And the Navy's not going to like this, Sophia. You got to be prepared for that."

"Listen, we'll take whatever they dish out. The main thing is I need to make sure that Mark's okay. And I can't reach him."

"I know we have friends up in Portland, and there's a former State Department liaison who is related to our friends. Perhaps Kelly can intervene, but I'm not sure. It needs to go through Kyle though. See what he has to say first."

"Yes, I get that. It's been five hours now, and I haven't heard a thing, and when I tried to go over to visit him, that's when they told me that he'd been moved. They did that without consulting me. And they took us off the ship without our luggage, so I have nothing. I just feel like I'm being treated like a criminal, and it's not fair for the girls either. I mean, is that going to be the next thing? They're going to say the girls must go somewhere else because I'm a criminal like Mark? I'm just grasping at straws."

"Now, there has to be a logical explanation. You just keep yourself and the girls occupied. Let me see if I can make some calls. I'm not going to promise anything, but I do promise I'll get back to you. And listen, if you need to talk to someone, I'm sure Devon, when she gets home, would love to call you back."

"Devon's not there?"

"No, she's down in LA at a training seminar. We're branching out into the Airbnb business, ecotourist. This is a license she wants to have for operating our facility here. She'll be back day after tomorrow. Otherwise, I'd put her on the phone now. But you take care, and I've got this number. What happens when you try to call Mark?"

"I saw them take his phone. They have his passport, and I really don't know what he has with him, but there's no contacting him. But I would gladly appreciate a referral if you can find someone."

"Will do. I'll spend the entire day, if I must, making calls and seeing if I can help. You just hang tight. I'm so sorry this is going on, and you know if I must fly over there and give Mark a hand, I will. He is my best friend. I know he'd do the same for me."

"Thanks, Nick. I really appreciate this."

"If I do come over, then I'm going to have to make arrangements for my kids, but we've got family in the area, so it's not like what you're going through. It will take me a day or so to arrange all that. But let me see what I can do, and I'll try to call you back before you go to bed tonight."

Sophia was slightly relieved but decided she'd stay proactive. She could follow up on the luggage, calling the cruise line and the police department. She did both. Crossing those off the list, she was told that a delivery was expected before the end of the day today and that the bag that Mark had packed for himself would also be returned to her. His other personal effects, like his cell phone and his passport, would not be returned to her until further notice.

With the suits the clerk delivered to her room, including a new one for her from the Hotel store, she took the girls downstairs to the indoor swimming pool and decided to put everything out of her mind and give herself just an hour of swim play. Her phone was nearby however, but it was more important that she give time to her girls.

About five o'clock in the afternoon, as they were returning to their room, Kyle called back.

"How are you holding up, Sophia?"

"How do you think? What's going on?"

"Well, we have a problem. I believe Mark is going to be charged. It's a difficult situation, but I have someone from the Navy Special Investigations who's going to reach out and get you a referral in Italy. The one thing we don't want is to have this appear in any media because that will complicate the whole thing. It's a sensitive negotiation, must be taken through the proper channels, and needs not to get distorted. I'm sorry to ask you this, but you're probably going to have to be prepared to be there for a day or two, maybe a week."

"Oh my God. This is getting expensive. But, Kyle, whatever it takes. We're here. All of us are here."

"I think that's the right thing to do. And we'll find out about why he was moved; I wouldn't necessarily disagree with the officer who told you he was being moved for his own protection. That's very like how they do things over there. The last thing in the world they want is for him to run into problems in jail. That certainly would cause an international incident. If the news media doesn't get hold of the story, which means you must be quiet about all of this, we'll just let channels take care of themselves, and hopefully, everything will be ironed out. I'm not going to be able to promise that I'll have an answer tonight, but I promise to call you in the morning if not. Are you okay? Do you need anything?"

"No, I'm fine. Thank you. What about calling the captain? He's a friend, isn't he?"

"I've already done that. I'm working on something there. But you just need to stay put and stay calm. Your job right now is to be level-headed and be able to react very quickly if something's needed. Again, I'm so sorry. The fact that he hasn't been charged and a court date set, that's all-good stuff. Let's try to be positive about it, and we'll see what kind of miracles we can make."

"Yeah, miracles. Is this going to mean the end of his career?"

"Let's handle that if it comes up to it. Let's hope it doesn't come that far. I'll probably talk to you in the morning. You be strong, Sophia. I know you're strong. Mark is counting on you."

"If you get a chance to talk to him, will you tell him we're here, and we're not going to leave him behind? I don't care what I must do, Kyle. I'm going to get him out one way or the other."

Kyle chuckled. "Yeah, I thought you'd say something like that. You're just like Mark is. He'd do the same for you. How are the girls holding up?"

"They're good. I'm going to find a babysitter recommended by the hotel. They have licensed services here, and I think I can trust them. Then if I must do the drive into the country, I can do that. I just don't want to take them all over Italy. It's hard for me to do that with all three of them."

"I understand. You work on that, and let us do our job on our side. Keep looking up. Keep praying and having good thoughts."

"Thank you, Kyle."

"Thank you, Sophia. You're one hell of a woman. Thanks for supporting your man. He's worth it."

CHAPTER 15

C ARLA GUALTIERI, THE regional prosecutor, sat down across the table from Mark.

"Special Operator Beale? I am going to ask you a series of questions about the incident that's been reported to us. It's a complaint. And I'm going to ask your indulgence to give me absolutely the truth, no matter what you think I might have of that. I need to get to the bottom line of what exactly occurred. Can you do that?"

"Absolutely. I've been waiting to have my chance to tell my side of the story. I'm completely innocent."

"This is going to be your side of the story; you are completely innocent?" She lowered her glasses on her nose and stared at him with her huge blue eyes, drilling a hole all the way to the back of his skull.

Mark shrugged, with eyes downcast, and said, "Well, that's not entirely true. I did push the kid. I pushed him up against the wall so I could grab onto him. I was fighting off several of his buddies."

He raised his eyes to try to determine whether she believed him. His opinion was inconclusive.

"How many of his friends were trying to stop your actions?"

"Three, maybe four. I'm not sure. I tried to fend them off as best I could by kicking and grabbing onto the kid and trying to reach them with my other hand. I was outmatched, but I didn't want to let the boy go. I was told his name is Samuel."

"Yes." She peered at the paperwork in front of her. "Samuel Collazo? I understand his father has taken on a position with the Italian government and will be residing in England."

"I didn't know who his father was. But my daughter was exposed to what I believe to be drugs that dropped out of Samuel's pocket. She tried to return it to him. She thought it was candy—they looked like a fruity cereal, multi-colored rings. She thought he'd want it back. They either didn't hear her or ignored her, so she kept it, and she put it in with her bag of candy we had purchased earlier."

"Did she ingest these drugs?"

"No, I think I would know that. She said she didn't. And we were with her the whole time. When she described Samuel to me, I started looking over the ship to see if I could find him, and I ran into him that night."

"Did your wife hear your daughter describe Samuel?"

"Yes, she did. So did my other two daughters."

"Okay, and what did you do with these supposed drugs?"

"I gave them to the captain, Teseo Dominichello. He is a friend of several of us on our SEAL team. We have been on cruises where he's been on board before."

"Yes, I understand there was a terrorist takeover of one of the ships in this Italian line? And you and your team were able to crush the takeover?"

"Yes, although the official story is that the passengers overtook them. We weren't really supposed to be there or be involved, but the passengers did assist us in finding the terrorists and holding them so that they could be arrested."

"Okay. That's a tall tale, Mark. May I call you Mark?"

"You can call me anything you like, as long as I can get out of this place as soon as possible."

"And why do you think you should be released?"

"Because I think this kid is a problem. I think he's not been supervised and was allowed to terrorize some of the other passengers on the ship. He's an accident waiting to happen. If he's got drugs on him or dealing drugs, it's something that should be stopped."

"And you took it upon yourself to do this?"

"Unfortunately, yes, I wanted to make sure he was apprehended so an investigation could be done and possibly he could be removed from the ship. Instead, this is what happened, and I'm here, and he's on the cruise. My entire family is in Italy and pulled off the cruise, my wife and three daughters, and he is allowed to run around freely on the ship. He's a danger to any other child or adult on that ship if he's dealing drugs. I don't know if his parents know about his activities, but I believe I was arrested so that they protected their son."

"That's a pretty damning assessment of their moral code, wouldn't you say?"

"Yes, I'm well aware of the fact that parents sometimes don't supervise their children as they perhaps should. Or have a different opinion of what's acceptable and what's not acceptable. I can see how they would be concerned that having a son who deals drugs or is in possession of drugs could jeopardize his father's opportunities. I'm not sure I would've done anything different had I known how connected his parents were, but I knew that he needed to be apprehended. And I thought I was doing my job to protect the innocent people on the cruise."

"Does your Navy talk to you about interfering with other government's judicial system, their laws, not inserting yourself since you are not sworn police or prosecutors? You are operators. You go in and handle riots and defend and rescue people in war torn areas of the world. But this is Italy. This is a civilized country with a constitution and a court system. You defied the authority of the security on ship as well as the police and the judicial system here in Italy. This is a very serious offense."

"I understand, and I'm very sorry for my actions. I probably overreacted."

"Probably?"

Shrugging and leaning over the table with his hands folded together, he added, "Yes, I overreacted. I should have been more careful not to hurt him. I was solely intent on making sure he was captured, and I should have paid more attention to the fact that I am stronger and bigger than he is, and I should have allowed other people to do their job. But that's the worst of it. I was doing it for all the right reasons."

"But if you thought someone was going to harm your family, would that give you the right to murder them? To cause a great deal of physical injury?"

"Under the circumstances, these circumstances, no. I made a mistake. This mistake could cost me my job. I could lose my trident over this. I was angry at this young boy's actions. I'm angry that I'm being charged for something that I really didn't intend to do. I am angry that my wife and children are not able to talk to me, that I'm not able to have representation or talk to my commanding officer or the naval liaison or anyone from our State Department. It appears that all my rights have been removed and Samuel's rights—well, he's allowed to run free and do whatever the heck he wants to do. It hardly seems fair to me. But that's your determination, not mine."

"You say the captain of your ship is a friend of yours? Why didn't he intervene?"

"If I had an answer to that, I would give it to you. I didn't even get the opportunity to speak to him. I was told by the security team that I had to remain in my cabin, and after I gave him the drugs, I no longer had any communication with him. Just because we are friends, I would've thought I would be given more choices. I was moved to this facility because I was told it was for my benefit. I don't understand any of this. Nothing's been explained to me, and it just seems that I was the victim here. Granted, I used perhaps more force than I should have, but I'm the real victim. And there are going to be other victims if he's not apprehended. That is something I'm most concerned about, and I suppose Captain Dominichello is focusing in on that. As he should."

"What do you think should happen from here on?"

"Well, if I've caused battery or some kind assault, I will have to pay the consequences. Whether it's justified or not, that's your determination, not mine. I didn't mean to cause him harm. I just merely wanted to apprehend him."

"But what is it that should happen in your opinion?"

"In my opinion, I should be released. I also think a team should be sent to the ship to investigate the drug use, to interview the boy and his parents, and to determine—perhaps by interviewing other passengers on the ship—if the boy and his friends are in fact a nuisance to other passengers. I know that there are people we talked to who complained about those kids. I have their names. If you like, you could interview them. I think after you investigate what went on, you'll see that I'm telling the truth. I'm not proud of it, but I'm telling the truth."

She looked at Mark without revealing any emotion. She asked him about his family, his upbringing, what his specialty was on the teams, how long he'd been a SEAL, how long he intended to remain in the military, and he answered all her questions. By the end of the interview, Mark was not sure if he was believed.

"Are you going to charge me with an offense, officially?"

"I haven't determined that yet. I do need to speak to the parents who lodged the complaint. Of course, it's going to require that they leave the ship to come here for the interview. That may be a problem for them. We will do our best to investigate. In the meantime, though, you are going to need to stay here. I will allow reasonable use of phones. You'll be housed in an individual room, by yourself, and your meals will be delivered to you. I'm not going to place you in the general population or allow you to have communication with other prisoners here. If what you said is true, I don't believe a lengthy stay or international incident should be created over this. But it's very important that we get to the bottom of why it was that you were so angry at this boy and verify that he either is or is not dealing or possessing drugs. Like you said, if he is a danger to the other passengers, we are concerned about that, and we need to do something before they leave Italian waters."

"They're supposed to be in Capri all day today. I believe they're headed out in the morning for France. I think the next stop is Nice."

"I will contact the captain immediately, and I will ask permission to come aboard to conduct a cursory interview if the passengers are unable to come to us. But I will ask that this be done before they sail farther. I'm sure the captain is not going to want to delay the cruise. But it is going to be his decision."

"Well, I thank you for listening anyway, and you can look up a couple of passengers there. Mr. and Mrs. Clopton and Mr. and Mrs. Brandon, both couples discussed with us their displeasure with this band of boys that seemed to run into everybody and cause problems. I'm sure there are others as well, but we did discuss it at length. There were also a series of thefts the cruise ship was handling, where people had fraudulent charges added to their shipboard account. You should ask them about that."

She handed Mark a business card and wrote her cell phone on the backside of it. "You may be receiving visitors our government might arrange for you, an attorney to help represent your interests. Please have him contact me directly before he speaks with any other members of the police force or the prosecutor's offices. It will be to your advantage that he does so."

"Thank you, ma'am. Now, can I call my wife?"

"Yes, I believe we are arranging for a phone to be brought in here, and you may give her a call now if you wish. I will also allow you a call to your naval representative. We are going to need their help in sorting all this out as well."

Mark was heartened. There was a tiny glimmer of hope burning in his chest. He prayed to the god of SEALs that he escaped this situation relatively unscathed. If so, he would devote the rest of his life to his family, his wife, and kids, even if it meant he had to give up the teams. Whatever it took, he'd made enough mistakes in his life. He wanted to make sure that he kept Sophia and the girls out of it. It was the most important thing in the world to him.

Nothing else even came close.

CHAPTER 16

T HE SUITCASES WERE delivered to Sophia's room, and much to the delight of the girls, they began dressing up in some of the new clothes they had brought with them for the cruise. The little time they spent down at the pool had refreshed everybody, and even though it wasn't normal, life had sort of returned that way, temporarily.

Her cell phone rang with a number she didn't recognize, and when she answered it, she was ecstatic.

"Hey, sweetheart. It's me."

"Oh my God, Mark!" She was speechless, bumbling, tears brimming over her cheeks. She felt like she was going to pee in front of her daughters.

"I'm good, and I just have a couple minutes to tell you I love you, and they allowed me a couple of calls. How you guys holding up, sweetheart?"

"I've been worried sick. We've not had any news. You say everything's okay? Are they going to release you?"

"I wouldn't go that far yet; I haven't even talked to anybody else. I'm not sure what the strategy is, or if there is one. But I didn't want you to worry. I think this is a safe facility, and for whatever reason they decided to house me here, I'm grateful. I'm in Montepulciano—"

"I remember it so well, Mark. It's such a beautiful little town."

"Haven't seen much of it, since I'm in the prison, which apparently is a high-level, not exactly maximum-security prison, for government and corporate offenders. I'm not even sure whether there's anybody who's done serious crimes here, but it's a little bit like a hotel, except there are bars and I have to wear the prison uniform."

"Do you have any chance of talking to Kyle or an attorney? Have they explained charges or if there will be?"

"I'm not sure. And I may have to ask you to get hold of Teseo. We may need his help."

"Kyle said the same thing. I know he's trying. He gave me the number. I left a message."

"Oh, that's good. I'm glad you've talked to Kyle. How did he sound? I'll bet he was a bit pissed about all this."

"Not sure about that."

"Is he working on something? Because I haven't heard a damn thing."

"I just spoke to him today around noon. That's the first he's heard of things. It takes time. But yes, he promised me an update later tonight or tomorrow morning. I talked to Christy as well. And I hope you won't be angry with me, but I also called Nick Gunn. He said if he had to, he'd come over here and help you break out. That was a joke."

"That was funny, but we can't do that here on these lines. It might get construed as something else. It looks like there are several things being put into motion. I sure would like to talk to an Italian attorney. And I have concerns about using anybody they might recommend to me here, so Teseo and Kyle, those are going to be our best bets. Since you speak Italian, you can interview them and kind of get an idea what they're about, and perhaps by then, they'll let you see me. But I just don't know who to trust. You should be careful too. But I wanted you not to worry and—"

"Daddy!" Carrie Ann had overheard Sophia's conversation with Mark. All three girls ran over to grab their turn at the phone. It was a shoving match, eventually the phone winding up on the floor and scooting to the other side near the sliding balcony door.

Sophia rescued it before it went into the street below.

"Sorry about that. The girls are so excited. They keep asking for you, and they don't understand everything. We're all concerned. God, I'm so relieved to hear your voice. You sound good, really good."

"Where are you staying?"

"I'm at the Savona Hotel. You remember it? It's very nice. They have invited me to sit in on a special dinner tomorrow night for Christmas Eve. And the hotel clerk has been wonderful, found some bathing suits for us until our luggage arrived."

"Oh, your luggage did come? Any idea where my bag is?"

"Yours and my bags came with the luggage as well. No worries there. Anyway, we're going to go to the candlelight vigil and the children's choirs at the cathedral that's within walking distance from here. It's a custom in Naples. I think it'll be nice, and if you're back, I would love nothing more than to have you join us. But in the meantime, we're going to have that little slice of Christmas anyway."

"Love you so much, and you're doing such a great job. I'm just waiting for instructions. One of the things that is going to be important is investigating that kid before they leave Italian waters. I believe tomorrow is when they head out for France. I'd like to get some representation or get hold of Teseo before that happens."

"Yes, Kyle said the same thing. I'm sure they're doing everything they can. Do you need anything? Is there anything you need me to verify? Papers, anything at all that proves who you are?"

"I have my military ID and my badge. They know who I am, and they have my passport. I think it's something else they're waiting for. But we'll get there. I just want you to know how much I love you and how much I'm thinking about you and how much I wish I could be there with you. If this turns out to be a long event that will take days or weeks to resolve, I want you to go back home and muster up the resources we have there, rather than spending time here waiting for answers that just don't seem to be coming. I'm sure they're doing everything they can."

"One thing Kyle said is that it was important that the media not get hold of this story. I guess that's more a warning for me than for you."

"He's thinking about the SEAL community. I'm not worried about my career, Sophia. If it happens, it happens. I know Kyle's probably worried about it. But if the media gets hold of it, in my way of thinking, it would be more a blemish on the new ambassador to England than it would be on me. I would think they wouldn't want that. But I'll let them tell me I'm wrong."

"That's a good point. And I think I agree with you. Well, I'll be here.

You make your calls, and if there's anything else I can do, please text me or call me or have someone else leave me a message. We're safe, people here have been wonderful, and the main thing is I'm just trying to give the girls some Christmas spirit," she whispered into the phone. "They still think we're going back on the ship."

"Gotcha. Well, I love you, and I'll be in touch soon."

"Love you as well."

"And, Sophia, things are going to change. One thing I've been doing is thinking about things. I'm partially responsible for all this. I should have made a different choice. From now on, I'm going to do things differently. You'll see."

"You try your best."

"This time, it wasn't good enough. I got distracted, and I put you all in jeopardy."

"Lots of time in the future to talk about that. For now, just get yourself out of there. I want you home. You belong with me."

"I sure do. I'm going to make that my sole priority. I promise."

THE HOUSEKEEPING STAFF brought back their washed, ironed, and folded clothes, and Sophia asked for a recommendation for pizza, which had been the choice of the girls. She showed Sophia a brochure on the desk with the phone number of a pizzeria that came highly recommended.

Sophia ordered an extra-large pizza because she was feeling like she could eat the whole thing herself. She was so relieved and famished. She put a movie on for the kids and prepared a bottle for Domenica after she managed to smear pizza sauce all over her pink cheeks. Resisting being washed, the toddler finally settled in for the night with her bottle, the girls next to her in the hide-a-bed.

Sophia double-checked the lock on the door and then took a quick shower, getting ready for an early bedtime. She was glad that, so far, the news was good. Now she needed to rest. Tomorrow, they'd start putting together a team and a plan. God, she hoped Nick, Kyle, Teseo, and all the rest of them, her friends and Mark's brothers forever, would come to Mark's aid. She wondered if she should attempt to stir things up a bit with the ambassador and his wife or ask the local police if they were looking into the drugs on board the ship but decided she would let others do the work they were better at anyway.

The girls were asleep, and the TV was turned off. Sophia grabbed the toddler, brought her to bed with her, and promptly fell asleep.

At 2:00 a.m., her phone rang again.

"Sophia, this is Teseo Dominichello, and I understand Mark has been transferred. Forgive the early morning call."

"No, it's okay. We expected him to stay here so that's where I am. But he's in Montepulciano, at the federal prison there."

"Yes, I know of it. I have some acquaintances there. You must be beside yourself with worry."

"That's good of you to say, Teseo, but Mark is the one who needs your help. I need an attorney that I can go visit with and can give me some direction on what we should be doing and if there should be petitions filed since I don't understand how the system works here."

"You best just leave things the way they are, since sometimes things happen unofficially. I think he's in good hands, although the ambassador and his wife are still forcefully demanding charges be filed. The main reason for my call is just to let you know that, so far, the prosecutor has not decided to charge. But that could happen at any time."

"That is good news. I will take any bit of good news I can."

"Well, there is one other thing, and I hesitate to let you know, but they have made a complaint against not only Mark but Carrie Ann. And that's a whole other issue. Family court—anything having to do with minors—is a very tricky situation here. If they don't become reasonable, and I'm sorry I couldn't appear to be coming to your aid, but if the ambassador and his wife don't turn their thinking around, I may have to ask you to do something your attorney probably wouldn't recommend."

"What is that?"

"I'm sorry. I'm not at liberty to say. But you'll know when I call you. I'm only going to ask you to do this if we've lost any other leverage we have. Just understand that. Everyone has Mark's welfare at heart. If there's a way to get him back soon, rather than have this drag on for weeks and months, that's what we're going to do. I am meeting with Kyle via Skype tomorrow. We are not going to pull out of port until I know exactly what we're running into. The ambassador and his wife are demanding that we keep to our timetable. We'll see what happens."

"Thank you, and I appreciate your cooperation. I wasn't sure."

"No, my dear, Mark is a dear friend. You, well, you light up the whole ship with your smile and your dancing. I just want to get you back doing that again. I just know this must be extremely difficult. So I will pray for you. Please have heart, and we'll talk probably tomorrow in the morning."

"I'll talk to you whenever you call, but I'm going to need a few hours to catch up with my sleep. Thank you so much for calling, Captain."

MARK WAS AWAKENED early by the sounds of shouting and arguing coming from down the hall. His room was a square ten by ten with windows facing the garden he'd driven past yesterday. Bars, of course, made it impossible for escape, but the door had a window in it and was not set up with bars like a normal jail cell.

It was also temperature controlled. He was given an adequate pillow and two blankets. He also was issued disposable slippers and a set of prison fatigues that turned into pajamas and were reasonably comfortable. He was allowed to turn the light on and off, although there were rules on when he could do this, and with no blinds or shades on the window, as soon as light came in, his room was extremely bright—he would have to say even cheery.

He'd been dreaming about something he couldn't completely recall. He was in a boat, a small boat, like the rubber boats they used to practice with during BUD/s training. But it was a holiday. He felt the bobbing of the water, lulling him in and out of sleep. But when he heard the arguing, he bolted straight up.

He didn't understand Italian, so the conversation was meaningless to him. There was an older gentleman who was dressing down two or three other people. He did hear several times the word "general," so he assumed that there was some military component to the argument. Then he heard the distinctive words "SEAL Team 3 from Coronado." That's when he knew the argument was about him.

He had not been able to get hold of Kyle but left a message. He was given a phone number Kyle could call back on—the cell on the prosecutor's card. As far as he knew, no one yet had contacted the Navy.

The argument got extremely heated, and then another individual arrived, putting an immediate stop to it. There was whispering before the entire group left the hallway off into a more secure, quiet room.

Mark decided to wash his face and put on his clean set of prison fatigues. The razor he was given was dull, and he wasn't given shaving cream but a bar of soap, which was of good quality. He felt better with a clean face and shave. He smelled better, and his clothes were clean. He set aside all his toiletry articles and sat on the edge of his cot, slipping his feet into the slippers. It was time to wait.

The books that he had decided to bring never made it to him. But he was glad to learn that several of them, signed copies from admirals or men he had learned special warfare tactics with, were not lost. Those were some of the most important books in his library, which was small.

Finally, he heard footsteps coming down the hall. At the same time, he thought it odd that he didn't hear any other prisoners, at least in this part of the building. He was going to ask about that.

He saw the face of one of the guards in the window. Keys jangled and the door was opened. Behind him stood an older gentleman in a full military outfit, not a dress uniform, but more a uniform of a politician with medals and ribbons overflowing. It reminded him of all the medals and epaulettes he'd seen on the cruise ship officers. Rounding out the group of three was the female prosecutor he had met with yesterday.

"Special Operator Beale, we have a request for an interview. You can refuse the interview if you like, but we are going to encourage you to meet with General Verasco, who is the grandfather of the boy you assaulted on the ship."

The guard was very serious, showing no sympathy and no emotions.

Mark studied the older gentleman and sized him up to be a blowhard, a fat, opportunistic, politician throwing his weight around. He didn't trust him at all. The lines of his face formed a perfect scowl.

"I wish to be told first when I am going to see my representation," Mark insisted.

The prosecutor came forward.

"Mark, as I told you yesterday, we are working on things. I don't have an exact answer for you. We are attempting to get in touch with your commanding officer and the Department of the Navy. We have reached out to the consulate in Rome, and we understand an official should be coming here today. One way or the other, you will have somebody from your side of the aisle visit with you. I'm not sure what that means yet, but we will try to get some answers for you."

"Okay, so if that's a promise, is it something I can count on?"

The general boiled over quickly, showing distain and a total lack of respect. "You have no right to demand anything. You have assaulted my grandson" he said.

"Not to be disrespectful, General, but in our country, we are inno-cent until proven guilty. I have not had a trial, and I have not, as far as I know, been charged. I am looking forward to my day in court. I'm sure everyone wants to get to the bottom of what occurred. Probably me more than anyone else." Mark saw that his delivery pleased the prosecu-tor, who stifled a small grin.

"Let's proceed down to the interview room where we can sit at the table then," the guard inserted.

Mark held his hands out as if he was going to have handcuffs ap-plied, and the prosecutor waved him away. "It's not necessary, Mr. Beale. You're being detained but not charged at this point."

He followed the group of three down the hall to the same interview room he'd been in the day before. He was given the seat at the head of the table. Everyone was given a bottle of water. He didn't realize how thirsty he'd been.

The general leaned into the table and folded his fingers together in front of him. "You are a trained killer, Mr. Beale. You have learned how to subdue and attack your enemies. You are no match for a sixteen-year-old kid, who may not understand how lethal a weapon you are. But I understand. I understand the threat to my grandson's life."

Mark considered whether he should reveal too much of what he thought would be his defense. He decided to give him just a tease.

"I saw your grandson break the law. If I am convicted and go to jail, I'm going to see to it that he does as well. He put my daughter in danger, and he knows it. I suggest you get the truth from his parents."

"This is ridiculous. What justification did you have for bruising his face and perhaps breaking his nose?"

"I didn't break his nose. Believe me, I know the sound a broken nose makes. Show me the medical report, will you?"

"He was treated at the medical bay. But I will get you the records if you like."

"I need to have that for my defense. I also would like to have him examined by an independent physician. Not on the ship but in Naples."

The prosecutor interrupted him. "Mark, I don't think we can ask for that."

"You need to check your priorities, Ms. Gaultieri. You almost sound like his own counsel. Your job is to see to it that justice is done. Nothing more."

She smiled, but Mark could see it was brittle. "I respect your opinion, General. That is exactly what I'm focused on, as we all are."

Mark could see that no further good would come of the conversation. Perhaps this is what they'd been arguing about. But he couldn't sit and listen to any more of it.

"Why do I have to sit here in this facility unable to appreciate my wife and three children, the youngest who is barely walking, my daughters who don't understand why their father, a war hero, is being treated so despicably? I am shocked that I am not given the same rights as your grandson. It is not the way you would be treated in my country."

"You think your country is so great? Your country has lots of problems, my son."

"I am not your son. I don't know anything about you, but I do know that your grandson takes drugs and sells drugs, and for that, I believe Italian law is quite harsh. Now perhaps your grandson is too young to serve in a detention facility, but then shouldn't his parents be held responsible for his behavior? There are several people on the ship who will bear witness to some of the things that gang of boys was up to. They were not just having a good time. They were bumping into people, they were stealing things, they were kicking bottles around on the deck until they broke, and I believe one of them pushed me over the railing. These are dangerous boys with substances that kill people. I'm surprised as a leader in your country that you're not even halfway concerned about that. I'm surprised that the new ambassador to England isn't concerned about finding out who had the drugs and why."

The older gentleman was clearly disturbed by Mark's remarks.

"I believe, General, it would be a good idea if your grandson and his parents came here to sit for an interview. I have some questions," said the prosecutor. "Perhaps that could go a long way to sorting everything out."

"That's preposterous. They're on a cruise for my son-in-law's new career in England. He's on official state business, and they have diplomatic immunity. They are not required to appear anywhere."

"I don't believe that covers the sale of drugs in international or Italian waters. I have spoken to the captain of the ship, who has verified that the contents that were purportedly dropped by your grandson, contained the chemical fentanyl. Do you understand what a serious allegation that is?"

"This is why my daughter has complained that this gentleman here has put his young daughter up to selling drugs to earn money on their cruise. This is why it's so important that he'd be prosecuted."

"If it's warranted, that is exactly what we'll do. On the other hand, if we find evidence bearing out Mr. Beale's statement of facts, we are going to have to open an official investigation. Perhaps the British government may have to be notified of this."

Mark was glad the prosecutor said what he dared not say. He did not know that Teseo had made contact. Things were looking up, but he wasn't out of the woods yet.

"I am going to cooperate 100% with any investigation you wish to have, Ms. Gualtieri, and I assume that General Verasco will do the same. I'm at your disposal."

CHAPTER 17

"**A**RE YOU SITTING down, Sophia?" Kyle Lansdowne asked her.

"No, I don't want to sit down. Is it good news?"

"I think it is. We found you a top-notch Italian attorney who's a law professor in Milan. He's agreed to take on your case pro bono, and he knows several of the players and has represented international soccer stars and businessman who have been detained in Italy on a whole host of situations from visa issues to extraditions, sanctions, and prisoner swaps."

"Music to my ears, Kyle. I knew you'd come through. Any idea why all this crap is happening to Mark?"

"Sometimes grudges are formed. Cabinet ministers and officials throw their weight around and create havoc for foreign nationals who get victimized and caught in the crosshairs. I believe he is exactly the guy you should have."

"Okay, so when does Mark get to see him?"

"Well, he would like to come pick you up in about two hours. If you can get a sitter for the girls—"

"I have one already arranged. Just in case. Two hours, that makes it 10:00?"

"Yes, ma'am. He will pick you up at the hotel, and the two of you will discuss the case as he's driving you up to Montepulciano. Teseo was able to get permission for the three of you to meet. Mark, of course, has to agree to all this, but I'm going to call him next and tell him to start making some notes if he can. They've told us they're going to give him pencil and paper so he can start working on his defense."

"What about charges? Are there going to be charges?"

"Our hope is that there will be no charges filed and the whole thing will just go away. However, we still have the issue of the drugs, and once the two of you and your family are back home in the States and on base, I believe Teseo's company is going to go after the grandson of General Verasco. But that's a little bit out of my hands. In the meantime, the kid and his family are going to be pulled off the ship and will be sent to London for his new job appointment. The company does not want that family on the cruise ship any longer."

"Wow, so they must have talked to some of the people we talked to then."

"It was reported by several people that someone was dealing drugs. Teseo has every single account. However, your little bag of tricks that Ophelia had is what's really driving this case. It is complete evidence, and if the baggy and wrapping and other things are put into forensic analysis, we're certain that his fingerprints will be all over it. I think they're going to be in a lot of trouble. But my main concern is getting you guys out of the country."

"Well, I have the babysitting taken care of, and I was going to attend the dinner here at the hotel. Then we were going to go up to the cathedral and listen to the children's Christmas Eve service. Are you sure I'll be back in time?"

"We'll make sure of it. I think you're going to like this guy."

"What's his name?"

"Antonio Garibaldi. Turns out, he's a distant relative of the famous Garibaldi who is credited with uniting the Italian country as one. It's a long story but an interesting one. I have a couple JAG officers here that have spent a lot of time with this guy. I think he's our man."

"Thank you so much."

Sophia quickly raced down to the desk and inquired about the babysitter who had been arranged for a future date. The clerk was a new girl Sophia had never seen before.

"Can she watch the girls for just a few hours this afternoon? I have to go see my husband."

She checked paperwork. "I see it here. I will call her right away. And you said you were meeting someone? May I have a name in case they come looking for you?"

"Antonio Garibaldi."

"And what time do you need to leave?"

"He's picking me up here at 10:00. I would say from 10:00 a.m. until maybe 3:00 at the most? I fully intend to be back in time for the dinner and the candlelight vigil."

"We will have her show up at the room at 10:00."

The babysitter arrived early, which Sophia was grateful for. The girls were given books to read and told that there would be no TV until they finished some writing exercises that Sophia had given them. And she had asked them also to draw a picture of their adventure in Italy.

"When are we going back to the boat?" asked Ophelia.

"Not this time, honey, but I promise we'll do another cruise someday. This time, something else came up that was unexpected. But it's all going to be okay, so don't worry."

Sophia waited for the attorney down in the lobby. At five minutes before 10:00, the gentleman arrived. Bringing an umbrella, he parked in the front and walked straight over to Sophia.

"You are Sophia Beale? Mark Beale's wife?"

"Yes, sir, and you are Antonio Garibaldi?"

"At your service, ma'am."

Sophia stood, hoisted her computer bag over her shoulder, waved to the clerk at the desk, and exited the front of the hotel. Garibaldi held the umbrella for her and opened the car door. He had a small new Mercedes coupe.

With all the rain, it was difficult for Sophia to recognize the roadway, but as they traveled, she saw the distinctive peak of the village of Montepulciano with the three churches and one castle perched on the top like crystals. They were still more than forty-five minutes away, but the peak of the extinct volcano, which had shaped the area, could be seen for miles around.

"Kyle says that you have a lot of experience with immigration or foreign businessmen and their issues with the government, similar to what Mark has here. I understand you're from Milan?"

"That's where my office is."

"And where you teach."

"That is correct, ma'am."

He was impeccably dressed. His nails were buffed and trimmed, his haircut looked fresh, and the interior of his car was immaculate. Sophia had always liked the attention to detail some Italian men adopted. Even his shoes were well polished, and there wasn't a speck of lint on his dark charcoal gray raincoat.

"Why don't you tell me in the few minutes we have left here, what is your defense, Sophia? What is it that you are going to be wanting to present or you want me to help you present?"

"Well, first of all, the boy was in possession of drugs, and we saw this. My daughter saw it, and I understand the captain has had the substance tested and it tested positive for fentanyl. I guess Mark's defense is going to be that he was acting for the good of the passengers, even though it wasn't his job. He's just wired to protect the innocent. He especially has a hard time dealing with people involved in the drug trade or human trafficking. I think what happened to him is his reflexes just kicked in and he overreacted a little bit. Like he was on a mission with his SEAL team."

"I was not aware he was a SEAL."

"Is a SEAL. He's still active. Didn't you talk to Kyle Lansdowne, his LPO?"

"Yes, yes, I did."

Sophia wondered if she'd heard Kyle correctly but put it out of her mind. "What else do you want to know?"

"I think what you have is a good start. What about Samuel's parents? Had you run across them before? Did you have any confrontations on board ship?"

"I don't believe we have. We heard from several people that there was a band of boys running around misbehaving, including one with Samuel's unique. We also heard that there had been a rash of hacked accounts on the cruise line, charges from the stores or the liquor store added to somebody's cabin bill. Our table mates said on a tour they had taken that several people on the bus had been hit with fraudulent charges. Also, with the percentage of elderly people on the cruise ship, the way those boys ran up and down the hallways and the outside decking, it was dangerous. So I think it was something that Mark thought was important enough to act quickly. He did not intend to cause him any harm, certainly not to draw blood."

"I'll need the names of those witnesses and people who had their accounts hacked."

"Happy to do so."

"How did this escalate into Mark's arrest?"

"He hasn't been arrested. He's been detained."

"Pardon. Yes, detained."

"The boy's mother went crazy, accused Mark of really battering Samuel. I didn't see him, of course, but from what I understand, it was just a bloody nose."

"Ah, but blood is blood. If he draws blood, there are certain rules and paths going through our criminal justice system that must be adhered to. Was anyone present who saw the altercation?"

"I don't know the answer to that because I wasn't there. I know that the boys' friends probably were there, because Mark told me they were trying to interfere, trying to pull him off Samuel, and they were punching him and kicking him while Mark was trying to hold Samuel and stop him from escaping."

"Okay, so we're going to have to find witnesses if we can. That will greatly improve our chances."

"What is your strategy going to be?" Sophia asked him.

"Well, first, I think there is a gentleman I work with who has some questions, and he's sort of an expert witness, so if you'll indulge me, I'd like to pick him up on the way."

Sophia was slightly concerned for this new development and wasn't a hundred percent willing to take on another stranger in the vehicle.

"That wasn't the arrangement. Will the prison allow another person?"

"It's no matter, if you're uncomfortable with it. We can do it another time. But I just thought it would help us get to the bottom of Mark's situation."

"If you think it will help Mark, if you think they will allow Mark to have three visitors instead of just two, I don't see where it would hurt. Who is this person?"

"Ah, he is a forensic accountant. I use him when we are discussing cybercrimes of various natures. He may want to ask you about your banking, about your income, that sort of thing. What we're trying to do is show a pattern that you're law-abiding citizens, you don't make a lot of money, and you're not interested in selling drugs. You don't have a background or a history of that, and you have no ability to manufacture the cybercrime of fraudulently charging other people's bills. We must create the groundwork of reasonable deniability; we need to make sure that the judge in this case sees that you are the least likely people to be involved in anything like that. And perhaps to convince him, as well, that this is the type of crime—drugs, credit card fraud—that young teens often find themselves involved with. That's a pattern that we're looking for."

"But I thought the main issue was the bodily harm, the assault charge?"

"What we're facing here is multi-faceted. We want to be prepared."

"I think Mark would be all right with that. Is it very far out of our way?"

"No, not really. Maybe ten minutes."

Sophia sat back as he turned off the two-lane country road leading to Montepulciano and followed the signs toward Florence.

"We're going to Florence?" she asked.

"No, we're stopping before there, but it's in the same direction."

"How long is your normal winter break?" she asked.

"Winter break?"

"For school. You teach at the law school, Kyle told me. How long do you have off between semesters?"

"We break the end of November. Many of the students go skiing in winter. We come back and start the semester the first of February. It's customary, however, for students to take summer classes, so in a way we have a nice vacation the beginning of summer and then again in the middle of winter around Christmas. Are you a religious person, Sophia?"

"Oh gosh, that's a difficult question. I was raised in the church, but aside from special performances and weddings and funerals, Mark and I don't really attend. We may be reconsidering that decision."

"And how do you like Italy? Is it your first time?"

"You know I am half Italian. My mother is Italian. My father was a serviceman killed in combat when I was young. We lived in California at the time, but after my father's death, my mother moved back here. I've been raised in two cultures, and Italy is not really what I consider home, but it is my family's home. I consider California home to us now."

"You ever considered living here as opposed to living in the States?"

"You mean going back to work for the cruise line? Or opening a dance studio, something like that?"

"Yes. Raising your family in ancient cities of Europe is a great cultural experience. Don't you feel unsafe living in the United States with all the crime?"

"Up until this situation with Mark, I always felt safe. He was always there with me. I never had reason to doubt my safety. I guess I took a lot for granted."

They continued driving, following a narrow roadway that barely had room for one car. On several occasions, they had to pull over onto a muddy shoulder to allow opposing traffic to pass them. The beautiful rolling hills and vistas of olive trees and vineyards disappeared, and they came through a section of land where it was heavily forested. At last, they drove up to a large estate home with an automatic iron gate that opened when the Mercedes stopped just in front of it.

Sophia extricated herself from the car just as the attorney was rounding the front side to help her. She had her computer case strapped over her shoulder, and he showed her the way to the front door. They were greeted by an employee in a uniform, directing them toward the living room.

"This individual is very wealthy, I take it. What is his relationship to you other than to use him as a consultant?"

"We are colleagues. We work together on many things, but it can be said that I work for him as well."

Sophia examined the tall ceilings with oil paintings depicting military men, some with metal armor, showing life as it was perhaps two or three hundred years ago. There were pictures of horses and portraits of beautiful women in flowing gowns, hired portraitures done by professional painters. The interior was filled with antiques, beautiful glassware, a collection of crystal goblets and whiskey glasses to one side, vases, china teapots, and vintage spirit bottles behind leaded glass cabinet doors. There was an assortment of clocks mounted on the mantel piece over the fireplace. It was a very masculine room, obviously set up to impress, which it did.

"This is quite a place."

"This house has been in their family for nearly four hundred years. They are descendants of royalty in a way," he said.

Sophia checked her watch. "I certainly hope he'll be down here soon. I don't want to worry Mark by making him wait."

Behind her, Sophia heard shuffling, and then a deep booming voice said, "He's going to have to wait, my dear. We have some questions for you."

She whirled around on her heel and saw an older gentleman in sweater and slacks, appearing to be close to her mother's age.

"You must be Sophia?" he asked, holding out his hand.

"Yes sir. And I'm sorry I didn't catch your name."

"General Verasco. I am the Deputy Secretary of Defense. We are discussing the way your husband abused my grandson."

She must have flinched, because the general added, "I'm not your enemy, Sophia. I just would like to make sure that proper justice is done."

Sophia stared at the attorney who avoided eye contact in return. "What's going on here? Are you an expert witness helping us with a case? Or is this something else? I feel like I've been lied to."

General Verasco began again, "I want to impress upon you that it would be wise for you to settle this particular matter outside of the authorities. If we must pursue a trial, if we must pursue what my daughter would like, which is have your husband charged with assault, and perhaps have a very public trial, it's going to be expensive. It will take a lot of time, and I'm hoping we can circumvent this."

"What is it you want from me?"

"There have been some allegations made against my grandson that I need to have corrected."

"Sir, I'm not the one making the allegations. My husband saw the drugs and, turned them in. Those items are outside of our control. They've been given to the captain, and I believe that's all been turned over to the police already."

"On the contrary, I have it on good authority that the drugs are under lock and key and will not be allowed outside the police station unless there is a very good reason why. In the absence of evidence, you really don't have a case."

"What exactly are you getting at? I feel like my husband should be part of this conversation. And don't you think it's wrong for you to insert yourself before I've even had a chance to talk to my husband after he was taken away? This was our ten-year anniversary gift to ourselves. We're traveling with three children, we've been forced off that ship, and my husband is being held against his will. Why is it that we need to have you intercede on our behalf? Your side is the one making all the claims against him. If you were to stop that, this all goes away."

"Not exactly. The allegation has been made that there are drugs, that my grandson either sells or takes drugs. And nothing could be further from the truth."

"I'm sorry, but I must object. I would like to go now, and I would like to see my husband. That's what I was promised, and that's the basis on which I got in the car with Mr. Garibaldi also."

"Oh, so he told you his name was Garibaldi?"

"That's who I was to meet."

"Well, there seems to be a little mix-up with that. And I apologize for contributing to it. Sophia, unfortunately, we are going to need to hold you here until we can secure your husband's promises and support for our cause."

"What you're telling me is now you're kidnapping me? First, you had my husband taken in, and now you're going to restrict me. I have children, Mr. Verasco."

"General Verasco, please."

"No, this is all wrong, and I must demand that you return me to my hotel immediately. Or to the prison there. I never agreed to this, and you got me coming here under false pretenses. I don't understand what you're looking for."

"You are right about one thing, Mrs. Beale. You aren't the one we should be talking to. You are, however, our leverage. I'm sure that your husband will be most cooperative when he discovers this. Again, we don't wish you any harm or ill will, but my son-in-law and daughter's reputation, as well as the reputation for their son, is extremely important to us. Certain things were said that must be retracted. I'm not asking. We are demanding this as a condition of yours and your husband's freedom."

CHAPTER 18

ARK WAS PACING in his small room, inquiring every few minutes about the meeting with Sophia and the attorney. He was told continually that there had been no calls and no news. He had been allowed to make a call to Sophia's phone, but it went directly to voicemail.

He asked if one of the guards could telephone the hotel to see if she had left, and the report came back that she had been picked up and was on her way to see him with the attorney.

He knew something was wrong. She would want to be on time. She would be just as antsy to have the meeting, as he was. He called the prosecutor's cell phone and inquired.

"I'm sorry, Mark, I haven't heard a thing. Let me see if I wrote the attorney's name down."

"But I understood him to be a colleague of yours. Is that not true?"

"Well, we deal with a lot of defense attorneys. I may or may not have run across him. If he is a law professor as you say, then of course he must be excellent. But honestly, I don't know the man." She shuffled some papers on her desk and then came up with a note. "Here it is, Antonio Garibaldi. Ah yes, I have heard of him. And I do believe he's a very good attorney. Would you like me to call his office?"

"Please. She is over an hour late now, and I'm concerned. Especially since she was picked up by him and isn't driving herself. I just want to make sure something hasn't happened."

"Of course. Let me call you back."

Roughly a half an hour later, Mark got the call from the prosecutor's office. "I have some bad news, and I'm going to send someone from our Naples office over to the hotel to check on the children. Sophia arranged a babysitter for them, and she left on time."

"So far so good."

"Hold on. Mr. Garibaldi had to cancel the appointment at the last minute. He had a conflict. I wasn't told this, and I don't understand why he didn't call you."

"Who is she riding with then?" Mark asked.

"That's the thing. I don't know."

"There is absolutely nothing I can do sitting here in this room. You must understand, my wife could be in danger. I need somebody who I can trust to go check and retrace her steps. I need to know exactly where she went and who she's with, if she's not with Mr. Garibaldi. Is this a kidnapping or just a miscommunication somehow?"

"I understand fully. I will send two uniforms over to the hotel to do a welfare check. We will question the staff, and I should get some answers for you. Please, Mark, if she does show up, please call me so I don't waste unnecessary manpower."

"You got it. You know where I'll be."

It was past one o'clock in the afternoon when Mark received a call from the police station in Naples.

"Mr. Beale, your children are at the hotel. They're being watched by one of the hotel staff. They appear to be in very good shape, very happy. Is there anything else we can do?"

"That's wonderful to hear. But I want to know where my wife is. She left with my new attorney, or who I thought was my new attorney, and she hasn't arrived. It's about an hour and a half past due. And that's not like her at all. This is a very important meeting, and she had to be back in Naples for another event this evening. I just don't know what's going on. Can you check the cameras and see who this person is who picked her up. Can you get a license plate?"

"Listen, Mark, we don't exactly have the resources to check on that, and you would have to file a missing or suspicious person report."

"But I'm sitting in a fucking prison in Montepulciano. I can't file that notice, and I need to know where my wife is. She could be in danger."

"I understand. Let me see what I can do, and from the communication we had with the front desk clerk, it appears she left in a white Mercedes coupe with a well-dressed individual. She appeared to know the person and left willingly. This is not a case of kidnapping."

"I understand that, but perhaps they had an accident on the way to visit me. It's not like her to be this late."

"Let's see if we can check the security cameras and get a license plate. That's the best I can do at this point. Do you have anyone else in the area you could employ to do some searching for you?"

"No, everybody on my SEAL team is back in Coronado in California. My only other friend is a ship's captain, and he is apparently docked at Capri, waiting for information on being released to continue with his itinerary, but that was the ship we were supposed to be on. Other than the captain and my wife's elderly mother, I have no one here to rely on. Absolutely no one. Do I need to get my State Department or the Department of Naval Affairs involved? Is this what I need to do?"

"At this point, it's not verified that this is a kidnapping. So there's a limit to what we can do. But let me check with my superior, and I think we can study the camera footage from the front of the hotel. And I'll re-question the desk clerk."

They had positioned Mark in the interview room, which gave him more space and enabled him to use a phone. The prosecutor had begun to be very generous with the phone time. Mark's next call was to Teseo Dominichello. He was told that the captain was in a meeting and would return the call shortly.

Frustrated and angry, feeling that time was slipping away, he made a call to Kyle Lansdowne.

"God, Mark, it's great to hear your voice. Hey, I tried to call Sophia this morning, and she doesn't pick up."

"I know, Kyle. That's why I'm calling you. The attorney that you put us in touch with—"

"Garibaldi?"

"Yes. Apparently, there's been a mix up, and she was prepared to go ride with him to come up to see me and did apparently get in a car with someone she believed was Garibaldi, except that Garibaldi's office has said he had to reschedule. I'm not quite sure why we didn't get the message, but my wife has gone off with somebody else. I just smell a rat. Kyle, something's wrong. I know it."

"Oh geez. I need to get hold of Teseo. Has the Department of Navy stopped by or the State Department yet?"

"I haven't seen or heard from anybody. At least they're letting me make some calls, but I'm shooting blanks here. I need to find her. And the local police say it's not a kidnapping case yet so there's a limit to what they can do. What am I supposed to do?"

"Well, I think I better call Garibaldi's office and explain what's happened. Unless they're aware of it?"

"I have no idea. I've left a message for Teseo. Maybe he'll have something for me. I don't want to assume the worst, but I don't like the fact that she's been out of communication. If everything was up and up, her phone would be on. She would answer calls or make calls. She would tell me she was late and why. That makes me think they've either had an accident or something is definitely wrong."

"God, Mark, I worked on this thing halfway into the night, and I thought we had all this handled. I don't understand why the attorney's office didn't clear the schedule or make the communication, but maybe they tried to. If her phone's off or lost or damaged, maybe that's what happened, but you would think they would reach out. So let me do some checking, and I'll get back to you."

"Thanks, Kyle. Any word from the Navy?"

"Not at this point. Mark, that's a good thing. When they start to make inquiries and get overly picky about reports and forms and all that shit, then I know something's going to hit the fan. But so far, they're kind of taking it slow. I'm hoping that they'd just like this thing to go away. But God help me, Mark, I don't know what the fuck's going on. But something is throwing this whole thing off-kilter. We'll get to the bottom of it. I know it sounds self-serving to say don't worry, but under the circumstances, really all you can do is try to stay calm and know that we're doing everything we can."

"I hope somebody from state or the Navy can jump in and overrule some of these decisions. I don't know how much leeway they have, but I need some big guns over here, Kyle. And I'm losing time."

"Where are the kids?"

"They're with a staff babysitter at the Hotel Savona. I've had a welfare check on them, and the police confirmed that they're happy and everything looks fine, and the hotel was aware that she was going on an appointment to see me with the attorney, and as far as they're concerned, that's where she went. It's just that she hasn't arrived, and I've got to find out where she is."

"We'll get it done. I know you'd do the same for me. Hang in there, sport. What a vacation this has been, huh?"

"Don't ask me to go on a cruise. I thought third time was going to be the charm. If something happens to me on another cruise, it's because I'm a stupid dumb motherfucker and didn't listen to reason. I have no business on a boat or being a fucking dance instructor. Trying to make nice with a whole bunch of weird people. It's not my thing."

"Yeah, I know. Same thing happened to me the last time. You can't unsee some of the things you see. And if someone innocent is causing a problem, it's hard not to jump in. I get it. It's an occupational hazard for us. But I know you'd rather err on that side than on the side of not having any feelings for people or not wanting to right the wrongs that you can right. I think if it wasn't for the fact that this kid was the grandson of a cabinet minister and the son of an ambassador, it would be a whole other story. This one was a fluke, and how the hell did you know anyway? I'll get back to you as soon as I finish my calls."

"Thanks again, Kyle."

Antonio Garibaldi showed up after three o'clock, just as the State Department representative had arrived. They sat down with Mark, listening to his story, all the bits and pieces and now the situation with Sophia.

"You're going to have to launch a formal inquiry, Steve," Garibaldi said to the man from State. "I'm not going to be able to do that. It must come from you. And they better get their butts in gear, or it's going to be an international incident."

"I got you. Let me step outside and get that going," he said.

"Mark, I need to ask you a question."

"Like I've been telling people, I'm here I'm willing to cooperate. Whatever you want to know, just ask."

"Thanks for your patience, and frankly, I'm ashamed of what's happened to you. There must be something I'm missing here, because these types of things just don't happen in Italy. I mean, every country has its little quirks of the judicial system, but this, this smacks of politics. And whenever politics gets involved, no matter where in the world it is, you know how that is. It fucks up everything."

"If I'd known who this kid was, maybe I would've acted differently."

"I'm not going to lecture you; you obviously know you shouldn't have pushed him up against the wall. But no way in hell should you be put through this. I'm just not sure that we're getting a fair hand here. And the fact that they're holding your wife as sort of hostage? At least that's the way it feels to me. That's way over the top. And somebody powerful is pulling some big strings. Either that or they're dumb as shit. First of all, I apologize about the cancellation. I did leave a message with the front desk at the hotel for her, and I'm surprised she didn't get it."

"Well, maybe that's the source of the problem. Maybe somehow that information got out to the wrong people."

"Could be, but a couple of things I need to ask you about because we have some choices on how we're going to work this. I want to bring in the news media."

"Oh no, my LPO says no media. That'll fuck it all up."

"Normally I'd agree with you, but in this case, public opinion and scrutiny in the news media, well, it puts a spotlight on things and all of a sudden stuff just clears up. I think this needs to go on a local news channel, and I have a reporter friend of mine that I can leak it to, and if Steve here has lodged his complaint or inquiry, we have a reason to go to the press and ask for justice. From what I understand with the defense minister's grandson being involved in drugs, either that's a complete fabrication or completely easily disproven, or they're being dumb about this. I just think that we need some help outside of the justice system."

"You're my attorney, and I'm sorry about how you got drug into this. I don't know whether it's a good thing or not, but I trust your instincts. You came highly recommended."

"Have the police located the person driving the Mercedes?" he asked.

"No, I haven't heard back from them."

"Okay, so I'm going to have Steve ride hard on them. I've worked with him before, and he can be a regular son of a gun. I think we need to rattle some cages; I know it's only been a day, but I sure as heck don't want this thing to go on for much longer. Suddenly, people get ideas that you're trying to throw your weight around, that the US is trying to ask for special favors for their elite warrior—we don't need any of that crap going on. You're a victim. You possibly made a little error in judgment, but you're a victim. The sooner we can get the public to understand that the better it's going to be. I'm not so sure their side is defensible in the press. I'd like to see how they squirm and how they justify it. I think that's going to tell me exactly who's behind this and why."

"Then, Mr. Garibaldi, have at it. I'll sit and talk to a reporter; I'll do whatever you want."

"No, I don't want you making any public statements. Let me do that, but better still, I'd like Steve to jump in and put the weight of the United States government on their backs. We'll see what they're made from. If that doesn't work, then we'll go to plan B."

"What's plan B?" Mark asked.

"I have no fucking idea."

CHAPTER 19

SOPHIA HAD BEEN locked in the basement wine cellar of the general's estate. She was provided a sandwich, some water, a couple of blankets, and a pillow for the cot that was set up for her. She knew it was nighttime, because she could hear the cicadas chirping through the foundation vents.

There was no light until she found a small pocket flashlight on one of the tables in the storage room. It appeared they used this for bottling or labeling, and a small assembly line was set up.

She tried the door handle after she was locked inside and found it was a lock that took a skeleton key. It could be picked if she could find some strong wire. She needed to find copper wire, preferably small enough so she could insert two into the keyhole.

Searching several of the shelves, she explored under papers and boxes and scoured the countertops and the two folding tables. At last, in the corner, she found some plastic-coated wiring rolled up in a coil. That required she find a pair of pliers, which she did on the bottling table. She cut herself two eight-inch strips, peeled back part of the plastic so she could insert the ends into the keyhole, and was able to pick the lock very carefully with the flashlight in her mouth.

When it at last turned over with a loud click, she was concerned that someone would hear her. With her ear up to the door, she heard music and talking from a radio or a small TV echoing from the kitchen area. She also previously heard pots and pans and the smell of food being prepared and assumed the general's employee was making a dinner. The cadence and movement continued, and she was grateful for the loudness of the TV.

Slowly opening the door, it emitted a loud squeak. She stopped to listen once again for any kind of activity from the kitchen. Assuming it was clear, she stepped through the doorway, closed the door quietly behind her, and tiptoed to the right, down the hallway toward the front door. In the living room area, she found her purse hanging on the back of a chair and her laptop propped up against the front leg.

Slipping the laptop over her shoulder and her purse wrapped cross-body, she was able to exit the front door, scan the surrounding area and parking lot in front, and determine that no one was there, nor did there appear to be any guards. Carefully, she exited the stairway and checked both cars out, finding both locked with no sign of keys.

Her choices were to walk down the small path to the right or head straight down the driveway toward the main road. She chose the first since she didn't want to be viewed from the second story of the house, which would be possible. It was a full moon, so the road and shrubbery glistened in the moonlight, wet with rain. She headed right.

A storage shed appeared a few feet away from the gardens surrounding the house, and with the door slightly ajar, she pried it open and found it filled with tools. Very quickly, she turned on the flashlight only to get a view of what was inside and was excited to find a bicycle. Not only that, but it was also an electric bicycle, and it had been plugged in. That meant it had a full charge.

Again, securing her laptop and purse on the back of the bicycle in the basket holder, she walked it outside and realized she needed a key to turn it on. Inside, she found a key that matched the brand of the bicycle hanging on a hook with a small bicycle charm on its key fob.

The bicycle whirred to life, a red light flashing and then going solid green. She mounted it, started pedaling, then kicked in the electric feature. It was quiet, and she hoped that her escape had been undetected.

Sophia passed a garbage area with a dumpster and several recycling garbage cans next to it. There also was a pile of leaves and garden shrubbery being composted. The path turned slightly to the left, heading more directly to the roadway.

On her trip out to the house, she remembered turning at a small convenience store and gas station just before the long entrance to the estate. That's where she headed.

Setting the bicycle around the backside of the gas station, she tiptoed through the shadows, examining through the windows to determine if someone was in the store. A young skinny clerk with scruffy black hair and wearing blue jeans and a Beatles T-shirt was perched on the stool behind the counter, watching a small TV and smoking.

Leaving her computer case but bringing her purse, she walked inside and greeted the store clerk. In Italian, she asked him if she could use his telephone.

He solemnly pointed to the wall next to the freezer compartment where there was a payphone. She asked for change with her paper money and dialed Mark's number. She didn't expect him to pick up, since she was sure they had still maintained his papers, his passport, and his phone and wallet.

But she was surprised.

"Hello?" Mark's warm and buttery voice was a welcome distraction. She missed him, but more than that, it was reassurance that he was not being mistreated and was healthy.

"Mark, this is Sophia. I don't have much time, but I've escaped from the general's house."

"The general? What does he have to do with this?"

"I think it was one of his men who picked me up at the hotel, impersonating the attorney, Garibaldi. I'm sorry. I was tricked, and they've been holding me here at his estate."

"Oh, my love, it is so wonderful to hear your voice. I'm here with Garibaldi right now. We were just going to be searching some addresses we found on the closed caption TVs outside the hotel. We found the license plate of the Mercedes."

"These people are looking for you to recant the story about the drugs and his grandson. I'm going to try to ride my bicycle—"

"When did you get a bicycle?"

"Mark, just listen to me please. I don't have much time. I'm going to head down the road. I found a bicycle in the shed at the house. It's an electric bike so I should make some decent time, but I'm going to head back the way he brought me, which is the opposite of traveling to Florence. I don't know what the name of the road is or the highway, but

I'm just going to head back the way I remember coming."

"Gotcha."

"We turned from Naples. We were heading to Montepulciano, and then he turned off toward Florence to pick up his friend, he said. It turned out he brought me to the general's house, and they have kept me there since."

"That explains a lot, and oh my gosh, hold on a second."

Sophia heard some conversation in the background.

"I'm about an hour and fifteen minutes away, Garibaldi says. He's going to have the civil guard from Naples try to meet you on the roadway and have you wait there. I'll drive down with Garibaldi."

"So you've been released? That's wonderful!"

"In light of what's been happening, the prosecutor decided that now is not the time to pursue charges. She would like to do a further investigation, and I'm confident she'll have everything she needs to go after these people. I am so happy you've gotten yourself free."

"Well, keep your fingers crossed, because it's dark, and the general and his henchman probably will be coming down the roadway any minute now. I'm going to be dodging in the bushes, avoiding every vehicle, every person I see, but if they come to a little convenience store before the general's estate, they've gone too far. That means they've missed me."

"I will let them know. And thank God. I love you. And the girls?"

"I haven't been able to talk to them. Hopefully you have."

"Not yet. But Garibaldi had the civil guard over to watch. They did a welfare check earlier, and they were doing fine. The babysitter turned out to be a real asset. But the police are there now, and they're waiting for me or you. Waiting for further instructions."

"I hope I get to see you soon. I'll see you in Naples, is that correct?"

"If they don't find you in about thirty minutes, forty-five minutes perhaps, you give me back a call. Okay?"

"Of course."

THEY HAD A tearful reunion in the Naples Police Department. Garibaldi was introduced to Sophia, and he turned out to be exactly the type of ally they needed. Thank God, she thought to herself.

Mark looked great, even under the circumstances. Sophia was exhausted after the five-mile ride she had gotten in by moonlight before the police picked her up. She was starved, so the station sprung for pizza. It was always pizza, the universal food there.

"What's the next step?" she said, folded into his arms.

"We're waiting on the prosecutor. We're waiting on Garibaldi's information, and we're also waiting for the State Department liaison who has lodged a formal inquiry as to my treatment. It's certainly going to get a lot of attention."

"I thought Kyle told us to keep it tight. He didn't want publicity."

"Garibaldi felt it was a good idea to give the story to a local reporter so we could begin to get an advance on some of the local public opinion. With the general's influence, it's possible he has friends in high places. This is going to make it more difficult for him to maneuver."

Garibaldi stepped forward. "If they are going to do illegal things, they do it in secret in the dark. They don't like the press, and our general population does not trust the government."

Sophia understood that one completely. But kept her mouth shut.

"He doesn't think the general has anything to do with the drugs, but he's trying to save his son-in-law's job. Now his own. This is a big step to foiling anything he's got up his sleeve," Mark explained.

She and Mark were free to go, and they were given a police escort to the hotel to visit with the girls and get some rest. The local captain promised that there would be a guard placed in the hotel lobby, as well as in the hallway by their room, so they would be undisturbed.

After the girls settled down, all of them wanting to climb all over Mark, hug him, kiss him, even little Domenica grabbing his lower leg and kissing his knee, which had him in stitches, they were returned to bed. Everyone settled down.

Sophia took Mark outside onto the balcony where they could view the full moon and the village lights in the distance. "You remember when we were planning this vacation?"

"Absolutely."

"I said surprise me?"

Mark grimaced and winced. "Yes."

"I don't think I'm ever going to give you that answer again. Except in bed."

CHAPTER 20

ONCE THE INVESTIGATION began, things proceeded at a record pace. Teseo was notified of their release, which relieved him greatly. Garibaldi also mentioned to him that the civil guard in Naples would be boarding the ship to escort the family of the ambassador off.

"Mark, I thank you for this. And I'd love to speak with you a little longer, but I'm going to ask for clearance to set sail. I would like to get out of Italian waters as fast as possible."

"Understood. Well, I'll let you get that done then. The civil guard should be on their way to the port now."

Teseo had docked at Naples, where there were more facilities for onboarding passengers as well as supplies for the next stage of the voyage.

"You're sure you don't want to come on board again?" the captain queried.

"No, I've been set free, but I've been told I can't leave the country yet. We're going to make sure it's all done correctly, dot every I and cross every T. And if I'm going to save my Naval career, it has to be done that way."

"Are they going to charge the ambassador or his family?"

"My guess is no. I think the general, though, is in trouble."

"The general?"

"The ambassador's wife is the general's daughter. General Verasco. He's the Minister of Defense."

"Oh, I see. Yes, I would say he's in considerable trouble if he kidnapped Sophia."

"You'll be able to read a nice juicy story all about it tomorrow online. Smooth sailing, and God speed. We'll have to catch up sometime in the future. But thank you for a most memorable ten-year anniversary cruise."

"You never renewed your vows."

"Hey, it's Christmas. I'm going to do Christmas with my family. That's the most important thing of all. But second to that, my friends and allies and the brothers I've been fortunate to serve with. I consider you one of those, Teseo."

"Well, I hope your stay in Italy is uneventful now. Time for some sightseeing, maybe some good wine, and enjoy some of our fabulous food."

The hotel prepared a special breakfast for the family, since they had missed the services and the Christmas Eve dinner. Of course, neither Sophia nor Mark had done any Christmas shopping for the girls, so several of the cleaning staff, as well as the front desk and the general manager, got together and wrapped some toys and children's books in Italian and a few specialized purses and clothes for the girls. It was a different kind of Christmas than what they normally had. And Mark liked it because of its simplicity and the fact that it didn't take them four hours to open all the packages. The girls were happy, and they were all together.

The cook made the girls special animal-shaped pancakes done with a cookie cutter. There were delicacies from the bakery down the street, the fresh espresso coffee served twenty-four seven in the bar, and Italian Christmas music, mostly choral groups.

After checking in with the prosecutor and Garibaldi, Mark and Sophia and the girls decided to walk on Christmas morning down the cobblestone meandering street to the cathedral nearby. All along the way, shops displayed their finest decorations, pastries, their known specialty meats, and brightly wrapped gifts.

When they got to the cathedral, the morning church service was over, and there was a choir rehearsal. Oddly, it was a children's choir.

"Look, girls, we get to see the children's choir after all. Don't they sound beautiful?"

Domenica blurted out, "I want to."

Several members of the choir started to giggle as Domenica's voice carried, echoing throughout the tall ceiling and balustrades.

Sophia's face and hair showed the reflection of the colorful stained-glass windows of the church, and it was fitting that, on Christmas Day, they'd be sitting here together, not on a boat, not running into crazy teenagers or gossipy adults, but just being a family and listening to the joy of the holiday.

They headed out toward the narthex to return to their hotel. The parish priest stopped them on the steps. "My children, thank you for gracing our doorway. I hope you will come back."

"Thank you, Father. We're from the States, and here on business for just a few days. But thank you for letting us listen to the beautiful choir. The girls loved it."

"It's a miracle, isn't it, how all those little voices come together and make one beautiful sound?"

Mark shook his hand and then posed a question. "Do you do marriage vows? I mean redo of marriage vows?"

"Not often, not as often as I'd like to, but yes, we can do that. Is it for you, my son?"

Mark looked at Sophia. "Do you want to do that today, on Christmas?"

"Are you free, Father?" Sophia asked him.

"Why don't you wait, and after the choir is finished, we'll do a private service for you. Would you like the girls involved?"

Neither Mark nor Sophia was able to answer since all three of the girls jumped up and down and cheered for the idea.

It was a special Christmas, a special way to celebrate ten years being together and the family that they'd grown together, and nearly lost. It underscored to them the true meaning of Christmas, a time for the celebration of the birth of one very special child.

It was also the time to celebrate one very special family and marriage.

DESTINY OF LOVE

SEAL Brotherhood: Legacy Series
Book 6

SHARON HAMILTON

CHAPTER 1

"HEY, SON, IS Julie home?" Mr. Christensen's voice was softer than usual. Luke was barely able to hear his father-in-law.

"No, she's still down at the school. It's parent-teacher night tonight. What's up?" he asked.

At first, there was silence. Julie's dad was normally very talkative, quite chatty, and always upbeat. Luke's antennae began to pick up something dark and ominous.

An involuntary sigh preceded the older man's gradual high-pitched whine followed by a collapse of his voice altogether. He started to sob into the phone. Luke plugged his right ear so he could make out the mumbling words. "I-I don't know how to say this."

"What is it? Is something wrong with Melinda?"

"No, not Melinda. It's Colin and Stephanie."

Luke and Julie's two girls were playing in the backyard in their new blow-up pool they'd bought the day before. September could be warm in San Diego, and the new pool gave them comfort, as well as occupied them for hours. The happy splashing and screaming, like two young sisters who competed in everything, sounded normal. But Luke knew this was not a normal call, nor a normal day. If Julie's dad's call was just a hello to touch base, Luke would've been out the back door screaming at them to be quiet so he could listen. But with Mr. Christensen in his current state, Luke dared not do that, and he halfway didn't want to even hear him.

Oh, shit. Here it comes.

"I'm sitting down, Dad. Tell me what it is." He steeled himself for news he knew was going to be horrible.

"Stephanie and Colin were at that convention in Las Vegas, and on their way back—they were almost home…" He broke down again.

"Take your time. Breathe, Dad."

"We've been having a marvelous time watching the kids for them. They've been little angels, bless their hearts." His voice hitched again, and he began to tear up.

It was hard for Luke to listen to his struggle. He wished he was there to comfort him.

"They needed this getaway so badly. They've been working so hard."

"Yeah, Stephanie was excited about it. She said they needed some alone time." He didn't want to think about his baby sister *that way* so he continued. "We couldn't offer to babysit this time, due to the beginning of the school year."

"Well, we got a call."

Again, silence on the other end of the line. Luke was careful not to let his heavy breathing carry over the phone, but now he was shaking.

"Luke, they were in a traffic accident, T-boned, just outside of San Jose. Stephanie was brain dead, no signs of life, no chance, and then she passed. Colin was, well, he was killed instantly."

Luke's veins filled with ice water. It was absolutely the last thing he ever thought he would hear. His little sister, the mother of three beautiful children and whose wedding he was best man for, was gone. She was such a sweet person, such a vibrant soul. And Julie's brother, Colin Christensen, had been one of his best friends when they lived in San Diego. A really solid guy. On board with the big family and hoping to have more.

The four of them as couples had been very close; the cousins—all girls ranging in ages from ten to six—were even closer. Now there were going to be three children without a mother and a father. Aging grandparents, also grieving. It was the worst that could happen, absolutely the worst.

He felt the foundation he'd been building, all the work he'd been doing, begin to crumble. It set him on the dark path he thought he'd recovered from.

"Oh, Dad, I'm so sorry," he said through his tears. "We'll get up there. We'll bring the girls if it isn't too much on everyone."

"No. That's fine."

Mr. Christensen was trying to be strategic, but his thought processes were failing. He was going through the motions, trying to inform, give details, but Luke felt his pain, his utter devastation. It was something he recognized easily with his own struggles with depression and PTSD.

"What do you need right now, and what can I do to help until I get there?"

"Reverend Dobson has been here already, or I'd have called sooner. I know Colin and Steph have a will and a family trust. I just have to find everything. You could help with that if you come. They have all kinds of papers and things, you know. There's the house. I mean, Melinda and I, we just don't know what to do with everything, and it's just such a terrible tragedy. We don't know where to start. No parents should ever outlive their children. And to see your grandchildren filled with pain…"

"Do they know yet?" he asked.

"No, we were going to tell them this evening. Tonight, the kids were supposed to come home. I'm sure it's going to be on the news. I just don't know how we're going to be able to keep it from them. So we'll tell them tonight, and I think, if you came up with the kids, maybe being around their cousins would be a good thing. If you can arrange it."

"Oh, absolutely. We could come right now—"

"No, I know parent-teacher night is an important event for a school principal, and Julie should be there. Once that's over, when she comes home, you can tell her. But don't spoil her evening. There really isn't anything she can do right now. I know she'll want to tend to Melinda. That will be great comfort to her to have her daughter close by."

"We'll hop in the camper van and come on up there. Probably to-morrow morning, but I have to talk to Julie first. How have the kids been? I'll bet they had a great time. You probably spoiled them to death."

"Oh, you know us, Luke. That's our job, our mission in life. The business, Colin's part of it, that will all sort itself out, but it's the kids and all the things that Stephanie and Colin wanted for them, we're going to have to figure that out."

"Knowing Colin, he organized all that down to the last detail. But we'll help any way we can."

He knew it was all in their will. The four of them had even discussed it several times. He knew it would mean moving the three girls down to San Diego. But Luke also considered what Mr. Christensen's reaction to that would be. Here he had just lost his son and daughter-in-law, and now he would be losing the proximity to his grandkids. Even though Luke and Julie lived in San Diego, it was still Southern California, a good ten-hour drive plus. Mr. and Mrs. Christensen's lives that centered around Colin, Stephanie, and the grandkids in Sonoma County were going to be disrupted.

But at least it was still California.

Amy and Jessica came in from the backyard, dripping water all over the kitchen floor. He didn't have the heart to yell at them. Instead, he grabbed a couple of towels and demanded they shed their suits and clean up the water. Sending them up to their room without telling them the news, Luke focused on preparing a good dinner, spaghetti and meatballs, which was their favorite.

He picked lettuce, tomatoes, and a couple cucumbers from the garden and had already made the meatballs and the pasta. At the last minute, he put in a frozen berry pie he'd bought. After the pasta was cooked, he covered it with the homemade tomato sauce using his secret stash of frozen herbs—leftover from making his own herbed vinegar. The heady basil, thyme, oregano, and spearmint added a wonderful flavor to his legendary sauce. He was a real Martha Stewart these days, and it gave him a chuckle, a brief release from the heaviness in his heart.

Cooking for the family had been Luke's job in between deployments. He was Mr. Mom when he was home. Things had been tight, but they were planning on having him quit the Teams and find something local, even perhaps work in an internship for a physician's assistant with his background and training as a medic.

He pondered the changes about to consume them. He remembered the long talks they'd had with Stephanie and Colin by firelight on their numerous camping trips together with all the girls. Each had agreed that, if something happened to the two of them, the other couple would take the children.

Luke had never thought it would happen this way. He always

thought the odds were that something would happen to him and Julie would need help with the kids. It never occurred to him that Stephanie and Colin would be the ones to meet a tragic end.

After he put the spaghetti and the sauce in the oven to stay warm, he made some French bread, finding odd comfort in chopping garlic and melting butter. He left part of his insides enclosed behind that iron door—unfortunately, he was too familiar with Dr. Death. That wasn't what would rattle his cage. Right now, he was calm and told himself it was what he was trained for.

You got this, Luke. You're strong. You've been working full time on this stuff. Going to be a piece of cake... He told himself all the things some of his buds might say if they were there to comfort him. It was his self-talk.

Their deaths weren't his fault. He wished he'd been there to protect them. And he knew as soon as it popped into his head that idea had to be purged.

Easier said than done.

He was supposed to deploy in two months, and they were working up to a detail in the Caribbean, and perhaps Central America. If he had to re-up, that would be the time to do it so his bonus wouldn't be taxed.

When he'd become a SEAL, he had never thought about what it would be like to have a family, to have people depending on him. He was just a young, dumb, randy, and extremely horny young man, no cares really except getting home from the next deployment or making sure that none of his friends and buddies were left unprotected. His job as a medic was to keep everybody alive and deal with emergencies—surgery, if he had to—but keep them alive until they could be evacuated out of there.

The missions were getting more and more dangerous, although considerably shorter than they used to be ten years ago when he first joined. Julie's career had taken off too. She had worked her way up the ranks to school principal and was in line to perhaps become the district superintendent. That was a discussion they agreed they were going to have soon. His biggest concern before today was how Julie's career might interfere with his job being a Navy SEAL.

But now there was this. A whole new set of decisions to make.

The girls ran downstairs in their flannel jammies. Amy was nine, nearly ten, and Jessica was six.

"Spaghetti!" said Amy. "My favorite!"

Luke studied the two of them, smiling. His precious girls. How their lives would change forever now that their cousins might be coming to live with them. He didn't want to tell them without Julie being present, so he pretended that it was a normal Thursday night—Dad's night to cook spaghetti while Mom worked late.

He served up dinner and enjoyed the banter of his girls' small talk, gossip from school, and comparing notes on some of the new teachers arriving this year. Jessica was in second grade, the same school and grade Julie used to teach. Amy was in fifth grade. Both heavy readers, they were going to be excellent students, Luke could tell. They'd certainly not copy his scholastic achievements.

"Do you have any homework yet?" he asked.

The girls looked at each other and giggled, both of them missing one of their front teeth, on opposite sides, almost looking like twins even with the age difference. They shook their heads no.

"School's just begun, Dad. It's too early!" said Amy.

"I wish I had some homework," sighed Jessica.

"Okay, well, you can watch a little TV tonight if you like. Mom will be home about 8:30 or 9. When she gets here, we'll have a little family meeting and then bed. I want you to brush your teeth and wash your faces, and if you didn't shower, this would be a good time to do that."

"Family meeting?" asked Amy.

"Yes, that's what I said."

"Is Mom going to have another baby?" asked Jessica.

Luke frowned at the comment.

Where the hell did that come from?

"What makes you think that?" he asked.

"Whenever we have a family meeting, it's always something important. Remember when Gramma Christensen got sick with cancer?" Jessica spouted.

Amy shouted back at her. "Stupid. Mom's too old, Jess. She can't have more babies. Her boobs don't work anymore."

Jessica looked at her older sister with admiration, as if she was obviously right in everything. Luke was losing it and nearly burst out laughing.

"I think your mother is going to have to explain a few things to you girls. Things I can't quite do right now. But it is an important meeting."

"Can I read on my iPad?" asked Amy.

"I think you can do that, yes. As long as it's a book, not a TV program. I don't approve you just opening up and watching anything."

"No, it's my app from school, the books we're supposed to read this year."

"Then that's fine with me."

The girls dashed upstairs to their bedrooms, and that's when it hit him. In this small house of theirs, how were they going to fit three more kids in? They would have to share, but Colin and Stephanie's kids were nearly the same age, so more than likely they would have to take one bedroom together, and his two girls would have to share the other spare. He was anxious for Julie to get home so he could start figuring out some of the logistics. He wondered if she would be able to take the day off tomorrow.

Recognizing he was obsessing over little things, he knew this was the beginning of a spiral he didn't want to take. He stopped, took a big drink of ice-cold water, and just stared at the garden, the flowers, and Julie's vegetables. He saw the mess with the water and the pool, but he just observed it, didn't judge it, or get anxious about cleaning it up. He drank another glass of water and began to feel better.

It was a win, after all. The old Luke would have downed a six pack or some whiskey.

'Pick your battles carefully and celebrate all your wins, no matter how small,' Dr. Brownlee had told him.

He cleaned up the dishes, turned on the dishwasher, and had thrown all the dirty towels and bath towels into the washing machine, just about to turn it on, when the front door opened, and Julie returned. She was dressed in her Navy blue suit, looking the part of the professional she was. As she slid off her shoes and set down her briefcase, he was suddenly so grateful and proud of her. She was the best mother and so patient with the girls, and though it was difficult for her at times, she had stood by him in his darkest hours after his difficult deployments and issues with PTSD. He never heard her complain. She was firm and laid boundaries down, but she was always in his corner. That was something he could count on.

"Welcome home, Sweetheart," he said, approaching softly and giving her a hug, holding her tightly, a little longer than usual.

Julie quickly pushed away and stared into his eyes. "Oh my gosh, are you on some new kind of medication or you're just happy to see me?" It took a couple of seconds, but she did break into a quick smile.

"No, I'm just happy to see you." He hesitated. "But, Julie, we have to talk."

He was going to lead her over to the couch to sit down next to her, but she stopped him.

"Luke, what is it?"

He stared down at his feet even as one arm wrapped around Julie's waist, pulling her closer. Looking back into her soft, beautiful face and getting lost in her chocolate brown eyes, he had to tell her the truth. "Julie, Colin and Stephanie have been killed in an auto accident."

He didn't need to say anything more. Her reaction was immediate. Stiffening, she clutched his shirt at his back, almost digging her fingernails into his flesh beneath it. Tears started pouring from her eyes, and she would've leaned over and shouted or screamed, but he held her firm.

"No!"

"Your dad called. And I think it would be a good idea if we went up there this weekend. Tomorrow, if you can make it."

Through her tears, she asked him, "How?"

"I have no idea, Julie, except that they were coming back from that convention in Las Vegas. They were close—in San Jose—and I guess somebody hit them. I didn't get many details, because your dad was pretty upset. He did mention that your mom really needs you."

She wiped her eyes with the backs of her hands, tried to straighten her hair, and adjusted her skirt. She wiggled loose from Luke's arms and removed her jacket, setting it on the back of a dining room chair. At last, she turned toward him, mumbling, "Of course. We'll go tomorrow."

He could see she was all about healing, making things better, comforting her mom. It was amazing she could just do that, Luke thought.

Then another wave of tears hit her as she bent over, the grief overtaking her.

"Oh my God, those poor kids!" she sobbed.

Luke traversed the room and held her in his arms again. He found himself tearing up as well. He remembered his vibrant sister, smiling on her wedding day—the day that brought him and Julie back together again.

"We need to tell the girls," he whispered to the side of her face. "You want to wait until the morning?"

Julie shook her head. "If we're going up tomorrow, I think tonight would give us more time to talk it over and help calm them. Tomorrow, we'll be getting ready for the trip. I'll have to make some calls first, but we'll pack everything up and then head out as soon as we can." Tears filled her eyes again. "Poor mom," she said, beginning to shake, her hand over her mouth.

Luke thought about his parents, both gone now, and how he was grateful they didn't have to experience the loss of his sister. Stephanie had been their pride and joy.

In a daze, Julie walked over to their living room couch and collapsed, putting her face in her hands resting on her knees.

"Can I get you anything, Honey?"

"I need a whiskey."

"Coming right up."

He brought her a small tumbler with one giant cube of ice. He decided not to join her but sat next to her, holding her left hand.

"How are we going to make this work, Luke? My mind is going crazy. I want to fix this, and there just isn't any way to do that. Of course, the girls have to come here, but we don't have any room. Where will everyone sleep?"

"I know. We'll sort it."

"And we were going to have you leave the Teams. Maybe—"

"Hey, let's take it one step at a time. Let's see what's set up and what we must figure out. I know Colin probably has a bunch of stuff prepared. Let's see what we're facing first and take care of the girls and your folks. Help our girls adjust to it all. Then we can make our minds up. I'll do whatever needs to be done."

"Maybe I should come home—"

"Honey, no. Let's not do this now. We'll figure it out as we go along. The right path will come to us."

She smiled up at him through her tears. Even with her cheeks red and blotchy, her eyelids already getting puffy from the tears, she was beautiful—the most beautiful woman in the world to Luke.

"Look at you, calming *me* down, Luke. I like seeing you strong. This changes everything for us—for all of us."

But then her smile turned into worry, bringing on more tears. He nodded, knowing exactly what she was thinking.

Their family of four was now going to become a family of seven. Money had been tight these past couple of years especially. If one of them quit, how would they be able to make it?

For now, they would be raising not two, but *five* girls.

All their best-laid plans had suddenly flown out the window.

CHAPTER 2

JULIE WATCHED AS the girls made their way down the stairway, taking a seat on the couch on either side of her. Luke was sitting across from them.

She took a deep breath and began what she hoped would be a speech that would make sense to them. She placed her hands on the tops of their heads, and they leaned into her. She knew they had no idea what was coming next.

"First of all, I'm afraid we've got some bad news."

At that, both girls sat up straight, turned in her direction, and searched back and forth between her face and their dad's.

"What's wrong?" asked Amy.

"What kind of bad news?" asked Jessica, already crying.

Julie drew Jessica to her chest and kissed the top of her head. "Sweethearts, Colin and Stephanie were in an auto accident, and unfortunately, Lindsey, Maron, and Kiley have lost their parents."

"But where will they go now? Will they live with Gramma and Grandpa?" asked Jessica.

"Well, it probably means they're going to come live with us. We will be sharing our house with your cousins. We want to give them the home that they've lost."

"That would be super cool, Mom. But they must be very sad," Jessica said spontaneously and then buried her head in Julie's side. "Mama, I don't ever want anything to happen to you or Dad."

"I don't think you'll ever have to worry about that, Sweetheart. And it would be a wonderful thing to share your life with them, wouldn't it?"

Jessica nodded, satisfied with the answer.

Amy was curious, wanting all the details, but Jessica was pensive.

"Sweethearts," Luke began. "We're going to go up there tomorrow, and you'll get to see your cousins. We're going to see Grandma and Grandpa, and we'll probably have to stay a few days up there to get things sorted out. I think you will be a great joy to your grandma and grandpa. You could probably help Grandma especially with some of the things she needs to do, and your cousins, they're going to need your love and support. I know I'll be proud of both of you. It's a very sad time for our family, but we are a family, and we are together in this."

"Why wouldn't we move to Santa Rosa? There are three of them and two of us," asked Amy. "They have a huge house."

"No, Sweetheart, I have a job here. Your dad has a job here. San Diego is our home. I don't think it would be a good idea for us to disrupt that at this time," Julie answered. "And your aunt and uncle talked to us about what they wanted if something should happen to them, just as we did for you two. It was all agreed to in advance that if something happened to your dad and me, you both would go to live with Colin and Stephanie. In this case, the opposite happened. And they asked us if we would raise their girls if they weren't here to do it. We gave them our promise and our commitment. We are family, and we will stick together. We don't want the girls to not have a loving home, do we?"

Both girls shook their head back and forth and agreed with Julie.

"Tomorrow is going to be a busy but important day. We want to make sure we talk about this. I'd like to hear what your thoughts are about it, and tomorrow morning when we get up, we're going to pack a few things for a few days, and we're going to leave and drive up there in the camper. It will be like most trips we've taken. And you know there's a lot of things we must do to get ready for it. Mama's going to take a few days off, and Dad's going to let the team know, and we'll gas up and go. You know Grandma and Grandpa are going to be so happy to see you both. And so are your cousins."

"So this is your chance to ask questions," Luke added.

"Will I be sharing my bedroom with Kiley or Maron or Lindsey?" asked Jessica.

"Yes, I think you will share your bedroom with someone. Maybe initially you and Amy will stay together in Amy's room."

"So our cousins will take my bedroom then?" Jessica continued. Julie picked up a little bit of territorial insecurity on Jessica's part.

"It's just a guess. We haven't worked it."

"Are they going to go to our school then?" asked Amy.

"Yes, I think they will, and it will be good for them to have you there to introduce them to all the kids there. I think that Jessica and Kiley might be in the same class, but I'm not sure. You and Maron probably will be as well. It'll be important that you are good ambassadors, and you can really help them in this difficult time by being good friends, sharing all the great things about living here in San Diego with them, so they can begin to have a new life and enjoy living here even though we know they're going to miss their home and parents and everything they had in Santa Rosa."

Julie's heart was breaking at the expression she saw on both her daughters' faces. They were trying to be brave, but Jessica was having a hard time with her lower lip and the steady stream of tears from her eyes.

"What else do you have questions about?" she asked.

"Will Grandma and Grandpa come live with us too?" asked Amy.

Julie looked at Luke, who all of a sudden had a puzzled look on his face.

"That's something I've never thought about, Amy. I don't think so, but of course, they'd be welcome. They'd have to sleep in the backyard in a tent though." Julie kept her demeanor straight, and several seconds later, both the girls giggled, catching the joke.

Luke inserted, "There're going to be lots of things we have to decide and work out. And we're going to ask that you be patient with us and just understand that your mom and I are going to do everything we can to take care of your cousins and to include them in our family, and we may make some mistakes, but we're going to work really hard to try to make this work."

Julie was concerned that the girls weren't more talkative, but she understood they were still processing. Amy still had not shed a tear. Julie suspected she'd be crying herself to sleep.

Both she and Luke tucked the girls into their bed, and Jessica asked if she could sleep in the same bed with Amy, who agreed. Luke read them a short story while they began to doze off, the sniffling and crying subsiding. Finally, little Jessica rolled over to the side holding her teddy bear and was fast asleep before the story was finished. He leaned over and kissed Amy on the forehead and gave Jessica a peck on the cheek.

Julie was proud of her warrior husband, the one who had learned to adjust more than she did, finding the space and the capacity to help the family now that this crisis had begun. She loved him even more watching how tenderly he loved the girls.

They stayed up for an hour talking over different scenarios and throwing out different ideas. Luke said he would give Kyle a call in the morning and try to figure out some way he could get some time off, perhaps miss the next deployment, if it was deemed necessary. All talk of her quitting her job Luke stopped mid-sentence and wouldn't let her speak about it.

"You've worked too hard, Julie, to get here. My days on the Team are going to be numbered anyway. I'm an old man now with sore knees and a sore back. I shouldn't be doing this kind of work much longer, but whatever we need to do, we'll do it. I'll adjust."

She was grateful for the man she'd met that night on the beach in San Diego. He'd been in a state of grief over the loss of his friend from their last mission, and he had worked hard to hold himself together, to get the treatment, and to not give up on himself in the process.

"You've worked hard to get to where you are as well, Luke. It doesn't seem right for me to ask you to quit the Teams. To do what? Be Mr. Mom?"

"Well, it's not that bad."

She knew he was lying through his teeth.

"You are a terrible liar. Come on, Luke, you never thought of yourself as being a professional babysitter, Mr. Mom full-time. You didn't even like changing diapers when they were little."

"Whew! I did it, though. You have to admit, it was a humbling experience."

She laughed at that.

"My hero. Always there. Always protecting the innocent. Little did you know that your protection detail would expand so."

"Comes with the package. It's what I do."

The next morning, they packed up their camper van and headed north for the ten-hour trip to Sonoma County. It was quiet. Amy didn't want to read. Both girls sat in their seats, staring out the window. Luke made several attempts to tell jokes or funny stories, which fell flat.

At dusk, they finally arrived in Santa Rosa. Julie's mother ran from the front door to the van, her face in a wide smile, focusing her attention on the girls. They hugged then the girls took off, almost bypassing their grandfather on the way to the house to greet their cousins. The three girls were standing in the doorway, none of them smiling.

Julie hugged her mom. "How are you holding up?"

"I'm finding the strength. The girls have been a lifesaver. To be honest with you, I've welcomed the distraction of fussing over them. It's been good for me. I'm glad you're here, though, because there're so many decisions that have to be made, and I just don't know what to do." She frowned and then sobbed softly. "I go fine for a while, and then an hour later, I'm crying again. I think that's normal, but the girls are quiet. A little too quiet. And, Julie, I'd like you to talk to them if you could please. I know they have some questions they probably don't want to ask me. They miss their mother."

"I planned on it."

"I know you and Luke are going to be good for them. If there's anything we can do to help, in any way we can, we'd love to. Your dad and I have talked, and if the girls need any financial help at all, we would be happy to contribute."

Julie knew her father was planning on retiring this year and giving his business to Colin, who had moved from San Diego several years ago to do so. All that would have to be on hold now.

"Mom, don't worry about all this. We'll sort it out. The main thing is we're all together and we're family."

All five of the girls were laid out in the upstairs guest bedroom, where Mr. and Mrs. Christensen had a double-sized bunk bed so that the girls could sleep close together. Amy and Lindsey took the top bunk, and Maron, Kiley, and Jessica took the bottom bunk. They ordered pizza, tried to keep the language upbeat, and turned in early.

After the girls fell asleep, Luke and Julie and her parents had a sit down and discussed the funeral arrangements.

"They used our attorney, Edmond Anderson, and I've got his office putting together the copy of their will. I'm supposed to get that tomorrow. I think he set something up with a funeral home, but not sure. He said he would bring it by. There's the house, there's some savings, and Stephanie had her little side business, her little cosmetic business, which I don't think she was doing much with anymore. I sure am going to miss Colin at the office." Her dad sighed.

"Let's wait to see what Mr. Anderson says when he comes, and hopefully, he'll sit down and go over all the provisions in the will," said Julie.

Her mother brought out a questionnaire that the funeral home had given them. "They have all these packages—" Julie's mother couldn't continue.

Luke inserted himself. "You know, I don't think any of us are up to this right now. Let's just turn in, and let's deal with it tomorrow. It's not going to make any difference. I don't feel like dealing with this right now, and I don't know how the rest of you feel, but this is just not something I want to do. Let's wait. I think that's best."

Julie agreed.

Julie and Luke took Julie's old bedroom, and a flood of memories growing up in this house came back to her. She remembered her first prom night, her first kiss on a date, the first time she had someone up to her room to listen to music and do homework. She used to sneak a kiss here and there. She remembered getting ready to go off to college and saying goodbye to her room, knowing that something was about to change in her life. When she came back for vacations and during school breaks, she had felt she didn't belong but was glad they hadn't redecorated the room. She remembered the graduation party her parents held for her and roughhousing with Colin in the backyard, playing football with some of his friends before he moved down to San Diego.

Julie had followed him down there and got her first teaching job after she got her degree.

There had been a lot of happy memories in this room, and she found those memories helped her heal right now. And with Luke's presence, it was easier for her to face her future. He was the man she'd always dreamt she would marry. He was strong and fiercely loyal, and he worked very hard to repair himself and to get help with his PTSD, making huge strides.

They had just begun to level out to the point where they could consider maybe living on one income so that Luke could stay home and take care of the girls or take a regular job that didn't require he be out of the country for huge blocks of time. Something less dangerous perhaps. But she didn't know what he was going to want to do, and right now, it would be hard—especially facing raising all the girls—to only have one income.

As they lay in bed looking up at the reflection of the leaves in the window, Luke put his arm around her and, with his feet sticking out at the bottom of her bed, said, "You know, I've never spent a night in this room before, Julie? I kind of feel like I'm the cat that ate the canary. I sort of feel like I'm in high school, and I snuck into your room or something."

"You're being silly. Really silly, Luke."

"But your parents… I feel like I have to be quiet, try not to snore. Like having sex would be forbidden." He laughed. "Yeah, I am being silly. But I'm having to think about things I'd forgotten a long time ago."

Julie suddenly was concerned perhaps he was pulling back memories of his first wife, Camilla, and their unborn baby, who'd been killed in a car Luke was driving. She was on alert to stop him in case it led to some of those dark, guilt-ridden places he'd found it hard to dig out of.

"Well, we planned for this, Luke. It's why we had all those conversations. Think of how bad it would be if we hadn't done that. We didn't know if we'd ever need that plan, but we made the promises and commitments."

He hesitated for a few moments and then answered, "Whatever we need to do, I'm going to do it. I know I can do it."

"We need to be realistic, Luke. I don't think it's going to be in the cards for you to quit. And if you re-up, you get a bonus, so that might help, but I just want to make sure it's what you want to do. I will quit my principal job if you're going to continue on the Teams."

"So if I decide to stay in, you're going to give up your career?"

"Not exactly, probably not permanently, but maybe temporarily."

"I'm going to have to take that into consideration. That kind of puts a little more pressure on me. You make a lot more money as a principal than I do as a SEAL. I could find something else to do."

"Like what?"

"I could join the police force, Sheriff, private security. There's lots of stuff I could do. Fitness training, security consulting for corporate groups, helping kids get ready for BUD/S training or military service."

"Okay, those all work. But it's going to be a full-time job taking care of these kids. They're at the age where they have things they're going to want to do, softball, soccer, dance—whatever. I'm not exactly sure what all the three girls are going to want. It sort of requires that somebody be home on a regular basis."

"I got it. And that's what I'll be. Mr. Joe Regular."

My Navy SEAL husband a Joe Regular? She couldn't help but chuckle then tried to hide her amusement.

"What? You don't think I can adjust?"

"I know you can't adjust that much. Throw down your body armor for an apron? Seriously, Luke, you think that will work?"

"Try me!"

Julie knew this line of discussion wasn't going to get her anywhere. His stubbornness was a strength on the Teams, and yes, he'd been trained to be adaptable, to a point. But to shift his whole focus to doing housework and shuttling kids around San Diego County? That was a different skillset, and he wasn't trained in that. And if he gave up something he loved doing so much for something that could put him over the edge, was that smart?

"I mean it, Julie. You can depend on me to do whatever it takes. I will make this work. I will have the cleanest house, the best-dressed girls, the most on-time taxi, and join the ranks of stage mom, soccer mom, whatever is required."

Although she wasn't convinced it would work, she loved it when he talked about wearing an apron and nothing else. And that gave her other ideas.

She rolled over in the small full-sized bed, pressing herself against his hard body, front to front, and whispered, "So let's see how adaptable you can be. Make love to me without waking my parents or the girls, Luke. Please?"

CHAPTER 3

C OLIN AND STEPHANIE'S attorney went through the provisions of the will that had been created, confirming the arrangements to have Luke and Julie care for the three children. Everything else was rather mundane. A good friend of Stephanie was going to handle the sale of the house, unless the Christensens or Luke and Julie objected and wanted to occupy the property. The assets would be left in care of the children for their health and safety but under the full control of Luke and Julie.

Luke had no idea what the estate was worth. Colin did have some savings, stocks, and shares of his father-in-law's firm, but most of the assets were tied up in the house. He was uncomfortable with the idea that Mr. and Mrs. Christensen were left out of the equation. Their loving selflessness had been demonstrated over the years toward all of them. He made a note to discuss with Julie, if they could, his desire to perhaps leave something to them, as her dad was planning to retire this next year. Now, without Colin, he might have to work a few years longer. Maybe they could help them too, without taking anything from the girls.

"Basically, what we have here is a pretty straightforward will and the trust. Julie, you are executor. You can make the decision where the children are to live, whether you move up here or they come down there to San Diego, and if you want to occupy their house here in Sonoma County or want it sold and the assets applied to the children's welfare. You basically have free rein, as long as you don't co-mingle the funds with your own personal funds. Now having said that, I realize that's sometimes a tricky proposition. So I'm going to request, and it's volun- tary but recommended, that we have an annual meeting to go over what monies from the trust have been spent. I'd like to do this up until the time they're old enough to inherit their portion, but you can discontinue at any time. It was Colin and Stephanie's express condition that the children not inherit a large sum of money until they're at least twenty-five, unless it's applied to college tuition or a training program."

Luke affirmed that Colin was as anal as he suspected he would be. He secretly thanked his lucky stars it wasn't the other way around, because his finances were a complete mess. Even with Julie's promotion to principal, they were living paycheck to paycheck. He'd never been very good at managing money, but he was going to have to learn. Of course, now they were hopefully going to have the money to manage.

The other issue that became clear to him was that the choice to leave the teams was now a real issue. He was hesitant to make the decision today with everything else going on, but he knew it would be the first thing he and Julie needed to discuss.

"My office is available any time you have a question. Of course, we bill you for it, but it's a lot cheaper if you ask a question rather than wind up doing something that might find scrutiny either with the tax man, the federal government, or an interested party. I don't anticipate the two of you will have any problems, however."

Julie accepted the records, statements from bank accounts, and mortgage statements in a huge manilla envelope labeled: Christensen Trust. They could hear keys jangling at the bottom. He then handed Julie a preliminary title report to the beautiful custom home Colin had designed and finished not more than a year ago. It was a stunning architectural masterpiece on five acres.

Luke was wary. Because it was Colin's and Stephanie's home, even if Julie and the kids wanted to live there, Luke would not be able to do so. It creeped him out.

Mr. and Mrs. Christensen agreed to watch the kids for a short while so Luke and Julie could stop over at the house and be alone for a private discussion. Luke was nervous even stepping foot in the house, almost as if it was a bad omen or stepping on a person's grave. He hoped they could be quick, grab a light snack and some good strong coffee, and be back at the Christensen house within minutes.

On the way, Luke got a call from Kyle.

"Finally, Landmine. I was beginning to wonder whether the team deployed and I somehow missed the flight," Luke barked.

"Well, I'm sure if you guys have a couple more kids you'd understand how it feels to have three. They sure keep us busy. And, Christy? Well, if it wasn't for the kids, she'd probably ignore me and work twenty-four seven. She is so busy these days."

Kyle did make a good point. There was a way for a Navy SEAL to be married to a career-oriented working woman without the kids suffering. Ye, Kyle was always to the point of exhaustion every time he had to spend the whole day or two with them without any help from his spouse.

But Kyle's comment about the kids hit Luke the wrong way. Managing three was one thing. Managing five quite another. But it irritated him all the same, and he couldn't let go of it. He warned himself that it wasn't a good idea to react to his LPO.

Kyle coughed into the phone. "So what's up, Luke? You said you had something personal to talk to me about?"

"I didn't want to tell you on the phone, but Colin and Stephanie were killed in an auto accident two days ago. We've just come up here to Sonoma County, and I was trying to give you a call letting you know I was going to miss a couple of days of PT."

"Oh, Geez. I'm so sorry, Luke. My condolences to Julie, the girls, and Mr. and Mrs. Christensen too. You all must be devastated."

"It's hard on all of us."

"Of course it is."

"We need to stay up here with Julie's mom and dad, because there's a lot we have to decide. Julie's the executor of their estate. Accounts have to be closed, safety deposit boxes opened, funeral arrangements made, and all their things organized. It looks like we'll be bringing the three girls back home with us."

"Oh, wow, where have I been? I didn't realize they had three. That's a shame. How did it happen?" Kyle asked.

Out of nowhere, Luke was suddenly furious with his LPO. His anger flared as his body began to sweat. His blood pressure exploded. Before he could take control of himself, he went straight into attack mode.

"Why does everyone fucking want to know what happened?" He felt the familiar irritation like an old grudge against some imaginary villain. It was uncharacteristically aimed at Kyle, but it was more like he was angry with the whole world for being lopsided, for leaving him alive to experience it all.

"Wait, Luke, that's—"

"Everyone wants the gory details. They were killed, smashed up. They died. He went right away, and my baby sister lingered and was brain dead and then died."

Just then, he noticed he wasn't alone. Julie was sitting right next to him and had heard every nasty word. Luke had gone off-planet, way into the Twilight Zone.

Julie urgently motioned for him to pull over, and he shook his head, waving her off.

"I said, pull over, Luke."

Instead of stopping, he handed her the cell phone. "You talk to him." Before she could speak to Kyle, Luke squeezed the steering wheel and shouted "Fuck!"

Julie jumped right in and nervously tried to save the communication like he used to when they first began dating. "I'm sorry, Kyle. He's been doing great. He really has. We drove all day yesterday getting up here. Today, well, it's been a long, painful day. We're all stressed. This is going to be a big change for us—all of us. I know it sounds selfish, but please give him a little bit of time to work it out. We don't know exactly what we're going to do. But he needs some time to figure it out. None of us want to rush into anything."

She held the phone from her ear so Luke could hear what Kyle had to say.

"I see. Well, I'm glad you're there, Julie. Because that didn't sound at all healthy coming from Luke. I have great sympathy for what you all are going through. I don't know who the fuck was that guy I just talked to, but I'm going to forget about it and just hope and pray he gets to a meeting or talks to Brownlee, something. Don't let him dangle with all this shit. And I don't want him saying something to me I have to report."

"Understood. I'll tell him."

"And I apologize if I reacted harshly. You take all the time you need.

Have him call me when he's got some of this sorted. And, Julie, we're all here so sorry about this. If there's anything you need, you just let me know. When you get back, Christy and the ladies are going to be all over you guys. Hope you don't mind, but it's what we do."

"I know it. I'm grateful."

"Luke's mental health is important to me. Until he decides to go off the Teams, he's my responsibility. So make sure he gets help—lots of help. He's not going to like you insisting, of course, because that's the way we're wired, but you make sure he gets help up there."

"I certainly will. Thank you. We'll be in touch."

Kyle hung up.

Luke had heard every single word Kyle said. He completely agreed with his LPO. And he'd just made a huge mistake. The anger came without warning, out of nowhere. Like all of a sudden, he was unbalanced, capable of doing anything, and that scared him big time. He knew what it was. He knew the feelings that he had inside, the survivor's guilt, and knew it came from a place of not being well. Sick people focus on themselves. Healthy people focus on everybody else and try to make things better. He knew he was going to have to fucking suck it up and get his shit together right away or he would lose everything: his career, his wife, maybe even his whole family.

"I screwed up, Julie. I'm sorry."

Julie set his phone in the holder up by his right hand and crossed her arms. He could feel her irritation.

"I'm not going to lie to you. That was very unfortunate."

"You think? I'm shocked at how fast it came upon me."

"Yeah, well, that's what the doctor told you. That means that you have more work to do."

"But I've—" He started to object.

Now it was Julie's turn to get upset. She turned in her seat to face him.

"There it is again, Luke. You have to understand that's coming from a place that's only in your mind, doesn't exist. You need to talk to someone, even more than before. We don't want this to spin you out."

She placed her hand on his arm.

"I'll be with you. We'll do this together. Don't shut me out, even if you think I've done something you don't like, because all I'm doing is caring for you, loving you. But I have a lot on my plate, too, with all these decisions. I need you whole and beside me. Do that for me. I think the rest will take care of itself. And don't reject Kyle's suggestions. I know you don't like it, but he's right. You even said he was right. He's your best friend in the whole world. You need him, too, Luke. Don't push us away now."

Luke was filled with regret. But that was part of the symptom of his PTSD. Everyone screws up, he thought to himself. He needed to stop beating himself up over it. He needed to be present.

"I'm going to try harder. You see things coming off the rails, if I don't see it, you point it out and remind me, okay, Julie?"

"Understand you don't have to suffer alone, Luke. I'm right there beside you. No matter what, just like you'd do for us, I won't abandon you. I'm here for you always. Do the best you can, and I'll try to meet you in the middle. That's all I ask, Sweetheart."

Luke felt his anger organize. He put it in a box, like he'd been trained, and double-wrapped it in duct tape, and saw it go smaller and smaller until it was filed away somewhere out of his frontal cortex.

"I know that you are hurting—we are hurting—but right now, the girls are the most important thing. We BOTH have to be strong. We lost two of the most important people to us, but those girls lost their entire world. Until we can give them a firm foundation, we have to hold it together. So get your anger out now before your grief consumes you. Then we go back to being the strong protectors our five little girls need."

Luke's eyes began to water until he sucked in air so deep his lungs hurt. But it made the tears stop, and that was the one thing he wanted to do. She was a hundred percent right. He'd been feeling victimized, not by any one person, but by the world in general.

"How did I manage to marry someone so perfect when I'm so flawed?" he asked her.

He was fully aware that life gave all kinds of lemons to all kinds of people, and it was his fucking turn. But it wasn't fair to make everybody else have to carry his weight like the boat crews on Coronado. Like those jerks, the VIP SEALs, reviewing the BUD/S training, never pulling their weight, and always made it harder for everybody else around them to get any task done when they were on a team. That wasn't going to be the guy he was.

"You're not flawed. You've seen things most people never see, and it's affected you. But you can heal. You have been healing. I'm so proud of you, Luke. Just remember that when you get feeling down. We love you dearly and are all proud of you—all of you."

She began to tear up. "Now our reality and focus will be taking care of my brother's children as well as our own. Five little girls need us, Luke, and like I told you yesterday, I like feeling your strength. That's the Luke I love and the Luke that I married."

He wished he hadn't taken her there, worried about his mental state, but he needed to be honest with himself about his fragility. Thinking about that made the tears stop again. He'd been slipping a little, not carrying his load. Time to man-up and find gratitude in his day. Be humble enough to ask for help.

He was going to be solid. Absolutely rock-hard solid.

"Julie, I'm going to ask for your forgiveness. When I get some time to myself, I'm going to call Dr. Brownlee and see if he can schedule a phone appointment with me."

"You do that, Luke. So glad to hear that, Sweetheart."

They turned to drive up to the subdivision where Colin and Stephanie's house was, winding up the gentle hillside until they reached the top where the property was. The beautiful copper-roofed home was extremely modern and looked like something Frank Lloyd Wright could have designed, utilizing lots of granite blocks, colored metal window frames, and the copper roof and gutter throwing a golden patina almost as if it was lit up from underneath all over the outside of the house. Attractive lighting here and there highlighted some of Stephanie's prize roses and their professionally landscaped front and side yards. Luke was surprised to see a light on in the home.

They parked in the driveway. Carmen, the lady who lived next door, the street gossip, immediately ran over to Julie and gave her a hug. She was an overweight Pacific Islander or Filipino woman dressed in a bright muumuu, and she'd been barefoot in her front yard watering her colorful flowers.

"Oh, Julie, I am so sorry. If there's anything I can do for you, please let me know," the neighbor said.

"Thank you. We have a lot to think about, but thank you. We're just going to go look around a little bit, and I'll let you know okay?"

Luke wondered how Carmen had found out about their accident. So he decided to ask her. "Is it in the news already?"

"Oh, yes, front page of the paper. Everybody's been out on their driveways talking about it. The paper said it was a car accident, is that right?"

"Yes, it was."

"When is the funeral? We'd all like to come pay our respects."

Julie sighed, nodding her head. "Yes, of course. We'll make sure you get the details. Probably Monday, but we're still waiting to make the final arrangements."

"Lovely couple. And those darling children. You know, I asked Stephanie if she wanted me to help her clean house or do anything. I don't know how she did it. She had those three girls, and she had her mail order business going on. She's just amazing. And Colin, so handsome and so talented."

She had her hands together clasped over her heart. Luke was having a hard time keeping his shit together watching her performance, which was the only way he could classify what she was doing.

But of course, Julie took it in stride.

"Excuse me, Carmen, but we only have a few minutes, so if you don't mind, we'll talk to you later."

She was much better at this than he was. He was going to have to learn to temper his irritation, because everything in the whole world irritated him. Just being alive irritated him.

He followed behind Julie as she dug into the manila envelope that contained the keys, some other small handheld pieces of equipment, a cell phone for her business and such. Finding the key to the front door at the bottom, she opened it and, after Luke stepped in, closed it behind him.

The large foyer was two stories tall, and the sound of their footsteps on the polished concrete floor, even though covered in exquisite oriental rugs, made him feel like he was at church. Light poured in from stained glass windows on the second floor, creating a Scrabble-type design below. They heard sounds of birds and airplanes outside, a lawnmower, a leaf blower, and other things indicative of a normal early afternoon in California.

Being in the house was hard for Luke. Especially since everywhere he looked he saw the attention to detail that was so much a part of Colin and Stephanie's lives. They walked through the kitchen and found two coffee cups, one with lipstick on the edge, still sitting in the sink, rinsed but not put in the dishwasher. Evidence that they had been together here, sitting, having coffee, not knowing their lives would be cut short.

The beds were made. The fireplace in the family room was clean and stacked with wood. Even the carpets had been freshly vacuumed. Someone had placed fresh flowers on the dining room table, obviously their housekeeper, welcoming them home.

Julie didn't say a word, just walked slowly from room to room, down the stairs, out onto the patio, and sat on one of the stone retaining walls overlooking Stephanie's garden.

"Such a beautiful place here. They were so happy. The girls… oh my God, Luke, how can we possibly provide anything that looks anything like this down in San Diego for them?"

Luke knew exactly how she felt. Trying to be helpful, he said, "Well, that's not really what makes a home, is it, Julie? It's the people in it. It's not how big it is or where it is or how fancy it is. Even though everyone wants a beautiful house decorated tastefully in a lovely setting to honor who they are. I think our house is beautiful. Small but beautiful. I'm going to say something that you probably won't understand."

"What?"

"I'd rather live in our house than this house."

"Oh, I understand that completely," she said. "I do. I get what you're saying."

"Okay, so the question's going to be for us, what do we want our new family to look like? Does this mean we buy something else, or we somehow remodel our place and make it into something that would suit everybody?"

"God, Luke, there's no room. I mean what do we do, add a third floor?"

"Yeah, maybe it's a project we can talk about later. I don't know how we'll do it. But if we can somehow stay where we are, keep our expenses just like they were, and use the money that Stephanie and Colin have in the house to help the girls with their college and their lessons and anything else they want, I think we would be okay. I think that's what they'd want us to do. They didn't choose us because we had a great big house on a fancy hill. Steph wanted the girls to be down to earth, not spoiled. They chose us because of how we live our life, Julie."

She immediately stood up and ran to him, wrapping her arms around him so tight while she sobbed into his chest.

"That's my Luke. I needed to hear that, Luke. You're so right. Thank you."

CHAPTER 4

J ULIE WAS TO meet with several realtors to give her an opinion of value for Steph and Colin's house. She asked her dad to come along with her, because he was the most qualified to explain the architecture, the design elements, and the features of the house, because he had helped Colin draw up and engineer the design.

One by one, different brokers stopped by, an hour apart, giving their opinion of value and getting the grand tour. Out of the four that she met with, one of them didn't want to give her a price, wanted to call it in the next day. But from everybody else, she got detailed market comps, which is what she was looking for. The prices had risen dramatically since her days in Sonoma County, but more or less fell in line with what Julie had guessed they would be.

In between the appointments, she'd brought some sandwiches and soft drinks for her and her father to sit at the dining room table and wait for the next interviewee.

"You know, Dad, one of the things we might need to do is remodel the house in San Diego. Just so we could accommodate all the girls. It won't look anything like this, but maybe you could help us come up with some kind of a plan that would make sense."

"Boy, I don't know, Julie. You've got a tiny lot there, as most of those are, and you already have a two-story. I'm not sure how much coverage they'll allow you there in San Diego, but I'll take a look and see what I can dig up as far as the zoning and building codes, especially the setbacks. It would honestly be easier to just scrape the lot and start from scratch. You could get a much bigger house out of it. But I also think it would cost you a lot of money."

"Well, that's in short supply, Dad. And of course we don't want to touch the money that goes to the girls. Until the house sells, as a matter of fact, we're going to be very tight. But I think we'll do okay."

Mr. Christensen looked at her admiringly. "You know, Julie, we never doubted you were going to be a great teacher, and now look at you, an administrator, a school principal. I'm so proud of you, and I think you and Luke are going to make wonderful parents to those girls. It's amazing to see how close they are, and now they'll get to live together, which is what they'd always wanted. Remember when they used to beg for this?"

Julie did have fond memories of the tears shed when their visits were over, all the girls begging to be able to go live with their cousins. It was ironic that it was now going to come to pass. But she had to tell him her doubts.

"Well, their time together was special, because in the past, they only got to have face-to-face contact two or three times a year, Dad. If they're going to be living together in our small house, I don't know how exciting or happy it'll be. But we aim to make it work. Trust me on that."

"Good enough then."

After she and her dad concluded their interviews, she picked one particular broker, even without a callback from the broker who didn't have an opinion of value yet. She chose a young aggressive agent who seemed eager and was very experienced selling high-end properties. And, more importantly, she'd sold the neighbor's property. She didn't come in with the highest recommended price, but Julie felt she wasn't afraid to tell her the truth, either. Not wanting the house to sit a long time unsold, she wanted to be realistic, gather a lot of attention, and maybe obtain multiple offers.

She exchanged email addresses with the young agent and promised to sign the listing as soon as she got the paperwork. But she also needed to make sure Luke was on board with it.

Julie did a rough calculation of the proceeds. With a listing price of $1.7 million minus the mortgage of eight hundred thousand and funds set aside for three college tuitions at two hundred thousand each, that would leave, by Julie's estimation, roughly three hundred thousand for the girls' needs growing up, placed in a trust and managed but spent frugally. She was going to double-check with the realtor the next day, because the realtor had picked up a business loan that had been placed against the property recently, and there was no evidence that that had been paid off.

But these were her rough numbers, good enough to have a cogent conversation with her husband.

At home, Luke was talking to Dr. Brownlee upstairs in her former room, so she left him alone until the call was complete. Later, she told him what she was going to list the property for and what they would be netting. She showed him the paperwork.

"Holy cow. That's terrific. The girls are going to be set."

"It's really not a lot of money, Luke. Not much at all. There may be some credit card debt we have to pay off and a car loan, which will be paid off when we sell it. It's a lot of responsibility to manage that college fund, make sure it keeps growing, but I think we could do some proper investing for them. And I'll have to check with the attorney about using some of the funds to enlarge the house to accommodate the girls. But I want to know what you think, Luke?"

He shrugged. "Sounds reasonable. I don't see why not. It is for their benefit. It would be much easier for them and for us if we had at least two more bedrooms. But I don't know where you're going to find them. Let's think about it, Julie. The house probably won't sell right away, but once it gets close to closing escrow, we'll have to make that decision. You should talk to the attorney now, though."

"Yup. I'm on it."

Mr. Christensen hooked up Julie's computer to his Wi-Fi so his wireless printer could print out the contract when it came through. While everything was being printed, she called the other three brokers and informed them of her decision.

Luke added, "One thing we didn't do, Julie, is look at all their stuff. There are clothes in the closets, filled pantry shelves, Steph's china and crystal. Some of it came from my mom and dad."

"Then we should keep those. That's part of your heritage too."

"There is a garage pretty full of boxes—stuff—not as bad as ours, but still pretty full. I think we should line somebody up to help with the move, so we'll be ready when the house sells. Did they have a storage unit or any other place that they used or was everything there at the house?"

"I have keys to two deposit boxes down at the Bank of Sonoma County and a key to a lot I think he kept an old car in. I'm going to try to find that. But I'll check it out. Other than that, I'm not aware of any other location. Colin had a few things at Dad's office, but I think most of everything is at the property."

"Still, it would fill a U-Haul van. That's more than we can handle. I'll get some help when we get down south from the Team guys."

"Good. Oh, and the realtor told me I needed to declutter and perhaps get it staged. I told her we'd try to remove some things, but I didn't want to pay to have it staged."

"I think you're right about that. The house is going to sell itself. It's such a beautiful piece of property, and the yard is just stunning."

"We'll arrange a work party, then. Maybe you could contact Zak and Amy, Nick and Devon—see if we can hire out their farm crews to give us a hand."

"I'll give them a call."

"How was your call with Brownlee?"

"He was concerned, and we had a good talk about looking for warning signs. He didn't buy that it came on suddenly, and I didn't have any advance notice. He said I wasn't paying attention and to be more aware of what my body needs. There's no such thing as a flare-up or an anger event occurring without stuff building ahead of time. And the long drive and all the stress, it just added on more layers. I have to be careful about my rest, and I honestly haven't been sleeping well lately."

"I've been a little on edge as well. You're probably like I am, wondering how we're going to make ends meet. The money isn't ours, and I know you know that. But there won't be much coming in until after the house sells. We're going to have to be very careful on what we spend."

Luke agreed with her completely.

"I guess I better call the old man then. Kyle's expecting it. I hope this dustup from yesterday doesn't affect my position on the team. But the fact is, Julie, if I don't stay on the team, if they toss me, so be it. I mean, I'm not going to fight to stay. I want to stay at this point, but now we have some options, and nobody can predict the future. As long as you're working, I think I'd like to try handling the load taking care of all five girls. And that's what I'm going to tell him. So if he won't give me several months off, then I'm going to let him know that I'll start the paperwork to disengage."

"Can I have an opinion about this?" Julie asked.

"Of course. Always. I shouldn't have said it that way. I meant to ask if you agreed with me."

"I think you ought to take a look at what you see yourself doing. Raising children and being a stay-at-home parent is not the easiest job in the world. I did it off and on, I guess, but this, with all five of them, this is a full-time situation. We could probably get help by using a bit of the money, take some of the stress off of us having to work ourselves to the bone twenty-four seven. But I want you happy, Luke. I don't want any regrets. And if you decide to leave the teams, I don't want you to come back later on and tell me that was a mistake."

"I understand. But none of us knows how this is going to affect us all. I might really take to it, or I might hate it. I don't know. But what I do promise you is that I will give it a good try for several months at least, and I think that's the time I'll make the decision—after I actually see what it's like to not be working out with the guys, getting ready to deploy, go overseas, and then come back. I need to see what that's going to feel like if I can."

"And the beauty of all of this is that Colin and Stephanie have set it up for us so that we do have that choice. That's a blessing. Most people don't have that."

Julie could see her words were hitting home. Luke's eyes were filled to the brim with tears, again.

CHAPTER 5

"**S**O HOW ARE you, Luke?" his LPO asked. Luke didn't detect any residual frostiness, even though he deserved it.

"I think I'm okay, Kyle. There's a shit pile of decisions we have to make. God, I've got so many lists, and so does Julie. Every hour that goes by, we think of something else we have to do. We put it on the list. Being a teacher, she's good with the visual aids. We got some of those big Post-it notes and started listing things, making categories of decisions, people we had to call, forms to fill out, things to do. We got the funeral arrangements taken care of. We even spoke to the girls' schools and inquired about the school our girls go to in San Diego."

"You guys go to Mission Viejo?"

"No, Bell City. It's a private school. I think the kids are going to love it there."

"Well, it sounds like things are progressing. What do you think happened the other day?"

"I knew we'd get to that. Julie and I talked about it afterwards, and you need to know, Kyle, she really brought me to my senses. Boy, she's direct."

"I think that's good for you, Luke. You want someone with boundaries. That's gonna save you in the long run when perhaps you forget."

"Oh, definitely. Anyway, she said that I was probably tired from the drive, and neither one of us had been sleeping very well, even before all this happened. Brownlee's backed her up and completely agrees. Being perfectly honest with you, money's been tight. And I've been a little bit worried about my future, whether I want to re-up or whether it's time to get out."

"Well, I'll tell you this, Luke, I would hate to lose you. I need medics. I can do without the bang buddies and some of the communications people. We've got to have sharp shooters and medics."

Luke chuckled. "I remember when Julie asked me why I was also a sharp shooter, and I told her it was just something I was good at. Then she asked, well, are you killing people or are you keeping them alive?"

"What was your answer?"

"A little bit of both, I guess."

"Yeah, that's funny, even though I'm not laughing. Most people would never understand, would they, Luke?"

"That's for damn sure. And I think about not being on the teams, and I just, I don't know if I could handle it. I mean, I've seen a lot of guys go down in flames. I just don't know."

"Yeah, disengaging can be a bitch."

That was putting it mildly, Luke thought.

"Well, I'm not going to press you. But I'd like to keep you on the team. And it sounds like you need some time to get things sorted, taking a note from Julie's conversation yesterday. I think I can sell it to the head shed. Get you some special circumstances temporary detachment. Do you think four or five months is enough?"

"Yeah, I think that would work, but I was hoping for six."

"I'll see what I can do, and I'll let you know. But I know I can get you four or five. After that, I'm not sure, with our recruiting numbers down. People aren't signing up for the military in general, but with these special ops programs, it's worse. Sometimes I think we show too many horribly disfigured vets on social media—it kind of scares the nineteen-year-olds, know what I mean?"

"I do. Not interested in a good death or dismemberment."

"Roger that, Luke. But the reality is that it's very dangerous, and you know they're getting more and more dangerous. We have more and more refinements to the rules of engagement. It's getting to be really hard to do what we do. I'm just waiting for the first team to get nailed with a bunch of lawsuits and investigations by Congress or the military brass, not that we're all choirboys. Knock on wood, that hasn't happened yet. But we're the ones using the lethal force if it's necessary. It's never pretty. But it's necessary. We do what others can't or won't. God forbid we ever stop funding the Teams because it's unfair, too violent, or some shit like that."

"I believe in what we do, Kyle. No worries there. I think we make the world a better place. I just want to make sure the toll it takes on me doesn't destroy me in the process. Julie doesn't want that either."

"What does she want you to do?"

"She wants me to do what is best for me. But she doesn't want me to decide and then change my mind or regret the decision."

"Well, you tell me how that's done successfully, Son. If I had the answer to that one, I'd be rich, filthy stinking rich."

"I think, if the Navy doesn't give me the time, I'll be telling you I need to start the paperwork. So you arranging that is going to make it possible so I can stay."

"And that's exactly how I'm going to sell it, Luke."

The next day, Kyle texted Luke to let him know he had his six months. His LPO said he wanted regular check-ins, and he wanted to hear Luke was talking to Brownlee on a regular basis. As his friend, Kyle said, if he needed anything or felt himself slipping, Luke had to promise Kyle he'd give him a call before all hell broke loose.

Luke was grateful for the wise man who'd been his team leader ever since he joined Team 3. Kyle was legendary. He was tough, but he absolutely cared about every single one of his guys. He knew about their families, their kids. He knew everything between the information he got and Christy got. They were the glue of SEAL Team 3. Kyle was more brother than he could ever have. All of the guys were right there with him too.

Luke wasn't going to do anything to disappoint Kyle. He was the finest warrior Luke had met. If he could be half as good a leader as Kyle was, he wouldn't even consider leaving the military.

Next, Luke began making phone calls, arranging a work party with the help of Nicholas Dunn and Zak Chambers, both former teammates on Team 3. Nick said he could drive a U-Haul down to San Diego and follow the camper van if that was what he needed. Luke didn't want Julie driving on her own so accepted his offer gratefully.

There were six other workmen, field hands of Zak's, who showed up one morning the following week. Luke was beginning to feel more normal. The funeral was over; the operational planning was nearly finished; tasks were distributed to others where they could be. As time distanced him from the tragic events earlier in the month, he found it easier to laugh and enjoyed swearing, getting sweaty and dirty loading boxes, and sorting and removing furniture to get ready for the house sale.

He dropped a file-box sized pink mailer that came from Stephanie's mail order business. Julie had discovered that Stephanie had closed her business account, pulled her website, and stopped her mail order business, but some of the items were still in her garage. When one of the big pink boxes labeled Gardens of Delight fell open, Luke, Zak, Nicholas, and several others whistled as several assorted vibrators, lubrication creams, feather whips, satin handcuffs, and sexual toys rolled out at their feet.

"Holy shit! Your sister and Colin were into this kink?" asked Nicholas.

"Well, this is tame compared to some of the things I've seen, and you know it. But no. I don't even think this belongs to Stephanie. I can't see her using any of this stuff. It's kind of play stuff, not hardcore fetish tools. And I know the difference."

The men laughed.

"Maybe they're Colin's," someone said.

"Well, you fellas do know how they're used, right? It's usually for the couple, together. But give me a break. I don't know what got into her head, but I'm glad she stopped it."

One of the helpers indicated he'd seen some of these items before when his wife had attended a home party where many of these were featured, and his wife bought some.

"You mean like a Tupperware party?" asked Luke. He was throwing things back in the pink box, annoyed that his family's dirty laundry was displayed for all to see.

"With an F. And they don't have to walk into those specialty stores. Some ladies just won't do that," added Nick.

"Exactly," agreed Luke.

Zak needed to add his opinion. "No, it's quite legit, Luke. Girls get together and drink a bunch of wine, and they model skimpy nightgowns and show little things, little toys that are kind of fun. I won't lie. I didn't mind when Amy went. She likes to experiment. It's kind of the rage now," he said.

"Well, if this was her mail order business, no wonder she shut it down. I mean, I wouldn't want the girls to see this crap. Like I said, I wonder what the devil got into her," Luke mused.

"Hey, Man, don't beat yourself up. It's the way things are these days. She was probably just trying to make a few extra bucks on the side. And if it was really taking off, well, I think you'd hear about it, right?" said Zak.

"I suppose. But look at all this stuff, I mean, look at all these boxes. She had a ton of inventory." He pointed to nearly a dozen large square boxes with the flowered designed logo in pink, along with a couple of ledgers she had prepared for sales on top. Luke looked them over before setting them back down on the stack of boxes. He could see that she had a healthy profit every month, stopping just around when they went to Vegas. She was very clearly going to quit, so Luke didn't worry about it, understanding that Stephanie had obviously changed her mind and had been getting out.

"So now what are we going to do with these? We certainly can't turn them into Goodwill," said Nick.

That got another chuckle from the group.

"I wouldn't take them to the county dumps either. You probably would get a ticket for it," added Zak.

"Yeah, that's just what I need, right? I can see it in the papers now, *Navy SEAL and his elementary school principal wife continues sister's sex toys business.* No, we can't have that. I'll find a way to dispose of it. I certainly am not going to leave it in the garbage down at the Christensen's. If they found one of these boxes, they're liable to have a heart attack."

"So I'll just put them over to the side in the U-Haul then. You want to hang on to these ledgers?" Nick asked as he handed the books back to Luke.

"Yeah, I'll give it to Julie. She probably has to make a note and keep track."

Several days later, the purging had been completed. At the last minute, several of the workmen's wives were called in to wrap, box, and tape things, especially some of the China and crystal, so that they could be transported safely back to San Diego. Mrs. Christensen had been asked if she wanted any of it, and she took a few bowls and a pair of crystal candlesticks, but Colin's mug collection and several of the other pieces they had on display, she didn't have room for. Her husband passed on them as well.

"Needs to go to a beer drinker. Some of these are valuable. You might be able to sell them too."

Luke was going to have to rent a mini warehouse, because their garage in San Diego was already full to capacity, such that they couldn't park their cars in it. But with the help of the estate money, that shouldn't be a problem.

The realtor did a final walkthrough, approving of all the empty closets in the bedrooms and the dishware purge in the kitchen as well as things in the baths. She also indicated that several potted trees and plants should be removed eventually, as there would not be anyone living here to take care of them.

"I'll tell the folks. Maybe they'll want them. We've got the truck completely filled."

The realtor had a landscaper come in and plant extra flowers in Stephanie's flowerbed and trim several of the bushes, and he agreed to a weekly lawn trimming that Colin used to do himself.

With only the bare minimum of furniture left for that lived-in look, things he'd have to come up and remove later or donate to charity, it was ready. He took one long look again, so he could remember this unique place that held their happy family.

"At least you got to build it and live in it for a bit, Colin," he mumbled to his friend. "Good on you. Now it goes to someone else to do the same. You created a masterpiece the next owner will love."

Closing the door behind him, he wasn't sure he'd ever need to come back. The finality of the impending sale created a shudder down his spine. And then he remembered, "You can't take it with you. Nothing belongs to us forever, even our families. Rest in peace, Colin, and give my sis a big hug and kiss."

The house was put on the market the day they left for the return trip to San Diego, stopping by their school one more time so the girls could say goodbye to their classmates and their teachers. There were some tears, but Luke saw in his little family, they were bonding together and helping each other. He was so proud of his girls. They were becoming sisters more and more every day. Lindsey and Amy were inseparable, and Maron and Jessica had formed a close friendship, but Jessica and Kiley were closest in age and had a special bond. He saw them holding hands more times than not. Luke saw a huge future ahead of them all just by watching them learn to be sisters.

It was a bright late morning when the two vehicles hit the road, headed for their new home in Southern California. Luke knew this was going to be the real test.

He was hoping for the best, and he was suddenly optimistic.

CHAPTER 6

JULIE TURNED AROUND to view the five girls sitting on the couch in the back of their Sprinter van. They were reading books, playing on their electronic devices, or coloring on a small table they had bolted to the floorboards. If someone were to watch them, you wouldn't know that, just a couple of weeks before, they lost their parents and now were going to be uprooted, would be attending a different school, living in a different town, and making new friends.

"Would you look at that, Luke?" she whispered to her husband sitting behind the driver's wheel.

"I can see them. I've been watching them, Julie. They're great kids. It feels like it's going to work out." He winked as he glanced over to her and gave her a quick smile. Then with eyes back on the road, he checked his mirrors, making sure they hadn't outpaced Nicholas in the large cab-over U-Haul truck.

"I've been watching Nick also. It's too bad we can't go faster, but it is what it is," she said.

"Well, theoretically, we could, except we'd probably get four miles per gallon in that beast. They didn't have any diesel trucks, but even with the difference in price, we would save probably a few hundred dollars. If you're okay with it, maybe I can spell him so he can have a nice comfortable ride in a leather seat, sitting next to my beautiful wife." He chuckled, pleased with himself.

"That's nice of you, Luke. I don't mind driving the big truck, though. I did my share of moving in my day. I'm not completely helpless."

"Oh, you don't want to drive that thing. It's filthy, and you can smell gasoline. I was lucky to get it, since it looks like all the moving vans are going east to Texas and Florida these days. It was hard to find one to take us to Southern California. I'm glad we got something."

She scanned the scenery, enjoying the comfortable ride and the huge windows. Above all the traffic, this was going in style, she thought.

"So how are your calls going with Dr. Brownlee?" She'd meant to ask earlier.

"Good. He definitely is a leveling influence on me. Wants me to take up tennis or something else like golf. God, I don't think I have the patience for golf." He shook his head, made one of his legendary faces.

Julie loved him for even considering it. She knew, if she begged him, he would try.

There had been some issues in the school district she had to spend time on just before they left, and she was anxious to get back to work. If they didn't get in too late, she wanted to report for work tomorrow. Her meteoric rise to principal was nearly unheard of, but she was the most popular teacher in the whole school, and many of the parents who were influential in the choice had had their children tutored or taught by Julie over the years, so she had quite a stash of supporters. The district was making signs they would be looking for a new superintendent, and even though she hadn't applied for the job, they let her know her application would be welcomed. She decided it was time to discuss it with Luke.

"What do you think about that superintendent job? You know it's not as secure as a principal's job, and they often move you around."

"How would that work?"

"It wouldn't. I'd have to tell them that with all the kids, especially now, moving would be a non-starter. But what do you think if I can negotiate it, would you be in favor?"

"I think it would be less taxing on you than your current job, Julie. You know, dealing with all those parents and then the curriculum issues, the personnel problems, and teacher issues. I mean, you have to manage the whole school. You even help decide what they plant and what goes in the playground for heck's sake. I think those superintendents kind of have light duty, and for all the money they make, wow, it's a no-brainer."

"Okay. So why do I think there's a but in there somewhere?"

"This is what I really worry about," he said as he looked at her carefully. "I worry that it would be too distanced from teaching. Like I'm not sure any of our superintendents have actually been long-term teachers. They come from a management background, a curriculum background, or even a publishing background for some of them. I'm not sure that's what really sets your heart on fire. You like being with the kids."

"But it would give me the opportunity to perhaps help formulate the direction that our schools would go in, and I'd have more resources available to me. I wouldn't have to be distant if I chose not to. It's just some of those superintendents are careful, so careful about not making favorites that they wind up appearing that they don't care at all."

"You're right. Being in the upper echelons is not the respected profession it used to be, but it's that way with everything these days, Jules. Nurses don't get the credit that doctors do, even though they do sometimes so much more. They just don't have the training and the respect. We have plumbers and electricians doing great work for large companies, but it's the company that gets the glory for it. We all know that. I remember the advice you gave me. 'Search your heart and make sure it's what you really want to do.' And if you want to do it, I'll support you 100%."

Julie was so grateful for Luke's support, although it made her nervous. The decision was hers to make, right or wrong. There would be no one else to blame. It was going to fall squarely on her shoulders. She sat back in her seat and pondered his comments.

She was pleased they'd bought the Sprinter van, although it did tighten their finances. It was perfect for taking the girls camping. It wasn't a four-wheel drive vehicle, so it rode very nicely on a Mercedes Chassis, a very smooth ride with leather heated seats and all the bells and whistles. They'd bought it used so they had only paid about half of the original sticker price.

Usually at gas ups and rest stops, Julie would get out sandwiches and get cold drinks out of the refrigerator, but they tried not to use the van's restroom and shower except for emergencies. That way it was easy maintenance; they didn't have to worry about draining tanks, the level of their gray water or black water or fresh water, and they could just drive.

She and Luke often took turns being the driver so they could make great time getting to places without having to stay overnight. One could drive while the other slept, and the girls had the bed in back.

If they needed a longer rest on trips, there was always a chain of restaurants and big stores that allowed overnight or temporary non-hookup campers. So as long as they stayed to the main highways, the routes were direct and simple. They saw a lot of beautiful countryside, and it was the cheapest way for all four of them to travel.

They stopped at a local truck stop to gas up the U-Haul, and Luke topped off the Sprinter. She accompanied the girls to the women's restroom, always wary of strangers in these roadside rest stops. But this one was clean and nicely shaded, and this time of year in the early fall, the traffic was fairly light.

She set up sandwiches and waters at a picnic table nearby, and all of them sat together, the adults mostly listening to the girls banter back and forth, and just enjoyed the day. She was grateful she was safe, and they were coming home. She missed her own house most of all.

"We're going to show you the beach that's really close to our house. I mean, it's like ten blocks away, not far at all," Amy said. "You have to go with an adult, but it's really a nice walk. The beach is beautiful too. Did you ever go to the beach up north at your old place?" she asked.

Maron was the first to answer. "Oh, the beaches up north are terrible. I mean, you have to wear a wetsuit just to get your feet wet. It's so cold. Lots of rocks and windy. I don't like it. I like going to the country and going skiing. Are you close to skiing?" she asked.

Amy and Jessica stared at their mom, looking for an answer. Julie was glad to help them out.

"We're about the same distance you are to skiing in the Sierras. We haven't really taken that up much. With the beaches so nice, we hang out there. And we get together a lot with the other SEAL families. We have backyard parties and bonfires quite often. They're looking forward to meeting you, and I think you're going to love it there. It's a whole new lifestyle, though, I'll be honest with you."

Maron shrugged and attended to her sandwich.

"I love the beach," said Lindsey. "Grandma and Grandpa took us one time when they went to Santa Cruz, and we loved it. We loved it so much we all asked Mom and Dad if we could move there."

She covered her mouth quickly at the mention of her parents. Her eyes searched from side to side but didn't focus on anyone in particular. Julie reached across the table and took her other hand in hers.

"Lindsey, it's all right. I don't think that's a bad thing to talk about at all. You're going to have lots of really happy memories. And I want to hear them all. It's going to be new for me. So don't worry about what you share, okay?"

Julie could see that Lindsey was about ready to erupt into a sobbing session, but instead of doing so, she nodded her head and held her breath, staring down. Amy leaned her head into Lindsey's shoulder and comforted her.

"It's okay, Lindsey. We love you so much, and we are so excited to show you everything we love about San Diego. And of course, we're close to all those water parks and Disneyland."

Kiley immediately erupted. "Disneyland! Oh, please, could we go there soon? Please?"

Luke nodded. "I think we can arrange that. Weather's nice, and school's in session so it's probably a pretty good time to go. We'll do that soon. That's a promise."

A cheer erupted from the little crowd in front of the adults. Julie breathed a sigh of relief at the realization they had just skirted the sad subject of the loss of their parents. She hoped that, in the future, it would get easier and easier.

But today, sitting next to her husband and watching her five children, today was a good day.

THEY ARRIVED AT their home in Coronado well after dark. The girls were fast asleep, huddled together in the queen-sized pull-out bed the couch made at the rear of their van.

"Let me get upstairs and arrange things a bit," she said to Luke.

"Let me know if you need help."

"Once I get the girls inside, you and Nick can go over to the warehouse, if you want."

He gave her a nasty look. "Tonight? You really mean that?"

She realized her comment had not been thoroughly vetted. Of

course they were tired. Nick especially would be after having been jostled around in the U-Haul smelling of gasoline. "Sorry. I'll set something out for Nick on the living room couch, and you guys can do it tomorrow."

Luke bowed. "Thank you, ma'am," he whispered, feigning tipping his cowboy hat that didn't exist.

She tore upstairs, put the twin beds in Amy's room together, and added another pillow and an extra blanket. Then she went into Jessica's room with the bunk beds, straightened the sheets, and brought out another pillow and a thick comforter in case someone decided to sleep on the floor by themselves. She was going to let them choose tonight, and then they'd sort out a longer-term solution tomorrow.

The girls were rubbing their eyes, exiting the van. Jessica had her teddy bear under her arm and was holding hands with Kiley. The two of them ran inside. Julie heard Jess's excited instructions, ending with, "I've got bunk beds too!"

Maron followed behind them, and then Lindsey and Amy were next.

"Amy, why don't you show Maron and Lindsey your room while I get some soup going in the kitchen? We'll have a light snack, and then it's bedtime."

With the girls safely inside, Julie walked over to Nick and gave him a hug.

"Thanks so much for your help."

"No problem, Julie. You guys would do the same for us." He stretched his back, Julie hearing a loud pop as his spine adjusted.

"Ouch!" Luke barked.

"You think jumping out of planes is hard. Try working in the field all day or replanting lavender. I don't think I've sat so long in years. But those were mighty nice sandwiches, Julie."

"Oh, that was all Mom. And the cookies are Dad's favorite."

Luke wrapped his arm around her waist and drew her into him. "I'll lock up. Nick, you go inside. You smell like you need a shower."

"If only to get rid of the gasoline smell. A few more hours of that, and I'd be puking my guts out."

"I've got you set up on the couch and laid out some fresh towels," Julie directed.

Several minutes later, all eight of them were sipping warm tomato soup and munching on some carrots and celery they had in the refrigerator. Julie noted both Luke and Nick appeared tired.

She knew her parents would be worried they made it home safe, so she called them up with FaceTime so they could see all five of their grandchildren. After trying to control the phone, she finally just gave it over and let the girls tell their excited tales about the trip. They did what Julie and Luke could never do: reassure them that all was well. At least for now.

Luke was smiling warmly at her. He gave her a thumbs-up. But Julie could see he was dead tired.

The girls' conversation was degenerating, and after one of the girls accused another of having potty mouth, she confiscated the phone and graciously signed off, blowing her parents a big kiss. Luke was in the background with, "Bye, Mom and Dad. Love you."

She set the phone down. The boisterous, simple dinner was going to be a regular thing, she realized. It came with the territory. She wanted them to feel safe in their new home.

Luke looked like he was about to fall asleep in his bowl.

"Go on, you two. Get yourselves to bed. I can finish up and get them tucked in."

"No, I'll help," Luke insisted.

"Mister, get your butt upstairs, and you take that shower. No arguments!"

The girls giggled, excused themselves, and followed their dad to the second floor. Julie turned to Nick. "Again, I know I've said it before, but thank you."

"I'm good. The timing was okay. Another week and we'd have been too busy. Our next event isn't for another ten days, and Devon's got that so organized, it practically runs itself."

"She'll have to give me some pointers, then," Julie said as she brought the dishes into the kitchen. Nick helped her carry what she couldn't.

"You being a teacher, you'll do fine."

"Well, it's one thing to manage twenty-five precocious second graders and completely another to manage and care for five daughters, ages all within four years of each other, and three of them having just lost their parents. I have a lot of catching up to do. I have to learn their routines, their preferences. I want them to feel welcomed here."

"I thought Luke was going to stay home and take care of everything."

She stared at Nick as she slammed the dishwasher shut. "Are you mad? Have you ever known a man to be able to handle that, I mean really handle that? There's an old saying about two parents who work. Only the mother knows their shoe sizes, and she's always the one the school calls if there's a problem."

"Better not tell Luke you feel that way."

"No. Bless his heart. Luke will try his best. I'm not worried about that. Not worried about the girls either. I'm worried about Luke."

CHAPTER 7

JULIE WAS UP and out of the house by seven in the morning, which meant breakfast, showers, breakfast cleanup, and unloading all the boxes were going to be Luke's job for the day. That and, of course, caring for five little girls, ages six to ten.

Nick laughed at him several times when he came out to the dining room with a frying pan in one hand and a spatula in the other, wearing one of Julie's flowered aprons—and none of the girls paid any attention to him.

"Honest to God, Luke, I think you're crazy. Just batshit crazy."

"We try to watch our language when we have little ears listening, Mr. Dunn," Luke said, imitating a Mrs. Doubtfire-type character.

"My apologies."

Luke swirled his spatula in the direction of the girls as if it was a fairy godmother's wand. "And as you can see, they were not paying any attention to you, either. So there you go."

"You're used to getting things done, Luke. If somebody doesn't do something, you're used to yelling at them, shouting, demanding they finish the job. Think of all the times you've had to do things to restore someone's life or keep them from bleeding out. You weren't nice about it, and nobody expected you to be. Now, all of a sudden, you're gonna be Mr. Happy House-husband?"

Luke walked over to him, irritated all the way down to his athlete's foot crusting his little toe on the right side. He whispered to his friend, "That kind of talk is going to get you no breakfast and a quick boot from the house. You stop that, Nick. I'm not going to have it, you hear?"

"I got you. But if you boot me out of the house, who's going to help you unload that truck?"

"I have it on good authority that we have some gentleman SEALS on their way over to do just that. Not only that, but I've got a couple gorgeous SEAL ladies coming over to help watch the kids so we can complete that. So you see, it's all under control. All of it was arranged last night before I went to bed, and God bless Christy, she's coming through for us. You know how she takes care of Kyle's team."

Nick nodded. "Indeed, I do. She's one of a kind, just like Kyle is."

"I don't know who he is sending, and I don't think it'll be him because he said he had meetings today. But we're supposed to have five guys. I think it'll only take us about an hour to get this junk offloaded."

"Did you ask Julie about the pink boxes?"

"No, I was going to bring one home tonight and see what she wanted to do with it. I was going to ask for suggestions." Luke wiggled his eyebrows up and down, waving his greasy magic wand in front of Nick's face. He turned and headed back to the kitchen, still gripping the empty frying pan with his left hand.

"Okay, who wants another egg?" he asked the Peanut Gallery.

"I want French toast," said Lindsey.

"I want pancakes and bacon," said Kiley.

"Daddy, can we have smoothies too?" asked Jessica.

With a sigh, Luke threw the frying pan and the spatula into the kitchen sink and walked to the head of the table with his hands on his hips. He knew Nick was going to have a hard time keeping it all together, because he knew how ridiculous he looked in this flowered apron. But he was trying to keep it light and fun. He figured they would cooperate better if they were having fun.

"Look, you guys. I am not a professional cook. I am not your maid, and I am not your butler or the housekeeper. I am a sometimes cook, and I can cook breakfast, but only one kind of breakfast. We're not going to be making these orders for five or six entrees for all these meals, okay? Just want to make sure you understand that."

"Okay," most of the girls said.

"I don't eat bacon. I'm a vegetarian," said Maron.

"Good to know then. Do you eat veggie burgers or veggie bacon?"

he asked her.

"I like veggie burgers, but it has to be on multi-grain buns, and I might be lactose intolerant, so I have to have the vegetarian cheese."

"Well, I've never bought vegetarian cheese or butter, and I think we can find some whole grain bread, but, Maron, you're going to have to give me a break here, because we don't eat that way."

He realized too late he had probably come across too strong. Maron's lower lip began to pucker and protrude. Tears streamed down her cheeks.

Damn it. Got to be careful, Luke, he said to himself.

Her crying stopped.

"Look, Maron, you and I will have a special shopping day, okay? We'll go to the store, and you can show me some of the things that you like to eat and can eat, okay?"

She looked up at him meekly. Now he understood why she was so skinny. In Luke's opinion, anyone who was a vegetarian was starving himself and would die before the age of forty. But that was a conversation and an argument for another day. He was encouraged by her attempt at smiling.

"Okay. Can we go today?"

If Maron was a new recruit or a young medic trainee under Luke, he would've dished out a healthy dose of "don't try to fuck with me." But this was Maron, and she was nine years old, a vegetarian, and had just lost her parents. Luke knew he was not going to win that battle, and Maron knew it too. That's why she pushed the envelope. He realized that was probably one of her skills.

Everybody has skills. He thought her skillset was irritating the fuck out of grownups. And he had to admit, the world needed people like that occasionally. But right now, he was hoping he could turn her personality around a little bit, perhaps soften it. And she was probably reacting to all the negativity that had befallen her. Of course, she was going to take it out on the big old tatted bad guy wearing a flowered apron. So be it. He was up for the task.

He walked over to her, patted her back, and then knelt so that they were eye to eye. "I have a lot of things to do today. First of all, I have to unload all the boxes we brought down from Santa Rosa. I have men showing up to help me with that. We have a few other things I have to do related to your parents' estate then a meeting Julie and I have to go to this evening. I promise you, before the end of tomorrow, I will take you shopping. And you can pick out anything you want to eat, within reason."

That brought a wide grin to Maron's face, and Luke was finally satisfied he could please her. If it had been appropriate, he would've grabbed her and given her a big hug.

Of course, raising five girls meant no good moment was going to last all that long. Amy asked him if she could go shopping too and pick out some of the foods she liked to eat. Jessica agreed, thought it was a good idea. And so Lindsey and Kiley were all for it too. Before he knew it, he was going to have five little girls wheeling him around in this supermarket, possibly spending a week's pay on items they usually didn't carry. But this was day one, and if it made them happy, he was glad to do it.

"All right, I can see defeat when it stares me in the face. We'll try to get it in tomorrow. I don't think today's going to work."

He cleared the table and sent them up to the room to finish unpacking and, those that hadn't, to get a shower and brush their teeth. Maron held back, hesitant to go upstairs.

Luke looked over at Nicholas who was chuckling already, trying not to spill his coffee. Maron slowly walked over to him.

"Yes, Dear?"

"I don't like sleeping on the floor."

"Okay, so you slept in Jessica's room? In the bunk bedroom, right?"

Maron nodded.

"So tonight you should sleep with Lindsey and Amy. There's plenty of room for you there."

"All three of us in the same bed?" Her little devilish face did irritate him, and it was going to soon be time for him to start setting some boundaries and limits to how much he was going to take. But it wasn't time yet for that.

Very carefully, Luke explained, "We will make sure that those arrangements are all handled tonight or tomorrow. If we have to buy more furniture, more beds, we will. But right now, you know we weren't set up for this. I'm just going to ask you, Maron, if you just give it a chance. Three to a bed, especially at the size and the ages you guys are, is no big deal. There's more than enough room for all three of you, and if you don't like it, then you can sleep on the floor in Jessica's room."

"Why can't Jessica and Kiley sleep in one bunk bed and I sleep in the other one? I want the top one."

"Maron, let's not do this. I'm asking everybody to be flexible. We're being flexible too. Please, just try to fit in."

Luke could tell immediately Maron wasn't the type of child to do that. She was going to be testing his limits right and left until he caved or until he reacted inappropriately and got in trouble. He'd seen it happen with other kids. His Amy and Jessica never behaved that way, but he'd seen other kids set their little brothers and sisters up until they blew it, overreacted, and then they were the ones punished. He could see Maron was very skilled at manipulating adults and children. And she wasn't afraid.

"We're going to do things my and Julie's way here. And you can tell us as much as you like what you would prefer, and if we can, we'll accommodate you. But if we can't, you're going to have to accept that. Life isn't perfect, as you already know."

Maron looked up at his face, fear written all over her.

"I'm sorry. That was unkind. What I mean is, we can't always get what we want." He was hearing the song playing in his brain while he was going crazy trying to tamp down his irritation, practicing patience, understanding, and the alternative to shouting and ordering and reacting.

"If I don't like it here, can I go home?"

"No, Sweetheart. This *is* your home. Now go on upstairs, get your teeth brushed, comb your hair, and get ready for some new playmates."

She looked at him with a puzzled expression.

"I have a couple of ladies who are going to come over and bring their children with them. They're wives of other SEAL team members. They're going to babysit for a few hours until we get our work done. You're going to really enjoy them."

"Boys?" she said with a wrinkled nose.

He already knew Brandon Lansdowne was going to be one of them.

He couldn't wait to see how Brandon would handle Maron. "Yes, dear. Boys will be coming over." It gave him great satisfaction to tell her that.

Brandon arrived with several other children, all brought by Tucker Hudson's wife, Brandy. They had been told the girls had a blow-up swimming pool in the backyard, so as soon as they walked in the front door, shoes were kicked off, shirts removed, towels were wrapped around their necks, and they headed for the backyard almost without greeting the adults. Luke went upstairs and told the girls to get their suits on and join the others outside. In total, there were now ten kids in the backyard, the oldest thirteen and the youngest five.

Most of the kids knew each other so well there was little argument and a lot of cooperation. Luke had always noted that during those family parties and get-togethers on the beach. The kids probably inherited this from the way their parents treated each other, primarily the men, but most of the women as well. It was a culture, he realized. And as he saw this younger generation playing, talking, splashing, and teasing, none of them displayed bullying and meanness. They were well cared for, monitored closely by Moms and Dads and knew how to behave. Not that they were perfect, of course.

Luke remembered when he sat in on the preschool visit with Kyle and Christy, when Brandon was caught swearing and being belligerent with another child at the school. The teacher had threatened he'd be expelled, and Kyle was nearly beside himself. Brandon, now a lanky boy of twelve or thirteen, was beginning to spurt up in height and was taking on a leadership role amongst the kids. Although he was not always the oldest, he usually did a pretty good job of making sure the little ones were taken care of. Luke admired his athleticism and his respect for human life. He knew that came straight from Kyle and Christy.

Shortly after Brandy and Luci Begay arrived, several other team guys and former team guys showed up in a four-door Hummer. Danny was there. So was Jameson Daniels, Tucker Hudson, and two other prospects or tadpoles, as they called them, new guys to the team who hadn't been on a deployment yet. They rode over to the warehouse together, some in the cab of the U-Haul and some in the Hummer. Luke registered the load with the gentleman at the front desk at the mini warehouse complex. He was given keys after he paid the deposit and six-month storage fee and was shown where to take the van. It was a well-lit storage facility, although not in a necessarily good neighborhood, but it was locked and monitored with security cameras. The gates were only open during daylight hours, which was done to thwart any kind of criminal activity so common to some of the other complexes in San Diego. A big arms bust had occurred at one several years ago, with several regular Navy guys and a couple of Marines purchasing guns and ammo from detaching sailors and selling them on the black market to gang members desperate to get their hands on them. There were nearly twenty who got booted, including one SEAL who lost his Trident. Several of them were now serving time in jail.

They made short work of the boxes, stacking everything as it was labeled, making sure to keep the crystal on top of the stacks so they wouldn't get crushed. There were several comments made about the pink boxes, and Luke was tired of explaining what they were, so he just clammed up and asked them to keep going. However, at the end, he had Nicholas put one of the boxes back in the U-Haul.

"What's that for?" he asked Luke.

"I told you, remember? It's going to be an experiment. I want to show Julie. We'll see what happens."

"Man, you're way more daring than I'd be. Does she even know about this stuff?"

"I kind of mentioned it to her, but I don't think she paid attention. It was hard for me to believe. Anyway, we'll just have some fun. I'll joke around with it. I mainly want her to tell me what she wants me to do with it. I couldn't very well leave it in their garage, could we?"

"Nope, well, that's a story I'd like to hear."

The guys who arrived in the Hummer said their goodbyes, and he thanked them for their hour and a half service. "I owe you a good dinner. I'll make it a steak dinner too."

Several of the team guys gave him a manly hug and whispered things privately. Mostly, everyone said they had his back, they knew he was not going to be on the next deployment or two, and they hoped he'd be joining them again soon. They all asked to be remembered to Julie, and some of them knew the Christensens and asked to be remembered to them as well.

"You drew a bad card there, Luke. But I can see you're going to make this work," Danny Begay said. "Blending families together, we found out how hard it was when we adopted Ali, but you know what? It was the best thing that ever happened to our little family. Your heart gets bigger when you can take care of someone else's child. There's no greater joy in the world. And these girls need you. I'm glad you can be there for them."

"Thanks, Man. I really appreciate that, Danny. I appreciate all you guys. I may not be with you on deployment, but I'll be with you in spirit. My heart's always going to be with you guys. So you better come back, okay?"

Everyone chuckled, said their goodbyes, as Luke and Nick locked up, exited the storage facility, and headed back to Coronado.

"So you're going to stay over one more night or what are your plans, Nick?"

"I was going to hop on a plane, but I didn't make any reservations. I think Jameson's got a little gig going at one of the clubs. I thought I'd pop over there if I can borrow one of your cars."

"No problem. We'll get this puppy taken back, and then I'll return it to the yard tomorrow. If you could help me with that, that would free up Julie for work."

"Sure thing." A couple of seconds later, Nick added, "Can I take your camper van?"

"No late nights, just in case we have to take the harem some place in an emergency, okay?"

"I'll be home by ten, Dad."

Brandy and Luci were still overseeing the huge water fight absorbing the entire backyard and part of the neighbors. Luke had invested not in water guns but water cannons that could shoot fifty feet or more when properly filled. They enjoyed watching the war play out in front of them.

Nick used the downstairs bathroom to take a shower and get ready to see Jameson perform. He told Luke he promised Jameson they'd meet for a bite beforehand.

While in the shower, Luke got a call from a highway patrol investigator, who was looking for Julie.

"She should be home within the hour. Can I take a message? I'm her husband."

"I'm going to have to talk to her as well, but you can relay the information. We have ruled out accidental and mechanical trouble as the cause of the crash that killed your sister and brother-in-law."

Luke swallowed hard.

"We now believe it was an intentional act."

CHAPTER 8

JULIE WAS EXHAUSTED from her day at the office. She'd had more meetings about issues than time to help straighten out the issues themselves. There were reports due, her input was needed for the budget for next year, and she had several interviews on the phone, which were going to lead to future teacher hires. They also had several concerns about substitutes getting other jobs and not being available for the existing staff. One third grade teacher was going to be out the rest of the year on maternity leave and had requested a substitute who was approved by another school district but had never been approved in Julie's.

She'd had several inquiries from other principals as to her application for the superintendent's job, as Devin McNally was leaving at the end of the year, just before Christmas. Julie hadn't applied as of yet but intended to.

The private school system Julie's district was affiliated with was made up of thirty elementary-middle school combinations and four high schools, with a sports program that attracted great men and women athletes who had a chance to receive scholarship monies, based on family income.

The district stretched from the Los Angeles area all the way to the southern border. Although not all faith-based, some of the schools were and elected to join their system for the academic programs and scholarship potential. Their donor base was huge and generous. Each school had the ability to order specialized classes with approval of the school board, which governed the whole system, the parents in that school, and their respective principals, like Julie.

They even sponsored a home-schooling program, and students could flow inside and outside the physical schools upon approval, which worked very well during the pandemic. With the support of the school board, Julie's biggest collaboration was with the parent-teacher board she'd created and set up as an elected group of twelve. The district was impressed with this idea and wanted to implement it throughout their system, so her candidacy looked favorable.

At least that's what the buzz was. She didn't mind it one bit.

Parents had always been an important part of her effectiveness, unlike other principals who were often at a tug of war with them.

But the State of California exerted its power over even private schools more and more, sometimes requiring changes to their curriculum without notice and without sound implementation methods. And the educational goal definitions were very sketchy and not well-defined, therefore easy to unintentionally break, resulting in fines. It had gotten so contentious at times in other areas that the district had to hire their first lobbyist, who also worked for other networks of private institutions, both faith-based and not all over the country. He was based in California, however.

So far, no major problems had occurred. But it did tend to alter some of the creativity in their curriculum and methods, for fear of the "Big Bears," as the parent-teacher group called them, the administrators for the State of California and their teacher union reps that inserted themselves mercilessly on unprepared districts. Julie wanted to see to it that their excellent program flourished with as little interference as possible.

Sampson Biggs was one of the most power members of the governing school board. A former NFL star, he maintained a successful player representation firm, recruiting kids from the projects with a past like his was and giving them opportunities they wouldn't otherwise have. His job was to spot talent for the district to feed into the four high school athletic programs the public schools couldn't compete with.

He wandered into Julie's office at the end of the day.

"Got a minute?" he asked. Julie had been filing reports online and set aside her laptop, inviting him to sit in front of her at the desk.

"Sure. What can I do for you?"

Biggs almost didn't fit into the armed wooden chair he was offered.

"We've noticed you haven't applied for the superintendent's job. Is there some change in your plans? I heard about your brother and sister-in-law. I'm very sorry for your loss, Julie."

"Oh, thank you, Sampson. I appreciate that. Yes, it's been somewhat of a juggle, but we're getting adjusted. Luckily, Luke is between deployments, so he's been shouldering most of it. We've just begun the process of blending my brother's kids into our household. So far, no blow-ups, no major problems. But I'd be lying if I told you it was easy."

"I can't imagine. Knowing you two, I'd say those kids are lucky. Boys? Girls?"

"Three girls. So now that makes five. Poor Luke was outnumbered before; now he's completely crushed."

They laughed at that.

"So are you going to be able to take on the new position if it were offered to you?"

"I'm still very interested. Frankly, it's just been a matter of having the time to do the application. I haven't had to write an essay on my thoughts of teaching, management, and curriculum for years now. I'd like to take my time and do a good job of it. Make the board's decision an easy one."

"That sounds promising. I'm glad to hear that."

"No worries, but I appreciate you checking up on me."

"Well," he said, standing, "I just wanted to stop by and let you know how sorry the entire board is with your family's loss and to reassure myself that this hasn't changed your trajectory. I know I've said it many times, but you are the one I want in that position. Don't take too long, okay? Until I get that application, I doubt I'll sleep."

Julie was flattered with the compliments, even felt her face flush.

"Thank you, Sampson. That's very kind of you to say. I appreciate your support a great deal. Means so much to me to be working where I'm wanted."

"I think it's an issue of trust. Your husband being a Navy SEAL, we appreciate what it takes to be married to an elite warrior like that. Sort of like being married to a professional athlete, as my wife reminds me and did all the time back in the day—I wouldn't deem to compare myself to the work your husband does and how it must affect your whole family. But failure isn't an option in the Paulsen household, is it?"

Julie chuckled as she took his extended hand in a firm shake.

"No, it's not. I have to remind Luke about that sometimes when I have to overrule him. Let's say that this new phase of our family life is humbling and giving him an opportunity to stretch and grow in ways he never knew he needed. But you're right, he's made it a mission, and he's determined to succeed."

Biggs nodded, pointing at her. "You're special, Julie. Don't keep me hanging."

As soon as he left, Julie sat back in her chair and breathed a sigh of relief. Forces all around her were pushing her to only one outcome: she needed to take the superintendent's job, if she could get it. And with Biggs' support, while there were no shoe-ins in life, really, it was about as close as it could be to one.

But she wasn't going to celebrate just yet. Luke's job was what she worried about most. She was confident he'd succeed being Mr. Mom and was grateful he'd be out of the killing fields for a few months, perhaps longer if he quit, but she knew Luke. She was worried about all the litter he'd create along the way. He was, after all, a human tornado: unpredictable, capable of upending things and altering everything around him. There was a cost-risk evaluation going on in her head she sometimes found troubling.

When she got home, she noticed Nick's pillow and blankets folded on the couch, indicating he was probably going to stay over another night. She called out for Luke, who responded from upstairs that he was reading to the girls.

She set her briefcase down in the study, plugged in her laptop and phone to charge, and took the long stairway up to the bedrooms, holding onto the handrail. She was hoping they could turn in early. With one good night's rest under her belt, she would probably start to get her energy back.

Inside Amy's room, all the girls were seated around Luke, who was reading them Alice in Wonderland. It had always been one of Julie's favorites. Little Jessica came over and greeted her. Luke stopped briefly with a, "Welcome home, Sweetheart," and then continued on with the book. She retired to the master bedroom, stripped off her clothes, and took a long, hot shower. She was in the process of putting on her nightie when Luke entered the room, closing the door behind him.

"Where's Nick?" she asked.

"He's taken the van. I said it was okay obviously. I hope you don't mind. Jameson's having a little gig over at Pierre's Bar & Grill. I don't think you've ever been there before."

"Yes, I have. We had a bachelorette party there one time."

"Ah, you are so right. I forgot about that. Well, he'll be back before ten, and I decided to let him use the van because the U-Haul truck is just huge and hard to park."

"No, that's fine. You'll take the truck back tomorrow? You got everything done?"

"Yup. Got it all loaded at the mini warehouse. Filled the whole space."

"How was your day otherwise?" She slipped under the covers after propping the pillows up, grabbing her book from the bedside table, and putting on her reading glasses.

Luke sat on the edge of the bed and hesitated just long enough that it got Julie's attention.

"What is it?"

"I got a call from a highway patrol crash investigator. They've determined that Steph and Colin's accident, if you will, wasn't really an accident after all. It was an intentional hit."

"How did they figure that after all this time? How come they didn't determine this at the time of the accident?"

"Well, I didn't realize this until this evening, but the driver of the truck that hit them took off, and they only just found him. The truck was not currently registered, and actually, it had been reported missing from a construction site in Las Vegas several years ago. Now they have this guy in custody, and he's claiming somebody paid him five hundred bucks to hit them."

"Who is this guy?"

"He's a nobody. No record. Worked odd jobs. Bigtime gambler and drinker, I guess. But they didn't have a chance to get him tested that night, so alcohol isn't listed as a contributing factor."

"Maybe he just used it as an excuse to try to get some leniency. I don't know that I believe that. Who would want to kill my brother and Steph?"

"I just don't know what to say, Julie. I was going to call some of our friends, maybe Detective Riverton here in San Diego, see if he had someone he could recommend, but he's on vacation for a few days. Maybe Armando's step-dad, Sergeant Mayfield. I need somebody with some law enforcement background to look into this and see what they're really doing."

"Stephanie and Colin didn't have a care in the world. They didn't have enemies. I doubt it was intentional. I mean, they're just not the type of people who would get involved in stuff like that."

"I know, I know. I've told myself that a hundred times over since I got the call. But I'd like to have someone investigate on our behalf, someone who has some background or at least knows who this highway patrol investigator is, in case he has an agenda of some kind. And he sounded perfectly legit to me, but I would be easily fooled."

"So could I. But on that score, I think you're a better judge of human nature than I would be. This is so far afield for me I can't comprehend it. It just seems so impossible we're even having this discussion, Luke."

She set her book on the side table and leaned forward over her knees tucked under the sheets. "What does this mean, Luke?"

"Well, first, we have to find out who might have wanted to harm them or, worse, kill them."

"So you actually believe this dude?"

"I'm just checking out all the angles. You know me."

She smiled up at her handsome husband. "I do. I know you can't help it."

"No, it's a good thing, Julie. If it's plausible, and I don't know for sure whether or not it is, then we have to assess whether or not that leaves us and the kids exposed."

"You're worried that some of it would rub off on us?"

"We don't know, do we?"

"I prefer my pink bubble, the 'cone of deniability.'"

"That's why I just would feel a whole lot better if someone on the inside would get me some information. I need to know what they're investigating and who the players are. It sounds like it could be directed against either one of them. But I have a hard time thinking that a housewife and an architect would create enemies, do you?"

"You think they're investigating Steph and Colin?"

"That's what I need to find out."

"How could you possibly think some dark secret lurks there? Where do you get this, Luke?"

"It's my training. I don't trust anyone who wouldn't put down their life for me and my family."

"But couldn't this just be a rabbit hole? Maybe this isn't good for you, honey."

"That's why I need to know why the investigators are headed toward a murder investigation. That means there is a motive. We don't know what that is yet. Until we do, we have to suspect everyone, and that includes Colin and Steph."

"No, that's not consistent with who they are. Really strange. But you're right. Somebody who knows how things work and who can ask the right people the right questions, that's who we need. You called both Riverton and Detective Mayfield?" she asked.

"Yes, I left a message for both of them. I'm sure they'll get back to me as soon as they're available."

Julie noticed the pink box on the edge of the bed on Luke's side. "What's that?" she asked.

"Well, this is the other part of my suspicious mind working over-time."

"What is it?"

"Open it. It's from my sister's business. Did you know anything about what she was selling?"

She began to crawl over the bed toward the box. "It was like home parties. I thought it was like cookware or knives or plasticware, something like that. She said she was doing these parties in ladies' homes in the area, and she was apparently pleased with herself. Now, I'm getting this from Mom, because Stephanie never told me what she was doing."

"Do you think they had some kind of a shadowy second life?" he asked her.

The question offended her first, and then she reconsidered her position. His delving into the possible sources of this information would help put it to bed and settle everyone's nerves, eliminate the stress of too many unanswered theories.

"I can honestly say that Colin and Stephanie were very much in love, and I mean Main Street Love, no question. They were an ideal couple and loved their girls. I never picked up any type of strange behavior, but what are you hinting at, Luke?"

"Do you think they were swingers?"

Julie laughed. "Oh God, no. That's the last thing in the world I would consider happening in their house. I mean, I'm sure they argued, but I never saw it. And they just seemed very compatible, very much in love. I don't see the need for any kind of a shadowy existence, some kind of an alternate reality. Is that what you're asking?"

"Well, look at this box, Julie. This apparently was Stephanie's business. Selling what's in this box. I want you to look it over and tell me if this changes your opinion of them in any way."

She kneeled on the bed, hovering over the already-opened pink cardboard box. Inside, she was shocked to find the contents. There were all kinds of bright-colored gadgets, jars, tubes of creams, feathers, velvet handcuffs, laces, very skimpy underwear pieces, and vibrators of every shape, color, and size. She was completely speechless.

"We found this before our trip down here and just loaded it in the truck. I wasn't going to say anything, except for the sheer volume of boxes she had. I thought it was odd. But now, in light of this phone call I got, I'm wondering if there's some kind of a relationship between these two things. I mean, she kept this pretty quiet if this was in fact what she did on the side. I'm just wondering if she crossed the wrong people or if something happened, and it led to a misunderstanding, and somehow they got involved with some kind of nefarious group. I don't know. I just thought Stephanie would've told you or maybe Colin mentioned something."

"No, I've heard nothing. And I really do think Colin would've told me if there was something going on. We never talked about their sex life, if this is what this is. It's possible one of them likes this stuff, and the other just went along, and they made a side hustle of it. We know that she stopped the business and pulled down her website. I consider that kind of normal if you've all of a sudden decided you don't want to be involved in this. But Mom seemed to think she was doing quite well with her business and making a significant amount of money every month, which was helping to pay some of the school fees and camps for the girls. When she had decided to shut it down, Mom really didn't know why, because she assumed that Steph was quite happy with it. I'm almost positive Mom doesn't know about any of this," she said, pointing to the contents of the box.

"That's what I thought. I think we have to investigate further. I need somebody who has their finger on some of this kind of alternative behavior. On the surface, it looks fairly harmless. Just a bunch of colorful toys for party night between couples. I don't think there's anything wrong with that. Just a little experimentation. But the abrupt curtailing of her business and the accident that killed them coming under scrutiny just sets my antennas on fire. I can't just ignore it now. I have to find somebody who can help us get to the bottom line."

Julie reached into the box and picked out a pink penis-shaped vibrator, pressing a button. The vibrator buzzed, even lit up, started shaking in her hand, and then, as if waving goodbye, bent forward a few degrees before resuming the erect position again and stopped.

"Oh my. Luke. This is—is—"

"That wasn't the kind of investigation I was thinking of."

He took the vibrator from her hand, turned it off, and placed it back in the box. He picked up a little hand-held buzzer that fit over a person's middle finger.

He'd brought something like this home some years ago, and it had been fun, but over the years, they'd misplaced it. She knew what it was and how it made her feel, dammit.

"Appears to be a new model here. Maybe we could test a couple of these things?" Luke asked her.

She couldn't read his expression, except he focused on her lips. She felt her arousal, even though the timing of it sucked, was so inappropriate, was something she should easily purge from her thoughts, except it wasn't easy. Their sex life had suffered over the past few weeks, and she suddenly felt needy beyond desperate.

"Why, Luke Paulsen. I wouldn't know what to do with this stuff. I'm afraid you'd have to show me."

"That's exactly what I was thinking. It would be my pleasure, my dear wife."

CHAPTER 9

L UKE HAD ONE of the SEAL wives come over to watch the girls while he and Nick returned the U-Haul. Then he took Nick to the airport for the one-way trip home, and Luke paid for that ticket as well.

"You holler if you need anything, Luke. I wish I had more contacts with law enforcement, but if I run across anything, I'll let you know. After our run-in with the neighbor, we tend to stay away from the courts and law enforcement. We stick to weddings, the ranch, and making wine."

"You got it made, Nick. Again, thanks, and let us know if we can ever help you out as well."

"Be careful about volunteering. We might get you stomping grapes yet!"

Back at the house, Luke thanked Brandy and checked on the girls. He received a call from Gus Mayfield, the retired San Diego Police Sergeant, who had married Armando's mother. Indeed, Mayfield was family to the Teams, and many times guys would use him to obtain inside law enforcement advice and information. He was returning Luke's call.

"So what's going on, Luke?" His voice sounded even crustier than Luke had remembered.

"Sorry I had to be so cryptic, but I really didn't want to spell it out too much. I've got a situation with Julie's brother and my sister. You know about the accident?"

"Yes, we were all sorry to hear that, Son. How are you holding up?"

"Well, we've brought the girls here, and we're getting situated. We still have some trust things to deal with. But the biggest concern we have right now is the investigation into the crash."

"Oh? There's an investigation?"

"See, that's what I thought too. It's been a few weeks now, and nobody ever said anything about investigating it other than trying to locate the drunk driver who hit them. As it turns out, they've caught the guy, and now he's telling the investigators he was paid to broadside their car. And the truck was stolen, stolen off of a construction site in Las Vegas several years ago. Ownership of it is sketchy, and the guy who drove the truck is even more sketchy. I just don't have a good feeling about this, Gus, and I was wondering if you'd be willing to look into it for me. I know you still have contacts up in Sonoma County and the Peninsula."

"I do. I'm not sure what I can find out, but I can try certainly. Best to just let them do their job, though, Luke. It really isn't necessary that you get yourself involved in it."

"I know that's a good piece of advice, but it's more than that."

"How so?"

"Well, this is difficult to explain, but my sister had a mail order business—a side business, selling sex toys."

"Good Lord. That's a surprise. But I guess these days, I shouldn't be surprised at all. Still, I would never think Stephanie would do anything like that. And Colin? Boy, that's a big new one on me."

"We removed the boxes they had stored in their garage, with the house going on the market, and—"

"You're selling the house? You should keep it and make it into a rental."

"It's a huge, architecturally-designed house, Gus."

"Gotcha."

"We found a whole bunch of inventory, and frankly, I didn't think much of it, either, except that even Julie's mother didn't know exactly what the business was. We all assumed it was home fragrance or Tupperware or knives or something like that. She would have these parties at people's houses. I guess I can understand why Stephanie never said anything to me or Julie, so that part is okay, but she closed the business down abruptly right at the time they were coming back from a convention in Las Vegas. The timing of it, her closing the business and shutting down her bank accounts, is just odd. And then they have this accident and indications are that it was a paid-for hit. I mean, wouldn't you start to draw some conclusions there?" Luke asked.

"Well, the selling of the 'pleasure items' doesn't bother me. Hell, Felicia and I have been known to experiment a little bit, and I presume you and Julie are the same."

"I'm not saying a word. Not admitting anything. And I won't repeat that."

Gus Mayfield chuckled. "Well, a lot of things would surprise you. But we won't get into that. I do think it is worth looking into, and if you don't mind, I will do that and get back to you. Don't expect anything earth-shaking. They're going to strong arm me, and they're going to know I have a connection to the SEAL community down here. When they put it together, I don't expect they're going to open up their files to me or anything. But I would be cautious about who you tell about all this. Because the worst thing that can happen is something can get out there on social media and all of a sudden you got rumors. And rumors are really hard to combat. Let the police do their job unimpeded, and let's see what they come up with before you start disclosing anything to anyone else. And do not, whatever you do, talk to the media. Remember, the media is not your friend."

"That's sound advice, Gus. I've also called Clark Riverton, and I know he's headed-up several organized crime task forces here in San Diego. I'd heard he was getting ready to retire, but maybe he could look in different directions and help us out too."

"Well, I think he'd be more connected than I would certainly. Why do you think it's organized crime?"

"The Las Vegas connection. They were coming home from there when it happened."

"I see. Not sure it has much to do with it, but I'll do my best, and you can have Clark call me if he needs to. I'll share whatever I've got with him and with you guys. Now again, don't expect any miracles, because Felicia's got me doing all kinds of stuff to get ready for the holidays. Sometimes I think that's why she married me. She's planning to entertain her heart out here, and you know what she feels about her gardens, her flowers, and her house. So I don't think I can do this quick, but you let me know if you hear anything further in the meantime."

"Will do. Thanks so much."

The girls were outside in their swimsuits, nobody in the pool yet, but sunning themselves in the warm early fall sun. Most of them were reading. Maron had fallen asleep on a chaise lounge. Luke figured he had about thirty minutes before he'd have to start putting together some things for lunch, so he went to his computer to research bunk beds. He found a site that sold double and queen-size bunk beds, which he calculated might fit in Jessica's room, but it wouldn't leave much room for anything else. He also found a Murphy bed/desk combination in another catalog that might work for Amy's room.

Knowing Maron seemed to like the bunk beds, he figured that would be the best way to go, so instead of checking with Julie first, he went ahead and paid for the bunk beds to be delivered to the house with a credit card. It was more money than he wanted to spend, but he hoped that the trust funds would be coming through soon and he'd be reimbursed. One thing for sure, it would handle a huge issue, and that was sleeping arrangements, which he knew would only get worse as the days went by.

He and Julie were supposed to meet with several teachers who were going to have the girls in their classes, and that was all scheduled for tomorrow. The following week, his girls and Steph's kids would be resuming their classes at school. The teachers had all been notified that everybody was taking a few days off, and nobody seemed to object to what they'd requested. It also gave Luke a chance to assess what interested the girls and to try to make them feel comfortable and at home.

He thought about Kyle's conversation with him about staying on the Teams or not and was grateful that he had the six months.

Luke decided he'd take the girls shopping, so he could check that one obligation off his list of things he had to do. He called them inside and promised them they could go out for fast food, providing they could find something that Maron could eat, and the girls were thrilled at the opportunity.

He loaded all five of the girls into the van and made his first stop at an organic grocery store, figuring Maron would have the best selection. But as they browsed the aisles, all of the girls jumping up to grab things and place them in the cart like a virtual smorgasbord, he discovered that Maron was the one who was picky, and his other girls were actually going to be filling the cart with very expensive items they really didn't need to get. And he didn't think they'd enjoy eating some of the things they picked, but he went along with it anyway. Maron was able to find her vegetarian cheese, vegetable spreads, organic peanut butter, and sugar-free jams, also the imitation bacon and garden burgers. She also liked to drink kefir and yogurt.

Luke felt like they were a small storm of activity when they got to the checkout counter. He got some amazing smiles and laughter as all five of the girls were talking at once, chattering amongst themselves, dashing in and out of the carts and playing tag. They knocked over a display of new cereals, sending boxes all over the floor. Several times, Luke had to step in and quell the chaos. He lost Jessica just as they were ready to leave the store and had to have her name announced over the loudspeaker. She'd gone to the bathroom but hadn't told anybody. That was another lesson and a long conversation that resulted in some tears.

As he pulled the cart out to the van, the girls swirling around him like a bunch of bees circling a beehive, he again had to remind them about situational awareness, watching for cars, watching for people watching them, all the things that he'd been trained and were second nature to him. His intent was to arm them with observations and techniques and talents that they didn't now possess. But the truth was, they barely listened to him, and that worried him no-end.

Next, they went to one of the local grocery stores, and Maron picked out several exotic fruits including dragon fruit, papayas, and organic bananas. He instructed her to keep them in a special green plastic bag, because the rest of the family was not going to eat organic. He bought several staples and the favorites of the girls, some frozen things that would make life easy for him, extra spaghetti sauce, and pre-made frozen meatballs for his Thursday night dinners, and other things. As he was meandering down the laundry section of the store, he got a call.

"Hey, Luke, I got an inquiry from somebody from San Jose, an investigative team."

It was Kyle, and the conversation surprised him.

"Wait a minute, somebody called you about me?" he asked.

"Yeah. Just asking questions about your background, whether you were a SEAL in good standing, how long you'd been there."

The girls boarded a long flat cart, and Lindsey started to push the others, heading around the corner.

"Just a minute, Kyle." He shouted, "Girls. You come right back here! Get off that d—that cart."

Sheepishly, they returned to him, hanging their heads. The long cart was abandoned in the center of the aisle and had to be moved by someone trying to approach from the other side.

"Hey, Kyle, sorry about that. I'm shopping."

"So that's what's going on. You're one brave sonofabitch."

Luke sighed, both frustrated and beginning to feel exhaustion.

"Kyle, I just want to mention to you that we need to be careful about this. They're determining this was not an accident but that Colin and Stephanie were intentionally hit, as you know."

"Yeah, I know. Christy told me. I didn't give him much information. I just—"

"Who was this person who called you? Are you sure it was a police investigator?" he asked.

"Well, let's see. He gave his name as, let's see, Spencer Roberts. He's an investigator with… hmm, I didn't write it down or he didn't give it to me. I just thought he was from Highway Patrol or the Sheriff's office. Holy fuck, maybe he's a private investigator."

"That's what I mean. You see now?"

"I do."

"Well, I need to talk to Clark Riverton, and I've already talked to Gus Mayfield. I think we have to be very careful about answering questions until we figure out who we're actually talking to. With this turn of events, I don't trust anything that's going on."

"Okay, I got you. Damn it, Luke. I should have thought of this. I don't know why, I just thought it was going to help. I gave you a glowing recommendation. I said nothing about the troubles you've had in the past. I just answered his questions."

"What questions did he have?"

"Well, he actually asked if you had ever been involved in any altercations or fights on the Teams? If you'd ever exhibited behavior that wasn't up to the Navy standards. He also asked about Julie. And when that happened, I really clammed up. I probably should have before."

Luke didn't want to get angry with Kyle, but he knew the conversation was a total mistake.

"I think until further notice, Kyle, we ought to beg off any interviews unless they come to you in person. We're going to need to check their credentials first, and let me have Gus and Clark look into things first. And then we'll kind of know where we're at. But right now, I need you to be very quiet and very tightlipped. I know we're supposed to be honest, but you know when it comes to missions, we don't tell everybody what we're doing. And this is sort of turning into something like that."

"Are you sure it's not your imagination, Son? I mean, are you really sure?"

"I don't have anything but my gut reaction to it all, and if I think these things are related, then I have to check it out before I change my mind about it. You and I both know we stay alive because we stay focused on everything going on around us. This could affect our family if it doesn't go well. I have nothing to hide, but I don't want to volunteer to give information to a possible future enemy."

After they unloaded the van, the girls went outside to eat their hamburgers. They were able to find Maron fish tacos at the same hamburger stand he bought meals for the other girls.

Clark Riverton gave him a call. "I understand from Gus you got a situation brewing?"

Luke was grateful for this experienced detective and his no-nonsense attitudes toward law enforcement. He was glad that Mayfield had made the connection.

"Yeah, it's getting pretty crazy, Clark. I would appreciate it if you could come over and talk to Julie and me about this. Would that be possible?"

"Sure. What time does she come home?"

"Well, I assume you're back from your vacation—"

"Yeah, it was actually a seminar. Daisy went to a tattoo convention."

Clark had married the tattoo artist that most of the SEALS went to for their skulls and Celtic crosses and bands of barbed wire. Her studio had been left to her by the prior owner who had been taking care of SEAL Teams for twenty years and was a former SEAL himself before he passed away.

"I think about 5:00, 5:30 would work."

"I got it. I'll see you at 5:30, and if Julie gets delayed, no problem. I don't have plans for the rest of the evening."

Luke sighed, glad the team he was assembling was maybe going to help them stay out of trouble or, at the worst, get them some much-needed information. Watching the precious girls climb in and out of the pool, laughing and spraying each other with the hose, he wanted them to never know some of the deep, dark things of this world, some of the evil he was battling. And he knew evil existed everywhere. Even when you least expected it.

This new revelation about Steph and Colin had proved that, beyond a shadow of a doubt.

CHAPTER 10

WHEN JULIE RETURNED home, Clark Riverton's car was parked in the driveway. He and Luke were having a conversation in the living room. The girls were still having a water fight in the backyard, and at times, the hose sprayed the picture window in the dining room. Julie was upset that Luke had not been paying close attention. Their screams were echoing all around the neighborhood.

"Nice to see you, Julie. I'm Clark Riverton." He extended his hand. "I'm semi-retired, in charge of the violent crime task force here in San Diego County. Luke has asked me to come over and give you some advice and shed some light on what has gone on so far."

Annoyed, Julie spoke quickly, one eye on the mayhem in the backyard.

"That's fine, but—" She gave a stern look at Luke. "You're not paying attention to the girls. Do you know that kids and adults can drown in three inches of water? These girls are out there totally unsupervised."

Luke got up, quickly checked out the window, and turned back to her. She could tell he was going to disagree with her and wasn't happy with her criticism.

"Julie, I've been watching them all day. I took those fucking girls to the store, I bought a ton of specialty food, I've been cooking for them, and I've been cleaning the fucking house until my hands are sore and raw. I've been working my ass off. I can't even take a nap because there's nobody here to watch them, and—"

"Whose fault is that?" she asked him.

"Whoa, whoa, whoa, whoa. Hey, folks," Riverton started. "I don't want to intrude on anybody's feelings here, but I don't think this is a good time. I'll come back later, on another day."

"No. You stay right here," both Julie and Luke said in unison.

Julie raised one additional question to her husband.

"And I thought we were supposed to go down to the school tonight or did you forget about that, Luke?"

He was getting more irritated. Still standing, with his hands on his hips, he barked back at her, "I rescheduled it for tomorrow. You said it was going to be hard for you to make it tonight, so I rescheduled it, and instead, we're meeting with Detective Riverton. Don't you think that's a higher priority?"

Just then, they both heard somebody screaming in the backyard. Someone was in pain. Julie, of course, thought the worst.

"Goddamn it," she cursed as she raced through the living room and out through the kitchen door onto the patio. Luke and Riverton were left behind and had no time to respond before she was outside. All kinds of horrible thoughts went through her mind as she searched the yard and the patio and the pool and discovered that Amy had fallen down and skinned her knee, red blood flowing all over the place. She mumbled under her breath, "Where's a fucking medic when you need one?"

She looked up at the living room window and screamed, "Luke, get out here and bring your kit." Her peripheral vision noted the other four girls jumped and retreated to the edge of the lawn, away from her.

That started in motion the rumbling of the old house, as it shook. Even the windows rattled. That told her Luke had sprung to action, was opening the cabinet and bringing out his big medic bag halfway slung on his back. He ran to where Julie was and took a look at Amy's bloody knee.

Julie was trying to help her into the patio chair.

"Don't touch her, Julie. Leave her right there until I check out her bones." Luke's voice was sharp, rough, and cutting.

"She hasn't broken her legs. She just skinned her knee, can't you tell?"

"I don't make things up, Julie, I deal with certainties. And if she broke a bone, it could be worsened by making her stand up on it to sit in a chair. If you want her to sit in a chair, I'll put her there."

And that's exactly what he did. He picked her up and sat her in the chair.

Julie saw the other four girls suddenly go quiet, sitting together on the lawn in the shade, watching the fiasco of their parents argue over a minor wound. At least Julie thought it was a minor wound.

Luke felt from her hip down to her knee and then from her knee down to her ankle, squeezing and asking Amy if it hurt. He moved her ankle then raised and lowered her whole leg outstretched. When he moved the knee back and forth, she winced and complained.

"Ouch. Daddy, that hurts."

He touched and moved her joint carefully, getting his daughter's blood all over his hands as he did so. He dabbed the wound with some gauze from the kit and pointed to the scraped skin that had been bleeding.

Everything was negative, and Julie was relieved.

"Okay, so I'm going to clean this. You stay right here. I'm going to get some towels."

Amy started to cry. "I'm sorry, Mom. Why does he have to be such a terrible dad when he gets like this? I get afraid of him."

"I know, Sweetie. He doesn't mean it. He loves you. He gets worried. So do I."

"I didn't *mean* to fall. I was trying not to, but Maron tripped me."

Maron stood up and pointed back at Amy, "I did not. Amy's just so clumsy she doesn't know how to do anything without help. You slipped and fell because you weren't paying attention, Stupid."

"That's enough from all of you!" came the booming voice of her husband. "I have had just about enough with you guys. I have given you everything you wanted to do today, right?"

Nobody said a thing. Luke stood there with a dripping tea towel in his right hand.

"I said, haven't we done everything you requested to do today? I took you shopping, we went out for lunch, and you're getting to play in the swimming pool. I mean, you have a perfect life here. Be grateful for Chrissake, instead of a bunch of spoiled brats."

Julie looked up at him. "Stop it, Luke. You're being an asshole."

Jessica inhaled and put her hands over her mouth. "Mother!"

"Well, I can see I'm not the only one who loses it. You know full well what it's like to take care of this group all day, and today is just… I've had it. I've had all kinds of unexpected crises, and we're trying to just have a normal life. This is a normal life, right? Is it going to be like this every single day?"

"I'm sorry. Maybe it's the apron, Luke. But I think the girls think you look ridiculous. They aren't obeying you, following your rules. You have to change."

Luke looked down at himself as if he'd forgotten that he was even wearing an apron. He quickly removed it and threw it on the ground.

"Fine. I'll get my own fucking apron."

"Luke? What's gotten into you?" In the background were four little girls with their hands over their mouth, Jessica with her palms over both ears, and all of them looking shocked and afraid.

"It's okay, Daddy," said Amy. "I understand. I'm the one who slipped and fell. I'm the one that caused all of this." She started to cry. "I'm so sorry, and I really didn't mean to ruin your day. And I'm sorry it's so hard for you to take care of us."

Her husband acted like he'd just been shot through the heart with an arrow. They heard the back door open and saw Clark Riverton's figure on the patio.

"Hey, guys, I'm going to come back another time."

Amy looked up at both her parents. "Who's he?"

"He's going to help us with something, Amy," said Luke. "Clark, it's not serious. We'll be done in just a couple of minutes. They're going to have a timeout, and I think we'll be able to finish our conversation. Don't go, please, because I honestly don't know when we're going to have the time to fit it in again."

"You're still being an asshole, Luke," Julie couldn't help whispering.

Amy looked at her mother. "I don't like it when you use Dad's words."

Of course they are dad's words. They certainly aren't mine, but I've been learning these ten years.

That almost got her laughing. Her husband did start to laugh. He chuckled all during the cleanup process, as he carefully put soapy water over the wound, picked out pieces of dirt and a leaf, rinsed it with clean sterile solution, and then applied some first aid cream over the raw skin. He then applied a three-inch gauze pad that had adhesive around the edges, making sure it was loose enough so it wouldn't pop off when she bent her knee.

"Your mother has a very ridiculously wicked mouth, Amy. But I still love her," he said as he leaned over and gave her a kiss on her cheek.

She was going to back away, but she accepted the small consolation. Her insides began to melt as he stared back at her with those blue eyes of his.

The girls were allowed to come into the family room, wrapped in their towels, keeping their bathing suits on for a later trip outside. Luke put on an Avengers movie, and they all sat on the couch or the floor enmeshed in the action film.

Riverton looked like he was very uncomfortable and extremely out of place. But he kept his mouth shut and didn't offer to leave again, which Julie appreciated.

Julie addressed him as they walked back to the living room. "You know I always told myself that, when I had kids, I would never use the TV to occupy them. It's just not possible if you're trying to raise children these days. I mean, they do a good job entertaining themselves, but sometimes, you just got to turn something on that they can plug in to, and then they're preoccupied so they don't cause chaos. There are some days I had a hard time even concentrating on putting things in the dishwasher or emptying the laundry. And that was with just two. Now there are five."

"I'm beginning to learn some of those things myself. You get a routine going. It's not that bad. It's really not that hard," said Luke.

But Julie knew he had a new appreciation for all the years before she went back to teaching, when she stayed at home with the babies.

Julie put water on for coffee and asked Riverton if he wanted something else other than coffee.

"I'll have a glass of water. That sounds about perfect right now. I'm afraid, at my age, if I drink a cup of coffee I'm going to be up half the night."

"No problem." Julie got him a glass of ice water. She put her hand on Luke's shoulder, softening her tone toward him. "Honey? You want some water too?"

"Yes, please. Thanks." He grabbed her hand before she could remove it from his shoulder. Holding it to his mouth, he kissed her palm tenderly.

After the coffee was made and served, they settled in. Julie enjoyed the warm beverage and the half-and-half she put in it and asked the detective what his take was on their situation.

"Well, first of all, Julie, you need to know that we just started talking about it. So I don't even know all the facts of the case, although your husband has talked to Gus Mayfield, and Gus and I have discussed it a little bit. We really need to see what the background is of this guy who hit your brother and sister-in-law. We also want to see why they are giving a lot of weight to his testimony, saying that he was paid money to do it. It's just not normal. You don't take a big rig cab like that and T-bone a car. You could still be killed yourself. A car could explode. I mean, it's very dangerous to do. I just think, and I hope, he's just trying to cover up a DUI of some kind and using this ruse to try to get off or beat the charge. But I don't know."

"Did you tell him about the box of delights?" Julie asked Luke.

"You mean the Garden of Delights? The pink boxes?" he asked.

"You know what I mean." Hairs at the back of her neck began to stiffen.

"Clark, you wait right here. I'm going to go bring down the box to show you what my sister was doing in her spare time, and I'd like your opinion if you don't mind."

"No, I don't mind at all. I'm here to help any way I can."

While Luke was running upstairs and then back down again carrying the box, Riverton held his water glass up, "May I trouble you for some more, please?"

"Of course." She brought the pitcher of cold water from the refrigerator after filling his glass and set it on the table so he could help himself to more later on.

Luke brought a chair over from the dining room table and set the box on it, lifted the lid, and invited Riverton to look inside. "This is what we found, lots of boxes like these in Steph and Colin's garage. It appears she had a thriving mail order business selling these."

Riverton peered over the edge and began to chuckle.

"What's so funny?" Julie wondered.

"Pardon me, but if this doesn't look like the top drawer of my wife's bedroom vanity, I don't know what does."

Luke chuckled, but Julie wasn't amused. Luke immediately silenced.

"I think that falls into the category of TMI?" Julie said with a smirk.

"So I apologize. I'm probably dating myself, but we used to call these fuckerware parties back in the day. I guess they're still in style."

"You mean, this is a thing that's been happening for like years and years and years?" Julie asked him.

"Well, like anything, people are doing all sorts of home-based businesses to raise money these days, and lots of these cottage industry things are popping up all over the place. There's no harm in it. I'm looking at this stuff, and it's all pretty generic, pretty harmless stuff. It may not be the kind of thing that you guys would be interested in trying out, but—" He chuckled again. "You know, I think healthy couples probably can use some of this stuff. You know they say that, with all the crap going on in our society these days, people aren't getting it on as much as they used to."

"You view this as a sort of couple therapy enhancement. Is that what you're saying?" she asked him.

"No, Julie, they're toys, harmless toys. You ever wear a sexy nightgown for Luke? It's the same thing. Nothing wrong here. Nothing at all to worry about. And if it assuages your conscience about your brother and sister-in-law, I don't see how it harms anybody. They're just toys, and toys are not against the law. Now, if we're talking about some heavy-duty S&M stuff where you have to have code words and handcuffs you can slip out of in an emergency, well, that's a whole other story, but this stuff is pretty tame. I've seen much worse. And I wouldn't be concerned, if that's what you're worried about."

"So you don't think this company with a base in Las Vegas, where they just came from attending a convention when they were hit, is related? You don't think that the fact that she was doing this on the side, they were in Las Vegas, and they get killed on their way home... you don't see any correlation with any of this?" Julie asked him.

"Not really," Riverton said. "You know, this isn't organized crime stuff. This is a little bit sexy stuff, I would call it." Riverton was squirming a bit in his seat.

"I think what Clark is saying, Julie, is he's familiar with this. And forgive me if I'm assuming too much, but you've probably used some of these items, right?"

"Well, it's a personal thing. You understand people have different kinds of tastes. I'm not condemning it, and I'm not admitting anything, but I will tell you, I wouldn't condemn anybody for playing around, experimenting. She probably had a good time selling this stuff. You know the women get together and have a couple glasses of wine. It sure would be a more interesting party than getting drunk and doing oil painting or selling cosmetics or plastic storage bins. Don't you think?"

"I don't know what I think. I'm just upset with the fact that they've called Luke and told him that this is a criminal investigation. That it was a deliberate effort on someone's part to hurt them. Maybe not kill them but definitely hurt them. And the fact that none of us knew anything about this before just adds credence to it. It's all a big mystery. We would be so grateful if you could look into their investigation and put our minds at ease."

"I got you. I'll do just that. But don't be expecting anything grand. I'm not going to be uncovering a counterfeit sex toys operation here."

Luke leaned forward and nodded his head and then mumbled, "Well, maybe you can do this one additional thing for us, Clark."

"What's that?"

"Do you know what we can do with twelve more boxes filled with shit like this?"

AFTER RIVERTON LEFT, they put the girls to bed. Luke told them about the bunkbed he'd ordered today and Maron especially was excited about having her own bed. She even agreed to sleep on the floor again.

Alone in their bedroom, Julie's phone rang downstairs.

"I'll get it for you," said Luke, who sprung to action, racing for the den, grabbed her phone, and handed it to her while it was still ringing.

"Oh good, It's Biggs. Probably something more about the superintendent's job I applied for." She took a deep breath before answering. "Hello, Sampson. How are you?"

Julie noted the edge to his voice that wasn't there when last they spoke.

"I'd like a short meeting with you tomorrow after you meet with the teachers, if you don't mind."

"Sure."

"Fine then."

"Um, not sure if you noticed, but I applied online for the superintendent's job."

"Yes, I saw that. We'll discuss it tomorrow."

"Is—is everything okay?"

"Have you watched the evening news?" he asked.

"No. Why? What have I not seen?"

"Just watch the news." Biggs hung up.

She stared at her phone. "That was very odd."

"Why did he call?" asked Luke.

"He wants to meet. I thought it was about the job, but now I don't know. Can you turn on the news, please?"

Luke did so. Both of them sat at the edge of their king-size bed and watched a report about how the fatal auto accident in San Jose some weeks ago was now being investigated as a murder-for-hire plot, and it involved a possible motive of financial gain. The reporter added that the murdered couple had been involved in a child pornography ring, possibly murdered to keep from cooperating with the police in Las Vegas who were trying to shut the ring down. A local San Diego family was also being investigated concerning this crime. More results would follow.

CHAPTER 11

"**I**'M GOING TO go to work today, Luke. I'm not going to let this media falsehood interfere with my job. There are teachers, students, and parents counting on me. I'm not going to fold and go run away."

She was her usual stubborn way when she was convinced she was right. Luke knew there wouldn't be any way he could talk her out of it, but he had to try—for her own safety and sanity, he had to try.

"But, Julie, think of it. You're going to be the subject of conversation all throughout the school district. It's not going to be hard for them to focus in on you. You've never had this kind of negative scrutiny, and eventually, the news media could start coming here. I think it's inevitable. I think we need to get an attorney and start doing some damage control."

"I just don't know where they're getting this information. And now the idea that some family member has killed them for their own financial gain? That's totally pure BS. If somebody did that, it couldn't be anyone from our family. There isn't anyone who would do such a thing. No, I have to act, walk, and conduct myself just as if I have nothing to hide, because I don't."

She could tell Luke all she wanted about how it was the right thing to go to work, but Luke was the one who slept next to her last night, and he'd be surprised if Julie even slept more than about ten or fifteen minutes without waking up in a cold sweat. He held her while she cried, he rubbed her back, he suggested she have some hot chocolate and brought it to her, he rubbed her feet, he placed lavender oil on her temples to help her sleep, and nothing seemed to work. But this morning, she was showered and dressed and ready to take on the day. Luke loved her tenacity and her stubbornness, but he was worried she was headed straight into a buzzsaw.

"Julie, if anything happens, and you feel like you're in the middle of a situation, you give me a call, and I'll be right over there."

She gave him a warm hug, opened the door, and faced the day.

He'd let the girls sleep in, and he made a couple of calls so that they could get coverage during their teacher meetings and Julie's meeting with Sampson Biggs. Luke was going to insist he attend that meeting as well. There was no way he wanted her to be alone today.

He checked in with Kyle, giving him the update just in case he hadn't seen the news report.

"Yeah, I almost called you last night, but I thought, if you didn't see it, I'd let you guys sleep. But damn. Something's going on here, Luke. You got Mayfield and Riverton on this, don't you?"

"They're working on it."

"What do they say?"

"Yeah, I talked to Gus this morning. I guess Riverton's already called him. They're thinking of going up to Sonoma County or at least to the peninsula, to San Jose. There's a high-tech highway patrol investigation center in Campbell, which might be of help. But now they kind of have to be careful too, or they'll get somehow implicated. It's a very tricky thing, Kyle."

"Well, these guys know what they're getting into, Luke. You don't need to worry about them. The blue line still exists. God knows these guys in all departments have had to stick together. I say this in the positive sense of it, not what's on the news. There are rotten apples all over the country, but the good ones stay together and even try to get rid of the bad ones. Don't worry about them. You worry about Julie. I sure do."

"You know, I can't help but think how this is going to affect the superintendent's job. She was first in line for it, and now the guy who's the school board member handling the applications has called her in for a meeting. He did not sound his warm and fuzzy self like he was the other day, Julie said. I am not hopeful."

"Well, don't worry about it. It's all going to be revealed in time. Remember what you said. You two have nothing to hide. And you're sure about Steph and Colin?"

"God, I'd accuse Julie's mother if I ever got that far, Kyle. No way they've done anything wrong. It's just not like them. I know how they love their kids, children in general. I've seen it first-hand for years. Never in a million would I think that. I'm actually offended at the thought. It makes me sick."

Later, Brandy and one of the new Team guys' wives arrived in time so Luke could make the 2:00 appointment with the teachers at their school. He thought he'd done a good enough job cleaning the kitchen, but when Brandy walked in and saw what was left of his breakfast and then lunch preparations, she offered to finish.

"No, just spend your time with the kids. I can do this later," Luke said.

"I don't mind. I'm here to help. And the kids will be occupied. Besides, I have Peyton here. It'll only take me about ten, fifteen minutes. You go run along so you're not late. And I'll see you back what about 5:30, 6:00?"

"Yeah, I think so. I'll text you when we're on the way home."

"Good deal. Good luck."

Luke wondered what the new girl thought of his situation, since stories of Team family issues grew like wildfire between the members, primarily the wives. He was going to stop and make an explanation but just decided to let it ride. If Brandy felt they were involved in something nefarious, she wouldn't have come over and brought her kids. He had received lots of support from several phone calls earlier in the day, and Kyle had mentioned to him several times not to worry. He wished that he'd had an update from Clark Riverton or Gus Mayfield.

All in good time.

The school was filled to overflowing with activity. Children were being picked up, running down the hallways, bustling at a fast pace. The energy level in the place was amazing. He wished that growing up he'd had such a wonderful, vibrant place to attend school. He was so glad that his kids got the benefit of Julie's selection.

Julie was standing outside room 206, where they were to meet the first of three teachers. This was the second-grade teacher that was going to be taking Kiley. Jessica was also in second grade, but might be in the other class. They needed to talk about this. He hadn't met the teacher before, Mrs. Pierce, but Julie said she was very good.

"Hi, Sweetheart. How's your day been so far?" he asked her.

She was non-committal and finally looked up at him. "I kind of lost my energy about an hour ago, to be honest. Tonight, I really have to get some sleep."

"I think you will tonight. Don't worry about anything. I'll make sure everybody gets to bed early, and you just turn in whenever you're finished, okay?"

"Thanks. The kids do cheer me up just being around them. I'm reminded that, even if this is hard, it's for them we're doing this. And the outcome we want isn't for us; it's for them."

"Just keep remembering that. It's good perspective. I feel the same way, Julie."

She slowly began another line of conversation, seeming hesitant to bring it up. "By the way, I'm sorry about our argument yesterday. I got to thinking about some of the things I said, and I want to apologize."

"It's been tough on both of us. We'll get to the bottom of it. There's a reason all this is happening, and it has nothing to do with us."

Mrs. Pierce appeared in the doorway, inviting them inside. She was an older woman in her early sixties, Luke guessed, hair done in a bun and very properly dressed. Her room was immaculate, lots of activities posted on the wall, but a little sparser than any of the rooms Julie had when she was teaching. There was still a lot of curriculum displayed in a very organized fashion. There were checkoff sheets and charts where students could earn badges and buttons and stars for meeting certain milestones. What it told Luke was that there was going to be a lot of student participation.

"Have a seat."

"Thanks for seeing us, Mrs. Pierce. I am Kiley's aunt, and Luke is her uncle. My brother married his sister, and Kiley is the youngest of their three that we have taken into our home."

"Yes, I was made aware of this. So sorry for your family's loss. How is Kiley adjusting?"

"She seems to be doing fine. She's very close to our youngest, Jessica."

"Oh yes, Jessica, what a little dear she is. I get to see her third and fourth periods since we trade off with the other second-grade class. So what can I tell you and what can you tell me about her academic performance?"

"Well, I haven't tested her, because that really wasn't something I thought I should do. I didn't want to influence your decisions. But I think she's very bright. She reads quite a bit, even at seven. She has a tablet that she uses, but we're careful about what media she gets exposed to."

"I wish more parents were like you. That's a good thing."

"And she seems to have an interest in butterflies and gardens. Her mother was quite a gardener. Used to maintain a beautiful rose and wildflower garden for her butterflies. I think Kiley probably is missing that."

"Well, what I'm going to do is not assign her any homework for the first few days. Then I'll give her a series of workbooks to go through. Once she turns those in, I'll be able to find out where she is on the curriculum scale. And if she needs some remedial things, I will let you know."

"Thank you. That sounds perfect. I was hoping something like that would be arranged."

"I also have a book on butterflies. If you wouldn't mind giving her this to read? Tell her it's from her new teacher? She might like that." Mrs. Pierce searched a bookshelf at her back and pulled out a large book with huge butterfly drawings, handing it to Julie.

"This is lovely. Thanks so much!"

Mrs. Pearce searched both of their faces. "I do have to mention one thing, and you're probably going to hear this multiple times, so you may not like this, but it's the reality of the situation. Since we're a private school, as you know since you are principal of our sister campus, we are careful about who gets admitted. You probably know that as well."

"Well, yes, but I don't make the determination. As far as I know, we've never turned anyone away at my school—"

"Perhaps you've not seen that selection process first-hand, Mrs.

Paulsen. And I doubt you've ever experienced the kind of issue going on now involving your family."

Luke grabbed the arms of his chair and waited for bad news.

"It looks like there's some news breaking about your sister and brother?"

"Yes, we watched the newscast last night on Channel 4. Very disturbing. And I have to say completely hit us from left field. We have no idea where all this is coming from, but I promise you, it's a huge distortion and a manufactured story. I'm not sure whether it's coming from any reputable source either. So I just ask for your forbearance and patience in letting things play out how they're going to. I assure you, we aren't going to let this interfere with any of the kids' education."

"Well, just understand that we'll support you as much as we can. We're doing this for the children, after all. If it gets to be a problem, then we may have to look at other alternatives. We don't want parents pulling their children out due to unnecessary publicity."

"Other alternatives?" Luke asked.

Mrs. Pierce directed her answer to Luke. "We may request that she transfer to another school."

"Oh, really?" said Luke.

"This, of course, would also affect Jessica."

Luke's stomach started churning, and he felt like hitting something. This whole situation was blooming out of control quickly. He didn't like where it was going at all.

"Mrs. Pierce, Julie and I have discussed it, and it's very possible that there's some kind of intentional leakage of these crazy stories to somehow damage us. I assure you there is no validity to any of it. And we are very devoted and dedicated parents, working very hard to give these three orphan girls, our nieces, a warm loving family. It would be extremely disruptive for our kids to have to change schools and to have all five of them have to relocate and get used to something new instead of just the three. So I beg of you not to rush to conclusions until we know further what's behind all this. Trust me, there is someone or something pulling the strings behind this."

Mrs. Pierce appeared to be moved by Luke's argument. "I understand your concern, and we are going to do everything we can to help you bring all this to a conclusion. Thank you for stopping by, and we look forward to seeing Kiley in the class on Monday."

She stood, extending her hand. The meeting had taken less than five minutes, which was much shorter than any of the other meetings they had had with their girls' teachers. He felt she was being very careful and neutral in her stance, even though she professed to support them. He was worried and distressed as he walked out of the room but thanked her for her time.

Julie held the butterfly book under her arm as they walked down the hallway toward the second room, where Maron and Lindsey would be in the same classroom as Amy. They knew Amy's teacher, Connie Matum, and had enjoyed her tremendously since the school year had started.

But when Luke turned to Julie while they waited outside the door, he could see she was in tears.

"This is the hard part, Jules. We worry about stuff we probably shouldn't even have to. The news media is just crap. They just throw out anything they can find. But trust me, we've done nothing wrong, and I don't think Colin and Stephanie did either. It's all going to be discovered. Just have patience please. And don't worry about it."

"You could see how affected Mrs. Pierce was. I just don't know what to tell them. Of course we say that it's not true, but we don't even know who it is we're fighting or where they're getting this information from. It's just so odd. I am heartbroken for how this is affecting the kids."

"Isn't this a change, having Maron and Lindsey in the same class?" Luke asked her. They had received instructions that the appointments would only be with two teachers not three when they arrived.

"Well, if you remember, Amy's class is a little bit small, so they probably felt since Lindsey was new that they'd put her in the fifth-grade class instead of sixth grade. And I think having her in the same class with her sister and Amy is a good thing. So for whatever reason they changed it, I think it's for the best. I just hope it's challenging enough for her. But after she gets her bearings, we can request a change if we feel she can handle it. They don't have a special honors class here for fifth grade, like my school."

Connie Matum greeted them warmly, giving them each a hug and then ushering them inside. She sat them at her desk and quickly assumed the seat on the other side. Donning her red glasses which contrasted with her frizzy bright blonde hair, she pulled up her laptop and clicked open a document that she was reading.

Connie had been trained in Mississippi and had a deep drawl. "I've made a list of a couple of things here. I don't know what the school situation was up in Sonoma County. They went to public school?" she asked them.

"Yes," Julie said. "I believe it was a very good district, one of the best. At least that's what my brother said. He also told me that Lindsey had been recommended for extra advanced placement classes. And a possible star lane they called it, a pathway for gifted children."

"I see," Connie said, letting her red glasses slip down her nose. "What about Maron?"

"I don't know about Maron. I just was told that about Lindsey. Maron seems to be a little more sensitive and kind of relishes being the odd man out. At least in our group, that's the way it's worked out so far."

Luke thought Julie did a great job of summarizing some of the dynamics he'd been experiencing over the past week.

"And, Luke, you are the primary caregiver at home? Is that right?"

"Yes ma'am. I'm in the military, as you know, and I've been given several months to stay home with the girls and make sure everybody gets situated properly. This is a big change for all of us. I was lucky to be able to get the time to do so."

"Well, bless your heart. I respect the military. My first husband was a Navy pilot, my dad was Army, and we moved all over the South. So we're grateful for your service, Mr. Paulsen."

"Thank you. I appreciate that."

"How's that coming?" she asked with a dimpled smile. Her eyes flashed in his direction. "I know if my husband was taking care of the kids, well, let's just say I wouldn't allow it. But I got to hand it to you, you know these days, we have to be flexible, don't we?"

"Yes, ma'am. It's a lesson in being flexible and humble."

"How is Amy taking to all of this?" she asked the two of them.

"She and Lindsey are very close. The cousins have always loved spending time with each other. Now that they're together twenty-four seven, we'll see how it works out, but we're lucky in that our families were very close before, so hopefully, this will continue. I haven't seen any negative effects so far on either of our two kids. And my brother's kids seem to accept the life changes they were given very maturely for their age. I'm very proud of them all," said Julie.

"I like hearing that, Julie. Well, we're going to do whatever we can to make things comfortable for them and to challenge them with their learning. As you know, our curriculum is quite advanced, and Maron may feel at first that it's far ahead of where she's been taught before, but we'll deal with that as it comes, and if they'll need extra tutoring, I will let you know. It sounds to me that Lindsey won't have a problem at all with it, and if I feel she needs to be promoted further, I'll also let you know. I don't think you'll have to hire a tutor in either case since they've got the best one at home."

"Thank you, Connie. I appreciate that."

"Do you have any other questions for me because that's pretty much all I've got?" asked Connie.

Luke considered whether or not he should bring up the newscast from last night and decided to not mention it in case it was something she didn't feel was important. Unfortunately, Julie didn't agree and brought it up herself.

"I'm sure you've heard a little bit about the investigation into my brother and sister-in-law's deaths and certain implications that we were quite shocked to hear on the TV last night on the news. If you see anything occur in the classroom, our kids getting overly sensitive, or you sense any kind of teasing or bullying going on, which I would doubt would happen, but if there is anything like that that does occur, please let us know. Don't be afraid to contact us."

"Duly noted, Julie."

"I'm not sure how much we're going to tell the kids about the investigation, and not everybody is going to react the same way, so there's a possibility they could be told things that are completely inaccurate or distorted. I just want you to know, Connie, that Luke and I are working very hard to try to help the police get to the bottom of whatever it is they're looking at, and we're completely cooperating with them. We want to learn the reasons for our siblings' deaths just like they do. But if you were to listen to the newscasters, you might get another story. So if at any time you have a question about anything, please feel free to ask either one of us."

"Thank you, Julie. I didn't want to bring it up, but of course, it is the white elephant in the room, isn't it?"

"It is."

"I understand, and it must be extremely stressful not knowing all the facts and details. I'm sure it will all come to light. And I wish you the best of luck, especially for the girls' welfare. Consider me an ally."

Luke was delighted with this interview. When they left the room, he admitted, "Even if she should be passed up the chain, I like Connie, and I'd think hard before moving Lindsey. I think she's right where she belongs," he said.

"I tend to agree. It wasn't my decision, but someone was looking out for us with this change."

They were approximately forty-five minutes early for their appointment with Sampson Biggs, who hadn't arrived at the school yet. After checking with the front office staff, Luke and Julie decided to go grab a cup of coffee before meeting him.

They each had a small espresso and sat in the colorful coffee house, listening to the screams of the espresso machines in the background and the chatter of students and the clickety-clack of laptop keys. It was a great hangout for the college-age group with a junior college two blocks away.

Luke approached the subject of the interviews and asked Julie how they had gone.

"I'm not sure really. They're not saying a lot. They're trying to be nice, but they're not saying a lot. And that has me concerned a bit. I like Mrs. Pierce. I think she'll be a very strict but a good teacher for Kiley, but I'm glad Jessica has Donna Spencer. I'd almost rather the two be in the same class, they are so close."

"I was wondering the same thing. It's going to be more intimidating having her in a class all by herself. We could suggest a change, if that's politically smart. Do you think it's worth pursuing?"

"I think both teachers are excellent as far as their qualifications, and I think they will both be very sensitive to helping blend the kids in. I'll need to think about it. We can ask for a change if we need to. Let's talk further on it before we decide, okay?"

"What are you not telling me?"

"Luke, I've never been in this kind of situation before where I feel like I have to apologize for who we are or who our family is. I've never been on the defense like this, and it's a really icky feeling for me. Everything I did surrounding the schools and my teaching and my relationship with my parents was always smooth and respectful. Now I feel like there's this cloud over everything. It's just not something I'm used to. I hope the appointment, the meeting with Biggs turns out to be a little better than I'm afraid it's going to be."

Luke grabbed her hand and kissed it. "It is what it is, Julie, and whatever happens, like you told me when this whole thing began, we are family, and we will weather the storm together as a family."

"Thank you for that, Luke. It means a lot."

They returned to the school, and within minutes, Sampson Biggs asked Julie to come into the assistant principal's office. Luke stood as well.

"Would you mind if I sit in on the meeting, sir?"

Biggs stiffened and then returned a disapproving stare. "I'm not so sure that's a good idea, Luke. This is a private matter between me and Julie. If you insist, I'm going to have to allow it, but I strongly advise against it."

Julie turned to him. "It's okay. You wait here, and I'll be out in just a few minutes. I'll be fine."

"I know you'll be fine, Julie, and that's not what I'm worried about. But I want to be there anyway." Then Luke added, "As you know, we're going through quite a bit, and everything we're doing is a joint decision. I think it's a good idea that I sit in on the appointment, so I can help Julie deal with the decisions that she's making. *We're* making together."

"If you insist, I really can't refuse. Come on in." Mr. Biggs stood to the side after he opened the door to the office.

"I suppose you watched the news last night, didn't you?" Biggs started.

Julie and Luke took seats on the couch at the side when Biggs motioned in that direction. He took a chair at a forty-five-degree angle to them.

"Yes, we watched it. I'm in shock, Sampson, to be honest with you," Julie said.

"You haven't heard any of this before?" he asked.

"No. All of this is new."

Luke added, "We knew they were investigating this as a murder, but not that it was a murder-for-hire or that a family member was involved."

"I suppose police departments have their own ways of scoping out all theories. They have to investigate all possibilities, don't they? Maybe they were preserving their evidence, sources. We don't know."

"They certainly didn't do that," barked Luke. "Someone leaked a bogus report to the media, and we think it was done on purpose."

Julie's attempt to soften Luke's rant didn't appear to sway Biggs. "We're cooperating with the authorities. Anything we can do to assist them, we're going to do it all. We have nothing to hide, Sampson."

His icy demeanor was disturbing. "Well, the district office has received inquiries about your job here, your position as principal, the length of time you've been here, and whether or not there had been any complaints filed against you. I looked up your records, of course, and this would be routine anyway for considering you for the superintendent job, and I discovered that you had some difficulty with a parent several years ago, a decade ago I think. This parent actually caused harm to your union representative, isn't that right?"

"He kidnapped both of us. The man was insane, just insane," Julie said.

"And he fixated on you in particular, Julie, isn't that correct?"

"Yes, and it all started because I noticed some behavior in their child, Corey, that was unusual. It was also very sexual in nature, and it's the sort of thing that a teacher's supposed to report. You know, by law, I must report this in California. However, Mr. Miller objected to it. He attempted to sue the school district, as well as myself personally, until it was discovered that actually he was the perpetrator and was, in fact, a pedophile. I believe he's serving time today."

"It's a wonder you even want to teach with an experience like that. What can you tell me about that?" he asked.

"I did my job, Mr. Biggs. I didn't back down, even in the face of this horrible situation. I protected a young child from his father's preying actions. I don't need to justify my behavior."

"Yes, and I agree and commend you."

Luke noted his eyes were still cold. He was not convinced the man was telling the truth.

"I'm asking how you handle the stress of this?"

Julie thought for a moment and then answered. "Well, I compartmentalize it as being a fluke occurrence that, hopefully, will never occur again. I was right, Sampson. I did the right thing even in the face of unspeakable acts and behaviors of others. I like to think I was the calming person throughout all this."

"But you lost your colleague—"

Luke was livid. "What are you implying?"

"Have you ever had second thoughts? Do you take any responsibility for his overreaction that caused the death of another educator? Your union rep?"

"You mean, do I take responsibility for trying to shelter a young child who was being preyed on by a despicable human being? Absolutely not. My conscience is clear. If there were another way, I would have taken it. But how can I be responsible for a deranged parent? I stopped him. His daughter has a chance to be safe now, to rebuild her life. I hope she is getting the care she needs. She was the loser in all this, and I kept her safe."

Biggs paused. "And yet look at what has happened with your brother and sister. Have the police interviewed you at all about their claim of financial gain? Have you personally, you and Luke, profited from their deaths?"

Julie stood. Luke thought perhaps she'd clock him. He tugged on her hand but did not rise to threaten the man.

"Mr. Biggs, I'm sorry, but due to the nature of the investigation, we've been asked not to discuss it with other people. And all I could say is the sweeping generalizations the newscaster came up with last night are so bizarre, so completely inaccurate, we don't even know how to respond to it. But rest assured, we are going to get to the bottom of it, and we will find the person responsible for creating this situation. In the meantime, we want to let the police and the authorities do their job, so coming up with ideas or justifications for whatever may or may not have occurred isn't helpful. But just understand that we've done nothing wrong, and we don't believe my sister and her brother did either. But we will find out who is causing this."

Biggs leaned back into his high-backed swivel chair, lacing his fingers in front of him, glancing back and forth between both of them. "Well, I'm satisfied for now. Let's just see how things play out. I'm sure I don't have to tell you, Julie, that if there's any kind of controversy that follows you into the possibility of obtaining the superintendent's job, it's going to be a detriment to you getting that job. So let's hope it can all be handled quietly and quickly. And I'm so sorry all this is happening to you both. I truly am."

Luke wasn't sure he was telling the truth, but at least everybody knew where they stood. He hoped he didn't have to gear up for an emotional fight. But if it came to that, he knew he could step up to the plate. The most important thing in his life was his family, and nothing was going to touch or damage them.

Even if it cost him his Trident.

CHAPTER 12

J ULIE TRIED TO conduct her daily affairs as best she could but found herself fielding more phone calls than usual. Although people didn't come out and ask her what was going on, the increased frequency of their calls set Julie's radar on edge, and she knew the reason for their communications was partly to gain some information about the investigation without asking her directly.

She read over the trust documents she had taken in her briefcase, thinking it might make her feel better to do *something*. She found several things that concerned her and decided to call the bank to ask them about closing the account for Stephanie's business.

"I'm inquiring about my sister-in-law's closed business account, and I was wondering if you could help me with the details."

After giving the clerk some information, informing her she was the executor of the estate, she was directed to the branch manager.

"Who is this calling please?" the manager asked.

"My name is Julie Paulsen. My sister-in-law, Stephanie Christensen, managed this business account, and I'm in charge of the trust. I'm trying to figure out exactly where the money went when the account was closed. All I have is the checking account statement that showed a balance of about $34,000 in it. But I don't know where that money went when it was closed, and it happened to be closed on the day of her death."

"I see. Well, I'm afraid I'm limited in what I can give you, but if you are the executor of the estate, you can come in here with your paperwork, and I can see if I can release that information to you."

"Well, I live in San Diego, and your branch is in Santa Rosa. Do you have anything in the Southern California area?"

"We have several branches in Los Angeles, but none in San Diego. I'm fairly sure that in order to show the disposition of the funds, you would need to come to this branch where she opened the account. I'm not sure another branch would be able to give you that information, but I can check on it for you if you like. Give me your phone number and email address, and I will get back to you."

Julie didn't want to upset an already buzzing beehive so declined giving him any information. She knew it was probably something he might think about and question later on, but she wasn't interested in violating any of the rules that Clark Riverton and Gus Mayfield had laid down for them. She wanted to make sure they didn't get further embroiled. But if she could do some checking without making things worse, she figured that was not a bad idea.

Instead, this one appeared to be a dead end.

"I'm sorry, but let me talk to my attorney, and perhaps his office can initiate something for me. I apologize for taking your time. Good day."

Both she and Luke were interested in what Mayfield and Riverton had found out. She wondered if they actually did travel up to Northern California. She put in a call to the attorney who handled the trust in Santa Rosa.

"How are things going, Julie?" he asked her.

"Well, I don't know if you've heard the news, but the police are investigating Steph and Colin's accident as a murder. And they're looking for some kind of connection. If you can believe the newscasts down here anyway, it sounds like they're looking for somebody who thought they would financially gain from their death. The long implication of this is that I'm under some kind of suspicion."

"Oh dear. I am so sorry about that. I've been questioned as well, but they didn't give me this context."

"Who is 'they' anyway?" Julie asked.

"Well, he was an investigator with the State of California, I believe. I think I've got his card."

"He came to your office?"

"It's something that happens quite frequently when you handle trusts and estates. There are lots of other parties sometimes who don't want to surface right away. It could be someone, a distant relative just trying to do some poking around to see if they can find something they can make a case out of. I often don't divulge much information, and certainly in this case, I was very discreet. Let me see if I can find his card."

Julie waited.

"Okay, here it is. His name is Justin Hamblin, and I have his phone number if you'd like it."

"Please."

The attorney rattled off a phone number, beginning with an area code in the San Jose Peninsula area.

"Thank you."

"Do you recognize this fellow?"

"No, I don't. And I don't believe Colin or Stephanie has ever mentioned his name either."

"Anything else I can do for you?"

"Well, I was going through some of the bank accounts and documents, and I see that Steph's business account, which is what's causing all this issue in the news, had over $30,000 in it at the time of its closing. And I can see from the statements that the closure happened, oddly enough, on the day they were killed. I'm wondering if you can tell me where this money wound up, because I don't see it deposited in any of their other bank accounts."

"Maybe they cashed it. People do that."

"I thought of that, but the bank won't give me any details. And they're saying I have to show up in person in order to get that information, even though I'm the executor of their estate."

"Well, maybe he thinks that since it was something that happened before—"

"But do we know that, really? And if the police are looking into this as being a murder-for-hire, should I give this information to the police or should I just launch our own investigation?"

"I see. Well, I always tell my clients to fully cooperate."

"And I am. I just discovered this large sum of money today when I was reviewing the accounts. And I didn't notice before that it was closed the day of their accident, not before. So it really isn't a stretch. If they wanted to be fully transparent, they'd release that information at least to you, wouldn't they, as their attorney?"

"I hesitate to get involved, especially if I could be accused later on of trying to impede the police's investigation, so I'd advise you to contact the police. The problem is, who do you talk to? And you need to be careful about this. Not everything that's given to them is followed up on. They are understaffed and overwhelmed with cases. So you're going to want to be careful. But it's a valid question, and something you should know. And if there's thirty-some-thousand dollars cash missing, as executor of the estate, on behalf of the children, you owe them a duty to discover it. That's my opinion anyway. So I think you should try to do that and then turn over what you found to the police. But make sure you are talking to the head investigation team, not someone else."

"'Someone else' being this Hamblin fellow?" Julie asked him.

"Yes, I've seen cards like this before, and I can't tell you that I really think it's legitimate. He may not be working for the State of California. He may be working for someone else. And I didn't spend any time checking on him, but if you like, I can have our own investigator look into his background, and I can get back to you."

"If you would, please. Thank you so much. And I think I'm going to take your advice. My husband has some close friends down here in San Diego, one who used to be with the crime task force and another gentleman who's a retired sheriff. They have lots of contacts even in Northern California. I think I'm going to have them make some inquiries for us as well."

"Well, I'll let you know what we find out, and you take care."

Julie had to ask him one more question. "Did you ever get the sense that Stephanie and Colin were involved in something shady or nefarious?"

"What makes you say that?"

"We found a bunch of things for her home-based business that were... Well, she was selling sex toys, okay?"

"Oh dear. Really? That doesn't sound like Steph at all."

"I think it was just sort of a fun thing she did to earn some extra money, but she never told me about it. And it looks like she made quite a bit of money with it, especially recently. I'm wondering if all this is related. Did you ever get any inkling they were involved in something that could be illegal?"

"As in child pornography like the news media says?"

"Exactly. I agree with you, that's so out of character for them. Did you see anything that caused you to be suspicious?"

"Julie, I couldn't have been more proud of Stephanie if she was my own daughter. I never got even a wrinkle of an idea about her being involved in something. And Colin, well, he's just one of those good guys, a really great guy, and I doubt he would ever put his family in some kind of trouble. So I doubt he would ever be involved in something like this. Someone is pulling the strings here, and I don't think you need to take more than two seconds to even concern yourself about whether or not your sister-in-law and brother were involved. It's just impossible."

Armed with that information, Julie felt slightly buoyed. It didn't take all of the weight off, but he was a professional. He had worked with Colin and Stephanie before, and he could attest to their character in his long-standing position with them. He was going to be one of the good guys with the white hats on their side. She was lucky that they had such an ally.

She decided to come home early, cutting it off about two o'clock in the afternoon. She texted Luke before she left the school.

"Coming home early. I think I have a little bit of good news."

His return text upset her.

"That's good. Because my news isn't so good. Come home safely, and watch your surroundings. Eyes in the back of your head, Julie. We'll talk more when you get here."

CHAPTER 13

W HAT WAS IT, Luke thought, that made women so much more flexible and resilient to deal with family stress, horrible things, taking care of children, and maintaining the household? He wondered what gene they had that allowed them to carry on, because he was going completely batshit crazy holding all this negativity, all this darkness, this huge gray cloud of crap in his gut while trying to smile and laugh and participate with five little innocent girls he would die for.

If he didn't get it together, they'd pick up on all his worry and darkness. Julie always made everything look so easy, so simple. If she was upset about something, the girls were the last to know—unless she wanted them to know, and then she'd lower the boom, but somehow with a sprinkle of sugar and fairy dust. Luke couldn't do that.

He'd known guys who had cheated on their wives before, had gambling problems, or did drugs and kept it from their wives. They had a policy on the teams not to tattle on another man, unless someone's health and safety were at stake. If the law was being broken, if someone was headed for a fall, a suicide, or to commit a crime, it usually wasn't a hard decision to make, given all the circumstances.

He knew, in the end, all things were made clear, and a lot of wives had to put up with that crap and carry on as if their whole world hadn't just gotten blown up. He couldn't do that. He really couldn't do that. "Moving on" wasn't something he did, and he'd tried too.

Like the guilt he felt for the accident that took Camilla's life. He'd never get over that totally. It would be with him for the rest of his life. He'd learned to live with it. But moving on? No such thing in Luke's world. And if you did dumb shit, well, you'd pay the price forever.

Forever.

What they tried to train for was being able to endure forever, exercise and mentally plan for it, because it was the nature of his job.

He was trained to fight, yes, and be a warrior, but he wasn't trained to deal with the hot, oily boiling pit in his stomach while he was looking at five little girls sitting out on the lawn under an umbrella dancing to music, wearing sunglasses and laughing, lying on their bellies, and kicking their legs up while jumping in their little wading pool, just being normal little girls. And Luke was sitting here watching them with tears streaming down his cheeks, tears he never wanted to ever show them.

He was crushed, nearly to the point of feeling defeat. The problem was, he didn't know who to fight and how to find out about it. The waiting was killing him, and the maintaining a cool and happy "happy-happy" demeanor was just driving him crazy.

Even Riverton calling to give him an update didn't help. He didn't want to tell him about his concerns, about what he had seen on Stephanie's clipboard. He didn't want to call up Dr. Brownlee and tell him either. He didn't want to tell Julie. Why couldn't he just wipe all this out of his mind and play with the girls? Just be with the girls, clean the sink, do the dishes, do the laundry? He should pretend that everything was hunky-dory-Disneyland-sparkly-great. Why couldn't he pretend?

And that was the issue for him. He wasn't made for this. He was made for something else. And did that disqualify him from being a normal human being, a father, a husband? He wanted to blast whoever it was that had ruined their family life, however temporary it might be. Every hour and every minute, it got worse.

Before Riverton's call, he'd dared to look through the box he'd brought home from the storage, like he was drawn to it as a moth was to the flame. Why the fuck did he think this was a good idea? He picked up the clipboard he had taken, and underneath all the orders and paperwork that he had quickly glanced through earlier was a list of Steph's customers. It was a long list, and it also had numbers, amounts of purchases. His finger traveled down the list of unknown customers, mostly women's names, until he came to one particular purchaser who had made enormous purchases, like thousands and thousands of dollars' worth of purchases.

His hands shook as he read the entry. It was the Feathers and Tails Ranch, a well-known bordello in Las Vegas.

When he came upon it, his heart had sank down to his ankles. His mouth had been parched and he ached, just ached all over. He knew about this place, although he'd never been there. It was a raunchy, horrible, dirty place with despicable acts and girls who were clearly damaged. He'd heard tales about it, and nobody he cared for or spent any time with had ever been there, but they'd all heard about it.

Now he was ashamed to say he'd never done anything to try to interfere with their business, because they had talked about it before, he and his friends, about how it just seemed like the wrong kind of place and should be looked into. The girls were reported to be all foreign and very, very young. Perhaps illegal. But something had been protecting the business. Some cretin, some monster, or a group of monsters were making money.

But they also were buying from his sister. And that bothered him most of all.

Was this group Stephanie's secret partner? Were they the real people behind her business? Were Stephanie and Colin being used for their squeaky cleanness? His mind was racing with all the possibilities. He just didn't want to utter them to anybody for fear of actually making them come true. Like, if he mentioned it or he spoke about it, all of a sudden it became real. Whereas, right now, it was just some crazy ass idea running around bouncing off the sides of his skull.

He looked out at the little girls again and felt the hot tears drip onto his shirt. The person he needed to be and the person he was this afternoon were two completely different beings. He wished he hadn't seen so much of the ugliness that he had seen during wartime, the women and children caught in the crossfire, the little boys forced to stand up and hold guns that were big enough to make them fall over. He'd seen tanks overrun schools and villages, kids with their arms cut off after the SEALs had done a vaccination clinic.

But even those things he could compartmentalize and put aside for now. Because that was his training. Because he went out on the battlefield, and the lines were drawn clearly. He knew what side he was on.

This, all this stuff, this degrading bullshit that was going on and invading his happy family life, this was some kind of a ghost, an angry gray cloud that just wouldn't leave him alone.

It was almost like all the innocent people he couldn't save were pulling at his feet from the grave. He saw Camilla as he held her—his pregnant first wife, dying in his arms. He saw the boys overseas he couldn't save. He saw his SEAL buddies and interpreters who had been returned to their camp mutilated, bloodied, and tortured. It kept him awake at night, but he knew it was his ticket to play, the cost of his heroism forever. He just didn't like being that close to death.

But with this, this was just evil. He was on the precipice. It was like staring over the edge of a 15-story building and taking forever to decide to jump, causing pain, the worry of what will happen to all these little girls, what was happening to all the other people who were being victimized and subjugated.

It was proof he couldn't save everybody, and that was the biggest problem. He didn't know who to get help from, and to solve it, who to attack, who to kill.

"Luke, you've got to get a handle on yourself." Hearing his own voice didn't help, though.

When Riverton's call came in, he threw the clipboard on the bed and answered. "Tell me something good. I need something good right now, Clark."

"Oh my God, Luke, are you all right?"

"The simple answer? No. Please tell me you found something that we can go on something where we can help end all this. It's a nightmare, Clark."

"Hey, Luke, calm down. You need to settle yourself. You aren't going to be able to get through all this unless you can settle yourself. So let me tell you what I got, and then you call somebody who can be more warm and fuzzy with you, Luke, because I don't know if this is good news or bad news."

"Just spill, Clark."

"I reached out to some old contacts in Sonoma County, who are agreeing to cooperate with me a little bit. I can't get shit out of the highway patrol, but my source in Santa Rosa is considering bringing in the FBI. And I don't know if that'll make it better or worse, but at least we'll get some deeper roots and see if we can't find out where this is leading."

"Okay, so exactly what are you saying? Can you spell it out for me please? I'm having a hard time being logical."

He saw Maron doing a little ballet step, a performance for the other girls, and the four of them clapped for her while she took a bow. Such a beautiful sight on any other day except today. Those five little innocent girls deserved everything in the world, and Luke wanted to give them everything he could.

"So tell me now, dammit."

"Well, it appears that there were some problems with Steph's business. There were some accounts and orders that got placed under her name that she disputed with the company. Apparently, they were at a convention in Las Vegas when they discovered all this. Something they uncovered got them so upset that they canceled a scheduled speech. Steph was going to be participating on a panel for this company she worked for, and she decided not to show up. They left early. And it looks like they made one stop before they left. By checking her phone records, it looks like she went to a bank, and then they got in their car for the drive home. That's all I've got."

"Okay. What do they think it means?"

"Well, she closed the account, apparently, making a large withdrawal. And we have not been able to verify from the bank in Las Vegas why. They haven't been contacted yet. We're waiting on the FBI to do that. But they're about to."

"So her bank in Santa Rosa had a branch in Las Vegas?"

"No, not exactly. I'm not sure why they used that bank."

"So what is this BS about someone taking financial advantage of her, insinuating that it's Julie and me?"

"That hasn't come from the police. We don't think the police investigation is compromised. So I don't want you to worry about that."

"But, Clark, they're calling Kyle. We just found out yesterday they've contacted the school board. People are asking questions. There's all kinds of information getting out to the news media. Where is this coming from?"

"I can't tell you that. But I can tell you this, Luke, you need to get yourself a criminal attorney and right away. I can recommend somebody if you like, but you need to get a high-powered very visible attorney who is good with social media."

After Riverton's call, he straightened the bedroom and placed the clipboard back in the box, folded clothes, and put in another load of laundry. He took out food for dinner, hamburger meat and noodles for a stroganoff, and picked some tomatoes and lettuce in the garden for a salad, waving to the girls as he did so.

That was his shell moving. Inside, he was completely crushed. When he got Julie's text, he was grateful she'd be home early. But he was dreading having to tell her about what Riverton disclosed. This was not going to be a normal family dinner. Nothing about his life was going to be normal ever again.

He decided to call Dr. Brownlee, who was not available. He left his phone number and knew he'd get a call back sometime today.

When he heard Julie's car pull up to the house, he closed his eyes and put his hand over his heart. He wasn't going to persevere for himself. He was going to do it for her. She deserved all of the success and accolades she had earned for so many years working through the system. She deserved to be able to come home and have someone greet her at the door and hold the rest of their life together. He wasn't worried about Julie. He was worried about himself.

Am I really up to all of this? What if I fail?

CHAPTER 14

JULIE HANDED LUKE the piece of paper with Justin Hamblin's name and phone number on it.

"This is the investigator who's been sniffing around the edges. I talked to the trust attorney, and he confirmed he spoke with this gentleman and that he doesn't think he's legitimately involved in the investigation. I think this is where our leaks are coming from."

"Who is he?" asked Luke.

"We don't know. But I think it would be good to give to Mayfield and Riverton, although the trust attorney is putting his private investigator on it as well. He said he worked for the State of California, but his card doesn't say what division. It may take a while, but if he's legitimate, we'll be able to find him. If he's not, then this is a huge clue for us. I feel hopeful we're finally getting to the bottom of what's going on."

"That's good, Jules. That's really good news."

She saw that Luke was un-showered and hadn't shaved today. She checked the outside window and saw the girls sitting down at the table doing some workbooks and reading. Everything looked under control with the house. She smelled dinner cooking in the kitchen. It was just Luke and his appearance that bothered her the most.

She walked up to him and placed her palms on either side of his cheeks. "What is it, Luke? What's going on?"

"I talked to Clark today, and they've determined there was some kind of a convention change for Steph and Colin. They were supposed to speak somewhere, and instead, they left the convention early. They stopped at a bank on their way home. Except they never made it here, did they?"

"What bank?"

"Well, he didn't tell me what bank, just got it from the locator on her phone. That's what they're trying to find out. Riverton said the police in Santa Rosa are going to call in the FBI, and it's probably not one of the banks that Steph and Colin bank with. It's some other bank. But that was the last stop they made before they came home."

"Okay, well, that's good news then. I think we're getting closer to something, Luke."

"I don't know. There's something else, though."

"What?"

"I went through the clipboard and looked at her customer list, and I found an entry to a particular purchaser who happened to buy thousands of dollars' worth of goods this last month. It's all recent purchases."

"Okay. What are you saying?"

"It's not an individual. It's a ranch, a bordello in Las Vegas. It's a very famous one, in that it's on the lower end. There's been a lot of rumors and talk about it for years, but it's still in operation. And this particular bordello is known for having very young-looking prostitutes that work there supposedly legally. But most of them are foreign, and the thought is that perhaps many of them have been trafficked from other countries and are not really legal here in the United States. They are being used. It looks on the surface, Julie, that they could be Colin and Steph's secret partners. And somebody needs to know about it."

"Well, I think you should tell everybody. I mean, what did Riverton say?"

"Julie, he said there were orders placed under Steph's name that she disputed with the company. And when she stopped and closed her account out, she did so from a different bank. We don't know where the money went to. That's why they are bringing in the FBI."

"Well, that's good news. That jives with what I discovered. I was looking through the records, and I saw she'd made a $34,000 withdrawal. I also didn't know where that money went, so I asked our attorney, and that's when he told me about the investigator that came to see him. We've got this guy's name and number. Now let's go get him looked at.

Let's check him out. Can Clark or Gus do that?" she asked.

"Yes, and there's one more thing. Clark recommended that we get a criminal attorney. Somebody very high-powered. That's going to cost a lot of money, Julie."

"How much?" Julie asked.

"I talked to the office Riverton recommended. His assistant is insisting on a retainer of $25,000. That's going to wipe out our savings."

"Well, I'm hoping we won't need all of it. But if Riverton thinks it's necessary, I think we better do it. I hate to pay that much money for attorney's fees, but somebody's doing a pretty good job of smearing us, and I think it's the only way we can fight back. We can't do it ourselves, Luke. It'd be like sending me out on the battlefield with your equipment. I wouldn't know the first thing on how to use it. We need to hire somebody who knows what they're doing. We need to hire somebody who's competent and runs across this every day. Let's go see him tomorrow."

"Well, tomorrow's Saturday, so I don't think we'll be able to get in until Monday. But maybe after we drop the kids off, we could do that."

"Luke, I just want to say to you, however it works out, if everything goes away, we still tried to do the right thing. That's the most important thing to remember. We're not fighting for us. We're fighting for the girls." She took his hand and walked him to the dining room picture window so he could look at all five of them sitting on the patio.

"These are the kids you fought for when you went overseas. These are the kids we're fighting for now. I don't care who is behind this or how big and powerful they are. Whatever it costs us, I will willingly do it to keep them safe."

Luke grabbed her in his arms, and for the first time in their married life, he sobbed into her chest.

"I'm sorry, Julie. So grateful for you. I can't help it."

"This doesn't mean you're weak, Sweetheart. It means you're a human being. And I, for one, love you for it. We will get through this. I promise, Luke, we will."

THE FIRST DAY back at school for the girls was exciting for everybody. Luke and Julie took them all on a shopping spree over the weekend, buying new clothes, backpacks, notebooks, shoes, and socks, everything to make them feel like it was Christmas all over again. They had planned on perhaps overspending, but it wasn't just for the girls they did it. It was for them as well. Things had been so tight, they'd been so careful with the budgeting, they just decided to splurge, maybe one last time, on the girls. It was an all or nothing thing for Julie. Luke completely agreed.

There were no fights over the weekend over who was going to sleep where. They didn't care where their clothes were hung, which closet, or which drawer they got. The girls were just happy to have so many beautiful new things. And even if they'd had a Christmas tree in their downstairs living room, it wouldn't have felt more festive. It really was something Julie needed to see.

They walked Amy, Maron, and Lindsey into their classroom and introduced them to their teacher, Connie Matum. Amy did a good job walking them around the room, introducing them to some of her friends and some of their new schoolmates. Kiley and Jessica stayed behind, watching from the doorway, holding hands.

Then they took the younger two girls over to Kiley's room. Before going to the new classroom, she had Kiley return the butterfly book.

"Thank you very much, Mrs. Pierce. I really enjoyed the book. I read it three times over the weekend."

Mrs. Pierce was a little bit on the frosty side, but after it was explained why they were going together, she had fully embraced the idea that the two girls would be in the same class. Luke and Julie both gave a hug and kiss to Jessica and Kiley and walked down the hall toward their car holding hands.

"Well, my dear," started Luke, "this is going to be a very interesting day, isn't it?"

"It's always an interesting day with you, Luke. I don't care what anybody thinks about me or my family. All I care about is what we've done together and what our future looks like. Whatever this guy says, I'll somehow endure it, within reason."

"Well, look at it this way, Julie, if we had to, we could raise a little money selling off those twelve boxes, right?"

"Oh, Luke, you're so bad. I'm going to tell all your friends about that."

"They'd probably agree with me, Julie. But you go ahead if you think you're bold enough to do that."

"You bet I am. I need a little comic relief. I hope this guy is the right choice, but if he's not, I'm going to get the satisfaction of firing Mr. Cornelius Goodman. I never thought I would talk to that guy. I hate his billboards and commercials."

"It probably works for him."

"He's a trained killer."

"That's what we want, baby. He's attorney to the stars, to professional athletes, and celebrities. But he's a good friend of Riverton, so I think he ought to be a safe bet. Shall we go, my dear?" he asked, opening the door for her.

They drove up to Los Angeles and headed to a tall steel and glass office building off of Wilshire Boulevard. It had a sweeping view of the city, at least what they could see. Still, it was a dramatic skyscape. Cornelius Goodman's firm had over sixty attorneys on staff, every single one of them listed, taking up a whole floor of the building. They pressed floor 48 and were taken in an express elevator right to his offices.

The attractive young woman at the front desk could have been an actress herself or a high fashion model. She professionally greeted them by name, handed them a small questionnaire packet, and discreetly slipped them into a conference room overlooking the city. Then she drew the drapes so the rest of the office couldn't peer in. Julie figured that was probably the protocol she was trained to do in dealing with some of the high-profile clients he worked with.

"You know, with all those attorneys in his firm. I think we'll probably be dealing with somebody else. But we'll see."

"Whatever he recommends, I'm going to do it. Didn't you say that?"

"Yes, I did."

Roughly five minutes after they completed their forms, Mr. Cornelius himself entered the door. He was easily six foot six, impeccably dressed all the way down to his expensive silk tie and matching handkerchief. With his height and his extreme good looks, Julie knew that he was a formidable opponent in a courtroom.

The first thing out of his mouth was directing them to stay seated.

"I got you here. You're in my office. You've had all kinds of stress put on you, but this is going to be day one of your emancipation."

Julie thought it was a rather bold statement to make.

Luke chuckled. "Well, I kind of like that. That's almost worth $25,000 right there."

Mr. Goodman sat and slapped his portfolio book on the glass tabletop. "Mr. Paulsen, I understand you're one of the Navy's finest. And I want to let you know that I am also an elite warrior. I'll tell you two things about me. First of all, I was done a favor many years ago by a certain detective. I was headed on a path that wasn't going to get me what I got today." He turned around and displayed with his arms the beautiful view. "He told me that day that I better make good with the chance I've been given, and I had the opportunity to transform and help other people do the same. I never forgot that, and anybody who Clark Riverton recommends to me gets my special treatment. In your case, Mr. Paulsen, since you have risked your life to protect my freedoms, I'm not going to charge you for this."

"What's the catch? Who do I have to off?" Luke said, jokingly. "Excuse me, that was not serious."

Julie gave him a disapproving stare. "Luke, that's—"

"It was funny, but I don't joke about murder, Mr. Paulsen. I know you don't either, really. But you're probably nervous, so I'll let it go. But yes, I am going to tell you that you're going to do some work for me. I want you to show up at every press conference. I want you not to be afraid of answering questions, as long as I'm there to coach you or you answer exactly as I prescribe. Is that clear?"

"Absolutely," Luke answered. Julie felt relieved.

"I'm going to tell you what to say and what not to say, and we're going to let the cops do their job and find whoever's messing with your family. Once we find them, Mr. Paulsen, Mrs. Paulsen, they aren't going to stand a chance. In my world, I know how to get it done. You guys need to just be good parents. You need to show up and do what I've told you. Now, I don't want any questions, I don't want any argument or your opinions about anything. I just want you to do 100% everything I tell you to do. Is that clear?"

Julie watched as his smile slowly widened. In fact, it was such a bright, wide smile it was disarming. She also noted he was studying them both very carefully and watching their reaction. She wondered what he was looking for.

Luke and Julie returned a glance at each other. Luke spoke up next, "Mr. Goodman, we will be your grunts. I promise you, you're not going to get any flak from us. We know how to take orders. And we know when we're outmatched. I'm going to rely on you to be the expert. Both of us are. Whatever it takes, sir. Whatever it takes. As long as I don't have to get my long guns out and ruin my career or hurt my family, it's whatever it takes."

CHAPTER 15

L UKE PICKED UP Mr. and Mrs. Christensen at the San Diego Airport.
"How was your flight?" he asked them.

They looked tired but happy to have landed.

"Oh, they just keep making those seats smaller and smaller, don't they?" Melanie Christensen said to him. "And I told him we should spring for First Class, but—"

Luke finished it for her. "It didn't feel like a celebration coming here, did it?"

Julie's dad covered quickly. "No, Luke, that has nothing to do with it. I'm just cheap, that's all. Trying to make sure our money lasts until we kick the can, you know. It's just, you know you're not going to live forever, but your bills do. They never expire, do they?"

"Well, Julie's delighted you're here. I already texted her, and she's waiting for you at home."

"She's at home today? Isn't this a school day?" Mrs. Christensen asked.

"Not today. She took the day off especially because you're coming."

On the way home, Luke stopped for a couple of things Julie asked him to get. "Do you need anything at the store? I'll be right back if not?"

"We're good."

Her parents both sat in the back seat of his Hummer. They looked smaller than he remembered, but they were as in love as they'd been in high school when they met. Luke had heard the stories.

"Good enough, then. I'll be right back."

On the way into the market, he got a call from Gus Mayfield.

"Well, I'll tell you what, Luke, that press conference was one hell of a show. How'd you get Cornelius Goodman?"

"Didn't Riverton tell you? He referred him to us."

"Did you have to mortgage your house to hire him?"

"Not telling. I got secrets too. But he cut us a good deal. So you have news for us?"

"I do, and I've talked to the trust attorney. We're going to be launching an investigation into bank fraud, and I've let him know the bank in Las Vegas is very likely going to be served and raided by the feds. Now don't tell anybody, but it's due to happen in the next day or two. I can't believe how fast all of this has gone. I think the fact that you guys were so public and on TV so much really spurred a few wheels to start turning faster than they normally would have, if you get my drift."

"I get you. Goodman told us so. He said, 'the crickets come out of the field.' I don't think law enforcement likes a lot of publicity, do they?"

"Well, I like the way he did it, Luke. He didn't blame the locals who were looking into it. He just said the FBI had more resources than he did and it was going to be a much larger investigation. I think, when they hear that, they all go running back to their desks and make sure every I is dotted, every T is crossed. And what do you know, they found something. I don't know what they found, but apparently, they're pretty sure they found a bank in Las Vegas that has been participating in some strange activity. And that's all I'm going to say."

"Hey, thanks, Gus. We needed some good news."

"So how's everything else going?" he asked Luke.

"The girls are settling in really well at school. And they love their classes. I think Julie's the one struggling right now a bit. But hopefully, that'll be behind us soon."

"I heard she didn't get the superintendent's job. That's too bad."

"It's their loss. She would've been perfect for that job, and she's already had offers from other parts of the country. Not that we want to move. But it's going to be okay. We agreed when all this started that, whatever the outcome, it was going to be okay."

"Well, I don't want to take too much of your time. I just thought I'd let you know stay tuned to the news, because there'll probably be some pretty soon. Either that or Cornelius will think up something. I don't think that man wants to go a day or two without getting his face in the headlines. But whatever it takes. All I can say is I could never afford him. Must be costing you a fortune."

"Doesn't matter, Gus. Whatever, it's worth it. My family's worth it."

"That's great to hear, Son. Well, you keep me posted, and I'll make sure to let you know if we run across anything else that you need to know. My best to Julie."

Driving up to the home, Julie ran from the front steps, hugging her mother and father. The girls followed behind her, everybody jumping up and down to get a hug with Grandma or Grandpa. Everyone talked to them, interrupting each other almost to the point of arguing who could tell their stories first. Luke could see that Julie's parents were invigorated with the group, and their travel malaise was completely wiped away by the energy coming from the girls. Like a bunch of elves guiding a giant, the girls took their grandmother and grandfather up the steps, through the front door, and into the living room. Two of them carried their suitcases upstairs while the others led them into the bedrooms that they occupied.

Luke heard the suitcases hitting the walls, but he didn't care. All that could be fixed with paint and a little time.

He listened while they showed them the bunk beds and the posters and the coloring and all the things they had done to decorate their rooms. Luke stood at the bottom of the stairway listening to the happy activity. It was everything he'd thought about being together would be. The only trouble was, it may not last. But he decided to enjoy it for the moment anyway.

He walked into the kitchen where Julie had retreated.

She was bending over the oven, pulling some dinner rolls out, her rear end poking out of that flowered apron that Luke used to wear.

He was enjoying the view. *To heck with the dinner rolls.*

"I almost burned these darn things. You'd think I'd never spent any time in the kitchen. I'm actually rusty, Luke." She closed the door, setting the well-cooked rolls on the stovetop. She pushed the hair from her forehead and greeted him with her arms wide, both her hands encrusted in flowered, quilted oven mitts that matched her apron.

"Where did you get those?" Luke asked.

"They were in the bottom drawer where the apron usually is."

"I never knew they were there. I would've used them too."

She walked up to Luke, pulled her arms around his torso, and brought him in against her. Whispering, she said, "I'm going to buy you a manly pair, very manly, and a manly apron for you to wear. I think you need that."

"Well, I'll accept your gift of manly oven mitts and an apron, if you'll accept my gift I've left for you upstairs."

"Really?" she asked.

"While you guys were shopping for school clothes, I went to a specialty shop. I won't tell you which, but you'll know when you see it."

"In a pink box?" she asked.

"Yeah, but it's not one of Steph's. Trust me on that."

She hugged him close and whispered, "I didn't think so, Sweetheart."

He helped her set the table, and he was amazed that everybody could fit with the extensions they hadn't used since they'd bought the table years ago.

Julie's parents arrived with their entourage encircling them, everybody vying for position to sit next to them.

Julie lit the candles and brought out the beautiful turkey she had been cooking all day. Luke helped her with all the other things, including the rolls, which were still well-done but very warmly received.

Mr. Christensen remarked, "Is it Thanksgiving? That's not for another month!"

"We are thankful, Luke and me and all the girls. We're thankful we could celebrate this nice dinner with you people today. We're so excited you came to visit, and we can't wait to show you all the wonderful things we love about San Diego, right, girls?"

A cheer erupted from all parts of the table.

Luke said grace, but before he began to carve the turkey, Julie stopped him.

"I just wanted to take a couple of moments and think about Stephanie and Colin. I wish they could be here today. I know they would've loved seeing you guys so happy, loved seeing you, Mom and Dad, and it's one of the reasons why we invited you up this weekend. I have a special family, and I never knew it until this all happened. I never doubted we were raised in love, and I never doubted how lovingly you were raised with Stephanie and Colin. I knew our girls loved each other, and I knew it was going to work. And we have a long ways ahead of us, but I'm very grateful, and that's why this is Thanksgiving for me, and hopefully, you can share in it too."

Luke came around the corner and gave her a big hug. Little Jessica squirmed out of her chair and did the same, which was so appropriate and consistent with the way she gave affection.

As he began cutting the turkey, Julie added one more note.

"Next year, we're going to need a highchair at this table."

Luke dropped the carving knife and paring fork and stared at his wife.

The girls looked confused, but Mr. and Mrs. Christensen were up on their feet, giving Julie a hug. Grandpa Christensen explained it to the girls. "You're going to have a little sister or a brother."

"Probably a sister," Luke said, smiling. "I don't think we make boys in this family. We make girls. We make beautiful girls. And I wouldn't have it any other way."

CHAPTER 16

JULIE FINGERED THE beautiful white, lacy nightgown Luke had purchased for her, laid out prettily on her side of the bed. He came up behind her, wrapped his arms around her, and kissed her neck.

"I wanted you to look beautiful tonight. You're not only a wonderful mother, you're a wonderful daughter, a wonderful teacher and principal—"

"Well, we have to talk about that."

"Okay, it's been a busy day, Julie, but go ahead. Tell me now."

"No, I loved where you were going with it, so complete your thought, and then we can talk later. Okay?"

"Okay. It sounds good. I wanted you to wear this, because I wanted you to know that, in addition to all those wonderful things, you are the most sexy woman in the whole world, and you should be wearing beautiful clothes, beautiful nighties. I just wanted you to have something special. I love you so much, and I owe you so much. This whole family owes you so much. I just wanted you to know you are cherished. You are loved beyond belief."

She was sobbing, but until he felt the hot tears cross over the backs of his hands wrapped around her, he didn't realize it. She hid it from him. She turned in his arms and looked up at him, placing her hands up around his neck.

"Luke, I'm so glad to see you're back. My Luke is back finally! We don't even have everything resolved, and you're back—the man I loved then and still love. We've weathered the worst part. I know there will be tough days ahead, but this makes me so happy."

"I've always been here, Jules. I really have."

"Yes, but you've not been able to express it. You jumped in, yes, but you've embraced our life, such as it is. I can't tell you how relieved I feel. It's been my honor and my complete pleasure. I'm overwhelmed with the love you have for this family. I'm overwhelmed with how you treat me. I feel like I'm the luckiest girl in the whole world. No matter what happens tomorrow, whatever happens in the future, I am always going to be your girl. And I couldn't have chosen a better partner for my life."

He planted a long, deep kiss on her lips. She was so hungry for him, smiling inside her heart at the knowledge that their love created another human being. And he didn't even flinch with the idea of having six children, maybe even six girls!

When they separated, he whispered in her ear, "How long have you known?"

"I think I got pregnant right away after we went up to Santa Rosa, and normally, I would've waited longer, but I knew Mom and Dad were coming, so I decided to get the blood test, and it confirmed it. Now it's still early, so a lot could happen, Luke. But I just wanted you to know. I wanted everyone to get some good news. No matter what else."

"So what is this going to do with the work situation?"

"Well, today, when I got the results, when the doctor's office called me, the next thing I received was this little letter in the mail." She went over to her nightstand and pulled out a letter from the school district.

Luke hesitated but then saw the letter had already been opened. She watched him read the words.

"You're going to let them get away with this?"

"No, a suspension means that I don't have to show up for work. It's a suspension with pay, Luke. We can take our time getting ready for the new baby, devoting ourselves full-time to whatever's happening next with the police investigation, and monitoring the inquiry into Steph and Colin's murder. I really think it's a blessing. I already knew I was pregnant. Then when I got this, I thought, this is perfect!"

Luke chuckled and then drew her into him again.

"How did I get so lucky? You talk about being so lucky. I'm the luckiest guy around. You're the only person in the world who would say a suspension was a good thing. You've been my rock, Julie. I never would have made it if it wasn't for you."

Julie knew she would remember their love making that night like it was the first time. And she remembered that one too. He was so tender with her, especially now that she was pregnant. Even though there wasn't anything he could do to disturb the baby, she knew men worried about that, and so his tenderness was extra special. And from her previous pregnancies, she also realized she would be horny as hell at least until she got to the six-month period. She'd already begun to feel her breasts getting fuller and had wonderful sensual dreams about motherhood, breastfeeding, the whole nine yards. She was so pleased her girls were so excited, all five of her girls, because she had really started thinking of Colin and Stephanie's girls as hers now.

She gave back all of the passion and tenderness he gave her, making sure he was fully satisfied by doing a few extra things that drew his attention or brought a smile to his face. She showed him how much she worshiped and honored him. His beautiful, muscled body enveloped her and made her soul sizzle. It had been so rare these past few months to feel the strength of him, and that always came with the damaged parts. But for now, she was grateful for this one night of strength, and love.

In the morning, Luke was off at a team meeting, since the group was going to be deployed. Even though Luke wasn't going to be in this rotation, he was still required to attend.

She found her father with a big pad of paper and a pencil, making some drawings. Her mother was outside with the girls, picking flowers and planting a flat of small chrysanthemums they had bought at the nursery the day before.

"You want some coffee, Dad?"

"Sure. Julie, I'd love some."

She set the mug on a coaster next to where he was drawing, and she peered over his shoulder.

"What are you doing?"

"I'm just sketching a few ideas I had."

"You're designing a new house?"

"I'm designing an addition."

"It looks huge. Is this something in Santa Rosa?"

Mr. Christensen put his pencil down and stared back at her. "Julie,

I've been talking to your neighbor next door, and he's offered to sell me his property. I wanted to first talk to you before we actually execute something, but your mom and I have been thinking about something ever since the girls moved down here. With both of you working, we thought maybe we could help out, and living in Santa Rosa without Colin and Stephanie is just not what it used to be. We're constantly seeing things we did together as a family that we don't do anymore. It's actually been painful to be there all alone with all of you down here. So if you're okay with it—and please tell us if you're not, because we don't want to impose ourselves on you guys—we'd like to pursue purchasing the property and then perhaps design an addition for the house next door that would attach to this house. Or not. Whatever you choose. But if we combined the lots, we could do it and have room for everyone and have it look fabulous—a real oasis."

"You could actually swing that? Because our financial situation…"

"If we sell our property, we can pay cash for it. So we wouldn't have to ask your lender for approval. But we don't want to do that if you feel pressured in any way. It's just an idea."

Julie was amazed that he had come up with this and managed to keep it a secret from her.

"Does Luke know about this?"

He shook his head, "No."

"And you'd sell your house?" she asked.

"I've already had your realtor come over and give us an opinion of value. We own it free and clear, so we might be able to even carry paper and live off of the note proceeds. I think I'm done with that house. It did what it was designed to do. It was a nice place to raise you and Colin. But there comes a time when everything is behind and nothing is forward. I'd like something to look forward to. No matter what it is, Julie. Maybe we can't take care of the kids full time, but we could lend a hand. And it would perhaps save you having to hire somebody to come in on a regular basis to do that if you're both working. Your mom and I would like to do that. We really would."

"I'm delighted, Dad. I'd never even thought you'd consider something like that. The girls would be ecstatic."

"Good, and by the way, your realtor said to give her a call."

"What?"

"I think your phone's not charged, Julie. She's been trying to reach you since yesterday. You have an offer on the house. She said to tell you it's a really good offer, and you should give her a call."

CHAPTER 17

"**I**S THIS LUKE Paulsen?"

Luke was washing the van. Julie was inside, talking to her parents, enjoying her forced time off.

"Who is this?" He made a habit of never talking to someone unless he knew who they were. The fact that they called him on his personal, unlisted cell didn't make it any better.

"My name is Justin Hamblin. I believe you will recognize the name. I got your number from your trust attorney."

Luke wished he had a listening device he could click on, like when he was on special ops. He felt naked without his equipment.

"Luke?"

"Go on. What the hell do you want?"

"I have a proposition for you."

Figures.

"I'm not in the mood, Mr. Hamblin. You've done some very damaging things to our family's reputation. My understanding is that you may be wanted by the law."

"Not aware of that, but I'm not surprised."

The guy sounded perfectly calm, and that pissed Luke off.

"I understand you're having some issues with the law as well, Mr. Paulsen. Maybe I can help."

"I doubt that."

"Just hear me out. I think I can help all this go away."

"You good at raising the dead too?"

"That was most unfortunate. That never should have happened."

"Damn right. They were murdered. Something tells me you were behind that."

"No, that wasn't me. Someone else made a huge miscalculation."

"Fuck you, you motherfucker!" Luke screamed into the phone. Then he searched the quiet Coronado neighborhood they lived in to see if anyone noticed. He didn't see any curtains being shut, cars stopping, or dogwalkers stopping in the street. He hoped no one had noticed. He didn't need that right now.

"If you will calm down, I have a solution to this never-ending saga that's befallen your family. I don't admit responsibility, Mr. Paulsen, if this call is being recorded. But I'm going to give you the opportunity to meet with my colleague to discuss arrangements that can make some or all of this go away."

"I think we're past that. If it's a fight you want, you've got it. And for the record, you are responsible for the leaks. I've had that verified by someone who knows, and I do hold you responsible for my baby sister's and my brother-in-law's deaths. I can't be talked down from that assumption, nor will I be talked down from spending the rest of my life seeing to it that you pay for it. I don't care how long it takes."

"At what cost, Mr. Paulsen?"

"Excuse me?"

"What cost would be too dear to pay? Aren't you concerned about the health and safety of your family? Do I have to give you their names and ages?"

Luke knew he should have thrown the phone in the gutter drain and called Riverton or Mayfield, but he didn't. It was the last thing he knew how to do, protect his family. It was too late for Steph and Colin.

"You better not—"

"I'm not talking about anything I would do, Mr. Paulsen. I know certain people who require certain documents to be returned to them. Until then, no one, even you, no one is safe, Mr. Paulsen."

He counted to ten. He envisioned cutting this man up, peeling the flesh from his skin, pulling every single tooth from his fucking skull, maybe removing his fingers joint by joint. He'd never done any of those things. Only animals did those things to people. But today, on this bright, sunny Coronado day, today, he could relish becoming that kind of a man, knowing full well there would be no coming back from that.

His revenge was much larger than his control.

LUKE TOLD JULIE he had to pick up a few things for the van. She started to show him the drawings her dad had made. He pretended he was capable of actually looking them over, envisioning a life with all of them together, seeing the girls living with their grandparents and all together, welcoming a new baby in the house, even if he needed to do diaper duty.

But he couldn't. His brittle smile was wide and sexy enough, taking a huge amount of effort to get there, that it fooled Julie.

He knew he should call Kyle. He should call someone else from the team, but that would get them into deep shit, even though they always said they had each other's back. That didn't mean following each other into the pits of hell. No, it didn't apply in that case.

Not telling them was a huge violation of the code of their brotherhood, but it was the only way he could keep them safe. Instead, he called Kyle and told him he had to run up to Santa Rosa to pick up something he'd left in the move. And he'd ask his LPO if he could have someone check in on Julie and the kids, just casually. Let them know he'd be back the next day.

"Why casually? Don't they know you're going or how long you'll be gone?"

"Not exactly."

"Fuck me, Luke. What have you done?"

"Nothing. I'm just going to go pick up something."

"Who are you going with?"

"No one. I don't need anyone to go up with me. I'm fine, Kyle. I was just asking for your eyes and ears for the family. Didn't want to spook them, you know, with all the shit going on?"

"Why not Mayfield or Riverton? They could do that."

"They're busy. And—"

"They're old. You need a fighter to protect them. Listen, Luke, you're about to do something you don't want to tell me about. I can tell when you're lying. You can't go do this on your own. Either I go with you, or you take someone from the team I pick out."

Luke thought about it. Should he take a shooter, an explosives guy, a medic, or—?

"Can I take Danny Begay? How about him?"

"The sling-shot guy."

"He's a shooter, you know that. He's been a help to me and knows the place I have to go to pick up this item. And he's calm."

"And you sure as hell aren't. Still not going to tell me?"

"Nothing to tell."

"Not yet, you mean. Okay, I'm going to call him and give him my advice. I'll leave it up to him whether or not he comes. You better not get the two of you tossed or, worse, wind up in jail. I can't afford to lose you guys."

And I can't afford to lose my family.

Ten minutes later, as Luke was picking up some things from the hardware store, Danny called him and asked that Luke pick him up outside the Skupper.

"I'm not going to share a beer with you, Danny. Either you're coming or you're not."

"Oh, I'm coming. I'm here with a couple of new recruits who didn't pass BUD/S. And they're getting drunk. I'm not. Me and Coop are babysitting. I'll let Coop do the rest. I'm going with you."

"Good deal."

"Just a clarification, do I need to bring my duty bag?"

"You probably should."

DANNY'S GEAR WAS in the secret compartment under the driver seat of his truck. He grabbed it, tossing it to Luke with a sneer.

"Don't make me regret this," he mumbled.

"I'm only asking for your protection. This isn't an action, and it sure as hell isn't an op. I have to meet with someone I don't trust."

Danny climbed into Luke's Hummer, and they sped toward the freeway north.

"Why not alert the locals? There are others who do this, you know."

"I can't. That's all I'm going to say."

"So who is this person?"

"I'm to meet with someone who wants something that was stored in a storage facility we didn't check. I got the key from Julie."

"So she's okay with this."

"She knows about it, yes." Luke hated lying to Danny, but it had to be that way. He'd find a way to make it up to him. But Kyle didn't leave him any room. He was going to blow up everything. And maybe he should, Luke pondered.

"What are we looking for then? Who is coming to get it?"

"I'm not sure who. But there's a bag stored in the back of Colin's Thunderbird. You remember that turquoise and white convertible he bought when he was down here? I didn't realize he still owned it. I don't know what's in the bag, but it could be papers for the car someone wants. I don't care a shit about that. I want to get these people off my back."

"These the people who have been telling stuff to the press and calling Kyle?"

"I think so."

"Fuck," Danny said as he peered out the windshield. "This have to do with that Feathers and Tails shit in Vegas?"

"Maybe."

"Maybe as in you don't know, or maybe yes, Luke?"

"I don't know. I've been promised that the issues we're facing are due to the fact that they need something back. They've been pressuring us. They don't really care about us. They just want us to do something. If I can solve this without any violence, without any more violence to my family, I think that's a good use of my time. Don't you?"

"So you're not going up there to off the guy, then?"

"That's not the plan. Ball's in his court." He abruptly pulled over at a rest stop. "I gotta pee. But let me tell you this, Danny, you are not to do anything except help keep me safe. No one is going to shoot or kill anyone, especially not you. Do you understand? I don't care what happens. If you can't save me, you walk away, and let destiny take its course. You do not risk your career. And I'm only bringing you because Kyle said I had to."

"I know about that. He's gonna want to know."

"He'll know soon enough. Don't tell him until he's too far away to be able to do anything. Okay, now I really gotta pee. You coming or staying here?"

"I'm staying with the shit. I'll go after you return."

IT TOOK ROUGHLY eight hours for the trip. Luke was pressing past the speed limit and was actively searching the horizon for little black-and-white friendlies. Danny helped with the lookouts.

He'd brought a ring of keys with him and, driving down Santa Rosa Avenue, stopped at a gated and attended mini-warehouse complex. He stopped into the office and inquired about the space Colin had rented, holding up the keys. He'd showed the young man a copy of the trust that stated he and Julie had the right to access it. It even had been listed in the trust.

The clerk searched through the ring, picked out the key with the unit number stamped on it, and handed it back to Luke.

"Is there anyone else here, asking for me?"

"No. Haven't seen anyone. We got people using their units today, but no one looking for you, not that I know of."

"Okay, we're going to drive down there. You see anyone who shouldn't be here, you call the cops first. You hear anything that sounds like a scuffle, you call the cops, okay?"

"Like they'd get here in the next four hours. But sure, I'll do that. Look, is there some kind of problem here? Is all this legit? I don't want to get into any trouble."

"No, sir. I'm a Navy SEAL. I've just lost my sister and brother-in-law, and I'm here to retrieve something that's important to the family. I'm just trying to be careful, is all."

"So if someone asks for you, I let them in?"

"Yessir. I'll be ready."

The facility consisted of rear units with tall doors large enough to store a regular RV. Then there were four rows of twelve-by-twelve storage units, all with roll-up metal doors. Colin's was at the end of one of the middle rows.

While Danny got out and walked around to the other side of the truck, watching the driveway from both directions, Luke opened the rollup door.

Colin's beautiful turquoise T-Bird sat all by itself. It was dusty, and all the tires were flat, indicating he hadn't been to the facility to work on it or take it for a stroll. He searched the key ring and found the distinctive key. He wanted to fire the thing up, but wasn't sure it was operable.

He looked up at Danny.

"We got company."

Luke walked outside to stand next to his teammate.

An old four-door pickup drove slowly toward them, a single driver, a young man with a baseball cap. He looked like a high school kid, scruffy and a bit dirty, like his truck, but otherwise not threatening. All his windows were rolled down, Luke noted.

The boy stopped about twenty feet away, sticking his head out of the window frame.

"You Luke?"

"Yessir. Who are you?"

"I'm Justin Hamblin."

He didn't sound anything like the person Luke had talked to on the phone.

"No, you're not." Luke walked over towards the driver door, and the boy demanded he stop. Out of the side of his eye, he saw Danny assuming a shooting stance, without producing a weapon.

"I said stop!" the boy yelled.

"You packing, Son? You got a gun you gonna use?" Luke demanded. "It'd be two against one, and I already told the clerk up front to call the cops."

Someone rose up from the second seat, shoving a long gun in his face, but he growled in Jason Hamblin's voice, "No, it'd be two against two. Don't be stupid, Luke. That kid never got that call off."

If Hamblin lowered the weapon or Luke saw something from the boy, he was going to grab the Sig Sauer tucked into his back. But he'd have to move quick and shoot whatever moved. He didn't want to do that. Not yet.

He flicked his fingers, preparing himself for what he hoped he didn't have to do, and giving Danny a clue that he was ready, but he didn't encourage his buddy.

Just then, from each side, two vehicles drove in, with screeching tires and a cloud of dust and gravel scattering everywhere. One landed behind the old truck, the other on the other side of Luke's Hummer, effectively closing any of them from an easy escape.

Hamblin swung his weapon around to the back and took aim at the cloud of dust, but he was shot in the arm, forcing him to drop the AR-15 rifle he'd been holding.

He heard a familiar voice before the kid scrambled out of the front seat and ran past Luke and Danny. He ended up in the arms of three fully locked and loaded Navy SEALs who had driven behind them.

"You dumb motherfucker! I told you not to get involved in this shit. Now look at what you made—who fired on this poor gentleman?" Kyle Lansdowne barked.

Nobody answered.

Hamblin was writhing in pain on the ground, but he was trying to crawl slowly away until Coop came up to him and stepped on his arm, where the wound was, which made the man have an early conversion and pee his pants.

"This guy's all fucked up," Coop said. "Someone help this guy up while I get my kit."

Luke was frozen in place.

"Get rid of the guns, dumbass," Kyle said. "Put 'em away. The cops are on their way."

Both Danny and Luke did so, just as two Santa Rosa police cruisers came barreling down the alleyway with their sirens blaring.

"Thought you didn't want to get involved."

"No, you didn't want to get us involved, Luke, remember? Besides, we aren't involved. We came by just to make sure you were okay, with all this crap going on. I think this guy's buddy shot him by mistake."

"Kyle, you're a fuckin' liar."

"I'm a better liar than you are."

"Thanks, Man."

"I told you not to do this alone. You can't do anything alone. Not when you're on my team, Son. We're putting you on a plane tonight, Luke. Now you have to do something even harder. You're going to have to make up with your wife. She's not very happy, Luke. Not happy at all. You might have fixed this, but I'm not sure you can fix that."

CHAPTER 18

JULIE HAD TAKEN the news of Luke's trip with fury at first, then alarm, and then found herself drowning with a huge foreboding she couldn't shake. Her mother had her go to bed, rest, and wait, especially for the sake of the baby. Kyle had called her, letting her know what Luke was doing and why, and promised he'd update her. He told her not to doubt the team was going to do everything they could to bring Luke back safely.

But Luke's decision to take off had her worried he might have landed in some dark place he wouldn't be able to dig his way out of.

He'd worked so hard. They all had. How could he betray their trust, leave without saying goodbye? She was his partner, yet he called Kyle, his LPO, not her!

Was she married to a man or a team? Was this going to be their new life if he stayed with SEAL Team 3? Would she always have to worry forever that whenever he left for the store he'd never return? How selfish and unfeeling this was. Didn't he care anything about her or the kids?

Or was he going off to end everything? Had the stress of these past few weeks just welled up so much that he had to take himself out in a blaze of glory. Julie thought he'd been doing so well, seemed to be happy with the new baby on the way, accepted the idea that her parents were going to live next to them. What set him off and what made him decide it was a good idea to not include her in this drastic decision?

Luci Begay came over later on and stayed for a bit, trying to console her. She was told others would be coming. While being thankful, Julie wanted to hear from Luke. He was her whole world. And why couldn't he understand that?

Luci tried to help her with answers.

"I couldn't talk Danny down. But he discussed it with Kyle, and he felt, we all felt Luke needed backup to come home safely to you and his family. Many of his buds on the team didn't trust the local law enforcement officers, didn't have a relationship with them like they did here, so it was not a problem signing up for this mission, Julie. It was to save Luke's life."

"But why couldn't he tell me?"

"Maybe he didn't know what to say. Maybe he just knew nothing you could say would change his mind and he wanted to just go for it? Doesn't make it right, but I've heard about things like this happening. Julie, they never listen. You know they don't. They march to a different drummer. We have to trust that they're doing the right thing. But we never can control it. You know that."

Julie did realize Luke didn't do it for the excitement of doing something against the people they held responsible for Colin and Steph's death or the crap coming at the family right now. He did it for them, not for him. Either way, there was no satisfaction for him. Either way, he violated some trust.

And he chose to violate the trust between the two of them.

Why?

At dusk, when she hadn't heard anything, she tried to call Luke's cell and got no answer. Then she tried Kyle's cell, and the same thing happened.

And then she got the call she'd been waiting for all day.

"Hi, Babe."

"Luke! Oh my God! Are you okay?" Her steely resolve melted at the sound of his voice. Then the wave of fear she'd been holding onto splashed over her. "You know I'm angry at you. You violated your oath to me, your promise. How can I ever trust you again?"

"I'm so sorry. I will understand if you can't take me back. I felt I had no choice. Jules, I wouldn't be able to live with myself if I didn't get this guy out of our lives."

"What? Did you kill him?"

"No, I didn't kill him. I didn't even shoot him. He got shot by someone else. But he's locked up, and hopefully, he'll be put away for a long time for endangering all of us and for causing the accident that took Colin and Stephanie's life."

"What was this about?"

"It's a long story. Right now, I'm just about to go into a briefing. I got Kyle, Danny, Coop, T.J., Tucker, and other guys too. We all have to be questioned by the police. But I'll sit down with you and explain everything. I promise. I'm so sorry. It's the last time I'll ever do anything like this again."

She wanted to believe him, but she had to be realistic, as well. If she didn't face the facts, she'd always be wondering, and she'd always be a mess. The kids deserved to have a mother who was present, looked after them, and kept them healthy and safe. Not someone filled with rage and resentment.

"When are you returning to us?"

"As soon as this is over. Tonight. They're going to put me on a plane tonight. The rest of the guys are driving home, bringing back my truck."

"Where did you go? Where in Santa Rosa? To the house—which, by the way, is sold."

"That's good news. I was at the storage facility that housed Colin's Thunderbird. He'd stored some incriminating evidence in the trunk, and the guy needed it back. I also think he had designs to off me, as well, to solve another issue. The guys saved my life, honey. I would have done and will do the same for them."

Of all the things Luke told her, the last sentence was the honest truth.

"Soon, Sweetheart. And if I'm lucky enough to earn a second chance with you, I promise you won't regret it. I'll be a model husband, Julie. I'll do anything you want whenever you want it."

She was beginning to get ideas already.

IT WAS ONE o'clock in the morning when he returned to their bedroom. A taxi had picked him up from the airport. He walked in without his bags, which he left in the Hummer with Danny and the guys, and collapsed in her arms.

"I'm so sorry, Julie," he sobbed.

She found her heart needing to show him the tenderness and love she had for him. Her big, fucked up, tatted mess of a man, this self-proclaimed "killing machine with a heart the size of the ocean."

One thing she knew as sure as the fact that she was alive, Luke needed her. And he wasn't afraid to show it, either. It had not always been this way, especially in the beginning when they were first getting together. But without her, she was certain he'd be lost.

But as she held him, listened to his sobs, felt how he clutched her nightgown and clung to her like a little child, she realized she needed him just as much.

She stroked his head, kissed his forehead, then begged him to strip down and just come to bed. She wanted to soothe all his rough parts, cover the scars, and kiss and love away all the deficiencies. He was a complicated package, a man who hadn't started out strong like some of the other teammates, but who had fought for his own sanity, for his family, for his career probably harder than anyone else she'd met.

He wasn't perfect. But he was all hers. And every inch of her belonged to Luke and always would.

He was home.

EPILOGUE

JUSTIN HAMBLIN WASN'T his real name, which wasn't a surprise to anybody. He'd been a recruiter for picking up young girls to bring them into the trade as sex workers. It had started when he began running illegals across the border. Earned a lot of money doing it, and he looked for investments he could make with his new-found fortune.

He'd run across the Garden of Delights mail order business quite by accident. He was invited to a party by a raunchy hostess who was training young girls to pleasure their Johns better. He saw a way to legitimize his business.

Stephanie seemed like the perfect mark, until he discovered her brother was a Navy SEAL, and he almost quit right there. But he'd spent time recruiting her to the party scheme, without her ever knowing what he was really doing. And when she needed help with her successful business, he was only too pleased to introduce her to one of his recruits, who had actually aspired to become an office manager one day with her knowledge of computers. A runaway who needed a mother and would do anything for money.

When Colin and Stephanie weren't looking too closely, he managed to sell devices to other trailer camps and ranches with the help of his recruit.

And then his girl fell in love. It was the bane of any pimp. She fell in love with one of her regulars she was working on the side, and he took her away.

Under the guise that she was in trouble and needed money, she got Stephanie to empty her bank account. But not before she delivered a package of photographs he'd been storing. Disgusting child porn, videos of mostly immigrant kids being abused.

Of course, they wanted out. Colin insisted they terminate their relationship and held the photos over him. So it has been time to scare Steph and Colin, scare them into giving up everything, including the incriminating evidence, so they could never again be a thorn in his side.

Except his helper didn't do what he'd been asked. He'd used a semi cab instead of the truck he was supposed to use and killed them both.

It really was an accident.

Had he got the photos, it would have been fine. He already had most of the money and was expecting more. Colin had offered to take a mortgage out on the house and had started the process, and with all that money, he would have been set. He could retire to Mexico or Central America until things cooled off. And then he'd start anew. It would have been a fresh start. He would have learned from his mistakes of the past and looked forward to a lucrative future.

But this damned family—the Navy SEAL asshole who went off like a bull in a China shop, his doggedly stubborn marks who wouldn't give up no matter what he threatened, and the young recruit whose life was transformed by love, all these things worked against him.

And he failed.

But when he got out, he'd be back. He'd find someone else to latch onto and milk for their assets. There were always people trying to come to the U.S. for a better life. There were millions of people out there he could use and abuse.

And he could wait. Besides, they'd decriminalized prostitution in most parts of California. Nevada had legalized it. Nobody was watching the border, and everyone wanted to party and have a good time.

All except these damned Navy SEAL families. He wouldn't make that mistake again.

HEART OF GOLD

SEAL Brotherhood: Legacy Series
Book 7

SHARON HAMILTON

CHAPTER 1

D EEP YELLOW AND orange tongues of fire lapped up the sides of the old wooden structure, originally built in the late 1800's to service the railyards and shipping lines at the Columbia River in Portland's warehouse district. Once packed with frozen fish and sundries making their way from the Orient or Alaska, now the trendy area had sprouted galleries, high-end loft housing for young yuppies and artists, catering companies hosting exotic food trucks, eclectic restaurants that seemed to pop up and disappear with the same speed, dance clubs, and foreign movie theaters. It even had a live theater/playhouse converted from an old slaughterhouse by the same name.

The building was in a string of galleries that extended several blocks long on both sides.

Some housed artist collectives in a live-work environment, with the showrooms below. But like many of the old structures, this one was just a gallery, refurbished and benefiting from timeworn, wire-encrusted skylights thirty feet in the air, which gave the magic light that was so important to the paintings and artwork it housed.

But this night, midnight, it started in this building first, the fire like a wild snake, seeking out other places it could creep into cracks and overtake a new structure. The beautiful, polished white oak plank flooring buckled and popped nails as the fire traveled over the top like a tiny child's toy locomotive, leaving a fiery streak in its wake.

Glass broke as windows, one by one, burst open to the cold night air. Even the rain couldn't stop the spread, hissing and roaring like an angry animal ascending straight from Hell.

The paintings on the walls melted at first, their bright acrylic colors running down in bloody streaks past the canvas, over the walls, and onto the floor, pooling, igniting, and exploding in small balls of fire. Each picture was overtaken, and its demise was celebrated by the demands of the blaze. These works of art were abused, lit up for a few seconds, and then perished in flame.

One by one, the canvases dropped as their wires warped, as their frames charred, and the weight of the melted acrylic from the painting above it pushed them all down.

Within minutes, the entire building was engulfed, spreading to the one next to it and then another, until a paint factory caught and exploded. Oxygen temporarily removed from the air, a brief few seconds of darkness blanketed the landscape before the inferno came back to life with twice the strength.

If left unchecked, it would spread and consume the dozen or so warehouses all the way to the waterway. Sirens in the distance foretold this huge event would be coming to an end within the hour, already leaving behind black, smoldering partial walls while debris still ignited as new food for the fire.

And smoke. Thick, choking smoke so black the stars were invisible.

Diedre Gray was in shock when she got the call from the fire department liaison at one in the morning. Rushing to their bedroom window overlooking the river and downtown areas of Portland, she could see the blaze in the distance. She shared the gallery space with several other painters and a sculptor, but judging from the size and intensity of the blaze, she knew her work was all destroyed. And her paintings were the main draw of the gallery. She and the other artists held events in the space, all of them lovingly restoring and upgrading the building with the magical skylights.

Her heart broke, leaving only a thick, black, charred remnant of her former vibrant self. Twenty years of work, some pieces she never intended on selling, gone. Just gone.

Her husband stood behind her, holding her shoulders with his hands, while she wept. There were no words worthy of use. Nothing was going to stop her sobbing until she was good and done. The grieving process was beginning.

News reports flashed on their television as they listened for information. Her husband agreed with the department spokeswoman that going down there would be pointless and they would just be in the way. Since there wasn't expected to be any loss of life, pets, or items needing rescue, they'd let the professionals do their job undisturbed by their presence.

She called the other artists, one of whom had moved to San Francisco and was leaving the gallery, informing them of the sad news.

They continued to watch the reports. Earlier, a demonstration downtown in the financial district had left damaged vehicles and glass storefronts behind, including several fires which were quickly extinguished. Fire crews were blocked from entering certain blocks, and the police were relegated to pushing back the mob all the way to the grassy Dickenson Park in the center of the city, where they could be gathered up or dispersed. These demonstrations were now so common people didn't even pay attention as they re-routed their streets to avoid the confrontations.

Young people had poured out onto the sidewalk as one of the student housing units at Portland State downtown had been set ablaze. The newscaster wasn't sure what the demonstration was about, as no permit had been obtained and no spokesman had developed, which was also common these days.

The warehouse fire was deemed not connected, but arson was suspected. The protest crowd was trying to avoid the police and were headed that direction. Traffic and fire crews attempted to keep their work area cleared to further demonstrations, even onlookers, but were battling an angry crowd that seemed they wanted to burn down the whole city.

Deidre had cried so much she was now sitting in her flannel nightie in shock. Larry Gray brought her some of her favorite tea, and she sat, holding it, forgetting to sip, until he reminded her.

"Nothing we can do now, Deidre. What a shame."

"Why would they do that? The spokeswoman said it started with our building, Larry. Who would want to do that? Do you think it's related to downtown?"

"Makes no difference. A bank, a school dorm, a car dealership, a coffee shop, drug store—they all get hit these days. I just hope everyone gets out alive," he said, rubbing the back of her neck.

"This is unacceptable. This has to be stopped," she whispered.

"It would be easier to move, Deidre."

"No. I'm going to stay and fight."

"But you don't even know who to fight. They just want to destroy. It's a statement that they want it all burned down, ruined. They won't be controlled."

"People have died, Larry, so they had the right to protest. Why can't they leave us alone to just do what we love?"

"It's evil. And the evil is growing."

And then she knew what she needed to do next. She would call her son, Navy SEAL Tyler Gray, in Coronado.

But she'd wait until morning.

CHAPTER 2

NAVY SEAL TYLER Gray heard screaming through the connecting wall from his two boys' bedroom. It was way too early on a Saturday morning. He'd been out late at a bachelor party for one of the tadpoles, new guy on SEAL Team 3, Oscar Ramos, and his head was killing him.

Besides, Kate usually jumped up first on these kinds of mornings to keep the peace between their three children. The boys had been fighting nonstop for weeks now. Oliver was the younger of the two boys, at five, and he competed in sports against his older brother, Grady, who was eight. He could nearly beat his older brother in a timed run and kick a soccer ball farther than most of the kids in his age bracket, as well as several years his senior. It wasn't something Grady tolerated well. Oliver made sure Grady was in a constant state of irritation and cut him zero slack. If Tyler had had a brother, he'd have been the same way.

But it made for a very noisy household.

Another scream erupted from their room, this time followed by a thump on the floor and then some serious crying.

He reached over to give Kate a hug, but then he remembered she had left before dark, driving up north to attend a catering class taught by a celebrity TV chef. So Tyler was in charge of all three kids all day.

He darted out of bed, shirtless but wearing red, white and blue boxers, and pushed the door to their bedroom so hard it banged against the wall and bent the door stop.

The crying stopped immediately.

Grady sat in the middle of the floor with a bloody nose. Oliver's right eye was going to be swollen shut soon.

"What the hell?" Tyler barked, barely able to change his language at the last minute to something more appropriate.

That's when he noticed Oliver silently set a large hardbound book down next to him, which had apparently been the weapon used to cause Grady's bloody nose.

"He hit me with a book," Grady shouted, pointing to the Three Musketeers book at Oliver's side. "He broke my nose!" he said through his bloody sniffles.

Tyler ran to the bathroom between their room and Kendall's, grabbed a towel, and wet it down, bringing it back to Grady. Holding it up to his oldest son's nose, Tyler bent his head back.

"Keep this on it for a few minutes. Doesn't feel broken, Grady. Let's get the bleeding to stop, and then we'll sort this out."

Out of the corner of his eye, he noticed Oliver was slowly pushing the large book under his bed with his foot, removing the evidence.

"Ollie, you get your butt back on your bed, and gimme the book."

He did as he was told.

"Sorry, but he was pulling my hair. I had to stop him. He pushed me into the wall."

"I did not," Grady gurgled into the towel. "He called me a baby."

"Oliver, your brother is three years older than you. If he's a baby, what does that make you?"

"He wets the bed, and I don't," was Oliver's answer.

So there was the problem. Grady had recently had a bout of bed-wetting, and Tyler and Kate had been scratching their heads to figure out what to do to make it stop. It was infrequent, but obviously embarrassing to Grady. Tyler was suspicious of most child psychologists, but Kate had been working on him to get him to agree to some counseling.

He was hoping Grady would just grow out of it. But eight was pretty old for a bedwetter.

"That's not how we handle this sort of thing, Ollie. You need to apologize to your brother. And as for that shiner, you deserved it. If you can't take the heat, then keep your damned mouth shut, understand?"

"Yessir." Oliver hung his head.

From behind him, he heard the little voice of his two-year-old daughter, Kendall, "Daddy said a bad word."

She was standing in the doorway, holding her baby blanket and sucking her thumb.

"You're right, Sweetheart," he smiled and said to her. "Daddy made a mistake, and he's very sorry. It's okay to be angry but not okay to swear."

He stood, crossed the room to the doorway, and picked Kendall and her blanket up. Tickling her belly made her giggle. He sat her next to Oliver on his bed and tended to Grady.

The nose was going to be very red and swollen, especially up on the bridge, and he considered taking him to the emergency room to be checked but decided against it after examining him further. It would be a two- or three-hour ordeal, and he'd have to bring everyone with him. He also didn't want to expose the kids to the hospital crowd for fear they'd come home with a bug.

The bleeding had stopped. He grabbed the towel and rinsed it in the bathroom sink.

The boys were still staring daggers at each other.

"Come on. Both of you say you're sorry, and let's shake on it." He watched as the two barely touched each other with the shake and mumbled their apology. It was as good as he was going to get.

He suddenly thought of something that might change the trajectory for the day.

"Who wants to go get pancakes?" he asked them.

The cheers he got were unanimous. He checked the time.

"You two get cleaned up. Grady, carefully brush your teeth and rinse your mouth, okay? And if I hear any arguing, the deal's off, and we get oatmeal downstairs. I have to change Kendall and get her ready."

THE HAPPY TIME Pancake House opened early. A Chinese family owned the business, sharing the kitchen with their Chinese restaurant, Happy Time Chinese, next door, which opened for lunch when the pancake house closed. Over the years he and Kate had been taking the kids there, they'd gotten used to the red lanterns and Chinese music playing in the background, but at first, eating pancakes to the ancient stringed orchestra had been distracting.

It was an acquired taste.

While they were waiting for their order to come, Tyler's cell rang. It was his mother.

"Hey, Mom. You're up early."

"I hope I didn't wake you…"

"Not a chance. Kate's at a class so I'm taking the kids out for pancakes. What's up?" He suspected something important had happened.

"My gallery has burned to the ground, Tyler. It's just awful. What a mess."

"Oh my gosh. I'm so sorry, Mom. When did this happen?"

"Last night around midnight. They called to tell me it was fully engulfed. We watched it from our balcony. This morning, your dad and I went over early, but they wouldn't let us in. But there aren't any walls, and the roof caved in. Everything's destroyed. Gutted seven other buildings as well as damaged several others. A paint company exploded right behind us."

"Everyone okay?"

"One of the firefighters was taken to the hospital, but yes, everyone is okay. Nobody was in any of the buildings. Several people got out in time."

"I can imagine how you feel, Mom. You had a lot of paintings there as I recall. And—"

"I had just moved several pieces there to store them. They were my keepers, the ones I wanted to pass down to the family. Some of my favorites. And they're all gone, I'm sure of it."

"Well, I'm glad no one was hurt, except for the firefighter. Hope it wasn't serious."

"No, the news said he would be released."

"What caused the fire?"

"They suspect arson. But there was a protest downtown last night earlier. Several places were set ablaze. Nothing like this, though. The investigator and the news reports say there isn't a connection. I just don't know why anyone would want to burn down a gallery."

"You don't know that. Could have started elsewhere."

"No, they said it began with our building. We'll be told more later, they said."

"Maybe this is a sign, Mom. I've been asking you to move down to San Diego to be close to us. The kids would love seeing you. Now that Linda and the girls are down here too, it just makes sense to be where both your kids are. Dad could get a principal's job down here no problem. Or retire. I don't like what I'm hearing. I don't think it's safe there any longer."

"But we've been here our whole lives. We met here, went to college together, and started the gallery. My roots are here."

"Except now they're soot and smoke, Mom. Promise me you'll think about it."

"Your dad is just like you. No, we'll have to straighten out things here with the insurance, and then we'll see where we are. I'd like to be able to get inside the place."

"You won't be able to until it's safe. You don't want to interfere with the investigation, either, right?"

"Right."

Then Tyler heard her voice quiver and knew she was softly crying.

"What's wrong with Grandma?" asked Grady.

"I'll tell you in a minute. Eat your eggs first then the pancakes. Everyone, eat your eggs first," Tyler instructed his brood. He addressed his mother. "We've just been served, so I'm going to have to go. Is there anything I can do?"

"I was wondering, both your dad and I were wondering, if you could talk to the fire inspector and just get a feel for—"

"Look, you know I can't interfere."

"Yes, but you sort of represent the family. I guess you could call and talk to them on the phone, but I was hoping you could come up for a couple of days and help us sort out what has to be done."

"Well, I'm not trained in that. But if it will make you feel better, sure, I can try to come up. I won't be able to talk to Kate until tonight when she gets home, and I'll have to check with Kyle. You know I have to be careful not to step on any toes, and I don't know anything about fires, but if it will help you and Dad, I'm willing. I am curious about why they think your building was the first one. Must have found something that led them to that conclusion. I would like to hear more about that."

"Oh, thank you, Tyler. It would be a great help to have you here."

Tyler spent the day cleaning up the mess in the boys' bedroom, washing sheets, and making sure the house was straight for when Kate got home. He called Kyle and got approval to take a couple of days off, since they weren't going to deploy for another couple of months, but there was a training coming up, preparing them for another trip to Mexico, possibly Central America as well.

He made a reservation for the one direct flight to Portland from San Diego, which he could cancel without penalty. He'd gotten the last seat and knew they would oversell the flight, so he'd get to the airport early tomorrow to make it.

He searched the internet news reports about the demonstrations that turned ugly in the downtown region and saw pictures of the warehouse fires, recognizing his mother's gallery roasting like a huge marshmallow.

It crossed his mind to contact Bryce Tanner and even perhaps Bone Frog Protection, an international security company who recruited former military, police, and rescue personnel for high-value hostage rescues. He wondered if they had any intel on groups who were involved with the violence.

Then he remembered the cautionary advice he'd gotten from Kyle and others. The first reports, just like the first reports of any military action, were always inaccurate. In an uncertain world, that was one thing he could count on.

As if sensing the trouble and danger to their grandmother, the kids were well behaved the rest of the day. They were seated at the dinner table when Kate arrived home, exhausted from the traffic and long drive.

He let the boys tell her about their fight, since she noticed the wounds, especially the shiner on Oliver's eye. Tyler added that everyone shook hands and apologized.

She smiled up at him. "Sounds like an ordinary day. Grady's nose is turning a little blue. Should we get it checked?"

"I think we should watch it. If you insist, I can do it tomorrow, but I was hoping to be able to go up to Portland to see Mom and Dad."

And then he told her about the fire. She agreed he should go.

As she sat down and Tyler served her dinner, little Kendall made sure she heard her news.

"And Daddy said a very bad word, Mama."

CHAPTER 3

KATE LOADED THEIR Suburban with the three kids, adding Tyler's duty bag, minus the weapons and rounds. He'd brought several sets of folded jeans and tee shirts, and one nice shirt and cotton pants with his leather shoes he hoped he didn't have to wear. They'd gotten used to wearing flip-flops between deployments in San Diego, and it always hurt to wear lace-ups or heavy boots. He told her he was usually medically treating blisters the size of his palm during their first few days overseas.

She and Tyler had talked until late in the evening what their future plans could be. It made sense for Mr. and Mrs. Gray to relocate to San Diego, but Tyler warned her that his mom was going to be resistant.

She answered, "I know she wants to be closer to the grandkids. Your dad can always find a good job down here. But he's almost seventy, Tyler. Don't you think he's considering retiring?"

Sitting next to her on the front seat, Tyler searched the windshield, thinking. "My parents have always done their own thing. You know they were hippies in college, right?"

"Oh yeah, we've talked about it. I think your folks went a little bit further than mine did, but it was the times. Your mom has never really grown out of that hippie phase. I mean, look at her paintings—"

And then Kate was reminded that most of her paintings were now destroyed in the fire. "Oh gosh, Tyler, I'm sorry."

"Well, it removes one root they have there in Portland. They spent so much time and money fixing up that place. Even though she loved it, now that it's gone, I'm just not sure my folks want to go through the whole thing again. I mean, it was one thing twenty years ago when they were a lot younger. Now, if Dad is going to retire, I don't think they have that much in savings. She does okay with her sales, but you know, I don't think they have the money."

"Well, you know a lot of artists up there live above their studios, and I, for one, would not be in favor of them selling the house on the hill and doing that. I think it's dangerous for them. So if that comes up, count me as a no. And I think your sister would feel the same."

"I think you're right. Linda is not really sure where she wants to land after her last divorce. She can live anywhere since she's supporting herself with her writing now, but I think she's headed to Florida. Still looking for Mr. Rich Guy. Maybe she'll find him there. With her two kids in tow, I doubt Mom and Dad are really going to see their grandchildren very often. But it is what it is."

"You know, when I first met your folks, they were so lovey-dovey to each other. It was a little off-putting to be honest with you. I mean I never asked my parents how often they had sex, but your parents, hell, I think they have sex twice a day at least, right?"

Tyler threw his head back and laughed until they both heard their two boys unanimously shout out, "Ew," from the second seat behind them.

"Now you've done it, Tyler," she chuckled.

"I guess I have. And boy, if you're right about Mom and Dad, we've got to up our game, Kate. I can't have my seventy-year-old father outperform me in the bedroom."

"I doubt that's the case, Sweetheart," she said, giving him a sexy grin.

Tyler leaned over and placed a kiss on her cheek. "Later, Sweetheart, when I get home, I'm just going to show you. And that's all I'm going to say."

She turned the corner, following the signs to the airport.

"Do you think they'll rebuild then?" Kate asked him.

"I don't know. They seem to think they're in their twenties, that they'll be young hippies forever, live forever, and I don't know what it's going to take to change their minds. Maybe this is a good wake-up call for them. Maybe this will help them cut those ties, dig up their roots, and spread out a little bit. Maybe they will come down to San Diego. Although, it's going to be a lot more expensive."

"Maybe they could move in with us?" Kate asked. She wasn't excited about the idea, but she was willing to help at least until Deidre and Larry could get their bearings. "Just for a year or two, until they figure out what they want to do?"

"Well, I'll tell you one thing, if there's no insurance proceeds, their choices are going to be limited. And one of the first things I'm going to do is check their policy and make sure they get every penny that's coming to them. Insurance companies often try to scam unsuspecting homeowners into thinking they have less coverage than they have. I've heard stories."

"Yeah, I have too, Tyler."

"And if this is some kind of a crime investigation, it's probably going to delay things."

"I think it takes a month or two or maybe longer for the insurance company to settle up. They have to get prices and—"

"Well, the building structure probably wouldn't be a big deal, but those paintings, I just don't know how they'd value them. They're her paintings. They're probably going to say she could always duplicate them, which is stupid, but that's what they're going to say. They are worth probably more than the insurance is going to cover. But it all depends on how they insured them. I just hope to God my mom didn't let it lapse. She's known for being a little absent-minded with the bills now and then."

That worried Kate. Her silence seemed to be a red flag for Tyler.

"You okay?"

"You raise some worrisome points, Tyler. I didn't even think of all the questions I had about the fire and how they're going to go forward. I didn't even think about them not having proper insurance. And you're right, that does limit what they can do."

"I'm not going to worry about it until I know I have to. My biggest problem, my biggest job is going to be convincing my stubborn mother that she could paint down in San Diego. She just might not be painting a lot of trees, rose gardens, rivers, and woods. She might be starting a new chapter in her career, painting beach scenes, the Coronado Village area, landscaping around the little cottages down by the beach. I think she'd like it. I really do. It's a beautiful area, lots of color, and I think it would be good for her."

Kate agreed and added, "Maybe it'll be a new chapter for all of us."

At the drop off, Kate hugged Tyler at the same time the kids surrounded him. He picked up little Kendall, who was crying.

"Don't go, Daddy. I don't want you to go," she said, sniffling.

"Listen, Sweetheart. I'm putting you in charge! You watch your big brothers, and you keep track of how many times they argue, okay? It's your job to monitor them."

"Okay, Daddy."

"Before you know it, I'll be back."

She nodded her head as Tyler handed her back to Kate. The boys gave him one last leg squeeze. Kate kissed him hard on the lips, wanting to make a lasting impression. She watched him walk away, surrounded by their three children. That long sexy gait of his carried him away, as he slung the duty bag over his shoulder and disappeared into the bowels of the airport.

It was always the same. Each time, she wondered if it would be the last time she'd ever see him. She tried to soak up everything she could about watching his backside vanish into the crowds. In the meantime, she would pray, hold her breath more often as she thought about him, and attend to their three kids.

Like he'd said earlier, no reason to worry until there was something to worry about. Until then, the goal was to just live with gusto, pray for a tomorrow, and get ready for a stellar reunion with all the stars and stripes and the marching band. It was all about celebrating the now for as long and intensely as possible.

And never let fear, mistrust, or worry interfere with their love.

CHAPTER 4

H IS MOM AND dad met him at the Portland International Airport. When the plane left San Diego, it finished its final ascent into the skies just about the time it had to begin its decent. The flight was slightly longer than an hour, and Tyler really didn't have much opportunity to get properly settled before they were on the ground.

"Great to see you, Tyler!" his mother said, grabbing him and placing a big kiss on his cheek, while his dad patted his back and waited his turn to give a hug.

"Boy, son, you bulked up. You lifting weights again?"

"Oh, we kind of have a healthy competition going on. I'm training some new medics, and I've been taking them out for runs and showing them the ropes. They think they can kick my butt, but at thirty-seven, I'm still stronger than almost all of those guys in their early twenties. I love showing them that, too, and since they have to go through extensive PT, I've been doing it right alongside them. So yeah, I guess if I ever stopped being a SEAL, I could go do WWE or something."

Both his parents laughed. Tyler noticed his mother had dark circles under her eyes, and her cheeks looked a little gaunt. He knew she probably hadn't slept since the night of the fire.

"Let me take that," his dad said, grabbing Tyler's duty bag.

"Nah, Dad, I got it. I know you can do it, but let me take this."

"All right, but just so you know, I work out too."

Tyler stopped and examined him from head to toe and back up to his head again. "God damn, Dad. You have been working out. I can tell."

"Well, probably not like you, but we go to the senior center."

"I do Aquarobics while he does the machines," his mother added.

"Good for you. You know what they say, either use it or lose it. None of us are getting any younger."

Downstairs, they walked through the pedestrian traffic area, over to the parking garage, where his father had driven his vintage 1969 Volkswagen bus. It was his father's prized possession and was inoperable during most of Tyler's growing up years. But his parents had lots of stories about that van, the places it went, and the romantic escapades his parents used to have. As a young kid, it used to embarrass him. He figured that's where his sister got her jive to write romance novels, although she never wrote about the sixties or seventies.

The moss green colored van was shiny, having been freshly polished, and stored in the garage. It had a cream white top with little moon roof windows along the ceiling, and the original plastic straps instead of armrests on the doors in the second and third rows. His father had souped it up a bit with a new engine several years ago, but during the first years they had it, the van was legendary for holding up a stream of twenty to thirty cars as it tried to climb the hills leading to their house.

"Would you look at this thing? It's perfect still. You must be out there every day washing and waxing it," Tyler remarked.

"He loves it more than me, I think," said his mother.

"Aw, I call foul. Deidre, you know that's not right. The only reason I've kept this van is because of the wonderful memories we made in it. And still make in it too, I might add." He winked at his son.

Tyler put his hands over his eyes and then covered his ears and shook his head. "La, la, la, la, la, la. I didn't hear that. I don't want to hear that. TMI, TMI."

When he looked up at his folks, they were beaming from ear to ear. He hoped that, as the years went by, he and Kate could have that kind of a relationship. His father adored his mother, allowing her to paint and be the free spirit that she was in her heart, while he was the main bread winner as a school principal.

He was one of the most revered members of the Portland public school system and had passed up the opportunity to become superintendent several times, because he didn't want to be removed from the classroom, which is where he developed the love of teaching. A very tall and handsome man with bright azure blue eyes, his white hair and salt-and-pepper beard made for a striking combination. He often disarmed people just by the way he intently studied them, and his casual, conversational dialect was pleasant and often welcoming.

Of all the people in Portland, Tyler could not understand how anybody in their right mind would ever wish either one of his parents harm. He figured the arson must have been an opportunity crime, someone who wanted to make a statement. He knew it couldn't be personal.

His dad fired up the old bus, and they headed out from the parking garage, twisted around several turns, and finally made it to the freeway for their approach to the hills overlooking Portland where the house was located. Before he turned to start climbing the road, Tyler stopped him. "Can you drive me by the warehouse?"

"Well, we haven't been given the okay yet. They are still doing their investigation, removal of evidence, and some minor cleanup. The city has to make the streets and the surrounding areas passable. So there've been road crews out there, and they've had it barricaded off. But we can go try if you want. Is that okay with you, Deidre?" He looked at his wife and asked.

"Doesn't hurt to try, Larry." She turned to address Tyler. "They might not allow it. So don't get your hopes up."

As Mr. Gray turned away from Palatine Road, which wound up the hill, he headed toward the Columbia River, which soon became a mixed-use neighborhood of residence-converted flats, businesses, and industrial warehouses.

Tyler asked, "So have they told you anything new?"

"Not a thing. We're just letting them take their time, do what they need to do. We don't want to get in their way, but yeah, it would be nice to know. My insurance office already has the claim. I'm supposed to get a call and an appointment in one to two days, they said. He said he was going to try to go over and take some pictures, but I doubt they're going to let him in."

"Well, Dad, you want to be there when he takes his pictures and does the inspection. And you want to overhear the conversation he has with the fire marshal or inspector. You just don't want any surprises, okay? One of the things you have to realize is that these adjusters make their money by keeping the claims low. One of our SEAL buddies had parents who had a fire, and the adjuster came over the next day and wrote them a check, which was great, except that it only covered about a third of the expenses of rebuilding their house. They learned too late that, had they not accepted that check, they would've been able to apply for more and were entitled to quite a bit more. So don't jump on everything just because they offer you some money."

"Yes, our neighbor told us that as well. Funny thing, our insurance agent said that the first offer is usually the best offer," his mother said with a sly smile.

Tyler shook his head. "That's BS, Mom. You know that, right?"

"We do now. Thanks, Son," said his dad.

Several blocks away from the fire scene, the streets were blocked off with bright orange barricades. Several of Portland's police and public safety group manned the barricades and only allowed rescue and city workers inside. The place looked like an anthill to Tyler, there were so many vehicles driving around. People were consulting in small clusters of two or three, power crews were restoring telephone and electrical lines, and even the gas company was there. A large debris box had been ordered and sat right in front of Tyler's parents' former warehouse. There were several other debris boxes further down the street until he could see barricades at the end, about eight or ten blocks away.

They were stopped by a policeman who leaned into the car, his arm on the windowsill. "Can I help you?"

Tyler noticed the policeman was searching the inside of the vehicle, probably trying to assess whether or not the passengers had weapons or some kind of contraband.

His dad spoke up. "We're the Grays, and the warehouse over there is—was—my wife's gallery that belongs to us, or used to anyway. My son is up here from San Diego, and we wanted to see if we could just walk around the outside a little bit, not interfere with your work at all but just see how bad it is. We haven't been able to do that yet." Tyler watched the policeman frown.

Then he pulled out a list of owners' names and addresses and put a check mark next to theirs.

"I have you on the list. Can I see some identification, please?"

Both of Tyler's parents reached out the window with their IDs. Tyler brought out his special forces' ID and handed it to the policeman as well.

"Oh, so we have ourselves a regular hero here. Is that it?"

"Not really, sir," said Tyler.

At the same time, Tyler's folks agreed with the policeman. His mother added, "He sure is. Very proud of him, sir. He's up here from San Diego to just help us sort this out."

"Well, I can allow you to park down the street in the makeshift parking lot, but you're going to have to walk, and you can't really enter onto the property. You can just stay in the street and take a look at it from the street level. I can't let you go into the back or walk through the building. And if a delivery or energy or rescue truck shows up, you're to give him complete right away, is that understood?"

"Thank you, sir," Tyler barked back at him from the second seat. "We appreciate that. No worries here. We're not going to interfere with anything."

"Well, Son, I figured as much. Be sure to check back with me before you go, so I can mark you off. Now, if you go down about a block and a half, you'll see several cars parked in a row. Please park right behind that first line of cars, and I'll meet you back here as soon as you can make it down the street."

"Sir," Tyler asked him again. "Is there a senior fire inspector or incident commander available here? Do you see anybody in position of leadership here that we might be able to speak with and ask questions of?"

The policeman scanned the area, squinting as he looked farther down the street. "I don't see them. They were here earlier for a briefing. We had news media here, of course, as you might imagine. The mayor was here, and I understand the governor's going to be here later on today. But no, I don't see him right now."

"Thanks, Man."

"No problem, Son."

They drove to the parking lot, Mr. Gray not quite obeying the policeman. Instead of parking in the grassy field, which was dusty with whirls of sooty debris blown all over, covering windshields and everything else in front of them, he went an extra block and parked at a gas station that was closed. They left the car there, locking it up.

The policeman let them through, and slowly, they walked over broken glass, pieces of metal strips, partially charred tree branches, sooty leaves, and some concrete rubble and fallen trees. Several of the rescue vehicles had driven over these, so scoring the whole area were dusty tire tracks of the engines and city vehicles.

The trees were all gone. The denuded fire site made the burned city blocks look like a scene in hell. The fire tended to equalize every color that previously inhabited this area, and it had been a fairly colorful area too. But now everything was black or dark gray; nothing in this several block long area survived. They did find a couple birds that somehow had gotten trapped in the smoke, and a squirrel tried to hop in front of them, appearing to be slightly injured. Its tail was scorched on one side, knocking his balance off.

"Was anybody living here at the time?" Tyler asked them.

"They said not. I know there were some lofts farther down they were working on, but I don't think they were ready to go on the market yet," his mother said. "They're standardizing this whole area and changing some of their zoning requirements, so my understanding is that the project took a lot longer than they expected to fully develop. And a lot of the people who own warehouse space here weren't really excited about a large yuppie population moving in. But what can you do?" she said, shrugging her shoulders.

When they stood in front of what would've been the entrance to the warehouse, they noticed the plastic fencing that had surrounded the property had melted and looked like marshmallow sauce on an ice cream sundae. No windows or doors or anything of any significant-sized timber remained. It was all a pile of ash, long ribbons of grey reaching to the sky. Everything was soaked, flooded. Several rolls of straw that Tyler had recognized from flooding on freeways in the San Diego area were diverting the black sooty water from the lot and down into the storm drain and gutters. The air still had an acrid bitter scent to it, even with the wind and promise of further rains. It would take weeks before that would go away, he knew.

He watched his mother stare at what used to be her beautiful gallery. Suddenly, her tears erupted over her lower lids and silently trickled down her cheeks. Tyler thought about all the work and the love she had put into those paintings that now were gone forever. He decided to find something positive and not dwell on the bad.

"Mom, at least you weren't here working late. I know you like to do that sometimes, so count your lucky stars."

"He's right, Deidre," said Tyler's dad.

"You're healthy. You aren't injured. This is just stuff. I know it's horrible to think about it that way, but the finger of God touched this place, and he decided you had too much. It was time to get rid of it. I think he knew you were going to putz around with it and it would take you a long time to decide what to keep, what to store. So he gave you a hand. He just touched the building, and he took it all."

As he said this, he noted his mother gasped and inhaled sharply, shaking and trying to grasp how this could be a good thing. Maybe he'd gone too far. Maybe she wasn't ready.

He wrapped his arm around her shoulders, placed his cheek next to hers, and whispered, "It's all good, Mom. There's a new future out there. And I'm going to help you find it."

She let him hold her for several minutes before she could respond. He once again felt the frailty of her body, yet she stood firm, heels dug in, not wavering. Her steel and resolve began to show. He withdrew his embrace, allowing her the freedom to build on what she'd started.

"I just have such a hard time saying goodbye to so much. I have never lost so much. I feel so violated. Just devastated. Oh, I wonder how we are going to deal with all this, this hurt, all these decisions we must make. I just, I'm—I'm overwhelmed. I think once I get past that, I'll cry myself to sleep for about two weeks. And then, I think I'll be all right. But this, this is not what I ever expected would happen. And I'm still asking myself why."

He was proud of her, of her strength. His dad's loving arms encircled her, whispering encouragements, patting her back, and giving her little kisses at the side of her face. She was holding up, all things considered, well.

"Mom, this isn't anything you can't recover from. Like I said, God took all this stuff away, so you could start a new life. The only thing we need to figure out is what that's going to look like. But thank goodness you're okay."

CHAPTER 5

K ATE BROUGHT THE kids home after dropping Tyler off at the airport, so they could work on their chores and Grady could finish his homework. Oliver had books to read but no formal homework yet. She set Kendall down to watch some animal movies while her two older children busied themselves with their work.

She put her notes from the catering class in their office, stored in a binder along with all the other research she'd been doing. They had considered several different options as far as their future—a future after Tyler left the team. She knew he was beginning to feel they had reached that point. All the SEAL wives knew either age, injury, family priorities, or sheer exhaustion would force their men to leave the job that they all knew was perfect for them, tailor-made for these strong warriors and big-hearted guys. Tyler had put in more time than most, since the average was a "one and done" tour of six years.

At one point, they'd seriously considered moving back to Sonoma County after his retirement, but since the kids were involved in so many San Diego activities and were used to playing with the other SEAL kids, they thought it would be too disruptive for the family. Now with the possibility of some kind of different future for Tyler's parents, they would have to consider things they hadn't before, including buying a house large enough for all of them to live in.

But Kate discovered she'd developed a deep love of entertaining and wanted to try her hand at setting up a catering company or a lunch wagon that served high-end office workers downtown and in Old Town. She envisioned making healthy sandwiches, soups, and salads.

With the heavy Hispanic population in San Diego, there was no shortage of taco trucks. Kate hoped to also have a full menu of ethnic foods but wanted to try her hand at cooking them in alternative ways: low-calorie, meatless, keto-type recipes and juices.

The class she had taken in Los Angeles on Saturday had really piqued her interest. She'd been dreaming about her new business venture, making it almost impossible for her to sleep. So while Tyler tossed about in bed, focused on his parents and the fire, Kate had dreamed about her future. Was this wrong, uncaring, or too self-centered?

No, she thought. It was her way to safeguard the future for all of them. She was happiest building things, creating a sustainable income stream they could rely on, and planning something that she enjoyed.

She decided to give Devon Dunn a call since Devon and her husband owned a winery and lavender farm up in her old stomping grounds, Sonoma County. They operated it as a wedding center, which was by far the most profitable portion of the business. Kate liked the idea of perhaps purchasing a piece of property down in San Diego or the Coronado area. She could also picture a larger home with a beautiful garden setting where she could Airbnb the property and make it a destination wedding venue. Since their budget would be limited, she considered that they'd probably have to look for heavy fixers.

Devon picked up on the first ring.

"Kate, how's it going?"

Kate could hear activity in the background. It sounded like she had a crowd and had picked up the phone in their large rental hall.

"Did I catch you in the middle of an event?"

"Well, yes, but I have a couple of minutes before I must be front and center. Hosting a silent auction and benefit luncheon for one of the private schools, raising money for their sports program. So, go ahead, I'm all yours for about five."

"Thanks. I'm doing well, although Tyler has flown up to Portland to be with Larry and Deidre—I don't know if you've heard, but their gallery burned down Friday night. They suspect it's arson, but there were also quite a few demonstrations in the downtown area, so we don't really know whether this was a satellite demonstration or just troublemakers.

But the fire inspector is certain that it is arson. And it took out another eight or ten buildings, even a paint company."

"This is the first I'm hearing of it. Nick has been to that gallery. I think they even might have had a work party before we got together. I'm so sorry, Kate. They must be devastated. And she has such beautiful paintings. Did she lose very many?"

"Yes, I believe she said it was around forty. Over half of them were paintings she never intended to sell, just kept for herself or to pass down to the family. That's the most heartbreaking part of it. And also, they loved putting together that center, housing other artists, and having events there. Kind of like what you do except on a much smaller scale and for the artsy crowd. It's part of their lifestyle, and now we don't know what their future holds. We don't know if they have the money to rebuild or if they even should. There're lots of decisions we're making."

"I have been hearing some of these reports about Portland. What a shame. Such a fun city to visit. All those quaint little shops and the bookstore. What's it called?"

"Powell's?"

"Yes, that's it. Great restaurants. Lots of churches, as I recall, and movie theaters. Beer halls. It's a city that even in the rain it's fun to be out walking in. Lovely rose gardens, wild rhododendrons, and views of the beautiful Columbia river, all the river traffic. Now there's crime and homelessness spiraling out of control. Not enough personnel and police and fire to protect the public. I don't know—I just don't know if I want to go see it and experience what's been happening up there lately. The news pictures are horrible. Do you feel safe?"

"Not any more, Devon. Tyler's been working on his parents to move down to San Diego."

Devon was quiet on her end of the phone. Finally, she added, "So I guess you are no longer considering coming up here and helping us with the winery?"

They'd had serious discussions about buying into Nick and Devon's complex, perhaps moving there and becoming partners. The fire had changed everything.

"Well, that's partly what I wanted to talk to you about. I think that scenario is probably a long shot at this point. But we don't really know.

I've been taking some classes and researching the catering business. I kind of like the idea of starting a food truck and creating healthy foods, an alternative to all the lunch wagons we have here. Some of the big office buildings who can't all go out to lunch or bring in their food would love gourmet, healthy foods, juices, maybe soups. I really think I could make a go of it. What do you think, Devon?"

"Well, I love to cook, but I don't think having a catering truck or a lunch wagon would be anything I'd want to do, but who knows? I think it's a good idea. And there are probably a lot of very health-conscious people down there. You might have a winner there, Kate. Although, I still think having a place, an event site, and then doing catering would make you more money. But that's just me."

"You think so? We can't do anything like what you have."

"We have the winery, and we have the lavender farm, but mostly because Nick inherited it from his sister. Otherwise, I'm not sure we could have pulled it off. A tragedy-turned-miracle. But, oh my gosh, it's so much work. It's wonderful work. And it's been good for the whole family to be involved, but the events and the ecotourism we're doing now pays much better. It's sort of an expensive hobby, I guess, the winery production is. Zak and Amy up in Healdsburg probably are doing a little bit better as far as that goes. But they're smack in the middle of Dry Creek Valley, world famous for outstanding wines and sort of on the highway for the wine tourism industry. We've had our setbacks as far as the winery and the lawsuits. But I think we're on firm ground now. But expanding the winery is so expensive, and it's hard to calculate market trends. You plant and then don't have a decent harvest for seven years!"

"Ouch! I get it."

"But tell me how you came to this idea of a catering truck."

"Well, when I was sitting in class and they were going over business models, profit and loss and proforma statements, and all the different food-related businesses that one could try, I just got really excited about the idea. And it's not anything I ever expected to do."

"It's a calling. It really is. Very artistic, in a way, like gardening. You don't know what you'll get, but you love experimenting with things, making things beautiful. Think of the people you'd serve, who I think would spend good money to eat more healthy. Not everyone is satisfied with a deep green milkshake for lunch!"

Kate had to laugh. "And all the burping and farting afterwards that would drive the office batty."

"You're right about that."

"But seriously, Devon, I'd love to come up and shadow you for a while. Maybe bring the kids if it isn't too much? We could come up during Thanksgiving or Easter break when they're all out of school?"

"Sure, anytime. School breaks are some of our busiest times. I'll put Oliver and Grady to work. Customers love seeing kids in these events. It's great training for customer service skills, and I'm sure Nick could put them to good use out in the fields too. Depending on when you come, we could be doing pruning or the crush or tying off some of the vines, weeding, I think they'd enjoy driving up and down the rows in the tractor with Nick and the girls."

"Oh, I think they'd love it. Kendall is going to be a bit of a handful, but I think she'd enjoy it too."

"Do you have any specific dates in mind?" Devon asked her.

"No, not yet. I want to wait until Tyler gets home to finish the discussions we've started. Don't want to plan something he's not completely behind."

"Sure. That's wise."

"And now, we have to talk about his parents and see what is what about their insurance and whether or not they're going to rebuild. It may be that, if they have enough of a settlement, they could buy their own place down here. But prices are rather high compared to Portland. There's just a lot of things we have to consider. But I mainly wanted to tell you that I'm interested and I'd love it if you could mentor me and show me the ropes, especially around the Airbnb."

"I'd be happy to, Kate. And you don't even have to come up here. I can show you everything I do with a Zoom call. You could get your computer out, and I could help you get set up online at some of the places I advertise in. It's really very simple. The time-consuming part is being connected to your computer and always making sure you get back to people right away. That's where I think a lot of businesses fail."

"Well, I'm glad to hear things have settled down and are going well.

I hope we can make it a family trip. I know Tyler would love to talk to Nick about his detachment. It's a big question in his mind, whether he could find something he loves as much as being on that team. We all know that the more times they deploy, the greater the likelihood they'll get injured or hurt or possibly worse. We always worry about that, don't we?"

"Oh, I remember those days. I probably wasn't the most supportive wife. I think Kyle still blames me for Nick retiring so soon. But it was the right choice. No way could I handle this by myself. And I still sell real estate as well. With the girls, the center, the winery, the lavender farm, and all the advertising, invoicing, and personnel issues I have to take care of, Nick winds up monitoring and working with the seasonal employees. It's an eighty-hour week for each of us. I just don't think there would've been a way for us to survive after all those lawsuits and problems with the neighbor unless he was fully detached. It was the right choice for us. But I'm sure Nick would love to talk to Tyler about it. It's a big decision. I know Nick misses the guys terribly."

Kate agreed. "You know, I think if we stayed in the Coronado San Diego area, Tyler may not feel so bad about the detachment."

"Yes, but there's the other side of that too. He'll see all his former teammates getting together and talking about their missions, and he's no longer a part of it. That could be frustrating as well. There's a lot of things to consider. Does he have any idea of what he wants to do other than the catering gig?"

"He says he'd like to help me. I think he could do anything he set his mind to. I'm just glad he's going to allow me to try something. And we'll have to wait and see how everything shakes out. But I'm so lucky that at least he's considering doing a project with me."

"Well, you know my opinion of these guys—they're the best of the best. And just because they're no longer on the teams, that ethos and that way of looking at the world and the way they treat people doesn't go away. I'd say you've got the best of both worlds if he wants to help you. I'd let him come on up here and explore it in earnest. And, Kate, I will do my very best to make it look fun and to enable him to fully engage. That would be my honor."

They ended the call with Kate agreeing to keep Devon and Nick informed and to touch base more often.

Next, Kate gave her mother a call, catching up on things the children were doing. And then she brought up the gallery fire in Portland.

"Oh dear, I saw the riots on the news, but I didn't know it had spread to their area. Deidre must be heartbroken," her mother said. "I just don't know what I'd do if something like that happened to us. Have they determined what caused the fire?"

"The fire inspector thinks it's arson. And it started at their warehouse and moved on down the street. They were able to stop it eventually, but it did a lot of damage to the neighborhood. Tyler's up there now going over all the insurance information and helping them file paperwork. At least he wants to be involved in talking with the adjuster. He's a bit anal about that score."

"I think that's a good idea. I'm glad he's able to and wasn't overseas. That should be a lot of help to them. What do you think they'll do?"

"You mean, will they rebuild?" Kate asked.

"Yes, do you think they'll build another gallery or maybe construct apartments or something else on that land? What do you think?"

"Tyler's dad is going to be seventy next year, and he's past retirement age, but he really likes what he's doing, and the district isn't enforcing it, so I think if they were to do anything drastic, he'd probably retire. Then they might have some additional choices. Tyler and I would love to have them come down here, so they could be closer to the grandkids."

Her mother went quiet then continued. "Oh, I envy that. We're just not ready to make that kind of a move, but it would be nice to be closer to you. I don't know if your dad will ever retire. He's really driven."

"We're just thinking about everything." Kate felt the need to change the subject.

"And on another note, I went to a class in Los Angeles on Saturday. It's a series of lectures about forming a food industry business, like for people wanting to do catering, specialty restaurants, bakeries, or setting up some kind of a lunch truck. And the idea really intrigues me. I'm seriously thinking I'd like to try that."

"A lunch wagon. Really?"

"Yeah. What do you think?"

"I think you'd do great with that, Kate. You're such a good cook, and I know you'd enjoy doing catering, but it's a lot of work. I thought you were considering moving back up here, helping out with Nick and Devon's winery."

"We were. Still might. And you're right. It is a lot of work. But now things have shifted slightly. It might be hard on the kids to uproot them. I'd like to do what Nick and Devon do, but do it down here, along with the truck. Mom, there are so many possibilities. Now I want to fully explore all of them! Probably not on such a grand scale like they do, but maybe purchase something in need of work, fix it up, and create a venue. Make a wedding center out of it, create beautiful, lush gardens, and do the catering around that. Possibly rent the house out for international travelers and do a modified Airbnb with catering as an option."

"Wow, your head is really spinning."

"I got my eyes opened at this seminar. Tyler and I have talked, and he's open to the idea of maybe helping me. But nothing's set in stone yet. And we certainly have to figure out what his parents are going to do first."

"You know my theory about all that, Kate." Her mother began to sound stern.

Here comes the lecture.

"You should put yourselves first. Don't change your plans because of Tyler's parents. Of course you're wonderful to consider that, but you have to live your lives. They've had a wonderful life, but yours is just at the beginning stages. Those kids are going to grow up fast, Kate. If it's something you could do together, I don't see how Tyler could stay on the teams."

"No, you're right. He's considering not re-upping. He's thirty-seven. It's time. It's time for somebody else to be a Boy Scout."

Her mother laughed. It warmed Kate's heart to hear that. She wished her mother was closer and was able to spend more time with her three children, but as she so aptly said herself, she was pursuing their own dreams, and right now, staying in Santa Rosa was what they wanted to do.

"Mom, I have to run, but I just wanted to let you know, and I'll update you as soon as I have some news. If you think of anything that would be helpful in dealing with the insurance company—I know Dad has had to deal with insurance companies for his business—we'd be grateful."

"I surely will. How's your sister Gretchen been doing? She still enjoying San Diego?"

"You would think with all the news, she'd feel she got out of Portland in time. But you're not going to believe this, Mom. She's actually thinking of moving back. Trace is also thinking of detaching from the teams, but they're just in the early stages of looking at it. She never sold her house there on the hill. I don't know why she'd want to move back there, but she's considering it. And I guess Trace has an offer from a company where a lot of the employees are former SEALs or Special Forces guys. That's life. Things change."

"I don't have to remind you that if you ever wanted to do your catering business here in your hometown in Sonoma County, your dad and I would help as much as we could. Just let us know."

"Thanks, Mom. Love you."

"I love you ten times more, Kate."

CHAPTER 6

A S TYLER'S DAD drove back through the warehouse neighborhood, rounding the damage site by two or three blocks away and looping down to the waterfront, he could see the homeless encampments. These camps encroached on the patios of restaurants getting ready to serve late lunch/early dinner, small business manufacturing companies and stores where employees would have to thread between a line of tents with the required thirty-six inches apart from each other, which was the law. He saw a group of school children coming home from one of the local elementary schools, walking past derelicts and drunks, one little boy even pushing a syringe into the gutter with his tennis shoe. It broke Tyler's heart that there were so many addicted, hurting people. It also broke his heart that so many innocent people were forced to be part of this community. He had to say something.

"Geez, Dad. I'm not so sure I want you driving. Can you pull over and let me get behind the wheel for a bit?"

"Tyler, we've been putting up with this for several years now. They don't really care about me. They're going after expensive cars."

"Dad! This *is* an expensive car. Have you priced it lately?"

Tyler's mother looked over at her husband, "He's right, Larry. Why don't you let him drive?"

Tyler could tell his dad was under stress, because he never swore. But this time he let out a string of words he'd never heard him speak before. Rather than making note of it, he ignored it, opened the door, and traded places with the older man. That relieved Tyler's own worry and tension, but just a little.

"I had no idea things had gotten this bad. And, Mom, you were coming down here at night by yourself?"

"No, Silly. Larry would come with me. Or I'd meet one of the other artists down here. I would go out, have a cigarette in the backyard, and watch the sculptor throw some pots on the wheel. He worked out in the backyard at night, even in the light rain. We just didn't think anybody would be interested in our property. We were always kind to these people."

From behind the seat, Tyler's dad leaned over to him. "She brings sandwiches down for the guys that are on the corner asking for work or food. She brings them chocolate milk sometimes, and you know she's nice to them. We aren't the problem here."

The scene was all too familiar to Tyler. Should he tell them about how many innocent people were being abused all over the world? He just didn't expect to see it in the United States. And it really bothered him. There was something happening that was eating away at the very fabric and soul of the country.

"It's always that way with people who prey on innocent people. I understand why they're trying to make a living by panhandling here. Housing is expensive, and if they're a mess medically and we don't have hospitals or housing for them, they're going to want to stay on the street. Besides, I think a lot of them trust the street better than they trust our own government to set up something for them. But there's an element I can see here that's growing, based on all the tags I'm seeing on the buildings. Some young punks have moved in, muscling for space and control. I see it in how they look at me when I drive past them. This isn't a healthy environment at all. In fact, I'll bet if you really got into trouble here, it would take quite a while for the police to show up. In that amount of time, you might be dead, both of you."

He looked in his rearview mirror and made eye contact with his dad. He didn't flinch but stared right into his eyes. He was hoping his dad would take it to heart.

"What you are saying is we should only come down here in daylight, not at night?" his mother asked him.

"Mom, and this is the God's honest truth, I don't ever want to see you down here, especially by yourself, at any time of the day. I had no idea it looked like this. I feel like I've been living under a rock. This is horrible. This is a war zone. And I think I'm qualified to tell you what one looks like."

Tyler's father inserted himself into the conversation.

"It's only gotten bad the last couple of years since the pandemic, Tyler. It's just everybody's so stressed and city services are maxed out. We're the lucky ones. We have a house that's free and clear. We had this nice gallery. I've got a good job, and your mom makes money on her paintings and teaching. At the time, this was all we could afford as far as a large warehouse building. But, Tyler, I hear what you're saying, and maybe we should consider when we rebuild to relocate in a better neighborhood."

"Well, that would be a start. I want to see what the rest of Portland looks like and I want to see what your neighborhood looks like now. Is it my imagination or has everything just gone downhill?"

"You haven't been here for, I think, over two years, Tyler. No one has been doing much traveling," his mother said. "We're just digging ourselves out as a city from the pandemic.

"Except that's not true. I've been traveling. I've been going to lots of places. There's no sense of safety here. There's no organized protection. They had more police guarding the barricade to keep looters out of the fire site than I see in the rest of this district. Honestly, I'm surprised that there isn't more of an objection to the way this is being handled."

"Well, you know our political views, and with my family's deep roots in the Quaker community, we thought we were helping by non-violently just going about our own business. We thought that would help the community better than to do anything else. We were investing in the city's future. Other than that, there really isn't anything we can do."

"You can vote, right?"

"Tyler," his dad said from behind him, "we aren't into social action—"

"Dad, voting is not social action. Voting is making your voice heard. And no, I'm not saying I want you to protest or march or do an anti-march protest to what they're doing. I just want you to help this neighborhood by voting in the people who will keep you protected. And it has nothing to do with politics. It has nothing to do with any political party. It's just wrong. They don't have Republicans or Democrats in Nigeria, Venezuela, or the Caribbean. They have different names for their different parties. That's not the problem. It's the lack of people being willing to step up and protect the innocent."

Tyler's chest was shaking. He was so angry. All of this had been going on for the past couple of years, and he had been completely unaware of it, wouldn't have known about it until something like the fire happened. He kicked himself for not checking on his parents more often. He was certainly going to check in with the Bone Frog Group, a private security and protection company. This part of the States was going to start looking like what he'd seen in Brazil, where women and children went shopping in blacked out Suburbans with bulletproof windows and doors, accompanied by armed guards with semi-automatic rifles. That wasn't the country he expected to see here, and he didn't want it to be the future of Oregon or anywhere.

He gripped the steering wheel and softly apologized. "I have friends who gave their lives so that we could be safe in this country. It feels like such a waste when I see this. There is no excuse for it. I can't insert myself here because we're constrained against that. But somebody's got to do something, and I don't like the signs. I really don't want you to rebuild here. Please, if you can just promise me that, I'll shut up."

"I guess we should have told you. But honestly, we thought it would get better now that people are going back to work and trying to reconnect with their lives. The pandemic appears to be subsiding, hopefully."

Tyler looked into the face of his mother and realized that she was trying to help him, but there wasn't a blasted thing she could do.

And she didn't even realize it.

The downtown financial district of Portland was cold and windy, the sun being blocked by a combination of rain clouds and tall skyscrapers. It felt to him like San Francisco, without the beautiful blue San Francisco Bay and sunlit, colorful bridges spanning it. Again, there were gang tags, streets littered with trash, and several businesses in a once-thriving downtown that were boarded up. Some posters advertised a resistance movement touting all kinds of different ideologies and theories that Tyler didn't pay any attention to. But although it wasn't as bad as the warehouse district, it still didn't paint a very secure picture to him.

He began to understand the enormity of the problem. He knew he was going to work very hard to get his parents out of the city and get them somewhere where he could check on them and where he felt they'd be safer. He just wouldn't be able to live with himself if something horrible happened to them. Here they were exposed. They probably didn't realize it because the changes had come on so gradually they didn't notice or told themselves it still wasn't as bad as it was elsewhere. It was the frog in the water scenario. By the time the frog realized the water was boiling, it was too late to save himself.

He took Palatine Boulevard winding up the hill in switchbacks until he got to the top. There was a large hospital there, and just down the street from it, facing the Columbia River, was their house.

His mother had always chosen bright colors to paint it, and this year, the color seemed to be golden yellow. It had white trim on the extensive porch. The steps were painted white on their risers, all the trim and the handrails were white, and it looked like they'd reroofed the house with green asphalt shingles.

Parking the van in the garage out back, he followed his mother in through the kitchen door. She gave him a hug as he dropped his duty bag.

"Well, I guess that wasn't exactly the kind of welcome you expected. I'm so sorry, Tyler. I really should have thought about warning you."

"Mom, it's not about me. I'm worried about you and Dad. I'm worried that you're not worried. But look, let's just forget about all this for right now. I think what I'd like to do is lie down, take a little nap, maybe get up, and take a shower. I have a few calls I need to make, and then I'm all yours the rest of the day and the evening."

"When do you want me to schedule the insurance agent to come over and speak to us?" his dad asked, coming in through the doorway.

"Well, I guess the adjuster is probably the one you want to speak to first."

"Oh, our agent says we can go through him. He said it's a very long, detailed process, and he could help streamline it. Grease the skids so to speak," his dad said.

"I'm not sure that's the case. I really want to talk to the adjuster. What the adjuster writes down is what you're going to get, and if he writes down the wrong things, then it's going to make a difference. But one thing you can do is get out your policies and let me look them over when I get done with my nap. Okay?"

"Fair enough."

"I've got to call Kate and let her know I arrived safely, that I've seen the property. Then I have to check in with my LPO just to let him know also what I see here. And finally, I have a couple other friends in the area I'd like to call. Just to touch base. It's been a long time since I've seen them."

"You go right ahead, Son," said his father. "We'll give you some privacy. Come down when you're ready."

He dashed up the stairs, like he had done as a child growing up. He went to the second door on the right, which was his old room, and discovered things had not changed since the last time he'd been here. He had brought Grady to a soccer tournament up in Portland, and the two of them had spent the night in his old room, which impressed Grady no-end. Tyler's trophies were still lined up along the windowsill and in the cabinet his dad had to make to house all the later ones, which kept getting bigger and bigger as his wins increased. Grady was just starting out and had visions of becoming a great soccer player like his dad. It had been a fun father-son event. Tyler let him take home one of the trophies to remember the trip by. Of course, he chose the biggest one, parading it through the airport on their way home.

He stripped out of his clothes and jumped in the shower, feeling that if he could just wash the stench of the fire, the travel, and the community that he'd just driven through, get the sweat out of his armpits, he'd make a lot more sense talking to Kate and Kyle and Bryce and some of the other people he needed to speak with. It was funny how that happened, but often he wouldn't return calls until after he got clean. It was just his thing.

He dialed his wife.

"Hey, Kate, I'm here in my old room, but boy, do I miss you."

She giggled. "Oliver and Kendall are taking a nap, so I'm going to whisper a little bit."

"That sounds kind of sexy."

"You think so? You're chicken to just turn around and come back."

"Well, that's what I want to talk to you about, Kate. I have to make this short because I need to make a few other calls too. But I wanted to let you know first that I got here. Also, I need to tell you this place looks like a war zone. I mean, I've seen villages in Nigeria that look better than that district where she had her gallery. Did you have any idea it was so dangerous here?"

"Not really. I mean, you know I don't dwell on the news. I just make it a point not to because I worry too much, especially if you're overseas. But it's hard to get the perspective, isn't it? You see it on TV, and yeah, it looks horrible, but you're sitting in your living room with your slippers and your flannel nightgown on, and somehow, it doesn't touch you. I can see it affected you. And I'm sorry it's worse than you thought."

"Well, I'm even more convinced than ever that they need to get out of here. They're being a little bit stubborn about it, but I just got here. There's a lot of moving parts. And I really need to speak with a fire inspector and their adjuster. Then I'll kind of get my bearings and be able to tell you how long it's going to take. I can't stay too long, because Kyle wants me back there. But holy crap, I had no idea that Mom and Dad were so vulnerable, and I think they're wrong about the arson."

"You don't think it was arson?" she asked.

"Oh, I think it was arson all right. But those warehouses that burned were not derelict buildings at all. They were some of the nicer buildings, the ones where people had come in and refurbished them, turned them into beautiful offices, galleries, studios. It sort of feels like somebody targeted some of the best buildings in the area and left the derelict buildings alone. It just doesn't feel right, Kate."

"I get it. Well, I trust your judgment, Tyler. You know better than anyone else in our family about that sort of thing, unfortunately. Am I allowed to share any of this with the other wives?"

Tyler was glad she asked permission. It was something they had forged together, this protocol.

"It'll be fine. I'm going to give Kyle a call now, so he'll be in the know. If this turns into a bigger project than I'm hoping it will, I may need some help from some of the guys, but I'm also going to talk to

Colin Riley's old team and see if I can get a read on what's going on downtown. So just hang tight for a few days, maybe two or three at the most, and I'll update you as soon as I have things to tell you. Until then, don't worry."

"Said Tyler never."

She giggled, and it felt good to hear her laugh. Tyler couldn't find the space to return her laughter with some of his own.

Next, he called Kyle but had to leave a message.

"Hey, Kyle, it's Tyler. I just got to Portland. Mom and Dad are fine, but the studio is, well, it's leveled. And I have other concerns I'd like to talk to you about—not leave a message. So give me a call when you get a chance. I think two or three days is what I'm going to need, but one of the things I'm very clear on is that I've got to get my parents out of Portland. This area isn't safe for them any longer. And I have to tell you it reminds me of some of the war zones we've seen overseas. So give me a call back, and let's talk. But everything's fine, no changes in my ETA, and haven't spoken to the inspectors or the insurance people yet, but I need to bounce some things off you, and you're the first person who I think can help me with some advice. Take care. Kiss Christie for me, on the lips."

He smiled, figuring Kyle would get a kick out of that last comment. When he hung up the phone, he knew that his LPO would call him back within the hour unless he was in the middle of a briefing or a meeting of some kind.

Next person he called was his friend Bryce Tanner, a former team guy and former San Diego police officer who had taken over the reins of Colin Riley's Bone Frog Protection Services, now owned by his daughter and daughter-in-law. Bryce had been on a hiring blitz ever since Mr. Riley's death a year ago.

"Hey, Tyler, boy, you're one of the guys I've got on my list to call this month. You interested in getting your separation orders?"

"No, not that. I don't know if you saw it in the news, but did you hear about the warehouse district fires that happened on Friday night?"

"Yeah?"

"Well, my mom's art gallery got burned to the ground. I came up here to help them. The fire investigator is saying it's arson. And I just frankly don't feel very comfortable with Mom and Dad rebuilding in that area or even being in Portland for that matter."

"Jesus Christ. You're fucking going to have to keep your damn mouth shut, Tyler. I've got several guys you used to work with on the team who are about ready to sign a contract with me. They hear you talking like that? They're going to back out. You can't do that to me."

"Well, if they have eyes in their head, they're going to see what I saw. It's an unstable situation. If we walked into a village like that, that's the first conclusion we'd come to. There's no welcome wagon here or people with flags—American flags greeting us or parades or anything like that. Everything looks normal until it all goes to hell, but there're little signs— the tag marks, the trash, the needles, and all the homeless, sort of an underground economy here. I'm just not at all happy with it, and I don't think anybody knows who's living here or what they're doing. It's just awful."

"I agree with you there. Part of that makes what we do a little more lucrative, but yeah, it's gotten pretty bad, I will admit that. Just don't go talking my new recruits out of it, okay, Tyler?"

"Deal. So I got to ask you, who do I need to talk to if I want the straight story on what's happening downtown and over at my mom's old warehouse?"

"Well, there are some really great cops still left in the city. We have a sheriff of a neighboring county that's probably better than the one who has jurisdiction here, but I think the police force and arson investigators on the fire department, they're probably your best guys. Most of them are real senior, and I think they pretty much can be trusted. We don't hold a very tight friendship on purpose, because we don't want to jeopardize their jobs, but I could get you a couple names if you want me to look into it."

"Hey, thanks, Bryce. I don't want to engage in conversation with the wrong person and then find out I started unraveling something I don't want to unravel. I want somebody to tell me the truth. I'm going to do that with the insurance company, but I need to figure out whether or not my parents were targeted in this arson or was their district targeted. And that's an important distinction. It means there's a different degree of safety that's required. I'm trying to figure out whether or not I need help."

"Well, Brother, we never served together on SEAL Team 3, but I got a lot of your buddies here, and we have a rule that we take care of our own. If you need us, you just give me a call, and I'll get some solid guys over. And we're not going to charge you either. I mean our business is good. Too good. You get my drift?"

"I do. So that explains why your offices are in Portland and not in, what?"

"Well, that's getting harder and harder to distinguish, isn't it, Tyler? I have to tell you that important people that have nice things are targets. I can't imagine your parents generating any kind of hatred or scorn against them, but just because of the fact that they are successful, took an old building, and turned it into a work of art, just like perhaps some of the other people there, makes them a target. I wouldn't worry too much about their safety. But I do think you're spot on about keeping them out of that neighborhood. If they were my parents? I wouldn't allow them to rebuild there. And I think things are going to change, but it might take a while."

"Well, my parents are getting up there in their seventies, so ten years won't make any difference to them. But thanks, Bryce, and I'll keep in touch. If you run across somebody you think I ought to talk to, you be sure to let me know. Text me if I don't pick up."

"You got it." He paused, and then added, "You knock up your wife again? You had two, I think it was, the last time?"

"Yeah, we got the two boys, eight and five, and now we have Kendall. She's nearly three."

"So Kate's got her little girl."

"Yes, sir. Otherwise, I'd be raising a small SEAL team. She's got her girl, and we're done."

"Well, good for you. I got two girls in college. I don't think I'm ever going to be able to retire now. After college comes weddings and maybe grandkids. I'm going to be working until I'm eighty years old, Tyler."

"Well, let's just hope things change before then. I got to go, Bryce, because I need to spend some time with the folks, but you take care and thanks for helping me out. I'll return the favor, Brother."

"Roger that, Tyler. Stay safe."

CHAPTER 7

K ATE HAD A visit from her sister, Gretchen, who brought her youngest child, Angela, with her. Angela had been one of their go-to
babysitters over the past year and was a very responsible fourteen-year-
old. Her two older sisters were on their own, both in college.

"Mom gave me the news about Tyler's parents and the warehouse.
God, Kate, that's horrible. Did they find out anything more?" Gretchen
asked her.

Kate noted that her sister had great survival instincts, like a cat landing on all fours after a fall. She'd had some tough years, mostly raising
her three daughters without much help from her first husband, a
professional basketball player who broke just about every rule in
parenting a dad could. She'd moved to Portland when they first got
married to be near his team. Their very public divorce after Tony
Sanders was caught on social media dancing and later dating several
women outside his marriage, including a stripper, had been humiliating
for Gretchen and the girls.

With Gretchen's oldest daughters in college, only Angela was still at
home. When she started high school, Gretchen and Trace moved to
Coronado, ending the commute and long patches away from the family
between his deployments. It was challenging, but her sister adjusted first
with the long-distance marriage and then the relocation and had even
thrived under it all. Kate knew Trace was one of those rare breeds of
man who became a father in every sense of the word to those three girls,
who loved him dearly in return. He was madly in love with Gretchen
and completely devoted to her happiness.

Gretchen was living her happily ever after, just like Kate was.

"I know he arrived safe this afternoon, and he's with his parents. I presume I'm going to hear some more tomorrow or maybe later on tonight. As of the time he called me, he hadn't met any of the fire inspectors or the insurance people yet. So his work is just starting."

Kate motioned to the living room couch and chairs, where they both sat. "You want anything?"

"I'm fine. Thanks." Gretchen was pensive then added, "I'm glad we moved out of Portland when we did. It had been such a great place for kids when they were growing up. Schools were good, and there were so many nice neighborhoods. They have a fantastic Children's Theater, youth symphony, lots of recreation department classes in dance, painting, and music. All that still exists, but now the whole downtown is just a mess. If we still lived there, I wouldn't allow the girls to take the bus like they used to before. Remember, we used to take the bus and go shopping? You came with us on a couple of occasions."

"I do. We could go everywhere by bus. It was very safe."

"Safe. That's what's missing now," Gretchen said, shaking her head. Kate noticed Angela was mum on the subject but looked as though she completely agreed.

"Tyler is going to try to convince them to move down here perhaps."

"I think that's an excellent idea. They must miss you guys and the grands. I don't know why they aren't camped at your doorstep twenty-four seven."

"His mom is so connected, and that gallery has been a great source of joy and inspiration for her. I don't think they ever would have considered leaving or rebuilding elsewhere if it hadn't been for the fire. We'll see. That's what he's helping them do, sort it out."

"They're lucky to have him. Glad he could get time off to do it." Glancing around the room, she noticed one of Mrs. Gray's bright paintings hanging over the fireplace mantle. "Is that one of hers?"

"It is. Beautiful, isn't it? So vibrant, alive. Makes you feel like you're standing in the middle of a tropical garden, doesn't it?" Kate said, admiring the huge painting.

Gretchen agreed. "So what else is new?"

"I have to tell you about this great class I took. It was an exploratory—all the different food, entertainment, and catering businesses that are available these days, everything from restaurants to onsite catering, even showed us a proforma about actually manning a gourmet food truck."

"A food truck? Wow."

"Yes. I'm really excited about it, enough to start looking into it. I've got more research to do, obviously, and Tyler hasn't completely signed off on it yet, as we haven't set up the logistics—you know how he is, planning things over and over again until it's perfect."

"God, Trace is the same way. All those guys are."

"We have to budget carefully, but it's either that or perhaps find a place down here where we could set up a wedding center, do sort of like what Devon and Nick are doing up in Santa Rosa."

"That sounds like fun. I could see you getting one of those vintage school buses and turning it into a lunch truck. Or maybe one of those old vegetable trucks. You remember those things you see occasionally? Mom used to love shopping there, remember?"

"Andy—the fruit produce guy, his name was Andy—used to come through the neighborhood, right?"

"That's right. And he used to flirt with all the housewives when their husbands were at work. But the vegetables were very fresh, and Mom swore by it."

They both laughed. Kate noted Angela rolled her eyes a bit.

"Anyway, there are a lot of things we used to do growing up that simply isn't around anymore, so as I was listening to the lecture about all these different options, I just fantasized on having this catering business and doing really healthy food truck choices, like healthy sandwiches, soups, juices, and some delicious keto, vegetarian, and gluten-free foods as well. I think people would pay a little bit more for good quality foods that help them with their diet or just for good health."

"I'm sold, Kate. I think you could do a great job. Yeah, an old vintage school bus, decorated shabby chic. Something really unusual with pretty curtains in it—maybe put in a table or two."

Kate shook her head. "There are certain health department things that are required, and I can't really have a restaurant on wheels, but I could set up tables outside and cater that way. I'm going to spend some time with Devon and Nick and really investigate all of that. Of course, first, we have to figure out what Tyler's parents are going to do. If we can get them down here and they can afford to buy, I think it's really the best solution."

"You're right, Sis. It's no place for them any longer. Too dangerous."

Kate wanted to include Angela in the conversation. "How's school, Angela?" she asked.

"Good. I made the varsity volleyball team, and I decided to quit basketball and just focus on volleyball. In the spring, I'm going to join a traveling team, so I get lots of exposure to college coaches."

"Good for you. Where do you want to go to school?"

"Well, San Diego State would be great, and they have a huge volleyball program. But I think anything on the West Coast here would be good for me. I'm not exactly sure what I'll be majoring in, getting my college paid for and playing volleyball are top of my list. I'll figure it out. Probably some kind of business or communications major."

"Well, if you're going to stay in the area and I do this food truck thing, maybe you can do some student research, come work for me part-time, maybe get school credit. I don't want to interfere with your team or family life, but we could sort of learn together, if you're up to it. I'll bet you'd whip your aunt pretty good in business. Probably teach me a few things," said Kate.

"What do you think of that, Angela?" Gretchen asked her.

She shrugged. "Sounds good. When are you going to start?"

"Oh, we're just making dreams, but maybe early next year if we can get the funds together to get the truck or buy the building. We're still looking at which way we want to go."

The two sisters caught up on other family business. Clover had met a nice boy from Colorado, and Gretchen expected there would be an announcement of an engagement coming soon.

"Is Trace going to walk her down the aisle? Or is Tony in good enough shape to do it?"

"No, Tony is out of their lives completely, even though he keeps trying to insert himself. I think Trace would be the one she'd ask, but it's up to her really. It's her wedding. And I'm probably putting the cart before the horse, so don't say anything to her if you happen to run across her.

Also, Angela, don't tell your sisters I told your aunt this."

"Your secret is safe with me, Mom. Don't worry."

"And how's Rebecca doing? She's in junior college, right?"

"Actually, she's working on her pilot's license. She was considering going into the Air Force, see if she could get some flying experience, but there's a good flight school, not the same as military training, but a pretty good flight school here, and she's already started taking classes. It's easier for a woman to get a pilot's license these days, so she's hoping she could start with one of the charter services and then work her way up to a large commercial airline. I've got a friend who's a triple seven pilot and loves it. Travels all over the world. Rebecca is all about travel and adventure."

"That sounds exciting. Good for her. I can see her being a pilot someday, although Rebecca and Clover are both over six feet. Don't they usually like pilots on the smaller side?"

"I don't think anything will stop her. Rebecca also coaches volleyball at the junior college to help pay for some of her fees. She's in an apartment now with four other girls, so Trace and I are almost empty nesters. Couple more years and Angela will be on her own somewhere. Not far away, we hope."

Kate smiled at the two of them. Gretchen had sworn off men completely until she met Trace on a celebratory vacation with several other SEALs and their wives and girlfriends. Tyler had introduced them. Gretchen had roomed with Linda Gray, Tyler's sister, who was a romance novelist. The two of them couldn't have been more different in personality.

"I'm glad things have worked out for you, and I'm also glad you moved down here. I imagine Trace is happier too."

Gretchen winced. "Well, he's actually considering getting out. You know he's forty-four, an old guy. I think this is going to be it."

"Tyler is thinking the same thing. Not quite having made the decision yet, but we're getting closer."

"Don't you have an enlistment coming up? It's always so tempting to take that bonus."

"It really is hard to turn down. But he feels like his body is giving out on him and one of these days he's going to hurt himself on a jump. His knees already cause a lot of pain, and he's going to probably have to have a new hip by the time he's fifty. So it takes a toll on him. I think he'd like to get out before he gets injured."

"So many of them retire on disability. It's just crazy how they survive. Tough guys."

"They are. They're the ones that get it done."

They heard some crying upstairs, and Kate recognized Kendall's voice.

"Uh-oh, I think we have a meltdown in process. I'll be right back—"

"I'll take care of it, Kate. Let me go see if I can help," said Angela.

"Really? That's nice of you, thank you!" Kate sat back down as she watched Angela mount the stairs two at a time. "She's such a good girl, Gretchen. So responsible, and it'll be interesting to see what she winds up going into."

"They scatter all over, don't they? I've seen families posted to far regions of the world, and yet we all still stay so close. Even the kids like to stay together. I think it's from years of bonfires and backyard picnics and team gatherings."

"I know the other teams are not exactly like Team 3. Trace and Tyler are lucky," added Kate.

"Tell me about it. Trace came from Team 8. He's never regretted that decision. That's why, when we first got together, he didn't mind the commuting. He had three girls to get to know, and he wanted to be home on the weekends. We made it work. He's the dedicated father that they should have had from the get-go."

"You're all lucky to have him be part of your lives. I'm so happy for you. You look healthy, excited. I've never seen you happier, Gretchen."

She gave Kate a quick smile before it disappeared. She began slowly. "So… if Trace gets out, he's looking at that security company several of the members of the police force and other teams, special ops guys have been joining lately. He told me Tyler also thinks very highly of the group."

"Yeah, he's setting up for an interview when they get back from the next deployment. I guess it's Mexico again." Kate said.

"That's what I understand too. God help us."

Kate hesitated to ask but knew that Tyler would be asking himself if he were there.

"Gretchen, Tyler may need some help up in Portland. He doesn't know for sure but he did tell me that he's planning on only being there two or three days. If it gets more involved or if he needs some help, he might be reaching out to several guys that are either from the area or familiar with Portland proper. I just wanted to give you a heads-up. You might mention it to Trace."

"Will do. I know he'd help any way he can. I'm so sorry about that warehouse and all those lovely things ruined. Your mother-in-law is one of the nicest ladies I've ever met. The first artist I've met who really wasn't weird, you know what I mean?"

"I agree. Our mom calls herself a hippie all the time, but Tyler's mom, she still is. She's the real deal."

The two had a good laugh together, then embraced, called upstairs to Angela who brought Kendall downstairs in her arms.

"Here you go honey, here's your mom." Angela handed the three-year-old over to her mother.

"What was it all about?" Kate asked Angela.

"I think Oliver pushed her off the bed. He didn't want to come downstairs because I think he suspects you're mad at him."

"Well, thanks for the heads-up. You think you'd be available this weekend to babysit? I'm hoping Tyler will be home and we talked about going to a game."

"Yeah, I'm free. Just let me know. Send me a text."

"Okay, Kate, you take care and please update me if you hear any news. You want me to set up some meal deliveries or something like that?" Gretchen asked.

"Oh, no, this isn't that type of a thing. And besides I'm home and able to care for the kids." She checked her watch. "Oh my gosh, I've got to go get Grady at school."

"Give our love to Tyler. We'll be praying for Deidre and Larry. And you too, Sis. Please let us know if we can help in any way."

Kate called for Oliver to come downstairs. She quickly strapped them both into car seats in the Suburban. On the way to the pickup, she thought to herself how lucky she was to be able to live in a beautiful place like San Diego, with a loving husband who was actually considering joining her in business. It put an extra bounce in her step, the thought of all the new possibilities, giving her energy, and a lightness of being she hadn't felt for several years.

Change isn't always bad. It depends on how you manage it, she thought to herself.

Of course, being married to the right man, a true and loving partner, didn't hurt either.

CHAPTER 8

"**H**EY, TYLER, HOW'S it going?" Kyle was returning his call. "Really nothing to report, except I'm looking for solid guys that I can talk to. Kyle, you wouldn't believe what that place looks like. I don't think there's anything standing more than about two or three feet tall. It's just smoke and ash charcoal. It's awful. And it affected a whole string of buildings going down several blocks. What a mess."

"How are they holding up?"

"Pretty good. I think they're still in shock."

"I'll bet. I know I would be, that's got to be a tough one. But at least nobody's hurt."

"Yeah that's what I told them too. The part that kind of gets to me and this is what I wanted to talk to you about Kyle, my folks are incredibly naive. I mean, you know they traveled all over during their hippie days in the sixties and seventies. They had a good time and they're used to being and talking to a lot of people—being free spirits, you know?"

"I got you. They've had a good life. They've seen it all."

"Yes. And they've always been great supporters of causes, they've helped the poor and they've worked with different groups. They're very socially responsible people. That's kind of why this whole thing bothers me, because I mean, my parents are the good guys. They're the guys with the white hats. It just is so unfair that they would be the ones who would get the brunt of all of this. Understand?"

"Since when is the world fair? Tyler, you've seen some shit overseas, there's just no rhyme or reason to it. Even when we think there is we go over there and you know, it's just a mess. Sometimes I think we're just glorified policemen, keeping people from blowing each other up, but I don't know if we really solve anything."

"True. You're right there."

"Your parents are just dealing with the world in a different way. I mean no offense Tyler, but we don't want people like your folks running things right? We don't want to have to go to them for our protection. That's why they got guys like us."

"Yeah, I agree with that a hundred percent. And I guess if it was just a random attack, I wouldn't feel this way. But I have a gut feeling that it's not. I have the feeling that they were targeted and it's just, you know when we get those hunches?"

"Hunches keep us alive sometimes Tyler. I say listen to them. But logically, why do you think they would be targeted?"

"It was something that the fire marshal told my dad the first day. He thinks that it started at their building, and then went on down the blocks from there. And all the buildings that were targeted were the ones that had been recently renovated, fixed up. So if this was some kind of a protest against economic opportunity or protesting some kind of inequity of some kind, why would they target the buildings that were improving the neighborhood?"

"Well, think about it Tyler. All these people coming in and fixing up the area, makes it less affordable for other people. Who knows, maybe somebody has an ax to grind on that score."

"Well, I didn't think about that actually. But it does make some sense."

"So are they going to be okay with the rebuild? Are they going to get reimbursed for what her art is really worth?" Kyle asked him.

"I've read the policy. Boy, talk about putting you to sleep. It's worse than reading a dictionary. The way they've got all the fine print everywhere. And right on the top of the policy it says this is in plain English, easy to read. I say bullshit."

Kyle chuckled. "Welcome to the world of owning real estate."

"So do we have orders yet or timing set up?"

"We do. It's going to be sooner than we thought. I'm thinking the middle of next month. They're trying to coordinate some treasury department things first before they go after this particular cartel. They don't want to send us down there unless they've got all their ducks in a line. I was meeting with the head shed today as a matter of fact. We'll take a tight group, not a big team at all. You can put in for a skip over if you want, but if you're going to re-up, you could do it in Mexico. And I didn't say that."

It was Tyler's turn to chuckle. "I haven't gotten there yet Kyle. I just am not prepared to make a decision. You know that Kate has been kind of on me to consider doing something else. She's got her heart set on getting involved in a business like catering or running a food truck."

"A food truck? Why the fuck would you want to do that? You mean like spreading mayonnaise all over white bread and shit like that? You think that would be fun compared to what you've been doing the last ten years?"

Tyler had to admit Kyle had a point there. That was the one part he hadn't considered, since it would be hard to find excitement in operating a food truck. He'd considered it because Kate was so over the moon about it.

"I keep telling myself, and I guess it's really repeating what Kate has to say, that I need to do something that's less dangerous. But doing dangerous is what I do."

"Doing dangerous is what you do well, Tyler. And I got to tell you, I would miss you a ton. So don't be thinking about that too lightly. I mean if she wants to go do the catering and stuff let her do it. But man, standing in a hot kitchen or a little cramped food truck space inhaling all that gas, wearing a dirty apron and having your face and fingers all greasy, just doesn't sound like any kind of fun I'd like to do. I'd rather go get a $5 an hour job at the YMCA and lifeguard rather than do that."

"Yeah. You're right. I knew it was the right thing to call you."

"God damn it Tyler. Did I just talk you out of becoming a professional chef?"

"Well, I think you might have. Anyway I will give you a call before I come back. So far I don't see anything that's going to take me any longer. But you never know. I'm going to try to wrap it up tomorrow if I can."

"That sounds good to me we'd love to get you back home. You take care now. Give my love to Kate when you talk to her."

"Roger that Kyle."

TYLER WAS STILL thinking about Kyle's words long after he'd showered, and tried to lay down for a short nap before dinner. He finally just got up, got dressed, and went downstairs to help his mom prepare.

"You get all your phone calls in?" his mom asked.

"Yes, I did. Had to leave a message for Kate, but she'll call me back later. How are you doing?" He placed his arm around her shoulder and pulled her to him.

"I think I'm going to be fine, Tyler. You know, it just is what it is. Oh, and your dad has the adjuster coming over tomorrow. I think he's sent Dad a list of things, a piece of paper he needs to fill out for the claim. Maybe you could help him with that after dinner."

"Happy to. So does he sound like a pretty reasonable guy then?"

"I have no idea. I'm beginning to think I've been living in an alternate reality. I get so involved in my paintings—all the color, form, and structure—it's like I'm in my own world. I think this whole situation has actually been beneficial for me."

Tyler leaned back against the kitchen countertop and examined his mother cocking his head to the side. "Mother, I never thought I'd hear you say that." When she looked up from her food prep, he gave her a huge smile. "I think you may be right. Sometimes change is good."

She blushed. "The good news is, your dad keeps pretty good records. He never throws anything out, so it's just a matter of going through things. That's what he's doing now in the study. But I think we'll be able to justify all of those pictures. The good news is we had them all photographed for the color catalog we were going to be making. That was just a stroke of genius. And Tyler, I've been thinking a lot about what you told us this afternoon at the warehouse. I probably have been awfully naive when it comes to spending a lot of time down there, especially at night. I guess I should be thankful that it's just a fire that destroyed the building, when it could have been much worse. But in my mind, I'd like to see the world a perfect place, where these things don't happen, where people treat each other respectfully. But that just isn't the case is it?"

"You've got that right, Mom. That's why they have to have guys like us. It's hard for people to understand the need for real protection. People only take it lightly until they get affected themselves."

"Well, I certainly have a newer appreciation for what you've had to go through. And I love that you call yourself a force for good. That's just brilliant." She followed it up with a warm smile.

Tyler's dad entered the kitchen. "So this is where it's all happening right?"

"Nah, I'm just kind of distracting her a little bit. I'm really not much help."

"I thought you were going to go into the catering business with your wife?"

Tyler was quiet for a second, realizing he wasn't really very good in the kitchen, in fact, he was horrible unless it was serving a beer or barbecuing hamburgers or a steak. Kate had done all the cooking, knew everything there was to know about wines, and was a real foodie. Tyler never acquired that.

"I kind of like the idea of spending a lot more time around Kate. I'm not so sure I'm going to be much help, but we'll see. We're still talking. Nothing's set in stone yet. First thing in our order of business is to figure out what's going on with you guys up here. And then we've got lots of time for the rest of it."

"Well, I put together a list for the adjuster. He's coming tomorrow, by the way."

"Mom told me."

"I have all the receipts for the remodeling, and I have the escrow papers from when we bought the building back 15 years ago, I even have a full rundown of all the expenses outside of the remodeling. I couldn't believe how much money we spent on permits and fees, inspections, engineering. We had to make sure the structure was sound in order to allow events in the building where people would come and food would be served. We worked our asses off."

"There's always one person in the family that has to be good with the records. For us it's Kate, I admire you, Dad. The more records you have, I think the better this will be for you."

They spent the evening eating slowly, talking about what it was like to grow up in Portland, all the memories they had raising the family. They even talked about Tyler's first school dates, and the time Linda's prom date backed out so she took her best friend, a girl. Caused all kinds of ruckus in the school. They talked about some of the camping trips they'd been on, and the first time Tyler had seen a butterfly when he was a toddler.

"You were such a beautiful boy, people kept asking me if you were a girl. Those blue eyes, and your curly hair, I have to admit I let it get a little bit too long. But by the time you made it to kindergarten, Tyler, you were all boy, active, running around. I remember being called into the teacher's office when you were in second grade, she told me that you were hyperactive. She mentioned that she thought you should be evaluated to take medication to calm you down. I knew that that would ruin your spirit. I knew that would be a huge mistake. I wouldn't let them test you."

"You should have, Mom. Who knows what they would've found?"

They all had a chuckle over that one. His mother added, "No I think you were intended to be exactly how you are, right in the middle of everything, saving the day and showing everybody else how to be strong. I can't tell you how wonderful it is to have you help us Tyler, to have you come up here and give of yourself, just spend some time with us. I guess what happens when you get old is you start becoming the child and your kids start being the adult. I used to think I wouldn't like that, but it's rather pleasant. I like seeing you in this leadership role. And with this family, that's going to happen more and more."

"Mom, that's very astute. I'm not offended by that comment, and that's why it encourages me because, and I know I've said it before, probably more than four or five times now, I really want you to consider not rebuilding on that site. And as a plan B to that, I really want you to consider moving down to San Diego with us. All the things that you do here you can do there. The difference will be I can watch out for you guys, you've got your grandkids to spend time with and Kate, and the weather's better. I won't worry so much when I'm overseas. There's a lot of really good reasons for you to do that. But I won't force you into doing anything."

His mother was always emotionally more astute than his father, Tyler thought. He was satisfied that things were going in the right direction just by hearing her comment.

He went to bed satisfied, and was able to fall asleep immediately.

Of course, that's when Kate called back.

"Tyler? Is that you?"

Tyler realized he had answered the phone and it was placed to his ear, but whatever he'd said to her didn't make any sense whatsoever. "I think you just heard part of my dream. I think I was dreaming in Ferengi?"

"That's funny. That's really funny, Tyler. So how is everything today?"

"Well, we're seeing the adjuster tomorrow morning. He's coming to the house, and I think I'm going to head back home maybe tomorrow or the next day. I need to touch base with the inspector, but you know, Mom and Dad are actually coming around to the idea of maybe moving to San Diego. Maybe Mom could help you in your business, Kate."

"Oh, that's not necessary. I'm going to have a big strong former Navy SEAL to help me. Besides, I think just having you in the lunch wagon or with me at catered events is going to be good for business. I'm going to show off those tats, those shoulders, and I'm going to let you bat your big baby blue eyes all you like."

He wanted to laugh at the comment, but he found it a little offensive. Was it all coming down to that? He was some kind of Adonis who would be paraded through town? He hoped she was just being lighthearted and making fun of the situation. But he wasn't really sure he wanted to do something he wouldn't be very good at. That bothered him. So did that make him a monster then?

"Tyler? Are you okay?"

"Sorry. I had tried to take a nap this afternoon, and I was just wired, couldn't do it. And I fell asleep tonight, and it just felt like I went into a coma. And then you called. I'm just not thinking straight."

"Well, you call me tomorrow. I won't keep you, and I've got a sitter lined up in case you want to go to the baseball game on Saturday. I have someone that'll give us a couple of tickets. Do you think you'd want to do that?"

"Sure. Are we taking the kids?"

"No, that's who the sitter is for. I figured just you and I go do something fun."

"That's probably a good idea. Kyle told me today that we may be leaving the middle of next month. They've bumped everybody up over a month."

"Oh, that's too bad. I was hoping we'd have a decent summer."

"Well, it is what it is, I guess we don't want to go down there unless they're ready for us, right?"

"That's true. So when will you know for sure?"

"I think it's for sure already. We'll know the exact date probably in a week or two. So I've got to sign off here, but before I do, just want to let you know I love you, and I think we'll make this work somehow with my folks. I really do think I can convince them."

"I think the kids would be ecstatic. Maybe this fire was a good thing, Tyler. It gives us all a chance to look at the future. I talked to Gretchen today, she came over."

"Oh really?"

"She said that Trace is considering joining that group up in Portland. And she told me that you were interested in it too. Is that true?"

Tyler wondered where they had gotten that impression. He did have favorable feelings about the group. He knew that Bryce was running a tight ship, and he knew it was a pleasant alternative to staying in the military, and he'd probably make a lot more money. He hadn't quite resolved the situation of living in Portland, however. That was a non-starter to him, especially now.

"I really didn't give Trace or anybody a positive read on doing that. And I don't want to live in Portland, Kate. Especially now. Trace, well, it's different for him, you know Gretchen spent a lot of time there and the kids are familiar with it. It might make sense for him, but honestly we haven't talked that much about it. Just a little. No, I'm happy where I'm at."

"Except you're going to be leaving the Teams, right?"

Little bells and whistles were going off in the back of Tyler's head. She wanted an answer in the affirmative. He wasn't going to be able to give her that. He inhaled deeply and decided to just suck it up and tell her what was going on with him.

"I've just got to be sure, Kate. I've got to be sure whatever it is I do next, if I leave the Teams, that I've got enough in my tank, that I stay the same man I am now as a SEAL. I don't want to lose that. My goal isn't to be Tyler Gray light. My goal is to be super awesome protector of the world Tyler Gray. As long as whatever I do after I leave the Teams, as long as I can still say that, I'll be happy. Until then, well, we're just going to have to let time reveal itself to us, okay Kate?"

"It wasn't what I wanted to hear, but I do understand. It's hard doing this on the phone. We'll talk about it when I can see you face to face. I think I understand what you're saying, and I don't want Tyler light either. But I was hoping that you would give me a chance to show you what I can do. I really want to try to do something, have my own business, have our own business. It's important to me. But if it's not something you want to do, you're right. You shouldn't. And I think we'll know in time. So waiting to have that discussion later, that's okay."

"Thank you Kate. I love you more every day. Thank you for always supporting me. I'm going to do whatever I can to try to return the favor."

"You already have, Sweetheart. But I don't mind you trying even more."

CHAPTER 9

THE INSURANCE ADJUSTER arrived at Tyler's parents' home at 9:00 a.m., sharp. He was younger than Tyler expected, appearing to be barely 30 years old. Tyler showed him to a place on the couch, and kept up a light banter until he started honing in on the man's experience.

"Wait a minute, I know you are their son, but this is really between my insurance company and your parents, Tyler. So if you don't mind, I'd like to ask them some questions and go over their paperwork and then we can have a little chat afterwards if you like. But I don't have to take up a lot of your time if we can just do it that way, please."

Tyler consented.

Mr. Gray showed the adjuster all the information he'd gathered on the pictures, as well as sharing with him the folder with all the fix-up receipts he'd collected during the 15 years they'd owned the building. They had renovated it twice, once to make it habitable, installing air conditioning and an adequate heating system. The second installation was to finish off the walls and install the beautiful hardwood flooring. He also demonstrated to the adjuster his tax base, reflective of the fact that they did all the work with permits, as required, and hired a contractor to do so. Except for some painting and sanding, none of the work was done themselves, but was organized and run by them.

"Well, you've just made my job much easier. We have you insured for a million dollars for the building, which may be more than the replacement cost, but as far as retail value it's probably underinsured for value. So, if you can accept the value at a million as a payoff, we can perhaps build in some other things to get you more money in other categories. You have policy limits for relocating your business, and also policy limits for medical expenses if someone had been harmed in the fire. We don't have to use those funds, so we may be able to earmark some of that unused portion for something that you really need so that we can get you the accurate amount."

Tyler was impressed with the way he ran the meeting.

"You're actually going to help them get what they think is fair, is that correct? There's no right or wrong way to do this, it's just you're going to try to get from the insurance company what my folks are asking or needing to get. Is that right?"

"That's right, I'm a private adjuster, not an insurance representative. We do it differently here and we think it's better for the homeowner. Technically I work for your parents not the insurance company, even though they assign me and pay my fees. But I do know how the insurance company works, and I'm like the go-between between them and the customer. If we can come to terms quickly, then we don't have to get involved in any other preliminary rulings or decisions. We can just move forward. It's kind of a new approach to handling claims and losses. We really have a hard time doing it when it involves somebody who has died or there's been a major accident with the claim. Those can be quite expensive because there's wrongful death, other liabilities and court proceedings that can occur, and can delay the claim payout greatly. But in this case, since we're just talking about replacement value of a building and property of a certain value, it should be fairly simple."

"How soon before we get the proceeds?" asked Tyler's mom.

"It depends on what we agree to. It's my job to negotiate that for you. You could sell the lot at a salvage value, be paid for the loss of the building and not rebuild it, take the money and do something else with it, or you could get some plans drawn and build the building all over again, which may take a while because you need to have permits, you need to hire an architect, engineers, all that sort of thing and it can take months, sometimes even a year to get started on that. It really depends on what your future plans are. If you need this building and you want this location, then that would be the route you would take. If you don't, my recommendation is going to be take the money and then use it elsewhere."

Tyler still had questions about the findings of the fire report.

"So what if they find out this was intentionally set?" Tyler asked him.

"That only complicates things if there's some kind of suspicion that your parents or someone they hired torched the building. I'm not hearing that at all, and frankly I'd be surprised if they were blamed for it. We all know what's been going on downtown. Our insurance company is in fact re-evaluating carrying insurance in Portland, so we may be looking for ways to disassociate ourselves. That might mean settling quickly. That's a good thing for your folks."

"So, you'll leave this market then?"

"We may not be writing new policies. Not every insurance company can insure against demonstrations and protests, riots, we're not supposed to discriminate on the basis of that, however, if losses and claims are high in a particular city, it's very common for an insurance company to roll back their new policy goals."

Satisfied, they'd received everything they needed, the adjuster told him he would take the copies Mr. Gray had given him and would write up a report that he wanted them to approve before he submitted it.

"After it's submitted, we have approximately 14 days for the company to answer, they will do so in writing, and if what they propose is acceptable to you then based on what you choose, we'll go forward."

After the gentleman left, Tyler felt extremely positive about the meeting. "Good job, Dad. You nailed it." Tyler said.

His father shrugged. "I'm one of these people that if I don't have the paperwork filed properly in the right files, I can't sleep at night. I never thought it would be useful in this kind of situation. But I get great peace of mind out of being organized, Tyler. Believe it or not."

Tyler's parents received word that they could meet with the fire inspectors down at the property later in the day. The three of them took the VW bus again, parking it several blocks away to keep from picking up debris, glass, and nails, and walked the distance to the site of the old building.

Several fire officials were having a small conclave in front of the former structure. One of the gentlemen stepped forward extending his hand to Mr. and Mrs. Gray.

"I'm Craig Moorehead. I'm in charge of the investigation, sort of the liaison between our department and the city. How do you do?" He shook both of their hands. And then he addressed Tyler. "I understand you're still serving in the armed forces?"

"Yes sir, I'm in the Navy sir."

"God bless you son, and I thank you for your sacrifice."

Tyler noticed Mr. Moorehead was a no-nonsense type of guy, probably with some military training, and got right to the point.

"We believe that this particular incident started very close to the stroke of midnight. You will see we found evidence that an accelerant had been used, and it appeared to have started in this corner of the building, with additional accelerants added all along the far wall that came up close to the dead shrubbery for the adjacent property. I can't walk you in to show you, but I can give you pictures, if you like."

"No, that's not necessary," said Tyler's mom.

"Okay good. This shrubbery probably ignited right away, and we had the fire traveling down the street. This person or persons who did this is very familiar with setting fires, probably has been trained, and while we don't know what they used as an accelerant, we believe it's a derivative of gasoline of some kind, possibly a thick pasty mixture, that could be painted on the side of a building and ignited. It's very expensive to use. It's used in fire control for controlled burns, and in some military operations, but it's a derivative of the gasoline refining process, and is actually something that we dispose of."

"Who would have access to this?" Tyler asked.

"Other than the folks who transport it to superfund dump sites, someone who has worked in forestry, or the military. But most of this product is disposed of, not used."

"That leaves it kind of open, then," he said.

"Perhaps. Only certain people are licensed to handle this type of material, so it narrows down who the suspects could be. However, I'm going to guess that we're going to find some site or manufacturing plant that has reported recent theft of this material. It's very sophisticated, and this is not created by a homeless person or someone who was looking to break in and use the building for shelter. That's going to rule out 99% of the people who live here."

"So what you're saying is it's someone from the outside?" Tyler asked.

"Yes sir, I am saying that."

Tyler and his parents shared expressions of wonder and disgust between the three of them, and then Tyler added more questions.

"So, it appears that this could have been created by somebody who was protesting downtown? Is that what you're saying, that there's a link between the two?"

"I am. We found some of this accelerant painted on several automobiles, used to fully engulf a car and cause an explosion. It works quite well with that. We also have some surveillance video that shows someone with a paintbrush and a paint can painting some pasty liquid on places that were later ignited. So we're fairly sure we're talking about one individual since that's all we've got on surveillance footage and he's obviously a trained professional fire starter. That's not a technical term folks, it's just how we say it, fire starter."

"So this was done after the demonstration downtown, which I understand was kind of completed by 11 o'clock or so? Is that right?" Tyler asked.

"There were still some loiterers and people that were being watched, but yes more or less everything was over by 11:00. I would say they knew that they were going to come over here and although it doesn't appear we had huge crowds, just a handful of people here, I would say they had it all planned that way. This was not a protest. This was pure destruction of property."

"Man, I didn't realize you could figure all that out from the evidence. That's amazing." Tyler said.

"Well, sir, I'm just giving this to you verbally because you are the property owners and because of your service, Mr. Gray. I always treat my military families like they should be, like they deserve. However, our investigation is still ongoing, and by the time I issue the final report, many things could have changed. So please don't quote me, please don't give this information to anyone outside of this little group here, and I will make sure to keep you informed as to how we're investigating, and ultimately, hopefully when we catch someone. I'm going to tell you right now, after working several of these types of incidences up in the Seattle area, which was my job before I came to Portland, I would be surprised if this particular person who did this is still in the state of Oregon. They're probably long gone."

"So do you call in the feds then?" Tyler wondered.

"Already done. They have an extensive lab, a lot more resources than we have here in Portland, so that will be the next step. And we also haven't finished our surveillance search. Not much in the way of camera footage here in this neighborhood but of course downtown, there's lots of footage. With facial recognition software, and you didn't hear that from me, we feel fairly certain we'll find the person or persons who are responsible for this. I just want to reassure you."

"You think that the fire started at their building and then moved down. Do you have any idea why they chose my parents' building?"

"Yes and no. I think it was targeted because it was one of the nicest buildings down here. I think it was not intended to cause body count loss, done carefully in such a way that it wouldn't cause any loss of life. They did it at midnight. This area has no surveillance cameras set up, and possibly they had scoped out the site ahead of time and determined that. They may have even been inside the building itself. I think it's a combination of all those. Opportunity, making a statement, getting the biggest bang for the buck so to speak."

"So do you think it's possible this is *personal* against them?"

"No I don't. I really don't. I think they were unlucky enough to have done a good job remodeling the building. That in and of itself made them a target."

CHAPTER 10

K ATE WAS DELIGHTED when she got the call from Tyler that he was coming home early. He had missed the flight for today, but was scheduled to be out tomorrow, and would be arriving home in the middle of the afternoon. She spent the day cleaning the house, changing the sheets on the bed and getting her nails done. It had been several months since she'd indulged in such delicacies, and without the help of Angela, providing babysitter services for Kendall, she would not have been able to do it. She came home with sparkly red polish which she hoped her returning hunk of a husband would thoroughly enjoy.

She purchased a couple of Tyler's favorite steaks, bone-in rib eye and had spaghetti fixings out so the kids could have their special food as well. She rented a movie for them, and washed her hair, shaved her legs and did everything she could after the cleaning and cooking, to make sure she was more than presentable.

Gretchen had asked if she could help, but Kate wanted to work on the house by herself, listening to all her favorite music, singing to the songs, and even managing to get a little bit of gardening time in to refresh the flowers in her front yard.

She got the kids to retire early and set herself up in the bedroom, reading one of her new books.

She'd been concerned about Tyler's comment about perhaps revisiting the idea of leaving the teams. Her hope was that she could convince him that leaving and joining a partnership with her, would be something not only better suited for their family, less dangerous too, but something he would actually enjoy. She knew he loved his job as a Navy SEAL, but she also knew he was concerned about his physical capabilities and didn't want to retire on a disability.

She reviewed some online courses on the catering business, and even explored several resources for purchasing either used food trucks, or brand-new retrofits. The brand-new vehicles were going to be out of her price range, but there were a decent number of trucks that had come on the market recently, due to the pandemic, and she flagged a couple of them to show Tyler when he got home. It was all doable with the money they had saved, and if they got a small home equity loan, that would be all they would need to finish equipping not only her home but perhaps renting a kitchen space downtown. She even talked to a commercial Realtor about doing so and he was on the lookout for such an opportunity.

She got a call from Christy just after the kids went down to sleep.

"So Tyler's coming back. I was going to call you and just say if you needed to have coffee or get together, I'm available. But now that he's coming home, I guess I was a little bit too late," Christy said.

"You've got so many other things to do, Christy, I'm good, but boy, I'm so impressed by how much you do for us. Thank you for thinking of me, but please don't waste your time here. I'd love to have coffee with you, but I know you're busy and you have your career as well."

"Well, it can be done you know."

That's when Kate suspected that Kyle might have put Christy up to the phone call.

"Yeah, I understand. I don't know that I could do it like you do though, since you've got your husband to take over the kids on a regular basis, I don't see how he does that either, but I don't know if I could concentrate doing real estate, and then also managing the kids. I mean I guess I should ask you how you do it?"

"Well, you get used to it. Remember when I first got together with Kyle, I was a successful Realtor or trying to be, and I had it in me to make it go long before we had kids. I think that with your experience in the wine industry, and what you know about customer service and catering at the wineries, you would be a good fit. So you actually have worked in the field you want to pursue. As far as Tyler being part of it, I'm just not sure about that. You're going to have to wait and see."

Kate noticed she didn't accuse her of trying to get Tyler off the teams, but she also didn't want to appear to be confrontational or against the move. It was very smart of her, and if Kyle coached her, he did a good job.

"Well, I realize this would be all on me. Part of me thinks I should try to get it up and running first and then bring Tyler in. But the other part of me realizes that I need help. And I can't do it by myself. Unlike you selling real estate I don't think I could do this just myself."

"I know you've thought about this, Kate, but maybe there are others out there that could give you a hand. However, one thing you're going to have to look at: he's a man of action. And sometimes these things don't work out the way we expect them to. I mean Kyle, I will tell you, is not the best person to babysit the kids but we do it to save money. And it forces him to spend more time there. Otherwise, he'd be down at the gym, he'd be talking to the guys, he'd be exploring ways he could run his team better. And I have to pull him back and make him do things that bring him into the family, even though I know he loves us all, I have to force him to stay involved."

"Like I said, I'm in awe. You actually have to remind him to stay involved?"

"And he knows that, so he puts up with it. But boy, there are some days I come home and Kyle is just a total basket case. Those kids have driven him up the wall and down the other side. And they know it too. He's a pushover. Not with the team, but with his kids. So we'll see."

"I never thought about that. Tyler has told me some stories, though."

Christy laughed. "Oh yes, we have the stories. You remember the one when we found Gunny's ashes delivered to the house with the lost luggage?"

"A classic tale. I've heard the story from both of you. Hilarious!"

"Truth is, the kids will eventually leave our home, at least the first two in just a couple of years, and he's going to have to face his future without them. I don't think he's going to make a good Realtor though. I would never make him do that."

Kate could see what kind of a salesman Kyle would make. She giggled.

"I think that's funny, Christy. And thank you for sharing that. By the way, I wanted to ask you about commercial spaces. I've been talking to another broker who had a sign in a little off-street that I thought would be perfect for renting a kitchen. Do you ever run across those?"

"Not often. I'm mostly specialized in residential sales. But I'd be happy to get one of our commercial guys to give you a call and maybe show you around if you want."

"Well, let me first talk to Tyler and maybe he has some thoughts. I don't want to waste anybody's time. There's also the possibility that something may be happening with his parents moving down here. I mean we can only hope and dream, right?"

"I loved my mother to death, I really did. I never knew my father. But I loved my mother with all my heart. She wanted me to come down to San Diego long before she passed, and I just, I wanted to make it on my own, you know what I mean?"

"I know exactly what you mean, Christy."

"But I think if we had lived together, honestly, it wouldn't have worked. She needed her space, and I needed mine. And yes, we loved each other, we were so close, but sometimes you can be too close. And I think that's the way it would have been. Life has a way of working itself out and honestly, Kate, I don't have the answers, but if you just keep your eyes open, the right opportunity is bound to happen. I don't think we should force it. At least that's my philosophy."

"Wow—"

"Okay, and I'm sorry. Lecture over," said Christy.

"I didn't take it that way, but you gave me a lot of things to think about, and I promise you I will take it to heart."

"I understand Angela's been babysitting for you. Is she good and is she available like for other SEAL families?" Christy asked.

"I think so. Up to her of course. She doesn't drive so you have to pick her up or have Gretchen drop her off, but she's very responsible and the kids love her. She likes to read to them and do coloring projects and things. I haven't had her take the kids outside of the house because, well, she doesn't drive. So I haven't tried that but for just straight babysitting at home, I think she's ideal. And I don't like the idea of hiring older kids even though I know several SEAL kids that would be fine. I just think she's the perfect age and the right temperament to do what she does. And I think she appreciates the extra money."

"Boy, that's good enough for me. I've had some inquiries, and I don't want to allow Brandon to babysit. It's just a whole different thing with having your son babysit other people's kids. Kyle and I have been against it. There's lots of other things he can do to earn money anyway. But I will certainly pass her name and Gretchen's phone number around with that recommendation and maybe you'll get some calls for references. Thank you, Kate."

"Happy to recommend her. Okay, well, I'm going to turn in early. I've got a few errands to run tomorrow morning early before I pick him up."

THE NEXT MORNING, Kate kept Kendall in the Suburban after dropping Oliver and Brady off at school. She drove to the store picking up a few last-minute items she'd forgotten to do the day before, took them home and then headed to the airport. She got a text from Tyler saying that the plane had actually arrived early, so he was already waiting at the pick-up station when she drove up.

Putting the car in park, she burst open the driver door and ran to his arms.

"God, Kate. I think I'll go away more often if this is what I come home to," he said as he kissed her.

She was pleased that he gave her the response she was hoping for.

"That wouldn't make a bit of difference, but it's wonderful to see you again and I'm glad it didn't take longer. Everything okay up there?"

"As good as it can be. We're still a wait and see."

They heard some honking and the traffic control officer was asking them to move along. Tyler threw his duty bag in the second seat, kissed Kendall who was screaming with her arms outstretched to hug her daddy, and then took over the driver duties as Kate slid over. He started the Suburban and carefully maneuvered them onto the freeway.

"I've got to pick up Oliver, and do you suppose we could do that on the way home?" she asked.

"Of course. I'm all yours."

"So will you have to go back up there soon or is this it for now?" she asked.

"I don't know. A lot of it depends on what they find, and if the adjuster comes in with a number that Mom and Dad can live with. They stand to walk away with quite a chunk. But they're going to have to decide where they want to live and what they want to do. And, you know how I've tried to encourage them, but I just have to let them make up their own mind."

"Of course you do. I'm so glad you were there though to give them a hand."

"You know I was kind of wary of what kind of support we were going to get up there, but the police and fire, the detectives that I've spoken to, they're all pretty darn good. And I talked to the Bone Frog Group, Bryce, who you remember right?"

"Oh the former SEAL and who became a policeman?"

"Yep, that's him. He said that the senior members of the police and fire departments up there are very qualified, very good, and he said that many of them are pushing to retire early, due to all the turmoil there. But for right now, we've got really good people on the case."

"So have they determined why their place was burned, I mean was it part of the protest then?"

"We still don't know. They are looking for suspects. Once that happens, then we'll probably know further but it's just a guess at this point. It doesn't really matter one way or the other except that they'll get their money, and I think it will affect where they invest it. And that's kind of the way it's going to be for them."

"I see. They wouldn't want to go back to an area where they had problems, is that what you're saying?"

"Exactly."

"How did it look?"

"You know I had déjà vu in my old room, and you remember when Grady was learning to play soccer and we came up for that tournament?"

"Yes, he was so excited. His first road trip with his dad."

"While I was laying there in bed looking at all my trophies and I thought about what it was like growing up there. I really have a lot of happy memories. I hope they can get it together to quell all this protest or at least you know make it more peaceful. Portland was such a beautiful city and I got to see some of that. We had a couple sunshiny days, little bit of rain, of course, but you know I have some wonderful memories of the way the city used to be. It was a nice place to grow up."

That stopped Kate's excitement. She didn't like the fact that Tyler was feeling an attachment to his old hometown. Of course she had an attachment to Sonoma County where she was raised, but it put her on red alert and perhaps he wasn't telling her exactly what he was thinking, but it did open the possibility that he was considering joining the group at Bone Frog, like Gretchen had mentioned.

"Gretchen says that Trace is seriously considering the job offer he'd received. I know we talked about you interviewing with him, but honestly with all this going on with your parents I kind of thought that went out the window. Does this mean you changed your idea a bit?" she asked.

"Well, like I said on the phone, we do need to sit and talk, Kate. I want to make sure that I do the right thing. I'm not going to do anything that you're going to have a problem with. And I'm assuming you'll be the same way, right?"

"Of course, I think we can both figure out what's the right path for us. But I want to put a pitch in for us working together on something."

"I'm open to anything, as long as we thoroughly explore what those things are. But no worries." He smiled and leaned over to her, putting his right hand on her shoulder, pulling her toward him so he could give her a kiss. He quickly refocused on his driving as they swerved slightly, generating some neighborly honks from passing drivers.

After they pulled up to the school, Kate got out to go pick up Oliver. Grady would be returning home with one of his friends as part of the carpool. Oliver was burdened with several paintings, and a note that was safety-pinned to the front of his shirt. He looked funny trying to juggle all his things, all his prizes he wanted to show his mom and dad.

"Hey there bud. I missed you," said Tyler to his son.

"I made all these paintings for you, Dad." He shoved the crinkled paper in Tyler's chest, releasing them at the last minute. Kate watched as they fell to the ground and started floating all over the yard.

"Whoa there! Hey buddy, we got to pick these up before they get wet. Come on, help me," Tyler said to him.

Kate watched the two of them run around picking up the papers, as well as the brown paper bag that had some of his craft items in it and some paperwork from the school district. All of that was brought inside the Suburban, Oliver was strapped in next to Kendall, and Tyler resumed the drive home.

She smiled as she looked at the face of her husband. How lucky she was. How lucky they all were. She hoped that it always remained this way.

CHAPTER 11

A LL OF TYLER'S concerns about Kate, about their future, melted away in their long and patient lovemaking that evening. The one thing that he appreciated about Kate more than anyone else he'd ever cared about, was that she was not afraid to show him how she felt. It had been a leap of faith for her to fall in love with him in the first place, being engaged to someone else when they met on the plane that fateful afternoon. He knew something about her was what he'd been looking for his whole life. And although they'd had their differences over the years, the last ten years since being married and the birth of their three children, had only deepened his desire and respect for her.

Now it was all about making sure neither one of them caved in or settled for second, since they both were in effect racehorses. Neither one of them were plodders. Neither one of them wanted a life that was just ordinary. Tyler had always been someone with stars in his eyes and a tremendous amount of drive in his soul to protect the whole fucking world. He laughed to himself as he kissed her smooth skin and luxuriated in the smell of this divine woman, he was lucky to have love him. He never forgot that and never stopped being grateful for it.

But Kate on her own, also was a racehorse. She wanted things in her life to be perfect. She wanted to be a great mother, she wanted to be a strong partner for him, always supporting him. And even though sometimes they'd get tired, or the stress of life, or him being gone for long periods of time, especially when the kids got sick or there was a money issue, all these stressors would wear her down when he wasn't home sometimes. Or sometimes when he was home and he was spending more time with the team than he was spending with her or the kids. There were always things coming up that wore on them, both of them.

But it was always their love that took front and center stage. It was like when they met each other they found someone else that could do great things with their life, but not forget their commitment and the power of the love they shared between them as primary. In fact, all of his strength now came from that love. He would be devastated without her.

As he explored and worked on all the little things he knew she loved as they made love, the way she liked to take it slow and have her orgasm build, build until she had no control, because for Kate, losing control in this positive way, was refreshing and needed. It wasn't the frantic kind of losing control when your whole world is exploding. He wanted her to let go, to shatter beneath him, to give him back what she felt and all the intensity of the love she felt for him. She was always willing to give her very best all the time.

He chastised himself a little bit, maybe just began worrying about it, as he was making love to her how could he be thinking about all these other things? And he decided that it was part of who they were as a couple. They were entangled just as they'd been entangled in bed, couldn't help themselves, jumped over boundaries that other people would never do, this was their life. And loving her body, loving her soul, loving the way she loved him back, that was what he wanted and that's what she wanted too. So he felt for her, felt the love and the desire physically with his body, but he also understood that love. It wasn't just sex, it wasn't just passion, it was how she loved him back, how he loved her.

"I wish I didn't ever have to leave your side, Kate. And that's probably pure folly. I want you to know that I miss you, I even miss you when I leave to go to team meetings. I miss you when I take the kids to school. I can't wait to see you every time I come home," he said to her.

Her face was still sweaty from her fitful orgasm, her breathing still ragged, deep, her eyes nearly delirious. He loved seeing in her eyes how his words affected her all the way to her core. He traced her lips with his finger, kissed her again whispered in her ear, "I love you so much, Kate."

"I am the lucky one, Tyler," she whispered back. "I think about it every day, what would've happened if I hadn't trusted myself enough to know the difference between where I was headed and what significance meeting you on the plane caused for me. You made my life a miracle. It was fate all the way from start to finish. And we're not done yet." She said and smiled.

"It's an adventure right? That's what they say about love, it's the best suspense out there. It's a mystery, just like any good mystery story. The love is the mystery, how it unfolds. And for me, I know it grows stronger every year we're together. And now I see the kids growing, some of you and some of me, the blending of our personalities, and the way they honor us as our children, because their hearts are pure, I can't tell you what joy it brings me. And I know it's a lot of work on you when I'm gone, but I want you to know I appreciate it so much. I look into the eyes of our three, and I see your magic in their eyes too, Kate."

Of course, her eyes teared up, because Tyler's eyes were tearing up. He felt his tears stream over his cheeks and down onto his bare chest. God help him, he wanted this relationship to last forever. He wanted to live forever in her arms.

IN THE MORNING, Tyler was grateful she didn't force the serious discussions about their future on him last night. Now, having coffee in bed after another quickie encounter, her lying tangled in the sheets still naked, and the room still smelling of her and their lovemaking, he sat with the two mugs heavy in whipping cream, presented it to her, and decided to flay open his soul.

"I know what you did last night, Kate."

Kate looked puzzled as she sipped her first sip and then closed her eyes and licked her lips. "Mm, this is the best coffee you've ever made."

Tyler thought about that. "This is the best morning of my life. I am so lucky, Kate. Honest. But I still know what you did."

He tried to look serious, maybe even alarm her slightly but he had to break out in a chuckle as she began to worry.

"I'm not sure what you're saying, Tyler."

"I want you to know that I'm willing to have that discussion this morning about whether or not I'm going to leave the Teams. I know you've worried about it. So can we do that? And Honey if you don't want to, I'm fine with that. But I feel like I promised, and I put you off on that phone call which I really am sorry for, and now I need to keep my promise. So here I am, let me have it."

She looked at him over the rim of the coffee mug. "Be careful what you wish for Mr. Gray."

"Are you going to do a 50 Shades on me then?" he said.

"Let me put it to you this way." She adjusted herself, coming up to sit, her knees and legs wrapped around her torso, the sheet pulled up to cover her breasts, but her lovely arms and fingers that held the coffee cup could have just as well been holding Tyler's heart the way he felt for her. He was addicted to her inside, outside, in the air, everything that she touched or breathed he loved. There would never be a time that he wasn't devoted to her.

"Yes? I'm waiting," he said.

"I first want you to know that I am worried about you taking your next step, because I know you get so much satisfaction out of what you do, even with all the dangers, because that's just the way you were made. It's the way you do everything, you do it full tilt, all out, no reservations. And while neither one of us are perfect, you have so much discipline and training, it comes natural to you."

"Well, I think you're the same way, Kate."

"No, not exactly the same way. I try to figure things out too, but I am driven more by inspiration. I like to do things that make me feel good. Like this catering business, like raising the children, like gardening. Like making the house a beautiful place, those are things that bring me joy, they bring me energy pennies."

"Energy pennies not energy silver dollars?" He asked, playing with her.

"No, I got that from someone I've heard speak about it, and it's energy pennies, doing things that put something back into your vessel." She said this while tapping at her chest. "Inspiration is my motivation, to create beauty and health in abundance. I'm not sure it's inspiration for you, but you are driven to protect and to keep safe and to cherish. It's a different thing."

"And is there something wrong with that difference between us?" He wondered.

"No, not at all. But I have to understand your motivation just like you have to understand mine. And if we are going to do something together it has to include both of those things for us to work together as a team. We do that in raising our family now, Tyler. You protect and provide for us, I watch over the kids and keep them safe and make the house a home and keep the home fires burning so when you come back you don't have to be handling projects or problems that I haven't taken care of. That's the beauty of how we work together in raising this family, in having this partnership. Because a marriage really is a partnership isn't it?"

"Yes it is. I never thought about this the way you are. So what you're saying is my need to protect and defend is part of what I should be doing if I'm no longer on the Teams, is that what you're saying?"

"I think yes, and that can take many forms. If we do something together, you have to be able to live in that world and love it, while I'm living in my world and loving it. And that's what we both bring to the partnership outside of the family and the marriage. And if it's done right, it can be a great enhancement. I don't want to take you away from your brothers, and I see things and I hear things and I've heard wives that do nothing but complain about you guys. I understand what they're saying, and I probably think some of it's justified. But I can tell whether they are of one team, when some of these conversations come up and it turns into like a bitch session. Not all the wives do that and I've, for instance, never heard Christy do that. I don't know if the guys do, but I can tell which relationships are really working and which ones aren't. I would like to have the kind of relationship that works and I think we do have that, Tyler."

He was incredibly proud of her. The delivery was flawless. He wished he'd had a recording of what she said so he could just play it over again and again and again, especially if he was out in some distant area in the shivering cold or worrying about getting shot somewhere. He would love to be able to hear her voice like this, affirming the best parts of him and noticing the best parts of her.

"You're incredible Kate. How did I get so lucky?"

"You sat next to me, and you looked at me with those blue eyes, and you reached right in and grabbed my heart. You didn't even hesitate. And you didn't even act like you knew that's what you were doing. I didn't know what was going on. But something triggered in me and I knew from that day forward if I didn't follow you or follow my instinct to be with you, my life would never be the same. We were both lucky, Tyler."

"Okay so this is all good and nice, but how do we make that decision whether or not I stay on the Teams are not?"

"Well, that is your world, and that is a decision you are going to have to make. Let me remind you about a few things. You've lost teammates, you've had teammates come back disabled, missing an arm or a couple of legs, blinded, severe cases of PTSD, some of them addicted to opioids and other drugs, coming back and making messes of their lives, getting divorced and financially in ruins. You've had all kinds of things in your Team and other Teams that you've seen. Accidents during training, being told by the Navy that you're no longer qualified. All these things can and do happen every day of every year. So we know that the longer you stay, the more chance this could happen. That doesn't mean you don't do it anymore, it just means that now you're 37 years old, you're not 27 years old and things happen to a 37-year-old body that perhaps don't happen as easily with a 27-year-old body. And now you have three little ones who you love dearly, that look up to you, and they'd survive, but they'd be devastated if you were harmed, or if you didn't come back. And I know you've seen those kids at SEAL funerals, you've seen the wives and the parents, you've seen the impact of all of that on the community. It's a question that only you can answer. I can't do that for you. I think you need to look at that first. I think that's where it has to start. And while you're doing that, I need to be thinking about what kind of an operation I could do perhaps on a limited basis until you are done with your commitment here, and whether or not I like it enough to even do it by myself if you decide you don't want to join me. The long and the short of it is, Tyler, I don't want to have you leave the Teams and then find out later that you gave up your whole life. I want you to be with me the best version of yourself that you possibly could be. I don't want you to hold back. I want you to take risks, but I want you to take calculated risks. I want you to love what you're doing, no matter what it is."

If he could bottle up her energy, her confidence, the love she held for him sitting sipping her coffee tangled in their bedsheets, stark naked, beautiful, lips that could sink a battleship, words that made his heart flutter, if he could just bottle it up and take a shower in it every single fucking day, he'd be a much better person.

Why did he worry so much about what she wanted or whether or not the changes were going to be good for them? If they just paid attention and moved from the point of what they loved doing, there wasn't anything in the world that could stop them.

CHAPTER 12

K ATE AND TYLER decided that Kate should run up and spend a couple of days with Devon and Nick at the Winery and Lavender Farm in Sonoma County. That way, she could have some of her questions answered, and they could have another discussion about some of Kate's ideas before Tyler left for his deployment. Nick and Devon's kids were at camp, since it was spring break for them. Her kids were involved in several sporting events, and Tyler was prepared to handle all three of them. Although Oliver and Grady were in school, Kendall started a new preschool, which took three-year-olds, but with certain exceptions, would accept somebody younger if they were fully potty-trained. Tyler wound up enrolling her in the preschool that Kyle and Christy's kids went to, having remembered some of the programs that school provided that he liked. That also gave him more leeway in the workups and meetings that they had, freeing him up a little bit.

Kate flew up on a Wednesday, planning to return on Saturday. They were still waiting for further information from the adjuster and the insurance company, so it was a small break in the all-consuming disaster and resolution project that had been Portland. They both decided not to overly pepper Larry and Deidre, Tyler's parents, about moving. They were experiencing some resistance there.

Devon picked Kate up at the Sonoma County Airport, named after the famous artist, Charles Schulz.

"I forgot how beautiful it is up here, Devon. I mean, we fly in and it's green and with the beautiful vineyards dotting the landscape every-where. I love it in San Diego, of course, but it's just so lush and gorgeous up here. I'm really excited."

"Well, I am delighted that you even want to come and talk to us about what you want to do. Of course, there's a part of me that hopes that you decide you can't do it on your own, and you agree to come here and stay and help us. You know that option's still out there for you." Devon said.

They drove down the freeway until a turnoff to Bennett Valley Road and the winery site.

"I think one of the biggest decisions we have to make is what's best for the kids too, Devon. They are pretty connected down there, and I don't know if I have the heart to dislodge them. But you know, they'll be out of the house in another 10 years and we'll probably be in a different situation."

"But what are you going to do in the meantime? Has he made a decision?"

"I'm leaving it up to him. But the answer is no, not yet."

"Well, the event center is, as you know, our biggest source of income. The winery is great and with the additional acreage we were able to get from our neighbor, we've got it planted, because all of his vines had to be removed, they were diseased and half of them were dead anyway from his lack of water. But we've put in some good varietals as well as a good healthy dose of Merlot, which we're known for here, and it's going to be six, seven years before we're going to see anything for it. So it's good that you're coming now, you can see what it's like at the beginning, if you decide you want to do a winery down there. I know the weather will allow it, but you're going to have to grow different things. And as far as setting up a center, well, I will show you everything we do, and I'll tell you about some of the things I'd like to do if we had unlimited resources."

"That's good. I want to see what you would do if you had unlimited resources. I'm sure it would be pretty fantastic." Kate said.

They both laughed.

"But you know reality is reality. Gravity is gravity. What goes up does come down, and if you make mistakes, you pay for it. That said, I wouldn't have it any other way. But the climate here as far as what you can do with your land is perhaps a little bit restrictive and becoming more restrictive every day."

"What do you mean, Devon?"

"We have rules placed on us now as far as the event center and having tastings and parties that weren't in place when we first started. In fact, I don't think we would've been allowed to have a winery here, on the edge of town, encroaching on housing. And of course the big buzzword here is low-cost housing or low-income housing. I mean, a lot of our political leaders would like us to just rip out everything and put in apartments. And you and I both know what that would look like."

"I see what you mean. So you're saying nothing stays the same. It's always changing." Kate answered.

"You got it. That's lesson number one. And you got it Kate."

They drove down Bennett Valley Road until they got to Sophie's Choice, the Lavender Farm and Winery. Driving down the gravel road, lined in yellow roses, the vines leafing out and beginning to spread, the floor of the vineyards well tilled, the rich dark brown soil warmed by the afternoon sun, she imagined that a couple of centuries ago when the first settlers came out from wine-producing regions in France and Germany, they saw this as a true paradise.

It was a spiritual experience for Kate. She had enjoyed working at Heller Winery prior to moving to San Diego, but had never really been involved in the day-to-day operations. She was just part of the management team that ran the event center. They were strictly a winery, not an eco-tourist place, and not a wedding center. Although they did occasionally have weddings there. Most of her experiences were selling club memberships and catering to tourists who had no clue about what they were tasting. Her goal was trying to convert a few of them to being long-term buyers of the wine.

What Devon and Nick were doing was something entirely different. She wondered, if she had married Randy and been involved in the winery, would she have taken them to a different place? She decided to pose the question to Devon.

"Do you ever wonder why somebody like Randy's parents didn't create something like this with their winery? They certainly have the room, they have the name, you would think they would try to do something like this and expand into more of the experience. That and the fact they're in Dry Creek Valley for starters. It's world famous."

"I'm not sure about them. You heard the news, didn't you?"

"No, what?"

"Well, as you know, their former employee left with hundreds of thousands of dollars. They found even more things after she was captured, and then just three weeks ago she was released, all charges dropped. None of us can figure out why. Mrs. Heller has had a recurrence of her breast cancer, and she's bedridden. Mr. Heller, I think, has taken his eye off the ball a bit, because the vineyard is in terrible shape. Randy's trying to do what he can, but he is such a mess. He's been married and divorced twice now, and I just don't think he's a very good business person. Everybody's talking about the fact that the vineyard's going to be for sale. I'm sure it's going to be many, many millions of dollars, and Nick and I wouldn't have anywhere close to the resources, nor would we really want to take it over. But people are starting to show up, and the wolves are coming out."

"That's a shame. That wine was just fantastic. I mean, they won so many medals."

"Well, their old reputation isn't helping now, because I guess they've lost several winemakers over the years. I think they are running short of funds. They were concerned about losing the business altogether from what I understand, but they were able to get some investors in and it just didn't get managed properly. I don't know why they lost interest, but there's something about this investor pull that has kind of taken the fire out of the bellies of the Hellers. I think they're not long for this area. I expect that they'll be moving somewhere else and selling."

"That's amazing. So why did they let Sheila go? I mean, why did they release Sheila?

"You mean Joan? That's her real name, you know. Joan?"

"Yes, she tried to kill me. The trial was over, she was serving time, I thought everything was settled. Why would they turn her loose?"

"Well, somebody has messed up what's going on and apparently some people who were witnesses or had testified against her are now changing their story. She's apparently claimed that someone else put her up to it, I don't know. But they let her go. And nobody's seen her, so she's not around the winery at all, not around Randy I mean, that lasted like a hot minute."

"Oh I knew that. That happened before she was convicted," said Kate.

"Well, she's onto other things. The $400,000 or whatever it was, plus the new stuff they found, was never seized. She was never required to turn it back or didn't have it. It's hard to get the straight story from the news media, but it's just a big puzzle. She's gone. She's gone with the money, the Hellers are failing, and everything about their life has just gone to pot."

"That's too bad. No, I didn't know anything about it. Do you think my folks know? They never said anything to me. And we've been up here visiting."

"This industry of ours is a very close and incestuous type of group, gossip and insider information is just all over the place. Some of it's accurate, most of it is not, so I don't really know that I've got the straight story either, but they try to keep it all within this group and if it wasn't for the fact that we attend some of the same meetings and some of us have used the same accountants and attorneys and salespeople, services, word gets out. And we've also interviewed a few of their employees for work at our place. I'm telling you, Kate, it's a hellhole. And I don't even know how much control the Hellers have. Because they completely rebuilt that place and it looks like a great big warehouse. It lost all the charm after the fire. It's just a metal building with a tasting room. I mean, who would want to have a wedding there?"

"I suppose there's some kind of a business model for somebody who's the investor but I agree with you, nothing I'd want to be involved in."

Kate didn't want to say it but she thanked her lucky stars she never did.

AFTER KATE AND Devon arrived, she was shown to her bedroom, and Nick appeared at the doorway, greeting her. She was unpacking and pulling out a couple of trays she had brought from San Diego as a gift.

"Hey there Kate, now I'm asking myself why the heck didn't you just bring the whole family? I mean, we could put them to work."

Kate ran over to him and gave him a deep hug. "Great to see you,

Nick. I understand things are going very well for you guys. And I'm so happy."

"Well, the kids are going to be excited to see you and I'm busy that's true, but gosh that guy Tyler, he slips through town and he doesn't stop and come in and see me, I'm going to get after that guy. And I understand he's considering leaving the teams, which I can wholeheartedly accept, so when's the date?"

Kate knew she had to straighten this out. "Actually, Nick, he hasn't made that decision yet. We want to make sure it's the right decision before we do it."

"Well, maybe you ought to just make it easy and come up here and help us. You know, join in with us. We'd love to have you guys."

"As you've told us many, many times, Nick. But I'm afraid even I can't make that decision for him. It's something he must do on his own. And if he doesn't make up his mind for another month or two, even if he comes back and hasn't resigned, I'm just not going to push him. I think we've come to a really great understanding, and it's more important that it's the right decision and something that we don't rush into."

"Sounds good to me."

"I was really surprised to hear about the Hellers. Do you know anything different about the situation, and the release of Sheila, or Joan, her real name?"

"No, it is kind of a mystery. I'm sure eventually we will. It just happened, you know just what, two, three weeks ago? I know they're still looking for her and unless they bring additional charges, she was released on time served. Apparently there were defects in the charging that made it so that she has in fact served the minimum amount of time and was able to be released. I don't know how they make these determinations. I'm glad I'm not the person in charge, but that's the way it wound up being. And thank God, they say she's left our area. Let her go prey on somebody else."

"That's just amazing. I can't believe it. Well, that doesn't really affect us. I'm just here to soak up what you know, take it back to San Diego and present the facts, make my case with my husband, and hopefully we can come to some kind of a conclusion and a compromise that'll work for both of us. And of course you heard about his parents, right?"

"Oh yeah, he called me about that. What a shame. I am so sorry for his mother especially. Her life's work up in smoke. I mean, I lived through the fire here at the winery. I don't ever want to do that again. I mean, if it happened to us again, I'd be done. I can't do it again."

"I think you'd find a way. After all, you have a piece of paradise here, don't you?"

Nick stood in the doorway with his arms crossed, scratching his chin with his fingers, a little sparkle to his eye.

"Yeah, it is paradise. And you're right, I would never let it slip away."

CHAPTER 13

G RADY HAD A baseball game after school, so Tyler took Oliver and
Kendall, sat in the bleachers and cheered him on. He got three solid
hits and played third base without an error. The team won by one of the
runs that Grady hit into home.

The team afterwards were cheering and jumping for joy, as they so
far had been undefeated. Plus, Grady's team was on average four to five
inches per player shorter. The others weren't older, or at least they said
they weren't, but Tyler suspected there was some funny business going
on and some birthdates were altered.

The coach for their Giant's team came up to Tyler afterward, shaking his hand. "We would sure be obliged if you would help us out with
the training next year. I mean we're looking through the season and
figuring we're going to place pretty high, so there'll be a lot of kids
wanting to get on the team. I just would love to have an additional
coach, and with your athletic experience and you being a hero, we just
thought it would be wonderful if you could help out. And we understand you have to be gone for long periods of time."

"Well, that's an honor, sir. I'll see what I can do. I always make it a
habit not to promise anything until I check with my better half, though.
She may have other plans for me."

The coach chuckled. "I'm sure she does!"

The kids wanted to go for ice cream, and although they hadn't eaten
first, Tyler relented. He took them to their favorite custard shop, and all
of them, including Kendall, got a single scoop with sprinkles on top. It
had been quite a process to get Kendall to agree to something, she

wanted to have them all, but at the end, she elected for the same combination that her two older brothers did.

They came home for dinner, Tyler having put together some of the things that Kate had set aside and frozen in advance, a nice macaroni and cheese mixture with bacon, which was one of their favorites. He sat down with them and had a salad himself, and a small piece of steak from the night before. He made sure afterwards that they got cleaned up, that they changed into their pajamas and did homework for Grady, Oliver and Kendall were given books to read. No TV. That was a sore subject but they agreed in the end.

It had been a good day, Tyler had made several phone calls, he'd been able to have a workout down at the Team room, Kendall was enjoying her preschool, although it was only two and a half hours long, but she loved the other kids and the teachers. That was making him happy that she had something other than just being home alone with him to occupy her day. He felt it was good for her.

He updated Kyle on what he knew, called his parents and didn't get an answer. Then he called the insurance adjuster.

"I'm sorry I don't have numbers for you yet. The insurance company's kind of dragging their feet though. Not like them. I'll try to get something for you and give you a call by the end of the day."

Well, since that didn't happen, and as life seemed to click away, the minutes and hours of the day were gone, and Tyler knew he'd have to call them tomorrow.

He dialed Kate to check in on how she was doing.

"Oh Tyler it's so beautiful up here. I'd forgotten how pretty it was. I've gotten a lot of information just from talking to Devon and Nick this evening and I got a good tour of the facilities. Tomorrow we're going to go over all the books and how they handle the bookings, how they do their ordering and hiring. It's really a work of love for them, and I didn't realize that they actually make more money on the event center than they do the winery."

"That makes perfect sense. I know they always say if you want to make a small fortune in wineries start with a big fortune. But I know it takes a while to get going. They've been around over 10 years now though, it should be starting to take hold."

"Well, remember they bought the new property last year and it does take six, seven, maybe eight years to have a full harvest out of new vines. And they've gambled on the varieties. There's a lot to wine making that I never realized. Oh, and the Hellers have just more or less imploded on themselves. They're in horrible shape I guess."

"Really? How so?"

"They took on partners to try to stay afloat after the theft of all that money, and I guess missus is sick again with her cancer. Randy's been trying to run the winery but he's proving to be a very incompetent manager, which I could have told them."

"No kidding. I wouldn't put him in charge of anything. Not even the wait staff or the trimming crew."

"Well, here's the other thing, they've released Sheila from prison. Apparently, she was sent up north to some super-max prison? But something was discovered with her case, and she was released. They said she'd already served her time. I think she only served seven years."

"All that money and she only served seven years?"

"It was some kind of an error with the judge's charging orders, a technicality, and she got a good attorney, and that's what happened. She's off. She's free."

Tyler heard the little bells and whistles going off in the back of his head. "So where is she?"

"Nobody's seen her. Nobody knows. She doesn't have any probationary period, so she doesn't have to check in with anyone. Except for the fact there's still an ongoing investigation as to where the funds are, which she claims she doesn't have and always claimed somebody else had put her up to it, there isn't anything they can hold her on until they have proof. And that's the problem."

"Wow. That's one dangerous person out there. She's a really good con artist. One of the best I've met. I wonder what the hell she's up to."

"Well, apparently, she's made some friends, because her connections helped her get that high-priced attorney and get her off the hook, and she's not doing anything as far as anyone knows. But as long as she stays out of everybody's way, hopefully the Hellers will win out the suit on the insurance claim, which is still ongoing. Devon told me there was some talk about Sheila claiming that money because of her wrongful prosecution, although that hasn't been ruled. She's just been released for lack of evidence. So she's sticking with it all until the Hellers are driven into the ground."

"She's diabolical. They weren't saints, but they didn't deserve that. What a vampire."

"I could see how Mr. Heller would be despondent. Not helping Mrs. Heller with her cancer either. All this has just killed the two of them. So unfair."

"And yet, they caused some of this themselves," Tyler said.

"It's true. Came out of pure hubris. Remember when they thought they could order everyone around?"

"There's a saying about that."

"Been a problem for them financially. But maybe eventually they'll get paid off. In the meantime, they have partners that have rebuilt the place and it looks terrible—at least that's according to Devon. I'm not going to set foot on that property ever again."

"That's my girl. You stay as far away from Randy Heller and his family or anyone associated with that winery. And Kate, if you see Sheila, you stay away from her too. Now that she's out and about, that kind of gives me a whole new perspective on my parents' fire. Do you suppose she would stoop to something like that? I mean you were friends with her for several years."

"Tyler, I don't even know if I ever really knew her. She's an odd duck, and has just strange reactions to things. I mean look at how she went off on me to try to get to you. She's just odd and damaged some-how. And blames everybody else I guess. Now going after the Hellers when she was the one who caused their demise in the first place. Give that woman some money, and you're right, she's almost evil. Dangerous is too mild a word."

"Like I said, stay clear away. If you see her, let me know right away."

"I've washed that whole scenario of what we went through 10 years ago, I've washed that out of my system. I don't spend any time thinking about it."

"Well, that's probably good. But keep a lookout for any little sign that doesn't make sense. You may be done with her. Maybe she won't be done with you, and she knows a lot about you, Kate. Look at what she tried to do with me?

"You're right. I promise."

"I need to check with the investigators then and maybe give them a heads-up. Thanks for that, and just remember, I can't wait till you come home on Saturday."

"Me too."

"Oh I almost forgot. Grady's team won tonight. They're so excited, that makes them undefeated. And this was the best team in their league so they have high hopes for taking the championship. The coach has asked me to help with the coaching next year. I told them I would have to check with my business manager, you."

"Thanks, Sweetheart. Say, I've got to run, but I'll check in with you before I come home. In the meantime I'm safe, I'm having a great time, I just love your friends Devon and Nick. They've treated me like a queen. Nick even asked why I didn't bring the whole family. I think the next time I'd like to do that if you're up for it."

"We'll get our calendars cleared out so we can do that. Maybe after I get back from deployment. We need to have a nice long trip to wine country. I know you'd enjoy it, it'd be great to see your parents, and there's lots of fun stuff to do. But you take care and stay safe, and don't go streaking off doing anything on your own okay?"

"Yes sir. Roger that!"

Tyler placed a call to the investigator he had spoken to at the site, and had several follow-up calls with.

"I just wanted to let you know that someone from our past, a woman who professionally embezzled I think over a half a million dollars from this winery in Santa Rosa, has been released unexpectedly and was in one of your prisons in the north, my wife said it was a maximum-security prison, and I am just calling to let you know that she's been released about three weeks ago and kind of has an ax to grind against our family, but mostly me. However, she did exhibit some rather dangerous behavior against my wife, and I don't know if this would have anything to do with the arson, but I sure would like it if you would add that to your list of things to check out."

"What's her name?"

Tyler gave him her name, as well as the name she went by, and explained the two. "She's apparently made friends with certain people in prison, she never returned any of the money or they couldn't find it, as she claimed it was somebody else who was behind her thefts, but apparently she bought herself a high-powered attorney, which tells me she might still have access to the funds. And the fact that she's only served seven years out of a 15-year sentence, not because of good behavior but because of some kind of an error, that just smacks as something wrong. My wife just mentioned it to me or I would've told you earlier. We thought she was safely tucked away and wouldn't be a problem for years. I doubt though that the time in prison has made her any less ardent about coming after us. But maybe I'm just being paranoid."

"I remember that case, and I remember hearing that she'd been released too. But my understanding is she's sort of disappeared into the woodwork."

"That's what my wife understands as well. There was some talk when she was behind bars that she would go after the owners' insurance claim, if you can believe such a thing. Just when I thought I'd heard it all, something like this happens, and makes me wonder."

"Yeah, try being in my line of work. You see much more than you ever wanted to."

"Please, just put your feelers out to check it and see what you come up with. I know you can't divulge everything, but let me know if there's anything else I can shed light or background on, and I just would be curious if you have any sightings or anyone has had any communication with her or her attorney."

"Who's her attorney?"

"I have no idea. I'm sure you could find it in the record, but nobody informed us, reached out to us, and I don't even think Mom and Dad know. I'm going to call them so they know that Sheila's been released, just in case they see her. It would surprise my mother especially if she was on the street. And I don't think she'd stay anywhere close to where the prison is so she's probably long gone. But I just want you to know."

"Thanks Tyler. I'll put the word out. You take care then."

CHAPTER 14

K ATE AND DEVON poured over the websites Devon used to advertise the wedding center, also showed her a list of vendors that she had cultivated over the years running the place.

"You want to have a newsletter sent out to all your former attendees. When they do make reservations online, we get their email addresses and ask their permission to be placed on the list. We also give referrals to people who refer others to our center, and that has really generated a lot of business, because families of families who have attended here love it and then want to use it for their wedding sometimes years later."

"Got it," Kate said. "Makes total sense."

"The winery is a different story altogether and it's not as fan-based run as the wedding center. So in that event we have our winemaker help us to enter into contests and things so we can get recognition and notoriety. We do every celebrity chef-type activity in Sonoma County we can, any wine tasting that we can be invited to, we do. I think it's very important that we both are the front and center spokesman for the winery, the lavender farm, and for the events center. And one kind of cross pollinates the other."

"What do you mean by that?" asked Kate.

"Well, when we're at a tasting event, we're also advertising the wedding center. When we're doing the wedding and taking reservations for that we make them an offer to use our wines at a discount, so that it's in essence a wine tasting for a captive audience while they're at the event. And one does compliment the other. The lavender farm we have contracted with a group of women who have a nonprofit setting up homes for battered women or women with children or women with young babies, and I've allowed the proceeds from that, and they're not tremendous, but it's something, we've allowed the proceeds to be a write off for us and allowed the ladies to use our lavender to make their oils and creams and sprays. It really does my heart good to do that for somebody, and it also is good for business. So it shows that we're trying to do good things for the county, for the area, and for these women in particular."

"I knew about the lavender farm, but I didn't realize you did that," said Kate. "I'm amazed at all of this, Devon."

"Well, it's taken a while to build and to develop, and for a number of years you know we were wrapped up in this lawsuit with our neighbor. That kind of took us off track for a few years, but it's now solidified to the point that we are able to do solid growth every year, and barring any unusual event that would say wipe out our grapes or, you know, some weather event that would be difficult to absorb, the center still goes on. As you can see from my reservation list we're now booking things two years out. And those places have to pay in full at least 12 months in advance."

"So what happens if they decide not to get married, or they cancel for some reason?"

"That happens, and it's a case-by-case basis. If it's a hardship where one of the parties is ill or has passed away and that's happened to us unfortunately, or perhaps the parents have fallen on hard times and the money is not there to complete what they had promised their son or daughter, those are hardships that are tough. Now if it's a case of the couple behaving badly and being children, or parents trying to book something to lock them into a wedding, and you know, we see that all the time, we really do, it's a different story."

"But you charge for it, right?"

"Yes, we always do charge a cancellation fee, but we don't ever keep all of their money. That's just not fair and it causes too much ill will. There are some places that do though, and some of the big hotel chains are not very good about releasing people from their obligations. But we try to work it on a case-by-case basis and give them terms or give them a discount so that they can still go forward and have the event but have it impact them less. You know, at the end of the day, we're all people in this together, and you won't get referrals if you treat people poorly."

"Okay so I see you've got these sites. These are pre-made websites that you can lock into?"

"Yes, there are a number of wedding shows, wedding programs, there are many places where you can advertise, I mean, we could spend a fortune on advertising and we do as much as we can, but we don't want to get overloaded. We attend all of these shows, we've tried to get a film crew here to do a destination wedding type of project, but so far that's still in the works and hasn't come to fruition. But you can see we've got like 15 or 20 places we can advertise online and just like Vrbo, they can click through and see the different places. Some of these sites are even international, so you're getting people from all over the world who want to come to Sonoma County and book a site. When we first started, this wasn't as extensive. But now, with the absolute birth of all these destination wedding venues, people are building hotels next to wineries and doing all kinds of things to really enhance the whole experience."

"You make it look easy. A hotel? Like Hotel Dunn?"

"That will never happen. While that's not something we want to do, this is a growth industry. And there's no stopping it. Some people spend obscene amounts of money for their weddings. A little less for anniversaries."

Kate and Devon went through the bookings, how the bookings were handled, she showed Kate her website, she told Kate they even had a full-time website manager and reservation manager who monitored the traffic and made it so that Devon and Nick were not stuck on the computer all day long.

"That's a very important hire, when you get to the point where you're just going crazy and you can't handle everything, you have to make that hire very strategically, has to be somebody who's well-organized, who knows how to check things and gets right back to people. We get bookings because we contact people right away. You'd be surprised how many people just never get back to their clients and then a week or two later they've found another site. So it's a very important position."

She showed Kate into another office area.

"You can see the gal over here," Devon pointed to a cubicle encased in glass, where a young woman was sitting at a desk with two large screens side by side, a pair of headphones and microphone on her head.

"Molly is our go-to gal, and she also majored in computer science in college, so she was a great find, and she loves doing this job. In fact, she doesn't want to expand her operation at all, doesn't want to take on additional duties, and we'd probably give it to her if she wanted. But we're happy with her, we're not going to mess with success."

Kate wanted to visit her mother and she asked if Devon would like to come.

"I'm afraid I can't, I've got too much to do here. But you can borrow my car and go see her if you like. I'm just not going to be available, and I have to do some errands downtown."

"Why don't I agree to meet you somewhere, and we'll have lunch then?"

"Okay, I'll drive one of the company trucks then and I'll meet you."

They chose a small delicatessen downtown that had been one of Kate's favorites growing up.

After visiting her mother and father, Kate headed for the late luncheon with Devon. Walking up and down the downtown area of Santa Rosa, Kate was flooded with past memories of her childhood, her high school years, and her early years working for Heller Winery. She remembered her first pair of tennies and colorful socks she bought from the eclectic gift center catering to teens. The used record store was gone, but in its place, was a nail bar and beauty salon. A couple of Shabby Chic designer stores sat side by side, as well as a bunch of new bistros, wine bars and children's clothing outlets.

She knew she wouldn't recognize anyone, and most of the stores were new to her. There were a few more boarded-up businesses than she had remembered, and a few more people hanging out in the park than she'd remembered. But all in all, it was nothing like the Portland scene. And she hoped it never would be.

Out on the patio of the deli, she got a table, had a light spritzer soda, and waited for Devon. About ten minutes later, she arrived.

"Wow what a morning. I just got back from the insurance company and it looks like we're going to be saving some money on our insurance because of our lack of claims. And that's such good news because it's a huge cost to us," said Devon. She sat and leaned into the table.

"I haven't ordered yet so choose whatever you like. It's on me."

"So how do you like downtown Santa Rosa? Does it bring back memories?"

"Oh of course it does. I am accustomed to San Diego now though, and it feels like home, mostly because the kids feel like it's their home. It took me a while though. This was a beautiful place to grow up. I don't regret living here at all."

"That's what I thought too. I mean we looked at other places and we thought, oh maybe we should go up north or maybe we should go south, maybe we should even consider going down there to San Diego, but with my business also real estate, which is now kind of phasing out—I've turned a lot of things over to another agent in the office—I work with some of my key clients on very large projects, but I wouldn't have that additional business. Now that the winery and center has taken off, I can give up some of that and it won't impact our future. It's kind of nice when you can transition from something you loved but had to do into something you love and love to do."

"That's what I'm looking for, Devon. And thanks for all this. It's been an eye-opener. I see how you do this, and I see what a difference it's made for you guys, and I'm just amazed at your operation. Nice thing is that you do most of it, don't you?"

"I wouldn't say that. Nick is in charge of all the work, the labor part of things. I just manage the publicity, the books, the office and the customer relations. In a way, it was something I was always good at before when I did real estate full time."

"I would not have known there was so much to do."

"You'll do it your way, Kate, if you do it. And you know, I have to say it, the opportunity is still there for you to come in and join us. Never feel like you have to be a stranger."

They started reviewing the menu when a shadow fell over Kate's end of the table. Looking up, she stared into the red rheumy eyes of her former fiancé, Randy Heller.

"Oh my gosh!" she said, startled. And then she realized she shouldn't have reacted so strongly, but the fear was real. She looked at

Devon, who was puzzled and turned to see Randy, and quickly turned around and kept her back to him. Devon watched Kate carefully as if looking for a sign they should leave.

"Randy you scared me I'm so sorry. And I just didn't expect to see you."

It was obvious he was drunk, smelled of urine, his clothes were disheveled, his hair was uncombed and looked like it had been uncombed for several days. He frankly looked like someone who slept in a park all day long, wasn't the son of a prominent winery owner. His pants were too long for his frame as his frame had gotten skinnier, he smiled a weak smile and revealed yellow, crusty teeth, which absolutely turned Kate's stomach.

His appearance reminded her of someone who might be asking for money at the side of a roadway, a supermarket.

"To the woman who ruined my life."

Kate reacted to this with a combination of offense and fear. It was such a wrong characterization. She couldn't let the comment go unchallenged.

"I wasn't the one that ruined your life, Randy. That was Sheila. Sheila did that to you and your family."

"But if you hadn't decided to break off the engagement, I would've never gotten involved with her."

She stiffened further. "Also not true. As I recall it a little differently, Randy, you told me you'd been involved with her before. Sheila is the one who stole all your money, and made your life hell. All I did was decide not to marry you. And I'm sorry if you blame me, but that's unwarranted."

"If you can sleep with yourself at night, I guess everything's okay." His voice wafted out into the ether, fading. Then he redirected to her. "You know that Mom's sick, right?"

"I've been told. I've also been told your dad's not doing well."

"No, they're not doing well at all. I'm not doing well, either."

"I am truly sorry. Your parents were very nice to me always. And none of my decisions had anything to do with you. They had more to do with where I wanted my life to go. I just changed my mind about it. But I worry about you, Randy, and I want you to know I did care deeply about you."

"But you didn't love me."

The waiter made a point to step in and insert himself in the conversation, probably watching the communication and the expression of the customers standing nearby. "Excuse me, sir, I'd like to ask you not to bother the customers please."

Kate was glad he was a rather tall, muscular man, easily outmatching whatever strength Randy had left. Randy smirked, shrugged his shoulders, and held up his right hand, twinkling his fingers in a silent goodbye. He turned around and left, disappearing around the corner.

Devon reacted first. "Oh my God, I had no idea it was that bad, Kate. What a mess he is."

"I think he's gotten into something, probably some substance abuse of some kind, and he's not himself. I mean, that's not the Randy I used to be in love with. That's a shell of a person. And I feel sorry for him, and I guess I do feel a little bad."

"Oh, absolutely not, Kate. He put you through a wringer. And the parents, pushing their way around, I heard your mother talk to them several times, and I even talked to Gretchen about it too. They were not exactly nice to you like you say they were."

"It doesn't matter now. It's just how they were. I'm sure they never expected to fall on such hard times. That's what happens when you get involved with a con artist. The real culprit in all this is Sheila. She's the one that should have paid. Everything she touches rots. I don't understand people like that."

"Don't be naive, Kate, you have to be careful. With all this going on, you need to distance yourself from all of it. Yes we care about our fellow human beings, but we have to stay away. And I'm sorry, but they chose the path they took. They have to have a certain amount of responsibility for it. Maybe Mr. Heller is not only saddened by his wife's illness, but he's probably very saddened by what's happened to Randy. You know every parent wants to do the best for their kids, and look at where they are now. That is a very heavy burden, but don't blame yourself, Kate, please don't blame yourself. It's not healthy."

Devon leaned across the table and took Kate's hand.

"It's the drugs, Devon. The drugs destroy everything. Everything good about a person. It sucks people dry. So sad."

"People who go that path are dangerous, Kate. They can't help but use and blame others. They need treatment, not your pity."

"I never thought I would see this creep into my life, I never thought I would experience this firsthand. This is always something that happens to somebody else, not me."

"But Kate, you know, in our community, we have lots of happy couples that wind up in some kind of trouble, sometimes he doesn't come home, sometimes there's injuries and the happy ever after doesn't happen for them. I think what I'm saying is you want to be careful, but you also don't want to forget to be grateful. We have the best life possible, Kate. We're married to heroes, to men we can count on, to men who will protect us. And yes, not every man is a hero, not every wife is a supporting loving wife, a good mother. But we have the best of what there is and I will always respect the years that Nick spent on the Teams, but I am so grateful he is done with that. And thank God he loves what he does now."

It gave Kate a lot to think about. The appearance of Randy took her appetite away, but she picked at her food a bit, and then their conversation just stopped. Her heart was broken, not because of what had happened in her life, but what had happened in their life. She felt sorry for him even though she probably shouldn't. She still did. She wished there was something she could do, but she also realized, if she did it would be violating her agreement with Tyler. There was no way in the world she was going to do that.

CHAPTER 15

TYLER BEGAN TO be concerned when he still could not reach his parents. He wanted to let them know about the possibility that Sheila was out there. He wished that he was in Portland to check on them physically, so he called the fire inspector and asked if they could do a welfare check or send somebody from the police department to do a welfare check on them.

"They're older, not elderly, but they've been through a lot. I would just appreciate it if one of your guys could go up there and just make sure they're okay. God forbid something would happen and they had a fall or one of them had a stroke and the other one got injured trying to take care of them."

"Do you go days without talking to them?"

"Of course. But right now, we're in the middle of this investigation. It's very unlike them to not answer my calls. And they know there's lots of people involved in this whole affair, so they would be by the phone. That's just who they are." Tyler said.

"Were they planning on going anywhere?"

"No. Absolutely not. Also out of character."

"Okay. I think you have a valid point there. I'll send one of the deputies over to do a welfare check then, and I'll call you back."

"Thank you so much. And is there anything further about your investigation?"

"Well, the only thing that we are a little bit stumped about is the fact that several of the cameras in the warehouse district, and there weren't a lot of them, were disabled. It looks like they were taken offline the day before, which begins to look like a planned event, right?"

"Of course it does. And what about the suspect or suspects?"

"Well, the main suspect who was seen during the painting during the demonstration, and we don't have a picture of the suspect at the warehouse, but the suspect that was at the downtown demonstration was very slight, and wore all black, including a black beanie and a black face covering. I would even offer to say that it was probably a teenager of some kind or young man. It's just odd that we have only one person doing that and everybody else running around setting fires to garbage cans, bashing in windows, and shouting and carrying signs. This particular person was definitely laying the groundwork for a lot of future damage. And the face recognition software doesn't work when they cover up their faces, and they frequently use umbrellas to cover their actions as well, so it's even hard to assess their body type. But I'm still of the theory that this isn't a huge, organized effort, and I still think it's the work of one individual."

"So, can I ask you about the release of Sheila, the lady that was involved in the fraud and embezzlement of the winery in Santa Rosa, the lady who accosted my wife? Do you think she might have had something to do with this or could that figure in the movie be a woman, not a man?"

"You gave me the heads-up, and we are still investigating those possibilities, but at this point I don't think so. It's just not something we see every day. I think it's just some kid who's disgruntled. And somehow got access to the materials. I wouldn't go that far as to say there's some kind of big conspiracy going on. You want to be careful about that Mr. Gray. And our resources are limited, getting smaller by the day, unfortunately."

"I understand. Well, please, after you do the check, have my mother call me, so I don't worry so much? Otherwise, I'm going to be flying up there and I'm going to be your worst enemy."

He chuckled. "Well, you'd have to join the line, son. I appreciate your tenacity and I'd probably be the same way if it was my parents, but please don't interfere with what we're trying to do. We're trying to do the best job possible. And there's a lot of loose ends here and unfortunately some politics involved as well."

Twenty minutes later, Tyler got the call he'd been dreading. "I'm sorry to tell you this, Mr. Gray, but your parents aren't at home. Now there is a vehicle there at the house. It's a small Volkswagen Bug, but it doesn't look like it operates. Do they have another vehicle that they could be using?"

Tyler gripped the side of the chair in the living room. His kids were running around the backyard having a normal day, and Tyler was all of a sudden descending into the pits of hell with worry and concern over his parents. And it wasn't only just over his parents, if there was something happening with them, it was only going to be a matter of time before it engulfed all of them.

"They have a van, a Volkswagen van, a vintage one. And that's what they use, I just don't understand, did it look like the house had been lived in?"

"Well, here's the thing, their cell phones were in the kitchen on chargers. It appears they left without taking them. That's damned odd, don't you think? With an investigation going on, why would they not bring their phones with them?"

"And the house, was it damaged at all or tossed or was it, were there dirty dishes?"

"No, everything looked clean and neat, it looked like their bed hadn't been slept in or maybe they just make their bed early in the morning when they get up, I don't know. The neighbors say they haven't seen them since yesterday morning and they did leave briefly in the van, and then came back, and then somebody came back late last night but nobody saw any lights on in the house and the van's gone this morning. So I am going to put out a request for all units to be on the lookout for the van, and I have one other thing I want to tell you about."

Tyler braced for the worst.

"Okay."

"Remember when you told me yesterday about the attorney that handled the charge for Sheila?"

"Yes, I do."

"Well, I checked the court records, and they've used a gentleman by the name of Gregory Poplin, who's a big wig attorney out of a firm back east somewhere, but he specializes in helping protestors beat convictions for damage and loitering and all of that stuff. You're going to love this. His parents served time for blowing up a bank building years ago when he was a baby."

"Oh shit."

"No kidding. He's also a homeless advocate, and he's been quite vocal and nasty to our local police force. She used him, partially funded by their Rights and Justice League, it's a group that helps bail out trespassers and people who are doing protests for certain causes. And they have every right to protest, but this group was selected to help people in that situation, especially those charged with violent insurrection."

"Great." Tyler was getting sicker by the minute.

"This gentleman did handle her case and was able to get her released. Now, normally he would cost a fortune to handle something like this, but with the foundation, she probably got some help. I don't like that he's involved in this, I don't think he's involved in anything criminally, but he represents a lot of people who we think have been involved in criminal work. So, it's possible that if there's talk about going after insurance proceeds for this winery like you told me yesterday, it's possible he's behind it. And what that means is Sheila may be local now. It may be that we're looking for her as well as whomever else was involved in this protest. And I hate to tell you this, Tyler. Because it opens up a whole new avenue of issues, I'm afraid I'm going to have to leave it in the FBI's hands—let their good people work on it. This is going way beyond what I can do."

Tyler was shaking when he hung up the call.

Even though the inspector had apologized, still offered to help on a limited basis, he just felt like his swim buddy had turfed the class and quit. He didn't have any allies left, at least not at first.

And then he thought about the Bone Frog Protection Group and the words Bryce had told him when he called him a few days ago. He picked up the phone and dialed his number.

At first, a recording came on the line, and then Bryce picked up.

"How you doing Tyler? Are things getting resolved?"

"As a matter of fact, I'm calling you, because I think I'm going to need your services. You were nice enough to offer, but I'm going to just get right down to it Bryce. I think my parents have been kidnapped. I haven't talked to them since the day before yesterday, and I just had the police go over and do a welfare check on them and they are not home. And they've also left their cell phones in the kitchen charging. That's not like them. I have a really bad feeling about it. I am about ready to jump on a plane and get up there but I have the kids and I promised that I wouldn't get involved. I promised Kyle, I promised Kate, I just need some help."

"Okay, man, we've got your back. I'm going to have to do a full incident report."

Bryce began grilling him on all the details of what Tyler knew, what he'd been told, and the timing of everything.

"Is there anything new in the investigation that I should know about?"

"They've brought in the Feds."

"That's a good thing, Tyler. They have resources the locals, even big city locals, don't have. Anything else?"

He also filled him in on the past confrontation with Sheila, the Hellers and the attack on Kate.

"She's a very sly, shady character. She embezzled money from the winery where Kate worked and has almost put that winery out of business. She was convicted of embezzlement and was due to spend fifteen years in prison, but she's been released now in seven, and she was befriended by some individuals while incarcerated, and put in touch with a high-powered attorney who got everything dismissed. It looks like and just feels like her hand at play here."

"Wow, you got a lot going on there, Tyler. How the hell did you think you could help your folks out with all this?"

"At the time, it wasn't with all this. It was just a fire. But things have been developing quickly and as I started to learn more details, I got more and more concerned. I'm smart. I know when it's more than I can take on."

"Yup. That's what a smart man does. We have sources you don't have, can sometimes find things others miss. It's why business is booming. If it comes to that, we do hostage rescue, and negotiation, too. You know that."

"Of course you do. Now Bryce, I don't want to be a crazy conspiracy theorist, and that's what the local police and fire chief thinks of this theory, but you and I know when we have a gut feeling, a hunch, we have to follow it up. So I'm looking to you to jump in and see what you could find out about this attorney, about this person, and see if she's left any tracks or if there's any evidence at the house that my parents live in that would indicate where they are?"

"I'm happy to do so, Tyler. You stay put though, you don't want to jeopardize your career by jumping into something you can't do. That's why we're here. And I will get the guys together and we'll put together something, do a little bit of legwork. You let me know the instant you get a whiff of something going on I don't know about, you hear?"

"Okay, thanks man. I love you brother."

"Right back at you, Tyler. Don't worry until you have something to worry about. We're going to do whatever we can and even a little bit more."

CHAPTER 16

KATE'S UNEXPECTED MEETING with Randy still bothered her, even after several hours. It was a face-to-face confrontation with pure evil. He was a stranger to her, a dangerous one, too. He had fallen so fast, so hard, so far to the bottom, that it scared her. It also scared her that his once powerful family, although extremely obnoxious during their heyday, had lost nearly everything now, including their own health, their own family unit. It was such a shame, and she was filled with grief and sadness.

Life can be a fickle lover sometimes, she said to herself. It was a phrase Tyler had used many times. It demonstrated how differently people reacted to negative things: some leaned in and made things work, or lessened the blow with their attitude, and others allow the situation to ruin them.

She'd also read in a self-help book, "Circumstances don't make a person, they reveal a person." And that was equally true. Some people reacted to small hiccups like it was the end of the world, while others could manage something huge and devastating, and learn from it, heal from it.

She knew which personality trait Tyler was. She hoped she was the same.

The fact that he blamed her for his troubles was a complete surprise. It showed Kate how devoid of reality he really was. She had done everything she could to let him down nicely, but in hindsight, she knew all along that being beside him, with that family, was going to be a mistake. She had no idea how right she'd been. And that also scared her.

One thing was for sure, the only thing she wanted to do now was to go home. She'd done the investigation, enjoyed spending time with Devon and Nick, and could see herself running her own business, like Devon did, and it excited her. Everything was on a positive lane until she saw Randy. Was he some sort of soul sucker who liked to put clouds in everyone's day? His refusal to see his own flaws and choices made it so no one else around him could survive either. He was in a downward spiral until he crashed and burned. There was nothing for him now.

But she'd gotten her answer for now. She could see the possibilities available to her, but only if it was the right time. And the answer very clearly was that this wasn't that time. And although she could have been disappointed, she chose to be strong, to face it head-on, "live for another day," another one of her favorite sayings. Now was the time to just stay together as a family unit, strengthen that unit, and not make any big changes.

What was most important was to help Larry and Deidre figure out what the rest of their lives were going to be first before she really started making any big plans for her family. No matter what happened, if they came to San Diego, if they rebuilt in another area, or even rebuilt at that location—even if they had lost it all and wouldn't be able to rebuild—discovering the way of that and the impact it would have on the whole family had to come first. They still had lots of time to plan. And although Tyler was open to the possibility of leaving the Teams, she wasn't sure now that she wanted to even ask him to do that.

When she turned into the gravel driveway, her phone rang, and it was Tyler. Her heart fluttered and instantly she was energized, filled with joy.

"Oh, Sweetheart, it's so good to hear your voice. I have had one hell of a day," she said to him.

"Well, that makes two of us, Kate."

He was direct and wasn't looking for chit-chat.

"Look, I'm going to ask you if it would be possible for you to come home. There are some things that have come up."

Kate noticed how cold his voice was, and that scared her.

"What's happened, Tyler?"

"We can't find Mom and Dad. And we are now shifting into the mode that something has happened to them. And I hesitate to ask you this, Sweetheart but I just have to. I know I said I wouldn't get involved, but I just cannot stay down here and wait for other people to do things that I could do. I want to go find them, I want to be part of that process. I just would not live with myself if I didn't."

"Well, of course. I would expect nothing less, Tyler."

He sighed and finally answered her. "You don't know how much that relieves me. You know, I took an oath to you when I said that I would not get involved and would let the authorities handle this, and I promised Kyle as well, but this is turning out to be a real mess. Much bigger than I thought it was. And I kind of feel like I'm in the center of it, like I'm the center of the wheel, not responsible for things, but somehow everything goes through me. Like someone is using everybody else around me to get to me. Does that make sense?"

"It does. But wouldn't it be safer if you just stayed in San Diego, stayed out of it, out of their way?"

"Let's look at that for a second, Kate. Me staying safe while my parents could be in peril? You think I could let that happen? You know I couldn't."

"I got it. That was me not thinking. Of course, you have to go, and of course, I will come home. I'll be home tomorrow. I'll get a flight somehow even if I have to go to LA and take a bus home." She hesitated and then added, "But are you going to be there?"

"Well, that's the thing, Kate. I want to get up there as soon as I can. So what I was thinking is I would drop the kids off at Gretchen's, and Gretchen and Angela could watch them until you could get home. I'm afraid I won't be here when you get home. But I'll check in with you. I've got a whole team of guys that said they'd help me here, and Bryce and his team are up there combing around looking for clues, so we'll see what goes on, and hopefully, we'll be able to find out what's happened and who's involved and get them brought to justice. I just don't know how long it's going to take. It bothers me I can't make promises."

"I understand, Tyler. I really do. We'll be good. And don't worry about me. My afternoon was quite an eye-opener. I'm not quite sure I want to be looking at making other choices right now."

"I'm in the same boat, Sweetheart. Let's just get to a level playing field first. And then when we can, we'll make those decisions, okay?"

"You got it. I love you so much, Tyler. Please be safe."

"Now that's a promise I'm going to keep."

She couldn't help but be disappointed, but at least she would see the kids. Then her logical side kicked in. "Where are you going to stay? Do you have some place safe?"

"I wish you had seen the Riley Estate, it's a fortress. Bryce and a whole bunch of his guys are there, old teammates of mine, some from other teams, some from other special ops groups, and then I'm going to bring three or four guys from here. We'll all be together, just like when we do an op overseas, which is how we figure stuff out. Not only will it be safe, the combined use of our brainpower is how this mystery is going to be solved."

"Okay, God speed. And please let me know when you get there."

That settled it for Kate, and she was not displeased she had to go home early. She might have even requested that anyway. She was done for now, considering all the possibilities that could be. She wasn't ready to give up the dream, but the timing sucked completely. And until Tyler's parents were helped and found and escorted to safety, there wasn't going to be any talk of running a new business, risking money, or risking more than she had to spend.

Once inside Nick and Devon's house, she sought them both out. "It looks like there's a problem with Tyler's parents. They've gone missing," she said.

"Oh no!" screamed Devon.

Nick was stoic in his answer. "That's not good."

"I'm going to try to get a standby flight out if I can tonight or tomorrow."

"So Tyler's going up there tonight?" Nick asked.

"Yes."

"And he's taking guys too, I'll bet."

"Yes, he said so."

"Where are the kids going to be?" asked Devon.

"They'll be at Gretchen's, until I get there. So I just need to find a flight, the soonest one out, and I'm even okay if I fly into LA and then take a bus back, but I need to leave as soon as possible."

Devon approached her carefully. "Here's what I think. It would be easiest on you if you spend the night, get some rest. The kids are going to be fine if they're going to be over at Gretchen's, and just take care of yourself. We'll take you to the airport in the morning. Let me get online and see what I can find for you and then I'll give you some choices, so just hang on a few minutes."

"You know, the kids are going to be really upset they didn't get to see you this time. I promised them when I talked to them this morning, that we would make sure they weren't away at camp when you visited. They love you and call you Aunt Kate. Did you know that?" Nick said.

"No I didn't."

"So Devon told me about your meeting with Randy. Gosh he sounds like a real mess. And she picked up some vibes about him being possibly dangerous. Did you get that at all?"

Kate had to admit that she did. And told him so.

"I guess he's a desperate man then, God I just hate to see somebody throw their whole life away. But I think that's what substance abuse does to people. It makes them crazy."

"Unfortunately, yes. Thank goodness they didn't have any kids, I guess he was married a couple of times and wouldn't that be awful if there were children involved?" Kate said.

"Amen to that. All right, so let's get the dinner together and we'll figure out what so you go on up and get yourself showered and changed and if you need me to do any laundry, well, we could do that before you go."

"No I'm fine. Don't worry about me."

"Well, one thing's for sure, there is a devil out there, he grabs people, he shakes them around, he causes terrible things to happen. But the good news is, we don't have to fall for his tricks, Kate. I mean if you look at all of the luck and all of the things we have to feel grateful for, it's a lot more than the other way. I'm just sorry to see someone else go through so much trouble. And I hope he gets help before he starts becoming a further detriment to himself."

"I feel sorry for him too Nick. I sincerely hope that's the case as well."

In the morning, Kate was able to get a flight from Santa Rosa to the

Central Valley, and then a puddle jumper direct to San Diego, which wound up adding about an extra hour to her flight time. She caught a cab, taking her home, where her car was still in the driveway. Tyler must have hitched a ride with one of his buddies because his truck was parked beside hers.

She'd gotten a message from him last night that he had arrived safe and sound. She didn't expect to hear much from him today.

She gave Gretchen a call and arranged to go pick up the kids. It was Easter vacation, their spring break, so the schools had been out for a day and would be out for the next week.

Oliver and Grady were excited to see her, little Kendall was playing with dolls at the corner, some that Gretchen still had from her brood. She walked with Angela, holding her hand, clutching a doll tightly.

"I missed you Sweetheart."

Kendall looked up at Angela, and then back at her mother. She held the doll out to her.

"Angela says I can keep this doll. I've named her Angela. She's pretty don't you think?"

Kate took the doll in her hands and examined her. "She's beautiful, Sweetheart. She's pretty just like you are." She looked up at Angela, "Are you sure this is okay?"

Angela smirked and shook her head. "I got to get rid of some of my dolls anyway, my mom's been after me to do it. This was one of my favorites, and I think it's perfect for Kendall. Right Kendall?"

Kendall grabbed the doll, held it to her chest and nodded her head, yes.

"Okay then, let's get your things together, and where's your mom, Angela?"

"She's on the phone but she'll be right here."

When Gretchen walked in the room, it was obvious she'd been crying. "God damned men!" she sniffled.

"What is it?"

"Well, that big lump of a husband of mine, he told me he was going to take them to the airport? He did, but then he fucking got on the plane too. I just talked to him. I am so pissed at him."

"Don't worry about it, Gretchen, Trace will be fine. He wants to go.

He also knows Portland better than some of the others, I think."

"Yes, you did ask me about him and I did say that he'd be willing to go but damn I didn't think he'd do that. Now we're all alone here. Do you want to just stay here at my place and we can all be together? I mean I hate to have you be at your house without a man and me be at my house without a man. Why don't we just all stay here for a few days until they come back?"

Kate thought about it and it actually sounded pretty good.

"I'll have to go back to the house to get more of their clothes, some for me, but that should work."

"Cool deal. We can stay up all night and watch romance movies."

They both laughed. It was exactly what Kate needed this evening. She needed her kids, and she needed her sister.

"On one condition, Gretchen."

"What's that?"

"You let me buy delivery tonight. I'm starved for pizza," Kate said.

All the kids, including Angela, jumped for joy.

CHAPTER 17

"**Y**OUR MARRIAGE GOING to survive this, Trace?" Tyler asked his buddy. They were traveling in Fredo's truck toward the military transport hangar.

"I think so, she's in tears. I'm glad that Kate's with her. It's tough but she has to understand. I mean, you're my fucking brother-in-law. You think I'm going to let you go through all this crap by yourself? These are your parents for Christ's sakes."

"Oh Trace," said Fredo. "You better be careful with that my friend. I hope you smoothed it over pretty good. Otherwise, you may be sleeping on the couch, and that's one step toward divorce."

Danny laughed. "You probably should listen to Fredo, Trace. He knows whereof he speaks."

"Listen to you fuckhead?" said Tyler. He wanted to draw them into focusing on the mission at hand.

"Okay, we've got a whole lot of things to strategize, and you guys are worried about getting laid? So let's just cut it out and let's pay attention to completing the mission without any major sacrifice."

Trace leaned in and pointed to Tyler with his thumb as if hitchhiking. "He says he's going to quit the Teams, but I think he's going for Kyle's job don't you think?"

The rest of the guys spent the next few minutes giving their highly valued opinion about that.

The transport plane they picked up was a sheer bucket of bolts. It had something wrong with one of its stabilizers, so the darn thing listed a little bit to the left, which was not going to be acceptable if they were delivering high-valued equipment, but for a bunch of raspy old SEALs, it would be fine. There was something perfect about taking the most antiquated behemoth of a ship they could take. *As long as it gets us there,* Tyler thought to himself.

They landed in the private military airport, which was just adjacent to the private airport outside of Portland. There, a military Jeep was waiting for them to escort them out of the field. Though they were all active duty, they didn't have clearance to actually use the site, so they needed to be escorted away, and it would be reported that they had been delivered on time.

There was an old Suburban left for them to use, something that Bryce had arranged. He was to meet them at Riley's compound, and he promised them he'd have some beers and some food for them.

Tyler was anxious to get the updates.

"Hey Tyler, I did bring some fire power. I know we're not supposed to, but I did anyway. Is that going to be cool or do I have to leave that behind at Riley's place?"

"God I don't care. I'm going to let Bryce answer that one. But I will tell you the gun laws here in Oregon are just super strict. You're going to have to be careful about that. No open carry, and as far as the concealed carry, well if they don't know about it, you just don't want to get caught."

"And I have the same question with some of my explosive devices. I know that's why you asked me to come along, so I packed a nice little wad of charges that might come in handy. Do we have any idea where they are? What kind of building they're housed in?"

"No, gents, we don't even know that they've been kidnapped. They could have fallen down in the supermarket and helping each other get up the other one fell down and they could be in the hospital for all I know, but that's just not how it's playing out. So we're going to treat it like it's a regular hostage situation kidnapping. And that's what the Bone Frog group does so well. That's why I asked them."

They drove through downtown Portland and Tyler veered off to the side and took them down through the warehouse district just as it was turning dusk. He didn't want to be down there in an old Suburban with just men in the car, which could flame some kind of gang activity. But he pointed to the strip of charred earth that extended down several blocks, and the big crater behind the Grays' warehouse where the paint manufacturer blew up.

"Was this an intentional set-off or did it just combust?" asked Fredo.

"We're thinking it was just a coincidence, it got hot, and it just combusted. I'm not sure anybody has said anything about explosives, and so far there haven't been any rounds fired either, but somebody did paint this substance and that is highly flammable. But it doesn't explode."

"Sure I've heard of that. It's called boat paste. Originally used to burn barnacles off ships' bottoms. They also use that shit when they want to ram something and cause further destruction. They used to use it in Vietnam believe it or not on some of those little rubber boats. You paste that stuff on the front of it, it hits a tree and just goes up like nobody's business," said Fredo.

"It's funny I've never seen it before. But the fire marshal knew all about it. It's a derivative of some kind and we have some refineries nearby, but he thinks somebody might have picked it up during the disposal period, because that stuff he said isn't used as much as it's dumped. They take it to the Superfund site."

They veered to the left and skirting down along the banks of the Columbia River drove past ten or twelve train track lines, passed the station and large storage yard, and then turned left to head west, and began to climb several hills, winding back and forth until they got to the top.

Tyler showed them his parents' home. "I got keys to it, so we can just do a quick run through here, I don't want to spend very much time because I don't want anybody to know that we've been here. Just do a quick run through, we can do it better in the daylight. I don't want to turn on any lights tonight."

They spread out over the house, everybody searching individual things, of course the first thing several of them looked for was any arms, and Tyler confirmed that his mom and dad didn't own any. There were valuable items that were still left in the house, so it didn't appear to be a robbery of some kind. Mrs. Gray even had her wedding rings in a little ceramic dish by the side of the sink in the master bathroom.

Tyler knew his father kept a safe with some important documents in it, and he found it to be intact in his father's side of the closet, behind the shoe shelves. Nothing appeared to be touched but he didn't have the combination.

Trace brought some baggies to pick up little bits and pieces of things. He pointed to the cell phones that were still charging, and Tyler nodded that yes, he should take them both. He also instructed him to take the charging cords since somebody would have used their thumbprint to get it attached to the wall, and it might make for some good evidence.

"What are we going to do if the police say they don't have it, when they come back and it's gone?"

"I think there are so many cooks in the stew—there's FBI and the local police, even the county sheriff, fire department, the fire inspector— they're probably just going to figure that somebody else picked it up and bagged it. We're not going to touch it. We're just going to see if there's anything of interest on it. I don't think I have any of my mom's passcodes, but I'm going to look through my list just in case. And the biggest thing is going to be who's leaving the messages right now. I want to know who they are."

"Roger that," said Trace.

The four SEALs piled into the Suburban, holding the few items they'd taken from the house in a paper lunch bag. Fredo stowed it underneath the second seat and placed an old blanket in front of it to hide it from view. Within ten minutes, they were driving through the metal gate of Colin Riley's castle on the hill. The gate opened as they approached it, and Tyler drove through very slowly, coming to a halt near the front door entrance.

"Would you look at that?" said Danny.

The lights were stunning from the top of the hill, and the air was so fresh and free of pollutants from all of the rains and the winds that Portland got, the stars appeared to be extra bright this evening. It was a pretty awesome sight.

"Wait till you see the inside of the house, guys. I mean if you think this looks like a castle now, just wait till you see it."

An interesting landscape display was in the garden area just before the front door. There had been pots and trees planted in pots that had been tipped over and cracked and made to look like some kind of a

Roman ruin. Flowers draped over all these broken pieces, and to the side, without the aid of any protection, was Colin Riley's old wheelchair. Someone had cut out the seat of the chair in a circle, and placed a wandering petunia plant there, which took over part of the back and one side of the arm. It was a very touching and fitting memorial to a man who lived larger than his body was capable of carrying him. He spawned the organization, having lost his son to a drug overdose and almost losing a daughter as well. The SEALs were responsible for returning her to him. He lived a brief period of time after the rescue and died a happy man knowing that his legacy would be continued and that some of the very SEALs who had rescued his daughter would be joining his team.

Before Tyler could get to the front door, Bryce Tanner and several other men came barreling out of the house. He could see in the distance several huge flat screen TVs, one of them with a basketball game playing.

"Hey, Tyler! Welcome, Brother. And all of you guys, I know I met you, Trace. I've met you, Danny, I think, but I haven't met you before, have I?" He looked at Fredo.

"I think if you had met me you would remember me. I sure as hell have never seen this place before. Nice digs."

"Well, this belonged to Mr. Riley, of course, and he left this as a training ground, dorm, strategy session think tank, if you will. He left this for all of us to use for as long as we keep the business going. It's been nice to have one place to congregate."

"Are Jenna and Kelly about?" asked Trace.

"Jenna should be here tomorrow. I'm not sure who else is going to be dropping by. Sven Tolar is back in Norway right now, dealing with a family matter."

As soon as they got inside, Bryce showed the men their rooms and let them select the sleeping arrangements. And he also showed them the equipment they had, where they could store any equipment they brought, explained to them they could help themselves to any of the food in the kitchen, and advised that no business was ever talked when the house was being cleaned or the food was being prepared by outside chefs. Then he began the process of updating everyone as to what he'd discovered.

"I found out this Gregory Poplin character is the product of two radical hippies, who got involved in protests during the civil rights movement in the sixties and seventies and wound up going to prison for blowing up a Bank of America building down in Silicon Valley years ago. I guess Gregory Poplin was a child of three at the time, so he was raised by his aunt, his mother's sister. Both of his parents have since passed on, his father in a prison riot and his mother of cancer in prison. He has always been an advocate for lawlessness and lack of police protection; he's an anarchist. A very dangerous one, because he has collected a large war chest of many millions of dollars. It's part of the shadowy underworld of donations that come in and don't get reported, that swing elections. They're bad people. I'm all for making the prison system humane, fair, honest, clean, and danger-free. I'm not for attacking police and fire and burning down buildings and ruining people's lives and their livelihood. This gentleman doesn't seem to quite know the difference between the two."

"So he got this woman out of prison then, correct?" asked Danny.

"Yes, he did. And if I'm not mistaken, there may be some kind of a romance going between the two of them. This is just a rumor. She seems to spend quite a bit of time in his penthouse apartment. And, oh yes, this is the rich part. He claims he is out to support the people, but it's only known to a handful of people that he owns a very fancy $5 million apartment that's roughly 3,500 square feet at the top of one of the insurance buildings downtown. He can see firsthand every single riot and what it does to the downtown area. With binoculars, I'm sure he could have watched the warehouses burn. There are a lot of politicians, especially small local ones, assistant DAs, school board members, people who don't have a lot of political clout, there's a lot of people afraid of him. And they should be."

"Bryce, so you say Sheila was seen going in and out of his place?"

"We've had somebody over at the building ever since your phone call, Tyler. She is a regular visitor, and she frequently spends the night. That's why I believe there is a romantic connection. She is quite a bit younger than he is, but you know how that goes."

"What about my parents?" Tyler asked.

"We're still working on that. I'm trying to get some more information from the inspector's office, but they've all of a sudden gotten pretty tightlipped. I have a feeling they are onto something, and they just don't want to share it. Were you able to pick up their phones?" he asked Tyler.

"Yes, sir, we have them right here." Tyler spread the phones in their baggies on the counter in the kitchen.

"Ronnie?" He called to the other room.

A young boy with frizzy brown hair and huge thick horn-rimmed glasses came running in. He didn't look like he was more than fourteen or fifteen years old, but Tyler recognized him as being one of the sons of one of the Marines who had joined the team. "Okay. This is Ronnie, and he's our electronic specialist. There isn't anything he can't hack or get into. He's going to take these phones and try to get a pattern of where they were up until the time they were plugged in. If my hunch is correct, they may have picked up whoever it was that located them at a store of some kind, perhaps shopping or having a lunch downtown. My feeling is they were recognized, followed, and then they were abducted. As far as we know, there is no ransom demand and no statements have been given to the paper."

"Does the FBI believe they are kidnapped or does the FBI believe they have been killed?" asked Tyler. His comment brought a hush over the group. Tyler, realizing he'd suddenly shut down all conversation, gave his justification, "Hey, I want to know what everybody thinks. I need to know going in what their approach is. If they think my parents are dead, I want to know that. And I want to know why they think that, because that's a clue."

Bryce nodded his head. "Actually, Tyler that's a very good point. I know from my years on the force, if it is believed that the hostage is alive, there's a lot greater care taken to not be discovered. If it's a question of where the bodies are, then it's a full-scale snatch and grab. They go out and they snag everybody they can, they ask as many questions as they can, and hope that they've found somebody that has some kind of knowledge of it. So far, we think that they're assuming that your parents are still alive. But they don't know where they are or who took them."

"Ronnie, I want you to trace where these phones have been, where these phones have gone, and give me a physical map of the Portland area where they traveled to at what time of the day, okay?"

"You got it, sir," said Ronnie. He grabbed the bags and disappeared.

"Just so you know, the police are probably tracing this as well. They have the benefit of having a cell tower to get information from. We're getting it from the source. They don't really physically need the phones to get that information, whereas this is the only way we could get it. The one thing they don't get clearly is messages, people that called and left a message on their phone. That's what we're also going to look at."

Bryce made mention that the men could help themselves to sandwiches in the refrigerator. He suggested everyone shower, get ready for bed, and that first thing in the morning, at daybreak, they would resume their activities.

"That should give Ronnie enough time to get all the data out of these phones, and if any of you get any messages or calls from anybody else on the outside, if it has to do with this investigation, I want you to let me know about it. There's going to be some people that'll snoop around innocently trying to find out what we're doing. They may not all be innocent participants."

"Any other questions?"

Tyler spoke up next. "Bryce, I want to thank you. I want to thank all of you for doing your jobs here. And, Trace, I'm sorry about your marriage."

Everybody chuckled.

"It means a lot to me that you're here. If at any time you guys have to leave, don't feel like you have to stay. This is a non-paid situation, and Bryce has been kind enough to donate his buildings and his services, so there is no burden financially on me or on my parents' estate. That said, I want you to clean up after yourselves, cook for yourselves, and don't be a burden to everybody else. You're going to meet the rest of the team in the morning, and I think you'll find them a real solid group of guys. Except for a couple of people you will be the only other ones staying at this house. Everyone else lives off campus. But for this particular operation I'm going to have all of you stay here, even I won't be going and staying in my parents' house. If anybody comes to the house, Bryce is the only one that answers the door. Are we clear about that?" Everybody nodded their heads.

"Once again guys, get some rest, and let's kick it in gear tomorrow."

CHAPTER 18

I N THE MORNING over coffee, the men sat, laid out all of the places they needed to cover, and the timing of it.

"How you want to do this, Tyler?" asked Bryce. "You want to be lead on this? Or you want us to assign and be point?"

"My ego isn't attached. I want to do whatever's going to get them out safe. I'd say our mission is first to verify that they're there where they are, who's guarding them, and then who's going to stand by and make sure the attorney and Sheila are detained so that the authorities can grab them."

"Sounds good to me. Anyone with questions so far?"

"Let's hear the plan," said Danny.

"Let me begin," Tyler said, "by saying we don't want any loss of life, on either side. We want to incapacitate not kill." Tyler looked at the eyes of the team around him. "I know I don't have to say that, and you guys will be appropriate. But I also don't want any of you harmed, so the use of lethal force is only necessary if it's going to save the lives of one of our team or one of the hostages." He shrugged his shoulders. "That's how I am and I think Bryce you can take it from there."

"Okay. Good reminder of the rules of engagement. So it's going to be a standard cover all the points operation, we follow and identify all the moving parts so we don't encounter any unexpected consequences. I got two men downtown in front of the attorney's building, and I've got one guy up on the floor. We'll be getting good intel about whether or not the attorney and Sheila have left the building. We assume there will be others there, but whoever comes out of that building this morning, we're going to follow. All of them."

Bryce laid out the teams in twos, indicating that each moving part would have coverage of some kind, and that once the holding location for Tyler's parents was identified, they would be verifying proof of life first, and second of all how much manpower they were going to need to conduct the rescue. All in all, they had ten men present and another five out in the field.

Ronnie had identified locations used the day before the Grays went missing, through their cell phones. He was invited to explain and show on the map where they went that day.

"It looks like they went shopping at a supermarket here and they went down to a bookstore in this area here. I believe this is Powell's. Then they bypassed the area where the demonstrations were, and several blocks to the west they stopped at an art supply store, where we believe they purchased some items. They were there for quite a while, almost forty-five minutes."

"That sounds like them," said Tyler. "My mom probably wants to paint. She does that when she gets nervous. She probably went to the arts supply store to buy something."

"OK, good. One of two things happened, either their house was being watched and they were tailed the whole time, or they picked up somebody at the supply shop, at the grocery store or at Powell's. My money's on the fact that they were monitored from the minute they stepped out of the house," said Bryce.

"So how does that jive with the appearance and disappearance of the van? The witness from the neighborhood who saw it come and go?" asked Tyler.

"I believe they came back and then were forced to leave, and someone went back to get something. Perhaps some clothes, perhaps some medication. Something."

"My dad's on quite a bit of medication and takes about six pills every day," said Tyler.

"So that would explain it then, they were told where to come in and where to get the medication, and that shows to me," Bryce barked, "they intended to keep them alive. Or at least for a period of time. I'm not quite sure what the overall game plan was but at least for managing their health, they needed to go back and get his meds. So that would make total sense to me," said Bryce.

"Do you suppose they would be housed in the penthouse?" asked Trace.

"We've been monitoring the penthouse for several days now, and there has been no indication that either of his parents are there. But there have been people coming and going, probably members of Mr. Poplin's inner circle. I don't think he'd be so stupid as to keep them there, because it would implicate him. He's smarter than that."

Tyler agreed with Bryce's opinion. Unfortunately, he didn't like the waiting part.

"So how do we arrange ourselves? Where do we wait? Staying here is too far away," he said.

"I think they would stay pretty close to the downtown area. I'm going to guess and again it's just a guess, that they want to stay mobile, they want to stay in an area where they feel comfortable, and the downtown area that has been taken over, is good cover for them. I mean some of his team could even be sleeping in tents down with the homeless encampments. It would be very hard to find them in that crowd. Also, they wouldn't stand out as being police or military or the good guys, and I think the homeless people would give them cover willingly."

"So, with three at the penthouse, and two or three at my parents' house, where are you going to want us stationed?" asked Tyler.

Bryce showed certain corners where they could have access to buildings, they also suggested that people stay in vehicles where they could be kept warm, and if they needed to move quickly they would have wheels. "This is his home," he said as he pointed to the location of the penthouse building. "And this is his office one block away. Somewhere between there is where I need the rest of you located. We need to cover anybody at any time moving between those two places."

"If you want any fire cover, I'm going to need some kind of a building with windows that open so I can do that for you guys," said Danny. "Any suggestions, Bryce?"

Bryce pointed to a building four doors down from the lawyer's office building. "This has a balcony on the fifth floor with a cafe that sometimes is open there. That would be a good place because it has a slatted railing, and you could see through if you were belly on the ground. It also has a good vantage point to several areas. However, you'd have to avoid being observed from the top of the penthouse which is directly perpendicular to this building. So, this area and this area." He demonstrated with his finger. "These areas would be visible. You'd want to avoid them. I would go there Danny."

"Roger that. And who do I take?"

"I want a volunteer."

One of Bryce's men raised his hand. "Okay. You two take one of our trucks and go make it down there. And please inform me when you're in place. And Connor," he addressed his man, "The security guard at the bottom of this building is a friend of ours, all you have to do is show your card and explain that there's a surveillance detail that we want to do from the rooftop. He'll be cooperative."

"Roger that." Danny and Connor left the room.

"Okay. That leaves these teams," and he demonstrated who was going where. "Tyler, I'd like you to stay with me. Trace, you and Fredo to stay together. But make sure you stay in radio communication with your Invisios, Fredo, if we need some firepower, I'm going to ask you to bring a small pack."

"You got it, sir," said Fredo.

"Nothing too flashy, just something that would get attention or bust open a door if we need it. This time of the morning, a lot of the downtown is going to be just completely dead. There will be some big trucks making deliveries, there will be janitorial services finishing up, it's busy from a commercial side of things but inside the offices, most of them except for the stock brokerages, will be completely empty. It'll be a good opportunity for us to get embedded."

Everyone agreed they understood where they were going and left in pairs.

On the way downtown to their vantage point, Tyler needed Bryce to answer a couple of questions. "You've been here, what? Three, four years now, Bryce?"

"Yes sir. About four years now. We moved the whole family here about six months after I started, just trying to make sure that it was going to be a good fit."

"So how do they feel about this now with all the stuff going on downtown?"

"Well I don't have to tell you that it's good for business, we have done a lot of little jobs just protecting bank presidents and CEOs coming in to attend board meetings and things of that nature, with the climate being the way it is. The police really have their hands full and with the numbers of cutbacks that have gone on and their hesitancy to stir things up, they really can't be counted on for protection. So we've been really busy with these small jobs."

"But you didn't answer my question."

Bryce turned down one of the main streets leading toward the bookstore, heading right through the center of the free zone where there were barricades, posters and even occasionally armed protestors manning the perimeter, dressed in full body armor.

"What does that remind you of?"

"Fuckin' A. You name the city. Djibouti, Ngala, Cape City."

"I'm not going to lie to you and say that my wife loves it here. It's probably not safe for her to live anywhere else though. I don't want to have to defend her from a long distance. So in order to take this position over and run this team, it was important that she move here. If she didn't want to willingly, then no way was I going to take the job. Since then, that's been the biggest problem in recruiting. I can't get them to come. The guys want to, but the families don't want to live here anymore. At first, it was just a nuisance. Now it's a real health and safety issue. There's so many companies leaving that the condition of the downtown is not going to improve. It's just going to get worse and worse. Not until they start voting in some people that want to do something about it. So that's where we're at."

"Sounds like the perfect profile for your team is experienced older guy, divorced, with grown kids. Doesn't have a family to protect, right?"

"That's about right. You probably know that's the biggest attrition for SEALs—the families they leave behind. Takes a special guy to do what you guys do and have loved ones at home. Changes your perspective real fast, doesn't it?"

"Is that why you left Team 5?"

"Yup. My wife thought it would be safer to go work for SDPD. How about that decision? Couldn't even protect my little girl."

Tyler didn't want to pry. Bryce had told him a lot right there.

"No regrets. My wife and I are as tight as we've been. She knows I love this work. And we have an axe to grind with the bad guys."

"Are you glad you did it?"

"I am, my daughter was so severely traumatized with the kidnapping and attempted slavery caper, she is still going through therapy four and a half years later. No kid should have to go through that. If I can save somebody else from having to experience that level of violence for their kids, I want to do it. And I wouldn't do it if I didn't have the support of my family. She sees things in school still that just makes my wife and I shake our heads. I just don't understand why we don't protect our kids anymore."

"Word there, Bryce."

"Why did we decide to turn on them, quit supporting them, quit keeping them safe? When did that happen? When did that become an American thing? I will never ever accept that. And if I have to fight the rest of my life to see to it that people who just want to live, go to work, and be safe… If I spend the rest of my life doing that, it's good work. And in a way, it's better work than police work. We have resources and assets and information, most of the departments are cooperative with us. And we soon learn where the stumbling blocks are, so we have coopera- tion because people in the police and rescue communities know we're trying to do good. We're trying to make their job easier. I think it's worth it."

"You know Bryce, if things don't improve, I can see us facing some- day the fact that our inner cities and our societies are torn apart by some of these people, trying to destroy the fabric of the family and everything we hold dear, you may find that it's even more challenging more dangerous than what we did overseas."

"No doubt, Tyler I think you're right. Overseas we had the brother- hood, we had the team behind us, we had guys on either side of us that were willing to die for us. Here when you're in a backup position, you're working with people who didn't sign on for that. They want to go home to their families too and they aren't in it to solve the problem, they're in it to manage the problem for now. Not their fault. It's just set up wrong.

Their hands are tied. Maybe someday that's going to be us overseas too I don't know. I just hope that we all remember that famous quote."

"Which one?"

"Evil exists when good men do nothing."

Tyler nodded his head. He knew now, even before their little mission began, that this was not going to be the hill he wanted to die on. There were other things he was being called to do. He couldn't ask Kate or Oliver and Grady or Kendall to be exposed to all this. He just could never do it.

Once they were in place the check-ins began. Movement was noted, pictures were being transmitted to cell phones, there was still no trace of the attorney or Sheila, but several of Mr. Poplin's staff were seen going back and forth between his residence and the office. A van left the office building and two teams followed carefully at a safe distance behind. It headed down toward the railroad tracks and the warehouse district, and pulled into an old packing plant, with a chain link fence all around the perimeter. The fence was guarded with two armed guards, opened for the van to be let in, and then closed behind them. Three men got out of the van with boxes, and went inside.

Pictures were sent to Tyler and Bryce.

"That's going to be my pick. Bryce I think they're there. It's just a hunch I have."

"The fact they went from Poplin's office to this warehouse, does point to that doesn't it?"

They phoned in to Bryce's office the license plate of the van, and it was registered to a nonprofit that assisted homeless. It didn't appear that the building housed homeless population, at least there wasn't a license registered to do so, which was city-required.

Two other teams followed other individuals who blended into the crowd downtown, some were passing out food stuffs, others were passing out blankets. They appeared to be homeless paid staffers, and could have been messengers used to distribute money and communication to other teams that could be down on the ground in the tents. Tyler and Bryce stayed put, until the sun had fully risen, and people started arriving at work. The city's population expanded to double what it was before dawn.

The team watching the warehouse was ordered to put up a drone, and to see if they could get some kind of video of what was located inside the building. As the footage came in to Bryce's computer, he and Tyler watched as they saw a large area set up with tables and piles of food stuffs and blankets and water bottles and other things related to the homeless crisis. There also was a portion of the downstairs set-up as a meeting room with metal chairs in rows facing a small dais in front. There were several offices that were at the far side of the building, facing the wharf, where the drapes were pulled and there was no interior light. While the drone was shooting the footage, one of the doors opened revealing a small lighted cubicle and, on the floor, several mattresses. Tyler looked closely at the mattresses in front of him on the screen and recognized the long gray hair of his mother.

"That's her. She's there. Is she alive?" He asked.

"I'm fairly sure if she wasn't, they wouldn't keep her here," said Bryce.

The drone was instructed to move around the building one more rotation, and then attempt to find a window on the outside that might have access to this office. From the outside they could see about ten feet up was the height of the window. It was going to require a ladder or scaling tools to get a man or two up in there. But the drone could only see through parts of it, as the blinds were twisted and crooked, and only revealed part of the room. But there was no mistaking the fact that Tyler's mother and probably father were moving. They were in sleeping position and rolling from side to side occasionally.

"Well, that's a sign of life then. That's a go for us." Bryce whispered commands to several others on the team.

Tyler thought in his heart thank God.

The rest of the teams were alerted, several were pulled off the downtown surveillance and switched over to the warehouse district. There were six, two that would scale the fence and cut the electrical power, two more that were going to be ramming the fence with their truck, and coming from the back of the truck two more to run in and face any opposition they'd find in the building. Other than the one person that moved in and out of the office, the building didn't appear to be very well guarded.

Tyler and Bryce moved positions just as the six-man team went forward. Within a minute, the gate was disabled, both of the guards were restrained and given a tranquilizer, the two-man team who scaled the wire fencing, successfully cut the electrical power to the entire area, and managed to go in through the main door. Scanning for any additional guards inside. They found two near a makeshift kitchen, crept up on them and disabled them, giving them a nice sleepy-time dose. They marked their location and confirmed it was clear.

"Don't see any gremlins, gents," they heard Danny say over his Invisio.

"You want to go in Tyler? I don't think we've got any resistance right now. Unless somebody's watching the site."

"Hell yeah. I'd like me to be the one my mom sees first."

They were alerted to an additional van headed their way from the office building. A team was re-routed, and the van was detained several blocks before being able to see the warehouse site. The driver was detained, disarmed, zip tied, and tranquilized. The second passenger met the same fate. In the back of the vehicle, they found containers of gasoline, rags and material for making Molotov cocktails. They took pictures and sent word to their police liaison what they'd discovered and where they could come find the van. This would also give them additional backup in case things didn't go well inside the building. The police would be close.

Tyler and Bryce walked through the open gateway, crossed the gravel yard and into the building. It was eerie and cold, drafty. But silent. Tyler ran to the door he'd seen on the drone footage, opened it while Bryce covered him from behind and then above his head. He used his gun light, with no electricity in the building.

Tyler called out. "Mom? It's me."

He could hear rustling in the corner and then her faint voice, "Oh my God Tyler you're here. I knew you'd come. We're okay. We're scared to death but we're okay. Your dad's not doing very well right now but now that you're here, we're okay."

CHAPTER 19

K ATE GOT THE call at around ten in the morning.

"They're safe, Sweetheart. As soon as I can, I'm coming home."

"Thank you for letting me know. Are you okay?" she asked.

"I'm much better now."

"Was it that group that was holding them? Were they in fact kidnapped?"

"Yes, they were. And hopefully, we got them all. We've got Sheila, and we found her attorney there too. The police have detained them, but they're not likely to be able to hold them. At least they were found. And a whole bunch of the attorney's staff were found implicated, and there's going to be a huge investigation of this. I'm not sure it's going to make much difference, but for now, his network, his gang is a little bit out of action."

"Of course he is. I would not have expected it any differently. I'm so glad that you went up there, but I'm going to be so much happier when you get back here. I've been doing a lot of thinking, Tyler. A whole lot of thinking."

"Me too, Sweetheart. But I just wanted you to know I'm coming home. I'll text you when I get a flight out of here."

Gretchen was sitting up in bed, waiting to hear confirmation that everybody was safe.

"Did he say anything about Trace?"

"All he said was everybody's safe. I'm sure he'll call, Gretchen. Don't worry."

"I hate it when we fight before he goes off and does something. I just feel like a complete heel. You would think I could just watch my mouth and not say some of the things I say. And he does it too, so I'm going to work on that," she said.

"It's all good, Gretchen. If you didn't care so much, it wouldn't bother you at all. But he just did something heroic this morning, and I know you're going to celebrate it. And whatever happened before he left, I'm sure he didn't mean to offend you or make you angry."

"But he promised me he was just going to drop them off."

"Yeah, and then he looked at his buddies, and he saw them, and he decided, hey, they're going to put their life on the line to go rescue somebody and why the hell can't I go too? And he just did it. And he's also family with us being sisters. He's family. He's doing it for you. He's doing it for me. He's doing it for all our kids."

"You're right. You're right. I guess I better call Mom."

"Yes, please do. And would you also tell her that it looks like they've found and captured Sheila?"

"Will do."

Kate went downstairs and began preparing coffee for her and Gretchen. While she was waiting for the water to boil, she called Devon.

"Oh, I've been thinking about you guys. Is everything okay?"

"Yeah, they went up there. They found Tyler's parents. They used the Bone Frog Group and a couple of the guys went from Team 3, but they got it done. They found everybody, and nobody got hurt. They found Sheila, too, and her attorney-boyfriend, I guess."

"That's wonderful. Oh, I'm so relieved, Kate. You must be too."

"I am. I just want to see him. I just want to physically see him and hug him."

"I understand completely. Listen, I won't take more of your time. You just tell him we're proud of him. I will let Nick know. He's going to be thrilled. And when you're ready, let's plan that trip. I want you guys to come up and spend just a few days with us. No talk about business or wineries or anything. Just come for vacation. You need it."

"You know, Devon, that's probably the wisest piece of advice you've ever given me. And I think the answer on that's going to be yes. But of course, I got to check with the boss."

"Yes, you do. Yes, you do. Thanks for letting me know."

She finished the coffee, and one by one, the kids started getting up, and the TV went on before permission was given. Gretchen walked past the big screen, rolling her eyes but making her way to the kitchen. She looked like a zombie, her arms outstretched and grabbing the coffee cup. She pulled the whipping cream from the refrigerator, poured nearly a quarter cup of cream into her Happy Mother's Day mug, and then guzzled half of it down before she got the refrigerator door closed.

"Okay, so now I'm going to be normal. Thank God I had my first sip of coffee."

Kate set her mug down and walked over to Gretchen, the two sisters hugging each other in front of the refrigerator door, still open.

"Thank you so much for your strength, Gretchen. Thank you for letting me stay here. Looks like we're going to be leaving sooner than I thought."

Carefully, Kate moved her sister away and closed the refrigerator door behind her. She took Gretchen's hand and brought her into the dining room table, where they sat.

"I can't wait for them to get home, Kate."

"I hate this part. I don't do waiting very well, Sis."

"That's what Trace says all the time."

"So does Tyler!"

TYLER CAME HOME about five hours later. He'd texted Kate, and she informed him that she and the kids were back home, waiting for him.

The sight of him at the door instantly had her heart fluttering and her knees wobbling. It was always like that for her. That first sighting, the first time they looked at each other after they'd been gone even for short periods of time. But especially if there was danger involved, some kind of an op or a training. It was so sweet to have him back. She ran to him, and he dropped his duty bag, grabbing her by the waist and planting a big kiss on her lips.

"As I said before, it's worth it to go away for the welcome I get when I'm home." He smiled, and she buried her head underneath this chin.

"Thank you, Tyler, for doing that for your folks. I'm sure you want-ed to stay with them longer, but thank you for coming home."

"Well, they're going to be fine. They admitted them both to the hospital, and they're going to do a full check on both of them to make sure they didn't get exposed to something. They didn't eat very much, and he was off his meds for a day, but they're in the same hospital room, I'm sure driving the nurses crazy."

"Probably teaching painting lessons."

Tyler chuckled. "I wouldn't be surprised…"

"Any idea what's happening with the insurance, and have they made any plans about rebuilding?"

"I think I'm going to let my mom talk to you about that."

"What do you mean?"

"Oh, that's her story to tell. She'll get around to it. She wants to do it her way. I want her to have the opportunity to do it. I just want to be home. I don't want to talk about insurances or anything. I just want to be home."

"Well, the kids are out back. They'd love to see you."

"I'll do that, and then I'd like to take a nice long shower with my girl. If she'll have me?"

"I would love nothing better, my love."

She knew he was probably dead tired, the adrenalin of the op having worn off with inactivity. He was either on full tilt or off. There wasn't any in-between. Still, he ran outside and greeted his kids and didn't show a speck of the fatigue she knew he was feeling. It was what he did and did so well.

In the next few days, Tyler and Kate jumped into their old routine. The boys were climbing all over Tyler whenever he sat down. Kendall asked him to read stories to her, and they took a small trip to a Lego store and purchased a big space shuttle model that was going to take them the better part of a week to put together. The boys were rapidly spilling all the pieces all over the floor, and Kate knew they'd be lucky to get it put together without missing parts showing. But it was fun watching them play, seeing Tyler patiently work with his boys. His boys were just like him, she thought. Exuberant, full of energy, curious, and bright. It was like three little boys working on that space shuttle rather than a father and two sons. It warmed her heart just watching them.

Kendall had been extra cuddly and extremely motherly with her doll. But after the first few days, the newness of the doll wore off, and it was relegated to several of her other stuffed toys. She had a small zoo: a stuffed dinosaur, a pig, a snake, and a big red rooster with a floppy top knot. The doll sat right in the middle of the jungle team, looking like she ran the place.

Kate started working with Kendall on drawing pictures between the lines, doing fine motor skill type activities. She even bought a set of special markers and scissors so she could make her own stickers. And for several days, the boys had little stickers on their butts or on the back of their shirts, little reminders of sunflowers and smiley faces all over the bathroom mirror and even on the shower curtain.

They went to the farmers' market and picked out colorful eggs. Someone was there selling green and brown and purple eggs, which delighted the kids completely. Kate thought of Devon and Nick's chickens. She thought of Zak and Amy's farm and her chickens and her vegetable garden. Kate decided that even though their lot size was small, it was large compared to the rest of the neighborhood. She'd try her hand at doing some vegetables herself.

The next day, she and Kendall laid out an area with the small hoe she bought that was Kendall's size. She had her make divots in the soil and then helped her plant peas, which were large enough for her little fingers to carry. Of course, she didn't plant them evenly, and Kate left them just the way they were done. They covered the peas over with planting mix soil and then watered it down.

It turned out to be one of Kendall's favorite jobs, to water and then accidentally spray her mother as well.

About five days after Tyler returned, the Team started their workout for their next rotation in Mexico. And then one day, when he was off with the team, she got a call from his mother.

"Kate, this is Deidre."

"Hi, Mom. How are you doing?"

"Oh, I'm fine, my heart and my liver and all my vital organs are those of a forty-year-old, they tell me. So I guess I'm going to live to be a hundred and something."

"Well, that's good news. How about Dad?"

"It's a little more complicated for him, but they're adjusting some of his medication, and they're hoping they can get rid of the cramping he's getting probably from the hypertension pills. But they'll get it straight. He's also gotten a clean bill of health. So we're grateful."

"I love hearing this. You gave us quite a scare, and I'm so sorry you had to go through all that."

"Well, the way I look at it, Kate, it's just like what I thought after the fire, and you said it as well, God just wanted me to lighten up and maybe change what I was doing. I missed my painting, but I've started getting back into it. Larry doesn't like the smell, but we'll fix that in time. I think now that the people who did this have been caught, hopefully they'll be incarcerated, and in a way, it's safer here than it was before."

Kate inhaled and held her breath. She really didn't want to hear what she feared her mother-in-law was going to say. "Well, I think it's a good wake up call for all of us to pay attention to what's going on around us, and hopefully, we've learned some lessons, and we'll put into place some things that will keep us all safer. I'm going to try to look at the positive side of things. But I am also very glad that those who went after you guys will be punished. And I hope they make it stick."

"Larry and I have talked, and we are thinking about what we'd like to do. I think one of the things I miss most is being close to my grand-children. Being close to you and Tyler. And I can't ask you guys to move up here, so Larry and I have decided that we will put the house on the market and maybe use the funds to buy something down there. You know, they gave us an unbelievable offer. I think with the abduction happening, they threw in more than they'd planned on doing, not that they had to. They should have settled before! Who would have thought that would happen?"

Kate chuckled, glad to hear the happiness in her voice.

"Now Devon has told me, because I had her help me find a good realtor locally here, that you were looking for spaces in Santa Rosa."

"Well, that was before, I think we're going to stay put now. I think we need to stay here until the kids are done with school."

"Well, that's good, because that's what I want too. And I've been thinking we could still do a wedding center, except it would be different than the other ones. It would be filled with artwork and big stained glass windows, a big building with beautiful sunlight coming in from all directions, and maybe it would be the type of place that would be sort of eclectic and different. Close to the beach perhaps? It'd be lovely if we could make some beautiful gardens around it. And we could display artists' paintings and sculptures. We could have gallery events for local artists, benefits for the arts community. But most importantly, we could use it as a wedding center and a catering office for you."

Kate was shocked. "Are you serious?"

"Of course I'm serious, Dear. I want to propose that you and I become partners. Not Tyler and Larry and you and I, just you and I. I'd like to be your partner. And if your sister Gretchen is interested or the girls want to be involved, I'd be in favor of that too. I just think we should work together and make those dreams that you had about creating a beautiful place to gather in, that we could make that happen in San Diego. I think we'd still have enough to buy a little house, not the size house we have now, but something comfortable, perhaps near your place."

"Are you sure? Portland has been your home for decades now."

"And we're done with being here. I'm ready to move on. I think it's healthy to move on. I like the fact that Tyler will be closer to us in case we need him, as we age and need more help. So would you consider my proposal?"

Kate didn't want to talk because she felt like she would be blubbering like a baby. Her chest was wet already from the tears streaming down her cheeks. She inhaled and exhaled several times, trying to quell the torrential rain coming from her eyes.

"I'd be delighted, Mom. I think it would be a lot of fun. I'm not sure how much we have to spend, and that was bothering me because I couldn't see how we could have this, keep abreast financially, save for the kids' colleges, and all of that. So if you invest the money in the building and we have that built, then that solves that question. Perhaps in our partnership, we could put a portion of the proceeds to pay you back for your expenses."

"No, no, no, no, no. I want to make a donation to this partnership. The insurance money would be a donation from us and our future. To our family really. That money does not have to be repaid. Now if we decide to fix it up further or add on or expand it, then we can talk about sharing the costs there. But I'd like to have a gallery again, and you need a place to show what you can do with your catering and create income from setting up these destination weddings."

This was an unbelievable offer.

"Who knows where this will go? And I even think it would be fun to start that food truck. I rather think our Volkswagen van would be an excellent little food truck. Pull it right up to events, festivals. People would love it. It's beautifully restored. We can set it up so that we travel around to different places and show up at events, and it helps showcase some of your catering skills. I don't think you have to buy a big old school bus or a vegetable truck in order to do it. The van would be perfect. The other thing that's perfect about it is it's something I can drive. I'm not sure I can drive a big old truck. And I'd like to help."

"Mom, I had no idea you and I thought so much alike. But you blindsided me with all this. I never knew this was even in the works. I can't tell you how excited I am. Thank you for your offer."

She gulped in a deep breath.

"Your offer is gratefully accepted!"

CHAPTER 20

FOUR MONTHS LATER, Kate and Tyler had purchased a used Sprinter van and took off for Sonoma County for that visit with Nick and Devon and their kids. Kendall wouldn't stop jumping on the rear seats, which folded into a huge king bed they all could sleep in, with some squirming. Kate went back and strapped her into the seat and then made the boys do the same.

There was a TV in the rear, as well as near the front of the van, a full bathroom with a shower, and an efficiency kitchen with microwave and a huge refrigerator-freezer. In fact, this model was chosen because of the size of the refrigerator-freezer.

They were going to drive all day, taking turns, and would arrive later this evening.

They drove up, passing through all the different climate zones of California, some areas bucolic and green with farmland, others dusty and grey where they raised cattle. And, as they approached Sonoma County, the appearance of vineyards dotting the hills like corn rows started changing the scenery. Without wildfires, which had plagued them in years past, the sky was as blue as Tyler's eyes, just like the beautiful day when she first met him on the plane.

"You remember that plane ride, Tyler?"

"How could I forget?"

"Do you suppose any of our kids will meet someone that same way, like we did?"

"Hard to say. But if Kendall begins to read my sister's books, I think she has a good chance of becoming a hopeless romantic. And I wouldn't have it any other way."

She didn't want to ask about his plans, because they'd discussed it, and she promised she'd give him all the time he needed without trying to convince him one way or the other. It was so hard to do.

"I know what you want to ask me."

She was shocked. "Now I can add mind reader to your list of accomplishments?"

"Do you want to tease me with those lips of yours, your sparkly eyes, that sexy expression? And would you look what's happened to your skirt? Almost indecent, Mrs. Gray."

She glanced down at her lap and smiled. Had she done this on purpose?

"Do you want to hear?"

"I would. What do I have to do to earn it, though? I'd like to earn it."

"Oh my, Mrs. Gray. My pants are getting tight."

She glanced over her shoulder and saw their three kids glued to the dragon movie.

"Just wait until I get hold of you tonight. You best be very good and very careful," he said and showed his handsome smile that made her panties wet.

"So I have to wait, then?"

"Not at all. Kate, I'm in full agreement with the center, and you and Mom and Gretchen working on that. I think Linda wants to be a part of it too so she can sell some of her books, but don't give her anything to do with money, promise?"

She giggled. "I promise."

"I'm going to sign on to one more rotation. Then I'm going to ask Kyle for my papers. We're losing a lot of members, and recruitment is way down. I'm going to give Kyle a long window to get more members onto the team. He'll respect that decision. He may even be looking at doing the same, but that's his gig."

Kate wasn't disappointed, because he said he was willing to leave. Now she had to check on the rest of it.

"Are you doing this for me or for you? Is this decision something you'd make on your own?"

"One of the things I did and didn't tell you was about going into the

VA and having myself evaluated. I'm going to need a hip replacement, and sooner than we thought. My elbows are killing me most of the time, due to a fall. And my knees are getting close to bone on bone. Every day, they hurt just a little more. I don't want to be on pain meds my whole life. I want to be active. Having a hip replaced before you're forty is really bad. But in our line of work, it's very common. Knees too. So I want to separate, have the surgeries, and then spend a nice long recovery period with lots of physical therapy. I want to be healthy and active."

"I want that too. So you're doing it for you. I like that most of all."

IT WAS A balmy evening as they walked down the vineyards, heard the crickets chirping, felt the cool breeze in their faces, and could smell the faint hint of grapes growing on the vines. Baby grapes. Not the big black luscious ones or the tiny currant-type ones that would be coming up later. It was a nice, pleasant scent unlike any other kind of orchard, farm, or garden.

"I love it here too. And we do have choices," he said as he stopped and kissed the palm of her hand. "If you ever think you'd like to come back here, just say the word."

"Thank you. But anyplace you are is my home. Always, Tyler. I wouldn't mind visiting more often, and now with the van, maybe we can. It won't be as expensive with the kids this way. We can trade off with the driving duties. Bring our own food."

"Specially prepared gourmet food."

"That's right. Maybe you and I could work some festivals up here, too, expand our brand, like Devon and Nick do."

"I was thinking the same way."

"Your parents have the VW van. We have our Sprinter."

"And I like making love to you much better in the Sprinter," he said, drawing her into him.

"Yes, I like the leather seats and the room. It's perfect for us."

He kissed her then ran his finger down her lips. "So you're okay with this arrangement?"

"Which one are you talking about?" she asked. "The one where we come up here, do festivals, and you stay on the Teams for another rotation, or the one where you screw my brains out in the van tonight?"

"Both. I want it all, Kate. I want all of you, and I promise to give you all of me."

"Always, Tyler."

"Forever."

FATHER'S DREAM

SEAL Brotherhood: Legacy Series
Book 8

SHARON HAMILTON

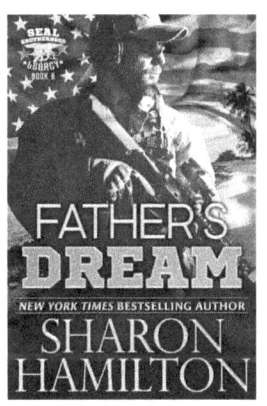

CHAPTER 1

FREDO CHAVEZ AND the rest of his unit on SEAL Team 3 waited in the bushes for nightfall. Reportedly, the cartel boss, Alejandro Ochoa, was a former cop who was caught embezzling US funds designed to put the cartels out of business and who served several years in prison for his crime then was pardoned by the Mexican president as a favor to the local governor. He took up his new job as representative of the cartel, helping migrants make the trek to the US by being their sponsor, collecting fees, and arranging the coyotes to deliver them to the Rio Grande for a border crossing.

It was also said he always showed up at dusk the night before the travel and they often started their trek at night. He was known for wearing bright green alligator boots.

As the team waited, Fredo readied his camera. The light began to dim in the sky, bringing with it some coolness, which was welcome. His job was to take pictures of the cartel boss, send them to the head shed, get confirmation a transfer of cash or other collateral occurred, and then have the team move against Ochoa as soon as he left the band of migrants.

The forty or so migrants in this particular group were mostly young men, women, and children, some appearing as young as two years old.

Fredo inhaled deeply and bit his lip as he watched through the telephoto lens. The terrified faces of the young children haunted him, their eyes wide. Hushed, afraid to make a noise, they hovered close to their mothers, those that had them. Others who were strays were quickly adopted into a family unit, rarely with a male member. He could see there was a great deal of distrust among the migrant children for any of the males, even the trafficked males in this group.

Some crying caught Fredo's attention, and he moved the camera so he could see the young child, a girl, crying next to her presumed older brother, who was about ten. The kid was searching all around him while he held her hand, trying to convince her to stop crying, but she was clearly upset about something. It didn't take long before they all realized what was causing the children so much anxiety.

Through the bushes came a bloodied female, someone who'd been obviously beaten, pushed, and prodded by being kicked in her rear end nearly to the point of making her fall by two coyote guards, who laughed at her stumbling. All of a sudden, a cry went out, and the entire group was yelled at and asked to form a line. The woman was sobbing. Bloody tears ran down her cheeks, leaving red stains on her white shirt. She collapsed and fell at the feet of her children.

Fredo's heart lurched, and he felt his stomach drop to his ankles.

"Fucking assholes. These people are animals."

He knew this woman would pay dearly for her passage, and that didn't include the horrific cost of rape that had probably just occurred. It may not have been the first time, either, as several of the other women looked like they were sporting bruises to their eyes and arms, and a couple of them were limping. There was general suffering all around. Their State Department liaison had warned them the condition of the migrants could tear their heart out.

They were right, Fredo thought.

No one in the group looked at each other, the most common trajectory was either to their own family members or the ground. And everyone tried to stay as quiet as they could as they formed their bloodied, sad, ragtag line.

The woman with the two children could not stop her sobbing, but she managed to do it in silence, holding both of them close to her thighs as she stood tall, wiping the tears from her face and the blood from her nose with part of her apron she wore over her skirt. She had no shoes, Fredo recognized, and that was going to be a problem. There was no way she was going to be able to trek across the desert-like area populated with cactus, broken shards of rock, and animal carcasses that would be their trajectory until they got to the Rio Grande valley crossing, where it would begin to soften and green up slightly. Her feet would long be in shreds before then.

Fredo looked at the two men who had escorted her from the bushes, and they were talking to themselves, sharing something, and he wondered what they were looking at. They appeared to be examining papers. Had they had possibly stripped them from the woman? Fredo didn't know, and he could not hear their words. Once in a while, he could catch some of the louder conversation. He wished he had a voice accelerator to hear everything, but for this mission, they were traveling very light, and it wasn't required.

Now he wished he'd insisted. He could get better intel that way.

The lead gunman, one of six guards who were traveling with the group, with an AK-47 strapped across his midsection, shouted for their attention.

The whole team heard a vehicle approach. It sounded like a Humvee, and they recognized it as the sound of freedom in their battles in Iraq, Afghanistan, and Africa.

But instead of being the sound and sight of freedom, it was a black Humvee customized with extra chrome and huge wheels, lifted, and Fredo was sure it had been stolen from US forces somewhere or driven across the border as a stolen vehicle. This had to be Alejandro Ochoa.

The whole team had been made aware Ochoa liked to collect the fees himself, oftentimes accepting extra monies and tips that he shared with his guards, but the guards were not to collect the money, probably because he didn't trust them. As soon as the vehicle stopped, Ochoa got out of the passenger front seat, his green boots clearly visible, even though the dusty and dusky night air was oppressively bearing down on them.

Fredo adjusted his lens to get a closeup of the boots and then the man himself, the side of his face, the back of his hair, and his hairline, which contained a large white scar he'd received with a blade of a knife during his incarceration, but it was as telltale as a tattoo on a man. Then when he turned around, Ochoa was chewing on an old cigar, as he was known to only smoke Cubans. His eyes were mean, he had several days growth on his beard, he was fatter than the pictures they'd shown the team earlier, and he appeared to be having some discomfort as he walked. Perhaps his boots were becoming too small for him. His face fashioned a nasty wince. He wore army fatigues, starched and pressed, and a gray shirt probably from his police days. It still sported oak leaf decorations on his pocket with black bars atop his shoulders from earlier days.

One by one, Mr. Ochoa visited each person, reviewed their paperwork, accepted their payments, sometimes in cash. Sometimes it was a note of some kind. One or two people brought bars of gold, which were obvious with their weight and the way they clinked inside the heavy bag as it was lifted to him. All kinds of contraband, including drugs, were turned in to him. Ochoa, when he received drugs, tossed it to his guards, but he accepted it as payment, nonetheless. When he came to the woman and the two children, she sobbed and said something to him, trying to explain a problem. Fredo could barely understand in a dialect, not from Mexico, but possibly El Salvador or Guatemala. It was obvious she was not a woman of means, was short the funds required, and Fredo wished he could record her voice.

"Are you getting this Fredo?" asked Kyle, his LPO.

"Roger that, Sir. I wish I could record it—that's something we must do next time—but she appears to be telling him that she was robbed of her money and she has none."

Fredo's stomach churned as he knew the culprits, but he wasn't sure how this was going to play out for her or her children.

Ochoa grabbed her by the shirt and pulled her face up close to his as he yelled at her that she was a whore and that her need for sex has compromised her life as well as her children's. He screamed at her using several gutter words, and Fredo carefully translated as best he could.

"He's telling her that she is a whore and that because she needed sex, she got robbed. That it was her fault. I think the two gentlemen, one with the one with the green T-shirt over to the left, are the ones who raped her, and I believe they stole from her as well. But she says she does not have the money, and she insists she is not a whore and that she was a victim."

Ochoa slapped her across the face and continued to lecture her, but he let go of her blouse and showed her his forefinger as he screamed back, making the children shudder behind her skirts. One of the earlier migrants who had already paid offered Ochoa to pay her fee and was butt in the stomach by one of the guard's rifles before he could reach Ochoa.

Ochoa seemed to take great care in lecturing her how dangerous it was for her children and that she might have to pay the ultimate price in order for them to go across the border.

Fredo began to translate again. "He asks her to choose which child shall live. He says that he will take her and one child. The other one can live, but she has not paid the fee, and for her services to his guards, he will allow one child to go free."

There were several murmurs and expletives whispered amongst the team. Fredo knew every single man in that unit wanted to just go take them out, and they could, but they didn't have the authorization until they got the verification that it was okay to engage. Things had changed so much in the past five years since they first started working cartels south of the border.

"I should send this up to the shed, Kyle. I think we need to request action. Something is going to happen. Someone is going to die."

"Roger that, Fredo. Send it up. Coop, you get your cellphone out and take some pictures while he's uploading."

Coop used his specially enhanced cellphone, a small gadget he had invented himself. It did not have the confidential link to the head shed that Fredo's did. It took less than thirty seconds before Fredo was back in action.

"Delivered. No acknowledgement yet but delivered."

Fredo continued filming as did Coop, when Kyle got the ping in his ear.

"It's a no-go. No engagement. Only target is Ochoa. Not the guards, no matter what they've done."

Again, several members of the team swore. Somebody called out for Mother Mary to protect them. Someone else used the name of Jesus. Every single man would give their life for that woman and child, and while Fredo continued to film, he was struck with the fact that he was serving with the finest men he'd ever met in his entire life on this SEAL Team 3. On his team, under such horrible circumstances, the very best of the team came alive. They had the duty to serve and to protect, but only after receiving permission. This wasn't the time to break out and go rogue, ruining all of their careers.

As tensions escalated, the woman pointed to the two men who had raped her, accusing them, and again was beaten to the ground. Before she could clamor up, Ochoa pulled out his pistol and shot her in the head. Several of the women and men in the migrant group screamed and the children began to cry—all the children in the group. The woman's two children stood by but were frozen in shock.

Finally, his little sister collapsed into her ten-year-old brother and appeared to be almost ready to pass out. She was hyperventilating and had gone white as a sheet. She began to vomit, and Ochoa tore her from the arms of the young boy and shot her in the head right between the eyes.

He turned to the boy who looked up at him with wide eyes but who did not flinch. He stood with his chest out, ready to accept the bullet he was sure was going to be his. Fredo had never seen a young migrant child show so much bravery. Ochoa began to lecture him about the lesson he had learned and the fact that his mother had risked her life for him.

The boy nodded. Ochoa leaned into him with a nasty sneer and cocked his ear, putting his hand up to it.

The boy answered, "*Sí, señor*. You are correct. Thank you for my life."

That seemed to move Ochoa slightly. He appeared to soften, smiled tenderly, reached over, though the boy flinched, and tousled his hair. The guards around him unceremoniously dragged the woman and carried the dead child into the jungle where, apparently, she was frisked. One guard returned, holding a cloth bag, which was brought back and dropped at the feet of the boy.

Ochoa barked at the boy, as Fredo translated, "'This is your legacy, now all that is left of your mother.' What an asshole," Fredo added.

He heard several people squeeze their fists together, slip their safeties on and off, and touch their weapons, each one trained on an individual, carefully. If it came to that, they'd all go rogue if Kyle asked them. There would be no hesitation.

Ochoa went down the line and continued collecting his bribes. Another duffel bag of drugs was tossed at his guard's feet, and a squabble ensued about a certain amount of payment received, where a gentleman behind a mother and children paid for their shortfall so they wouldn't have the same outcome. When Ochoa came to the gentleman, he had payment in full, but Ochoa asked for more. Fredo relayed all this to the group. The gentleman said he had no more, but he could deliver some to his relatives waiting on the other side of the border if he would trust him to do so.

What that gentleman got for his efforts was a bullet to the head as well. Fredo was beginning to think that Ochoa routinely killed several of the migrants after he received payment or received mostly all of the payment. In this case, he'd received everything he'd required, but he still wanted to take the man's life. It was like an example to the rest of the group. You only look out for yourself, and if you try to help someone else, it may cost you.

As the man was being dragged off, the woman and three children suffered in silence and looked down at their feet. One of the family members was a teenage young girl, far too pretty to be on this dangerous trip. Fredo knew they wouldn't get across the border before she was raped multiple times. Not all of the groups suffered this way, but it probably depended on the guards that went with them and where they hooked up.

The line was over, and Ochoa began to pass out money to the guards, of course saving the largest sum for himself. He saved the gold bars and had someone take them to the Humvee, but he passed out dollar bills and peso notes, generously greeted with grins and nods and great approval. He turned to go back to the car.

"Kyle, you've got to get an answer from them."

"I've just relayed the information that he's about to leave. I'm hoping they'll split us up so we can go after him while a few of you follow this group, and we'll catch up later."

Ochoa got into the Humvee and slammed the door.

"Oh, shit. Okay. The answer from above is we follow Ochoa. We grab them, and we bring him over the border. That's our mission. We have to leave the group alone."

Fredo looked at the young boy, who now was missing his younger sister and mother, obviously no money, no skills, and probably no additional resources. He slung the bag over his shoulder and began to walk with the guards. One of the guards was taking a leak behind some bushes and had left his rifle standing nearby.

Fredo grit his teeth. "No, no, no, no, no. Do not do that. Very stupid."

As the Humvee took off, the young boy grabbed the rifle and managed to shoot two of the six guards. Two of the other guards tried to disarm him, and he struggled but finally was beaten to the ground and then shot in the neck. A huge spurt of blood arced across the dusty field. Fredo's heart sank.

The group left him in the clearing to bleed to death, if he wasn't already dead.

Fredo knew Ochoa must have heard the gunshot, but at this point, he'd been paid. He didn't care who died, even if it was one of his own men. He was the cruelest son of a bitch Fredo had ever seen.

The group quickly disappeared into the scrubby forest. Kyle gave the go ahead to follow the tire tracks, and he told the group that a bird was launched so they could get some night vision tracking, and they would figure out a way for them to stop Ochoa before he made it back to his compound.

"May I check on the boy? What if he's still alive?" Fredo asked.

"How are we going to be able to take care of him, Fredo? He's more than likely dead."

"We can try," said Coop. "Let us go check him out. We'll catch up. If I think he can be moved, I'll carry him on my back," said Coop.

"I'll do it too. We'll take turns," said Fredo. Several others on the team stepped forward to agree to the same. They would all take turns carrying the child until proper first aid could be administered if he was alive.

"Okay, Coop, go quickly, but only if you're sure he'll make it."

Cooper, who was their team medic, and Fredo ran to the boy. Cooper searched for a pulse and nodded his head. He'd been shot in the shoulder, not the neck, but it had nicked an artery and he would be bleeding out quickly. Cooper stopped the flow with Fredo's help. They tied off his upper arm with a tourniquet underneath his armpit up to the brachial artery on top of his shoulder.

He tightened it so hard that the boy began to stir, probably from the pain. But he was alive and able to respond, even if slightly.

"I got to tie it tight, otherwise, he won't make it. When he wakes, he's going to be howling. If he makes it that far."

"What do you think? Can we take him?"

"Did you see that kid? He's a fighter. There's no way I'm going to leave a fighter in a jungle after losing his mom and his sister and let him bleed out. No fucking way, Fredo."

"Agreed. So he's going to make it then, right?"

"I will say whatever it takes. And you too."

They picked him up carefully. He had a huge bruise on the left side of his cheek where he had fallen on a rock, but there was no breakage of skin. They saw cuts and bruises on his legs probably from the long trek. And other than that, he was generally malnourished and overly skinny but in fairly good shape.

Cooper fashioned a seat sling so he could be draped over the backside of Coop's tall frame and cinched it around his waist, holding the boy's wrists together, his arms draped over his shoulder, with one hand while he used his other hand to be ready in case he needed his weapon. Fredo carried his medic kit and his communication box, and they ran to catch up to Kyle and the others.

By the time they reached the location where Ochoa was going to approach his campground, it was nearly dark. The compound was well fortified, and their team of twelve would have no luck breaching the doors or getting through the guards. They counted more than fifty armed men. But a further wrinkle was a compound in the middle of the fortress that held some hostages in cages who were being processed. Some were probably held for the lucrative sex trade, others as servants or perhaps being used to negotiate a ransom. But it was not a situation that would get Kyle permission to engage. There would be the possibility of too much innocent loss of life, and there was no verification of the nationalities of the prisoners in the middle of the compound. In other words, no US civilians that could be verified.

Kyle instructed them to make camp and then asked Cooper how the boy was doing.

"He's still alive. I can tell he's breathing but barely, and he peed down my back, which is normal. I'll give him something for pain and get some antibiotics into him for now. I'll set him down and have a good look. Anyway, can we phone something in to pick him up?"

Fredo looked as Kyle shook his head no. "Like I said, if he can't travel with us, then we should have left him back there. I don't want him to cause us to slow down and not be able to get our job done. That's a mistake. I don't want to endanger the team just to save one person, but we'll do what we can, and if there's a way, we'll get him out. I think, at this point, our best…"

"That means we get to steal a vehicle or two," said Fredo.

Several of the others liked the idea and told Kyle so.

"You said they wouldn't allow us to engage, but would they let us steal equipment?" Coop asked.

"I guess if it was considered life or death, anything is possible. We're going to have to wait for the next caravan to get Ochoa. In the meantime, we'll get this kid home, get you guys back, and let's get some better equipment for next time. I say we grab a truck or two, call in some coordinates, and get picked up," whispered Kyle. "And watch out for patrols. We are defenseless if we get spotted."

He sent out two from the team to do reconnaissance, looking for likely vehicles they could easily steal, and hope they could find something that had fuel and was operable.

"I'm going for the Humvee," said Andrew.

"Better not hit the beehive just yet. Just a couple of trucks will do just fine. One if we have to. But make sure they run."

The two SEALs disappeared into the night as Cooper worked on the kid and the rest of the team made camp. Sentry assignments were made by volunteers. They switched everything to night vision and double checked their equipment.

For the first time today, Fredo had hope that something good was about to happen. And he'd been dreading just the opposite all day.

He hoped saving the life of that brave kid would be that something. Right now, after what they'd seen, they needed to experience a miracle. It would be years before he'd get those visions of the deaths out of his head.

CHAPTER 2

S INCE FREDO WAS away on his mission, Mia had received some free tickets to watch the baseball game and took the twins, Diego and Luis, as well as Ricardo, her oldest son. The twins were ten, and Ricardo was thirteen—a gangly preteen boy full of energy, who was an excellent baseball player and all-around athlete.

While Ricardo was athletic like Fredo, his stepdad, the twins were more bookish, which came as a great relief to both Mia and Fredo. After years of trying to get pregnant, they had finally conceived, only to have twins. She had always wanted a girl, but that apparently was not in the cards. And she didn't feel she was made of the right stuff to raise four boys, especially with Fredo being gone so much on missions for SEAL Team 3, so she went back on the pill, and they stopped trying.

Ricardo was tapping drumsticks to everything he could find in the house, wearing his baseball cap backwards, even messing with the twins, tickling them, and joking with them. It was all a result of his excitement over going to the baseball game. The tickets were in a private box space. Someone in the Seal community had been invited but couldn't go, so Mia grabbed the chance to be able to take the boys for free, even though it wouldn't be truly free. They could eat her out of house and home, and she knew it was going to cost her over one hundred dollars just to get them hotdogs and sodas.

In the box seat, food was provided, but they were more the hors d'oeuvre type, so Mia allowed Ricardo to go grab some hot dogs for the three of them. There were ample drinks available, healthy juices and sodas, as well as fresh water, which Mia took advantage of. Several minutes went by.

"Ricardo's been gone an awful long time. I'm hungry," said Luis.

"I'm sure there's quite a line. I wish I could have just ordered it here, and then Ricardo wouldn't miss any of the game. But he'll be back soon. It's only been fifteen minutes," she responded.

At the half hour mark, Mia began to worry. Roughly five minutes later, Ricardo entered the box, sheepishly holding several hotdogs, with mustard and ketchup smeared onto his T-shirt. He looked like he was out of breath and apologized. His face and hairline sweated profusely. Mia took a damp towel and dabbed his forehead and cheeks. He was bright red.

"What did you do? You ran the whole way back or something?" she asked him.

Ricardo was rather glum and rolled his left shoulder, like Fredo did on many occasions, and bashfully told her he was just hurrying to get back. And he was sorry it took so long.

The boys were happy with their dogs as they watched the rest of the ballgame, Mia paying more attention to her boys and how they cheered and shouted with the other guests in the box suite than the baseball game. In fact, if Fredo were to ask her, she wouldn't have remembered the score. But one thing she noticed was that Ricardo seemed to be affected by something, and was more quiet than she'd expected. She suspected something had happened in his adventure to get food for his little brothers.

After the game, she thanked the box holder for donating the tickets and spoke to her and her husband for several minutes, indicating that Fredo would be very happy to learn about their generosity.

Mrs. Johansen gave her a hug. "Oh my dear, it's the least we could do. After all, he's out there fighting for you and me. I think a little fun day with his wife and kids is entirely in order. Your boys are growing up strong, Mia. Very handsome young men," Mrs. Johansen said, winking.

"I'm very proud of them. And, of course, I'm proud of Fredo too." Mia blushed, trying to suppress her embarrassment.

She said her goodbyes to the rest of the group while she shepherded her three boys out of the box seat rows, down the hallway, and into the general population of fans leaving for the parking lots. She noticed

Ricardo was searching his surroundings frequently as if looking for someone, and this alerted Mia to the fact that she was going to have to sit him down and have a discussion out of the ears of Diego and Luis. He didn't seem to connect with anyone in particular or notice anything in particular, so she wasn't alarmed, but he didn't stop searching, turning around and looking up and down the lines of people as they made their way out into the parking lot, until he sat in the car and she began to leave, which automatically locked the doors. Ricardo leaned back in his seat, his arms folded across his chest, closed his eyes, and was asleep in mere minutes.

When they got home, the boys were sent upstairs to shower and get ready for bed, while Mia asked Ricardo to join her in the kitchen.

"Have a seat. I want to talk to you about something," she said to her son.

Ricardo's expression was one of wide-eyed disbelief, and then he added a shrug and deposited his lanky frame in the chair at their breakfast table. He didn't make eye contact but focused on his hands folded on the Formica top.

"You want some milk or some ice water? Or some fruit juice, Ricardo?"

"Just some water, I guess. Are you upset about something, Mom?"

"No. Not at all," Mia lied. "I just want to have a little talk about something. I'll be right there."

She poured a tall glass of ice water for both of them and sat at a 45-degree angle to her son, placing the two glasses on metal coasters. She watched him take a long drink and set the glass down, but still avoid eye contact.

She prayed for strength, hoping she could extract the information she sought without causing a scene.

"I can tell when something's happened, Ricardo. And I do believe something happened today. I don't want to guess, and I don't want to worry, but you seemed disheveled and preoccupied with something after you came back. I would like you to tell me the truth about what went on today."

He looked startled for a minute before gaining composure to answer her.

"Nothing. I mean, there was just a lot of people, that's all. It was hard to find a place where there wasn't a line that was going to take an hour to get through, but I finally did, and by the time you order and then it gets given to you and you put all the fixings on, it just took longer than I expected. Thank goodness I didn't have to get a soda."

"Ricardo, I mean it. I want the straight scoop. I need to know what went on. And don't tell me nothing did. Your mother has a sixth sense about these things, and I'm especially alerted to danger or negative things. Something happened. You need to tell me now. Or when your dad gets home, he'll be all over your case about it. I think you'd much rather talk to me than to Fredo. Is that right?"

Ricardo took another long sip on his ice water, chewing an ice cube with a crushing jaw motion. He swallowed and set the glass back down. He began to nod his head. "Okay, you're not going to want to hear it."

"All the more reason you should tell me. Come on, Ricardo. You know I'm doing this for you, for all of us. I don't like to be left out of something important. And if it's something that's got you upset, I need to know about it."

"Do you know that Caesar, my sperm donor, is getting out of prison?" After his comment, he chanced a look at Mia's face and probably got the expression he was expecting. Mia was truly thrown off guard with this reveal.

"How do you know this?"

"I ran into a couple of guys. They told me." Again, Ricardo looked down at his hands, at the glass, anywhere but up at Mia's face. He didn't want to make eye contact.

Mia leaned forward, and she grabbed Ricardo's wrist in her palm, begging for him to look up. "Who are these guys?"

"They're kids, like me. Except their dads are in the Scorpions. These guys are newbies, wannabes. Assholes, really."

Mia withdrew her hand and stared at the ceiling, wondering what in the world had been created today. She missed not having Fredo around, and she was devastated with this news. She wondered whether the boys sought Ricardo out or, which would be worse, he sought them out. She hoped to God he answered her question the way she wanted. She had to ask.

"So you started the conversation then?"

"Nah, like I said, they're assholes. They're delinquents. In and out of school, you know. They're headed in their father's footsteps. But they like to make trouble, and they pick on people. They like to pick on the weak ones."

Now Mia understood why Ricardo didn't want to tell her. Was he ashamed he was considered weak?

"Well, not exactly fair, especially when there's more than one of them and there's only one of you, is that correct?"

"Yes. There were four. And I guess their dads and older brothers are big and important in the gang. They asked me if I wanted to check it out, and I told them hell no. Then they asked me again if I wanted to meet my father, my sperm donor, but I told them no. I already had a father. And I mean it too, Mom. I have no desire to meet him. And I didn't know what to do so I pretended that I was going along with things. Until they started hassling me. They ordered a couple more hot dogs and soda and some candy, so that the guy taking the order added their order to mine. I decided not to protest and just paid for it, and I'll reimburse you out of my allowance, but it was an extra twenty bucks or more."

"You did the right thing. The best thing is not to escalate. And I'm glad you told them you didn't want to have anything to do with Caesar, but you need to keep your distance from these guys."

"Yeah, except they're at school, and they're bullies. I mean, that's all they do. The administration doesn't do a damn thing about it. They're handling all these kids with kid gloves. It's not fair on the rest of us, but I don't want to make waves."

"Well, I'm glad you told me, Ricardo. And you are very brave to do so. You stay away from those boys, and let's sit down and talk about it when your dad gets home. I think it should be pretty soon now. Christy called me to let me know they were on their way. I'm sure Fredo's going to want to know about it."

"Mom, I don't want Dad getting involved, because with his job and everything, he could get in trouble."

"Thank you for that, Ricardo, but you know your dad would do anything to protect you. If it was required, he'd be there for you."

"I know that. I also know that I have no desire to become one of their newbies or to have any kind of a relationship with the asshole who got you pregnant. I look at him as being pure trash. I just hope there's not as much of him in me and more of you. And I hope he doesn't want or pursue finding me. That makes me uncomfortable, Mom."

Mia stood from her chair, came around the side of the table, and gave Ricardo a hug, kissing him on the cheek. "You are so special to me, Ricardo. I will not let anything happen to you. You need to be honest and tell me everything that happens regarding these boys. Don't underestimate their evil. You know your dad is working on cartel business down in Mexico, and these guys here in San Diego are like cartel-lite, wannabe gangsters, but they cause a lot of havoc. Given the chance, they could be dangerous. At some point, we're going to have to tell your administrators that you've been harassed. But not yet. We'll talk to Fredo first."

"Okay. Thanks, Mom. Can I go now?"

"Of course."

Ricardo stood and, even at thirteen, was nearly as tall as Mia was. He gave her a chaste hug, not a needy one, just enough to show his developing affection for the human race, and she knew he didn't want to appear weak. Mia hugged him back harder and then let him go, watching him run upstairs.

The twins were showering together and probably making a huge mess in the bathroom, judging from all the sounds they were making. Under the circumstances, Mia decided to let Ricardo sort it out. In a few short moments, she heard him lay down the law, and Diego and Luis were muted.

She smiled to herself. He sounded just like Fredo.

CHAPTER 3

T HE TWO SEALS assigned to stealing a vehicle were able to hot-wire a covered personnel carrier, and the ride across the border area—over three hundred fifty miles, plus or minus along the Texas border alone—was bumpy, hot, and extremely dusty. It was also one of the most dangerous parts of Mexico, not only for Americans or American soldiers, but Mexican citizens as well.

The goal was, even though they would have to travel a great deal in Mexico, to cross the border at a large designated area as close as possible to San Diego, close to their Team base, where they could have their State/Homeland liaison meet them, rather than a remote outpost elsewhere. It was going to take them nearly eight hours to make the journey.

Of course, everyone on the team was worried about the survival of the child.

Just outside of San Diego proper, after having driven most of the night, the sun was beginning to show a pink-orange-peachy glow. They'd arranged to meet the Department of Homeland Security liaison, who was also a State Department special agent, who could take them from Mexico and, with his badge, get them through the border crossing with the child without questions being asked.

Kyle and Fredo had relayed all of Fredo's photographs, as well as some of Coop's, identified the sighting of Ochoa, and were told their intel agencies were still trying to determine when the next trip would be, but that it probably would be soon.

There were changes going on within the US State Department, and those changes were going to have an effect on the size of the migrant caravans, as well as who would be coming. The State Department was interested in the fact that this particular group was made up mostly of women and children. That was not usually the case. More and more, it was becoming solid groups of military-age males, some with apparent military training or former police training, and although they didn't have anything specific to point to, the SEALs were told that those groups were indeed extremely dangerous. In fact, State told Kyle they were starting to view these groups as armed militia successfully getting across the border and hiding out in Texas and Arizona. It was a new game, all the same players, but the heat level had ratcheted up tremendously.

The boy moaned occasionally, and Coop monitored him carefully to make sure he didn't overdose him but needed him comfortable so he wouldn't go into shock. His pulse was getting better, and he had been given fluids intravenously, so his organs and body could stabilize and generate the additional blood he needed to heal. But he was far from well, and it wouldn't take long for a huge infection to not only take over his upper shoulder region, but it was close to his heart, his lungs, the blood flow to his brain. It was not looking good, but he was stable for now.

As agreed, their liaison, Carlos Gutierrez, met them at the little villa in Mexicali, a safe house for State Department's special agents from time to time. Since the truck was without call letters, even without a license, they were not easily identified, but the fact that it was a large truck and could carry some twenty men made them a target anyway. Kyle was able to relay all this information to the State Department, and Gutierrez brought a California license plate and new registration papers for the truck to hand to the border guards.

"Glad to see you, Gutierrez. This wasn't the plan," said Kyle to the agent, who had sweated through his white shirt, making it stick to his torso.

Gutierrez pulled back the canvas flap and examined the child. "He's awfully white. You sure he's still alive?"

"He is. But he's going to need surgery right away," said Coop.

Fredo placed his hand on the boy's forehead, searching for signs he could be picking up a fever, and actually, the boy felt clammy and cold.

He didn't know whether to feel good about that or not. But Fredo knew it wasn't normal, and the sooner he could get medical treatment in a sterile situation, the better.

Gutierrez continued. "Okay then. I'm going to hop a ride with you and leave my car here. I'm going to need to be driving when I get to the border. They aren't going to listen to you, and they aren't going to want to bribe me, so that's the way it's got to be. Anything I need to know about this vehicle?" Gutierrez asked Kyle, who had been driving.

"If it's all the same to you, I'd like to go shotgun," said Kyle.

"Fine by me. But we're going to be speaking Spanish. Try to keep up." The salty agent gave Kyle a cheesy grin.

"*Sí, sí.* I got you." Kyle continued, "She sticks a little bit going from second to third, maybe there's going to be a future issue with the transmission. I'm just guessing they don't service these things. And it's been out in the hot desert probably more days than it's been in the jungle, but either one is a truck destroyer. I doubt they ever change the oil either. Every available man in Ochoa's camp carries an AK-47 and a side arm. I doubt any of them are mechanics."

"Thanks for the heads-up. I've got Scripps on my phone here, and I'm going to let your medic do a video call with them so they can be ready for the kid." He handed the phone to Coop, and immediately, Fredo heard the crew from the ER on the line.

"What's going to happen with him?" Fredo asked Gutierrez. "You know that he witnessed the death of his mother and little sister. She was only about three years old. I don't know if he has any relatives in the rest of the group, nobody he paid attention to before she was shot. But what happens to a kid like this?"

The agent shrugged. "He'll be processed. It's going to take a while. He'll probably be placed in a foster care situation if we can find one. There are NGOs that are picking up these kids, but we're being careful to make sure they aren't funneled right back into the hands of the people that kidnapped them or caused their injuries all over again. And that's happened a lot unfortunately."

"I think every man here would help with the care of this kid," Kyle added. "But I don't know what the State Department's stance is on it. You'll let us know, though, right?"

"You bet. I'm just a phone call away. And if I'm not answering, well, then it means I'm south of the border doing something I can't reveal my location by phone. I will make sure to mention to my upper tier your concerns."

Gutierrez had his phone returned and then walked to the front of the truck. Fredo followed the two until he realized there wasn't room for three in the front seat.

"Will we be able to see him?" he asked.

That drew an inquisitive look from Kyle.

"You've kind of formed an attachment to this kid, Fredo," Kyle added.

A shout came from the back of the transport. "All this is nice chit-chat, but we got to get this kid to a hospital and fast," yelled Coop. "Let's dispense with the niceties and get him in the US of A. I just don't want to be doing a fire fight with him in the back."

"Roger that." Kyle handed Gutierrez the keys. "It's all yours, Sport. Don't get a speeding ticket or we'll all go to jail." Fredo headed to the rear, but not before he heard the agent give a smart retort.

"Not a chance in hell that it's going to happen." Gutierrez reached in his back pocket and brought out a huge gold badge. It wasn't lost on Kyle that the big letters rounding the top of the badge said special agent. State Department of the United States of America on the bottom. Even from a distance, the letters stood out like they were neon.

"That must be a get out of jail card then. Will that hold for all of us?" he asked.

"I have the full backing of the United States of America. They don't fuck with these. Trust me. Even the low lives don't fuck with these."

Fredo hopped in the back. The truck had already started moving so he got a couple hands up and then plunked himself near Coop.

Barely five minutes later, they were stopped in a long line of cars coming to one of the largest points of entry in the United States. Gutierrez moved the truck out of the line and advanced, coming up to a kiosk and stopping briefly before exiting the truck. Immediately, several semi-automatics were trained on him. He quickly got his badge out.

While Kyle and everyone else tried to listen, Gutierrez was speaking rapidly, waving his arms and pointing back at the truck. The sentry called for permission, and soon, a senior official with several colorful metals over his breast pocket advanced on them, listened to Gutierrez's narration, slowly studied the truck, and then glanced back to Gutierrez. After some further discussion, he nodded, and a barricade was removed so the truck could advance through to the US side. As the truck began to rev up, everyone in the back breathed the sigh of relief. Fredo's peephole in the canvas soon showed nothing but road and cactus. Several others used holes in the canvas cover to look at the situation they had just left.

"Thank God. It worked." And then louder, T.J. shouted to the front, "You're all right there, Carlos. Hey, do you have an extra one of those I could borrow sometime?"

It was time for some levity, and several of the guys chuckled. Coop was still attending the boy. Fredo used a cold pack on his forehead, around his cheeks, and especially around the bruise near his eye. The bruise was getting huge and quite purple, but other than that, his lips were red and his coloring was beginning to pink up a bit. It was an improvement.

In twenty minutes, they were at Scripps, Coop had relayed the kid's vitals to the team, and a crash cart and gurney were all prepped for them as soon as they drove up to the emergency room. Fredo counted two doctors and four nurses or orderlies, who quickly picked the boy up, placed him on the gurney, kept the drip going for his fluids, and ran, literally raced through the emergency room doors down the hallway toward what Fredo knew was going to be the surgical center.

Coop shook his head. "Lucky kid. Just under a lucky star. Of course, you saw how he reacted," he said to Fredo.

Fredo nodded yes.

"No kid should have to see that, and I'm sure as hell glad she didn't see the death of her daughter. I just don't understand why these people risk so much. They must have been sold a bill of goods about how safe it was. If they only knew what the numbers were. It's awful," said Gutierrez. "I'm going to go inside and fill out the paperwork and get some things started. Kyle, you want to come in and give your information in case he wakes up and I get permission for you guys to visit him?"

"That would be awesome. He has a lot of information—where they started from, who the men were, maybe even their names or who some of the migrants were. I'd like to get that information from him so we could use that on the next stop. I'd be most grateful if you'd allow that, Sir," said Kyle.

"We're all on the same team here. He's one lucky kid."

"That he is," said Fredo. "And again, sir, I want you to know that there'd probably be a line in this team here of people who would agree to help take care of him. If he needs a sponsor, one of us could probably do it. In fact, we'd probably have to fight each other over it."

Gutierrez laughed at that. "Well, at least if that's the way it goes, we'd be pretty sure he wouldn't be trafficked or sent back to Mexico. Not unless he's a child murderer."

"You're still doing the DNA testing?" asked Coop.

"We are. But not officially. And you didn't hear that from me. We have to have a database, otherwise we don't know what we got. And of course it's not enough to do disease or health testing, but at least we can tell familial strains and perhaps find somebody here in the United States that he's related to. But you're going to have to question him with me there. I don't think they'll let you talk to him by yourself."

"We'll abide by the rules, sir," Kyle said.

Fredo elected to stay behind and talk to the boy in case he was conscious, so he placed a call to Mia and had to leave a message. He figured she was still asleep.

He gave his information to the emergency room and made sure the comment was left that the boy had intel that was going to be most valuable to their job following up and attempting to deal with the coyotes and the cartel members. He didn't want that noted in the kid's file because there was no control over who looked at his records, but he let the head nurse in on the importance that they get a chance to talk to him quickly. But nothing that would interfere with his health.

Fredo and Gutierrez sat in the surgery waiting room. He'd never met someone from Homeland so senior, and he asked Gutierrez how he managed to get his job.

"That's a long and tangled story. I was on a gang task force in Northern California, San Jose area. That's in Silicon Valley."

"I know where it is. So you were a local cop or Feds?"

"SJPD. Anyway, we kept seeing the same things over and over again—kids recruited, especially young males who were too young to go to jail but would get off with lighter sentences. Some were mules, bringing in contraband. But more and more, that part was ending since that was more or less for small timers. Now they were coming in with trucks and planes and boats. It's gotten a hundred times worse than when I first started. So the real contraband now with the border crossings is the human trafficking. These girls are sold, convinced that all they have to do is work a year in a rich family's home with glossy photos that they show them. I've seen those photos. Those assholes. And they get parents introducing them to their daughters willingly and letting them come, thinking that they're sending them to a better life. It's a shame. And it's hard to get ahold of, especially these kids that come from the small villages where internet and TVs are spotty. There are always tales of people who came back to small villages rich and rolling in dough. All it takes is a few of those people, and suddenly, the whole town wants to go. It's a shame," Gutierrez said, shaking his head.

"So how'd you get with the State Department from the gang task force?" Fredo asked.

"I had a buddy from high school who got into doing border guard duty for Homeland Security. Unfortunately, they found him way out in the middle of the desert somewhere, executed. He'd been tortured too. It broke my heart, but I was furious. I wanted to kill someone. I mean really kill someone. I didn't think I was going to be calm enough to go back to my police duties, so I applied through Homeland Security for a special agent job. I didn't want to be driving migrants across the border, changing diapers, and feeding babies. I wanted to go after the criminals, and I wanted to have the kind of authority where I could really do something. The problem with my police work was all our efforts were interfered with, depending on the jurisdiction. We have such a wide variety of judges and district attorneys… it depends on where the busts happened. Sometimes they'll plead they're from a different locale, and you have to use something outside of San Diego or San Jose or maybe way up in the mountains. We get a change of venue all the time. And I'd have to drive all over hell and back to these court cases, and most of them, we lost. And guys that were set to be deported just disappeared on us. I wasn't doing anything. I mean, the percentage of guys we caught and actually deported was tiny compared to the amount that got through. I just couldn't work there anymore and see the numbers rising, see the carnage, and not have the authority to fix some small part of it."

Fredo knew Gutierrez was one of the white hats, a good guy, like his SEAL buddies.

"Well, that's kind of why I joined the SEAL teams. Same thing. Difference is we do ops with multiple men, and each guy would die for me. We don't always achieve our goal, but we know how to keep each other safe, and we know we can depend on each other. It's a group thing, not an individual thing. It's dangerous to do it on your own. But I think we are a force for good. Otherwise, well, the risks are too great, and now that I've got a wife and three kids, she needs me home. Now more than ever."

"Sounds like you have your priorities straight. If I wasn't so old, shoot, I would've become a SEAL. Or tried to. I don't know if I could have passed everything, though. You guys are iron men."

"Nah," Fredo sighed. Then he smiled and stared right back at Gutierrez. "We just don't quit. We're dumb like that."

The surgery took well over two hours, and it was nearly noon when a doctor walked slowly down the hallway and gave them the news.

"He might actually lose his arm. Whoever tied that tourniquet did a hell of a good job stopping the bleeding, but man, he damaged that tissue. We have a collapsed artery we had to repair and all kinds of other things going on, but if we can get that circulation going, he'll be okay. I'm surprised it didn't nick anything else. I mean, there's all kinds of stuff there in his chest. I think it ricocheted off his clavicle, because we got a fracture there, and if it had gone the wrong way, shoot, it could have gone to his spine. But I think he'll make it. He's pretty strong. He's a fighter."

Fredo was relieved. "Thank God. So is he put in a coma? Is that what the next step is?"

"No, I think he's stable enough to get some painkillers, but we're going to have to go in again probably in a day or two just to make sure he's doing well enough, and we'll have to repair that clavicle and check on our other work. I don't want any bleeders going on. We'll get his vitals and just track him for a while, but he's going to have to have a couple of surgeries. I'm glad you brought him here, because I don't think many of the emergency rooms down here could have handled it," the doctor answered.

"Thanks, Doc," Gutierrez said as he shook his hand.

"He's going to need a lot of care. Some physical therapy and, if he loses that arm, prosthetics. It's going to be a long haul for him. We'll see how he goes if he wakes up, if he's cooperative, and if you can convince him to be cooperative, it'll go a lot better for him. Does he have any next of kin?"

"That's just it, Doctor. He witnessed the murder of his mother and his three-year-old sister. That was hard to watch. And he tried to kill the guys that did it, and that's how he got injured. He was home free—he could have just stayed with the group, but he fought back. So yeah, he is a fighter."

"Well, he's lucky then."

"We've all been saying that. He's the luckiest little kid around. At least for today. Until the next time we find one. And that'll probably happen soon."

CHAPTER 4

MIA AND HER mother, Felicia Guzman-Mayfield, were making fresh tortillas and tamales in Felicia's newly remodeled kitchen. It was something she'd enjoyed doing many times during the year, something she and her mother started when Mia was barely walking. Her mother would put her in a highchair and give her some dough to roll out, even giving her dull knives to have her chop tomatoes and other ingredients for the tamales Felicia was famous for.

Mia figured it would be nice to give Fredo a nice home-cooked traditional meal, since tonight he would be home. It also gave her the stability, standing next to her mother for nearly a half day, gaining strength and courage to discuss with Fredo the reveal about Caesar's possible release. Felicia had that quiet courage, forged through many years of adversity in Puerto Rico, when Mia's father was still alive. Now, Felicia was loved again, this time by Gus Mayfield, her second husband.

"You enjoyed the baseball game, yes?" Felicia asked her.

Mia was hesitant to answer, not wanting to engage her mother further with some of her concerns, especially since she hadn't talked to Fredo yet.

"They loved it, and I enjoyed it because I loved watching their faces. It was very generous of them to donate those tickets. We had private box seats in a suite area, catered. Oh, there was good wine and all kinds of fresh fruit smoothies. It was delightful. Hardly felt like a baseball game though. My recollections of baseball games were sitting in the sun, getting sunburned, and dropping mustard all the way down the front of my chest."

Felicia laughed. "Your father loved taking you to soccer games in Puerto Rico. He wanted you to play soccer, football, you remember, Mia?"

"I'm not an athlete, Mother. I don't like getting bruised and muddy. Some of my friends in school were banshees about football. I didn't want to get my clothes or my hair or my makeup messed up. It's amazing that I even married a man of action."

"Well, that's because he was one of your brother's best friends on SEAL Team 3. You met him through Armando."

"How could I forget? He reminds me every time I see him."

Felicia smiled and paused, before adding, "Armando is doing better these days. Sambra has brought some new life to his eyes. He's not all the way over Gina's loss, but I think, in time, he will settle down. Sambra wants to have children, and I think Armando's a little bit concerned since he and Gina had had so much trouble. He's worried that she could be too fragile."

"Oh, these men. These team guys all think we're so darn fragile and we're going to break if they squeeze us too hard. We're just as strong as they are in other ways, and we endure so much. I just don't get where men have to treat us like we're porcelain teacups or something. It sort of annoys me. The fact is, we can handle a lot more stress and pain than the men can. And some of them, I have it on good authority, faint at the sight of blood. Can you imagine that?"

"Oh, no. Who?"

"Well, I know this new guy Crane, he did. Plus, at their in-doc session, he fainted when he got a shot. It's so funny. These big macho guys can do so much, but the sight of blood or needles drives some crazy."

"Well, I'm sure if Crane is married—"

"No, he's not. But I know what you're going to say."

"Yes, he will never make it in a delivery room, will he?" Mrs. Guzman answered.

"Nope. And he shouldn't even try."

They worked in silence until Felicia's husband, Gus Mayfield, entered the kitchen.

"Oh my gosh, it smells heavenly in here. Do I have a couple of Puerto Rican angels stirring up some kind of a heavenly dish for me tonight?" Mayfield had been a detective and lived alone after his unhappy marriage and divorce. Felicia's husband had been killed in the line of duty in Puerto Rico, and she never remarried after she came to the United States with her two children, Armando and Mia. Their love match was something Mia and all the rest of the wives from SEAL Team 3 were touched by. Big huge Mayfield treated Felicia like she admired her prized plate-sized dahlias in her front yard.

"That's what we are, Gus. Angels. Fredo gets back today, so I thought I'd give him a little treat. But there's going to be plenty for you, don't worry about it. And my boys love tamales as well. In fact, I think the twins could eat them for breakfast, lunch and dinner."

"I don't see anything wrong with that." Gus came over and gave Mia a peck on her cheek, wrapping his arm around her shoulder. He was careful not to get any of the cornmeal on the sleeve of his shirt or his protruding belly.

"So Fredo's been gone for—how long were they gone for?" asked Mayfield.

"This one was a short op. They're after cartel bosses who are trafficking women and children at the border. I think he left three weeks ago Sunday. But they're done, and Christy told me they'd be back today."

"They get their man?" Mayfield asked.

"I'm not sure. I wait for Fredo to tell me. If it's important. But you know they usually do."

Just then, Mia's cell phone rang. It was Fredo.

"Hey, sweetheart. I'm sitting in an empty house," Fredo barked.

"Well, the boys are in school. It's only two o'clock. I pick them up in a half an hour, unless you want to."

"I'll do that. So where have you been all day? I've been trying to reach you for two hours."

Mia looked at her phone and noted that he had left several messages. "I'm sorry, you're right. I don't understand. We must have been in the store, or we were out in the garden. I must have left the phone inside and missed your calls. Not intentional. I'm not avoiding you. I have something special for you tonight."

"Well, does it involve getting naked and swimming in the pool?" Fredo asked.

"Remember, Fredo, we have three boys. And I haven't yet shown them what I look like naked. I don't think you want me to do that, or did I get it wrong?"

Mayfield and Felicia laughed.

"So you're at your mom's house? What the hell are you doing there?"

"That's your surprise. And you're going to love it."

"Okay, so I'll get the boys. Do you need me to pick up anything at the store?"

"Nope, I'm almost done here, and then I'll be home in about forty-five minutes to an hour. Make sure the boys get started on their homework right away. I know Ricardo has a report due early next week. I doubt he's done enough research."

"Will do."

Mia signed off and sighed. She knew it was a good idea to cook Fredo a special dinner, which would allow them to linger together while the boys go for a quick swim and then head to bed early. That would give her the time she needed to explain to Fredo what had happened yesterday. She decided to quiz Mayfield about it.

"Gus, I received some disturbing news yesterday. It seems Caesar is going to be released from prison. I was under the impression he got a thirty-year sentence. Do you know what's going on?" she asked him.

Mayfield's face elongated with a worried wrinkle in his forehead. All of a sudden Mia thought he looked ten years older.

"I have my contacts, but no, I didn't hear that. I don't think anybody on your legal team knows it either, because weren't they supposed to call you if he got early release?"

"They're supposed to. I haven't seen anything in the news, not that it would be news, but you know with his reputation and the gang so active, even more active now that he was behind bars, I just am not very happy. If you could, I'd like it if you could look into it a little bit for me. I didn't get many details."

"Wait. Where'd you get this intel from?"

Mia didn't want to tell him it was Ricardo and also didn't want to tell her stepfather about the confrontation with Ricardo. Eventually, it was going to have to come out, but she wanted to discuss it with Fredo first. That was always a rule for them. Their family came first, and then by agreement, they could share it outside the family. The release of Caesar might be a hoax, so she didn't think it was inappropriate to tell Mayfield.

"I'm not at liberty, since I'm not sure the information's accurate. But if you wouldn't mind checking into it, if you can, that would help. I want to talk to Fredo first. I'll let you know. But I'd like to get it verified. Would you do that for me?"

"Of course, Sweetheart. I could make some calls right now if you like."

"Gus," Felicia started. "Why don't you do that, while we're finishing up here and putting everything away. I think it would be a good idea for Mia to have that information before she sits down to talk to Fredo."

Mayfield mumbled something as he left the room and headed for his office located in the back bedroom of the little house.

"Is he upset, Mom?" Mia asked.

"No, he's just tired. All the years and all the tragedies he saw, it wears on him. And he's going to worry about this Caesar thing. Let's hope it's false information, okay?"

"I agree with that. But something tells me, with the money and the people in his organization, he can afford to get himself out of jail somehow. I just don't know how he does it."

The kitchen was clean, and the tamales were placed in a glass baking square with a plastic snapping lid for easy transportation home. The dishwasher was turned on, and the kitchen towels were tossed in the washing machine. Mrs. Guzman took Mia's apron from her, added her own to the handful, and dropped them in the washing machine, turning it on. Her last act as kitchen monitor was to sweep the kitchen floor. Mia held the dustpan.

Mayfield came in just as Mia was coming back from making a second trip to her car, loading up supplies. He had a pensive expression on his face. It wasn't a happy one. Mia braced for something she knew she wasn't going to like.

"Well, I've just talked to the warden over at the county facility. He verified that Caesar got an appeal, and his conviction was overturned, partially on the testimony of somebody who confessed to the murder.

I'm not sure how he could get around all the other charges, the kidnapping, the brutal treatment you had at his hand, but it's probably easy for people to recant since that's what the gang does, they intimidate. It's probably more a case that without the murder charge he'd get off quickly with the other charges anyway, so probably better to just release him. The warden says the state can always recharge him, but he doesn't think they will."

"So he's already out then?" Mia asked. She looked at her mother, who was standing next to Mayfield, her palm over her mouth.

"It appears that's true, Mia. I'm sorry to say, if he wants to, he has the right to see Ricardo. I'm not sure what your standing's going to be, but you probably better plan on getting a good attorney and taking some precautions."

Mia's eyes teared up. "Well, I'm going to go home and have this nice dinner. I'm going to greet my husband and watch my kids play outside. I'm going to have a tall sangria, and then I'll face the music. It's been a delightful afternoon over here. I'm so glad you were available, Mom. We'll have to do it again. I needed this."

Felicia melted, stepping close so she could take Mia in her arms. She spoke to her in little cooing sounds whispering little things in her ear, just like she always had done.

"Well, the good thing is she's married to a Navy SEAL. And he's got a lot of buddies, and she couldn't be in better hands. I'd offer to have you guys stay over here, but the house is so small, and I actually think you're safer with Fredo. But if he has to leave again quickly, I'll help you make some other arrangements."

"Christy Lansdowne will probably have a say in that, Dad."

"Of course. I forgot about that." He gave her a brisk smile. "Somehow, we'll figure it out. But don't you hesitate to let me know if you need anything. I'll probably get some more information later on, and if it's important, I'll call you. But otherwise, I'm not going to spoil his first evening home with you. Just try to relax and forget about it. We can always deal with this tomorrow."

Mia stepped up to her stepdad, wrapped her arms around his neck, and allowed herself to be enveloped in his huge arms.

"Thank you, Dad. I love you."

"Me too, Kid. Me too."

CHAPTER 5

FREDO PICKED UP all three boys at St. Cecilia School. The twins came out first, and then Ricardo showed up at the parking lot, coming from the gym. Everybody had their backpacks stuffed with books. The twins had checked theirs out from the library, and Ricardo had brought home a large encyclopedia borrowed from his history teacher.

"Boy, you guys have some homework. Ricardo, you are using this for your report?"

"Yup. I got to do some work before the weekend. Otherwise, I don't think I can finish it in time."

As Fredo took their backpacks and loaded them in the back of his Hummer, the three boys sat as they usually did, Ricardo in front and Luis and Diego in the second seat.

"We good to go? Anybody need to get something on the way home?" Fredo asked them. He wasn't expecting a huge celebration since this wasn't one of their long ops. The boys had gotten quite used to the routine of Fredo being gone maybe eight or ten times during the year. Not like in the old days when he would be gone for three or four months. Many things about the SEAL community had changed over the years. This was easier on the families, doing short trips usually lasting no more than two weeks or a month at the most.

"I'm good," said Diego. Luis agreed. Ricardo shook his head and didn't say anything.

"Okay, well, I think your mother has something special planned. I'm not quite sure what it is, but she was over at your grandmother's house today."

"That means a nice dinner." Ricardo said. "That's what she does when she goes over to Granny's house. They cook. They talk and they cook. And they gossip and they cook. And they tell stories, exaggerations, and they cook."

Fredo grinned. "Yup, that's my Mia. She is a mother's daughter."

The boys came racing through the front door as soon as they arrived. Mia stepped outside to give Fredo a big hug. She even offered to carry his duty bag.

"No can do, sweetheart. Rules. I got rules. Now, what's this surprise?" he said as he kissed her on both cheeks and then gave her a quick kiss on the lips. He studied her face, which caused him to ask the question, "Are you okay?"

"Yes, but there is something we have to talk about. I'll do it after dinner, after the boys go down. But we have to talk, Fredo."

"Is this bad news?"

"I'm not sure. Please," she put her palms on Fredo's shoulders, "please, let's just have an early dinner, let them play in the pool, and then you and I can have that talk. Don't try to get it out of me. I really don't want to do this in front of the kids."

"Should I be worried?"

"Fredo, I told you, I don't want to do this right now. I want to wait until after dinner."

"Can I bribe you?"

"You're impossible. If I tell you what it is, it's going to ruin your dinner."

"Well, then, you have to tell me now. There's no more getting out of it. What is it?"

She looked at her feet. "Caesar has been released from jail." She searched his face, reading him like a book.

Fredo stared back at her, watching her beautiful brown eyes now tearing up and tears overflowing down her cheeks. He was flabbergasted. "How the hell did that happen?"

"We don't know. When I was at my mom's, I asked Gus if he could make a call or two, verify that information."

"Wait a minute. Where did you get the information, Mia?"

"Well, it gets worse, Fredo. Ricardo was confronted at school, and one of the boys in some of his classes, they're acquaintances of his, are younger brothers or sons of Caesar's gang members. They told him. And they told him that he wanted to see Ricardo. I don't know if that's true. I think they just tried to scare him. But Ricardo is quite upset about it. As he should be. So Caesar is released, and we got it confirmed by the warden. Gus said he'll help us however he can, but he suggested that we get an attorney. Perhaps—and this came from the boys again—perhaps Caesar is going to try to make a play to get partial custody of Ricardo. I don't know the first thing about that, so we're going to have to game up, right?"

Fredo was staring at the ground, feeling the insides of his stomach churning, helpless, lost as to what to do. He knew it wouldn't be wise to just pick everybody up and leave, leave his job and all the other team guys behind. He knew the best thing would be if somehow Caesar was rearrested and recharged. And now it was his time, his turn to do some research.

"Mia, well, I'm glad you told me. I'm going to put it out of my mind for a little while until we get through dinner. Thank you for letting me know. I'm going to sit with it a bit, and maybe I'll have some better ideas in an hour or two. Gosh, I was so looking forward to just going to bed early and being in your arms. I can't help but feel that Caesar is going to want to come between us. I'm not going to let that happen."

"But you better not do something stupid, Fredo. I can't have you arrested or out of the picture. It's too dangerous. I need you by my side. I know, together, we can make it work."

Fredo had been planning on broaching the subject to Mia about them adopting the little boy he'd rescued in Mexico, whose name was Ivan. He learned that later after the boy's admission. Now that was going to definitely take a backseat to this new wrinkle. The easiest solution would also be the most devastating. Fredo hoped Caesar would get involved in some kind of a gangland shootout, fall down, and never arise again. But that would be too perfect and something not likely to happen. But he knew also that people like Caesar who were bullies, only spoke truth to power. Unless Caesar knew Fredo wouldn't hesitate to take direct action against him if he interfered, he just wasn't sure what kind of show of force would be appropriate. And he was going to have to give

Kyle a call just to get some guidance. He had thought, just like Mia had, that they'd never have to worry about Caesar again.

"Don't worry, sweetheart. We'll figure it out."

THE DINNER WAS delicious, true to its billing. Fredo stuffed himself, and so did the boys. Something that was supposed to be leftover for one or two nights later in the week turned out to be perhaps a snack and not enough for a full meal for any of them. Fredo spoke little, thinking about the situation with Caesar and wondering who from the team he could take with him to go talk to the guy. Maybe he didn't quite have the fight in him that everybody was expecting. Maybe he just wanted to live the rest of his life outside the boundaries of the violence that he had perpetrated. It did happen occasionally, but Fredo didn't expect it.

Ricardo no longer liked to be hugged and kissed by his dad, but he did allow Mia to give him a loving kiss. And at last, all of the boys were in bed.

They came downstairs, and Mia fixed both of them a sangria, adding plenty of orange juice and ginger ale. Fredo was glad that the alcohol level had been tamed.

They sat outside by the pool in lounge chairs, enjoying the warm late spring night and the stars that were starting to poke out from the turquoise sky. All during their time in Mexico, he kept scanning his phone for weather reports of San Diego, and he knew that they'd had a nice mild weather pattern, but mostly with sun. He was so lucky to be living in San Diego. He almost needed to pinch himself.

Finally, he reached out to Mia with one hand. Her legs were stretched out on her lounge chair, and as she gripped his hand, she turned slightly on her hip so she could study him.

"I think this type of clown is going to have to receive a warning pretty quickly. There's always the possibility it'll make it worse, but if he's changed at all or he's not going to be interested in actually being Ricardo's father in any way, shape, manner, or form, maybe it won't be a problem, Mia."

"I just don't see that. He thinks he owns everything. He thought he owned me, he thought the baby was his, and now Ricardo is a young man. He's going to want Ricardo to follow in his footsteps. And that's the strange thing about this whole thing. He knows this isn't good for him. Ricardo has a good life being a good kid, a good student, and has a brilliant future. You would think if he cared about his son at all that he would just back out and leave us all alone."

"But that's not the way of it, is it?" Fredo asked.

"No. I'm sad to report that I think you're right. So how do we go about approaching him or letting him know we're not afraid of him or of getting the authorities involved so that he would risk going back to prison?"

"Well, we need to find out what the DA is going to do. If he's going to re-arrest him, we want to help him along with that. I don't want to kick the hornet's nest or anything, but when he gets upset, he kind of does just that. That's a good reason to keep him behind bars. On the other hand, if he's learned some kind of self-control over these past nine years, I suppose supervised visits with Ricardo might be in order. But definitely not for a weekend. And we're going to have to work on that. It might be a fight."

"That's exactly what I was thinking. We have a lot of work to do to figure it out, Fredo."

"Do you have any information about what he will be doing if he comes back here?" he asked her.

"Oh, I know what he'll be doing. He's going to run drugs."

"And he's going to try to sell off the kids that he's still holding. The good news about our situation now is that they will have to catch him doing something illegal, and we're going to have to strategize. How's Ricardo holding up about this? He seemed okay to me."

Mia nodded. "He's a good kid, Fredo. You've instilled in him some good values. He's not a hothead. I'm guessing there was a lot more bravado because of who told Ricardo about the release."

Fredo agreed. "They probably built it up to be something way bigger than it is. I'm sure he's going to have to check in daily, maybe wear an ankle monitor, if they still think there's enough evidence to charge him."

"Do you think perhaps you should talk to the warden, ask him some questions about his behavior?"

"I could do that. I just want to be very careful, though. I don't want to worry about something that isn't going to happen. That's the main goal."

Fredo admired his beautiful wife, the only woman in the whole world Fredo could have ever loved, the woman he had to work so hard to woo and who had rejected him over and over again until finally she saw the light, and since then, they'd been one of the happiest couples of all the Team couples. Fredo would be devastated if something ever happened to Mia and, of course, Ricardo as well. He halfway wished he could just pay someone to get rid of him, but that was only a fleeting thought and not anything realistic. It would be certainly something that would cost him his career and possibly several of his friends' careers as well. He couldn't let that happen. And he'd wind up in jail on premeditated murder. Unlike career criminals, Fredo would be locked up, and they'd throw away the key.

"Is he safe at school? I mean, do they have these boys in the same classes?" Fredo asked.

"Yes, I believe the morning class is three days a week, and the afternoon session is twice a week. As you know, the twins are split up."

"So what has Ricardo said about all this. I know he's a good kid, but you'd know. You told me he was acting quiet, upset. Any idea his thoughts?"

"He's okay. He's a really strong kid. But you have to promise me, Fredo, you will not use him as bait to lure Caesar out of some dark hole. I don't want you to put him in harm's way. If we have to, we should move."

Fredo could not come to any conclusions, since he just didn't have enough information. The thought of moving scared him now that they had put down such deep roots in the community. They'd been saving for years for the pool and, last summer, finally had it put in. It kept the boys at home, and they brought their friends, so both Mia and Fredo could check on who they hung with. Not spying, just being strategic, Fredo thought.

First thing he was going to do tomorrow was get some of those answers, and then they could make a decision on which direction to take. It was always about that, assessing the risk and weighing it for the reward. She didn't want direct interaction between him and her ex, but if that was the only way to keep his family safe, he knew he'd do it, even if it cost him his freedom.

As he looked at Mia's beautiful body, all the softness, the peaks, and valleys of her feminine mystique he could never get enough of, his heart expanded and then melted. He was awash with his love for her, every single cell of his body craved her more than he thought possible, and it was growing stronger year by year. He could easily get lost in the aura of her love. He would gladly die to save her and Ricardo. But his real mission was to bring the entire family into safety, including himself.

First thing tomorrow, he was going to need to talk to Kyle.

CHAPTER 6

MIA WOKE UP to the first light of day, initially startled with the panic that perhaps she'd overslept. Last night had been a wonderful celebration, a welcoming home of the love and support she gave and received from her man. Fredo had always been an attentive lover, never stopping to show her how much he worshiped her body and soul. He never once, even after this almost decade of marriage, dialed that back or got tired of letting her know how important she was to him. It was just something she never expected. And their relationship had bloomed in all aspects of their life. They enjoyed teaching their children, they enjoyed projects together, and they just plain enjoyed everything they did together, including sex.

She smelled bacon cooking, and with the obvious conclusion it had to be Fredo, since his side of the bed was now vacant, she was grateful he had let her sleep, gotten up, and from the sounds of it, gotten the boys up and ready for school. Now she was the recipient of his warm love.

She fell back into the pillow and scanned the ceiling. Fredo had never complained that she didn't bring home a paycheck. He wanted her front and center with the boys, all the way up to doing homeschooling. But since Mia's knowledge of math and English, which had become her second language, was limited and left her feeling inadequate to teach, she resisted the homeschooling. Several of the SEAL wives had begun groups of teaching pods, which interested her, but she was concerned that she wouldn't be able to contribute and since the boys loved St. Cecilia's School, for now this was the logical choice.

Taking a deep breath, her hands shot up above her head on both sides of her ears as she stretched and luxuriated in the few extra moments of sleep Fredo afforded her.

And just at that moment, he walked into the bedroom with a steaming cup of coffee.

"Ah, I see the princess has awakened."

"Thank you, mi amore. It smells great downstairs. I'm assuming the boys are all ready?"

"You've got that right. Got you covered, so why don't you just stay in bed and hold that pose for a while. I'll be back in about a half an hour to forty-five minutes, and maybe we can find something else we can do in this room. Do you suppose this can be done?"

Fredo grinned at her, a lascivious grin only he could make. It was quite obvious Fredo felt they were ready for round two.

"That sounds like a lovely idea. Maybe I should take a shower and put on a new nightie?"

"Why don't you just take a shower and not put on the nightie? I like that too."

"Your wish is my command."

"Oh, don't get me started. I can make a lot of demands on you. You ain't seen nothing yet."

She drew her feet to the floor, stretched, and took another sip of her coffee. "Fredo, I was thinking we should talk to the administrators at St. Cecilia, maybe let them know about this situation with Caesar and his minions? What do you think?"

"I could do it after I drop them off. It's probably something we should schedule and sit down together though. I'd feel better if you were there. Why don't I make an appointment? Then we can kind of sort out and strategize what we're going to say. How about that?"

"Works for me."

Mia took her shower and then gave Christy Lansdowne a call. She thought it would be a good idea if their "team mom" knew about the situation they were facing with Ricardo. She knew that Kyle would want to know and notifying him would be Fredo's job. But it was also important to notify his wife, Christy, and that was her job.

"I'll bet you're glad he's back," said Christy on the phone.

"Always. He even let me sleep in this morning, made breakfast and everything for the boys, and took them to school."

"You know, I knew the very first time I met Fredo that he was just one of those guys who would do anything for his family. Not that Kyle isn't that way as well, but I think the way he demonstrates his love for you, his patience over all those years of angst he had to endure—"

"You mean all the crap I put him through?" interrupted Mia.

"No, it was just something you had to arrive on your own. You decided to change your lifestyle, and I respect that. I think Fredo saw it in you before you did yourself, and if there ever was a couple where marriage enhanced everything about them, you guys would be the poster children for it."

"Wow. Oh my God, Christy. You're making me embarrassed now."

"Okay, I'll stop. So what's up?"

"I'm sure Fredo's going to talk to Kyle about it, but Ricardo had an incident at school the day before yesterday, and Caesar, his biological dad—"

"I know who he is. The cretin who fathered Ricardo?"

"Exactly. Even Ricardo calls him the sperm donor, which I rather like. Anyway, it looks like Caesar has been released from prison, without any notification to our side. I'm not sure why and how this happened, and we're looking into it, but some kids that are younger brothers of gang members and wannabees on the periphery of the Scorpions, sort of intimidated Ricardo and told him that his dad wanted to have a relationship with him or something like that. Anyway, it scared the *cajónes* off my son, and he's upset, as he should be. He's thirteen, he's not a grown man, and he has no interest in having a relationship with his father, who really isn't his father. Fredo is. But he's afraid of this man who supposedly wants to now be part of his life. We haven't verified all of this, but we're just sort of wondering what we should do and looking for advice."

"Oh my God, Mia. This is horrible news. And of course you can't just sweep it under the rug, can you?"

"Hardly. Even my mother is concerned, of course, and Gus as well. I've spoken to him yesterday, and he's about ready to put his belt on and go after the guy I think. Fredo is right to not want to kick the hornet's nest, as he calls it, but we're also concerned that if we don't say something that Caesar will take advantage of that or perceive it as weakness.

You know what I mean?"

"Yes. Makes sense. Bullies and bad guys are like that. The good news is when they're like that they're stupid, and they don't think things out. But they have evil minds. You've definitely got my attention. And I'll make sure Kyle hears about it from me. But you're right, Fredo needs to talk to him himself."

"So we're going to contact the school, I think, and then we're going to need a good attorney. Might I ask you if you have any recommendations?"

"Geez, the only attorneys I deal with are real estate attorneys. I'm going to have to ask around. And I just don't know anybody right now who's going through some kind of a custody battle. It's like a family law attorney you need."

"No, we really need a criminal attorney. We need somebody to go after this guy and get him put back behind bars. I don't know how he got off, but it was a poor decision at best, and at worst, somebody got paid off. I would love to be able to find out."

"Well, Mia, let me put some thought into it, and I'll also ask Kyle. Sometimes he knows more about what's going on with some of these families. You know the guys talk. I just don't recall having any of the wives go through this type of thing. We've had divorces and custody battles but not like this, not when someone's come home from prison and wants to insert himself into a family that he nearly destroyed. I just gotta have faith in our justice system, Mia. Why would they allow somebody who almost killed you and your son, why would they allow him to have any kind of access?" Christy asked.

"Money talks. But yes, I agree with you. I'm going to hang my hat on that. Anyway, thanks for picking up. I know you're busy, and I'll let you know if I have any news."

"You do that. Please, Mia, if you need anything at all, if you need a place for the boys to come stay for a while, anything at all, you let me know, and we'll be there for you. Don't worry about that. How did Fredo take the news?"

"Well, we're in the 'let's think about this and strategize' phase. I'm grateful that my husband has matured in his fifteen years as a SEAL. I have a feeling when he first joined, his reaction wouldn't have been like that."

"Oh, yes, they do like to figure things out. Ad nauseum. Not all of them, of course, but it's nice to see that even men of action can mature. And they do that because they have more at stake with wives and kids. They stop doing stupid things."

Mia chuckled, and added, "Except they still jump out of airplanes in the middle of the night at 13,000 feet."

"Touché. Yes, they still do that."

Just as Mia hung up the phone, she heard Fredo's distinctive greet.

"Hello, Lucy, I am home!"

Fredo did a perfect imitation of Desi Arnaz, from the *I Love Lucy* series, which was one of the old TV shows both she and Fredo loved watching.

He tore up the stairs, probably taking two or three at a time, and was in the doorway casually leaning against it, eyeing the sight of her naked body sitting on the bed.

"So this is what I like, a beautiful woman, no clothes, not even a nightie, sitting and waiting for me to come home. I like this, Mia. I like it more every time I see it."

"Well, then why don't you come over here, and I'll show you how excited I am that you're back?"

Fredo made it to the bed in less than a minute, and during the time he was traversing the room in a bunny hop, he was getting rid of his clothes, including his canvas slip-ons.

CHAPTER 7

FREDO WAS IN the shower, getting his first of the day, while Mia soaked off his backside, getting her second. With soap everywhere on both of them, Fredo heard his cell phone ring. He would let it go, except that he had placed a call to Kyle and guessed it could be his return call.

"Oh shit, I think that's Kyle."

"No, no, no! You have to rinse off first, you're not going to be running across our floor with soap down your ass," Mia said.

He quickly turned his back to her, and she used the wand to rinse him off, instructed him to turn to his front side, and repeated the motion. "Now go." She spanked him on the butt cheek as he left the shower, running for his telephone.

"And don't fall!"

"Oh shit, shit, shit," Fredo whispered while he tried to run carefully until he reached his phone.

"Hello, hello, hello, I'm here," Fredo shouted.

"I was just going to hang up. I figured leaving you a message was going to be useless since you never listen to your messages, Fredo. How the hell you doing?"

Kyle's familiar voice barked at him in a pretend dress down.

"Dammit, Kyle we've only been home, what, thirty-five hours?"

"That's a long time to the life of a fruit fly."

"Very funny. I happened to be taking a shower with my lovely wife. So let's make this quick. Otherwise—" He noted Mia wrapped in a towel standing in the doorway to their bathroom. "Oh, crap. It's too late."

"Okay then, Fredo. You'll have to find time for that later. I think it's admirable that you extricated yourself in time to talk to your old LPO. I did listen to my message you left, and I'm concerned. But I'm calling you back to give you the benefit of some information."

"You heard something about Caesar?"

"Yes sir, I did. I also talked to your father-in-law, Gus Mayfield, and he has some connections in the prison system. Turns out, he got himself a judge who isn't going to be up for reelection for another four years, and they've suspected that he's in the pockets of the cartels. They're not pulling any punches anymore. They're not letting anybody get away with not being loyal, so Judge Mathers has granted Caesar a dismissal of all charges and vacated the judgment to time served. You do know he was due to get out in twelve years, not thirty as you told everyone, as we all thought."

"I didn't know that. So he got out three years early then?"

"That's about it. Apparently, he was a model prisoner, and he's convinced a lot of people he's going to turn his life around. I'm not holding my breath for that. His gang still says they hang with him, and well, we know all the crap he pulled. So it's a good cover, but I don't think it's going to fool any of us. Might cause you a problem, though."

"I hate to hear that. So in that situation, can somebody who's served time for endangering a child actually get rights back to have visitations?"

"Well, I'm not an attorney, but I've got a couple names for you. There is such a thing as court-supervised visitation, but you're going to need help with that. And you don't want to be the one paying that bill. It's expensive. I'll text their numbers over in a few. Give them a try—I generally try to stay away from them."

"You got nothing to worry about, Kyle. But I hear you on that one. So do you know anybody who's been through this, like what we're walking into here?"

"Not on the Teams. But hey, I'm sure it's happened a lot. The way things are down here, well, let's just say it's not getting any healthier. Next, they'll be asking us to pack up and ship out to Norfolk or something. It's not going in the right direction. So I want you to be smart, Fredo. Don't go off doing something you know we'll all regret. And I really don't want you dragging any of the guys into this. You hear me on that?"

"Yes, Boss."

"I get that they would probably come and help you, but I just don't need that shit right now. I know you guys would back me up in a firefight if we were overseas, and that's what the brass tries to do—keep us out of trouble—but these types of things, these interpersonal things, husband and wife, even though her ex is a dickwad, we just have to keep our hands out of the cookie jar. So I'm telling you right now, Fredo, don't do that. You stand down."

"And what? Get ready for something to happen before we can go after him?"

"You know I can't give you that kind of advice, Fredo. I don't dare tell you to go get even. At the same time, I know what I'd do in that case. But we have to be smart. There's all kinds of really brilliant people out there a hell of a lot smarter than you and me. Let's use them. And you know if it's money, we'll see if we can set up a fundraiser or something. I know you guys aren't rich. Got all those kids to support, and the attorneys are not cheap. But we'll see if we can find somebody who might be owing us a favor or is just grateful for something we did for them. They're out there too. San Diego has tons of great attorneys."

"As far as schools and all of that, Ricardo runs into these guys at school, and of course, the twins also go to St. Cecilia's. Should we consider transferring them? You certainly wouldn't recommend going into public school, would you?"

"Oh, I think public school would be worse, don't you?"

"Yeah, you're right. But these kids start causing a problem at the school and administration is apt to use the hatchet approach."

"Now that sounds like something we do. I can't see a bunch of nuns running around with hatchets."

Fredo chuckled. "You'd be surprised what they do. But no, not real hatchets. What I mean to say is they kick everybody out. Unlike school districts where they have to give warnings and counsel the parents and try to come to a peaceful resolution, the sisters don't mess around with this stuff. They run a very tight ship. Even though he's the one being picked on, they're just as likely to ask him to leave the school too. They hate press, and they hate other parents reading that there is some kind of gang violence at school."

"I can see that," Kyle said. "No controversy. Sweep it under the rug sort of thing."

That gave Fredo an idea. "So what if the kids got arrested or, you know, ran into trouble with the law somehow? What if it's not like a big fight involving Ricardo? Then they'd kind of be forced to do something, right? I mean, I don't wish them any ill will. Shoot, they're still preteens, for Christ's sake. They're not smart enough to realize if they just keep their heads cool it would work out better for them. But they don't have that maturity. If we could get these kids written up or get their names in the paper somehow, it would be easy to also request that they be released and say that Ricardo had been hassled by them."

"Well, that's a thought. Personally, I'd stay away from that as if my life depended on it. They don't like to be messed with, Fredo. If you're going to go with that approach, then you probably ought to keep all this a secret. You want the papers to tell them. You don't say a word about it."

"But if I don't warn them at the school, Caesar might show up and claim he's the boy's father and take him. Or strong-arm take him. I doubt they'd willingly let him go."

"That's right, Fredo. They'll stand up to him until it crosses a certain threshold, and then they don't want to have violence, so they'll cave, and I think Caesar's cohorts know that too. But maybe that's the way to go. You and Mia talk about it. I'm sure you're going to come up with the right decision. Your biggest problem now is going to be raising the money just in case you need one of those high-powered attorneys I'm going to get you. Oh, and by the way, thanks for the compliment."

"What?"

"Well, Christy said Mia told her that you were leading the charge to sit down and reasonably strategize and do a risk-reward type scenario. And she said you told her that it came from me. So thank you."

"You're welcome." But Fredo knew those words were never said. Christy was just buttering him up to make the phone call.

"So how's the kid?" Fredo asked.

"I was going to go run by there in a few minutes. Are you dressed yet or not finished in the bedroom?"

"Fuck you. I could have my share of the fun. I got married a lot later than you did, so get off my case. You know it's kind of ironic, I thought I'd never have any kids, except for Ricardo. But before Mia and I solidly decided to get married, and it was a real commitment not just a dating situation, I thought I'd never have kids of my own, and now I've got three. And now I'm even thinking about maybe adding a fourth."

Kyle sighed in exasperation. "So I'm going to guess, Fredo, you didn't tell Mia yet about the kid, right?"

"That's correct. We had this other thing to talk about."

"And that's important, it really is. But here's the thing, Fredo. She's the one that's got to do the work, so she's the one that's got to choose. I don't see how you can even put your hat in the ring until this thing with Ricardo is taken care of. And let's be honest with each other, Fredo. How would you feel if you were a ten-year-old kid coming into a strange family, not knowing how to properly speak English, new country, new people, new schools, new cultures. How would you feel if there was a whole lot of drama about some asshole drug dealer hassling your new mom and your new stepbrother? Don't you think he'd feel a little uneasy. Maybe a tad bit uncomfortable?"

Fredo thought Kyle made tremendous sense, but something in his gut still told him that this little boy who stood up to forces much greater than himself, this little boy deserved a chance, just like Ricardo had needed a father to step in and assume the duties that his biological father would never do. Fredo always considered himself someone who saved the innocent, and that's what he intended to do.

But there was Mia. And if she said no, it would be no. He was sure someone else would step up. He thought about going over to the hospital with Kyle and decided to jump in.

"Okay, Kyle, I'm on board. You can pick me up in just a few minutes. At least I'm showered. I might still have some soap on me, but I'm clean. I'll be ready when you get here."

THE HOSPITAL WAS busy today, even the main lobby was filled with people waiting. The hospital also had a physical therapy wing and prosthetic services for veterans. They were locally known as one of the best in Southern California.

"Geez, Kyle, if this is how busy the main lobby is, the ER room must be a zoo," said Fredo.

"I think you're right."

They inquired at the reception desk first of all to make sure the kid was still registered, and he was, and second to see if he was being allowed friends and next of kin.

The woman behind the desk pushed her thick, round, bright-red glasses back onto her nose. "You are relatives?" she said in a thick Latin accent.

"We are not, except we helped rescue him. We just want to check on him is all. We won't stay long. Can you check your notes and see if he's conscious?" Kyle poured on the sweetness as only he could do. Fredo had seen it hundreds of times.

"I see here that there are restrictions on his visitors. I will not be able to give you his status. But if you wait, I'll let you speak to his attending physician, who's still here from morning rounds. I'm sure he'd be glad to talk to you properly. I'm really not supposed to give out any information."

Fredo leaned forward and practically barked at the woman. "But he's still alive, right?"

"Sí, señor. He is alive. I think the doctor will be able to give you a much better idea of what his current condition is, so I will have him paged."

They sat on a round donut-shaped leather cushion with a hole in the middle. It did resemble a glazed donut, no question about it. Fredo was suddenly hungry for something sweet.

"You want to get a coffee, or you want me to get some?" Fredo asked.

"Sure. I'm going to wait here for the doc, but I'll text you if he shows up. You go grab something for yourself. If they've got bagels and cream cheese, I'll take it."

"Anything else? Coffee?" Fredo asked.

"No, I'm good. I got my water."

Walking down the hallway, it was common to hear multiple languages spoken, as several immigrant families used the hospital's emergency room for routine office care. He heard dialects from all over Central and South America, several he'd never heard before.

He hoped there was some improvement today, and he was looking forward to being able to question the kid about some of the things he had seen. He purchased a bagel with everything on it for Kyle and one smothered in cream cheese for himself, along with a coffee and cream. When he got back to the lobby, the doctor was speaking with Kyle.

Fredo handed Kyle his bagel.

"Perfect. Now my stomach will stop rumbling. So, Fredo, this is Dr. Halprin. He's one of the best surgeons down here, I think you remember him from yesterday morning?"

"Sure do." He extended his hand and shook the doctor's.

"Good to see you again. You guys did a hell of a job," Dr. Halprin said.

"Thanks for taking good care of Ivan. Do you have good news for us?" Fredo asked.

"Yeah, I was just telling your LPO here, he's making very good improvement. Of course, it's still too early to tell. He suffered quite a bit, the loss of blood is something that sometimes winds up being problematic later on, but even though he is skinny, he's healthy. Somebody's been feeding him."

"So he's eating then?" Fredo asked.

"Just a few bites here and there, not a lot, and that's normal. In time, after his surgeries, we're going to have to take a look at him and do some tests, but as of right now, I'd say he's well on his way to recovery. And he'll be a lot more comfortable if I can get him off the pain meds and get him something that won't be so devastating to him."

"You mean he's awake?" Fredo asked.

"Yes, he woke up early this morning. Well, he was in pain. He was having a hard time sleeping because of the pain, and he made us promise that he'd have no visitors. I wasn't planning on anything, but then when they told me last night after I went home that he woke up, I figured I'd better get down here first thing this morning and do some evaluations. I was about to go in. Do you want to come in with?"

"Hallelujah," Kyle said.

"Oh, the both of you?" The doctor looked puzzled for a few seconds. Then he continued. "Oh, what the hell, I'll have you both go in. Kyle, let me get you a lab coat, okay?"

"Fine by me."

The boy's face was swollen such that he would be difficult for Fredo to recognize if it weren't for the setting and the fact that he was familiar with his injuries. His head was bandaged above his eyebrows, and he had a cast on his right arm, but it was his left arm that had really suffered the brunt of the kicking and treatment he'd gotten at the hands of the guards. His eyes opened and closed softly. His focusing abilities took some time to kick in, but when he looked back and forth between Fredo and Kyle, he came up with a weak-looking grin. In Spanish, he said, "My saviors."

The doctor looked at Fredo, asking for a translation.

"He called us his saviors. That's nice." In Spanish, Fredo responded. "You're a tough kid, and I'm so sorry for what you have been through. We, all three of us," And motioned to the doctor, Kyle, and himself, "we're here to help make it so that you never have to experience that again." He paused, just to see if the boy had recognition of what he was talking about.

"Where am I?" the boy asked in Spanish.

Fredo translated the answer. "You're in the USA. San Diego. Scripps Hospital. I go here sometimes," Fredo said. "This here is your doctor, and he is one of the best surgeons in this whole area. You were lucky he was on call and here in the emergency room when they brought you in. He's going to try to make it so that you experience less pain, but he has told us that he can't do that until he does perhaps another surgery. But I will translate for him so he can tell you himself."

Ivan nodded his head, fully understanding.

"I am grateful you brought me here."

"We'd like to come back and talk to you about your trip," Kyle started, "But we don't want to tire you. Perhaps we could see you tomorrow? Is that okay?"

Fredo translated. "Sí, I would like that very much."

Kyle then asked if he needed anything.

The boy answered in Spanish, but everyone standing around the bed knew what he wanted.

"I need my mother and my little sister."

CHAPTER 8

WHILE FREDO WAS off with Kyle, Mia picked the boys up from school. Today, Ricardo wasn't talkative at all, and she tried to pry out of him if any additional hassling had been done by the boys. She soon realized her prying was not getting any results.

Ricardo's math teacher was a friend of Mia's, had dated a former SEAL for a period of time but still was single after the death of her first husband. She wondered if perhaps Adrienne could shed some light on how Ricardo was doing. She decided she would schedule a parent-teacher conference. But she wouldn't share what was going on with Ricardo's biological father.

"So no further incidents then, is that what you're saying?"

"Oh, I wouldn't say that. They glared at me. But those assholes, I think they glare at everybody. Maybe I blew it too much out of proportion, Mom. I'm just going to forget about all that shit."

"Ricardo!"

"I'm sorry. It's just sort of annoying, and I let it slip. I really am sorry, Mom. I don't do that very much."

"Well, I don't want you to do it at all, especially in front of your younger brothers."

"Well, they're going to learn it if they don't already know. You can't keep them as babies forever. They got to grow up. And they'll find out, the world's kind of a nasty place sometimes."

Mia wondered where all this modern introspection came from. It was hard to say what was influencing Ricardo these days. He'd been placed in an advanced reading class and was flying through the books he was given. The teacher told Mia he was the best student in the class. Yet, Ricardo never talked about those books or how come the love of reading had just taken off this year. Whatever was the reason for it, Mia was glad.

"How about this, then? If we decide to take a family vacation this year, and again it all depends on what your dad's schedule is, is there any place in particular you'd like to go?"

From the backseat came the unanimous shout-out, "Disney World!"

"I asked Ricardo. We'll get there. I don't want to spend that kind of money just yet." And then to Ricardo in a lower tone, she said, "Would you like to do something just you and your dad? You could go skydiving maybe or he could take you out shooting. Some of the guys go hunting. Does that interest you at all?"

"Sure, I love all those things, but guns? They make me nervous."

Mia knew what Fredo would say if he was here. She tried to paraphrase it as best she could.

"Well, that's probably because you haven't had enough training using guns. But it's not something you have to do. You wouldn't be expected to defend your family. It'll be another story after you leave the house, go off, and get married."

"Who said anything about marriage? I'm thirteen, Mom. I don't ever think about that one."

Mia quickly glanced over at her son, saw the expression on his face, and understood the addiction to girls had not yet begun. Perhaps it was better that Ricardo was a little bit of a late bloomer. God knows, Mia wasn't that way at all. And she'd driven her mother crazy. She should be grateful.

"Well, you think about it. It's got to be your idea, and if we can swing it, if it's something not all five of us can do but just you and your dad or the three of us, if it's within reason and not too expensive, we'll do it."

Ricardo stared at her. "Are you buttering me up so you can drop the hammer on me later? What is it you really want, Mom?"

"I just want you to feel like you can tell me anything. I want you to understand that we have your back. I know it's probably confusing, and a big part of it's my fault for having made certain choices perhaps I shouldn't have. But if I hadn't, you wouldn't be here today. So I guess good can come from bad. I'm just hoping we don't have to see Caesar very much in the future. We're working on that anyway."

"I don't understand why he wants to have anything to do with me. I'm not anything like him, from the stories I've heard anyway. I don't want to be a wannabe 'gangsta.' I don't want to be hanging around the shopping centers and cemeteries and parks at night, I don't want to get in trouble. That's just dumb."

"I'm glad you see it that way, Ricardo. That's healthy. I wish everybody had that kind of maturity."

"I think some of the guys at school who brag about some of the things they've done, they are trying to fool themselves into thinking they're big badass dudes."

"Ricardo, I don't like that tone of voice, and I don't like you swearing. What's gotten into you?"

"Nothing, I'm just like I always was."

Mia decided it was time to stop pestering him with questions, since it was obvious her probing was not getting her very far, and she needed all the connection with him she could get. If things got really heated, he didn't need to have both sides of his family turn into a nightmare. She wanted to remain close to him.

"You know I love you, right?"

"Yeah, I do. I think you and Dad have done a great job. You both work hard. I'm proud of our family. Some guys at school, their sisters or their cousins or sometimes their mothers, they embarrass them. I don't feel that way about you guys. And most people when they find out what Dad does, well, they're in awe. I mean, not everybody can do the kind of stuff he does."

"I'm glad you see it that way, Ricardo. Your dad's a very special man. Not everybody is physically capable and emotionally capable of doing some of the ops that he completes. He doesn't talk about it much because he doesn't do it for fame and glory or recognition of any kind. He does it because it's his calling, because he doesn't want to see innocent people get preyed on by cretins. So we're charged with keeping the faith, keeping the home fires burning, and making sure Fredo knows that we appreciate him. I think he'd rather have your respect than anything else in the world. I know he loves you, but even more important, he values you."

When they got to the house, the twins were sent upstairs to begin their homework while Ricardo was given the dining room table to work on his. He had a computer upstairs in his bedroom but the computer the whole family used downstairs was connected to the printer and Ricardo wanted to be able to make notes and print them out so he wouldn't forget the references.

"I know you've got a report for history. How's it coming?" Mia asked Ricardo.

"It's coming. I'm going to finish it this weekend, but that's why I got the book so I can work on it, because I have to turn it in on Friday. I can't keep it over the weekend."

"Good job, Ricardo. How did you pick the mission in Santa Clara to do your study on?"

"Remember last summer when I went up to play soccer at that tournament in Santa Clara?"

"Yes, Fredo took you. I don't think I went to that one, but gosh, I've been to so many."

"No, Mom, you didn't go to that one. Anyway we got to know the kids on the local United team. They were fourteen-year-olds kind of all puffed out and feeling superior, and then when we beat them, we came in second place in the whole tournament. Well, since we obviously were impressing people with the size and the quickness of our team, they started being nice to us and showed us around. One guy took several of us on a tour of the chapel at Santa Clara. Did you know, Mom, that they have Indians buried in the walls?"

Mia scrunched up her nose. "I'm not so sure about that. We call them Native Americans now. But they told you that?"

"Yes, they said some of the priests that were there, the fathers, and some of the elders from the village were buried within the walls because it took a couple of years to finish the whole mission complex. Anyway it gave me an excuse to go look up that theory, and I haven't verified it, but it's kind of an interesting issue."

"I could see how that would capture your attention. I'd take it with a grain of salt, Ricardo. I never heard that growing up, but then we didn't live on the Peninsula either. We lived for the first many years of my life in Puerto Rico. And trust me, they didn't put Indians' bodies into the concrete there."

"Well, we all thought it was kind of cool. Somebody said that when the organ gets played late at night, there's spirits that come from the ground up, singing. It's kind of creepy if you ask me. But I got enough material for a good report without having to bring up all of that. But you asked me why, so I just told you."

"Well, whatever reason you have to do a study of the mission at Santa Clara, I completely approve. As long as we don't have ghosts flying around, ghost stories, cattle mutilations, all that stuff. And who knows, maybe it was a wives' tale told just to keep people out of the church. I think it would scare me."

"Well, it does scare me. I think about it all the time. We'll have to go there sometime. I think you'd like the history of it."

"You know, we could do a long weekend sometime, come up and do that road trip. I'm afraid it's out of the cards before your paper's due, but I think you've obviously got a lot of questions, and maybe the sisters will put you in contact with a researcher there. There's a famous University there."

Just then, they heard screaming upstairs in the boys' bedroom. Mia banged on the door.

"Open up, this is your mother speaking. I want no more of that roughhousing going on."

She came back downstairs and started to load up the dishwasher, tidying the kitchen. She needed a few things at the store for dinner but didn't want to leave all the boys together without an adult. But then she heard Fredo's Hummer park in their driveway.

She brushed her hair, fluffed it out—long and wild was how he liked it—and then greeted him at the doorway.

"Well, Sailor. Are you going to be here long?"

"I think so. I'm sticking around your whole life, sweetheart. Trust me on that." He walked right past her into the living room and on to the kitchen. His routine, without the warmth.

But he usually smiled after that or gave her a hug, a kiss, or something tender. Even the boys couldn't elicit a wrestle or some high fives. It wasn't his lack of interest. It was something else.

Fredo was in one of those moods where she couldn't tell whether he was on solid ground or not. The boys greeted their dad when he entered the kitchen, dropping his duffel bag unceremoniously right by the kitchen rear doorway. It had been their tradition. Fredo was to give up his dirty clothes. This time he was late, but that had happened before, so Mia knew they'd be extra ripe sitting in the hot sun of the Hummer's interior. Then Mia would set upon getting everything cleaned and folded to his specifications, ready for his next deployment.

But today, he was distracted and didn't seem to hear anything Mia had said.

The boys finished their afterschool snack and headed for the pool. Every time she saw them jump in, every time she wrote that monthly check, she was grateful they'd splurged for the pool, even though they could not really afford it on Fredo's military salary. It was an investment in their happiness.

But not even the blue-turquoise pool could entice Fredo into a more playful demeanor. She decided to keep trying, but be very careful about it. Never push. Keep the criticism logical and with provable facts and details. Only things emotional Fredo liked was their lovemaking, and then she could come off the rails, and he'd be in the best mood ever. Funny how that worked. If she could show him how much pleasure he brought her, if he could feel it in the beating of her heart and her breathless pants after the exhaustive sexual encounter, he'd believe it. But just telling him or asking questions wasn't the way.

It wasn't really play-acting, although some might think so. It was fulfilling the role she'd chosen, why he'd chosen her, because she wanted to be all the things he wanted and limit the things he didn't. Far from submission, working hard to understand and be the best wife any SEAL could have had become her joy. He deserved it, and she did to. It worked both ways for them both.

Right now was going to be the heavy lifting time. Done with grace and showing her caring side, not her angry or critical side.

Showtime!

"You've been out in the sun. Go take a shower, and I'll get these started in the wash."

He nodded to the floor.

"Any snakes, scorpions? Any dead furry animals like last time?"

"Probably should have checked. Why don't you let me load the washer and I'll dispose of anything I find?"

She raised her eyebrows. "I'm a big girl. I've done this before a time or two. I was just making fun, but I guess my delivery and timing needs work."

That got his attention, and she could see him melt, realizing how he was coming across.

"God, Mia. I've been a fool." He stepped in front of her and grabbed her into his arms. "I was distracted. Forgive me?"

"As long as that distraction isn't a she, blonde, and with a bigger bust than mine."

"No worries there, Mia. No one could ever be anything but a cheap imitation not even worthy of my gaze. I look, but when I see something attractive it does nothing to diminish the joy and love I have with you. You are irreplaceable, one of a kind, and I don't begin to deserve you. I'm glad you listened to my poor pleas, took pity on me, and made me the happy man I am today."

The words were so beautiful, Mia's tears poured out. When Fredo heard her sniffle, he drew back, studying her face before placing a tender kiss on her lips.

"Mi amore," she whispered into his hungry mouth.

He rocked her back and forth, steadying her in his massive arms, rubbing her back up and down her spine with his calloused hands. His battle scars and all.

"The wash can wait. Let's talk," he said.

She brought two glasses of ice water to the table in the kitchen, where they both sat.

"Was this a difficult morning, Fredo? Something going on with Kyle?"

She remembered too late she was trying not to ask too many questions and silently cursed herself.

"No, that part's fine. I didn't tell you what we found in Mexico. I can't tell you the details just yet until after our debriefing, but we rescued a little migrant boy who had been injured by the men who were trafficking him and his family. We were able to medically evacuate him to Scripps, just in time. He's still very ill, but this morning, he was talking."

"So you went with Kyle to visit him, then," Mia said, suddenly understanding Fredo's mood.

"We did."

Fredo looked at the ice water, the drips of condensation traveling like tears down the glass, then continued. "He's all alone."

"But you said he had family."

"They didn't make it."

"That's terrible. Poor thing. Well, I'm glad you came to give him moral support. Good on you guys for doing that."

But that didn't move Fredo.

"What? What's going on?"

"The timing sucks, but I was going to ask you if we could apply to adopt him."

"We don't know him, Fredo. You just met, right?"

"Sometimes you know things about people instantly. Things like bravery, courage, how it feels to lose a parent, or, in his case, I think both his parents and a sibling. His whole world. He's going to be needing lots of medical help and his recovery will be long. But that little boy is a warrior, and he stood up to pure evil like few grown men do today. I think watching that had the same effect on the whole platoon. I even saw some tears on guys I've never seen cry before, Mia. Bravery comes in all sizes, colors, all nationalities, but once you witness it, you are forever changed."

Mia touched his hand, and he squeezed her fingers.

"Of course, it would change you. I wouldn't expect anything less," she whispered.

"It's the part of my job that I love because it masks some of the evil parts of my job. I'm not sure I'm suited to do anything else. But I do think I've never seen such a strong character in a child. I don't want that wasted, watered down, disregarded, or malnourished. He's all alone in this world. I don't know whether it's for me or for him, but I'd like to try to give a hand-up. And before you ask, it doesn't diminish my love for the boys, either. Or you," he said while squeezing her fingers.

"I understand, Fredo. If you are sure, I'll trust your judgment on this. May I ask that I get to talk to him first before the final decision is made?"

"Ah, Sweetheart," Fredo said as he knelt in front of her, his arms wrapped around her torso. "That is why I love you so much."

A few minutes later, as Fredo was trying to arrange a visit at the hospital for as soon as possible, his cell rang. He hung up and answered it.

"Mr. Chavez?" It was an older woman's voice.

"Yes, ma'am. That's me."

"This is Sister Mary Margaret from St. Cecilia's. You asked to make an appointment with me, and I have some dates and times I thought I'd go over with you. I do have some time this afternoon, if that works. About four? Or tomorrow at noon. And then there's—"

Fredo interrupted her. "How about tomorrow at noon? The boys will be in class, and we'll not have to hire a sitter."

"Very well. I'll put you down. Now, will both you and your wife be coming, or just you?"

He looked into Mia's eyes. She was nodding.

"She'll be with me."

"Good. And I understand you didn't want to reveal your reason for this appointment. Is there some problem here at school concerning one of your boys?"

"They love the school there. This has to do with some family dynamics going on, or what might be going on. We wanted to discuss it with you first in private, see if you had any recommendations for us."

"Of what nature, Mr. Chavez?"

"I think it's best we talk tomorrow. Thank you for being so available."

After Fredo hung up, Mia commented on something she'd noticed.

"You're serious about all this, aren't you? You left the afternoon open so I could possibly visit the boy, right?"

"I did. Still waiting for permission. Can you arrange a sitter?"

Mia looked out at their yard and the water fight ensuing. It was going to be hard to take them out of the pool.

"Let me get the youngest Bennet girl to come over. I know she's saving for college. She might enjoy a dip in the pool herself."

CHAPTER 9

F REDO TOOK MIA'S hand, and they walked down the corridors of the huge hospital complex to Ivan's room. Before they could enter, the head nurse ran over and blocked their entrance.

"You can't go in there without permission. Are you family?" she asked Fredo and then briefly nodded to Mia.

"I'm the fellow that rescued him from Mexico. We are considering filing papers of adoption, and I would like to introduce him to my wife. If he's well enough today. Is he?"

"Well, those aren't reasons that I can give approval. You're going to have to check with his doctor, and he's not here right now, so I'll try to get him on the phone, unless you have his number."

"I have his number. He gave me his card." Fredo pulled it out of his jacket pocket.

"Very well, I will trust you, but please reach him before you enter the room. And just for your information, he's eating like a horse."

Her once frosty appearance warmed quickly.

Fredo whispered in Mia's ear, "They have special rules about foreign patients coming in under an emergency situation. Many of the people who they get are not immunized for all kinds of diseases that we've eradicated decades ago. They have to be very careful. I'm surprised they don't have a sign on the room, so I'll have to ask about that. And so far there's no DHS guard, which is also unusual."

With Mia nodding, Fredo heard his line pick up on the doctor's end.

"Hello? This is Dr. Halprin."

"Hey Doc, it's Fredo Chavez. We met this morning and yesterday."

"Yes, Fredo, what can I do for you?"

"Your station nurse said I needed your permission to come see him. My wife wants to meet him since we are considering that paperwork that we discussed this morning. Would you be so kind as to allow her to visit?"

"You're at the hospital now?"

"Yes, sir. I went home, and we got to talking. She has not met him, and I think it's only fair that she get a chance to introduce herself. Also, I have some questions I need to ask him about the organization that he witnessed, and she can be my witness, if you'll allow maybe fifteen, twenty minutes of questioning. If we see he's in any kind of distress, we would gladly leave. But I need your okay on that if you're in agreement."

Dr. Halprin hesitated but then gave his approval. "I don't want to tax his energy, but we do not know everything about his system yet, and if something should pop up and it becomes an emergency situation, I'd rather have given you guys the chance to ask him your important questions. So I'll allow it, but under no circumstances, Mr. Chavez, are you to stay there longer than an hour. And I'm going to tell that to the nurse too. In fact, I'm going to have her monitor his stage of awareness and pain level, and if it agitates him at all, I get all his vitals sent to me directly, I'll be able to see it, and I will cut it off there. So please don't push. It's what's good for him."

"Thanks, Doc. I'm handing the phone over to your nurse here."

After giving the nurse his cell phone, Fredo pointed with his thumb to the door, which was closed, and he and Mia entered the darkened room.

At first, Fredo thought the young boy was sleeping, but then he noticed the front of his face was wet, and he'd been crying. He felt sad and a little guilty about witnessing the fact that he missed his mother and little sister. Perhaps they had pushed their luck too far, and Fredo certainly didn't want to cause him any more undue stress. But he theorized that the more Ivan learned about Fredo and his Team guys, the more he would like them and the more comfortable he would feel around them. He could only begin to guess what kind of crazy stories these people were being told by the cartels and also by the police in Mexico proper.

"Ivan? It's me, Fredo. Are you open to having a visitor or two?"

Ivan scooched up on the bed, bringing himself to sitting position with his legs extended out front. He did look like the pictures of children's books of *The Princess and the Pea*, where the princess was so tiny compared to the size of the bed with all those mattresses piled up to the ceiling. Ivan had a surgical bed that had more than twenty adjustments and positions to accommodate any kind of surgery, and it was also wide with side panels that pulled down or up or turned into rails, if need be. Ivan leaned forward and gave an inquisitive look at Mia.

Fredo wrapped his arm around his wife and pulled her slowly and gently over to Ivan's bedside. "This is Mia, my wife."

She extended her hand, and little Ivan timidly took the tip of her fingers and shook up and down. In Spanish, he said, "Nice to meet you."

Mia responded in Spanish that she was likewise charmed. Then she added, "I understand you were quite the little fighter. My husband is very impressed with your bravery. I am so sorry for your loss, and I wish you to know that this gentleman here, my husband, is one of the finest and bravest men I have ever met. Please don't hesitate to remain friends with him. He wants to help you. And you can trust him."

Fredo added, "One of the things you're going to need to do right away is to begin to learn English. That will help you get around much better, will help you find things, and you'll be able to be more involved in your own care if you do that."

Ivan nodded his head. "I am grateful, Señor. I have made some very good first friends. How long do you think I have to stay here?"

Fredo answered him back in Spanish as well. "As I think the doctor told you this morning, he has an additional surgery or two on your shoulder to repair some of the things he couldn't do the first time he went in. I'm going to guess that you'll be here for a few days anyway."

Mia touched Fredo on his shoulder, leaning toward the boy.

"Is there someone that you know that you would like us to contact for you, Ivan? May I call you Ivan?" she asked.

Ivan shook his head from side to side and then some kind of remembrance crossed his face because his eyes got big, and he looked to the right and the left on the floor for something.

"What is it? Are you looking for your bag?" Fredo asked him.

"Sí. I have it in my bag."

Fredo got down on his knees and searched under the bed and came up empty-handed, but Mia pointed to a closet door directly opposite Ivan's bed. When Fredo opened it, he saw the satchel that Ivan's mother had been wearing when she was shot. There was still blood on it that had not been removed. He tried to ignore it and brought it over carefully to Ivan, turning it around so he might miss the stain. But he didn't. A single tear ran down his left cheek as he zippered the top and rummaged through articles of clothing and some paperwork, one by one laying the things out on his legs when he thought they were important.

"May I?" Mia asked.

Ivan pushed the satchel in her direction. Mia rummaged through the paperwork that Ivan had been disinterested in, placing them all to her right, and searched for other paperwork to add to it. Finally, at the very bottom, something that surprised both of them, was a military dog tag. When Mia held it up, the little silver beads of the necklace hanging down touching the covers on the bed, Ivan perked up and pointed to it.

"This, this. This is my father. My father is in the US. He lives here. My mother was trying to go meet him."

Fredo was distressed with his information. It changed the trajectory of everything they'd been planning. If Ivan had a blood relative who was a US citizen, he would more than likely only be sent to that person. And unless the person was deceased or refused him, only then would there be some kind of an adoption recommended. He decided not to explain this to Ivan, or Mia, until he had time to properly lay it out and get answers.

"So where does your father live then? Where in the US, what state?"

Ivan shook his head and shrugged, holding his hands in front of him, indicating he had no clue.

"I think he doesn't know what a state is," Mia whispered in English.

"You have different regions in Mexico. In the US, it is the same thing. We have states like small countries making up the big United States, which is our US country. It would help me to find your father if you knew where he lived. And from the looks of this dog tag, it appears to be not new. It also appears that your father was a US Marine, is that correct?"

"Sí, sí. Yes, my father is a Marine. I never met him. I was only a baby when he went back home. My mother was his girlfriend for a period of time. She was a professional girlfriend. You have that in the US?"

Fredo shared a look with Mia.

"Ivan, it's probably also something that women do in the US. However, it may be more prevalent in Mexico. So your father was on vacation, is that what you're saying? What did your mother tell you?"

"She says he made her his wife while he was in Mexico. His Mexican wife. My mother thought that perhaps he had an American wife as well."

"And you don't think he even knows that you exist, is that correct?" Fredo asked.

Ivan looked down at the bag, his lower lip protruded slightly, looking sad and unsure what to say. After a few seconds, he shook his head from side to side. "No."

"Do you have anything else that tells where your father's house is?" asked Mia.

Ivan shrugged again. "Maybe the papers, but I do not read English. There are some papers there in English, I think. My mother paid much money to come here. It was required that it be US dollars. $8,000. That is more money than she made all year working as a housekeeper for a wealthy gentleman. I was surprised that she was able to find the money. And then it was stolen."

"We are going to look through this paperwork, and do I have your permission to make a copy of some of these things so we can help you find your dad?"

Ivan nodded his approval.

Fredo did manage to find Ivan's certificate of live birth, and on the certificate received from the doctor who delivered him, a form that the doctor filled in blanks, it did list the Marine as being Ivan's father.

That was certainly something he needed to get a copy of, and he also found a letter. It came from California somewhere, but the postmark was smudged. Without a return address, it really was no help. He took out the letter and saw that it was handwritten.

"Would you like me to read this letter? It is, I believe, from your father to your mother. Has she read this to you?"

"I don't think she read it. She does not read English. One of her younger sisters teaches in the school, and she was not able to read it either. So I have never heard it before. Can you read this letter to me so I can hear the voice of my father?"

Fredo stiffened and cleared his throat about to begin the reading, all the while feeling Mia's tense body standing next to him.

"May we sit down?" he asked the boy.

"Sí, sí," and Ivan pointed to the chairs.

"My dear Lupe,

First, I want to tell you how much you mean to me and how special our month was together while I was visiting Cabo San Lucas. I didn't expect to fall in love, but I did. Now that I am home, unfortunately, the reality of my fun time in Mexico has made me a very sad man. I was not completely honest with you, and I should not have taken advantage of your generosity when you offered to cook and keep house for me. But I will always cherish our April together, and although I probably will never see you again, I hope and pray that you find a wonderful man to make your husband, and I hope that you have a happy and successful life.

I was engaged to be married when I came down to Mexico on that fishing trip. My buddies had been coming down there for years, and they were the ones who said that I should find a girlfriend, a wife for a month. My wife here, as we got married soon after I returned, will never know about you, but I think she would have liked you. I just wanted you to know that because I developed feelings for you, I stepped over the line and took what was offered without taking the responsibility of knowing I had no right to ask that of you. Nor that did I have the right to break the promises I had made to my fiancée, Mary.

But I will always cherish the sunsets, the wonderful fresh fish dishes that you cooked, the homemade tortillas and tamales, and that amazing white pepper sauce that burned the whole inside of my mouth and throat the first time I ate it, but which soon became my staple, and I have yet to find it in any restaurant here.

I am leaving the military and going to work for a farming

concern here in California. My father-in-law has a large ranch, and he raises cattle, as well as apples, prunes, peaches, and sometimes other fruits. I have always liked farming, and I was fortunate enough to not be born on a farm, so this, even though it's a lot of work, is fun for me. I think if I had been raised on a farm, it wouldn't be so special.

Please say hello to Adela, to Maria, and Bernadette. I hope you'll remain friends, and I hope all of you find wonderful husbands. I will think of you always, and I think you will always claim a piece of my heart.

Much love, and God bless you,
Lance."

After reading the letter to Ivan, Fredo didn't have the stomach to stay longer and ask him questions about his life in Mexico or the long difficult trek his little family made at great cost. He wanted this to be the last thing Ivan heard before he went to sleep tonight.

There would be more times in the hours to come where they could discuss the nasty business of the smugglers and the heartache and ruin they were spewing everywhere.

He couldn't save Ivan's mother or sister. But he and Mia could give him a little bit of peace, and if it wasn't in the cards to have him come live with them, he could at least help him solve the riddle of finding a forever home he would feel safe in.

He placed his big, calloused hand on the boy's head.

"Goodnight, Son."

He handed back the letter and noticed Ivan pressed it to his chest and held it firm like it was a lifeline.

CHAPTER 10

MIA TEXTED THE babysitter, letting her know that they were on their way home. She asked if the sitter could stay an extra forty-five minutes so she and Fredo could stop and grab something to eat and pick up some pizza for the kids.

The Bennet girl agreed to it enthusiastically and said she was having a great time swimming with the kids in the pool.

Homework was going to have to wait, Mia realized. Tonight, they were just being kids.

Fredo took her to an Italian restaurant, and they ordered an early dinner light fare, selecting a table in a dark corner so they could have some privacy while they talked. They put in their order for the take-out for later, and it was promised to be brought piping hot.

"Fredo, did you have any idea any of this happened in the past? Did he mention it before?" asked Mia.

"Well, before, he was out cold. He was in pretty bad shape. And at the hospital, he didn't say anything about that, so I'm not sure what to think. I want to believe him, though, and I think with these documents, I'll start looking into it."

Mia noticed Fredo was not smiling, and she suspected all this new information threw him for a loop. He didn't do unexpected consequences well, she knew from nearly ten years of marriage now. But, in these cases, there were probably a thousand different scenarios of the same situation with other crossings at the border every single week.

"The one thing I was struck with, Fredo, is it sounds like he really loved her, but he didn't want to bring her to the States. Because he was already engaged. So first of all, he's kind of a lowlife for doing that to her. And second, I mean, if the guy was super responsible, he would've checked back with her. I'm sure he knew whether or not they'd used protection. So that's kind of irresponsible of him. I don't think I like that."

"No, I didn't like that either, but, who knows, maybe he was just really young." Fredo gave her a sly grin. "I mean, I don't know anybody who made some dumb decisions at eighteen or nineteen years old, do you?"

She smiled. "Oh, I have one little lady in mind. And yes, I know her quite well." She grinned.

"I'm going to check with Gus and see if he knows how we can quickly get a Marine roster during those years around Ivan's birth. One thing we know is that he had intended to leave the military about ten years ago. So that narrows the scope of investigation quite a bit. But what I'm most concerned about is, what if he doesn't want to see the kid? I mean, do we explain to Ivan that he may be walking into a hornet's nest of some kind? I'm just not sure I can explain it to him."

"Maybe it isn't necessary to. We should find him first and ask him how he wants to handle it. I think we'll come to that decision in due time. Let's first see if he's alive, let's see if he's in the general vicinity, because we don't have the money to be traveling all over the United States to look for him, and let's see if he wants to talk to the boy. At the least, after they finish their investigation, he needs to be told about her death. I go either way about letting him know he's fathered a child. I sort of think it also needs to be up to Ivan for that."

"That's good advice."

Later on that evening, as Mia was cleaning up the kitchen and getting the kids put to bed, Fredo called Kyle and gave him the news about the Marine and Ivan's mother. He put the phone on speaker so Mia could listen in.

"That's a damn shame. Man, this kid has been living under a thunder cloud for a long time too. The last thing we want to do, of course, is get him in some kind of temporary place and then have him yanked out or come into some bureaucratic snafu somewhere where he's bounced around a bunch of times. This is a type of situation where he's too young to be making important decisions about his living situation. And the way our government works, it's not going to be good on him at all to sit around and wait. But I think the worst thing for me is the father. I think he's a jerk. And the kid deserves something better, doesn't he?"

"Amen to that, Kyle," said Mia to the phone receiver.

"You heard that, Kyle?"

"Loud and perfectly clear."

"He does deserve more. Much more," Fredo agreed.

Kyle reacted. "Now don't go taking that on yourself. The law is the law, and we are not going to interfere with how it's working. I think we need to stay out of it as much as possible but just be informed where the process is. At some point, you're going to meet somebody who's going to give you the keys to the kingdom, how all this happened, someone on the Mexico side who knew the family. That will be valuable information, so even if we can't have much of a say in where he's placed, we'll have one more piece of the puzzle to help future orphans. It's not a perfect world, but damn, his family back home may want him back or, at the minimum, will promise to stay in touch. I think that's going to be really important for Ivan."

"I couldn't agree with you more, Kyle."

"So any more information on Caesar or the boys at school?"

"No, I guess they've not had any more interaction, or the gang boys are not going to school. It's somewhere between that and nothing. Even Ricardo told Mia in confidence that he thought that perhaps the situation with Caesar was blown out of proportion like Ricardo suspected. But we have to stay vigilant."

"You know, Kyle," Mia inserted. "Sometimes when the kids don't tell you things, it isn't that nothing happened. They just won't tell you. So we could be reading it all wrong."

"I got you. I'm on the same wavelength. It's too bad there aren't some good guys who we could get to help you, but we're still looking for a good attorney who is familiar with criminal work. I don't think you have to worry about a custody battle—I think you have to worry about your own public safety."

Fredo agreed. "You haven't seen the pool yet, Kyle. You should see how the yard looks, the gardens, and the flowers. It's just absolutely beautiful. You know, Kyle, it was a stretch to try to get that pool in last year, but I'm so glad we did it. And Mia's taken to gardening just like her mother. She's very happy there. I would sure hate to leave that behind or have to leave the community for our safety. But you know, Kyle, I'd do it if we had to."

"I understand. And hey, Fredo, thanks for keeping me informed. I'm going to be all ears if I hear anything, if I get contacted by somebody from the State Department or Homeland Security or our special agent friend, I'll make sure they let you know too, and I'll keep you in the loop as much as I'm allowed. That said, we're going to have to go in for a debriefing tomorrow morning."

"Fuckin' frijoles! Why did they wait three days? I mean, there's been so much that's gone on already."

"I don't know. You know Homeland Security's pretty busy these days. So I'd give them a little bit of slack. And the Navy? Well, the Navy's busy all the time, too. That never changes. No picnic there. I think the debriefing is mostly for Homeland Security, and they're probably the ones that triggered it. So you be ready with your facts—think about them tonight, and if they call me in the morning and say we got to come in, then we got to come in."

"Okay, but I got an appointment with Ricardo's administrator at school tomorrow at noon. We're going to be careful but have to give her a heads-up so that if something happens on campus we have somebody who's watching for that."

"Good idea."

After the phone call with Kyle, Mia pushed Fredo into the living room while she finished the cleanup of the kitchen and put in another load of laundry.

"Never-ending story of my life: laundry!" she whispered to herself.

She joined him while he surfed the channels looking for something they liked. She knew that Fredo didn't want to think about his debriefing tomorrow. He needed a little distraction, first with the TV and then a nice hot, erotic shower before bed. Well, maybe some play in there someplace, too.

While he was flipping through channels, he saw a news flash from the southern border in Texas where a large caravan of women and children had drowned in the Rio Grande River, all of them undocumented, and as Fredo put his face up to the screen, he thought he recognized some of the clothing on what was a drone shot of a couple dozen people floating in the water. The announcer was letting the public know that some of these had been intentionally murdered, gunshots to the head, and that most of them had no papers, so there was no way to identify who they were or who they needed to inform.

Fredo looked at Mia. "I think that's the group we saw. I think that's Ivan's group."

"Seriously, Fredo?"

Fredo grabbed his cell phone and put it to his ear. "I'm going to call Kyle again."

"Wait until the morning. You'll see him. Enough already, Fredo," she answered.

But she was too late.

"Hey, Kyle, call me back, or turn on the news. There's a story about a migrant group that drowned in the Rio Grande in Texas at the Texas border. I think you should get a hold of that footage, because I think I recognize some of those people. Not their faces but some of the clothing. Like there was this lady with this bright yellow skirt and a black sarong over her shoulders. I think I saw that in the crowd they showed on the news. You don't have to call me back, but see if you can get hold of that footage, and maybe it'll help Gutierrez nail that Ochoa butcher. Just trying to help out. Let me know if you want me to do anything else."

Mia knew that Fredo was keyed up, ready for action. It just seemed like the hits kept on coming. First, it was Caesar getting out of prison, then it was the harassment of Ricardo, then it was meeting Ivan, and now this, the death of all these innocent people. It was too much to handle, and two of those very important events directly affected her family.

And then she remembered, they had an appointment at noon to talk to Ricardo's director in addition to that already full plate. How was she going to keep a lid on all of this? And what would Sister Mary Margaret think about all these issues they were embroiled in?

She was going to take a soak in the hot tub, maybe have a little glass of something, and get good and sleepy before she tried to go to bed.

Otherwise, she would be up all night with worry.

And maybe Fredo could help with that, which brought a smile to her lips.

CHAPTER 11

F REDO WAS SURPRISED to see Special Agent Gutierrez at the debriefing the next morning.

"I understand you've been to the hospital a couple of times to visit our boy. Is he giving you good information?" Gutierrez asked.

Fredo noticed Kyle turning and heading in their direction. "There's a lot to this, and we found out that apparently his father lives in the United States. He was a Marine, maybe still is, but he was a Marine at the time he and Ivan's mother were together. Apparently, they were on their way to try to find him."

"Well, that's kind of a shock, isn't it? It makes it pretty easy then. That's where his final destination will be."

Fredo was afraid of that assessment, and he had a pang in his gut about that working out.

"Sir, if I can insert myself here," Kyle began. "Fredo and I have talked about this, and he's ready to put together an application to formally adopt Ivan."

"Whoa, whoa, whoa! Total cart before the horse here. You guys are jumping the gun. You can't poach this kid. He belongs to an American citizen."

Fredo was extremely troubled by Gutierrez's opinion. Before he could stop himself, he'd winced. He was glad Kyle spoke before he could open his mouth and say something inappropriate.

"Sir, if I could explain something to you. This little boy has been trafficked and damaged. He's lost his mother and his younger sister. However, he does have relatives back in Mexico, older siblings. And I'm not sure if his stepfather in Mexico is still alive. But one of the things we're concerned about is that perhaps he was convinced to travel with his mother and sister when he really didn't want to. Fredo and I came to the conclusion that it might be best if we check out the Marine father first, if we can find him, and then based on that, go forward with whatever we're allowed to do."

"Well, you can turn in an application for adoption. I can give you the form, but I think the likelihood it will be approved is quite small. We generally don't like to split up families. We all know he'll have a better life in the United States, but he won't be with anybody he knows. If he can be with his biological father, well, that's a little bit better than having him be a complete stranger here. But I don't see that it's anybody's place to seek his adoption. Can you explain your thinking about this?" He was looking directly at Fredo.

"I think what Kyle's trying to say is that maybe his father isn't going to want him. And before he gets shipped to some location where he doesn't know anyone, he and I or a couple of men who were there the day of his rescue could research, travel, and speak to the father first and then do what Ivan and the father would like. The father has rights, and Ivan has the right to not be bounced around the system. Gutierrez, you know that happens a lot. And I want your promise that you aren't going to hand him over to an NGO."

Gutierrez raised his eyebrows and then whistled. "Well, I'll say one thing for you guys, you do your research. But I can promise that deal. I don't think we have to involve the agencies. Most of them are Catholic charities. I don't think we have to put them in charge. And if you guys on your own time want to go find Mr. Lover Boy here, I'm okay with that. I really would like to see the kid get somewhere he wants to be. It wouldn't be the first time that a father disavowed having a child out of wedlock. So let's just do that then. But as far as promising you can be first in line for an adoption, Fredo, I'm afraid I can't do that. But you can go ahead and apply, and then you'll be at the head of the line if that should change."

Fredo was okay with that, and he told Gutierrez so.

The briefing was called to begin shortly, only eleven of the twelve SEALs who went to Mexico were available for this. Randy and his wife had booked a cruise several months ago, and there was no clause for a refund due to cancellation. Fredo had thought it was overkill to ask the entire platoon to show up, but he figured there might be something else going on, and he'd find out soon enough.

Kyle walked to the front of the room as team members took their places in the conference room. Fredo sat next to Cooper.

"How's it going there?" Cooper asked him.

Fredo leaned back and stared at the ceiling. "It's complicated, but the kid seems to be healing pretty quickly. They have to go in maybe twice and fix a couple of things, but he's really a trooper, and he heals remarkably fast."

"I heard about his father. Dumbass Marine, huh?"

"Well, a lot of our regular Navy guys are the same way, in all fairness," Fredo answered him.

"That's affirmative. A few Team Guys as well. But I hope it gets sorted. And I understand you're trying to effectuate an adoption if you're allowed?"

"Yep. Mia is behind it 100%."

"And what about your boys? How are they going to feel about this?"

"Well, we're not going to tell them until we know for sure we have the green light. That's always best with them."

"And Caesar, you run into him yet?"

"Not yet. I'm hoping that he's changed his mind or changed his ways. Honestly, Coop, we have so much on our plate. I'm glad he hasn't shown up yet. But we'll be ready if and when he does."

"How's Ricardo taking it?"

Fredo chuckled. "This is a direct quote, 'I don't want to meet that sperm donor. He didn't care anything about me, and instead of being a father, he decided to live a life of crime and go to prison for it.' And that's an exact quote from my son."

"Yep. You got your hands full, that's for sure. Well, you give my best to your lovely wife, and we'll see if we can arrange the kids to have a get together here. We're overdue, Fredo."

"I'm sure my boys are going to be happy to spend some time with Gillian. They're just barely beginning to wake up to the opposite sex. It's funny as hell, Coop. It really is. What an awkward time for a young man."

"You mean horndog."

They both laughed at Coop's comment.

"You were pretty funny, Fredo, when you went after Mia. I died laughing every day. What were you thinking? But nobody could talk you out of it, and look what happened. Now you've got three sons, and you're itching to make it a fourth. I'd say that is some serious dedication, Sport."

"And it has nothing to do with my sperm count, does it?"

"Thank God. Boy, I sure got tired of hearing about how yours had dented heads. You fuckin' moron, excuse me, mentally-challenged horndog. And I rest my case."

Kyle asked the room for quiet. "We're going to be calling you in one by one unless there's something specific they're going to need to talk to you about, and they will let you know in advance that the interview might go longer, but I've been told that these exit interviews are going to be a half an hour or less, which means you can break off early for the weekend. So that nobody gets their panties in a wad, we're going to go alphabetically, but we're going to go from Z to A this time. So sit back, you can calculate where you'll be in that pecking order, but don't leave the building, please. And, when your name is called, you're going to see these two gentlemen over here." He pointed to two regular Navy guys, both wearing headsets and wired. Both looked extremely young. The kind of guys many of the SEALs had a problem with—always messing with the rules and how it affected their careers. He hated the little infractions they occasionally had to endure on base.

"One additional item I'd like you to comment on, unless they ask you not to, how many of you saw the news broadcast last night about the migrants drowning in the Rio Grande?" Kyle had raised his arm above his head, looking for others. Only three of the eleven saw the news post, which included Fredo.

"So you might be shown a picture and asked if you recognize any of the clothing or the people in that picture. And I'm going to warn you, it's a little graphic. We're talking dead people here. People who have traveled over great distances and put their lives on the line, risked everything for a chance at freedom in the United States, if they're legit refugees. If they're lucky, they get to where they need to go, to a relative or an acquaintance who can sponsor them. But the vast majority of them get dropped off in a location, sent to a particular house to work off a debt that they didn't pay when they started their journey. And if they don't pay it, some of them don't make it, or their relatives back in Mexico or wherever they're from get visited and often hit up for more money or ghosted. So look hard at the photographs and see if you recognize anybody from the scene we witnessed live in Mexico three days ago."

They started calling names, and Cooper crossed his legs and his arms, leaning back into the metal chair, making it squeak. Fredo thought he looked extremely uncomfortable with his long gangly arms and legs, but he didn't want to criticize.

"Are you going to tell him you're interested in adopting the boy?"

"I'm not sure yet. I want to see what they're about first. That may be a detail that has escaped them. I am going to mention Caesar, though. It's not exactly germane to this particular operation we're being debriefed on, but all the same, it's something I feel I should disclose."

When Fredo's name was called, he discovered that the interviewers were not up to speed with what had happened during their mission. They were clearly way over their head as far as knowledge of tracking Mr. Ochoa. Fredo gave his account of what went down and his role in uploading the photographs and wishing they'd had a speech-modified long distance mic to pick up their communications.

"Duly noted, Special Operator Chavez."

They went back over the scene where Ivan's mother was killed and had him retell the incident several times.

"You're absolutely positive it was Ochoa who shot the mother and the little girl?"

"All the way down to his fuckin' green lizard boots. Unless the intel we were given was false or fake. He likes killing innocent people who become examples of the consequences of not following orders. Gentlemen, I don't have a dog in this fight, but it's dangerous for all of this to be going on at the border. It doesn't happen every day, but it's risky for all our own citizens there. Anything I can do to help protect the innocent, well, that's my mission too. And those poor guards down there trying to manage the border, you ought to be giving them all medals. With the international-sized flavor of the problem, I can't imagine it's something they signed up for in the first place. It's, in fact, probably something they don't want to have to do again. Kinda like hitting a ninety-mile-an-hour pitch with a teaspoon, if you get my drift."

He was shown a blowup of the drone picture he'd seen in the newscast. "You recognize this or any of these people?"

"Well, luckily, you can't see it here, but the newscaster said a few of these people had gunshot wounds to the head. That would be Mr. Ochoa's style, or guys he trained. Which makes me wonder if this wasn't supposed to be their intended outcome. Might allow the cartels to raise their prices to guarantee the next caravan. Get them to pay extra for their safety. But that's just how it comes at me, fellas."

"Anything else?"

"I'm trying not to look at it, if you don't mind, but I do recognize this woman here with the yellow skirt. I saw her alive before Ivan's mother was shot in the head."

"Ivan?"

"The little boy we rescued. You read my report, no doubt?"

"Yes, yes. Anyone else?"

"No, except that the ratio of women and children to preteen males is about the same as we saw down there. I could definitively say it's the same group. And that now means they'll be looking for us next time we go down there, unfortunately. And they'll be looking for drones."

"Oh, there will be drones, for sure," the investigator added. "They have them too. They are well-equipped, well-funded, not like our border operation who has to beg for everything."

That's a fact!

Fredo agreed with the gentleman completely. "My point exactly."

"Anything else?"

Fredo leaned back in his chair. "Are you researching the connection between these coyotes and the gang activity here in San Diego? Because there is one. I'm sure of it."

"Explain, please."

"It's like every gang member down here has creds with these bastards in Mexico. They go and come freely, bring in whatever they want.

Except now they bring it in in huge shipments, use diversion so everyone's scrambling to keep up with the traffic in one area, leaving another fully exposed. We've seen this dozens of times. Why isn't more done to crack down on that connection between the locals and these cartels?"

"Many of the cartel members, the higher-ups, are legitimate businesses that are licensed to be involved. They overtake weak NGOs. There's plenty of money to go around, as we discussed before. The criminal doesn't have the worry about funding or the jurisdictional red tape between agencies like we have. You ever see the movie *Fitzcarraldo*?"

"Not sure."

"About a Peruvian billionaire who brought a steamer over the Andes one piece at a time. Nobody thought it could be done. Sometimes the way we do things here feels a lot like that feat of the impossible. In real life, they actually did it. Here? Well, let's say we're working on it."

"Got it. Let's hope their better angels start showing up. We need some help. Everyone down there needs help."

"Roger that, Special Operator Chavez."

The other interviewer asked another question about local gang activity which gave Fredo the room to mention Caesar.

"My wife was married to one of these guys, when she was a rebellious teen and thought it was cool to hang with them. She had no idea what they were really into. This guy, who went up for it and has recently gotten a sweet deal to get out early, he's walking around here, free as a bird. His minions attend some of the same schools our kids go to. Now I'm the stepdad to a child whose biological asshole father wants to come 'back into his life.' What a family man, huh?"

The agents wrote down Fredo's details. "We'll bring this to the local director's attention, pass it along to the station chiefs. You may or may not hear from them, but thanks."

Then he produced a card, passing it along to Fredo across the desktop.

"Joel Bluestein," he read. "You live here?"

"Between here and LA."

"Okay, well, I'll let you know if I can use a hand-up. I'd like to find him in the middle of some dirty tricks and send him back to prison,"

Fredo said.

"Or the source," Bluestein added.

"Come again?"

"Don't you guys use that term? Sending them back to the source, back to the ground? Their holy place?"

"Oh, yes. I have my non-Middle East hat on. Now I understand what you're saying. Yup, that applies too."

Fredo was relieved that the debriefing was without an edge, making him feel like the criminal instead of the guy saving everybody.

He was told to prepare for another visit down there within a week. That didn't set well with him. He didn't see Coop or Kyle and decided not to discuss it with anyone else for now. Mia would be terrified he would be gone soon.

When he got home, he found Mia just stepping out of the shower, getting ready for their noon appointment at St. Cecilia's. It was a refreshing change, a holiday for his eyes and his heart.

"You could go that way. I think it would shock everybody in the office."

She came over to him, dropped her towel, and allowed all her pink parts do her magic to his very engorged pink parts. Fredo was urgent, but Mia stretched it out so long he didn't have time for a shower himself. He wished he'd never made the appointment. But even while dressing, he still had a boner after a fairly serious romp on the bed.

Which was exactly what he needed.

CHAPTER 12

MIA AND FREDO sat across the desk from Sister Mary Margaret, the director of St. Cecilia's School, where all three of their children attended.

"I'm glad the two of you came in together. We always try to encourage both parents to come, that way we don't have any miscommunications. In this day and age of social media, written instructions, bombardment of the news media, TV, cell phones, it's odd to me the older I get how much difficulty we have in communicating with each other. And I think there's just no substitution for 'together time.' I used to have a counselor I spoke to on a regular basis. She was a friend as her child was in our school as well, and she used to call it 'just bumping around time.' So thank you."

She gave a sweet smile and studied both of their faces one by one and then back to the other.

"Sister, we're grateful for your time. And we thought about this quite carefully before we decided to make the appointment."

Fredo turned and watched Mia's expression as he continued.

"We've had an unusual situation in the blending of our two families, and while the twins are mine biologically, Ricardo is in every way my son as well, except he was fathered by a rather difficult man. This gentleman had gone to prison and has been recently exonerated."

"I believe I was made aware of this," Sister Mary Margaret agreed. "But go ahead, explain what I can do for you two today. And for your family."

Mia felt it was perhaps her opportunity to step in and take over what

Fredo had started. She wanted to start with some admissions—things she wanted to get off her chest.

"Sister, I did not always live my life as a Christian woman. In fact, I wasted a lot of my youth chasing exciting, shiny objects, which landed me in quite a bit of trouble. And I am regretful of those years."

Mary Margaret interrupted her. "He who is without sin? From the Bible? I think we all can say we have trespassed, and a trespass is a trespass. There's no such thing as a hierarchy of good and bad trespasses. But I understand what you're saying. You're saying that you have changed and you weren't proud of who you were, but now I assume you feel like you're on the correct path. Is that correct?"

Mia was relieved that the woman was so easy to speak with. She also gave herself a red flag, Fredo's admonition not to share too much. Before she continued, she looked at Fredo to make sure he was in agreement and saw his gentle nod.

"Well, I thank you for that, and I'm really relieved at your attitude. So as I was saying, I made some mistakes, and as you know, God sends children into the world, and they are not mistakes, even though unfortunately we sometimes talk about them in that fashion. Like something we have to get rid of. That's not me. So while the relationship with my former friend was in all ways a mistake, Ricardo, my baby, was not."

"I understand. Quite a mature attitude, my dear," Mary Margaret said.

Mia took a deep inhale and hoped she was using the right words, but she knew Fredo would stop her if that wasn't the case. "Ricardo's biological father went to prison for, among other things, abuse we suffered at his hands. I was pregnant with Ricardo when he was arrested. I had been beaten, tied up, kidnapped, the whole nine yards. He was reacting to the fact that I wanted a different life for me and my baby, and it wasn't something he could accept. So now he's out, and something we thought was going to be a thirty-year sentence? Turns out the courts have reversed their decision, and he's only going to have served nine of those thirty years. Which means, as a minor, he wants to be part of Ricardo's life again. Now we've heard this from boys here at the school who are friends of Ricardo's or maybe not friends but acquaintances. We've also heard it from certain officials at the prison where Caesar was incarcerated, and we've heard it through several other sources, both Fredo and I have. So this is fairly well documented as accurate."

"And has he contacted you?"

"Well, not directly himself, which is how he operates. He gets people to do things for him, so he can claim plausible deniability. It's like he doesn't care if anybody else gets caught, as long as they don't tell on him. And he has told some younger brothers, who are kind of circling around the gang hoping one day to be accepted. Tthey are thirteen, fourteen-year-old-boys, and three of them attend this school. He's delivered to them a message for our son, Ricardo, letting us know that he wants to be a part of his life. And they have been—I'm looking for the word—it's not ridiculed but it's interfering with Ricardo's presence here at the school, in that he can't get away from them. And they're bigger and stronger, and they have the backing of their gang, which we obviously don't have."

"But I understand you probably have most of the SEAL community behind you," Sister Mary Margaret inserted.

"Well, yes, that's true as far as resources, but I'm sure you're aware that they can't be called to action just because of how they're trained for things in the United States. At least they're not supposed to. And I don't want to get my husband in trouble for anything he isn't supposed to get involved with. Having said that, I know what kind of a man he is, and in this particular case, we can't take a proactive stance. We can watch, and we can be vigilant. But there's nothing else we can do. Unless you could help us out Sister."

Mia hoped that her subtle plea was picked up.

Sister Mary Margaret glanced over at Fredo. "I think I understand Mia very well. What mother wouldn't be concerned in this situation? I'd like to hear your take on it, please."

"I have been involved in this situation ever since the beginning. I have been in love with Mia since before she even knew I existed. I met her through her brother, Armando, who is also a member of SEAL Team 3."

Sister Mary Margaret leaned forward, put her elbows on the desk, and created a church steeple with her fingers. Her wizened and wise look showed Mia that she had a backbone of steel. She noted that the director could be a valuable ally or a formidable enemy.

"Oh my, so your family is populated with all sorts of heroes then. Good for you!"

"As Mia has said, there are limits to what we can do here and remain an active Navy SEAL. However, when it comes to the life, the health, and safety of my family, I will not hesitate to do what's necessary. I don't expect anyone else to protect my family any better than I could. There are good police and fire rescue, sheriff's offices, staffing. There are good people out there that try very hard, but they don't have the training I have, and they don't understand perhaps the mindset of the pure evil that is this gentleman. And I've seen it over and over again in our missions overseas. Bullies, people who take advantage of others, men and women who like to flaunt their power, belittle others, and I've seen whole villages in Africa want to rise up and murder some warlord or leader who has been so horrible, but they're afraid to. So they use fear as one of their swords."

"There are plenty of messages in the Bible about that very thing. Fear is a powerful weapon. The bigger and more complicated society gets, the easier it is for individuals like that to hide out and not pay the consequences. So I think what you're telling me is you want to make sure your family is protected but not at the expense of your career."

"Exactly! I am so glad you said that. I was hoping that you would understand," said Fredo.

Mia could tell from just the timbre of his voice how grateful he was.

Sister Mary Margaret paused for a moment, reflecting on all her seventy or eighty years, and then said, "Well, my life is very simple compared to yours, although I do have roughly 2400 sets of parents I have to deal with, plus 60 teachers and teachers' aides, and I think, at exact count, we have 1,200 students. Some of them are remotely schooled, of course, but in the school, we have almost 1,000. It's a big school and very successful. But even that doesn't compare to the complications and the social forces you have to survive in, Mr. Chavez. And I thank you and respect you for that. I am not qualified to be able to strategize and create a plan that would be nothing more than just a guess. But I do promise you that I will watch. I will be careful how I discuss Ricardo with the other teachers, but I will suggest that extra care needs to be taken to watch him, as well as your twins, but I just don't feel comfortable orchestrating some kind of a plan beyond that. And I'm just trying to be completely honest with you, Mr. Chavez. This is way outside my wheel well."

"Sister, it's very brave of you and honest to admit that. I think there are a lot of people out there that just would like to have a couple private SEALs in their back pocket they could go send out and get even with all their enemies. I can see you're not one of those, and I'm grateful for that as well."

Sister Mary Margaret gracefully bowed her head and put her hands back in her lap.

"This is what I think would be ideal. Without making it obvious, I would like a journal kept of interactions between Ricardo and this group of boys or anybody else that happens to waltz on campus. There is to be no releasing Ricardo to his father under any circumstances, and I don't care what kind of paperwork is shown, he is not to go with anybody but Mia or myself."

"We'll put that in writing, too," added Mia.

"Understood, and I will make sure to alert the yard duty as well as the teachers. No problem with that."

"Frankly, we don't think it'll be very long before Caesar does something that could wind him back up in prison. It's difficult to just have to wait that out, and we certainly aren't going to poke the bear, but that may be what we have to do. He is very well-schooled in how to handle police, administrators, and the court system. Most of these guys who are leaders are very bright. They're just evil as well. I don't expect that he will do anything to harm Ricardo. You need to know that Ricardo, and you can verify this with him if you like, doesn't want to have anything to do with him. So if being at the school is a safe space for our boy, we want him to have that and always be under the attention of people that are looking out for his welfare, not policing him or spying on him, but genuinely concerned. I think that needs to be explained to him, so that when he sees people watching him, he knows. I don't think he will take it the wrong way, but we came here just wishing to open everybody's eyes and awareness to the fact that we could have a problem. And if we don't, hallelujah!"

Sister Mary Margaret smiled and clapped her hands, loving that comment. "Hallelujah! Amen to that."

Mia asked a question she'd been wondering. "Is this something, this conversation we're having, is this something that you are compelled to tell the police about?"

"Well, if it was threats of violence or, you know, a kidnapping situation, if that were something that had been threatened, then yes, we would be compelled. I would also call you and let you know. I cannot interfere with the police doing their duty, and their duty is to keep this school and every child, every teacher, every parent, every staff member safe. I'm not going to second guess them, and I'm not going to order them what to do. But this conversation we're having right now is not something they need to be privy to, unless we admit that we've discussed the possibility that Caesar will try to contact his son outside your home and this would be the logical place."

"I'm satisfied." Fredo reached into his pocket and handed Sister Mary Margaret his card with his cell phone on it. "You call me anytime you see anything that doesn't look right. And let me write Mia's cell phone on the back of that card please."

She returned the card to him, and Fredo added Mia's cell.

"I'm going to be out of the country again for a few days, maybe a few weeks. I'm going to check in with you. I can also leave you a message and just let you know when I'm gone. As far as when I come back, I won't have that information, and if I did, I couldn't tell you. And I couldn't tell you exactly when we're leaving except that it will be very soon."

"I understand. Where are you going?"

"Ah! Forgot that one. You see, that's part of my agreement with my boss. We can't tell anybody where we're going or how long we'll be there. That's a violation of my oath. But we will do our best to inform you when I'm gone, so that you understand and you take appropriate actions. In that case, you definitely need to stay in close contact with Mia."

"Well, I've taken some good notes, and I will go over these with my teacher liaison and also Ricardo's homeroom teacher. I'm not sure I need to tell others about it except perhaps our yard duty person, who is actually a teacher waiting to be hired, so she sees all the kids on a regular basis and probably is going to be someone I will rely on quite a bit when I ask questions. I'm excited to say that I have the full faith and support of just about every teacher here, so you'll find I can assure you their complete cooperation."

"Well, Sister, this has been a pleasure." Fredo stood and extended his hand. Sister Mary Margaret shook it very firmly. Mia also gave her a handshake but didn't squeeze her fingers blue like Fredo did.

CHAPTER 13

I T WAS NEVER easy to leave the family on these fogless early mornings in San Diego, and it was often considered by Fredo and his teammates the most difficult part of the mission. Nobody wanted to be away from their families for an extended period of time in harm's way, least of all the wives. The men understood and took the challenge, because it was what they were hired to do. But seeing the toll that it took on the children and the wives was something difficult for most SEALs if they were human.

But in this case, Fredo was exceptionally worried, and although it never bothered him before, this time it did. There was no set end date to his mission, and all kinds of things were being thrown at them. It made it hard to strategize, get a grip, maintain control over their home environment and the outcome of a possible confrontation with Caesar.

He knew why that was the case, and it wasn't something that he disapproved of, because that's the way the job rolled, but he disliked how it affected Mia and the fact that she wasn't sure from one day to the next when he would be available to come to her aid. And she was dealing with a lot of things this time.

On a normal day, the boys were often rambunctious. She'd gotten proficient at managing them by herself, but Fredo knew this was draining. She never complained, she rarely made some comments, and especially now, she was trying to be very respectful of Fredo's feelings, a routine they followed before a dangerous deployment. These days, they all were dangerous. It was no ski trip to the Fjords of Norway or trekking across the red desert in Morocco.

They had woven together their highs and lows, their risks and rewards so many times as he'd been sent all over the world. While there wasn't anything such as routine with the Team, she was more used to it than she was in the beginning. And if complaints were going to be made, they had to be made after he was home, after the job had been done or not done, depending.

"I will try to call. You know the drill."

He hated to tell her that, but it was necessary.

"Yes, I do. Now once you step onto that plane and once you fly away from me, your job, Fredo, is to not worry about me and the kids. Your job is to get your butt home safe. I want you to think about that every moment that you're awake. And maybe in your dreams too."

He pulled her to him and hugged her, chuckling. "I can't wait. I'm already homesick for you." He pushed the hair out of her forehead and kissed her there, then on each cheek, and then hard on the lips. He tried never to think of it, but he knew he was joined by all the other SEALs who were saying goodbye to their wives and girlfriends or parents, that maybe this was the last kiss he'd ever have. Those had been things that happened in their community. God forbid it should happen to them.

"I love you, Fredo. Please, I'll be fine, pay attention to what you need to do and then get home safe. I mean that with my full heart. And I promise to let you know if something major occurs over here. But until you hear that, don't worry and don't wonder, okay?"

He smiled back at her, feeling all those warm, wonderful feelings he'd been having especially these last three or four days. She'd been unusually affectionate, cooking his favorite meals and doing all his favorite things in the bedroom. There were several times he was almost reduced to tears, he had been so moved by how caring and loving she was. She was nothing like the woman he met over ten years ago, a spitfire, smart and gorgeous, with a body that could stop a battleship, start a war even, unflappable, and yet inside still a little girl. Now he was seeing the melding of that little girl and that saucy tart who would never give in to him and who honestly wanted him to just go away and told him so many times.

Now that melding had formed her into a warrior princess he had never imagined. She was fierce, loyal, and mean if she needed to be, but compassionate. And he could tell she loved being the woman she was, which meant she loved being his wife. And nothing in the world felt so good as having her to come home to.

"I am the luckiest man in the world, Mia. Who would've thought?"

She buried her head in his chest, and when he began to feel the tears stain his jacket and then his shirt underneath and then his undershirt, he knew she was just as moved as he was.

THEY ONLY SPENT an hour in the airport, because they were waiting for several Navy personnel, mostly ground support teams, who were bringing specialized equipment. There was a senator who was flying down there to discuss some situational things with their Spec Ops Lieutenant Commander who was stationed in Cabo San Lucas temporarily.

And there were also a couple of ladies who didn't identify themselves but appeared to be CIA or interpreters. They weren't State Department, because they would've shown their badges. So he guessed CIA. And he didn't know exactly what they were there for, but it was all part of the normal operation. This time they substituted the SEAL that couldn't go with another fellow on the team, Casey. He was a newbie, been in about six months, but was already skilled as a medic in training. Coop had been very impressed with him and had worked with him carefully.

Once they uploaded into the plane and took their seats, Fredo relaxed, closed his eyes, did some breathing exercises, and meditated, looking for that little spot at the very edge of the ocean, that place between the turquoise sky and the navy-blue sea. That line. That place of no man's land where sky and water blended, and it was so small the naked eye couldn't see it. As he focused on that seam line in the universe, he cleared his mind of everything and just saw the sea and the sky.

He was conscious of his heartbeat and his breathing. He still heard rumblings from the plane's engine and the rocketing that sometimes happened as they lifted through a heat spike, but more or less for the next twenty minutes, he was able to complete a thorough meditation, clearing his mind of everything except where he was and what he was there for.

They arrived in Cabo San Lucas roughly four hours later, offloaded into a couple of vans, which was their standard procedure, and headed down the narrow roadway, looking to traverse up the peninsula and then across to the border just south of the State of Texas. It was going to take them all day to get there, but they would get there by dusk.

The route had been circuitous, just in case someone had been informed of their arrival. They didn't want anyone in the know to be able to alert the bad guys. It certainly made the trip longer and more boring, but the strategy was that usually their teams were only tracked until they landed and deplaned. In this case, if the cartels were aware of their presence, they would not expect that they'd take the long track to the interior of Mexico.

A villa had been arranged for them, which didn't suck compared to the cactus and dusty hideout and night they had to spend overlooking the compound Ochoa had erected. They were about ten miles away, camouflaged in the little tourist village of artisans and specifically silver and inlay-work artists. As they wandered through the village at night, moving in groups of four or five so as not to alert the town that twelve Navy SEALs had arrived, store after store, most of them closed, showed beautiful intricate artwork and craftsmanship. Money had been tight for Fredo and Mia after the decision to put the pool in, but Fredo wanted to buy her something and found a pair of silver hoop earrings with a tiny etching looking like a flower vine all around the rim. He thought that looked like her. He made a note to come back and get it for her if it was reasonable.

He texted Mia to let her know he'd arrived safe and would be off the waves for a bit and to wait for his call to her.

They settled down for the night, but before they fell asleep, Kyle laid out what their plan was for the next day. He rolled out one of his famous maps, marked up and wrinkled. It was like the bible of what they'd been doing down there the past three or four years. Almost like a journal, except it was a map. It helped their orientation, especially with the new tadpoles.

"So we're here, and Ochoa's compound is right here, if you recall. We are going to just take it light the first day. We're not going to do any stealth night stuff for maybe a couple of days, and that's because we might find something we need to further inspect. So we're going to be casually watching this compound as we drive past it to another village, and we're going to be posing as business people, scouting for a remote location to perhaps build a factory. That's the story. Now don't get too detailed if you talk to the locals, because someone will blow it and say something that the rest of you aren't going to know, and then we're going to get discovered. They're watching for that."

To a man, everyone nodded understanding.

"But they aren't going to suspect you too much if you're looking to start a business in Mexico. They want the work, they want to be your conduit, and it's not politics for them; it's money. So we are not a threat to the common people, only to the gangsters and criminal elements. But mind you, every single person you're going to meet has a connection to a cartel member. It's just impossible to get away from them. You don't want to talk too much about this fictitious business. You want to make it sound like just formulating ideas and looking at different communities, and you can ask questions about the community and then focus on what you really want to know. That would be reasonable. But if you, of course, walk up to somebody and say, 'Hey, have you seen this bad guy Ochoa,' because everybody knows him, you'll immediately be reported. They'll be rewarded. More than likely, you'll be dead. Please remember that, and please keep your wits about you twenty-four seven."

There were a few questions, mostly from the newer guys, since the older ones knew that food would be brought in, as would happen if they really were businessmen scouting for a location. They would always keep their guns not visible in the house, and they would use their props that they were asked to bring. A few people brought fishing poles, others brought camera equipment, portable game machines, cards, and journals. They weren't going to look like the militia had just come to town. They were going to look like regular, straight businessmen looking for a partner in Mexico to do something that will help both sides.

"All right, let's get some sleep."

Fredo raised his hand. "Kyle, are we allowed to text home anytime? Or are we on emergency only mode?" He wasn't going to reveal he'd already done so.

"No, you can text. Keep it very short. Remember you're a player, so you aren't going to be tied to your wife's apron strings, right? So keep that in mind in case somebody's looking over your shoulder."

"Anybody else?"

"Are we going to be traveling with interpreters?" Riley asked.

"We elected not to this time. That usually requires a local person to be used, and this area isn't quite the population numbers so that we could do that safely and not have it get back to the cartels. But that doesn't mean you can't ask shopkeepers and people you meet down in the town square about places to go to eat or drink or buy gifts, that sort of thing. A business-class tourist would do that. And that was a good question, by the way. I was waiting for that, and then I forgot to mention it."

Fredo took a shower and righted himself for bed. He even shaved. When he came back into the room, Cooper, who was one of the two guys he was sharing the room with, looked up from his book.

"Everybody good at home?"

"She hasn't responded yet. But I'm sure she has it all under control. Are you worried at all about this guy? I mean, he's got to have a sixth sense, being a former cop. I just hope we get some good credible intel from that drone right away, get in and get out. What say you?"

"Yeah, same here. It would be okay by me if we got to come home in a week or less."

"What are you reading?" he asked Coop.

"How to make a pistol out of Legos in a hurry. It's kind of cool."

"My favorite was the artificial mechanized arm we used in the Middle East. Remember that thing? You'd hold your arm out there, and all we'd see were asses and elbows."

"Yeah, and you, asshole, had a hard time keeping a straight face. Trying to get me killed?"

"Nah. A pistol would be easier. Night, Bro." Fredo turned his phone off, which still left a small alarm buzz in case of an emergency, laid back on the bed, and pictured that ocean and that sky scene one more time.

Until Coop ruined it by calling out in falsetto, "'Nighty-night, Princess."

"Fuck you," Fredo whispered as he rolled over.

"Not. My. Type."

CHAPTER 14

MIA'S PHONE RANG, and she was surprised to find Special Agent
Gutierrez on the other end of the line.

"Is this Mia Chavez?"

"Hi, Agent Gutierrez. Fredo isn't here. He's on deployment. But can
I help you?"

"Well, we processed your husband's application. It's in both of your
names, for the adoption. At least we've put it on file, and the boy has, for
now, finished the surgeries that are required. Tomorrow, they're going
to release him from the hospital. I'm supposed to find a place to take
him, and I remembered our conversation. Do you want to take him for a
spell?"

"For a spell. What does that mean?"

"On a temporary basis. It could become more permanent. You'd get
the first crack at him."

Mia was quickly not liking Agent Gutierrez' tone. But this was good
news. She told herself to smile.

"Well, sure. Now is this a sure thing or is it maybe going to happen,
because I'm going to have to talk to my kids."

"Well, I thought you guys had already decided that you wanted to
do it. Now if something's changed—"

"No, sir, this is still the same. It's just that I didn't want to put the
kids through too many changes, so we decided not to tell them until it
was a sure thing. But there's no problem. I'll tell them today as long as
you're sure that this is going to happen."

"Well, in our line of business, we never can be sure of anything. I'm sure Fredo can relate to that."

Mia felt slightly insulted at his attitude.

"Have you ever tried to raise three boys on your own? I do it all the time, and the six or so times a year when Fredo's gone, he's not available to tell me how to work the washing machine or get the internet working, or who I should take the TV to or what happens if the car is sending colorful lights in my face."

"Okay."

Now Mia felt he was annoyed with her.

"Look, I will be happy to take Ivan, and I think what I'll do is take all the kids over to the hospital. Can we do it that way? They won't be in school tomorrow."

"I'll arrange it. You know the room he's in, right?"

"Of course."

"And you'll inform your husband?"

"Oh, heck, no can do. I was going to make it a surprise."

"Well—."

"It was a joke, Agent Gutierrez. I'll do it right now. I may only be able to leave a message. But he usually calls every day if he can, and if he can't, I usually shouldn't be calling him. But no worries. We'll handle it. What time should I be there tomorrow?"

"Well, they say they release at 10:00, but I am going to say why don't you pick him up right after lunch? Then he can get a good meal, and between 12:00 and 1:00, if you come at that time, he should be ready to go. He's going to move a little slow, because he's got a cast and a sling, and you know, he has to have help showering and all of that."

"Okay, so do I need to get anything to cover his shoulder or make sure it doesn't get wet?"

"I'd check with the nurses tomorrow."

"Thank you, and is there a checkout process or something I have to sign?"

"It'll all be there for you tomorrow. If I can, I'll come over. I may not be in town that day, though. But you have my cell. This is my direct line to my cell, and call me if there's any kind of a problem. And I want to thank you. I was going to have to spend four or five hours finding a home for him, since I promised both you guys he wasn't going to be taken to Catholic Charities. They are pretty good, you know, not all of them are bad, but boy, we have some bad agencies out there popping up all over the place."

"Well, that's because they smell the money."

Mia continued to be irritated at the special agent's sloppiness as far as handling details. It was quite obvious to her that he would never be the right kind of a parent to stay home with the kids, especially three boys who liked sports and wanted to do all sorts of extracurricular activities. Mia knew that many SEAL marriages were destroyed by the fact that there was this hierarchy, everybody was looking up to and admiring the SEAL members themselves. Meanwhile, the wife was at home running the show most of the time, except for when he got home and was Mr. Big Cheese again. She'd never had that problem with Fredo, but she'd heard others complain, and she agreed with it pretty much. This guy, Mia knew that he would not be a very compassionate partner. Maybe that's why he was still single.

Mia called Fredo's number and got the standard voicemail stiff arm. She left a message, even though there was a fifty percent chance that it wouldn't take. Then she called Christy Lansdowne.

"Oh my god, that's great news, Mia. Does Fredo know?"

"Well, I can't get a hold of him, I assume he's in place and can't answer, but if he listens to his messages or if you talk to Kyle, tell him to let Fredo know he's got a message, okay?"

"You bet. So you pick him up tomorrow at the hospital, is that what it is?"

"Yes. We're going to get there around noon. I'm taking all the kids."

"Well, if you need to drop them off here, if that's something you want to do on your own, you and Ivan face-to-face, then you could take him home and show him the house. If that's what you want to do, I'm available tomorrow. I'm not working."

"Well, I suspect you've got a house full of kids then."

"Yeah, we do. And I've got a couple I'm waiting to hear from, supposed to be a play date trade off, but you know how that goes. People get busy. It might just be my three. So drop them by if you need to."

"Thanks, Christy. I think I'm going to stick with my plan. My goal was to try to bring him into the family and let everybody be involved in that process, and the kids are pretty good about their behavior, especially in a hospital where things have to be quiet. I don't even know if they'll let them in the room. Sometimes they don't."

"Yeah, you're right about that. Some floors have strict rules about it."

"But we'll sort it out. I mainly just wanted you to know so that Kyle did, because if Fredo was here, Kyle would be the first person he'd call."

"I got that, thanks."

Mia had some of her mother's fresh tamales frozen in the garage, so she took them out, covered them, and left them in her refrigerator to thaw. She thought Ivan would enjoy those, but she didn't know what kind of food he liked. She made a list of a few things her kids liked and made some guesses on Ivan's behalf. She headed out to pick up things at the store nearby.

Then she remembered the twins had soccer tomorrow morning. It was a highly anticipated game, and they wouldn't want to miss it.

She telephoned the coach and asked if the game was still on and if the boys could miss it. She got an earful about the commitment his players' parents had to make to either play or go home.

"I've got an issue with transportation. I have some place I must be between twelve and one. Could you perhaps pick up the boys on your way to the field?"

"I'll have Mrs. Spencer do it. She's the Team Mom. I'll have her call you. This number?"

"Yes, please."

"Okay, calling her next. You let me know if it isn't arranged, and we'll figure something else out."

"Thank you, Coach Smith. I really appreciate this."

Julie Spencer called and agreed to pick up the boys at eleven in the morning. "It's a shame you are going to miss the game."

"Maybe I can drop by and see the end of it. But, if I don't make it, could you either take the boys to your house for a few minutes before I get there or drop them off at my house? I can try to get a sitter."

"Oh, nonsense. I'll bring them home if we don't see you. But this is such an important game!"

"I know. But I have to do an extremely large favor for someone. It came up last minute, and I'm so sorry."

"My, you certainly have a busy life, Mia."

"Fredo's on deployment. He's just left. I'm all alone."

"I understand. I'm happy to help out. Hope we see you tomorrow."

So that had changed the trajectory for tomorrow. Mia decided she'd pick up Ivan after she saw the boys off safely. Ricardo would want to stay with them and watch. But she'd let him choose. Perhaps he'd want to meet Ivan first. Either way, it was all set.

Everything had happened so fast. She hoped she didn't leave something out. She recounted each step of her plan and couldn't find any holes.

With the possibility another child would be coming to live with them, she was going to have to establish a routine, stick to it, and get the rest of the family to help her out. And maybe she'd need some special help from her mother and Gus.

Her phone rang, and once again, it was Gutierrez.

"Something's changed?" she asked. "Or am I suddenly your most favorite person?"

"I'm sorry. I've just been informed the application was denied."

"Wait a minute, you told me it never really was posted, just filed."

"Apparently, I was wrong. Now, I have a way you can still take Ivan, since all my initial instructions were to have CPS come get him tomorrow afternoon at Scripps. I've just talked to his doctor, and if you can get there this afternoon, say close to noon, would you be able to take him home today?"

Mia thought it was odd all of this had been so disorganized and poorly planned. And she was doing all the adjusting.

"H-how come, if our application was denied, I am given permission to take him home today? Why is one day make that kind of a difference?"

"Bureaucracy. That's all I can say. I'm really sorry. The excuse that the paperwork just crossed paths, adjusting the timing, is always a good one."

"Who is making these decisions?"

"It's DHS. And you are quite correct, it's all messed up, very fluid, and changes all the time. We're in full panic mode here, and it's getting worse. I only wish there were more wonderful people like yourselves to help. We are starved for those resources."

"Well, I have to pick my kids up at school at two. There better not be a delay when I get there, or you will have to find someone else."

"I promise. If I have to go over there myself and make it happen, you'll be able to pick him up at noon. Where are you now?"

"Why?"

"Just didn't want you to get there before I get the signoff delivered to the floor."

"I'm on my way to the store to pick up some things. Then I'll head over. I'm not far."

"As long as it's not before twelve. You might see me there begging the head nurse. It won't be pretty."

"Agent Gutierrez, I'm not doing anything illegal, am I?"

"No. Why would you say that?"

"Well, everything about this plan seems like a leaky boat. Now you might have to beg to have Ivan discharged today? I didn't think hospitals operated this way? I don't want to get caught up in some issue and have CPS after me or—"

"Mia, you have a very active imagination. Stop making yourself crazy."

Now she really didn't like his condescending tone. "Maybe you should let Ivan go into the system like all the other kids."

She couldn't believe that she'd just said that, but she had a knot in her stomach that was growing. All she saw were problems ahead, and no one to help her solve them.

And then she remembered the face on that little boy, the one who had seen his mother and sister murdered. Maybe she was being overly critical. Maybe this sort of thing happens this way, and perhaps that's the reason everything isn't working right now. Her guilty conscience was kicking her in the shins.

And then Gutierrez delivered the final blow.

"All he has is you, you and Fredo. You two have the biggest hearts of anyone I've seen. But I understand. You have limits. You're not used to this. So let's just forget it—"

"No. I'll pick him up. But you better have him ready. I've just rearranged my whole day tomorrow, I've asked for special favors to pull this off, and now I have to redo everything. But you're right, what Ivan is going through is far worse. But please have him ready. No problems."

"Fine. We'll be ready for you, then. Don't rush. You want to be safe. And thank you for your kindness."

Mia was liking agent Gutierrez less and less the more she talked to him. She wouldn't have anything to do with him if it weren't for Ivan. She decided to overrule her gut and go with the plan. She glanced at the clock and saw she had plenty of time, if she didn't dally. Luckily, there wasn't traffic yet for a Friday. She hoped Fredo would be pleased with her decision and that he was safe, wherever he was. She started to rehearse what she was going to tell the boys.

Just before she came upon the entrance to parking, she checked her rearview mirror. She noticed the same black car had followed her from the corner of her street all the way to the parking lot of the grocery. He must have realized he'd been spotted, because he parked several rows away from her and didn't exit the car. She thought he looked like an undercover policeman, maybe somebody from immigration, DHS, she didn't know. But whoever that person was, they were in some kind of official capacity. No uniform, no specialized plates, just a feeling she had.

She made a ruse of having to get one of the long carts which was stuck in a row of baskets near his car. As she headed over to the cart station, she kept her phone in the palm of her hand as if she was trying to hold it while she was steering the cart. She tried to take several pictures and then switched it to video to take sweeping videos as well. When she got home, she would research the license plate and phone it in to Gutierrez. Maybe she should call her stepdad Gus Mayfield too. Anyway, she had to get a good description of the car, the license plate, and the guy in it.

Taking the cart and making a big U-turn, heading for the front door of the market, she was surprised to hear the car door open and a man's voice call out to her.

"Ma'am? Can I bother you for a second?"

She whipped around and looked at him. He was dressed casual but nice. It still didn't give her a warm fuzzy feeling to get very close to him.

She stood behind the cart so that there was eight to ten feet between them. Her hand still operated the video feature on the cell phone, and she pretended like she didn't know it was on and looked for a place to store the phone but didn't have pockets. She didn't want to alert him that she suspected something.

"What do you need? Stay right there, please."

"Are you Mia Guzman?"

She froze in place, then whipped around, ditching the cart and sending it back toward the stranger, and ran to the front of the store. She could tell he was coming after her, the sounds of his shoes scraping across the paved parking lot was unmistakable.

She got to the doors before he did, but they did not close as fast as she'd hoped, and he was able to run through at the same pass she did. She ran to the first teller she could find. The lady always wore too much makeup and had bright red hair and painted-on eyebrows and lips that pursed in a perfect heart shape, looking like some kind of a morph between Cruella de Vil and the Wicked Witch of the West. She was already made up for Halloween; every day she looked like that.

The clerk's eyes grew large as she saw Mia in pursuit by this rather beefy guy running full tilt toward her.

The assistant manager thought he was taking good care of his other customers in the store and came over nicely to get Mia to slow down. He got between Mia and the guy in the parking lot, and they both tumbled to the ground.

The teller whispered to Mia. "Go to the office. The manager's there, and they'll call security."

"Thanks."

She knew where the office was, right next to the women's bathroom, and she'd been in there quite a few times with all three boys. She barely got through the door when the gentleman from the parking lot showed up, right behind her. And then the assistant manager behind him, holding his nose, bleeding down the front of his shirt.

"Call the police." Mia said.

The office assistant took too long to figure it out, and by the time she had picked up the phone, the parking lot dude had ripped it out of her hands and thrown it against the wall. In a big beefy voice, he yelled at all of them, "Somebody close that fucking door. You!"

He pointed to the bloody assistant manager.

"Nobody else move, and I want to see everybody's hands on their laps or on a desk somewhere."

Then the worst of the worst happened, he pulled out a pistol. It looked like Fredo's SIG Sauer.

"The first person to disobey me is going to get shot. You don't want to be that person."

The other two office helpers as well as the general manager himself walked in through an anteroom office in the back, completely uninformed as to what was going on. They quickly complied. When the general manager didn't know what to do with his hands, the fellow from the parking lot told him to face the wall and place his hands on either side of his ears.

Mia just stood there. And looking down at her palm, she saw that the camera was still rolling.

"Thank God," she whispered to herself. Unlike her pretense, she did have a pocket in her jeans, and quickly stowed the phone in front, hoping the man would not find it if she was alone with him. She needed that evidence, and she was going to do everything she could to protect it. It had his description, the license plate number, the make and model of the vehicle, and now all these threats. Everything they needed to find and detain him.

"This little lady and I are going to take a ride. And I'm going to count to fifty, because I think she looks pretty fast, so if we run, I think we'll make it in time. I don't want anybody here calling cops or security."

Right on cue, they heard banging on the door that the assistant manager had closed and locked. The two managers looked between themselves and somehow the message was relayed that the assistant manager should just unlock the door quickly and then duck. Because that's exactly what he did in the next movement.

The fellow from the parking lot raced to the other side of Mia. He shot the assistant manager in the chest twice and then grabbed Mia's arm before the security guard and several other tellers behind him could even enter the doorway. By waving his gun and grabbing Mia around the shoulders and neck with his other arm, he was a formidable character, and no one anyone would want to tackle. Mia heard screaming echoing off the walls of the store as people panicked.

They made it to his car. He opened the passenger door and threw her inside. She locked the windows and doors and tried to honk the horn, but without the ignition on, the horn was ineffective. She looked for something to break the windows and found another revolver in the glove box. She checked it, and it was loaded. She released the safety, and when the gentleman came to the driver's side, he got blasted in the chest through his driver's window and fell backwards into the carts.

Mia scrambled out of the vehicle. A group of bystanders encircled her and the man who was shot. She raised her arms and placed the gun on the hood of the car.

"He tried to kidnap me. This is his gun. Somebody, please call the cops. Please."

She felt lightheaded and woozy and wasn't quite sure where she was for a second. Disoriented, the parking lot started to rise up in the middle and presented an angled look. Everything was out of focus, sharp angles everywhere, people's faces were blurry, and she felt sick to her stomach. But the last thing she remembered before she blacked out was seeing the guy struggling in the carts, flailing, his arms and legs working, but with a huge wound in his abdomen, he wasn't going to be running anywhere.

"Asshole," she thought to herself before she passed out.

CHAPTER 15

O NE OF THE things Fredo learned early on in his naval career was that what was constant was inconsistency. Things could change in a moment, minute, an hour, or a day. They would go through a long dry spell with nothing to do basically, and then all of a sudden, it's like everybody woke up and took a dose of adrenaline, and the world started exploding again. That's when they were needed the most.

So when they saw the orders come through early in the morning, Kyle got them up at four and went over what task they'd been given. They had drone footage of several large vehicles, including one semi with a huge trailer, heading toward the compound where Ochoa was. It was believed, based on the intel they had sent back last time they were here, that they were transporting several hundred human prisoners to some kind of a crossing, and that crossing could have been anywhere along the Texas to California border. They could use drones, but there might be the opportunity to nab Ochoa, and that was what the SEALs were there for.

Fredo wasn't too worried about the mission, since they were obviously more trained than anything he'd seen so far of Ochoa's militia. But anything could happen, and with a trailer full of human cargo, it made rescue a little more difficult but not impossible.

Kyle had put a strict lockdown on all their cell phone use, which annoyed Fredo, since he was dying to check in with Mia. He also knew that if there was something critically important at home, somehow they would get him the message.

Everyone geared up, got their night vision equipment ready, and then also got their day packs stored in separate duffel bags. The two vans they had, both of them with the logo of a pleasure vacation outfit that was a legitimate tourist representative near Mexico City, was their cover. They did not use any local drivers, but Armando and Fredo, since they were native speakers, would be driving and act as tour guides if they were pulled over.

So before sunrise, they got in place near where they had spent the night before and watched carefully as the large semi pulled in through the massive gates of the compound. Behind the semi were three all black Suburbans.

With his night vision lens, Fredo was able to take fairly closeup pictures. However, the black tinting on the windows made it impossible to identify who was inside there. He took pictures of all of the guard stations on the outside of the compound, the turrets that were guarded inside, the guards crossing back and forth across the courtyard, which served also as an equipment staging grounds and turnaround, and the guards maintaining order in the cages that were open to the elements, tarps thrown over them in the hot part of the day. It was squalid conditions, humans being kept like zoo animals. Add to the fact that several of them were young children, it sickened Fredo's stomach.

Barely an hour transpired before one of the black limos took off from the gate, and after checking with the powers in San Diego, it was determined that the SEALs should stay in place and not go after what could be a decoy. They would find out soon enough if Ochoa had made his escape with the first Suburban, and if that were the case, well, there still was the issue of where they were taking the semi and how they could interdict and stop them, so that any hostages inside could be freed.

Fredo knew Kyle was calculating every scenario, even the almost impossible scenario that all this was a decoy or diversion and what was really going on was some main operation elsewhere.

As the light of day descended upon the compound, what became evident was that the semi-truck was not bringing human cargo, but bushels and bushels of drugs. White plastic bags were loaded into the back, floor to ceiling. Fredo couldn't tell if it was farm supplies, flour, or sugar. So possibly, Ochoa had negotiated a deal to expand his operation to include drug trafficking in addition to human trafficking. It was unlike him, and with the way he reacted to drugs being given to him as payment for passage, it sort of surprised Fredo. But he let it be.

Instructions were given to follow the large truck, even if it meant not following Ochoa. It was thought that this was an even greater prize, and since it had entered and exited the Ochoa compound, it could contain proof enough that he had expanded his operation and might be enough to get the Mexican government to capture him and turn him over.

That was the theory. Now came the execution.

As the semi pulled out of the gate, the team noticed that the two blacked-out Suburbans remained behind.

"Boy, that's odd. It's just not like what I expected at all," said Kyle.

"You think it's a trap?" Cooper asked.

"I don't know. I just never know with these guys. You know that the average lifespan of a cartel head is less than five years after they join?"

"You're kidding," said Fredo.

"Nope. They get involved, and they get used up. It's like fish eating the fish eating the fish, and finally, the whale gets them all, right? You've seen that cartoon."

"Oh, yeah. So what are we doing? Which fish are we?" Fredo asked.

Kyle looked through his binoculars again. "They're still in the cages. They don't look like they're getting ready to be transported, and with all those bags, it's almost like this is a warehouse. A truck's here to pick up goods and then deliver it to wherever. My hunch and my guess is perhaps somebody paid Ochoa to be giving them safe passage across the border, using one of his routes and all of his guys. And they told us to expect to find his guys on both sides of the border."

"Yeah, saw a program once they've infiltrated the police in LA and San Diego. Can you believe it? Gang members and cartel bosses as cops?" Coop said.

"If I can get closer, I could probably get license plates, maybe make out some faces. What do you think?" Fredo asked.

Kyle shook his head. "Nah, it's not that important. I think we just go when they say to go."

Kyle spoke into his INVISIO and gave the team orders to prepare themselves to leave on a moment's notice. The day camp was pulled down, all the supplies stored back in the vans. All evidence that they had ever stayed there was removed, even to the point of someone doing one last sweep with large branches tied to his feet, swishing over the rocks and sand and small cactus brush, even removing tiny pieces of paper with tweezers, paper that the SEALs probably never left. But except for the tire tracks, which they could do nothing about, everything was put back into its original position.

Finally, they got the orders to track the truck. A whole fifteen minutes had gone by, and no further action was seen from the compound. Coop had launched his drone carefully and notified Kyle that the truck was headed straight for the highway west and did not meet up with any other vehicles. But it was coming to a major village.

"Before we take off, can you run it by the compound, the prisoner area there?" asked Kyle. "I want to get some pictures, and they probably won't be good enough for facial recognition, but they might be able to digitally recognize people that have been reported missing or we know have been kidnapped. I'd like to be able to send that off before we leave."

Coop responded, "Will do. I'm on it right now."

Coop always scrunched up his mouth while he manipulated the bird, like how somebody would stand and move and make noises while they were using a pinball machine. If you jerked the machine around too much, of course, it would tilt, but people tried to do it anyway and never affected the outcome of the game. Coop was using his extra-long neck, his six-foot-four-inch frame and long fingers to arch himself, push forward and back and bite his lower lip when he placed the drone close to the perimeter of the compound, hovering just far enough out of eyesight. He even let it hover behind a tall pine tree that had been partially denuded, getting shots of the compound from two angles that they couldn't see from their lookout. All the footage, and there was quite a bit of it, was uploaded. Kyle was on the phone while he looked at Cooper's monitor, discussing what they found with one of the officers back in San Diego.

"Yes, sir, we're ready to go whenever you let us know. The truck's got about a twenty-minute advance on us, but Coop's drone has determined that they haven't hooked up with anybody else, and they are on their way to the highway. My guess is they're going to enter Texas or someplace remote."

He listened while he was given instructions. Nodding his head, Kyle signed off.

"So we're to follow. How much life do you have left in that bird, Co-op?"

"Oh, I got about six hours maybe. I've got the rapid recharge, though. All I need is about thirty minutes of downtime and she's good to go again. What's the question for?"

"They want us to just follow but not be detected. We have to follow enough behind them so they don't see us. And we're to look for drones when we get to the Managua Flats village. That's when we need to close the gap and pay close attention to where the truck goes. It's possible it'll be offloaded to another vehicle. I really don't know. But we're to watch and report."

"Okay, got that."

Kyle again turned on his comms, notified San Diego they were leaving, and then gave instructions to his men to load up in the vans in the same order they came in and get ready for a several-hour drive.

About an hour later, the truck started to speed up, and if they hadn't had the drone, they would've missed the fact that the truck turned off just before the village. It rounded a small mountain that looked more like an extinct volcano crater. In the next few minutes, all they could do was follow the curve of the road around the mountain, heading the opposite direction of the village. The roadway then traveled straight north, toward one of the border crossings.

"Son of a bitch!" Fredo said. "Where the hell is he?"

Several of the other team members in Kyle and Fredo's van swore openly. Everyone was searching the horizon everywhere, and there was no trace of the vehicle.

"It just disappeared into thin air?" Kyle said. "Did you get drone footage, Coop?"

"I got nothing, Kyle. She went for the village. I'm calling her back." Then he had an idea. "Why don't you head back the way we came, and I want to take a look at the side of the hill. We might have missed something."

There being no other vehicles on the three paths they could take, for as far as their eyes could see, they agreed and turned around and headed back in the direction of their villa. As they rounded the curve, which is where they lost the truck, everybody looked out the left side of the van. What was almost perfectly camouflaged was a large seam in the mountain, an actual door made of stone, even planted with trees, and apparently they had some kind of mechanism to open that door and store the truck inside. The fact that they had followed, lost the truck, and then come back and found the entrance probably meant that the team had been discovered as well.

Kyle notified San Diego about what had occurred and asked about their surveillance. He was told they had missed the pass of a satellite overhead, so had no record of the vehicle turning off anywhere. Kyle was given orders to return to the villa.

Fredo wondered why they would go back to that villa, especially if they were suspecting that they'd been discovered. Perhaps they were going to be readying for a firefight as maybe the militia from the compound mobilized and were going to greet them when they tried to arrive. Or they could get there and find everyone gone, including the prisoners that they all had seen.

There were so many things that could have happened, and he wondered also why all of a sudden the operation had changed from something that had been done day in and day out, practically like clockwork, into a rather unusual operation involving a semi that drove into a mountain for camouflage. And if they were going to be selling the material in the back of the trailer, why would they hide out in a mountain?

Coop let the drone fall back so they'd be notified if some convoy came from the direction of the semi to overtake them. It was dead as dead could be. In fact, there weren't even any animals out prowling around, dead ones either on the roadway. That was very unusual.

They made it all the way to their compound, but before traveling up the private drive, Kyle directed Fredo to turn off and take a back road where a small hill would give them a good view of their compound and Ochoa's in the distance.

"You're thinking we just need to wait a bit and see what turns up? Are we playing like bait now?" Fredo inquired.

"I don't know what's going on, but I certainly don't want to put you guys down in the middle of it there. I mean, there's no cover. They could bring in jets for all I know. It could be rigged to blow up. I just think we better stay here where we know Ochoa comes back to very frequently and watch what he's doing and not go chasing off after black Suburbans and large semis. And now I'm wondering what's in those bags?"

Danny piped up and added his two cents. "You know, they could have been bags of fertilizer, Ammonium Nitrate, like the stuff they make bombs out of? My uncle back in Arizona puts bags of that stuff on his farm, trying to get his fallow field to grow, but it has to be applied constantly every year, and they go through a ton of it. Maybe that's what it is. Maybe it's just for farming or maybe it is for bomb-making."

"Interesting," Kyle said.

"You know, Kyle, if they were making bombs, that would be the perfect place for them to do it. I don't think there's anything that could penetrate that mountain, as far as radar, and except for the few times when the truck's going in or out, it just looks like a normal hill, very expensively put together," noted Coop.

"So we're thinking maybe it's a bomb factory, not a delivery to the US?" asked Fredo.

Several of the guys agreed with this assessment.

"I'm going to run that up the ladder and see what they say," said Kyle.

Fredo pulled up into a small thicket of trees barely taller than the van and a large flat area next to it, covered with tire tracks, where he could park and they could surveil their own digs. Kyle motioned for him to stop while he talked to his LT back in San Diego.

"Sir, we've kind of looked at how all this feels to us, and I'm just going to float a suggestion or a what-if in front of you. You tell me what you think."

He listened for his instructions.

"Well, the bags we saw loaded into the semi could be farm supplies, fertilizers. It also could be something fairly easy to get but used for making bombs. And so we wondered what if that was not just a storage facility and that truck was not taking those supplies north of the border. What if it was delivering it to a bomb-making facility?"

Kyle listened as the rest of the team in the van stayed silent.

"Understood. I'll let them know."

"Guys, I think you are geniuses. They've just received word that there had been deliveries made to the compound in just small delivery vans for weeks. We thought it was food and supplies for the prisoners and the militia staying there, but apparently, they were also being delivered ammonium nitrate, and we know what they like to do with that, don't we? So I think we're on the money here. It's not drugs, and that would make sense based on Ochoa's proclivities, but it is indeed a staging or a bomb factory, and it's closer to the border than his compound, which would make his discoverability lessen. Nobody could accuse him of doing it at his place. I think it's a smart move, but we saw them."

Fredo said next what had to be said. "What we don't know is, do they know that we know?"

CHAPTER 16

MIA WOKE UP in an ambulance, screaming, while going like a bat out of Hell. She had a tube in her arm, and it appeared they were only giving her fluids. She checked her body to see if there was any pain, and other than a bruised lip and a small cut on her ear, she was fine. She had a bit of a headache, but otherwise, she was fine.

She opened her eyes and stared into the face of a paramedic.

"Ma'am, we're headed to the hospital, and we'll be there in just about five minutes. Do you have any medical conditions I need to know about?"

"Where am I?" She was confused and couldn't remember what happened. Then as she put her hand up to her forehead, she remembered that she had passed out and that she had apparently shot somebody.

"Did I kill someone?"

The two paramedics in the back chuckled. "Were you going for that or were you just trying to scare him?" the other paramedic said.

"Stop fucking with me. Did I kill him or is he wounded?"

"Ma'am, he died in his own blood. He's being transported to the coroner. Apparently, there were lots of witnesses at the store. Was this man chasing you? Do you know who he was?"

"Absolutely no idea. But I think I know who sent him. I'll give you a complete statement. But first, I need you to call someone for me. I'm supposed to be over at Scripps by 1:00 to pick up a patient who's going to be living with us. I need to go do that."

"No can do, and it's already quarter to 1:00. You aren't going to make it."

"Then I need you to call over there or, better yet, do you have my purse?"

One of the medics handed her the bloodied purse. She looked at it incredulously. "Whose blood is this?"

"The guy you shot. He almost made it over to you. At least that's what the witnesses said, and he grabbed your purse and then was going for you."

"Okay, well, inside the purse—and you can go ahead and open it— there's a card of a Special Agent Gutierrez. I need you to call him and let him know what's happened. And then I need you to call the surgery ward at Scripps and let me talk to the head nurse there. I'm supposed to be picking up a patient, and I'm going to be late."

"Ma'am, they may admit you."

"That's horseshit. I'm not going to stay in any hospital. I've got to go get Ivan. And I'm going to bring him home no matter what you guys say. Nothing is going to keep me from doing that. Now if you're not going to take me to Scripps, because I'd agree to be seen at Scripps, then you better release me as soon as we get to the hospital. I'll say what I have to say so the doctor lets me go. But this is a life and death situation, and you have to let me do this."

"So where's your car?"

"At the grocery store where this guy fell. I left it there. The keys are probably still in it."

"No, the police probably took the keys, and they're probably going to impound the vehicle as well as the gentleman's vehicle."

"Crap. Something else I have to straighten out." She tried to calm herself and then added, "Would you please call and get permission to take me to Scripps? I got to get there right away."

After checking, they did receive permission to have her taken to the emergency room at Scripps, and they arrived at roughly ten minutes after 1:00. It was late, but she'd made it.

As they rolled her into the emergency room lobby, she recognized several of the orderlies she had seen before on other occasions when she'd brought the children in for various things. They smiled and nodded, looking concerned, but finally, she recognized the smiling face of her neighbor, Anson Hernandez.

"Anson, Anson. It's Mia here."

The young attendant quickly made it to her side.

"Mia, what are you doing here? What happened?"

"There was an incident. Some man tried to kidnap me from the parking lot, and—"

"That was you?"

"Of course it was me. I told you it was me. Why?"

"The guy that was killed today a few minutes ago?"

"Yes, I guess. Unless there was another shooting."

She watched him tell her that it had been all over the news reports as an alert, and they'd sent alerts to all the area hospitals looking for anyone who knew anything about it, any eye witnesses.

"I am surprised that you were involved."

It was turning out to be that kind of a day.

"Why, you don't think I look like a serial killer? Well, it's not like I went after him. He came after me. He was going to take me in his car, and I found a pistol, and I shot him. That's all there is to it. But, Anson, I have another problem. I'm supposed to take a patient upstairs back to my house, and then I've got to go pick up the kids at school. I was supposed to bring them, but I was on my way to the store and never made it. So I've got my kids at the school waiting for me, and I've got the little boy I'm supposed to take home upstairs in the …"

"Mia, where's your cell phone? I can get the school's number out of your cell phone, right? And do you have someone else that could go pick the kids up?"

"I could try Christy or one of the other wives. There's Brandy and Libby Cooper."

"How about one of the soccer moms?"

"Good idea." She dialed the coach's wife, who promised she would have the kids delivered back home and would wait until she got there. "St. Cecilia, same as my Gordy goes to. I think I'm on file there and authorized to pick them up, right?"

"Yes. Oh, thank you!"

"Is everything okay Mia?" she asked.

"Well, now everything's fine, but we did have a near kidnapping incident. I'll explain it to you later. But please don't mention anything to the kids. Okay?"

The next call she made was to Christy.

"I saw that on the news. That was you?"

"Well, I didn't have much choice. It was his gun. I got it out of the glove box of the car. But, Christy, he tried to kidnap me. He tried to push me in the car and kidnap me. I'm here at Scripps, and I'm supposed to be taking Ivan back to my place."

"Oh, I didn't know that. I thought Kyle mentioned that he was going to go into some kind of a migrant camp for unaccompanied minors through CPS. I didn't realize you'd been given permission to take him."

"Gutierrez arranged it."

"Gutierrez? Did you know that Gutierrez has gone AWOL? Everybody's looking for him."

Oh, fuckin' crap-filled tamales. Why me?

"I'm missing something. I just talked to the man. In fact, he may be upstairs, here at the hospital. What do you mean?"

"Agent Gutierrez used to be an agent in high standing, but apparently, he works for the cartels now. Whatever he told you to do, Mia, he's probably directly put you in danger. I wouldn't trust him at all. The Feds are looking for him, and of course knowing that Fredo and Kyle had some interactions with him, half of SEAL Team 3 is looking for him too. He's moved out of his apartment. Apparently, he's just gone, disappeared."

"But I just talked to him…"

"On the phone, right? He could have been anywhere."

That told Mia everything she needed to know. They'd been completely duped. And she was all alone, hoping to rescue an orphan child, but she was the one that needed rescuing. And her children, now they were at risk as well. Her entire world was blowing up in front of her. And Fredo was on a mission, rescuing someone else's kids, probably.

It really wasn't fair.

She rolled off of the cart, almost falling on the floor, and stood on wobbly legs as Anson tried to help her. She was a mess. Her pants were torn, and her chest was covered in blood. Her hair was dusty and full of leaves.

"I've got to get upstairs to see Ivan. Anson, you've got to take me.

And guys," she said as she turned to the paramedics, "I will settle up with you guys later. There's no way in hell I'm going to be admitted to this hospital. You tell the staff to just keep their distance. I'm a woman on a mission, and I will not be deterred! I will settle the bill as soon as I can, but right now, there's a little boy upstairs, and his life is in danger, and I've got to get there."

They reluctantly let Anson take her in the elevator to the fourth floor on the surgery wing. She passed by the charge nurse, who looked surprised to see her.

"I'm here to collect Ivan?"

"Ivan was checked out two hours ago, Mia. His representative came by signed all the paperwork. It had all been arranged in advance."

"You mean he's not here?"

"No, Mia. He's gone, checked out."

"Did he willingly go with this person?"

"I think so. Another of the nurses took care of him."

"This was a man, sort of a big man? With a short mustache and dark black hair?"

"Yes, I think that was him. He signed it here. Right here, you see? It says Fred or Frederi-Fre—"

Mia read the name out loud. "Fredo Chavez. But that's my husband, and he's in Mexico."

"Well, they wouldn't have let him take the boy without a form of ID. How would they have that if your husband is in Mexico? Are you sure?"

"What? You think I would lie about something like that? I know I look a mess, but none of this is my fault. I'm being played here. Yes, I shot a man, but I was sent here to pick up this little migrant boy, and…"

Her tears burst out. She knew she looked crazy, and she did feel like a wreck.

"Would you like some juice?" the pretty candy striper asked.

"No! I'd like a pitcher of sangria!"

The young volunteer jumped back about two feet.

"I'm sorry. I know I don't make sense…"

Mia sat down on the leather bench, sobbing as she sunk into a deep despair. This was all wrong. She'd been outmaneuvered. They'd been too trusting, and the system had failed her. Now it was time to go around the system.

She called Julie Smith about meeting at her house, but the mother never answered her phone.

CHAPTER 17

FREDO AWOKE JUST before dawn when the valley floor was pink with the promise of a new day. At first, Fredo thought he would roll over on his bed but then realized they had not spent the night in the villa. They were still in the campout overlooking the villa and the compound beyond.

Hunching up on his elbows, he surveyed who was awake. People were beginning to stir, and close to the van, he saw Coop begin to get up and check his equipment. Fredo picked up his scope and aimed it down at their compound and didn't see anything unusual. There were no vehicles in the drive or along the roadway that led up to the villa. But as he scanned farther, Ochoa's compound was just beginning to come to life. He did notice one of the black Suburbans with its lights on, loading several people. He wished he had a better vantage point but whispered to get Coop's attention and pointed.

Coop had fashioned a special set of binoculars on his helmet, pulled them down, and took a look. He signaled that he identified something positive.

Fredo followed the roadway leading to the compound, and still everything was quiet. He listened for evidence of drone activity and wasn't able to hear a thing that bothered him.

He touched Kyle's bag and pointed toward the compound, handing him his scopes.

"Shit, something's going on. Okay, we got to go."

Kyle was up, and since they all were fully dressed, one by one, the team rousted themselves, patted Andy on the shoulder, thanking him for his night sentry, and began to mobilize. The best place for them to talk was inside one of the vans. It also was going to be the warmest place. The whole team gathered, huddled together, while Kyle waited for orders.

"Okay, so we got their attention. We're going to have to scope out whoever leaves this compound first. If it's one of the Suburbans, we follow it. If it's a civilian car, we follow it. I believe the theory is something has gone awry and Ochoa is leaving this morning. Coop, Fredo, anybody see what's happening with the cages down there?"

Coop responded first. "I see people spread out all over, sleeping, as best they can. But there does appear to be fewer people. Perhaps some have been taken away or loaded up somewhere. I'm pretty sure nothing happened last night, because I watched until the wee hours."

Fredo knew that Cooper had been tasked with getting all the rest he could since a highly trained medic was right now their most valuable asset if they were headed to a firefight. But he also knew that Coop had extra gadgets he'd brought, some of them not even Navy issue, and he just couldn't stay away from using all his "stuff," as he called it. He was also disciplined enough to operate with a lack of sleep for a few days, unlike anyone else Fredo had ever met.

He knew that all the tensions happening at home were beginning to weigh on him, and he was feeling his lack of sleep. Coop was the iron man, and he deserved it. He was the only one on the platoon today who didn't drink. Fredo thought perhaps he should give that a try as well. But damn, there were so many things coming down the road. And he stressed that he hadn't heard from Mia.

People began pouring out of the van, gathering their things, and they loaded up. Someone made some coffee that was poured around in tiny cups, which tasted delicious. A few energy bars were passed around, Kyle reminding them to stow the wrappers afterwards. That was going to be breakfast. Certainly wasn't like the breakfast he'd cooked for Mia a couple of days ago. He smiled at that recollection.

"God, I hope you're safe," he said to himself and to her.

Kyle sauntered up to him and whispered in his ear. "Fredo, I guess Mia called Christy. You've got some voicemails you need to check. But I'm going to tell you not now. Okay?"

"Everyone okay?" He was rattled.

"I think so, just some news about something. And it was really short, and Christy should not have texted me. But I want you to know as soon as I know, so that's why I'm telling you."

"I got you. I've been staying off the phone. I only did one text yesterday."

"That's okay. There'll be time later, but right now, we got to focus here."

"Roger that."

So that was a hell of a thing. Now, Fredo had to worry about what he didn't know, and he didn't understand why he couldn't check his messages, but maybe there was something there that would affect his performance, and Kyle didn't want him to hear it. Whatever it was, he kind of wished that Kyle had kept his damn mouth shut. He took three deep breaths and went back to checking on the compound with his scopes.

The Suburban was being loaded with people, but it didn't appear to be anyone from the prisoner cages. He wished to hell he had something higher power. He would've focused on all these images, but he was recording them, picking up his phone, and clicking the video on. Maybe if he sent it up to the LT, maybe they'd have a digital enhancement that could make out the faces of the movement he was watching.

"I'm going to send this up, Kyle. They're loading up one of the SUVs."

"Good." Kyle raised his own scopes and nodded. "Yep, I think it's going to be showtime very soon."

Then Kyle clicked his fingers, which got everyone's attention and pointed to his ear. Those who didn't have their Invisios inserted did so immediately, and he talked over the comms.

"So we got activity down there, and I want you to be packed up. If you don't have your bags in the van, get them in the van right now very quietly and very slowly. Remember, we're crab-like objects. Remember the beach training?"

A very soft groan arose from the group.

"I know, I know. But it got you to this day, and you're trained. And you're a badass."

Fredo heard a chuckle somewhere. They boarded the vans, and Fredo sat behind the wheel as he had before with Armando driving the other one. They turned over the engines and let them idle, warm up, and then waited.

Coop informed them that the Suburban was leaving the compound. The gates had been pulled back and allowed it to exit.

"That's our go-sign. Coop, can we send a drone or will that not be possible?"

"Not a good idea, sir. We're going to be traveling. I don't want to leave it behind. When we get to the road following the vehicle, I'll send it then if you want, but we'll have to stop. I got to make sure that she's locatable. If everybody's moving, it's going to be problematic. And if that drone drops and they see it, well, they're going to know everything. They're going to even get the camera that's on it. So we can't do that."

"I got that. All right, let's move out. Slowly."

They wound down through the back road, avoiding the turnoff for the compound they had been staying at earlier. Pausing at the junction of the official road and the driveway, however, even though both of them were gravel, Fredo checked right and left and then without seeing traffic turned left as he was instructed. Kyle was talking to his LT, and they had visual contact of the vehicle, which was helpful.

This time, the SUV headed due west, appearing to head to the village, not north to the area where they found the semi at the edge of the mountain. There was a detour that came up on Kyle's computer sent by San Diego, indicating the Suburban had turned and was going to circumvent the village, not go through the middle. He continued getting instructions from home, which he relayed to Fredo. They sped up slightly so they could close the gap, and Fredo finally saw the taillights of the Suburban way off in the distance. Due to the fact the terrain was so completely flat, except for small clumps of trees and swales, creek beds in wintertime, their visibility was as at least fifty miles in any one direction.

Kyle's instructions alerted a change in course, the Suburban heading due north.

"I think they're heading for the border, Gents. Looks like we might get our opportunity here."

Fredo was excited with the news. At last, perhaps something was going to be actually happening. He knew the waiting was always necessary, especially being able to understand their environment and where all the players were located. Waiting and studying was always a good idea, and when things happened spur of the moment, it often led to unintended consequences and a possible firefight, which was dangerous. But this team had twelve able-bodied men, and he guessed that there weren't twelve shooters in that suburban. Probably only a handful, if Ochoa was one of them.

They followed the van at a distance, but Fredo kept his line of sight since the light of the morning made it possible for him to turn off his headlights. The Suburban was traveling approximately eighty-five miles an hour, so Fredo had to floor the van to keep up.

Kyle got word that the vehicle was indeed heading for a border crossing, something not official, but an area where there was free passage if someone had a four-wheel drive vehicle and could traverse a small rivulet coming off the Rio Grande. He knew that oftentimes the cartels used dried up creek beds as highways, which would cover up their tire tracks after occasional rains here, and make numerous trips almost undetectable.

Kyle was alerted that they had a go for stopping the vehicle. "Can you catch up to him, Fredo?" Kyle asked.

"I'm flooring it now, but I'll give it some more if I can. These things don't have the power the Suburban does, but I'm trying."

The SUV began to slow and then pulled to the side of the road and drove down into a creek bed valley. This was a lucky break for the SEALs, because that meant the trip would be slower and it was now possible for Fredo to overtake them, if he could close the gap. They were following behind in clouds of dust, gravel, and rocks that had been spewed all over the area. It wasn't lost on Fredo that it was possible the targets didn't even know he was following them, there was such a dust storm created from its massive tires.

"We have orders to ram him. Let's go." Kyle said over the comms.

Fredo stepped on it, and within seconds, the caked back end of the Suburban and its red taillights flashed. Fredo drove right into him and knocked the suburban in the driver's side rear panel, knocking it at an angle and causing an overcorrection from the driver, which nearly toppled the vehicle, but it was still moving, and Fredo now was concerned about the condition of the front end of his van.

"How's everybody back there?"

"Good to go. Van B is right behind us. Thank God they didn't hit us, because I'm sure they can't see a damn thing."

"Okay, do it again. We have instructions to stop and board."

Fredo hit the SUV one more time, and this time bent the left rear tire, causing the Suburban to swerve back and forth, fishtailing, and finally resting, slammed up next to the side of the rivulet bank. Within seconds, the doors opened, and they were being fired on with automatic weapons. Van B flew past them and crossed the path where the shooters were taking some of the firepower, but enabling Fredo's van to unload. Everyone spread out and took positions so that when the dust settled, they were ready to mark and hit anybody they could see.

At this distance, Fredo didn't need his scopes, but he grabbed his MP3 and was wearing extra clips, rolled out of the van, but left the motor running. He followed Coop behind a couple of scrubs, surveyed the perimeter, and noted there were fewer shots coming from the area of the SUV. He also noticed two bodies next to the driver's side door, the door hanging open but riddled with bullets. Fredo knew Ochoa had to be there, and he also knew they were required to bring him in alive.

Kyle reminded everyone for a sighting. "Anybody, anybody see those green boots, you let me know. Everybody else here is expendable."

"Roger that," said Fredo. He took up a position quickly behind a small tree, which didn't give him much stopping power or protection but gave him a better vantage point. Then he saw movement on the opposite side of the Suburban. Grabbing his binoculars, he honed it at dirt level and saw the unmistakable green boots running in the opposite direction away from the vehicle.

"I got eyes on him," Fredo said, just as two others communicated the same thing.

They took off after Ochoa. Kyle and six others stayed behind and immobilized, pinning down the remaining shooters until at last there were no more shots fired. The desert was eerily quiet as they ran full tilt up a small swale where Ochoa had scrambled and dove over the edge.

They didn't know what was going to be there, but they had to follow.

Fredo took point, and the three others spread out maneuvering so that, when given the call, they could take the ridge. When Fredo got up to the top, he saw Ochoa scaling down a rocky riverbed wall, heading for a small stream, but he was all alone. He gave the order for the group to advance, and the SEALs were able to overtake Ochoa, mostly because of those damn green boots that were probably too small for him.

Vanity proved to be his undoing. Fredo grabbed the guy, faced him straight on nose to nose, while his team tied Ochoa up.

"Okay, motherfucker, you get a free trip to visit your Uncle Sam. Have a nice day." He said and ran to the side to report to Kyle that they had captured him.

Fredo noticed that his van was smoking when he reached the ridge line and surveyed the group. All of the shooters from the Suburban had been either incapacitated, wounded, or killed. The vehicle was not drivable. They were ordered to leave the dead and wounded in place. Kyle ordered the whole team to pile into the second van, get nice and cozy with Ochoa, and head for the point of entry at the border. Fredo was tasked to drive.

It had been arranged that a US representative would meet them after they got through Mexican authorities, but they would not have help until they got through the Mexican side. They were instructed not to show papers or passports, and if necessary to blow past the gates. The Mexican authorities were not going to be notified of their crossing, but once San Diego learned that they had blown through, they would do so immediately to stop any further action, if possible. But they were prepared for another firefight. Ochoa was covered up, and as they approached the gate, he began to yell in Spanish, swearing like a stuffed pig. Coop took out a tourniquet and a rag from his medic kit and subdued his mouth. He pulled the tarp back over the gentleman, and then everybody waited as Fredo slowed and eventually stopped at the checkpoint.

"Your papers please, passports, and destination," the border guard asked in Spanish.

Fredo told him that they had been messed with by Ochoa and his militia and that they were coming. He had to move his men through the border, and if Ochoa came, he should let them pass and not try to stop them. He explained to them that these were construction workers, all US citizens, and this was a rescue mission to free them from being captive.

The border guard looked through the windows and noticed the overcrowding situation. He didn't do much checking, so Fredo knew that his little story about Ochoa and his militia had created a good ruse. The border guard didn't want to have anything to do with Mr. Ochoa. Fredo suspected that he would take a vantage point and abandon his post until the militia or what he thought was going to be the militia came through.

Fredo traveled the stretch between the two borders. Kyle got word that the SOS had gone out to the Mexican authorities about a rescue operation and requesting they have permission to leave the country, which was unnecessary but part of the plan.

At the US side, they all breathed the sigh of relief. They were waved through, and Kyle had a visual map of an airstrip they were to wait for a pickup.

Approximately forty-five minutes later, they arrived at the airport or what could be called a farmer's landing strip, really. They were peppered all over the border area for light planes and even larger planes to take off and land from. It was almost like the whole region was perfect for an airport without ever having to build one.

Ochoa was given a tranquilizing shot and would be coming on board as a wounded passenger, but fully restrained by his wrists and ankles. He hadn't been wounded, that is, not his body. But he was furious. His red face and bloodshot eyes spewed hatred, and his language was vile, so Coop gave him another dose, and he immediately dozed off. Fredo and Armando laughed at some of his expressions, and they were grateful the rest of the group didn't understand them.

Finally, the small jet landed, not exactly a fine-looking specimen, but this bucket of bolts was going to be their lifesaver. The pilot taxied then turned around and headed back in the direction in which he came, ready for takeoff. They abandoned the van, loaded all the equipment, and three people took Ochoa on a makeshift stretcher. Everybody loaded up, and in less than five minutes, they were wheels up and headed to San Diego.

Kyle informed them that it was a straight shot, no stops, and they'd be home soon.

A cheer went up. Mission accomplished.

The one thing that Fredo needed next was to hear from Mia. He hoped to God she had some good news for him.

CHAPTER 18

G US MAYFIELD ARRIVED at the police station where Mia was being interviewed. A task force had been created from there to find Ivan and former Agent Gutierrez, as well as Mia's soccer mom friend, Julie Smith, her three children, and Mia and Fredo's three.

Mayfield slowly and delicately told Mia he'd been informed that three armed guards had shown up at the school just as her friend was leaving with the kids and diverted her and the children. It happened so fast there wasn't time for administrators to intervene. Someone had tried to follow them and got shot at on the highway so turned off and reported the incident to police. Numerous other parents and teachers also called in the event.

"Oh my God, oh please, please, please, please, please, they have to be safe!"

Mayfield held Mia in his massive arms, trying to reassure her, but she was inconsolable.

"And Ivan. Ivan is missing too."

"Well, I think they have ways of tracking Gutierrez, so I give that a pretty good chance of finding them."

What Mayfield didn't say and Mia feared was if the child proved to be too much baggage for Gutierrez, that he might damage him or worse.

"So he's headed for the border?" she asked.

"We believe so. But you stay here while I check around and see what I can find out. Have you heard from Fredo?"

"Well, he said if he didn't call me back, I wasn't to call him. They sometimes go places that they're not allowed to use the cell."

"Fuck that. You get him on the phone. This is important," Mayfield shouted.

Mia quickly dialed Fredo's number. Astonishingly enough, he picked up on the first ring.

"*Mi amore!*"

"Sweetheart, I just listened to your messages. I'm so sorry I wasn't able to respond. Are you okay? Are the kids okay? And how is Ivan?"

Mia didn't know where to start. Her emotions were beginning to take over again, and she stammered and sputtered. In between tears and moments of clarity, she tried to communicate all the facts as she knew them. "And all of this could be different now. It turns out, Fredo, nothing we were told was the truth. Agent Gutierrez works for the cartels!"

"Fuck it. That asshole. I just hope he gets justice, we get justice."

"No, Fredo. You don't do anything, okay? We have to focus on getting the kids back. We just want to find the kids."

"I'm going to see if I can get released. We dropped off Ochoa, and we're headed back to base. I'll get there as fast as I can."

She had given him the station name and address and looked for Mayfield so she could let him know that Fredo was on his way.

It was a long forty-five minutes. The police station was a beehive of activity, and Mia sat in the corner, wrapped in a metal blanket, because she was shivering. Finally, someone came over and felt her forehead, took her pulse, and determined she needed to lie down and rest until her husband arrived. All the questions she had for them went unanswered. They had to nicely tell her to stop interfering and let them do their job.

Mayfield escorted her into an empty office/storage room that had a cot and several fresh pillows and blankets.

"You lay down here and cover up, and I'm going to be right outside this door. I'm not going to leave. I'm going to stay right here until you wake up, okay?"

Mia was in a strange state. She needed the rest. But she felt oddly strong, mentally. Adrenaline was pumping through her big time, yet her body was still failing her. She sat on the cot and removed her shoes while Gus positioned the pillow for her head and covered her with a blanket.

Lying down had never felt so good.

Mayfield dipped down to whisper in her ear, "Mia, sweetheart, you just relax and let it all go. You're going to be safe, everything's going to work out, you'll see. Just wait here for Fredo. You're doing great, kid. You're doing really great."

As Mia fell into a deep sleep, she somehow could tell that her stepfather wanted to give her a kiss on the cheek, but he was awkward and unsure of himself, which was the reason her mother loved him so much.

"Thank you, Gus." And then she fell asleep.

FREDO'S WARM ARMS pulling her into his chest and squeezing her tight awakened every single pore in her body. She smelled his sweat, his unique scent, the sounds he made as he mumbled in her ear and pressed her close.

"You're safe. You're safe, and there are lots of people looking for the kids. Oh, Mia, thank God you're okay. What you have been through and what I have let you—"

Mia put her fingers over his mouth. "Kiss me, Fredo."

They kissed gently, and then her need for his reassurance overcame her, and she pressed closer to him. "Hold me."

"Of course, Sweetheart, I'm here. We will not leave any stone unturned."

"I don't know why I'm so tired. I'm exhausted from all of this. And we had such high hopes for Ivan and our plans for the future, and I just don't know what's going to happen."

"Well, we first have to find everybody. So you've got to help us. Is there anything you can tell us about the plans about where you think Gutierrez would go? Anything?"

She racked her brain trying to think of something that could help them. But nothing was coming. "I'm just blank. It's like I can hardly remember anything that's happened. It's all a blur. I have so much racing around my head…"

His palm brushed back the hair from her forehead. "You're just exhausted, and now it's time for others to do the heavy lifting. Your part is done for now. I know it's difficult, but we're going to have to wait until they finish, and they will find them, I know they will."

"I think of Ivan too, how terrified he must be. You think they'll coordinate somehow? They put everybody together somewhere? That's the only thing I can think of, Fredo. These two parts have to be working together, right?"

"I think that's what they're working on. Gus is out there trying to be a fly on the wall. He's kind of big, and he sort of sticks out, so we'll see how well that goes. But for now, at least, they haven't kicked him out. Gus said these guys here are really good. And he's worked with them for years. I think it's good that he's here."

"So how did your mission go?"

"Mission accomplished. Ochoa was delivered, hand delivered you might say. Boy, he was angry. It'll be interesting to see what impact that has. We still have to negotiate with the Mexican authorities, since he was a fugitive from them technically and a former federal officer. But I'm sure our guys aren't going to let him go home anytime soon, and he's probably going to spend quite a few years behind bars here. It sucks though. It'll be a lot more luxurious than it would be in any kind of prison in Mexico. Trust me on that."

"Sounds like he doesn't even deserve that. But I'm glad you got him. Any word on the caravan people who perished?"

"Well, that's gonna depend on him, and we did get some positive news on the photos that I sent out. It looks like that's verification that Ochoa had been involved with this group, so that adds an extra layer of depth to his future prison sentence. I'll just put it that way, because in all reality, it's going to take years before he'll be convicted. But he's going to remain behind bars where he can't hurt anybody else. But they'll find somebody else to run the operation. They always do."

"I'm so glad you were able to do that. Ivan is going to be thrilled with this. I can't wait for you to tell him."

Fredo paused for a few seconds and then delicately approached his next idea.

"You know, we have to prepare for the possibility that they may do away with Ivan, as he's not the package or the prize for them if they sell him, but he's also the problem. He's the only one who can link that group with Ochoa, on an eyewitness basis because he was there. We have the photos, but he can tell the Feds a whole lot more about the operation. In that sense, him being alive is dangerous. So I don't want you to expect it, but I want you to be prepared in case we get some bad news. That's how these things go. I've seen it myself many times overseas."

Mia's tears soaked her cheeks and the top of her blouse. But she was controlled. "I understand. We tried, we really tried, Fredo. I did it because I wanted to give him a better life. I will forever feel partially responsible for this."

Fredo tried to silence her, but she wouldn't be hushed. "No. Let me continue. I trusted the wrong people, and because of my actions and my need to fulfill that promise to myself, I acted without thinking. I was stupid, Fredo."

"No, Sweetheart. You were brave. You did what any caring mother would do, and more. I mean, you defended yourself against an armed assailant. No one lost their lives over it in that grocery store except for the bad guy. You got word to the right people, and now it's up to them to do what they do best. Ivan was never going to be a happy youngster in a wonderful, loving home. He was trafficked, Mia. Everything he had in life had been ripped from him. He was a pawn, being used still by the people who originally were responsible for his leaving his home to come to the States. His mother made that decision, bringing him all this way and exposing all of them to such danger. And look at what they aspired to, to find a man who may not know that Ivan exists and may not even want him? I mean, if you look at his odds, Mia, they weren't good to begin with, sweetheart. But don't blame yourself. It's why this whole trafficking business is so tragic. It's not only tragic for the person who's being abused, but everybody who tries to help them. Everybody surrounding that person, their family at home, other people, innocent people, get caught in that web. It's the nature of the business. It's brutal, it's bloody, and they absolutely don't care about you or me or our children or Ivan, for that matter. It's the reality of the situation, Mia."

She was grateful for Fredo's honesty and for the reminder that she still was a mother of three boys and that was her job, her only job.

The door burst open, and Mayfield's hulking frame blocked the entire doorway. "We got a hit. We know where Gutierrez's car is. They're going to see if perhaps he's met up with the others, but they're going to get him. It's just a matter of time."

Mia noticed his face was the most hopeful she'd seen. "Thank you."

"So I'm going to go check things out here and get a full read on everything. Mia, you stay here, okay?" whispered Fredo.

"Not on your life. I'm going to go everywhere you go. You're not leaving me behind this time."

Fredo smiled at her. "Of course, Dear." And then he smiled again.

Mia was reminded of the counseling session they had gone to at one time when they hit a rocky patch in their marriage. And the counselor had clearly told Fredo that the best thing he could do when his wife was upset about something was to first answer back, "Yes, dear."

"You remembered."

"Absolutely. I remembered all of it. I remember all the good and only this much," he held his thumb and first finger together to show how small, "this much of the bad stuff."

Within minutes, Gutierrez's car was located, parked at a motel about twenty miles from the border station near San Diego. It was frequented by relatives coming to greet other relatives coming across the border. It was explained to Mia and Fredo that when Gutierrez became a suspect, when they called in the FBI to surveil him and possibly do an assessment of whether or not he was compromised, they put a tracking device on several of the things he would be taking. One of them was his suitcase, which he had with him always, but the other tracking device, in addition to things planted at his home, was on the car. And Gutierrez had not switched the car out. Hence, they knew where he had been and hopefully was now.

As Fredo and Mia watched, they received news that a SWAT team had arrived, verified with the clerk at the front desk that, in fact, Gutierrez was there, and he also verified that he was with a young boy. The clerk said it bothered him to see how frail and scared the young boy looked. He suspected that he was either a runaway or had paid this gentleman or someone else to bring him over the border, and now was beholden to him.

They weren't able to see the videos, but the SWAT team did wear body cameras, and the police verified that, in fact, Gutierrez was in the room with Ivan. They were both very much alive. While they were processing the scene and separating Ivan from Gutierrez, his accomplice arrived with Mrs. Smith and the children, all six of them. Everybody was fine. The police stopped the vehicle in the parking lot, unloaded everybody, and arrested the three gunmen. They found directions, pictures, maps, and a ton of arms and ammunition. They also found some drugs. The kids were fine and anxious to come home.

"Even after all that's happened, Fredo, I still want to fight for Ivan. Now, I want to give him that American future more than ever. Can we do this?"

"As long as you don't get your hopes up. It might be difficult, but I agree. It's going to be tight, Mia. But I'm all for it, Sweetheart. He deserves you as his mother."

CHAPTER 19

FREDO WAS GRATEFUL beyond words as the big police van pulled up with his precious cargo, bounding down the stairs, high-fiving police and rescuers. Ricardo was right in the middle of it all, and the Smith kids couldn't stop talking about riding in the big tactical van and meeting all the officers who helped in their rescue. He imagined it was like living inside their favorite police movie. They had probably not really realized or considered how much danger they were in. He knew that, for weeks to come, they'd be the talk of the school. The director might even hold an assembly to talk about child safety and human trafficking—but all that was someone else's job.

The only thing that worried him was little Ivan, who had been pitched from one country to another, losing those he loved and getting let down by those he had quickly formed an attachment to who he probably felt had let him down. Again.

He kept to the sides and watched as their three children ran to their mother, and she embraced them with a big wide happy smile on her face, tears and all. It was quite a reunion, and Fredo would never forget this day.

He sauntered over to Ivan, stood next to him, and watched just like he did. He sensed if he tried to put an arm around the kid, he'd pull away. It was going to take a lot of time, and Fredo knew he could be patient. He'd seen so much about this kid already that he knew he'd survive all this. And if they let him, Fredo and Mia could turn his wishes into dreams.

He wished he could help every single suffering child everywhere. But of course, those lofty goals could never be fully achieved. And it probably would take some of these kids growing up and healing, if they could, to help such a project get off the ground.

But that was a wish and a dream for another day. Right now, Ivan had support around him that he wouldn't allow himself to accept. His fixation was on Mia and the kids, Julie Smith's kids jumping up and down, excited like they'd just been on a carnival ride. Nobody was paying attention to Ivan, but he saw it all, and he compared his life to theirs.

Fredo knew it was making him sadder by the minute. He was lost again.

He knelt down in front of the boy. He did not touch him. The scared look on Ivan's face told Fredo he'd been right.

"Ivan, I'm so proud of you," he said in Spanish. "This has been no picnic. You've been living with this uncertainty for weeks now, if not years. But I'm here to tell you that's going to be all over soon. Just like we promised, we're going to make sure you have a loving home, our home, if we're allowed. We'd like to include you in our family. I think there's a lot you could teach our kids about what life is elsewhere. They don't know anything but this. You know so much more."

His little mouth was still pursed shut, almost in defiance against his own emotions. Fredo knew Ivan wanted to be needed like his kids. Being left out was one of the first things he probably learned in his young years. He probably had no real childhood. Everything had been robbed from him and nobody really cared.

"Would you like me to help you find your father, the Marine?"

His attention immediately went back to Fredo's face, although he suppressed the glimmer of hope Fredo saw behind Ivan's eyes.

"No promises, but we'll do our best to locate him. If it doesn't work out, I hope that you'll consider living with us, allowing us to become your parents, legally. Unless you'd rather go back to Mexico to live with your siblings?"

He shook his head. His first words were, "I don't like that place anymore."

"Okay, then should we look for your father?"

He nodded his head, yes.

That hurt more than Fredo had expected it to. He would have much preferred Ivan to choose him over an absent father, albeit, a father who didn't know he existed. But that was Ivan's choice, and not one Fredo could make for him.

He was giving Ivan a taste of the freedom he so desperately wanted and didn't know how to ask for.

"You know, when I saw you standing there, facing that gun pointed at you, you stood tall. You are very, very brave, Ivan. Never forget that. I know what bravery is all about, and I've seen good and bad examples of it. That's part of what haunts me every day. But I believe, if we stay strong and we work together as a team, we can accomplish anything. Do you believe that, Ivan?"

The kid swallowed hard, and then Fredo saw the tears forming. Slowly, Ivan moved towards him and then fell against his chest and began to sob.

In that heartbreakingly wonderful moment, he knew what his real mission in life was. He was a protector, yes. A defender of his country. And he was husband to the most wonderful woman in the world.

But most of all, he was a father. He had been destined for that even when he thought he couldn't father a child of his own and beat those odds, with the help of Coop and his ridiculous smoothies and tofu. He won Mia's heart in the beginning, which started his journey. He'd been witness to some of the finest men ever created. He'd put away some real assholes. And he still came back, because he was father to these boys. And, even if Ivan didn't choose to live with them, Fredo would always feel like a father to the boy and would always be there for him, no matter what.

Ivan's little sobs died down as Fredo's palm rubbed his back and squeezed the top of his spine, speaking to him in his native tongue.

There would be time for speeches later, lessons on living, and reflections. Right now, he was just grateful today would end on a bright note. He hoped he'd lit a candle for Ivan so he could see his way forward when it got dark again.

And he hoped it never got dark.

ALL FOUR OF the boys were splashing in the pool. Ivan stayed in the shallow end, on the sand deck, and Fredo suspected he'd never been in a real pool before and probably didn't know how to swim. But he wasn't going to embarrass him by placing water wings on his arms or a life preserver. Fredo would watch vigilantly and protect him from that humiliation.

He thought perhaps Ricardo and the twins might have figured all that out, and they played gently in the sand deck area, not the deep end like they usually did. It made no difference as the same amount of water was splashed, just without all the jumping in and out.

Ricardo offered to share his room with Ivan, and that upset the twins. Fredo watched Ivan's face as he laughed at being the most popular one, for a change. In the end, he chose to room with Ricardo.

They didn't know in the days that followed if Ricardo ever told Ivan about his biological dad, or "sperm donor," but on the day when Caesar had made the appointment to come see Ricardo, everyone in the household was on edge with this highly anticipated meeting.

Mia especially was unsure whether or not they were doing the right thing. She'd discussed how she still feared repercussions from the cartel bosses or others who associated with the former agent, Gutierrez.

"You worry too much, Mia. Look at what we've been through. You think God would have put all of us through this if he didn't have a plan? We're not done yet."

"Whatever do you mean?"

"I don't know. I guess this has made me realize there is more to life than what I do. My family has always been important to me. But I look at little Ivan, and I'm inspired."

"What are you going to do if he finds his father and goes away?"

"Ask him about his mother. He'll tell you. He's very smart. It will be like the answer he gave me when I asked him if he missed her. He put his palm right here, on his heart," Fredo placed Mia's hand on his heart, "And said to me, 'she is right here.'"

They waited for an hour for Caesar to show up. He was supposed to arrive at two. Half past three, it finally dawned on them all, especially Ricardo, that his father wasn't coming. With no phone call, no message left, they didn't know what happened. Ricardo was in a slump for the next two days because of it. Fredo witnessed how Ivan was tender with him. Did little things to make him laugh. Ricardo could be glum around Mia and Fredo, but Ivan's personality was infectious, and he could not resist breaking a smile when the little one did his antics to cheer him up. They became closer than Fredo thought possible, each boy healing the other one's heart.

Mayfield one day revealed that Caesar had been arrested again for dealing drugs and pimping and was likely to spend another few years in prison.

"You suppose he ever intended to meet Ricardo?" Fredo asked.

"We don't know, do we? No father should put his kid through that. Something's wrong with a man who can't be a man."

"Roger that."

About a month later, as they were sitting around the dining table, the subject of fatherhood came up. One of the twins had used "sperm donor" in a derogatory way in his conversation, and Mia stopped him. Ricardo was shaken but tried not to show it.

Fredo called to him, and Ricardo sat next to him on the table's bench seat.

"I'm going to tell you something about fatherhood, real fatherhood." He spoke to the whole group assembled there. "Anyone, well, almost anyone can father a child. But a real father is part of his son's life. And he does things in life to make sure he gets to stay that way. Ricardo's biological father, I believe, really wanted to be a good father. Who wouldn't?"

He messed up the top of Ricardo's hair, and the rest of the boys laughed.

"But it takes someone who makes better choices to be a real father. And when you guys grow up, I hope you'll remember that. Fathers don't just happen. They're a complicated mixture of bailing wire, bravery, honor, duty, and…"

He looked across the table at Mia.

"And love." He smiled at her.

He heard her whisper *"Mi Amore."*

Ricardo put his arm around Fredo and gave him a hug. And then he heard the words he could not believe.

"I'm glad you're my real dad."

Ivan held his orange juice up for a toast. He stood on their side of the bench.

"To real dads everywhere, whether they know it or not!"

His English wasn't perfect, but it went straight to everyone's heart as they all toasted to the best of the days to come.

SECOND TIME LOVE

SEAL Brotherhood: Legacy Series
Book 9

SHARON HAMILTON

CHAPTER 1

G RETCHEN HAD BEEN flittering around the dressing room like a girl readying herself for prom, Trace thought. Their daughter—his stepdaughter—Clover Sanders was getting married today. The sun was out, and the birds were chirping just like they always did, especially in April. Coronado was the most beautiful in the spring, but it didn't compare to his wife and how cute and flustered she was, sparking off expressions he'd never seen before.

"Relax, honey," he said, stopping her spinning by placing his hands on her shoulders.

She didn't make eye contact at first, but Trace insisted.

"It's going to be lovely, you'll see," he whispered to her, trying to sound super mysterious and sexy.

"Damnit, Trace. How do you stay so calm?"

"Because I will it so. Because I did 150 pushups two hours ago and a ten-mile swim in the bay before breakfast. I can feel my heartbeat against the leather soles of my shoes, honey."

She gave him that look, the one he liked, that tried to show him she was resisting him, but he was going to win the war anyway.

"And because I wasn't the one making all the preparations and co-ordinating everyone to carry out this mission. I'm just support staff. That's what I'm doing now."

As he expected, when he didn't release her and didn't stop trying to lock eyes with her, that smirk appeared and then bloomed into a beautiful smile.

"There's my girl."

"No longer a girl. I'm—"

"Perfect, in every way. Inside ..." He leaned forward, kissed her ear, and whispered, "Deep inside and outside. And you taste good too."

Her lips were soft and moist and demanded things of him he'd been already thinking about, but they didn't have enough time to execute.

"Better?" he said as he pulled back and studied her face.

"Much. Thank you."

"Oh no, thank *you!*"

She took his arm, and he escorted her to the narthex of the church, where they waited with the rest of the wedding party without the bride, the groomsmen looking like kids on a little league team but taller, Trace thought. He'd probably seen a bunch of them in their hot tub over the past several years, since most of them were long-term friends of Clover's as well as Jack's, her husband-to-be.

Jack was nervous as hell and kept smearing down his hair, which had been unfortunately over-oiled. It still didn't keep his wayward locks from shooting out like he'd stuck his finger in an electrical socket.

"I passed out at my wedding too. Not recommended," Trace said to the wide-eyed boy who was going to be his precious daughter's better half and was barely shaving. The kids were getting younger and younger these days.

"Mr. Bennett, sir, I wish you wouldn't talk like that, because, well, I keep seeing visions of me peeing my pants, shitting myself, or passing out. My odds aren't good, so I don't need to hear that."

"Just kidding. You'll be fine. This isn't the end of life; it's the beginning of life, son. You're gonna look back on it and laugh. Trust me on that."

"Mrs. Bennett didn't tell me you passed out."

"No. I meant my first marriage. And I should have been scared with that one. It was my body's way of trying to protect me. But I was punch-drunk on love or sex or a bit of both. It took time, but, when we finally got to know one another, we didn't like who we were together. It's different for you and Clover. You've known her—what?—seven or eight years?"

"Actually, almost nine. I was in her first class in Coronado when they all moved down here to be with you. We met that day and have been friends ever since."

"See? I was right. This is just about saying your lines in front of your friends and relatives. Nothing about the wedding itself should cause you any fear at all. You're a match made in Heaven, and, if I couldn't see the love with my own eyes, I trust Clover's judgment. I'll bet she worked you over and made you beg, am I right?"

Trace smiled internally, already knowing this to be true.

"That's putting it mildly. But she's worth it. I used to think she was trying to push me away."

"It's a trait of the women in their family. Want to make sure you're a keeper."

Jack mumbled agreement, searching the crowd nervously.

"They signal her when you are all inside. Don't worry. You won't jinx it, son."

Jack gave him a nervous laugh. "Mr. Bennett, I was wanting to talk to you about something. Could you help me get into a BUD/s class? I'm thinking of trying out for the Teams."

"You talk to Clover about this?"

"Sort of. We—"

"Son, you need to learn that you don't need my permission or help. You need Clover's. You find out if you got her in your corner first, and then you come talk to me, but not before. It won't end well if you do it the other way around. Women don't like to be second."

"But lots of your teammates joined that way. They just joined and made the grade."

"Because they weren't married. It's not like taking a few extra classes at the junior college, son. Whole different world. It will change you. Clover has to be on board."

"Understood."

Gretchen had been coordinating some things with the photographer and came over to Trace and Jack.

"Ready? The music has changed, and they say we can begin. Jack, go escort your mom and then come back for me, okay?"

"You got it, ma'am." He burrowed through the crowd and took his mother's arm, and they entered the church.

Gretchen sighed. "So young."

"I was thinking the same thing," answered Trace, his arm around her waist. "He's a straight-up good kid."

"I agree. And she's gonna boss him around like crazy. Hope he's ready for it."

"If she's half as bossy as her mama, he'll love every minute of it."

He saw her sneak a finger under her eye to wipe away a tear.

"You're the most beautiful woman here, Gretchen. I knew the first time I saw you that you were a prize and just the right person to make my life worth living."

Kate and Tyler slipped in front of them with their youngest, Kendall, dressed in hot pink with a large, white bow at the top of her head, and her two older brothers steps behind. Kate waved, and Tyler punched Trace in the left arm as they quickly were ushered into the church.

Jack came back for Gretchen, and Trace sent her off with a kiss. His coloring was much better now, and, with the walking, he didn't look so pale and exuded more confidence. One by one, the other bridesmaids and groomsmen escorted each other down the aisle, turned, and waited for Trace to bring down Clover. They were stunning, the girls in shades of pink and rose, to the men in the Navy who wore dress whites. The other three wore white tuxes.

Minutes passed, but she didn't appear. As the music began again, Trace knew that Gretchen was going to be beside herself. Things could always go wrong. Although not a "runner" as some of his Teammates discovered occasionally, anything could happen. Could she have been kidnapped? With the way the world was, anything was possible.

He flew to her dressing room. With the phone to her ear, she sobbed. Her face was red and she'd smeared her eye makeup.

"Who is that, Clover?" he said as he wrapped his arms around her and pointed to the phone.

"It's Dad," she whispered.

"From prison? He's calling you from prison? That f—" He stopped himself before he uttered his favorite word.

"Look, Dad, I gotta go now. Trace is here and it's time. Thanks for calling, but please don't worry about me. I'll be fine."

Trace could still hear Tony's voice on the other end of the line when she disconnected the phone.

"Come on, Front Row. Let's get you straight. Everyone's waiting." While they hurried to the narthex, he asked, "What was this business with Tony? Why did that asshole—sorry, Clover, but that's how I think of him—get you so upset on your wedding day?"

"Trace, it's nothing. He's getting out soon, you know this, and he wants to spend time with me and Jack. Telling me all the things he wanted to do to make up for—"

And then Clover stopped and broke down and began to bawl.

Trace flew into a panic. If only Gretchen was here to make everything right. After all, as a Navy SEAL, he wasn't trained for *this* stuff. Ask him to do a snatch and grab, blow up a building, or stop a caravan of bad guys from entering a village? That he could do. But try to cheer up his stepdaughter at her wedding when her asshole father called from prison and victim shamed her, making her sad she had such a loser for a father? That wasn't something he'd trained for. That's what Gretchen specialized in. She'd know exactly what to do.

He grabbed her and hugged her tight, tighter than he'd ever hugged her before. He suddenly wasn't sure if he wasn't the one who needed strength.

"If I could take it all away, sweetheart, you know I would. But that's just the way things are. Life sucks sometimes. Sometimes the people we expect the most out of let us down. They treat us wrong, like your dad, and you still gotta love them anyhow. But it sucks. Just know, two hundred people are here who love you and can't wait to help you celebrate this beautiful day. This is your day, not his. He shouldn't have even called you."

"I know, but he's weak. He can't help himself."

"Right. And I'm going to be the gatekeeper until your mother tells me I'm wrong or going too far. No one is going to hurt my big girl. So you get yourself all cleaned up, just a little—"

He pulled out a mirror and handed it to her. Clover winced and nearly began crying again. With some of the supplies still in her hand, she worked on the makeup streaked under her eyes.

"The redness is already going away. Honest, honey. But they're gonna scream at me if I don't get you out there into the narthex. So help me out, okay? Help out this poor Navy SEAL from getting hit with a baseball bat by all the women here today, including your mother!"

"Oh, Trace. You're the best. I'll defend you." She giggled, dabbed powder on her face, threw the cosmetics in an offering bowl at the back of the church, and grabbed his hand. "Let's go kick some ass and take no prisoners."

"That's my girl."

IT WAS A beautiful ceremony, and the love that surged between Clover and Jack permeated the lovely April early afternoon, infecting the audience and wedding party with warm thoughts and magical wishes for the perfect life and union just beginning. Within seconds of the bride's appearance, her dress made of bright white satin covered in a sheer overcoat with pink butterflies and small pink rosebuds appliquéd and adorned with beaded pearls and crystals, the audience was stunned and immediately forgot the delay. As she walked, snickers rippled through the audience as they saw her favorite pair of volleyball shoes, died pink with hot pink laces.

The whole outfit was created by Clover and reflected her originality and her quest to celebrate life in all its forms. She clutched his arm and stood tall, bowing to the audience as they passed the aisles.

He savored this gift Gretchen had given him when he married her, because he never would have been able to walk a daughter down the aisle without her three beautiful girls. They were his, just as if he'd fathered them himself. He loved them all with everything he had.

The reception, even though he'd asked his teammates to keep it close and respectful, got a bit out of hand. A couple of the single Team Guys got drunk, one nearly getting into a fight with a Navy regular who was on the arm of a female guest, a friend of Clover's. Someone spiked the punch, and it had to be removed from the children's table, replacing it with another nonalcoholic punch. After that, someone made a store run for juice boxes and sodas, which were also consumed by the adults.

Some of the *Dancing with the Stars* type behavior was a bit risqué, lots of thighs and cleavages showing. People danced he never knew could dance, even with some stumbling and falling on the dance floor. It was always the same, whether the team was in full dress uniform or more casual. There was always the chance someone would embarrass themselves or someone else, but nobody got hurt, except for their pride.

The dinner was catered by the ladies auxiliary to save money, and the crowd stayed until the wine ran out. That had been done on purpose.

On the way home, Gretchen was exhausted but smiling, even giggling.

"I'm glad you had a good time, Gretch."

"Your buddies never disappoint. Those friends of Jack's came, the ones who just graduated from BUD/s. Nice boys who look you in the eye."

"They have no idea about the rest of the training. Deer in the headlights, my dear."

She smiled. "It must make you proud, seeing all these fine, young men going off to support and defend our country. You suppose Jack's thinking about that?"

"Like I told him, he better get Clover's permission first or he'll learn a very hard lesson."

She softly laughed. "Well, it's up to them. If he was my boy—"

"Well, he is, in a way," Trace interrupted.

"True, but I'm leaving it up to Clover, regardless of how I feel." She gave him a sexy smile. "You were most handsome, Mr. Bennett."

"Why, thank you, Mrs. Bennett."

"What do you really think about Jack going into the Navy?"

"Like you said, it's up to them now."

"Hard to see how he'd get veterinarian training becoming a Navy SEAL."

Trace laughed.

"What's so funny?"

"Oh, he'll get to work on, and with, some animals all right. Of the human kind. But if he's called and he uses his head, he could do it. It's all up here," he said, pointing to his temple.

"Oh, but, my love, you're so wrong. It's all in here," she said as she held her palm against his heart.

Trace moved her hand down into his lap.

"I like your ideas, Trace. And with Angie staying over with Mom and Dad, we'll have the whole house to ourselves." She kissed him on the cheek and tried to slide over closer, the gear shift getting in the way.

"I better hurry or I'll be banging you in the Walmart parking lot, sweetheart."

"That suits me just fine. But not under a streetlamp, please."

CHAPTER 2

G RETCHEN THREW HERSELF against the closed front door of their house when they returned. She hadn't recovered from their little tryst in the parking lot. Her head was spinning, and her breathing was still labored.

Trace's relentless lovemaking made her knees fold every time she thought of his determination to wring every last drop of energy from her. He demanded her full participation and then gave her complete satisfaction and more. Now ten years older, instead of being softer and gentler, he was even more driven and fully charged up, powered by his passion for their life together. It was impossible to resist him, and she never wanted him to stop.

He turned around, pulling her off the door and into his arms.

"That was fun. We should do that more often," he whispered.

Somehow, she drew up the energy to chuckle as she fell against him. "I'm beginning to think your first wife sent you away because she couldn't handle you anymore, strange as that thought is. How in the world did that woman let you go?"

"She tried to come back, remember?"

"Oh, yes, I hated that."

"I wasn't interested in the least. You know that's not who I am." He kissed her and, again, that sharp sizzle shot down her spine, making her heart race. "First time was a mistake. Second time, I hit the bull's eye. I mate for life."

"You just might kill me with your libido, Trace."

"Not a chance. I'm still waiting to love you hard enough to put another baby in your belly."

"Trace, I'm too old. I'm on the pill. You know this."

"Go off it. I want to make you pregnant. I want another little girl, but I'll take a boy. Maybe twins. Maybe one of each. Twins run in my family."

"Oh my God! Trace! You devil! That's not going to happen. Soon enough, you'll be holding your first grandchild, but we have to be patient with them. It will happen in time. That's going to have to be enough for us now …"

"I want more."

He began kissing her neck again, his knee pressing between her legs, making her quiver and ache again as she rode him. Even though she still had tender spots from their acrobatic lovemaking in the back seat of the Hummer, she was getting turned on all over again.

He abruptly stopped and spanked her rear.

"Go shower, and let me make some food to soak up all that alcohol. Then we'll get some nice rest and wake up lazy, but still horny, in the morning."

"Now I'm beginning to understand what my life will be like when all the girls leave."

After a long, deep kiss, he whispered to her lips, "Absolutely. Release the Kraken!"

He sent her off with another spank, and she laughed all the way to their bathroom, shedding clothes along the way. A good, warm shower would be good for her, she knew. It might help with some of the swelling and bruising she might have in the morning. Hummers were small spaces in the back, and the upholstery was rather unforgiving.

As the water sluiced down her body, she mused how exciting it had felt, like she was twenty again, and how her life had changed these last ten years, making the previous ten disappear—with the exception of the joys of birthing all three of her girls.

She rubbed her belly. Was there room for another in there? Would she be pregnant the same time as her daughter, Clover?

The answer to her query was *yes*. With Trace, all things were possible.

She dried her hair and slipped on a robe, cinching it at her waist. She could smell Trace's specialty wafting from the kitchen: hot scramble, which was eggs with salsa and lots of cheese, stirred quickly in tablespoons of real butter. This would be followed up with pan-fried French bread slices and fresh jam from the farmers market.

He pulled the chair out for her and took obvious note of the gaping wound that was the front of her robe, raising his eyebrows and giving her a low growl as he bent over to serve her up the hot midnight snack.

"You smell and look lovely, my dear."

"These eggs look fantastic, Trace. I had no idea I was so hungry!"

"I noted you didn't eat anything but a donut and coffee all day. Not good for your body, Gretchen. We have to keep you in fighting strength." He growled again.

She laughed. "I thought I did pretty well tonight. I was able to keep up with you."

He sat down next to her and watched her eat. "You definitely did." And then he just continued staring.

"What?" she asked.

"I meant it when I said I want to make a baby with you."

"Trace, we're practically grandparents' age. Don't you think we should act like it?"

"You mean I can't do this?" he asked as he slid his hand down her front and squeezed her right breast. "Oh, man, and no more of this?" He bent and sucked her nipple into a hard peak. "I want to taste you all over. I think grandfathers do that. Not in front of the kids, though."

"Aren't you going to let me eat?" she whined as he kissed her neck. "Or were you making this lovely food just to take it away from me?"

"Absolutely not. I just don't want you to forget what—"

Trace's cell phone rang.

"What the fuck?" He peered down at it and they both read: "A—hole" on the screen. "What the fuck does Tony want from us? He already ruined Clover's day."

"What? I didn't know about this."

He held his finger up. "Tell you later," he murmured before, "Hello, Tony. What can I do for you now? You out of toothpaste or condoms?"

Trace put it on speaker phone so Gretchen heard the profusion of swearing coming over the line, plus some background crowd noise.

"Same at you, man. Can I make your day worse, Tony? Just name it, and it will be incoming, special delivery right for you in a pail filled with dog shit."

Again more swearing. And then Tony began to sob.

That got Trace's attention. He sat up. "Tony? What's going on, man? You okay?"

"Like you care one thimbleful of jizz for me."

"It was your fault. You punched me first and you scared the crap out of your daughters."

"Shut up!" Tony yelled over the phone, which got a reaction from somewhere else in the hall outside his cell. "I need help, man. I need protection."

"Sorry, bud. No can do."

"Not here. I need you to protect me when I get out."

"The way I hear it, it's more dangerous inside, with all the gangs and the guards not making enough money for the danger they're exposed to. And my commitment to your family doesn't include protecting you, inside or out."

"I got people after me."

"But you're such a nice person, Tony."

"Shut the fuck up. I've only got another thirty seconds. I need you to pick me up on Friday when I get out. I'm supposed to get some money to some people that day."

"I see, so I need to drive you to the bank. Can't you take a cab?"

"You don't get the problem, you SEAL jerk-off. I don't have the money."

"I didn't realize toothpaste was that expensive. Are you using that many condoms?" Trace was having way too much fun and hadn't been watching Gretchen. Her anger began to boil.

Leaning into the phone, she asked him, "Who do you owe money to and how much?"

"There's this group called The Organization. They funded me an attorney to help with my appeals, and I signed with them so they could get me back on the court roster."

"That wasn't smart, not after nine years. You been practicing?" Trace inserted himself.

Gretchen put her hand over his mouth and frowned. "Tony, how much? We don't have anything we can give you."

"You can sell the house in Portland."

"That's your house."

"I owe more than the house."

Both she and Trace gasped.

Tony continued. "When the agency thing didn't work out, and it still might, but I thought I could earn some money with some of my gambling talents, and I lost. I lost big. Took a couple of bad chances I shouldn't have, and—"

Trace was holding his forehead and shaking his head. He made the gesture to Gretchen, his forefinger across his neck. Gretchen had to agree. Tony jumped in water so deep he was probably going to drown, his life ending over his bad decisions.

"I'd say more than a couple. Look, Tony, first thing you have to do is to get real with yourself and us, if you expect any kind of help. I can try to keep you safe, but you're not coming to live with us, and I can't protect you twenty-four seven. You'll have to raise the money. You'll have to negotiate time, and that might cost you something, probably more money. But you're in a spot, and, if you don't start telling the truth, you'll not only end your life, but you could endanger your family's as well." Trace was stern, deadly serious, and he wouldn't look Gretchen in the eyes.

"I understand," Tony said, drifting off into a whimper.

Gretchen shook her head from side to side, but Trace said it anyway.

"I'll be up there on Friday. We'll talk. Not going to promise anything, but I'll meet you as you walk out of there. The rest is going to be up to you."

The phone went dead, running out of time.

Gretchen knew Tony also was out of time. She feared this was going to have an effect on their whole family, and, with Trace being the protector he was, though he disliked Tony as a husband and father, he couldn't stand anyone who bullied people who were not capable of fighting back.

It was just his nature.

With a sinking feeling, she knew she'd never be able to talk him out of helping out the father of their daughters, for their sake, not Tony's.

CHAPTER 3

T RACE LANDED IN the Eugene Airport and rented a car, driving to the West Oregon Correctional Facility, a whole hour ahead of Tony's scheduled release time. He wasn't nervous about the visit, but he was concerned for the precarious position Tony had put himself in and how that would impact the family.

Gretchen had tried to talk him out of going, but he knew matters would only get worse if he ignored Tony, possibly spiraling out of control. That might be something no one could solve.

The facility looked more like a hospital. While gated and fenced, it was considered a minimum-security prison. All the same, psychiatric patients were housed there as well, and Trace knew that the criminally insane were probably even more dangerous than some of the hard timers in the maximum-security prisons. Their reactions were extremely unpredictable, and they could go for years on end without incident, suddenly having a crisis.

He'd promised Gretchen that, if Tony was a complete mess, he would try to deliver him to the proper authorities and get back home. He didn't like leaving Gretchen and the two girls alone. And he was missing out on greeting Clover and Jack when they got back from their honeymoon at the end of the following week. But if it took a week, Kyle had given him permission to handle it.

He parked at the main entrance, in front of the gate, but got out of the car and paced. A young woman and her infant were also waiting. The area looked more desert than the usual green of Oregon, even in April. The ground had been mowed extra short and had dried. The waiting lot itself was graveled with a light spray of oil, like he'd seen in the highway dividers for weed control. He heard occasional hawks overhead, but the nearest tree was more than a mile away, closer to the small one-church towns along the highway, just outside of Eugene.

He'd been told prisoners were never released early, but sometimes an hour or two later than their scheduled time. He checked his phone for messages and considered giving Gretchen a call but decided against it. He needed to wait in the desolate silence of a place no one wanted to be, and he didn't want to project any of that on Gretchen. He'd call her later, once he met up with Tony.

Retired SDPD Detective Mayfield, a friend of all the Coronado SEAL teams, had told him, "He has the option of staying in a halfway house. They're more set up for former drug addicts, but compulsive gambling is an addiction. He probably should try to get into some place like that for his own good, but most people don't take to it very well. It prolongs the stink of detention, and, as soon as they're out, they want their freedom. It's not a good idea, but that doesn't figure into the calculation, Trace."

Trace knew Tony wanted to stay in his old home in Portland, overlooking the river—the house Gretchen and the girls lived in alone after the divorce. His former lady was long gone after his conviction, so he'd probably live alone.

"He can't come here, Trace," Gretchen had told him. "I don't want him anywhere near the girls, and I don't care what he promises," she'd said.

"I understand, honey. But, as far as not seeing the girls, we may not have the clout to make that happen. If he wants to come to San Diego and is granted permission, he'll be on probation for a while, but we may not be able to do anything about visitation if he keeps his nose clean. I'll do my best, though. First things first; we got to get this financial thing off his back."

"Agreed. Have you made contact with the realtor in Portland?" she asked.

"No, that'll be my first call if that's what he's thinking." He asked her if she thought highly of the lady who sold them the house in the first place.

"Well, it was years ago, before we were married, and she's still in business, so I suppose she'd be the logical choice. But I don't know if she's followed things and knows what is happening with him."

Trace figured it would be hard to miss. He was sure all the local papers would be filled with the tall tales of Tony Sanders, wunderkind-turned-devil. "I'll check her out, and, if Tony agrees, that's probably also something we'll do—put the house on the market. Do you have any idea what it's worth?"

Her answer was quick and a bit nasty. "It's not worth anything to me. I don't even want to look at it. It's probably a mess, since I think he's rented it out to some tenants. I'd say six, seven hundred maybe? I really don't know what the market's all about."

Tony was released a hundred yards from the last gate. Trace clenched and unclenched his fists and said a little prayer.

Here goes nothing. Come on, Tony. Be a man and make it easy for me. I don't want to be here anymore than you want me to see you this way. Let's get it over with so we can all move on with our lives.

He remembered, when Gretchen kissed him goodbye, her message was brief, but stirring.

"Please be careful, my love. Come back to me soon. But watch your back. Nothing in Tony's world makes any sense or is very safe. Proceed like you're walking into a war zone; then, if you don't come under fire, you'll be pleasantly surprised."

I got you, Gretchen. Don't worry. It'll all be fine.

Tony's tall and now beefier form still had that cocky swagger he used to have years ago when he was actively playing ball for the Trailblazers. Trace figured he'd probably practiced some, maybe showed off a bit, but being incarcerated for these years didn't do anything to dampen his ego or his cockiness. That was a bad sign.

His sweatpants were brand new and baggy, and he wore high-top tennis shoes, not professional athletic shoes. He'd tucked his laces into his shoes and they had come undone and sloppy looking. He had on an oversized grey sweatshirt that was probably also prison issue, and, though it was huge across his chest and belly, the arms were about four inches too short.

All 6'6" of Tony reported behind the secure yard fencing. As if called to attention, his chin defiantly raised to the heavens, squinting at Trace and waiting for the gates to slowly roll open.

He slung his bag over his shoulder to the tune of the tired, old wheels carrying the gate, stepped up to Trace, and stuck out his hand for a shake.

"Thanks for coming, man. I know this was probably one of the last things in the world you wanted to do, but I just want you to know I appreciate it. You're a stand-up guy, Trace."

"That's all right. We all make mistakes, Tony. What matters most is what we do with the rest of our lives. And you still have a lot of living to do. Besides, I didn't do it for *you*, and I think you know that. I did it for Gretchen and the girls."

He gave a "huh" in answer and then spat to the side.

"So let's get you set up, and let's see if we can move some mountains and get you started on a firm foundation."

"You able to bail me out?"

"Hell, no. I told you that already."

"Just checking to see if things had changed."

It pissed Trace off that Tony still had that cocky attitude after he'd thought perhaps the ex-convict was on a different trajectory.

"Look, I'm not able to contribute a dime to your care, but I can accompany you. But you're going to have to earn yourself out of this hole you've dug yourself into. I'm just here for—well, just consider me an Uber driver, okay?"

Tony shrugged, which showed Trace a lack of respect, surprising him slightly. He would've thought Tony would've been more contrite. But then he had to tell himself this was Gretchen's fucking ex, never a wise man and never able to control his emotions or his actions. Brilliantly talented, he'd still ruined his chance at a multimillion-dollar basketball career that could have set him up for life. That was going to weigh heavily on him as the days and months progressed.

The bigger they are, the harder they fall.

"Do you have to make a call to set up a meeting?" Trace asked him as they headed for the car.

"Already done. I got to go stop by a place down in the university district. There's supposed to be a bar this guy, my contact, owns. They passed me a message inside. I'm supposed to go there and schedule an appointment with some asshole who is expecting me to walk in with a wad of cash."

Trace was concerned about the setup. "You didn't tell anybody on the inside about your lack of funds, did you?"

"Not really. My cellmate knew, of course, but I don't think anybody really cared about what was going on with me. And I was limited to what I could do on the phone, so whatever calls they heard, they didn't hear anything about that."

"Well, you were pretty agitated when you talked to me a couple of days ago. If they heard any of that conversation, then there are a lot of people who know, Tony. Remember what I told you? You got to stop lying to yourself. You're in grave danger if you're into some bad people for a lot of money. Want to tell me how much it is?"

"Well, let's just say it's more than the house is worth or more than the equity I have in the house, but I'm hoping he'll give me some time."

Trace noted that Tony still wasn't coming clean. And, again, he was disappointed and knew there was another red flag waving in the wind waiting for the war to begin. He hated situations like this.

"So we're on to Eugene?" he asked.

"Yes, sir. It's called the Red Hook Cafe and Grill. Someplace downtown, the Hippie District."

Trace put it in his GPS, and it found a location, indicating it would be twenty-five minutes to arrival.

Tony turned in his seat to face him. "So how's the happy couple?"

"Well, they've made it to Hawaii. Sounds like Clover really loves it there. They've got a condo overlooking a golf course on the rainy side of Kauai."

"I know it well. It's a damn good golf course if it's on the North Shore."

"I wouldn't know, but they seem to like it. It's rained every day so far, but they're having a ball. Of course she talks to her mother more than me, but Jack's a good kid, and I think he has the cojones to make a good life for her."

"Well, that's good. I hope that maybe I can help them. If I can get onto a semi-pro team—we call 'em 'G League'—I might be able to earn a little bit of income, do some coaching maybe. First I got to get this jerk off my back."

As Trace drove down the highway and then turned off to the signs of Downtown Eugene, he asked Tony about how he got involved in gambling behind bars.

"Prison's got TVs. They've got ways of betting on games. I mean, that's all we do is watch games, because the classes are shit. I'm never going to fucking learn how to take apart a motor or cook. I don't want to learn how to bake bread or peel carrots, for Christ's sake. The only thing I like to do is read magazines and watch the sports games. We were not really restricted so it was easy to make bets, even though we couldn't do it online, so the fees were high, and payout was difficult."

"Yeah? How do you handle that?"

"Two ways. First, you can get your wife to bring in some for conjugal visits, but you took care of that, Trace."

"Like I said, this isn't my rodeo, Tony."

"Other way is more expensive. The pros do it the second way."

Trace thought to himself that, of course, Tony thought he was one of the pros. And that nearly told him the whole story. Tony's ego wouldn't let him NOT gamble like a pro. They nailed him on that, Trace suspected. He'd fallen for it, and it would cost him.

"The pros, you gotta be worth something to do the deal this way. Gotta settle up after you get out, and that brings with it a whole other set of problems. There were also protection scams. Some guys were worth a lot of money if they paid out in the end. You get in with somebody and they protect you, for a fee, so you don't get knifed before you pay."

It hurt his heart to say it, but Trace couldn't resist.

"Sort of like the honor system, except with ridiculous interest rates, right?"

"Yeah, you gotta be approved for it. Only a few get that plan. If somebody was worth a lot of money but of course didn't have it, there could be things done on the outside to pressure them to pay up. It's a big racket just like it is anywhere. More dangerous though. The guards, they all knew what we were doing, and they didn't care really. As long as nobody got hurt."

"And how long did it take to rack up this huge bundle you won't divulge? I take it that it's more than the cost of a new Bentley?"

"Well, I was doing pretty well there. I was actually a couple hundred thousand ahead, but, all of a sudden, things changed in year four when it looked like these guys were able to secure me a spot on one of the eastern amateur teams of a big club. There was going to be a signing bonus, which would give me plenty of money to live on for the next few years if I was careful. All of a sudden, I started losing, and that bonus, if it ever really was there, got eaten up in less than a year. I think they saw me as a paycheck."

"Tony, that's always the way they treat you. Those guys always see suckers who bet on their games as paychecks. They win more than they lose. That's how come it's so lucrative. And people will take a chance at things when they're desperate. I'm sorry you didn't get some counseling or some help with that. Don't you have an attorney? A probation officer? They should have intervened."

"Story of my life, Trace. That was one thing my last coach told me just before I packed up my locker. He told me I would've been a much better player if I would've listened and been coachable. Hell, I played more basketball than that guy ever did and he was twice as old as I am. But I do have a habit of kind of learning my own way."

Trace turned off the highway toward downtown, noting how much seedier the stores and shops and houses looked the closer they got to the university. Protest signs were common on front lawns or draped on hand-painted posters hanging from the front porches. Unlike most of San Diego, the young college-age students dressed in colorful clothing with brightly colored hair, elaborate tats, a variety of piercings, and all sorts of styles. It was almost déjà vu for Trace, who had seen pictures of San Francisco during the Haight-Ashbury times, and this reminded him of those photos he had seen in an old Life magazine.

They pulled up to the Red Hook Cafe and Grill, and he accompanied Tony inside. The interior was so dark Trace wished he had night vision goggles to flip on, and he paused a couple of minutes to let his eyes adjust. A lone guitar player sat on a small stage in the right-hand corner of the dive. Hardly anyone in the audience in front of him was paying attention and—this being the middle of the afternoon—more than likely the spectators wouldn't improve until after dark. Tony sauntered up to the bar and asked the bartender his question.

"I am supposed to ask for Sam. I guess he's the owner of this place?"

The bartender nodded as he polished a shot glass and set it down. His face was bright red with a bulbous nose that screamed alcoholic like a neon sign.

"You guys want something to drink?"

"Not for me, thanks," said Trace quickly.

But not Tony. "Sure, this on the house?" His cocky manner hadn't been turned down one notch.

"You got to be fucking kidding me. You're here to see the boss and you're asking if it's on the house? I don't know you from anybody. Your money's as good here as anybody else's. It will be ten bucks for a beer, for you."

"Ten bucks! That's robbery."

"Well, that's because you kind of dissed the owner. Better not do that around here very much. These guys bite. When you were inside, didn't anybody teach you any manners? You don't go walking up to people in the box and treat them like that. Why would you do that here?"

"I'm sorry, man. I'm new to all this."

The bartender nodded his head and gave a smirk, then studied Trace, and angled his head back, examining Tony again. "I said you better be careful. These guys bite. You don't want to get bit by these guys."

Tony looked at Trace. "Can I borrow ten bucks?"

And so it began. Trace pulled out a twenty and handed it to Tony, who handed it over to the bartender. He got a light beer on tap, and the bartender didn't give him change.

"Mmm," Tony said after he took a sip. "The best fucking beer I've ever had."

Trace was going to have to have a talk with Tony. He was going in all the wrong directions and pissing off all the wrong people. He nudged Gretchen's ex. "Can I have a word? Let's take your beer over to the corner. I need to talk to you." To the bartender, Trace said, "I'll have another beer for another ten, and I'm sorry, sir, but there's no room for a tip."

The bartender handed Trace his light beer on tap, his face expressionless.

Trace thanked him and asked, "And are we going to be meeting this guy, Sam, or what's the program here?"

"I already messaged him. He'll be on his way ... ten, fifteen minutes maybe. You just go have a seat. He'll find you."

Trace headed to the opposite corner from the singer so he could give Tony some advice, if he was up for it.

"Tony, the bartender's right, and you're taking offense before you're even engaging. Remember that, when you're walking into battle, the enemy gets a vote. It's their territory. They know what they're doing, and they already have a plan and a strategy. You're walking into something, and you don't know what you're walking into, so you can't afford to be cocky or piss off somebody. So you better just swallow your pride and get with the program. Otherwise, you're going to get yourself in worse shape than before. There's a limit to what I can do. And I will not be dragged into your shit. As much as I want to help you for the sake of Gretchen and the girls, I'm not going to be mired in your mess. So don't do that anymore, or I'm out of here, and you can find your own way home, wherever that is."

"I just didn't like him taking advantage of us."

"It's not the greatest injustice in the world. You have to pick your battles carefully. You understand?"

Tony nodded.

"Why do you think they wanted to meet you here? This is their turf. You have no say in the matter. You gave up all your rights when you overextended yourself, when you paid them their ridiculous fees, when you agreed to pay them back and couldn't control yourself from losing more money. You gave up your rights. You have no rights here. They're letting you live. They're letting you in their establishment so they can fleece you some more. So, get ready. Because that's what they're going to do."

"How do you know so much about these people?"

"Look, Tony, I've seen evildoers all over the world. They don't change their stripes. They don't start out being assholes and then all of a sudden get real nice and reasonable. They get worse. So it's not to your advantage to piss them off."

"I just don't want them to think I'm afraid of them. They don't scare me."

"Well, now you're being downright stupid. Don't you remember that phone call you made to us? You were scared out of your pants. Don't sit there and tell me you're not afraid of them. You should be afraid. And, if you're not, you're even stupider than I thought."

"I just think I've got a certain amount of pride left. I got big plans to turn my life around. I just don't want them to think they're dealing with some spineless creature that is like all the other losers they work with."

Trace started to chuckle, shaking his head in disbelief. "All they deal with are losers, Tony. And you're at the top of the list. You're the biggest loser of them all. You gave up an NBA career, for what? What was the payoff for you so you could do it your way? So what are you going to do if they decide, okay, you can't pay us back? Maybe we'll just take a couple of your fingers or take your life or maybe hassle one of your kids? Have you ever thought about that?"

"Yeah, I've thought about that. I am not going to let that happen. I'm not complete scum."

"I want to believe you. I really do."

Trace and Tony exchanged a stern study of each of their characters. What Trace saw in Tony's eyes was total capitulation. He wondered if he had some kind of a suicide or death wish. And did that mean that Trace had just gotten himself in one hell of a mess?

"You just keep control of your emotions, Tony. If you think you have to show some of that bravado, sit on it like a fart when you're out with a pretty girl instead. Just be quiet, and let them do the talking. After we know what the plan is, then we'll know how to react. You're going to want to get the house on the market right away, and we should get up to Portland and do that. The sooner you can get them something, the better, and you're going to need some money to live on. You got anything else you can sell, liquidate?"

"I got a Bentley convertible, but it's been in storage all this time. Hasn't been run. I might be able to get seventy or eighty thousand for it. It's a sweet little machine, or it was."

"Okay, they set you up with any retirement plan or anything like that on the team?"

"No. Most of that went toward my legal fees. When I was done with the trial, I didn't have much of that left, and I was docked some early penalties, and I still owe a tax bill, but they've given me forbearance until I'm out."

"How much do you owe the IRS then?"

"It's about a hundred. Hundred and fifty maybe now."

Trace glanced at his side. How could one man so singlehandedly mess up his life by accident? No, Trace thought, this wasn't by accident. It was on purpose. Tony was on some kind of death mission, and that meant he was extremely dangerous.

"Well, first, we find out what's the deal here, and then we make our plan. Do you know this guy Sam at all or some of his colleagues?"

"No, they had a whole board of directors at the prison. I only worked through them. They told me Sam would get me hooked up with who I needed to talk to. I don't even know what this guy looks like."

Just then, a heavyset gentleman who wasn't more than five feet tall walked into the bar. His shirt opened one button too far, revealing a gold coin encrusted in gold filigree hanging around his beefy neck. He wore cowboy boots, which made him look like a small pixie, not a cowboy. His blue western-style shirt matched his jeans. But he did have an expensive haircut and fresh shave, and he headed right for their table.

Tony stood up to shake the man's hand, and Sam motioned him to stay put.

"You stand up like that, son, and I'll shoot you right there. That's an aggressive action. I kill people who do that."

Trace knew he was dealing with a pure amateur.

"So don't do that to me. You sit. Now, how much money did you bring with you today?"

CHAPTER 4

GRETCHEN AND KATE gathered at a restaurant to have breakfast, sending off their parents. Mr. and Mrs. Morgan lived in Palo Alto up north, and it was a long one-day drive for them.

"It was such a lovely wedding, Gretchen. You should be proud of yourself," said Mrs. Morgan. Her husband, Joe, seconded that.

"I've never seen her look so beautiful, sweetheart. She was just glowing. She looked like she'd been out in the sun, had a nice tan on her face," he added.

Gretchen knew that was from all the crying that Trace had interrupted shortly before Clover walked down the aisle. But she wasn't going to reveal her daughter's secret.

"I really think they'll be happy, Mom. Jack seems like a wonderful guy for her. He's going to be okay with her being headstrong, sometimes negative at times. She works hard, and so does he."

"What's this I hear about him perhaps wanting to join the Navy?" asked her dad.

Kate turned and stared back at her. "Oh my God. I didn't know that. Is that a real thing?"

"Well, I guess he discussed it with Trace, but, hey, you guys aren't even supposed to know about this. We don't even know if Clover has been asked, so we certainly don't want to create a scenario where the whole family knows it before she does. If she doesn't agree, both Trace and I will counsel him that he shouldn't go. But, if he enlists, we'll give them our full support, so all we can do is wait."

"She told one of her bridesmaids that her dad called her before she walked down the aisle and apologized for not being there," whispered her mom.

Gretchen shrugged, trying to appear casual about something that bothered her a great deal. "Yeah, well, we've had years to get used to that. Now he starts wanting to hang around, when he needs something. He's due to get out soon, and, well, it's just not going to be easy for all of us. So pray for us, Mom and Dad, please. Please pray for us."

"You got it, kiddo. Any of my cop buddies in Palo Alto, I'll let them know about it too, because if he's going to be hanging around your family at all, I'm going to let them know he's not to be trusted. I still don't trust him, and I don't think I ever will." Joe's face darkened with concern.

"It's not for me to say," Kate began, "but you and Mom taught us about forgiveness. And when we can, we should."

Gretchen knew her mother would react negatively to that and wished her younger sister hadn't mentioned it.

Louise stiffened her back. "No way. There's forgiveness, and then there's being stupid about it. I think we'll never trust him. You might forgive him, but I would never trust him to be alone with the girls. Surely, he isn't going to request that, is he?" Louise asked her.

"I don't think so. And, of course, being a convicted felon, there's no way he would get full custody or even partial custody. It's going to be supervised visitations, if anything at all. Of course, that's assuming the girls want to see him. Angie might a little bit, because she was quite young when all of this happened and he was sent away, but I don't think Rebecca would. And Clover, well, she's got Jack now, and I'm pretty sure Jack wouldn't like it either. So I think we're okay. It's Angie I probably have to watch out for the most."

"Hey, where is Trace anyway?" asked Joe Morgan.

Gretchen looked up at Kate before she answered. "Actually, I should have told you to begin with. He's gone up to Portland to help Tony get situated. He's being released today."

"Oh my Lord, just when I thought everything was going to be smooth sailing for a while, this little thing gets thrown in," her mother complained.

"Well, that's kind of why Trace is there. I mean, who else in the family could handle it? And, apparently, there are some loose ends that Tony needs to tie up. He owns the house outright, so he'll probably have to sell it and possibly sell some other assets as well to have money to live on. I doubt there'll be a chance any team in the NBA, even a nonprofessional training club, would take him. Maybe he could get a coaching job somewhere if it didn't require a background check, but anywhere on the West Coast, that would be difficult. Still, there's always a possibility someone would give him a chance somewhere. Perhaps a private school coaching job or athletic director. He does have a college degree and was well thought of in the day. Had quite the following. He would make a good coach. But the rest of his life is a hurricane. And I don't think it's getting better."

"You think he'd learn his lesson, that knucklehead," said Joe.

"Well, they always say 'you can lead a horse to water but you can't make him drink.' He had all these years to think about what he'd done and to try to make amends with himself, other people, but he really didn't reach out much. I thought, at first, he was just embarrassed for his behavior and maybe a little bit irritated that I'd moved on so quickly, but I've come around to the conclusion he just doesn't have the capacity to be caring for anybody other than himself. And that's sad, because he wasn't at all the guy I thought he was or the guy I first met. Remember those days?" Gretchen asked the table.

"Oh, I was so enamored with him. This big, tall, handsome basketball player all the girls wanted to be around. Of course, later, I learned about all that happened," said Kate.

"Not to mention all his extracurricular activities and his gambling problems."

Gretchen looked at her father after his comment.

"You knew he had gambling problems way back then?"

"I heard a couple of my buddies talking about how he was doing some interviews for an online gaming platform, talking about betting on games, and he was sort of a spokesperson for some group that was trying to get subscribers. I just assumed that he was doing that maybe to pay off some debts. That's a lot of times what athletes do. And they're not supposed to bet on their games or professional league games of any kind, but he sure was into it. We know it's an addiction. He *looked* like a gambler to me."

Gretchen thought that was interesting and pondered it carefully. This would be something she wanted to let Trace know about. Perhaps the people involved in the online gaming were also the ones he bought from.

Louise Morgan slapped her husband on the shoulder. "Well, Joe, I guess we better be on the road. I'm stuffed to the gills. I said my good-byes before Angie left for her game. And I said goodbye to Rebecca last night. I wish we could have stayed long enough to see Clover come home safely, but that's the luck of the draw, isn't it? Have her call your dad and me, okay? I'd like to hear all about the honeymoon. We also have a special wedding present we want to give them."

"Oh, thanks, Mom. I'll do just that. I don't think she's posting any-thing on Facebook, and Trace kind of schooled her on that—no TikTok either, not letting the whole world know they were young newlyweds on their own, but I'm sure she'll take lots of pictures and send them to you when she can. Don't worry, you'll see them. I haven't seen any either, but I have talked to her once, and she's having a blast."

"She was talking about snorkeling and doing some paddleboarding," Kate added.

"Yes, and she collects shells too. I know she's loving it. Away from Mom and Dad, they get to do the moonlight strolls down the beach, the little umbrella drinks out on the lanai. I have fond memories of Trace and I doing the same thing. But, of course, we weren't married then."

"Well, kiddo, your secret's safe with me. I don't know if you've told the girls all the details, but I ain't saying a single thing," said Joe.

"Thanks, Dad."

Kate and Gretchen walked them to their car, waving them off, and then left in Kate's car, heading to her house. They had about three hours before they had to pick up the kids. Kate's were at a birthday party for one of the SEAL kids who was new to the area.

"More coffee?"

"Oh, gosh, I'll never get to bed tonight if I do. I'll take some water, though."

"Coming right up."

The two of them sat in Kate's living room. She had decorated it with posters of Chez Panisse and other famous restaurants and little Parisian bistros she'd collected over the years. Some were truly vintage advertisements for restaurants long gone from all over the world. It was an eclectic and colorful room and reminded Gretchen of Kate's mother-in-law, Deirdre Gray. A well-known artist in Portland, most of her paintings had been destroyed in a fire in the Warehouse District several months ago, and they had moved down to temporary quarters in the Coronado area.

Kate told her Tyler's parents would've been invited to the breakfast this morning, but they were taking a gardening course.

"Gardening? So they're learning that now?"

"Well, sort of goes along with our plans, Gretchen. A beautiful wedding center, gallery, and event location, like we talked."

Gretchen smiled at the thought of Deirdre and Mr. Gray getting on their knees digging out weeds and planting flowers. Coronado was a special place and very easy to grow things, even citrus and bananas. She hadn't had the time, but she fantasized about Kate's wonderful ideas of opening a catering business housed at the center.

"What are you thinking about? You're smiling. I'll bet you're thinking about Trace," said Kate.

"No, I actually was thinking about your in-laws. Looking at the walls of your living room, I could almost feel Deirdre's presence here even though they don't live in this house. Can't wait to see what they find."

"I know. We are kindred spirits. And you get along with her too, right?" asked Kate.

"She's so much fun. I don't think I've ever met someone so full of life, and she wears her clothes and her big beads and jewelry and her hair things like she's a walking canvas. I'm glad to see she's moving on, and I really think she'll be a good partner for your little venture."

"I want to make sure you're okay with all of this, because I don't want to do this without you."

Gretchen frowned.

"I don't know how good I am at all this stuff, but I'm certainly willing to help. I mean, you usually want partners for two things, first for their money, and second for their talents. I don't think I have either of them."

"That's not true. I think you have a very good business sense, and I always run things by you that are financial. Gretchen, you know that. I trust your judgment. You read people really well. You were the one who warned me about Randy, and then you warned me about getting involved with Tyler before my engagement was over with Randy."

Gretchen nodded her head. "Yep, and, as for me, I made my choice, and he was the first person I fell in love with, and Tony was a total dud. Nice at first, but he turned out to be a wolf in sheep's clothing. Trace was only my second boyfriend. I don't shop around a lot, do I? Is that a good thing?"

"The best. You are an excellent study of people. And you know who the good ones are. I'm so happy you met Trace."

"And he came along at just the right time too. God love him. I never expected to fall in love again or to fall in love so hard. He says the same. Second time love is the best."

"No arguments from me. Oh! I almost forgot! We took Deirdre's VW van, and I found a little upholstery guy here who does wonderful things to the interiors. We made up a color scheme, Deirdre and I, and she drew out what we thought we'd like to have the interior look like— the cabinets, how the kitchen would work, place for seating and food prep. We have to install a stove, more like a griddle, storage for supplies, a refrigerator, and tiny all-in-one bathroom. We have a lot to do to meet current food selling standards. If we were just keeping it private, we wouldn't have to do so much. But look at these."

Kate showed Gretchen some of the sketches Deirdre had done for them. The cute little Volkswagen van with the ten light windows on top was outfitted in the drawing with yellow and white polka dot curtains. The interior appeared a beautiful blush pink color with light-stained cabinetry. The outside of the van would be repainted a very pale green. It all looked very fresh and sporty, and it suited Kate's energy and her ideas.

"This is what your bedroom looked like when we were growing up, remember? Same colors and everything."

"I know!"

"These are fabulous. You have any idea how much it will cost?" asked Gretchen.

"Well, hopefully, it won't be more than about fifty. Tyler thinks it'll go higher, but this little guy is going to give me a really good price. He does custom seating arrangements for restaurants with his signature tuck and roll. Works restoring old cars too. He's sort of a car buff, and most of the local car collectors hire him to restore interiors for shows. He's quite famous in the industry."

"What a find."

"He's very busy, but he kind of likes the idea of working on a food truck. I think he'll probably get business off it. Who knows? We could be opening up a new type of collectors' car! 'Food Truck Specials,' we could call it. What do you think?"

"Wow, I bet his shop is just awesome. It would be fun to see his work."

"No, not awesome at all. It looks like a typical garage mixed with a tailor shop, scraps of leather and leatherette all over the floor. He's got about ten tables and several full-time seamstresses, plus one apprentice he's hoping will take over his business someday. He has enough for someone to work full-time just maintaining the leather sewing machines and the other equipment they've got."

"I'm impressed."

"They are patenting a stamper, so they can do embossed work, and also a pattern cutter, instead of having to hand cut everything. But right now, except for the stitching, which is all done with machine, most of the rest of his work is done completely by hand. And he can custom do wood framing and detail work on the inside as well as metal accessories on the outside. Deirdre came up with the idea of a bumper in the back that highlights the name of the food truck."

"I can't wait to see the vision. You've got a winner there, Kate."

"I think the guy's really, really talented. He told me I should get a bigger van, so Tyler and I have been looking at old plumber's trucks, utility vans, you know, the kind that have built-in shelves?"

"Oh, yes. You know Mom used to tell us about Edy, the vegetable man, who used to come down the street and sell to all the housewives back then. His truck was painted up in bright boho decorations. The fruits and vegetables were all boxed in colorful little crates."

"I don't remember those stories. It was probably before my time. But

I wouldn't be surprised."

Gretchen checked her phone. "I think I need to go. Friday traffic."

"Hey, Gretchen, let's go look at spaces when you get free. Let me know. We can pick up Deirdre and do a little girl exploration. How does that sound?"

"I could use some distraction right now. That would be fun. Do you think Deirdre is free today?"

"When will Trace be home?"

"I'm not sure. Supposed to call me tonight."

"Maybe Angie could babysit over here while we go?"

"I'll ask her. I'm sure it would be okay. Her schedule with her practices and coaching the little ones is pretty full, but I don't think she had plans today. I can ask."

They hugged before each making a call. Gretchen knew she was going to go to bed tonight with colorful images floating around her brain, probably keeping her up way past her bedtime. But it would be a welcome distraction to replace the worry in her heart with the chance of such a colorful future.

CHAPTER 5

TRACE DIDN'T TRUST one hair on Sam's body, and he had a lot of hairs to choose from, even protruding from his nose. His beefy presence was not menacing as far as people went. He was used to seeing oddballs on deployments, but there was just something about the man he didn't like or trust. Not that Trace would ever like any of Tony's friends. Sam seemed like the type of guy who would just as soon steal your food as rip you open with a knife. He was that casual about the way he dressed, about the way he talked. Plus, everyone around him exhibited fear, which told Trace he'd probably done his fair share of murder and mayhem, and he wasn't anyone to fuck with.

"So who's your asshole friend here, Tony?" he asked Tony.

Trace noted that he talked to Gretchen's ex as if he'd known him for a long time.

"Sam?" Tony asked, caught off guard.

"No, fucking Santa Claus, you asshole. I asked you a question, and I want an answer. Who the hell is this guy?"

Trace started to speak, and Sam cut him off with a hand to the face.

"No, I said him. I want you to tell me, Tony."

"This is my ex's new husband. This is Trace. Trace meet Sam."

"No, I said who *is* this guy? Like who *is* he? Who is he to *you*? It ain't right that you're hanging around with your ex-wife's new boyfriend or husband or whatever he is. I need an explanation, Tony."

"I brought him for backup. I didn't know what I was running into here. Trace is a member of the military. He's a Navy man." Trace was glad Tony didn't mention he was a SEAL.

Sam looked him up and down but didn't ask him to stand. Of course, he noted Trace's tats on his forearms and then peered with dark, beady eyes right into Trace's. These types of men often measured bravado by whether or not he blinked, so Trace decided to let the guy off the hook and blinked early. This wasn't the time for a show of strength. That seemed to satisfy Sam that he was dealing with someone who wasn't as violent or dangerous as he was, and he liked that thought.

That made him very, very dangerous.

"So, Trace, you packin'?"

"No, sir. You can check if you like."

"No, thanks. But don't try anything here. So, Tony, I guess, has told you about his little situation?" He finally sat down at the table and turned toward the bartender, summoning him over.

"Yes, sir, what would you like, gentlemen?" the bartender asked after he scurried over.

"I'll take a whiskey," Sam said. He gestured to Trace and Tony.

"A whiskey will be fine for me too," said Trace.

"You can make that three," Tony added.

"Okay, so we have some numbers to throw out, my calculations are somewhere in the range of $950,000. Is that about what you came up with?"

Trace whistled in spite of himself. After all, any normal person would have the same reaction, and it didn't seem like a good idea to pretend that that chunk of change was easy to get.

"Holy shit, Tony, you didn't tell me it was that much."

Sam blurted out, "So you're lying to your friends too? You lie to your ex? I know you lied to the guys inside. I had to pay off some of them. They were damn angry you didn't pay up."

"I couldn't. Everything was tied up."

"Well, now you're out, and now you can be of use to me. You are going to get me the money. Let's talk about that, the important stuff."

"Well, here's the thing, Sam. All my money is tied up in the house. I have a few things I can sell, but I don't know how much the house will get, but it's free and clear, so I'll sell it and give you whatever I can get."

"Okay, so that's going to take three or four months. That's longer than a hundred days, right?"

"What's the hundred days?" Tony asked.

"It's what you promised my committee in the joint. You can't do that?"

"I can get you maybe fifty thousand, go get a line of credit, and bring you that in a few days, I think. I don't think I can get you more than that, because I'm basically unemployed, and I'm a felon, and I don't have a job."

It was the first time Trace saw that Tony was actually telling the truth.

"Okay, so you think you can get me the fifty grand within a week?"

"Yes, sir, I do."

"If you don't, you're going to lose a finger. I'll let you choose the finger, but I don't think it'd be a very good idea for you to be minus a digit if you're planning to play any kind of basketball ever again, do you?"

Trace saw Tony's face go completely white. "I'm a man of my word, sir. I'll get you the money. I should be good for it. There's tons of equity in the house."

"And because you're not paying me within a hundred days, unless you can do that, the interest is twenty percent a month, so in four months, five months, six months, you're going to owe a hell of a lot more than 950K. What are you going to do for the rest?"

"I have no means of earning income. Teachers or coaches, they don't pay anything, and I can't get a job in a regular school because they don't hire felons. I'm all ears. I can work for you if you like."

The bartender brought over the whiskey, and Sam's face lit up with delight. He threw his back in one large gulp and slammed the glass back on the table. He clapped his hands together and rubbed them, smiling with a huge Cheshire-type grin. "Now we're talking, I've got some special plans for you. So we keep on this schedule, you get me that fifty thou by … I'll give you ten days, okay? After that, it starts getting bloody. I don't like bloody, especially in my establishment here, but, after you get the house on the market and you get an offer, I want to see what you're going to be netting, and I want to make sure you give me all of it. I don't have to tell you that it's in your best interest to get the house sold quickly. We'll see what's left afterwards. I don't want to promise right now, but I've got some really good ideas how you and I can make some money."

"Is it legal?" Tony asked.

Trace sipped his whiskey and squirmed. He knew, of course, it wasn't legal. And it was only going to entrench Tony further in this guy's clutches.

"Sam, if I may?" Trace asked.

"No, but go ahead anyways."

"Is this money owed to you? What guarantee is there that he pays you off and someone else doesn't come after Tony for the money. Do you have something that proves it's your debt?"

"You obviously don't do this for a living, do you?"

"Obviously."

"The reason it's my money is that I'm gonna kill him if he doesn't deliver it. Now, does that clear things up for you?"

"Partly. If he pays you off, then he's free to go, no strings?"

"Where are your brains? He's done when I say he's done. You see, I'm the aggrieved party here. He's shown me no respect. If he plays by my rules, he gets off, but not until I say so. Now, if you don't mind, don't ask me any more fuckin' questions."

"It's okay, Trace," Tony mumbled.

"So now you're standing up for him? Tony, we're going to have to have some serious discussions about protocol. Or, maybe your ex wants this guy to get you shot. Did you ever think about that?"

"No, she wouldn't—"

"Jesus Fuckin' Christ. I think you're about the dumbest motherfucker I've ever met. Wake up and smell the coffee. The whole fuckin' world's for sale. You can do anything you want as long as you pay the price."

"Okay, got it."

"So back to whether or not it's legal. That's in the eye of the beholder. May not be exactly legal, but it'd be pretty hard to prove. You've got a lot of information, inside information about trades, and you got friends still, I'm sure. Some of that information leaks out, some of that information could be useful to me as far as placing my bets."

"Sam, I've been out of the game for a number of years, and none of my teammates have ever visited me. I'm pretty sure they don't want anything to do with me."

"Well, you're going to have to try then. You're going to have to try to make the rounds, see what you can find out about your old team. And, in a way, it's reasonable, because you're looking for a job, right? Ask your old coach if you can be the ball boy for Chrissake."

Trace rolled his eyes. He knew instantly it was a mistake.

"You've got a problem with that, Grandpa?" Sam asked him.

"You mean, do I think it's likely that a professional basketball player could turn around and be the ball boy for the team he used to play for? Is that what you're wondering about, Sam? I thought you were smarter than that." Trace knew he had to keep it light, but he just couldn't help himself.

"I see your friend has more sense than you do. So we'll find something for you to do, but I want you to get back into someone's good graces on the team. Maybe not the Portland team, maybe Sacramento, San Francisco. I don't know. I just want inside information, and that's how you're going to pay off the rest."

"Sounds kind of nonspecific. Can you give me any details?"

"You wearing a wire or are you just stupid?"

"No wire. Like him, you can check."

Sam stood up, and, for a second, Trace thought he was going to slap Tony across the chops. He took a turn, inhaled deeply, and then sat down, folding his hands in front of him on the table.

"We have a problem, unless you wind up with a sugar daddy who gives you all the money. Then we don't have a problem. You pay, you stay. You don't pay, you are permanently retired, and painfully."

Sam looked over at Trace. "I'd be kicking myself all over the place if I didn't ask. Are you his sugar daddy, Trace?"

"No, sir. I'm on military pay only, no side jobs, and my wife doesn't work. We're supporting one in college and one going to college. There's no money in my family to donate to this cause."

Sam scratched his beard, winced a little bit, and nodded his head, thinking. "I got you. I like your style, Mr. Military Man. I think you and I should talk some more about our futures together."

CHAPTER 6

K ATE, GRETCHEN, AND Deirdre spent the afternoon pouring over some of Deirdre's plans for a space she and Kate had discovered in a warehouse district close to the beach where new recruits for the SEALs traditionally trained.

"I love the idea that we can grow lots of beautiful gardens—flowers, flowering trees, veggies, and herbs—and also host wedding receptions inside or out that take place on the beach since it's so close," said Deirdre.

"It's really a perfect spot," Gretchen agreed. "I've driven through that area."

"I see festive and decorated golf carts and open-air buses shuttling guests to and from," said Deirdre. "The space has two stories, and, with a tilted roof, you have some really nice light coming in during the day or starlight for evening receptions. The walls are perfect for displaying paintings and other artwork. It's a painter's dream!" she added.

"I'd like to take a look if you've got time," Gretchen said.

Kate was enthusiastic for the idea. "Let's do that. And I'd like to show you what our little upholstery guy has come up with. We thought it would be kind of cute to have a soda fountain and ice cream store at the east end, set up for kids' parties and fifties-themed events. We'd have connected music boxes on the tables in booths with plastic padded seats in all the ice cream colors. He made a mock-up of one of the booths and several tables bordering in a retro metal trim, making it look just like an old-fashioned soda fountain. I can't wait to show it to you, Gretchen," said Kate.

The three ladies arranged for Angie to babysit Kate's younger ones and then took off on their adventure. Sunday mornings on Coronado were always mood-enhancing for Gretchen, and it was no different today.

Just as it had been described, Gretchen saw a long, warehouse-type building that even had a grain elevator on the inside, which she noted could be fixed up to serve customers on both floors since Deirdre had designed the interior so there was a second-floor ring that rimmed the building on the inside.

When she stepped farther inside the nearly five thousand square foot space, through the double glass doors, it felt like walking into a church of possibilities. "Listen to the acoustics in here. Boy, you could do some musical events that would be outstanding."

Deirdre gestured up. "From the second floor, if we add some side windows and doors and maybe a few small balconies on the outside just big enough for a couple of tables and chairs, you can actually see the ocean from the building. That's a million-dollar view from up top," said Deirdre, pointing to the ceiling.

"There's your way up," Gretchen said, pointing to the metal basket elevator standing near the wall on the south side. "You could design some wonderful metal sculptures for that thing," she mused.

Kate jumped in. "This being a steel structure, there's nothing in the middle to interfere, and no structural walls would have to be built. We're just talking about interior walls for the kitchen. Perhaps we buttress them against the elevator, add a classroom or demonstration kitchen, and make a place for storage as well as an office. We even thought about putting in an apartment upstairs for an office manager or caretaker at some future date. You and Larry could live here temporarily if you wanted to, although it's not the size nor the scope of what you're used to, but it would work for temporary."

"I like that idea, if we can get out of our lease. I'll see what Larry says. I love living inside my art. It's the *only* way to experience it!" she answered.

Kate demonstrated where they considered putting the soda fountain and booths, a sanded concrete dance floor extending the entire length of the building, which would expose the aggregate pebbles, enhanced with color. She indicated where the killer sound system would be housed, along with a small stage for performances. On the west side, with added windows and doors leading out to the patio and gardens, it would be perfect for sit-down dinners, wine tasting, and afternoon wedding receptions.

The more Gretchen looked at the space, the more excited she got.

They continued around the building as Kate showed Gretchen the property lines extending back nearly two hundred feet. "There's room for parking, and the lot to the back is also available."

"Amazing," was all Gretchen could think of to say.

"I'd like to put in some raised beds and grow our own vegetables," said Kate. "Maybe eventually we could have a cooking school here, but this area would be great for the catering trucks, getting them under a carport system that would also support solar panels. And the raised beds on sprinklers would allow us to grow all our herbs and vegetables for the business, maybe even set up a retail country store, even get a fruit orchard going, although that will take some years to develop," she squealed.

Gretchen gave her bouncing sister a hug. She hadn't seen Kate this excited since she'd discovered she was pregnant years ago. "I can see it all just as if it was finished. What a beautiful space and concept. When do you put the offer in?"

Deirdre shrugged. "It's in the insurance company's hands now. The adjuster is getting ready with his final numbers. Once we know what we have to work with—and we've already received some of the funds for our living expenses down here—but once we know for sure, then we'll know what we can offer. The property's been for sale for over a year, and there have not been any interested parties, so I think now is a good time to jump on it."

Gretchen noted the neighborhood was very tidy, especially for an industrial district with mostly existing cinder-block buildings painted with colorful murals built during World War II. At that time, arched ceilings, Quonset hut type open truss-beamed buildings were the style, and several had been car dealerships at one time. But now, most of the structures were light manufacturing or industrial companies occupying them, small operations that needed the space for production and storage. One of the neighbors was a wholesale nursery that sold palm trees and other tropical citrus and greenery.

Further down the road was the infamous flesh skin graphics, the tattoo parlor Kate said most of the SEAL Team 3 guys went. "It has a dubious reputation, of course, not sure if you've heard, sis."

That made Gretchen curious. "Single SEAL stories?" she asked timidly.

"Sacred ground. They have good memories of those days, as it should be."

Gretchen had an idea. "I think if you're able to buy the building and start the business, we should choose a logo and all of us get a matching tattoo maybe on our wrist or forearm somewhere. What do you think about that?"

"Like the guys do on SEAL Team 3," Kate agreed.

"Well, I don't have one yet. I guess, once you get over seventy years of age, it's about time, right?" said Deirdre.

"I love the idea," said Kate. "That's going to be your job, designing the logo. What should we call it?"

"Bone Frog something. Has to have that in the name," Gretchen suggested.

"Bone Frog Art and Garden Center?" added Deirdre. "But I think that's too long."

"Bone Frog Center. Just keep it simple. You could do a spin on the bone frog logo, maybe put flowers on her head … has to be a her," added Kate.

"I see T-shirts in our future," said Gretchen.

Next, they visited Jose's upholstery shop, which was on the other side of Coronado, a little bit north of the base. Also in an industrial district, instead of light manufacturing and commercial storage units this area was filled with auto body shops and engine repair and overhaul auto repair shops. It was not a particularly good part of town, unlike the warehouse they were considering purchasing. But it was a car-lover's haven with dismantled vehicles, including abandoned school buses, trucks, and classic clunkers just about everywhere they looked. For those who loved collecting and tinkering with old cars, it was truly paradise.

Jose greeted them as they walked through the roll-up door into his kingdom. He was wiping his hands on an oily rag.

"*Buenos días, señora,*" he said to Kate.

"This is my older sister, Gretchen, and you already know Deirdre, my mother-in-law."

Jose held up his dirty hands and begged off shaking theirs but greeted them with a curt nod. He motioned for them to come to the back of the shop.

"As you can see, I made a demo of your booth just so you could get an idea of the space and the colors I can do. I made it as a sample using all different colors in pastels on one side and the bright colors on the other side. I wouldn't make it this way, of course, but this is just an example of what you can have."

He pointed against the wall at a colorful booth with bubblegum colors on the right and bright fluorescent colors on the left, meeting in the middle, making a U.

"All it would need is a retro Formica tabletop. And we can attach it if you wish, but I think it's better that you can move it around. That way it's more flexible if you want to make an area for dancing."

Gretchen's fingers smoothed over the plastic upholstery, loving the richness of the texture and the colors.

"Jose, this is fabulous. It looks like something out of an old diner. You're quite a craftsman."

"Well, this is kind of fun for me, because most of the time I'm restoring old vehicles, and I have to use material that looks like the original, and much of it is with drab colors. With these, just like with custom hot rods, we can kind of go crazy. That's the real art of it all."

"Please show my sister the drawings of the van, how you're going to fix it up," Kate asked him.

On the wall over the upholstered booth was a blueprint of the insides of Deirdre's van, done in blue scale, but Gretchen could see where the cabinetry, the bathroom, and the kitchen were located.

"I'd like to put a pop-up in here; that way if you take this somewhere you have to travel, someone can sleep on top. The health department won't allow you to sleep downstairs in the kitchen. But if it's a separate pop-up area that's temporary, they will allow it."

"Good to know," said Kate.

"I've found some old panel trucks and utility vehicles that might work. I'd like to find something that needs total work," he said as he waved his hand through the air. "We put a new engine in it, we completely redo the insides, and I make the outsides open with a canvas canopy that can be locked down at night. That way, if you have things you want to sell, like food supplies or drinks, it can be a regular food truck but not like any food truck you see around here. I think, with more space, you'd have a better kitchen, and you could hold more products. You wouldn't have the bathroom, of course, but we can put in bigger refrigeration, make the drawers into coolers, and perhaps have some of them hold ice water. In Mexico, my cousin kind of patched together one of these, and he's going to send me some pictures. I'll show you later."

"So these are the trucks you were talking about, Kate?" asked Gretchen.

"Yes. But I think we should start with the van first. Don't you agree, Deirdre?"

"It all depends on the numbers." She addressed Jose. "Do you have any figures yet?"

Jose shook his head. "No, señora, not yet. I am just swamped this week, but maybe next week I'll have an idea. The nice thing about your van is that it's stock, already works, but you may find that if you use it much, you're going to need some upgrades to the motor."

"Oh, yes, that thing's a slug when it comes to hills," Deirdre agreed.

"With the cabinets we'd be putting in, it's going to make that worse. Quite a dog going up any hill. So you might want to consider getting more horsepower. But I understand your concerns about cost, and we will give you prices both ways."

"Thank you. That would be helpful. We aren't super rich, so cost is probably our most important element. I think everything else we can negotiate, even the price of the building. I'm hoping the sellers will be flexible enough so that perhaps we would make up the cost of the upgrades to the vehicles with the savings on what we pay for the building," answered Deirdre.

Gretchen could see that Deirdre had a keen eye for bargains, and, with her experience designing and building her artist gallery and workshop in Portland, she'd learned from her mistakes and was going to be using all that knowledge to benefit the project here in Coronado.

Afterward, they stopped for a light lunch, and then Gretchen picked up Angie, and the two of them went home. Angie was filled with questions.

"I'll show it to you after they get it in contract, honey. Right now, it's just sort of a pipe dream. It has to be something that's affordable for Deirdre, coming from the insurance proceeds. But I think it's doable, at least it looks like it is, and it would be fun to work on. Might be a good little part-time job for you too," she said to her youngest.

"I would love it if Aunt Kate could show me how to cook and do catering. I have friends at school who work part-time for catering companies, and they make pretty good money. I think it would be fun to do that and save up for college."

"Absolutely, sweetheart. This is an opportunity that most kids your age never get. You wouldn't have to be going off to an expensive culinary school to get the kind of skills that Kate has already. She's fabulous, and she's wanted to do this for, well, ever since she was in high school herself. She ran the Heller's wine-tasting room, and two SEAL wives she's friends with do this up in Sonoma County. You've been there. But way before that, she first started talking about having a food truck. I know it's going to be a success."

After a brief pause, Angie asked, "When's Trace coming home?"

"I'm expecting a call from him sometime today. It doesn't sound like it's going to take too long, but you know how your dad is, and there are always surprises when it comes to Tony. I'm glad we have Trace to help him out."

Angie was quiet suddenly. Gretchen used the opportunity to speak on the subject.

"I'm sure he's going to try to spend more time with you girls, and it's really up to you as far as how much you want to see him. But he is your father, and we aren't going to make you do anything you don't want to do. Just understand that."

"Is he different, Mom? Like do you think he got better?"

Gretchen groped for a way to keep her language civil. She scrunched up her nose. "Well, I haven't seen him, of course, but Trace doesn't think so. He's the same old Tony."

Angie sighed and sank deeper into her bench seat. "He embarrasses me, Mom. Some of the boys at school tease me about him. I try not to pay any attention, but they laugh sometimes and call him stupid names."

"What kind of names, sweetheart?"

"Double Dipper, Fuzzy Balls Sanders, that sort of thing. Worse, too."

She wasn't sure how to respond, but, before she could, Angie asked her, "Did he really hurt Trace?"

Gretchen realized Angie was talking about the fight Trace had gotten into with Tony, one of her ex's wild and crazy, alcohol and drug filled events where he was completely insane and out of his mind. Gretchen knew the girls worried about their dad, and she was so grateful for Trace's presence to help calm the situation.

"I'm sorry, sweetheart. I think we'll have to take it one step at a time. Trace will give us a good report when he gets home. Hopefully soon. Before your sister gets back from her honeymoon. I would try not to worry about it too much, Angie. There's a lot of people helping to look out after you guys. Especially with everything that's occurred. You've seen more of the seedy side of life than most of your friends have. Unfortunately, some of these things aren't very pretty and you've gotten closer to danger than any of your school friends will probably ever be. But I know you'll take it as a learning experience, and I know you will grow and understand more and more what families are all about. I know we will forgive your father, but we aren't going to give him too many chances to put any of us in harm's way. That's what Trace has promised to do."

"I know. It's not fair that he has to do that, but I'm glad he's there. I think I love him more than Dad. Is that wrong?"

"I'm proud of you for being honest about that, Angie. It's a natural reaction to the love that he's bestowed on all three of you. He's a good man, and we're lucky to have him in our lives. Tony's lucky to have him help with this transition, even though I'm not sure he completely understands the gift. But we'll forgive him anyway and hope that, in time, he'll get better, and then we can relax a bit. Right now, we're going to be pretty vigilant and limit everyone's exposure to him. So, no texting, no computer messages, no calls that Trace or I don't know about. Okay,

Angie?"

"You got it, Mom. Thanks for everything you do for us. I hope someday I can be just as good a mom as you are. And I hope I get to marry somebody just as nice as Trace is."

Angie's words warmed Gretchen's heart. She was going to love telling Trace about their conversation this afternoon.

CHAPTER 7

T RACE AND TONY traveled to Portland. On the way, they stopped by a branch of a bank Tony had banked with. They gave him applications to fill out and also showed him how he could apply online when he got home, if he chose to.

Tony wanted to stop overnight someplace, but Trace insisted they make it all the way back to Portland so they could spend the night in Tony's house. He needed to see what kind of a situation there was there.

"Well, I got tenants, and I guess I have to ask their permission before we can stay there. They could say no," Tony replied.

"Okay, we'll ask them, and, if they say no, we'll get a hotel. No problem."

Trace gave a call to Gretchen before they continued driving, just as it was turning dusk. He didn't have much to report and didn't want to report the few pieces of news he did have, because he didn't want to worry her. But he could tell from her reactions that she was concerned.

"Just wanted you to know we're on our way to Portland, and I got Tony. The rest are things we discussed about the house. I'll fill you in more later. I'll be driving until dark."

"Again, be careful."

He told her to give his love to the girls, even Clover if she talked to her, and then they said their goodbyes. He continued the drive to Portland, getting there just after eight.

Trace remembered the house that Gretchen and the girls had lived in, but he had never thought of it as Tony's house. Gretchen had said it gave her and the girls a nice stable place to live, and Tony had always promised the proceeds from renting out the house would pay for their college. Of course, that never came to fruition.

The house needed a lot of paint on the outside, and weeds taller than his waist reached for the night stars. He knew it would look even worse in the daytime. A couple of beat-up Volkswagens were parked in the driveway, blocking any route to the back entrance next to the kitchen.

Parking illegally in the street, he accompanied Tony up the steps to the porch, and they knocked on the front door. Heavy metal music blared from the insides.

As Tony's tenant opened the door, Trace was hit with a blast of smoke coming from inside the house. He turned his face away and swore, noticing the guy gripping a red bong in his right hand.

The young man was dressed in swim trunks and a dirty T-shirt. His long, blond dreadlocks were disheveled, their roots frizzing. His blue eyes were disarming but glazed over. He was very clearly under the influence.

"Can I help you?" He slurred his words.

"Hey, bud. Joel, is it? I'm Tony Sanders, and I own this house. You're behind on your rent, kid."

"Oh, really?" He scratched the back of his head, turned, and yelled to the rear of the house, "Hey, Nicole! Did you not send the rent in? I gave you the cash, didn't I?"

As a female voice shouted something in return, Tony added more information.

"Look, man, my records show you're behind three months, not one month, and I need a place to crash, and this is my house, and, since you're not paying, I'm going to stay here tonight with my friend here."

Joel put his hands up to his ears. "Whoa, whoa, whoa, slow down. I'm getting messages from both sides here. I can't talk to two people at once."

He studied Trace, and then lazily his gaze returned to Tony, who responded, "Yeah, I'm your landlord. And I need to stay here."

"I don't like that guy. He looks dangerous." He pointed to Trace with a whine.

Trace pulled on Tony's arm. "Hey, man, we don't want any scenes. Let's just go get a hotel."

Tony, being Tony, wiggled himself loose and confronted the tenant again. It was another stupid move.

"Joel, you're an asshole. I got some pretty powerful friends who are real bad asses, and they'd love to just fuck you guys up real big. So you get out of my way, and you let me sleep on your couch or your floor or someplace, because I just got out of prison, and I don't have any money, and I don't have any other place to stay."

The guy raised his eyebrows on the opposite side of the screen door. That certainly did get his attention, although it wasn't something that Trace would've recommended anyone do. But it was having good effect.

"Hey, man, I'm sorry about all this shit. How about me and Nicole just take off for a day or two, and we'll come back after you found a place to stay? Will that work?"

Hallelujah, he's seen religion!

"So when you come back, I'm going to change the locks, and, if you don't have the money, you aren't going to be able to get your junk. Get your ass moving and get your cars out of the driveway so I have a place to park, and you come back when you've got the cash. If you don't have the cash, I am going to fucking find you, and I'm going to take one of your fingers."

Trace's spirits spilled into his socks. He'd allowed Tony to engage against his better angels, and now could see it was a total mistake. But he was also concerned Tony would just get amped up further if he tried to stop him. So he decided it was two against two, and he wasn't going to start a fight, but he sure as hell would try to protect Tony if one started. And he didn't want to do that either, but he was not left with any other good choices. Pulling Tony off the porch was going to be a bad move.

Tony was relentless. "I'll take that as a yes. But I mean it. Or I could take one of your toes, one of your big toes. I'll even let you choose whether it's the right foot or the left foot, asshole."

Trace leaned into Tony and whispered, "I think he got the message, Tony." He stared at Joel, who put his bong down and pulled his dread-locks behind his ears, tying them together with a large rubber band. He was quickly sobering up.

"You've got about thirty minutes to get your stuff out, and we'll wait out here for a bit. We aren't going to touch anything of yours, but, if you call the cops, I think you're going to find that they will not take too kindly to squatters," Trace said.

Now Joel was getting defiant all of a sudden. "Oh, you think so? We don't have cops in this town anymore. And they don't care if squatters take over some rich guy's house."

Trace realized his mistake. He had to intervene, and he did so gently but with force in his voice.

"I don't think you understand. This gentleman is in a great deal of distress, and he's on a tight time schedule, reinforced by some threats from some very bad dudes, like he said. So you have thirty minutes, and then we're going to come in, and we're going to stay here, and I think we'll be done by Sunday, Monday at the latest. So find someplace, gather your stuff, and let us have the house. By the way, we are going to be putting the house on the market."

"Are you two a couple?" Joel asked.

Trace was beginning to lose his shit. Nothing about working with Gretchen's ex was turning out the way it was supposed to. Everything was harder than it needed to be, and he tried to remind himself about those little speeches he'd received his entire career about the enemy getting a vote. Now he felt like a goddamn fool for even volunteering for this failed or soon-to-be-failed mission.

"Look, asshole, I don't want to hear another word from you. All I want to see is asses and elbows, got it? You get out of this house in thirty minutes, and you can live to play another day. Okay?" Trace tried to give him his most angry, wretched look, and it appeared to be working.

The door slammed in their faces, and they could both hear the tenant giving orders to the mysterious Nicole, who at first didn't believe him that they had to gather up their things and vacate the house for a few days. She argued with him until Joel brought her to the front door so she could look through the window at the two guys looming on the porch. That's when she got it. Her eyes grew large as fried eggs, and she soon disappeared. Next thing they heard, both clunkers in the driveway backed up, screeched tires, and took off down the roadway.

"God, I hope they didn't lock the front door. I don't have a key anymore," said Tony.

"Let me know if you need me to break the window," said Trace without a smile. He was tired, he needed to lie down, and he wanted this day to be over. He wasn't going to call Gretchen again tonight, even though he'd promised.

SATURDAY MORNING, THEY filled out Tony's paperwork, then took it into the bank. The pretty, young assistant manager indicated they would have an answer by closing time that very same day. When the loan was approved, Tony asked if he could borrow a hundred thousand dollars instead of just the fifty he'd applied for and was quickly told no.

"We'd like to help, Mr. Sanders, but this is all we can do. We hope that when you get back on your feet, you'll come back to having a deposit relationship with us. That's why we're helping in this time of need," Trace heard her say on the other end of the line.

"How do I get the money then?"

The young woman at the bank explained the money would be digitally deposited to his account on Monday. And three days later, the funds would be good.

"I'm not sure what my account numbers are, and I don't have any credit cards with me. Can you make me a new credit card?"

"Surely, Mr. Sanders. A debit card. That's a good idea. I can do that and have it mailed to your home in about ten days. How's that?"

"Not good enough. I need it quicker than that, and I need the loan proceeds on Monday. I can't wait to have it clear the bank."

"Well, we don't hand out that large amount of cash, but I can make out a cashier's check for you. Do you have a person's name you want me to make it out to? That way he or she can deposit it in their bank."

"Sam. That's all I got," said Tony.

The assistant manager coughed into the phone.

Trace interjected, "Listen, ma'am, if you put the funds in there digitally, is there a way you can make them good the same day so he doesn't have to wait the three days? And will he be allowed to pull the cash out right away? Or can he pull it out in stages, say over the next three or four days?"

"Excuse me, Mr. Sanders. Who is this person?"

"He's my ..." He looked at Trace. "What do I call you?"

"Mr. Sanders, is everything all right?"

Trace cut in again. "Excuse me, ma'am, but I'm helping Mr. Sanders with getting his life back in order post-incarceration. I am married to his ex-wife. We are family in a way."

"I see. Well, let me check with my manager. Why don't you call me back on Monday and we'll see if we can make some kind of an accommodation for you? If I give you a cashier's check and it's not made out to anybody, it's dangerous to travel with such an instrument left blank. But perhaps we can request funds on special order. I'm just not sure it'll be available Monday. The easiest would be to deposit it to your checking account, and then you can write checks against it."

Trace could see Tony was getting irritated. It didn't bode well for his future that he couldn't even figure out how to access funds, get a loan, or work out details without Trace's help.

"I think that would be fine, right, Tony?" Trace said in response.

Having received the good news that his $50,000 was approved, the next order of business was to meet with the realtor they had called to visit the house this afternoon. Trace spent some time cleaning up some of the dishes, sweeping and vacuuming the floors, making beds, and trying to tidy up as much as he could, while Tony lay back on the couch with a cold, wet washcloth on his forehead, sporting a splitting headache, he said.

Trace figured the realtor would understand that, since it was a rental for several years, it might need some work, but, as they were in a hurry to get it liquidated, hiring people to do such a thing wouldn't be possible.

Shirley Ledbetter was right on time and held her diminutive, red fingernailed hand with the charm bracelet attached to her wrist for Tony to shake. He was nearly twice her size. But Ledbetter, from the advertisements that Trace had seen in his days visiting Gretchen in Portland, was an extremely successful agent and had a reputation for being no nonsense.

"It's nice to see you again, Tony. I'm glad that you called me. I think I have a couple who might be interested in this, depending on the price. Are you interested in something fast?"

"Hell, yes." He motioned for her to come inside and introduced her to Trace. They sat in the living room initially, and then she got up to do a quick walkthrough of the house without Tony or Trace hovering behind her. "I like to look at it the way a buyer would see it, not with you explaining things to me. I'm going to take some notes of things that maybe we should address, but I like to see it in the eyes of a potential buyer."

Trace was impressed, and they both nodded. He could tell that she questioned his presence, and, since Tony hadn't properly introduced them, he did so himself.

"Ma'am, I am now married to Gretchen, Tony's former wife. As you've heard, Tony's had a run of bad luck, and I'm here on behalf of Gretchen and the girls, to help him out a bit. Not financially, of course, but just to help him with the paperwork. He is in a bit of a financial bind."

Of course, before the agent could respond, Tony disagreed with Trace's opinion. "Oh, wait a minute. I've got money. No, we want to get the top dollar for this house. I would like to do a few little things so we can just really rake in all we can. So help me with this, Shirley. Okay?"

Trace worked very hard to control his anger again, already the second or third time today that he had to do so.

"Ma'am, that's not exactly true. He does not have a lot of time. As you know, he's been incarcerated."

Shirley quickly responded this time. "Yes, sir, I understand fully. And while fixing it up to get top dollar might be usually the best way to go, this couple who I have are young contractors, and he doesn't want to pay for somebody else's work that he'd have to rip out and redo anyway. So, in this particular case, the fact that we want a quick sale works very well for this particular buyer. He has all cash, and he's most anxious to find a place. They've lost just about everything they've tried to offer on."

"Okay, I'll let you do your job."

Trace sat back and let her do her walkthrough. Of course, Tony couldn't sit and wait for that to be over, so he got up and started explaining things to her, exactly what she told him not to do. Trace also heard him ask her for names of plumbers and electricians, painters, and people who could help spruce it up. He shook his head in disgust. Tony was never going to learn.

The two of them returned to the living room and joined Trace. "So, after seeing all of this, I think you can get close to eight maybe. This is a very popular part of town, it's away from the downtown enough with all the problems there, but it has the nice view of the river, and it's a close commute if people are going north to Washington state or south if they happen to work down toward McMinnville or Eugene. It's a lovely, older neighborhood, as you know, not a lot of rentals. I think if I explain to the couple that you've not lived here for several years and really hadn't been able to keep track of the tenants and the condition of the house, I'm pretty sure they will agree to take the house as is. But I am going to need to show them very soon."

"Sounds good to me," said Tony. "When?"

"Well, the good news is I'm showing them another property tomorrow morning early. Perhaps we could come over here afterwards? About 10 o'clock—or 11:00, if you need later?"

"Let's do 10:00. So how does this work then?"

"Well, I have prepared a contract for you, and I left the price blank until we talked. I would need you to sign this contract, and it doesn't obligate you to this particular couple, but it does give me the right to show the property and collect a commission. We can discuss a longer-term listing agreement if the two parties cannot agree. I did not prepare that."

Tony signed the single-party listing agreement with Shirley, and, as the two of them watched her navigate the creaky front stairs, her hand gripping the handrail on the left and her heavy briefcase slung over her right shoulder, Trace thought for the first time that perhaps this was all going to work out fairly quickly.

"Let's go grab some dinner. On me. Steak?"

"Sure thing, man. I could use a good steak. My cooking skills are shit."

"So are mine. On that we agree. Hey, I guess we're more alike than I thought?"

CHAPTER 8

G RETCHEN WAS INVITED to one of the SEAL Team 3 legendary bonfires, welcoming several new recruits to Kyle's squad. She went with Rebecca and Angie.

It was good to catch up with several of the other wives, many of whom had been present at Clover's wedding. She was rewarded with compliments and glowing accounts of how lovely Clover looked and what a great time they had.

Christy introduced her to Margarita Tamu, the wife of Isidor Tamu, both of whom were born and raised in Mexico and had been naturalized as citizens of the U.S.

"Margarita is also a gifted dancer and artist. They have three girls, just like you do, Gretchen," Christy let her know.

Gretchen shook the beautiful woman's hand. "So wonderful to meet you. Please, if you have any questions at all, don't hesitate to give me a call. I'm sure Christy has already given you the phone tree, and I'm Gretchen Bennett. Trace Bennett is my husband. I know how it felt being invited to my first one of these parties years ago, so I'd be happy to share my perspective on how this whole brotherhood thing works. Maybe you'll find some of it useful in navigating the society they've created here."

"Thank you. I would like that. You are very kind."

She was drop-dead gorgeous with an attractive smile and smooth accent while she spoke flawless English, with her "twist."

"Which one is your husband?" Margarita asked.

"I'm afraid he's not here tonight. He never misses these, but he's up in Portland helping a family friend." Gretchen felt the words stick in her throat.

"I understand."

"We can also share babysitting and other things as well. So don't be a stranger, and don't feel like you are bugging me, okay? It only feels intimidating at first. In fact, it's really very easy to get to know everyone, and, soon, you'll find a real family here. And if you have any trouble with the young, single guys who may not have the manners they should have, you let me know, and I'll have it fixed."

They both laughed.

"Thank you so much. Everyone is so welcoming here. I was told of this, but it's very nice to see. I'm sure my Rosie, Camilla, and my Angie will very much enjoy meeting your girls."

Both Angie and Rebecca were presented to Margarita, and each shook her hand.

Christy had been watching from the side, checking something on her cell phone, pretending not to hear, but she stepped forward. "Well, I'll leave you together," she said. "Gretchen, would you mind introducing her to several of the other wives? I've got a little reconnaissance I have to fulfill for my husband."

"No problem, Christy. Happy to do it. Oh, and does she have the phone tree? I'd like to highlight my number for her. She can use it as reference as she meets people."

"No, I forgot." Addressing Margarita, she said, "I'll make sure to drop a copy by your house tomorrow, okay? It was stupid of me. My mind is tired."

"You and me both, Christy," Gretchen agreed.

"Everything go okay up north?" she pried.

"Yes, I believe so. Just that I think Tony is more of a handful than Trace was expecting. But I'll fill you in tomorrow sometime."

Christy walked off and cornered a new couple who had just arrived.

Gretchen leaned into her new friend and whispered, "Christy runs a tight ship and is the perfect complement to her husband, Kyle Lansdowne, the Team's LPO. If Kyle is the glue that holds the Team together, Christy is the wire frame it's attached to. She makes it a point to know everything about everybody on Team 3, better than her husband."

"I see. She appears very confident and kind. She commands respect, doesn't she?"

"You bet. None of the guys would ever cross her, or they'd hear about it from Kyle. They are a matched pair, a real team of two. You'll find that you can trust her. And do yourself a favor and take her advice to heart. It will be a lot easier on you both if you do."

"Do your girls play volleyball?" asked Angie, Gretchen's youngest daughter. "Because both Rebecca and I have played, and we both coach. We'd be happy to have your girls sit in on one of our clinics."

"Well, that's lovely. I don't know if they have ever played volleyball. My husband has been playing soccer with them since practically before they were walking. You know soccer is more popular in Mexico?"

"Yes, Clover and Rebecca played soccer. I didn't care for it," said Angie.

"Are they on a team?" asked Rebecca.

"Well, we're still exploring, but I understand the United Club is quite good. Both my girls would like to play soccer in college, and this would help with the costs. They are a little bit younger than you two, so they have lots of time before they have to think about that, but soccer and sports for women is very important, no?"

Rebecca immediately answered her. "Oh, yes. Clover and I both received partial college scholarships for our volleyball. Soccer is also very big."

"I think it's good for women, because they usually recruit more for the soccer teams than they have to for any of the other teams. Maybe softball as well, but, for soccer, the teams are huge. In Mexico, sometimes they have a bench of thirty or forty girls. They have difficulty finding enough fields and coaches, so their teams tend to be very big."

"Well, you're going to have to bring your girls to one of our clinics. If they give it a shot, they might find they enjoy volleyball." Angie asked, "Are they tall?"

Margarita threw her head back, her beautiful brown curls flashing in the night air. "Oh, no. We are small packages. Very powerful, but small in stature."

Gretchen couldn't resist adding, "Good things in small boxes."

Everyone laughed at that.

Later, there was an announcement by one of the new recruits, Roger Valise—he and his girlfriend Vanessa were now engaged. Gretchen thought they looked even younger than Clover and Jack. She took Margarita by the arm and introduced her to Armando. "Armando is from Puerto Rico. My husband has nicknamed him the Latin lover."

"Well, Gretchen, in all fairness, I haven't been single more than a few months in decades." He greeted Margarita warmly. "Actually, they call me Armani. They think I spend a fortune on clothes, but I buy them at the discount stores. Very nice to meet you. I hope you will enjoy our little community."

"Thank you."

Gretchen added, "Armando remarried last year. His first wife was killed on the job. She was a policewoman. Lovely lady."

"Yes, Sambra sends her regrets, but we shall have to call on you some time and get properly acquainted. We have one child, Artemis, and we're always looking for new babysitters, if you have daughters of the right age."

"I have three. My thirteen year old loves babysitting."

"Wonderful. Sambra is also relatively new to the group. She'd love meeting you, I'm sure."

He said his goodbyes and wandered off.

"It's quite a lot to take in, and I'm sure you'll have questions. But, culturally, it's very important that the SEAL wives be included in the work. They are part of the job," Gretchen said as she brought Margarita over to Libby Cooper.

"I've heard about this. And I've heard about how the group stays together, how they help each other through good and bad times. I am so very proud of my husband. He always dreamed of living in the United States and working for the U.S. military. As a boy, he was fascinated with stories of World War II and Vietnam. When the opportunity came up for him to begin citizenship by applying for the Navy, he jumped at the chance. He's not regretted it since."

"Welcome, my name is Libby Cooper—this bag of bones is my husband."

Gretchen let Coop lean over, practically doubling over in half to shake Margarita's hand. "Very nice meeting you. Where's your guy?"

Margarita frowned and scanned the beach. "Oh! There he is. Isidor. He's there talking to the short one in Spanish."

"Tell him not to believe a word that guy tells him," Coop said and gave her a wink. "Anything at all Libby or I can do to help make your transition easier, you just let us know. There is this phone list. I assume Christy has—"

Gretchen interrupted. "Yes, we've already been over this. You're going to forget all these names, but once you get the list you can make notes. At least that's what I did."

"Awesome."

Libby and Cooper excused themselves, and that gave Gretchen an opportunity to ask Margarita about her artwork.

"Well, I do large abstract painting, acrylic on canvas. I am self-taught. However, I've been working under a tutor, and we talk online once a week. I have sold two of my paintings to the mayor's office in Chula Vista, which made me very proud."

"That's fantastic. Do you have pictures on you?"

Margarita took out her cell phone and flipped through several screens before she showed Gretchen a portfolio of some of her canvases.

"These are absolutely stunning. I have an artist you have to meet. Her name is Deirdre Gray, and she also does large acrylic paintings. They aren't abstract, but more modern cubist like a blend of Dali and Rousseau, if there is such a thing."

"That would mean jungle scenes and twisted figures, snakes and tigers and green leaves. Is that what she paints?"

"Well, sort of." Gretchen was at a loss to accurately describe Deirdre's portraits and landscapes. "They are huge, some of them eight or ten feet tall. And they're brightly colored, but you could stand there for several minutes and see so many different things inside. They're like little, tiny paintings within paintings, and I don't know how she does it, but it's almost like she puts a little painting in the middle and then paints around it or makes it part of the overall picture. She's also started to do some ceramic work and crazy quilt patchwork. You know, fabric sculpture?"

"Oh, yes, I love that as well. I don't have a proper machine, but, yes, some of the artwork from Mexico is unbelievably beautiful, with all the folklore and the festive colors. It's amazing how intricate and how creative different fabric textures and stitches come together to create a big piece. I've planned a trip to go to Kentucky to visit museums on quilting."

"Fantastic. We'll have to arrange a field trip, because I've never been. So you just have to meet Deirdre. We're in the process of buying a building and setting it up as a home for a catering business, as well as setting up a wedding center. Of course, Deirdre is going to be featuring a lot of her paintings, but she was going to be inviting several other artists to display their works on a rotating basis. I will certainly make sure she gets your name, because I think these would be gorgeous."

Margarita thanked her with a big smile. "When will you have the grand opening? I'd like to come."

"Well, I'm going to say it'll be at least a year. We've just made the offer or are getting ready to make the offer on the building this week. I think it's going to be a fabulous place, and it's very close to where the SEALs train down at the beach. You know, the course and the rubber boats?"

"Oh, yes, I've been told about those boats. And the little bald spot on the top of their head?"

"Yes. My husband has a bald spot that hasn't quite grown back yet, although he came to BUD/s a little bit older than some of the others. But, yes, they all talk of that, don't they?"

Gretchen had almost forgotten Angie and Rebecca had followed them around. Angie spoke up first. "And how their feet turn green when they take off their shoes."

"We had that as well, and, no matter how hard he scrubbed, that green color stayed with him for at least five days afterwards. My girls thought it was funny too," said Margarita.

Gretchen's cell phone rang, and it was Trace.

"Excuse me. My husband is calling." She stepped away but still within eyesight of her two girls. "I've been wondering what happened to you. I started thinking perhaps Tony got you into some trouble, but then I realized that would never happen," Gretchen whispered to him.

"Oh, if you only knew, Gretchen. He's such a mess and seriously wearing me out. I'm just not sure he's going to be able to do it on his own. He's like a big teenager who can't take care of himself because he was too spoiled by his mother."

"The answer is still no."

"No? No about what?" he asked.

"He's not coming to live with us, Trace. There's just no way in hell I'm going to let that man stay in my house. I don't even want him in San Diego."

"Oh, I get you. No, that won't happen. And I don't think it's what he really wants anyway. We got a buyer for the house, and we signed the contract this afternoon. Tomorrow, I'm going to accompany him to deliver some money to people he owes, and depending on how that goes, I will probably come home Tuesday, I hope. Tomorrow, if I can."

"Oh, that's wonderful news, sweetheart. I have missed you so bad."

"I think we have to be prepared for the fact that Tony has probably done so much damage to his reputation, not to mention his body from lack of exercise and all the things he's put into it, and he just doesn't seem to learn, Gretchen. I mean, sometimes I think he is really honest about wanting to clean his life up, and then—other times—it's like he looks at me like I'm crazy when I remind him of what he promised. I honestly wonder if there's some kind of a cognitive decline—because he just doesn't remember stuff."

"Maybe that was beginning to happen before he got in all that trouble. The coaches were pretty upset with him, and I know he felt the pressure."

"I don't know, but I'm doing what I can. The house got sold to a young contractor and his wife, really nice couple. They come from money, so it's an all-cash offer, and they want to close it quickly, so I think the timing's good on all that. I can't stay here too long, because we have the workup, and I got a call from Kyle, and I guess we're going to be deploying sooner than anticipated."

"Oh, pooh. And here I was hoping I'd have you for a month or two."

"Well, don't worry about it. It hasn't happened yet, but I want you to be ready for it."

"I will. I've got two little ladies who are dying to talk to you, Trace. They're standing right next to me."

She handed the phone to Angie first and continued talking about the wedding center space with Margarita while overhearing the conversation. Trace was having fun joking with their daughter. When Rebecca got on the phone, she mentioned to him that they had invited Margarita's children to come over to one of the clinics that she coached for younger kids. Gretchen knew it probably made Trace smile from ear to ear.

Angie grabbed the phone again and asked him, "Daddy, I just wonder if we would be able to have chickens?"

Gretchen stopped mid-sentence, did a double take, and stared at her youngest daughter. "Angie?"

"Well, my friend Cecilia from school, they have a little farm. She has a donkey. And they have chickens. Oh, they're so cute, and I got to hold them, and the mother chicken—guess what? She lays blue eggs."

Gretchen smiled as she listened to Angie, always the most expressive of her three, go into great detail about how the chickens were cared for. Margarita looked on with a big smile on her face too.

"She's really sweet, isn't she?"

"She's always been my live wire. This one here"—she put her arm around Rebecca—"is my athlete. I think if she sticks with it, she could play professional volleyball. She's that good."

Rebecca adopted a reddened, bashful face.

"Do you play, Gretchen?"

"Oh, I bump with the girls from time to time, but mostly, I just shank it, and they have to go chasing after the ball. I'm not all that athletic, but the girls have really enjoyed it, and it's wonderful conditioning."

"I'll make sure the girls watch a practice or two. What does a short girl do on a team? Yours are so tall!"

"The back row position, libero, usually is a short girl who's extremely athletic. Oftentimes, on the good teams, they have someone put in there who has actually done quite a bit of gymnastics, since they literally have to dive for the ball and often do somersaults trying to pass it to their teammates. It's a tough position to play, I think maybe the hardest."

"Really? So a shorter player would still, if she's athletic enough, be able to compete?"

"Well, if she can jump, like high jump type quality, then she can block in the front row. That's where they put the giraffes usually. I call them giraffes because they're all so tall, and they look clumsy as heck when they're teenagers trying to get down and dig a ball. But the little girls in the back row, as long as they get to the ball and can successfully pass, there's a spot for that kind of a player, and she can get things that the tall ones sometimes struggle with."

"I didn't realize."

"In fact, when Clover was playing, their team was huge. I mean, there were thirteen- and fourteen-year-old girls who were over six feet tall on her team. And if you looked at the parents, well, it was a conclave of the giants, if you know what I mean. Well, they played a team from Hawaii, and those girls, I don't think any of them were over five feet tall. Those girls never let a ball hit the floor. They would dive, they would do pancake saves, and they would do cartwheels. Oh my gosh, they were so athletic, and they never let the ball hit the ground. You can be serving balls and spiking them all you want on the one side, but, if the other side returns those balls every time, you don't have to jump and hit it really hard. You just have to not make a mistake, and they beat our girls handily in straight sets. So I have a whole new respect for short volley-ball players."

Angie handed the phone back to her mom, probably at Trace's prompting. Gretchen stepped away again and signed off to Trace. "I'm glad you're helping him. Thank you."

"You're welcome. I didn't do it for him, you know that. But I just couldn't live with myself. Leave him out there dangling. Tony doesn't really need a best friend; we need to get him a wife. We need to get him a wife quick. Do you know any prospects?"

"I'm just thinking through the list of our friends who I hate enough to recommend."

All of a sudden, Gretchen had an idea. "I've got the perfect woman for Tony."

"Yeah?"

Gretchen saw an odd couple sneaking off into the shadows.

"I can't wait for it. The suspense is killing me."

She grinned. "Shayla. Your ex!"

CHAPTER 9

T RACE GOT UP early, giving Tony a few extra minutes to rest. It had been a long couple of days, mostly due to the stress of Tony's situation, and it was beginning to take its toll on Trace. He could do action and danger and jumping out of airplanes at thirteen thousand feet at midnight. But this emotional stuff, not knowing who was in charge, who the real enemy was, caused his brain to be on alert twenty-four seven. There were so many aspects to Tony's complicated situation, and some were increasingly becoming more dangerous by the minute.

He straightened the kitchen and picked up Tony's shoes and other things he'd left strewn around the dining room table, made himself some coffee, and called it good. The rest of the place was going to have to wait until the tenants returned.

He took his cell phone and his coffee out on the porch to look over the Columbia River and just collect his thoughts. Often it was the best way to organize all the little loose ends and details going on about a mission, just like he did when he was working an op for SEAL Team 3.

It was beautiful here, cool at nights, unlike San Diego, and he remembered visiting Gretchen, meeting the girls, and falling in love with her in this house. He was a bit sad that it was going to be leaving the family, but it had been so overridden by these terrible tenants, it almost didn't even look like the same property. It was time to move on, he knew. After he married Gretchen, she and the girls were much happier down south with him.

He thought about all the things that could go wrong, not to depress himself, but just so he was mentally prepared if one of those scenarios happened to show its ugly face. He didn't really know much about Sam and The Organization, but he didn't really want to deploy any Navy assets to dig into it, and so the only other person he could talk to would be perhaps Kelly Fielding, who was living in Portland and working on her father-in-law's security company with her sister-in-law, Jenna Riley.

He thought about what he was going to ask her. He wondered what had ever happened to Sven, the Norwegian special ops soldier, highly decorated, they'd used on several missions in Africa, most notably the Canaries, which was where they were supposed to be going next. He hated that place. Last Trace had heard, Sven and Kelly were an item and made a good team.

Tony had turned out to be more of a handful than he'd calculated. He doubted even Gretchen knew how far out of control he was. He was cocky, argumentative, and more like an ill-mannered teenager with too much money and not enough common sense. He knew he wasn't going to be able to control him as much as he needed, and—especially during his deployment—it might be a dangerous time for Tony. If there was any way they could put this whole thing to bed before Trace left the country, that would be ideal.

Part of him regretted ever volunteering for the mission. But he also understood that evil had a way of breaking out just when you thought it was contained, and, when that happened, all bets were off. Bad news could just streak across anybody's life, embroil many more innocent people, like Gretchen and the girls, and would continue getting bigger and bigger until someone stomped it out with force. So it was better that he was involved, even though he just wasn't sure how this whole thing was going to end.

He dialed Kelly's number, and she picked it up on the first ring.

"Oh my God, Trace Bennett. It's been—what?—a year, two maybe since we talked last?"

Trace had thought for sure he would wake her up, but she was chipper and ready to work. She must have been using her spin cycle or went for an early workout.

"Yes, ma'am. None other."

"Does this mean you're in Portland?"

"I am. I'm up here with Gretchen's ex, Tony."

"The basketball player?"

"The same."

"I didn't think you two were friends at all. So what gives? You still sticking with Kyle and the team, or are you about ready to jump ship and come work for us?"

Trace chuckled. "Nah, I'd make too many demands on you, Kelly. The first thing you'd have to do is move your whole operation to Coronado because there's no way in hell I'm going to live in Portland."

"I get it. I wish he hadn't set it up here either, and we're looking. But I'm not sure San Diego would be our first choice. But definitely not the Pacific Northwest."

He heard sounds of a male voice in the background so Trace didn't want to intrude. "I see you've got company, Kelly. Can I call you back later?"

He heard the distinct voice of Sven Tolar growling behind her. "Kelly, what the hell?"

"You want to talk to him, Trace? Warning you. He's in a foul mood."

"Yeah, I'll talk to him."

Kelly and Sven had a battle over the cell phone, and Sven won.

"How are you, Trace? You're here in Portland?"

"Yep. I came into town on Friday. I'm with Gretchen's ex, Tony. He got released from prison, and he's got himself in a little bit of trouble, so I've picked him up and am helping him raise some money so he can get rid of that trouble."

"Don't you give him any money. From what I've been told, the guy's a loser. He's not long for this world, Trace. You need to go back home. But not before you see us, okay?"

"Well, partly the reason I called is to see if you or Kelly had any information about the group that's kind of got him by the cojones. It is called The Organization. Have you heard of them?"

"Oh yeah. Can I put this on speakerphone?"

"Are we secure?"

"We're not wired, and I sweep regularly, and it's just the two of us in the house now. So yeah, I'd say so."

"Knock yourself out then."

"So how did he get mixed up with The Organization? These are really bad dudes."

"Oh, I know. I've only met one of them, and I could see right away that they have something in common with Tony."

"What's that? Or is this a joke?"

"They're stupid, and they're dangerous. And that combination of the two makes them even more dangerous. I'm up here just because it's a favor to Gretchen and the girls. If I can't get him straight with this guy, not sure what to do. Wish I could just cut him loose. Even if I wanted to, I can't give him any money. I mean, we're hand to mouth as it is with two in college. Just finished paying the last check for Clover's wedding."

"Clover got married?" Kelly asked.

"Yeah, married a really nice kid who's studying to be a veterinarian, but he's kind of excited about all the SEALs he saw at his wedding. Oh gosh, he's asked me to train him. But don't you say a word, because Clover doesn't know yet."

"Ouch," said Sven. "That's a huge mistake. I hope you set him right."

"I did. I *think* he heard me."

"Geez, did you bring Gretchen and the other two with you?"

"Nah, Tony was in the facility just outside of Eugene, and it's really too dangerous for her and the girls to be involved in any of this. I want to keep them out as long as I can. We met with a guy who I guess is the money man. He gave us instructions. We're on our way to give a little down payment, and then Tony's going to give him the rest of the cash after his house sells."

"Here in Portland?" Kelly asked.

"Yeah, it's the one Gretchen used to live in. I think you've been here a couple times, guys."

"Oh, I know it now. Nice view of the river?" she added.

"That's it. Anyway, he's had it rented out while he was in the can, and we already got a buyer for it, a young contractor and his wife. They're going to pay all cash, take it 'as is,' and close it quickly, which is good news for us. Before he hands over all that money, I wanted to see if I could get more information about these people. I mean, they might take the money and then murder us both or set it up so that we get compromised somehow, and that's all she wrote, end of story, right?"

"No, you don't want to do that. Yeah, you need to find out who's really running the show. You need some help?"

"I just need information."

"I'll tell you what. You buy us breakfast, and we will meet away from downtown. I've got a favorite little diner called Betty's Butter Biscuits down in the warehouse district."

"Yes, I know it well. Tyler's mom and dad had that gallery that burned down. I was going to stop by and pay my respects."

"They moved down there, didn't they?" asked Sven.

"Yes, I meant, pay my respects to all the beautiful paintings that Deirdre lost in the fire. Just about broke her. But she's doing really well, and they've got a big project they're working on. I'll let them tell you sometime when we get together."

"Cool. Well, I'm hungry. I don't know about you," Sven said. "So we'll meet you down at Betty's in say thirty, forty-five minutes? Does that work?"

"If I can get Prince Charming up. He's been snoring up a storm, so I think he slept pretty good, but I sure didn't."

"Tell me you didn't sleep in the same bed with the asshole."

"No, sir. I would've slept on the floor. I would've slept in the garage, but I was not going to sleep in the same bed as Tony. Not to worry, Sven. And quit mothering me, for Christ's sake. I've got a wife and three daughters who do a lot of that. So just stop it, okay?"

"I get you. You want to go check on lover boy and let us know if it's a no-go?"

From behind Trace, Tony yelled out, "No, I'm awake. We'll be there. Thirty minutes max."

Trace turned around to see Tony dressed in a woman's pair of pajamas, the fabric colored in bright pink and yellow pigs, surrounded by daffodils and angels. He looked ridiculous in the outfit. However, he knew Tony didn't own a pair of pajamas because he only owned three pieces of clothing, and Trace had seen them all.

"Well, we'll see you down there then. It looks like we're a go," said Trace. He hung up the phone. Turning to Tony, he asked, "Goddamn it, Tony, what the hell's going on now? Are we adding cross-dressing to your list of transgressions?"

"It's the only thing she had that had long sleeves. It was dark. I couldn't see and I was cold, man."

"What'd you wear in the joint?"

"As many pieces of clothing as I could: sweatshirt, sweatpants, socks. I covered up, man. I was cold all the time. I tossed all that shit before I left. Didn't need the memories. I think the heat's turned off here. I was freezing."

"Well, let's get you fixed up. You like the coffee?"

Tony held his mug up. "Yeah, it's just the way I like it."

"I was going to apologize that we didn't have any half-and-half, but I was afraid to leave you alone. Wasn't sure you'd be here when I got back."

"Come on, Trace. You've got to understand I'm in this for the long haul. I'm trying to get my life turned around, and I'm not going to bail on this whole thing and become a fugitive. I got too much going for me."

Trace silently disagreed with Tony, but he didn't want to waste the energy trying to argue with him. "You just get your butt in the shower. I'll follow, and we'll get down there and talk to my friend."

As Trace pushed Tony through the living room and out to the back bathroom, he was peppered with questions from the former NBA star.

"Sven has a history of European Special Forces, and we've used him on ops before, outside of the U.S. He's now working with his fiancée, I think. I'm not sure they got married, but she helps run a security firm that she and her sister-in-law inherited, and they do all kinds of special projects for major players in business and political. And, on occasion, Uncle Sam has been known to task them with a few things. That's how we initially met them. Kelly has a background in State Department work. She was married to the owner's son, who died from a drug overdose."

"Nice people, huh?

"No, they are. Other than my SEAL buddies, I wouldn't want anybody else to have my back but those two. Someday, I might go to work for them. But, for right now, I'm going to ask them a favor."

"What kind of a favor?" Tony asked.

"I'll tell you at breakfast. Now get your butt in the shower and let's leave this place in about ten minutes max, okay?"

"You've got it."

Betty's Butter Biscuits looked like a hopping place at 7:30 in the morning, with a line of customers about twenty deep extending from the front door halfway down to the corner. The patrons appeared to be an eclectic group, some professional people in suits and others, students, dressed casual for school. It was a testament to how good Betty's biscuits must be, thought Trace.

"Was this here when you were with Gretchen?" he asked. "I don't remember seeing it before."

"No, I think it's new."

Trace looked for a parking spot and, after driving around the block twice, finally managed to snag one from a customer just leaving.

They didn't see Kelly and Sven in the line of people waiting, so Trace led the way and checked out the tiny dining room.

"Ah, there they are," he said. The two were sitting in a far corner, nice and private, just like Trace liked it. When he and Sven made eye contact, Sven got up, crossed the room in three oversized strides, and gave him a big hug.

"It's been way too long, son. God, you're getting old."

"Let's keep it honest, Sven. You're not more than a couple of months older than I am," Trace answered.

Kelly waved and remained seated at the table, sipping her coffee. Sven snagged the waitress and ordered a couple more coffees for Trace and Tony. "If that's all right?"

"And I'll have cream if you have it," said Trace.

Trace began his introductions.

"So this is Tony, Gretchen's ex. I don't think you guys have met yet, right?"

"No, I would've remembered it. Nice to meet you, Tony." They shook hands, and then Sven introduced him to Kelly Fielding. "Have a seat, guys," he said to the two of them.

The waitress brought their coffees, and Sven indicated they had already ordered so Tony and Trace added theirs.

"So what's going on?" asked Sven.

"I overheard part of your conversation, Mr. Tolar. I don't appreciate your opinion of me. But, just for the record, we just want some background information on this group, The Organization?" Tony's voice was laced with lots of attitude, and Trace noted that Sven picked up on it right away.

"Uh-huh. Now, son, there's a rule about dealing with people like that."

"You mean don't do it, right? Fuck, I know that already. You don't have to tell me that."

"Well, first of all, you don't go announcing it to a room full of strangers, okay?"

Tony turned in his seat and studied the customers eating all around him.

"So if you're going to talk about these people, I want you to be quiet about it. It's just not smart."

"God, you guys are all so touchy."

Kelly inserted her opinion, "That's how they stay alive, Tony. You could learn a lot from these two."

"Okay, so I get it. Let me say it over again then. We just want information. I mean, I think Trace has a point. We want to make sure—if we work out a deal with them—that they'll honor their side."

Sven pushed his chair back from the table, nearly tipping over, and laughed. "Oh, you're concerned they won't honor the deal? That's exactly what they do, Tony. They keep changing it on you all the time. They'll say, 'Oh, you got to do this' and then 'Oh, you got to do this' and then pretty soon you're in it so deep you'll never get out. As a matter of fact, we could sit here and talk ten years from now, and you'd still be stuck with them. And you would've paid them a lot of money."

"Well, I think they underestimated me."

Trace looked over at him carefully, and then he gave a blank expression to Sven before he answered, "Honestly, Tony, every time I think you say something stupid, you say something even more stupid. They're working with you because they think you're their bitch, Tony. They're going to milk you until you're dead," he whispered between his teeth.

Sven jumped in. "The only way we have a shot at it is if we negotiate, get them paid off, and perhaps make it not worth their while to hassle you anymore."

Trace wondered how in the hell that could happen. Their choices were limited.

Sven inquired further. "Tell me again who you're dealing with. Are they all local guys, or are you talking to people from out of the country?"

The waitress interrupted them by presenting their breakfast, which looked fabulous. Trace was going to have to restrain himself not to order double and triple orders of biscuits.

"I always did kind of like gambling a little bit, and I did some work for them. There was a group in L.A. I got involved with, to help them set up their online gambling platform and, you know, help them promote. Their thing was run from someplace offshore but, as long as I wasn't betting on my teams or anything professional in the U.S., I could still promote it. Or at least that's what they said. Anyway, it turned out that wasn't true either. When the team found out, I had to cancel on the deal or nullify my player contract, and, of course, that incurred fees."

"Of course," Sven said.

"And then, after things started unraveling with my coach and the team, I was kind of stupid. You know Gretchen and I split up. I just kind of went on a little bit of a spiral, and we had that altercation between me and Trace, and … Anyway, I got four years, and I was doing pretty good with that. In fact, I was even doing some gambling from the facility here in Eugene, and then things started to go sour. I got in a couple fights, and then I started losing bets. And then, what do you know? All of a sudden, I'm doing nine and a quarter years. Just hardly doesn't even seem fair. I was the victim here."

Trace noted Sven's glazed-over look. Tony was not making points with him.

"So then what happened? How did you pay them? They kill people who don't."

"Well, before long I was in it so hard that, you know, they had carried me. The interest was bigger than the original money they lent to me, so I'm stuck, and I got to sell the house, which we did, by the way. We've done a lot of work, haven't we, Trace?"

Trace nodded his head in full agreement.

"Anyway, I'm to give him $50,000 today. I got an equity line on the house, and then I'm supposed to pay him the rest later. In about two weeks, the escrow will close, and, after commissions and everything, I think they'll get about seven maybe. I'd like to have a little to live on, but he doesn't seem to be very interested in that."

"And who is *he*?"

"Sam, the guy I'm dealing with in Eugene."

"Okay, so it's his money that bankrolled you?"

"Yes, at least he's the one who owns the guys in the facility I was in. They all work for him, doing various things. I figured I was going to get back on the court, Sven, and it even looked like they had a shot for me at one of the G leagues, and there was going to be a signing bonus that was going to be good for me. I had retirement saved up, a little bit left over from my contract. But the rest of it they voided when I went to prison. And then it got spent on attorney's fees, as their guys tried to negotiate this deal."

"Don't tell me. They scared them off, right?"

Tony nodded. "In the end, it all fell through, and then I started losing, and the debts really started piling up. So I'm kind of in a pickle. I'm worried they'll come after me if I don't give them the money."

"So how much money are you going to be short after you sell the house?" asked Sven.

"I think about one fifty, maybe two? It's kind of hard getting specific numbers. He charges what he wants to charge as far as interest, like twenty percent a month, and, um, you know, he just more or less tells me whatever he wants to tell me, so it's hard to follow the plan."

Sven had been shaking his head during the last part of Tony's pathetic statement. His expression was pained.

"Of course, it's designed that way, Tony. You do know that they're not going to let you go, right?"

"Well, what about the thing you said. That we make it inconvenient or difficult for them to do business with us. Isn't that what you said?"

"Yeah, something like that. But you don't want to be dealing with these people long-term. You want to try to get out of it with the first offer and then walk away. I mean, I don't ever want you guys … I think it would be stupid of you to have anything further to do with them. You understand that, don't you?"

"Hell, yeah."

"So let me tell you a little bit about this 'Organization.' You may not know, but they also are involved in other things, prostitution, some drugs, and extortion. But their real specialty is providing young girls for businessmen, household slaves, sex slaves, and they get their girls from foreign countries that are embroiled in skirmishes. War is good for business."

"But nobody ever said anything about—"

Both Trace and Sven whispered tersely, "Quiet!"

Sven finished his coffee and sighed. "They're captured, sold to these guys, and these guys … I mean, it's just like a farmers market, right? They pick them up, clean them up, and sell them to the highest bidder. That's where they make the real money, and they hook some of their business clients, people like yourself with big incomes or used to have big incomes, to help them. Or to turn them on to their friends. Once they get their hooks in one person in the group, then they go after the whole group to try to be an indispensable addition."

"That's just pure evil."

"So is gambling, drinking to excess, many of those very same vices I believe you have, Tony. They're very dangerous. They're ruthless, and they are so good they're even working through some of this country's legitimate NGOs, so our Uncle Sam tax dollars fund some of their projects. Everybody loves to save children, right? Refugee children especially, and there's a whole lot of them being brought into this country right now. It's lucrative, and I don't think our government has the will or the brains to solve it. And there is an unlimited source of young children being orphaned by all the wars all over this planet. War pays. It also kills. But it pays well."

"So, Sven, how do we stop this?" Tony asked.

"I'll tell you what … I'm going to go with you and Trace today to deliver the first payment. We'll discuss the terms for the balance. I want to meet your guy. I want to see what he's about, and I'm going to make him an offer."

Trace immediately interrupted. "Sven, I didn't ask you to do this," he objected. "I didn't ask for you to bail him out. Don't do that. It's a losing proposition."

"It's just one poker hand, Trace. We do this one thing, and we lose the round, but we win the game that way. I have to get them off his back, and then we go back, and we create a little mayhem. Not so as anybody would notice, but just a little payback. And who knows? I might get my money back." He smiled.

Trace looked back and forth between Kelly and Sven. "You would do that for Tony?"

"No, Trace. I do that for you. Because you care most about the people they're going to ruin if we don't make this deal. Our job is to keep them away from Gretchen and the girls. Trust me when I tell you this, Trace, the only way you can have a prayer of getting them off his back is to pay them. Pay them whatever they want. And they'll go away for a while. That's when we play our second hand."

"And what's our second hand?" Tony eagerly asked.

Sven crossed his arms and glanced down at Kelly, who smiled back, and it was obvious to Trace that they'd discussed the whole thing. He knew the answer Sven was going to give them even before he said it.

"I haven't quite figured that out yet. But when I do, Tony, you're going to be a standup guy, and you're going to be right in the middle of it."

They finished breakfast, agreeing to meet back at Tony's house. Trace and Tony packed up what they had, including the cash Tony picked up on the way home. They left a note for the tenants that they'd need a couple extra days. When Sven arrived, they took Trace's rental to Eugene to meet with Sam.

"He's very pushy, Sven. So don't get pissed off if he disses you," Tony cautioned.

Trace cursed quietly as he drove on. He saw Sven smiling at him in the rearview mirror.

"No need to give me the particulars. I'm going to be checking out other things. Not to worry. This time, he gets a free pass and can say whatever he wants. Next time will be different."

The bar and grill looked the same as it did before. The light dusting of rain felt dirty on Trace's face and neck, but—when he entered the place—he felt the thick smoke of cigars and dope plaster to his wet face like a facial mask. It added to his irritation, but he quickly adjusted his mental state to stay alert to something he wouldn't expect.

Sam was already sitting at the table with his whiskey. This time he didn't offer any to Trace and Tony. His dark, squinting eyes bored into Sven.

"Who's this jerk?" he asked.

"Extra protection," Trace said before Tony could stumble through a word salad.

"Are you packing?" Sam asked him.

"Fucking A, I am," answered Sven.

Trace felt the tension in the air. Sam was considering his options.

"Anytime I carry more than a grand, I'm armed, and you would be too. So let's move on and get this thing handled," Sven continued.

"You a foreigner?" Sam asked.

"None of your business. Russian, if you must know."

Trace almost split a gut. Tony started to object, and Trace stepped on his big toe. Hard.

"So let's see the money."

"Let's drink first," Sven said, startling everyone.

No one moved. Even the bartender was waiting for instructions from Sam.

"You heard the man. Bring the bottle and some glasses, or are you a vodka drinker?"

"I prefer whiskey in this part of the country. The vodka you'd serve me would be horse pee," answered Sven.

The bartender started across the room with the three glasses rattling and a bottle, setting them down on the table, and was back behind the bar in a flash.

Sven poured the glasses, added some to Sam's and then they held their drinks in the air.

"To enemies becoming friends long enough to make some money. To ending conflict, with everyone walking away alive."

It was an odd toast, but Trace nodded and drank, as did Tony.

"Another!" Sven insisted.

Trace shook his head when the bottle was presented to him, but Sven argued with him. "It's required. Otherwise, you're out of this deal completely."

Trace knew it was a masking type of maneuver, showing a lack of respect, a little wrinkle or crack in their wall of defense, showing it on purpose. He was tempted to just agree and walk out. He wanted nothing more of this situation, but he went along anyway.

"Of course, if it's required, I'll do it."

They all toasted again, this time with Sam's call-out. "To the gamble of life. To burying enemies both foreign and domestic."

Trace was now grateful for the platter of ham, eggs and all the biscuits he consumed, as it was a good antidote to the alcohol. He had a few hours of driving to do, up to Portland again then back to Eugene and a possible flight out. All of this were the steps he had to take to get free.

"So you are Sam, no?" Sven asked.

"I am, and you may sit at my table now."

All three of them did so. Trace noted the room was nearly empty. Of the patrons who were there, none looked like part of Sam's gang or henchmen, but he guessed there could be some upstairs watching on a TV monitor remotely.

"How much does this asshole owe you?"

"Nine fifty, plus." Sam grinned, and Trace noted he had a gold tooth in front.

"Nine fifty. No plus. All interest stops for thirty days."

"No, sir, Tony knows and has already agreed to pay twenty percent a month on top of the principal."

"Except some of the principle is made up of carried interest, so it isn't principle at all. You're making profit on profit."

"What's it to you?"

"I'm looking out for you, Sam. Because if you don't accept the nine fifty in thirty days or less, then the next offer is going to be eight fifty. Then seven fifty … and so on. This is your best deal."

"You can't do that."

"I just did. So are you turning down the offer of nine fifty? You get all of it in thirty days, cash."

"What about today?"

"I'm taking that off the table next."

"Hold on there, asshole. I'm not agreeing to that."

"The kid's gotta live. He's gotta look for a job and get a car. He needs money for that. How much do you need today? Are you that hard up you can't give him a chance to conduct his business to get you the rest of the money?"

"I need fifty."

"I already told you that was going next. Now it's forty."

"I said fifty."

"Okay then, it's thirty. Are you ready to stop?"

"No, man."

"You go down to twenty. But today you're a lucky man, Sam. You get $25,000 today and the rest in thirty days. That's the best you're gonna get, or we go get our other negotiators, and we make some calls to the U.S. Marshall's office and the Eugene District Attorney. Ken Wheeler is his name. I know him on a first name basis. I think he'd want to know about this shakedown—"

"Fuck you. Okay, I'll take it. But you and me, we have a score to settle later."

"Looking forward to that, Sam. Can't wait. I do my best negotiations in a ring, or tarmac, or in a bar, like this one. Of course, there's always collateral damage. But you know that's part of the cost."

"You are a dead man."

"Really?" Sven checked himself out, padding his chest and frowning. "I think you're wrong. I'm very much alive, and, remember, I do have something that will put a four-inch hole in your chest. So play nice, Sam, and you'll be forced to take nearly a million dollars off this pathetic kid who happened to fall in your shithole. But you're gonna keep your hands off him after you get paid. Understood?"

"Just give me the twenty-five."

"You gotta give me your word, in front of all these people here. Otherwise, I let my little friend do the talking."

Several of the patrons left through side doors, unlikely to return, from their expressions. Even the bartender sat down behind the countertop.

"I promise."

"To kill me? Come on, to do what?"

"It's settled after I get the full nine fifty. Tony's hands-off."

"And you tell The Organization too?"

Sam smiled, obviously enjoying his lie. "Yeah, I tell them to keep their hands off too." He started chuckling.

Sven directed Tony to give him the money. He counted out the $25,000 and dropped it in front of Sam in wads tied in bank paper.

"You should be proud. I walked in here prepared to give you nothing. My Russian friends will think I've gone soft. So don't tell them if they happen to stop by just to check to make sure you didn't leave town."

Sam collected his money and, for a few seconds, looked like a little boy with all the money and houses in a Monopoly game he'd just won.

CHAPTER 10

G RETCHEN AND ANGIE were baking an apple pie when Trace quietly tiptoed through the front door and approached them in the kitchen, both of them covered in flour. Gretchen heard him come up behind her, heard his familiar, raspy breathing as her heart instinctively skipped a couple of beats. She turned just as he grabbed her.

"Trace!" Gretchen collapsed into his arms and was so grateful he had returned she wasn't going to chastise him for not making that phone call to let her know he was back in Coronado.

"Well, mission accomplished?" she couldn't help but ask.

"It's all been sort of worked out for now. As long as Tony gets the house sold, it's game over."

"How the heck did you do that?" she asked him as Angie gave him a careful hug, still depositing flour on his cheek.

Trace glanced between the two of them. "I'll tell you about it later." He paused and then smiled at their youngest. "Angie, how are your games going?"

"Really well, Trace. We've got a dynamite team this year. The new girls are awesome, and I think we could win some titles. I've signed them up for some camps and some festivals where they can play against some great teams from all over the U.S."

"Awesome. Road trips?"

"Yes. We'll be taking those in June and July. It's just amazing what these girls are doing. I wasn't half as good as they are at their age."

"Well, let's see. You're fourteen, and they're twelve?"

"No, Trace, they're eight and nine years old. But they're already nearly six feet tall some of them. I mean, it's amazing. And the parents are so into it. It's really a joy."

"So maybe you have future plans to go into coaching then. I mean, that's a huge career field. It would have a good, solid future."

Gretchen felt her stomach rumbling. She could feel a boundary being breached.

"Trace," she started. "She's having a great time. I don't want her to think that she has to do this for the rest of her life. Let her take the win and enjoy it, no pressure. She's got lots of time to decide what she wants to do. Love you, but sometimes a kid just needs to be a kid. Right?"

Trace nodded his head. "Yes, ma'am. Whatever you say."

With another kiss to both of them, he dashed upstairs to unpack and take a shower.

Angie whispered, "Mom, you're kind of hard on him sometimes. He just was trying to be nice."

"I'm aware of that, sweetheart. I just don't want him to push too hard. You've got your father as an example. I think Clover would still be playing basketball today if he hadn't pushed so forcefully."

"I get your meaning. He did do that a lot. It wasn't pleasant."

"It's just not at all like what it used to be. These sports teams are so competitive. And I get it, it's a good thing to go for, but not at the exclusion of family and just being a teenager, Angie. It doesn't always have to be coaching a winning team or coming in number one. That's what you go for, and, hey, I have no problem with that, but just because you're coaching eight- and ten-year-old girls doesn't mean that's going to be your trajectory. I want you to keep all your options open. And yes, Angie, I'm very, very proud of you. But you know that!"

Angie hugged her. "Mom, you're the best. I got lucky in that department, didn't I?"

"Thanks, Angie." Gretchen practically melted. Tears came to her eyes, which she quickly covered.

"I even got lucky with the men in your life."

Gretchen thought to herself that her taste in men had improved greatly since her very first choice of Tony. Now she understood what a real man was, and, now that she'd found him, she was all in. Nothing would ever change her mind.

Gretchen and Angie finished their pie and put it in the oven while Trace followed up with some of his teammates. He got a call from Sven and walked outside to take it. Gretchen suspected Sven had something to do with the outcome of Tony's deal.

There was a gathering later on over at the Brownlee residence, a pool party, and several of the couples were going. Gretchen told Trace about the new men who had joined the team and a couple of the wives that she'd met the day before.

"Your new Mexican recruit's wife, Margarita, and I had a good discussion about art and the project we're working on. She's also a painter. You should see her work."

"You point them out to me and we'll say hello."

Austin Brownlee was in a good mood, flanked by his new girlfriend, Melissa Murphy, and flatly put down rumors that they'd gotten engaged, but they were living together and, for all intents and purposes, were married in every way but one.

Gretchen, at first, had been resistant to the relationship, mostly because of the initial drama of their appearance in Coronado. Austin's twin brother, Will Brownlee, had been a SEAL killed in Grenada. Years later, Melissa and her daughter, Will Brownlee's child, had shown up on Austin's doorstep to get to know the family. Austin's wife had passed away over a year now, and the two were accepted into the extended family after everything came out. Knowing all the details now, it seemed like Austin and Melissa's attraction and love story were written in the stars.

She reminded herself that none of them ever knew what the future held for them. Things could change on a dime. Idea was, Trace told her, that they all keep on living, enjoying the freedoms the SEALs and many others they worked with protected for them.

"Best way to honor them is to live your life fully," he'd told her.

That wise advice had worked miracles in her life. Once, she'd thought her life was a mess and doubted any romance would ever come her way. Now she was certain the love she and Trace held for each other was borne out of the hardships of loss, feeling forgotten, and being alone. All that had changed. She feared not having him by her side.

The two of them made the rounds. Near the lounge chairs, Angie stripped off her clothes down to her bathing suit and talked to several of the other SEAL kids, who frolicked in the pool until a couple of the Team Guys came in and took over. They splashed and created such a stir the girls got out, yet the boys tried to compete.

On the way home, Gretchen told him how the project was coming.

"You gonna take me by to see it?"

She turned to Angie in the second seat. "You mind?"

"No, I'm fine. I'd like to see it too."

She directed the way to the warehouse just south of the base, and they got out to walk around the building. They couldn't see much of the inside due to the fact that the windows were taped over in some places and, in other places, just plain dirty. It looked like someone was in the process of painting it.

"So you got this building? All signed, sealed, delivered?" he asked.

"No, I don't think so. I am concerned about this paint though. This wasn't here a couple of days ago. But we're negotiating, I guess. I'm leaving all of that up to Deirdre and Kate. And they weren't at the party today, so I wonder what the heck's going on with that." Gretchen allowed the wave of concern to brush over her.

"Well, maybe they had it scheduled before the offer went through. Maybe the owners wanted to make it look more attractive to draw more interest."

They walked the grounds, and Gretchen pointed out the fact that from the second story you could see the ocean.

"Nice! That will be a winner!"

"The other thing we like, including the view upstairs, is the plan Deirdre drew up that calls for a big platform on top overlooking the center and the first floor down below, so it would be a place to sit or have tables for a small, quiet get-together during a larger party. It's also right across the street from where you guys used to train, if you remember?"

"How could I forget?"

"And around the back, we have lots of room for catering trucks and extra storage if we need to bring it in. I mean, Trace, you would just not believe the drawings I've seen, and it just looks like a perfect complex. It's a cooking school, a wedding or party venue, and an art gallery all rolled up into one. I'm excited they even want me to be a part of it since I can't contribute anything."

"You contributed a lot, Gretchen. I think it'd be really thrilling, and look at all the fun Angie would have working down here, don't you agree?" He looked at Angie.

"I told Mom I'd love to learn how to do catering, and it looks like she's going to start a school or something. I know I have several girl-friends who would take her up on the offer to be an apprentice. It's just something I never thought I'd be doing, but I love to cook just like Mom does. With all the parties and things that Mom and Aunt Kate could throw together, I think it's ideal for them. And I think the people would come."

"I'm proud of you, Gretchen. I really can see the vision here. You think big," he said as he bent down and kissed her.

"They are the inspiration. Honest. I'm just one of the team members."

Later on that evening, she sat with Trace and was filled in with further details about what went on in Portland.

"How was it seeing Sven and Kelly?"

"They're considering moving their operation. And, of course, they asked me to join them again. I didn't say anything or let them know that we talked."

She and Trace had talked about the someday when he might want to do something else other than be on the teams. He'd put in his six years, and that was good enough. He would be up for re-enlistment soon, and that was the time when they had to make a decision. They could use the bonus money, Gretchen thought to herself, as they were not exactly flush with cash, but it would mean that he'd have to re-up for another four or six and that would place him near fifty years old when he got out. She didn't think that was a good idea.

"So if you want to consider it, I'm okay with you discussing it with them, real numbers and figures. You know, I kind of think Tyler's in the same boat, and there're several others too. Being on the teams is kind of a young man's deal. What do you think?"

"Well, it would give me flexibility, as long as we can limit the days away and the danger. But I really don't want to live in Portland. I wish they'd moved down here. I'd like to find out what they're thinking first. But, you know, it's a possibility, Gretchen. I could see us staying here—"

"Oh, of course, I love it here, Trace. I don't want to move again."

"That's what I'm saying. We could stay here, and, you know, if I have to travel a little bit, well, that's okay. But I just don't want to spend more time than I have to up in the Pacific Northwest. It's cold and just not my place. Too much negative history there. If all that hadn't happened, I might feel differently. It is a beautiful area, but it's not for me. And you've found a place here, with people you love, and that will continue whether or not I'm still on the teams. I'd consider other places, but I think they'd be better off to be down here. This is where a lot of the tactical companies are, equipment manufacturers, and training centers. They'd have a steady stream of SEALs getting out of the business and looking for something to do, investing in things down here. I think it's a wise decision if they chose that. But we'll see."

"What are they doing these days?"

"Well, I guess they're doing some things in Europe and in Africa, but, with their success with the trafficking, I think they're gonna focus on the women and children being kidnapped and sold. And I talked to Sven a little bit about why he was so interested in helping Tony. It appears that this group that Tony got hooked up with is actually a major player in human trafficking, especially children and girls."

"Did he know that when he got involved?" asked Gretchen.

"No, I don't think he did. I just think he succumbed to his demons, and that led him down the wrong path. I don't think any of us realized how deep their roots went. They're all over the world, Gretchen, even in Europe and Africa."

"Geez, that's horrible. So you think Sven is interested in going after these folks after the fact?"

"I do. I think he's hoping he can find and target some of these people, get some financial help from those who want to also join the cause, and he could find more than enough work. I'm not sure working for the government is going to hold out very much longer. It's a little too dicey for everybody, and you don't have the protections we used to have when we did things. But for private foundations, like the one that they inherited, that's the way to go. They'll keep it legal, but they'll help remove that scourge."

"A worthy goal."

"Besides, the innocent public needs someone standing up for them, someone who can help train them to think like a warrior, teach them how to keep themselves and their families safe. The government is too busy putting out fires elsewhere."

Gretchen saw that his face was animated, his eyes twinkled, as the idea seemed to appeal to him. She made a note to make sure she asked all her questions, because it looked like her man was going to make some changes, and she just wanted him to be safe. It wasn't enough to just have money to live on; she wanted him to be safe.

As they made love that evening, she let the worries drift off and allowed herself to feel the power and love of an ordinary man who did extraordinary things. Someone who loved as hard as he worked. Who would always be there for her, no matter what.

It was an honor to bring to their bed all the passion she found deep down in her soul. He deserved this, and so did she. They were both lucky to have each other.

CHAPTER 11

TRACE PICKED UP Tyler on their way to a full workout at Gunny's gym. They tossed the irons around and spotted for each other, making cracks at some of the older SEALs who liked to frequent the gym early in the morning, and Trace was introduced to a couple of the newbies who were just starting their SEAL Team 3 journey.

"You know the thing that I love about coming here is I can see myself in twenty or thirty years. Like these guys," Trace said, pointing to several grey-haired, beefy men covered in tats who were laughing and enjoying themselves and their self-punishment. They grunted and groaned loudly.

Tyler nodded. "I don't know that I want to look like all of them but, yeah, some of them are in pretty good shape."

Trace laid down to work on a thigh extension machine. He asked Tyler to up the weight a bit and then began his reps.

"You know, nothing wrong with a white ponytail, little bit of a paunch, and muscles like that—look at those guys' muscles and their thighs. I mean, they don't look like the kind of guys who you would want to mess with, right?"

"Yeah, you're right. Certainly would make the women and children feel better walking around with old guys like that."

"I think of the way my grandfather looked in his seventies and eighties. Some of the older men in my family were strong because they worked for a living their whole lives, on farms and machinery and heavy labor work, but they didn't look anything like that. And I'm not saying I want to be a bodybuilder or anything."

He stopped the repetitions enough to take his breath and rest up for the next rep.

"I get what you mean. The ones we don't see in here, of course, are the ones who got injured. And there are some of those in wheelchairs or walkers or who can't stand up straight. Can't hear, can't see, can't sleep through the night from pain. Bad knees, hips, heart."

"Yeah. And that's too bad, isn't it, Tyler? I mean, they gave so much, and they get so little recognition for it."

"Hey, is this *you* talking?" Tyler asked. "When did you expect to get a bunch of medals or recognition for any of the shit you did? You know what it's like, Trace. We do what we do; then we fade back into the woodwork. We're not supposed to be drawing attention to ourselves. If you want to do that, well, go into politics or, I don't know, start a corporation or do a bunch of TED Talks. Write a book, a tell-all book about SEALs."

"Nah, not my style, but some who do, I respect it, if it's good work. Not trash talking. I don't think I have anything that I want anybody to follow me on. I mean, I just want to get my job done, make sure nobody around me gets killed, protect the family, and have a good life."

"You do have a good life, Trace. You found what you needed all along. Some of us get there right away, and some of us have to wait about twenty years or so before we get it. But once you get it, you get it. I once heard of a grandfather of a SEAL who got married again at eighty years old. Can you believe it?"

"Good for them. That's the way it should be, shouldn't it? We never stop falling in love, do we?"

Tyler leaned in and whispered in his ear. "Shh. You don't want anyone to know that. We're big, tough guys, but, inside, we're really softies, right?"

As Trace started another repetition, he boomed out, "Fucking A!"

The comment made the room turn around and take notice. Tyler gave him a wink and shot him with his finger gun. "Now that's what I'm talking about."

After their workout, they went for a run on the beach, passing groups of team guys practicing certain maneuvers, playing football, running in and out of the surf, or lying down and getting wet and sandy voluntarily.

As they ran past, both Tyler and Trace laughed at the ridiculousness of people even trying to do wet and sandies when they didn't have to.

"That would never be me. I don't want to see another rubber boat unless I have to use it for a training exercise or a rescue. No more rubber boats for me. Gretchen asked me if I should get a little Zodiac. We could go out fishing, and I said, hell, no. If I get a boat, it's going to be a big old fucking fishing boat. And then we can go out and anchor and spend all night making that thing rock and roll."

"Well, at least I can report back to my wife that her sister is being well taken care of," said Tyler, with laughter, barely able to get it out.

"Damn straight. No, Gretchen is one of those women who never thought she could get much, and, when you shower her with everything you've got, she just melts and blooms into some fantastic goddess. It's just amazing to see. I feel an ache in my heart at what she missed for so many years, but I'm also very proud of the fact that she's loving life now and that she sees more to the future than she thinks about the past. And that's a good thing, right?"

"That's right. That's the way it should be. So, speaking of futures," Tyler said as he stopped and they both breathed heavy to recover. "You think about what's the next on the road for you?"

"Well, we've got this deployment coming up, and Tony's things are hopefully going to settle down here in the next thirty days or so, I hope. I don't know. I'm sort of thinking maybe I will get out. What about you, Tyler?"

"I'm thinking the same thing. I mean, I don't have as much overall time in length of service like you do, but I think we're done. I've got the kids to think of and other things I want to do."

"I've been thinking a lot about the Bone Frog group. You know that they asked me again when I was up there."

"Of course they did. We'd make great additions to their operation. They've got some good solid guys on their team too. I'm just not sure what their deal is all about."

"One thing that's kind of a deal breaker for me is that they're up in the Pacific Northwest. I want to spend as little time up there as possible. I mean, there're parts that are beautiful, and there's a lot of just gorgeous scenery and lakes and rivers and fishing and hunting. I used to really enjoy all those things, but I want to stick to things that are a little closer to home and where I want to live. Plus, Gretchen and the girls love San Diego. I couldn't take that away from them. And I told Kelly it would be a deal breaker for me if they stayed in Portland. We'll see what they do."

"Well, I'm in the same boat, Trace. And I will seriously look at whatever you look at, brother. Kate's the same way. She wants to stay here. She loves the community and the wives, and it's just something that's hard to see when you're not on the teams. All the guys training and you run into them at parties and things, and I know I'd miss it, Trace. That's the thing I fear the most. What if I get out and I get totally bored with life?"

"Well, that's why I'm thinking maybe staying with the Bone Frog group is a good alternative. We are men of action. We don't just wait for the world to fall apart. When we're called or compelled to go forward, we do. That's what a good man does. He protects the innocent. I'm not so sure I could work for anybody except someone like their team. I've sort of lost my trust in certain individuals, if you get my drift."

"Oh, I feel the same way. I think the public does too. It's getting to be pretty crazy out there. But we have to be at the ready, and I guess, if we were private, we could pick and choose what we do. And that's different than being on the teams. But thank God for the teams. Without them, look at where we'd be at."

"Yep, we need them. And there's a lot of good talent that's leaving, pursuing other things. It's good training for whatever, but once you're a team member, you're a team member. You could lead a warehouse full of technicians or a computer lab anywhere. You know how to lead and how to be part of something bigger than you are. It is just a question of finding the right things that stimulate all your juices, you know? Balancing your age and your physical abilities with that wonderful thumping of your heart when you're doing something dangerous."

"I know. Remember when we used to almost not be able to sleep at night because we were so anxious for the next day to start a mission?"

"Yep, I do. Those are some of my best memories, Tyler. And I am glad I stayed in, even with all the problems I had with Shayla. We all run into these personal things that we get involved with, and sometimes it takes guys off track. I'm glad I stuck it out, and look what I got. I got Gretchen and the girls. I found my new north. And maybe that's what has got to me. I feel like they're paying the price for my being gone so much. I'd like to be around more. Lord knows they need the protection."

"Right. About that. I think about it every day." Tyler wiped down the machine. "Let's grab some grub. Okay?"

"Nah, let's do another five miles down the beach first, and then we'll get some food," answered Trace.

Tyler and Trace wound up at the Rusty Scupper, getting their usual cheesy scrambles, hooking up with several of the other team guys who frequented the restaurant early in the morning when they were off.

Every time Trace walked into the Scupper, he saw the line of Navy SEAL pictures, men who had forfeited their lives for their cause, young men, mostly, looking like high schoolers, handsome and brave, standing guard for their SEAL photos. They bore their Tridents proudly, looked clear-eyed, and stared straight at the camera. Trace could see the courage in their souls as he studied the pictures of the fallen warriors. One by one, he gave his respects to each of them, some who he knew personally, some with stories that he'd heard, and several new ones he'd never met and regretted that.

Tyler walked silently behind him as they maneuvered through the gauntlet of history behind the bar.

They situated themselves in the corner, which was often the place where several of the SEAL Team 3 members would congregate. They'd been out in the sun so didn't want to sit outside on the patio where the barbecue was and the fire pit, and this was still early morning so he needed his breakfast in silence and in the dark.

When their order arrived, Tyler broached a couple of questions they hadn't discussed before.

"What do you think is going to happen with Tony?"

Trace put his fork down and thought about it for a second. "Sven told me something that kind of sums up my fear. I wouldn't say that I expect this, but it is a fear."

"What did he say?" asked Tyler.

"He said he didn't think Tony was long for this world. I really don't want that to happen, for the girls' sake."

He stared into Tyler's eyes and saw agreement there. "I'm conflicted. I wish I was never tasked with helping him, but it was what I had to do, and now I'm conflicted because Sven has inserted himself so deeply into Tony's affairs. I just don't know how it's all going to end."

"Well, don't worry about Sven. He's solid. I mean, I don't think anybody could get to him even if it was something bad."

"I'm not sure he knows what's coming. This Organization is super bad, and they don't really have any code. It's not like a family. It's like an amoeba or a flesh-eating something that preys on society, sucks the blood out of them, takes their treasure, and discards detritus. It's an evil group of people. It's too much for one man or even one group to go after. It would be years taking them down. And I fear that all Sven has done is substitute himself for Tony. And I'm here to tell you Tony's not worth it."

"Except he is your wife's ex and the father of your girls," said Tyler.

"That's true, and that's why I got involved in the first place. But Sven is committing funds as well as manpower. He very clearly wants me out of it, but I can't let Sven take that risk in my place."

"But we've got the deployment coming up, Trace. You forget your job."

"And that's why I'm conflicted, Tyler. It's my job, agreed. But I'm worried about what's going on at home. And I never used to feel like that. It's like each time I go away, I worry more and more about the people I'm leaving behind."

"You better talk to Kyle about that, Trace. You know what he's going to say. He's going to say if you start thinking about it, worrying about it, then it's probably time to get out. He's going to tell you that, Trace. Do you want to hear that?"

"Not yet. But I'm getting closer, Tyler. I would just never forgive myself if something blows up while we're gone. I'm hoping and praying Sven can get this thing put to bed. I don't want it hanging over everybody's head while we're halfway across the world."

"I think you need to have a little more confidence in Sven and his capabilities. And it's not like he doesn't have a team. He's got Bryce, several SEALs from Team 5, and a couple of San Diego detectives and policemen, a couple of Marines, and some group guys. He's got a good crew behind him. If he needs it. And Kelly, well, she's still got weight, and they're smart, Trace. They have a lot more resources than you or I have, even being on the teams."

"Yeah, I agree. I just don't like that he's investing some money in Tony's recovery. Because Tony isn't good for it. He's not going to pay him back."

Tyler put his arm on Trace's shoulder. "Look, man, it's better that Tony owes Sven than owes those animals in The Organization. Take it from me. It's a much better place for everybody if that happens. Because Sven knows how to fight back. Tony? He'd just get mowed under. And you know how you'd feel about that."

CHAPTER 12

C LOVER ARRIVED HOME, loaded with bags of gifts she had bought for her two sisters, Gretchen, and Trace. Jack struggled at first getting things out of the car, but he brought up the rear with additional bags, leaving their luggage behind. Gretchen noted he didn't complain with all the stuff he had to carry, and it appeared he let Clover spend what she wanted on things to bring back. She smiled.

"Oh, so great to see you, sweetheart," she said as she hugged her daughter. "You look absolutely wonderful, a little sunburned, but you look fantastic, Clover!"

Gretchen saw the twinkle in her eyes, the happiness that was so much a part of Clover's spirit now blooming in her new life as a married woman. She hugged her son-in-law as well. "Thanks for taking good care of her."

"No problem. She's easy to please. A little bit of sunshine, some margaritas, some beach time, some snorkeling, walks on the beach, a lot of talking. It was wonderful, the perfect honeymoon. Very laid back too," he said with a chuckle.

"What was the highlight of the trip?" Gretchen asked.

Angie joined the group, and the excitement accelerated again as she gave Clover a full body slam with the two dancing up and down. Eventually, everyone sat down, and Gretchen served some ice water. "You want something else, Jack?"

"I think I'd like a coffee if you've got any made. I am kind of weary from the flight and time difference. I'll take a nap this afternoon, but I'd like some coffee now."

"Coming up."

Clover shouted across the room as Gretchen ground coffee and prepared the French Press. "We loved the waterfalls, and there were some beautiful hiking trails up at the North Shore. They're kind of dangerous when it's wet and slippery, but the views are outstanding. There's no way you can get to those places except on that hike. And the snorkeling at the Ke'e beach at the most north portion of the island, that was beautiful, and the Waimea Valley, oh, it was all so gorgeous. All the rain we got. I actually didn't even mind it at all," reported Clover.

"Trace and I loved it there too. I'd like to go back someday. Maybe for our anniversary sometime," said Gretchen.

Jack added, "There was a cute little needlepoint store we ran into. Clover, you have that package?"

She dug through her bags and handed Gretchen a thin, pink paper sack. Inside was a hand painted needlepoint canvas. She was overcome with its beauty and the thoughtfulness of the two of them. Her eyes watered up.

"This lady is eighty-something years old, and she just sits there on the beach in her bare feet and paints these canvases for this needlepoint shop. They're really beautiful. All Hawaiian scenes. You'd love it there, Mom. I know you would, as soon as you can get back."

"This is beautiful. I'll work on this one next." Gretchen wiped her cheeks.

Clover pulled aside a package for Rebecca, handing it to Gretchen. "I'm not sure when I'll see her again, but, if you could give this to her from us, that would be great."

And then Clover handed Angie a package of the same size. Angie tore it open with gusto, and it revealed a long, beautiful flowered dress with a ruffled edge.

"These are traditional Hawaiian muumuus, made by a local seamstress. She only makes these, her own creation and design, and you see people wearing them all the time. But they are certified 100% Hawaiian made. Even the material is patterned and dyed there on the islands using organic local dyes. You'll want to wash it the first time in cold water, maybe twice, and then you should be good to go."

"Thank you, Clover. I love it," said Angie. She danced to her bedroom to go try it on.

Gretchen handed Jack his coffee and asked him if he wanted cream, which he declined.

"Where's Trace?" he asked.

"He's back, came back last night, and had a successful trip up to Portland. He'll be back for a while, and then he leaves on deployment in a few weeks. So they're getting ready for that. He's out doing a workout with Tyler."

"How is your project coming, Mom?"

"Have you got news I don't have?" asked Gretchen.

Clover smiled. "I got a call from Aunt Kate. I'm sorry. I guess you don't know they made an offer on this building, and it got accepted."

"Really? I didn't *know* that. She didn't *tell* me."

"Well, she offered me a job, Mom, and she wants me and Angie to help her with the cooking school and helping set up the catering business. Along with you, of course. But she wanted to make sure I didn't feel obligated or forced into doing it. She wanted to make sure it was something I wanted to do, so that's why she called me direct."

Gretchen was a little miffed that Kate hadn't let her know, but she understood her sister's tactics. Her sister knew Gretchen would be overly protective of Clover, and she understood why she wanted Clover's permission first before it was discussed further. But Gretchen still didn't like it. She attempted to cover up her disappointment at having been left out of an important decision.

"Well, it's one thing to tell her that my girls are all excited, but I understand she needed to check it out for herself. There's a lot of planning going on, but it's such an exciting project, and I'm so glad they got the building. We were over there yesterday, and it looks like somebody's already started to paint it."

"Well, I didn't know that. But anyway, she called me in Hawaii just so you know. And I told her I'd see what I could do. I didn't want it to interfere with school, and she didn't want that to happen either. But we're going to work out some hours that will allow me to do both. But there are a few little changes that are going to happen here, and I just wanted to let you know some recent news."

Gretchen sat up straight just as Angie danced into the room with her new dress.

"I love it. I absolutely love it!"

"Come have a seat. Your sister's about to tell us something," said Gretchen.

Clover took Jack's hand, and they looked at each other, the love between them emanating brightly. "Mom, we just found out we're pregnant."

"Wait a minute? You haven't even been back a day, and you already know you're pregnant?"

"I know. It shocked us too! We were snorkeling, and I stepped on a sharp piece of shell. We had to go to the emergency room to have it checked out, or that's what the concierge recommended. While we were there, they took a blood test, and I guess one of the things I'd mentioned to the doctor was that I had been kind of stressed and I hadn't had a period for a couple months. Well, the doctor went ahead and did a pregnancy test on me, which I was okay with. And it was positive. We're going to have a baby in about seven months. I guess we weren't careful enough."

Gretchen was shocked.

Angie ran over to her sister and gave her a big hug and fell into Jack's arms as well. "Oh my gosh. Oh my gosh. I'm going to be an aunt. I'm going to be an aunt!"

Gretchen was delayed in giving Clover her response, lost in thought about all the repercussions of this news. She hadn't quite figured out how she felt about it. She hugged her and hugged Jack and then took back her seat. "So how is this going to affect your schooling? And now this new job with the project? You've got a lot on your plate, Clover. And, Jack, what about your schooling? I mean, how's this going to affect everything?"

Jack started slowly, "Well, we're delighted, and we can't wait. I'm going to continue and see if I can double up on my schooling and get it finished early, or get as much done as I can before the baby arrives. You need to know, Mrs. Bennett, I want Trace to help me train for the Teams. Clover and I have talked about it, and I'll get my degree in case things don't work out, but I think—maybe a year from now—I'd like to try out."

Things were piling up on Gretchen faster than she could deal with. She felt herself floundering, in an emotional freefall.

"But, with a new baby at home, you want to be gone for all those important firsts?" Gretchen knew she was beginning to show her worry and concern. "How are you going to do all this?"

"Mom, you always said to trust you, to trust in life, and this is one of those times when you have to trust me. I think I know what I'm doing. I can finish my degree before the baby's here and still work part-time for Aunt Kate, you, and Deirdre. I'd really like to be involved in that. And I'll give up my coaching. I could turn that over to Angie and Rebecca if they'll take it."

Angie nodded enthusiastically. "Rebecca and I would love to!"

Gretchen hadn't even considered this was a possibility. All of a sudden, she thought about all the moving parts—Trace leaving for Africa, Tony and his problems, now Clover being home and pregnant. What else could happen? She was filled with doubt and didn't want to rain on her daughter's parade, so she smiled and tried to show a united front.

"Sweetheart, if anybody can do it, you can. I believe in you. And Trace and I will support you however we can. I'm so happy that you've returned. And I'm so glad I'm going to be able to watch as your pregnancy grows and to be part of this new little one's development. New project, new life in the family, it's all good, Clover."

But Gretchen knew, inside, her worries were forming a dark cloud. This wasn't just going to be a change for Clover and her husband. It was going to cause an epic shift with all of them, the whole family. She was going to have to get ready for even more, even though she already thought they were on overload.

But with Trace, somehow, they'd pull it off.

CHAPTER 13

T RACE'S DEPLOYMENT TO North Africa and the Canary Islands came up as an emergency deployment. Kyle took with him twenty-five of the team members, since this operation was going to be carried out in various waves.

The State Department was concerned about a human trafficking operation that had just been discovered in the Canaries, which appeared to be rapidly growing in scope. There were questions about the national origin of the organizers, and the SEALs were tasked to go in and see if they could get intel, evidence of either Russian or Chinese assets being used to support this cause.

This particular mission wasn't a rescue but a fact-finding task in order to determine what, if anything, needed to be done. The fact that a huge number of new immigrants were sighted arriving at several ports in the islands and seen leaving in various crafts, including private jets—to parts unknown—was of concern to State. Due to the fact that there had been some unrest on the Canaries recently, Kyle got permission to bring a larger team than normal. There was always the possibility they would have to move on to the west coast of Africa. There were also military skirmishes spreading through Nigeria, parts of Benin, and Niger, as well as other parts of north and west Africa.

Trace was almost grateful for the new mission, since it took his mind off of the problems with Tony. In the transport, as they bumbled along across the Atlantic in the huge, very uncomfortable airplane, he thought about how he loved this part of the mission, the anticipation of the action, even though it was hot, noisy, and mind-numbing. Everyone went into their own space while they traveled. Everyone silently geared up and checked what they brought and made sure they were prepared for whatever the situation, listening on their devices, meditating, sleeping, or doing whatever they had to do to get their mindset into the game and flow of the mission, depending on their specialty. It was the quiet before the storm. Hopefully, the entire mission would be quiet. At least that's what Trace wanted.

He barely had a chance to congratulate Clover and Jack on their honeymoon, celebrate their news, and try on the aloha shirt that the two of them had bought him. It was adorned with palm trees and bright plumeria blossoms. He didn't want to tell them that the shirt was a tiny bit small, but he planned to wear it anyway when Clover was around. He'd beefed up these last few months working out, being helpful and active support to Gretchen and the girls, planning the wedding, probably overeating, and for sure overdrinking.

But he'd shed some pounds during this op since it was going to be hot and they would be eating on the run, not full sit-down meals. Often, in times like these, he would practically fast, if he was hydrated. It was better if he worked on an empty stomach than a full one.

He loved the glow in Clover's eyes and face, how Jack attended to her every need. And he was excited about the prospect of a new little one in their family. Unlike Gretchen, and she'd told him her reservations, he was pleased with the news. He thought Jack would make an excellent father. Trace planned on spoiling the dickens out of the new little one as well.

Kyle asked him to sit next to him so they could have a private conversation. It was difficult to do with the noise of the engines so loud.

"I just want to say in advance that I hesitated bringing you along on this mission, Trace, because of everything that's going on at home. You understand that there's no going back, even if something goes sideways?" Kyle asked.

"Yes, I got it. I appreciate it, sir. I'm all good. We've got another week or so before the escrow closes on Tony's house and the money gets delivered. Thankfully, Sven is involved. Never meant to do that to him, but, in hindsight, I'm glad I did."

"Damn straight. That was a good choice. Otherwise, you'd be wanting to stay home. I know you would. And I know you have some big choices coming up, Trace. Things I'm sure you don't want to mention. Let me just say, I want you here as long as you can be. I need you. I need experienced men, mature men who understand what this business is all about."

"Well, thank you, sir." He wasn't sure how to continue.

"You need to tell me anything now?" Kyle asked.

"Not the time, Kyle." He searched for something else to share and then found it. "Gretchen and I talked about me not checking my phone so often, and she's not going to bother me unless it's absolutely necessary. I plan to be fully present, Kyle, focused on what needs to be done, no matter what. Besides, it's really in Sven's hands, and I think he'd do a hell of a lot better job than I ever would anyway."

"Well, I'm not going to say that, but, frankly, you'll get no argument out of me. Sven's a standup guy. I wish he could get his citizenship taken care of, and I wish the Navy could have his butt on my team but that's not for Sven."

"He's an independent, sir. He's made for what he's doing now. He travels, he likes to roam, and he doesn't like to be tied down."

"Roger that. I'm just glad he's one of the good guys and he's on our side," said Kyle.

"He's a formidable enemy to any who try to destroy freedom."

They landed on Gran Canaria, and, before several of the team members were transported off island, Kyle called a meeting. Shortly, they'd be split up into three different compounds with groups of eight to ten men in each. Senior guys were embedded with each group so that those individuals could talk. Trace was put in the same camp as Kyle, so his leadership responsibilities would be minimal. But Cooper went over to one of the islands, and Tyler was tasked with leading another group at Tenerife. Fredo and several other long-termers were also sent to Tyler's group so he was provided with lots of assets.

When they got situated in the house that had been procured for them, Kyle gave the whole group an overview before the others were transported by ferry to their particular locations.

"This is a little bit different than some of our ops, fellas, in that we're supposed to be Uncle Sam's eyes and ears. We have some State Department help, but they'll be sort of invisible, on the sidelines. We aren't going to have as much direct and no on-the-ground communication with them. What we're supposed to do is look into this rapidly-growing smuggling operation that appears to have been formulated taking refugee ships from North Africa. Most of these are people who have traveled great distances, perhaps from Nigeria or more the interior of Africa, and they have secured paid passage to the coast where they take dinghies and arrive in the Canaries. It's a bounty system, similar to the operation going on at the U.S. southern border, with boat captains ferrying across migrants seeking to immigrate to the Canaries for probably no good reason. Maybe to participate in the human trafficking ring, the drug trade, or possibly to begin forming a standing militia that could be imported anywhere around the globe."

Kyle took a couple of minutes while the group took note of his message.

"Also, some of the larger ships are carrying human cargo. If we find one of those, we have authorization to stop it and then call in the Navy to board, unless they're being escorted by the Civil Guard."

"That's actually happening?" asked Jameson.

"Just what the rumor is. But, short of seeing actual evidence of human smuggling, we're interested in picking up stories and finding out who the leaders are, who's directing them, and who on the islands are supporting them. They can't run an operation without local support. We're supposed to find out where that's coming from."

Kyle showed the terrain of all of the islands and what they suspected was taking place in the various areas. "You have ship building over here. There's also a small factory we think is storing arms, but we are to check that out to be sure. Tyler and your group—you're going to be doing that. I want pictures, and I want names of people who come and go regularly. I want to know who owns the facilities if you can find out, and I want to know if any civilians like local police or militia are involved. That also would be helpful to the State Department."

Armando had a question. "Kyle, I need to ask you ... Why is it that State doesn't use its own assets or the CIA to look into this? Why are we being tasked with this?"

Kyle had an answer for that and acknowledged Armando's question.

"It's too dangerous, Armando. Things have just gotten to be a tinderbox over in Africa. We are not involved militarily except for some support staff and a SEAL Team. We have some operators embedded with the UN forces covertly. But they're not hardened, high quality assets, and we really don't want the diplomats or the CIA to get involved in a war. The diplomats aren't armed generally, and they don't have the ability to use force if it's necessary. That's why we're tasked with it."

Fredo asked another question. "I thought we're not supposed to engage?"

"Only if acted upon. Only in a dire emergency, to save one of our own. I'm not even sure we'd be justified in acting if it was a local person's involvement. I don't think we can do a rescue. At least we haven't been cleared for that. We're not supposed to start a war. We're supposed to report on what the status is before our government decides what approach they're going to take. It may be that there will be no military force at all, only economic. It may be that it goes through diplomatic channels. We don't know. But they need information that only we can get, and that will help them come up with a plan that works."

Trace had an idea. "What if we find local officials are compromised?"

"That's a very real possibility, Trace. In that event, we report and then we ask for solutions. We may just report and go home. I'm hoping it'll be something like that, that the gift of our intelligence will be enough to go on, so we don't get embroiled in a firefight. I really don't expect and don't want to do that."

One of the newer SEALs asked, "So how are we going about this? I mean, we're all on different islands doing different things. How do we communicate with each other? What happens if everything's coordinated with the traffickers going from one island to the next to the next? What happens if we see there's a direct correlation between all of these groups?"

"That's a good question, son. Your seniors will all communicate twenty-four seven. You report to your team leader. And it's definitely possible they are all connected. And that's part of our job. We sure as heck want to know what we're walking into before we do it. You don't want to hit the hornet's nest before you know how many are inside, right?"

"We usually do a lot of beach time, some cooking, we play a lot of cards, and minimal drinking, but some," said Coop.

"I'm going to say less on the drinking side, please. We're sometimes surrounded by people who don't drink, so you've got to remember that. That said, we are just American tourists, just a bunch of guys getting together to go fish or go play around. If we happen to go into some seedy bars and get firsthand information, so be it. That's what we do. We just be typical idiot American men. That's what they think of us, so that's how we'll play it."

Over the next two days, the team on Gran Canaria broke into groups of threes and fours, never less than three, and wandered the streets, oftentimes changing up who walked with who. When they got back to their mother house, they compared notes. Several of the men had been propositioned for prostitution, even offered underage girls, which was not uncommon in this region of the world. Those places that seemed to harbor individuals in that trade were noted, and a map was created. They set up a program of checking out those areas at different times of the day, even late at night, routinely changing up the guys, sending them out for one or two drinks and then pulling them back and sending another group later. It was like a scatter approach, a hit or miss operation, just to see what they could snag, kind of like throwing the net out to get fish bait for catching the bigger fish later on.

One of the guys in Tyler's group actually made contact with a hostess who had a whole house full of teenage girls, all of them Black, not native Canarians.

Kyle instructed them to send it up the chain and await the response before they did anything. Of course, they were asked to keep their distance until an okay was given.

On Gran Canaria, which was the seat of several government offices, a trio of the team members began a friendly conversation with several of the Guardia Civil officials, who seemed to be honest and talkative. The team members hesitated before they brought up anything about drugs or girls, wanting to see if the officials would bring it up to them first.

Later, Kyle asked the SEALs to find the Guardia Civil gentlemen to ask about their safety, if they wandered through the streets and looked for items to take home to their girlfriends and wives, if it was safe for them to travel in twos and threes, and if they were susceptible to smuggling or robbery.

The Guardia Civil were quite proud of the fact that they had greatly decreased the amount of drug smuggling, telling them so, in broken English.

In Spanish, Carlos, one of the newer SEALs, asked the police, "What about girls? Not for us, but if we brought our girlfriends or daughters, are they safe here?"

The local police all gave them the answer, in English, they expected to get. Yes, it was very safe there.

One of the guards offered, "The girls who are put into prostitution here have been smuggled in from other areas. We look for those people too, as they are breaking the law and making our shores less safe. Generally, the tourists and the population of Gran Canaria are safe from these people. They run houses for tourists or as a stop-off point for European and United States' destinations. But as far as girls and wives and daughters escorted by men, they would not be touched. It's sort of a code amongst the traffickers," the guard said.

"Where are these people from who do this?" Carlos asked.

"They come from all over. We have Russians, Ukrainians, people from Albania, Mauritania, Algeria, and several from Africa. African girls are the easiest, I think, to smuggle. They're often paid. They pay their parents to steal them. Or warlords, who capture families, kill the men and sell the women and children. Horrible business," the guard answered.

Carlos indicated to them that it was the same between the Mexican and U.S. border.

"You should not have a problem here as long as you are not dealing with drugs or girls. We want you to come to our islands and spend your money, have a great vacation, enjoy our beautiful blue waters and our lovely beaches and our culture. We have much in the way of culture, and we are like a bridge between Europe, Africa, Portugal, and Spain. A mixture of the whole world. We have a rich history of piracy and smuggling, but old traditions die hard. Things are much tamer now. We have order," the guard said.

After the SEALs made it back to their rented house, they sat around the pool, finishing their dinners, and talking about the day.

One of the Guardia Civil they had spoken to earlier showed up at the front door. This indicated, of course, that someone had followed them home. Carlos spoke to the gentleman and brought him inside the kitchen where Kyle and Trace were conversing. They didn't invite him outdoors to see the others.

"Please do not be alarmed. I'm one of the good guys," he said.

Trace wasn't sure he trusted him.

"Just in case you are doing something that is counter to the kidnappers and pirates who *do* frequent these islands, I'm available to be your resource."

"Why would you think that? And why would you put yourself out like that?" Kyle asked.

"I had a good friend who was working for the United States government and for the government in Spain. He was paid informant money, but, unfortunately, his status was discovered. He was murdered nearly a year ago now. He was my best friend. In his name, I would be agreeable to helping you find whomever it is you're looking for."

Carlos asked him how he took them to be anything other than just American tourists.

"I see the tattoos. I see the way your arms and shoulders are, the way you move. You gentlemen are trained, physically trained, and—just by watching you walk down the street—I can see there's something different about you. Most everybody who is attuned to that can tell the same. I will warn you, though, don't try to do anything on this island. The police have the backing of many of the kidnappers and money behind it. They're bought off, and they will disappear you. It's a very dangerous situation. I would not ask these questions unless you know who you're talking to. But I will help you all I can."

He shook hands with Carlos, and then Kyle stepped up, looking him in the eyes.

"I'm the leader of this group, and I don't deny those assumptions but won't agree with them either. I need to get your contact information. Do you have a secure line to discuss these things?" asked Kyle.

"Just my cell."

"Not secure enough."

"I have nothing else, sir."

"Then we'll get you something, but what about your family?"

"My family has gone to the United States. It is no longer safe for them here. I am waiting here for my mother's hospital operation. And then I will be escorting her to the States. I am not going to return, but the Guard does not know these plans. I can help you in the meantime, if you can get me some form of communication. That's why I came in person and alone."

"So be it. We'll get you that."

After he left, Kyle asked for and received word a set of phones that could be used on the island would be dropped by drone from one of their naval ships about twenty miles away. It would enable Kyle and the informant, Guerrero, to speak personally without interference. It was an untraceable number and had satellite coverage that was secure, untraceable.

They delivered the phones in a package at a predetermined drop-off in the city park downtown. Later on the next evening, Guerrero telephoned Kyle and let him know that he got the phone and that there was going to be a new shipment of young girls coming in the next day, and they'd been asked to not board or interfere with the cargo ship as it came in.

"You have the ship name and the time of arrival?" asked Kyle.

"Yes, sir, the Margarita Malaga." He gave the arrival and pier information.

"Roger that. We aren't going to interfere, so you will not be compromised in any way, but we are going to let the Navy know. Anything else like this you get, you let us know. Okay?"

"Will do. Is this worth some money to you?"

"I'm not a purser, Guerrero, but I'll see that something comes your way. We will let you know when we drop something off."

When Kyle relayed all of this to the State Department, he was told a package would be dropped off on the beach at midnight and given coordinates. It was to be given to the official to encourage him to keep the intel flowing.

Kyle placed the small envelope under the seat of the couch in the Hotel Don Pablo, on a public veranda located on the second-floor balcony off of the bar. It would be easy for Guerrero to get in there, pick up his package, and leave without being seen.

Similar pieces of information were collected from the other two groups. The name of the house owner—the madam of the young girls from Africa—was discovered and relayed. She was a recent Russian immigrant herself with experience running houses all over the world for various oligarchs and warlords.

A warehouse full of guns and drugs was located on Tenerife, not more than about two blocks from the famous beaches. All this information was relayed to the State Department. They were to wait the next few days to see if further action was required.

Trace asked for and was given permission to call home. He wasn't able to reach Gretchen, but he left a nice, long message. He missed her, he missed seeing Clover and the other girls, and he told her everything was safe, that he was good, and that they were fulfilling their duty and their promise, but, so far, no live action. He asked her to be patient and hoped that he'd be home soon.

He lay in bed and looked up at the stars through the window that night. He knew she was looking at a different set of stars when it turned night in California. He thought about the way they strolled on the beach there, the project they were working on, and all the things that were ahead of them at home. He hoped that Tony got his money settled, and he hoped that Sven was out of danger.

Now his job was to complete the tour and get his butt home, perhaps once and for all.

"Goodnight, sweetheart."

CHAPTER 14

"GRETCHEN! I'M IN trouble, really big trouble!" Tony said on the other end of the line.

Gretchen reared up from a sound sleep, glancing at the clock. It was nearly 2:00 a.m. "Why are you calling me?"

"Because I don't have anybody else to call. I've been trying Trace for the past hour, and he doesn't answer."

"That's because he's not here. Why are you calling Trace? I thought you had Sven helping you out?"

"Well, I don't want to get him involved. I didn't want to tell him."

"Tell him what?"

"I got busted. I got busted with someone I thought was a hooker. And I'm sorry to tell you this, but I got enemies here, Gretchen. I got to get out of jail. I got to get bailed out tonight. I'm afraid what's going to happen when people find out about it tomorrow morning."

"Wait a minute, Tony. You got money. You got money from the loan on the house. What's up with that?"

Tony mumbled something that didn't make sense to Gretchen. "Are you drunk, Tony?"

"Just a little, and, as far as the money, I'm not sure where it is."

The last part, he whispered into the phone, obviously trying to protect the information from others who might be waiting in line.

"I'm sorry, but there's nothing I can do. We're tapped out. There's just no money here for me to do that, and I'm not going to put any of our assets on loan until Trace is back here. I can't help you, Tony. You're going to have to call Sven."

"Do you understand what I'm saying? I'm in danger, Gretchen." He was slurring his words and getting more and more emotional by the moment.

"Tell me exactly what happened. You picked up a prostitute and then got arrested?"

"Well, she wasn't really a prostitute. She was a decoy. And I propositioned her, and, well, you know, she took all the money I had. I mean, I've got more. I just can't remember where I put it. It's somewhere in the house. Maybe the tenants took it, I don't know. But I'm in a jam, and my biggest problem right now is there are people who, as soon as they find out I'm in jail … I'm going to be toast, just toast."

"Not to mention what Sven's going to do to you when he figures it out."

"Don't bring up Sven."

"Why not? He was your guardian angel, Tony. All you had to do was stop being a jerk, stand up and be a man for a change. There's absolutely nothing I can do, and calling me was a mistake."

Just then she saw Angie at the doorway, then make her way into the bedroom and sit down on the bed next to her. She was sick that Tony's daughter was going to be privy to all this information. But they'd already had somewhat of a dose of reality. Gretchen figured she might as well just finish it off.

"You know your daughter's sitting here, next to me, and she's wondering why you would call me at two o'clock in the morning. Should I tell her that you tried to—"

"Don't tell her!" yelled Tony.

Gretchen had half a mind to just hang up on him, but, in looking at Angie's sad eyes, she thought better of it. "I'll try to reach Sven, but that's the only way you're going to get out of there. First of all, I'm not in Portland. You could just have them escort you to the house to pick up your money. It must be there."

"I'm not in Portland. I'm in San Diego."

"San Diego? What the *hell* are you doing here?"

"I needed a break. I just needed to go back, and, well, I have a couple friends here, and I couldn't find them, and I thought maybe I'd run into somebody I knew, one of Trace's friends or Trace or—or *you* maybe, or somebody downtown. So I just hung out there, and I guess I had too much to drink."

"Tony, you can't just drop in on us here. We're not here for you any longer."

"She's my kid."

"She's fourteen, and you are to stay away from her. You aren't allowed unsupervised meetings or contact, Tony. You know that."

Tony was breathing hard into the phone. It sounded to Gretchen he was about ready to pass out.

"San Diego should be safer than up there," said Gretchen.

"No, it's not. I got word Sam had me followed. Somebody passed me a message and said Sam is after me. He's coming to get me. What the fuck do I do, Gretchen?"

"If he's going to bail you out, let him!"

"He'll kill me."

She nearly said the unthinkable, but didn't. "You call Sven. I'll try as well. Which station are you at?"

"Central North, I don't have the address, but I think he could find it. Do you think maybe you could come down and try to talk to these guys?"

"Hell, no. I'm not going to go do that. They're not going to listen to me anyway."

"Okay, well, at least I tried. Hey, Gretchen, I'm sorry about all this. I'm sorry about everything."

"You should tell your daughter. I'm done with you, Tony." She hung up the phone.

She sat there with her elbows on her knees, her face buried in her hands. She wanted to burst out crying, but, with Angie sitting next to her, she held it all in. Angie's sweet words helped her mood somewhat. She placed her arm around her mother's shoulder and drew her close.

"Mom, it's okay. Dad's a full-on creep. And he shouldn't ask you to go down to the station and bail him out."

"You heard all that?"

"Of course, I couldn't help but hear. He was yelling in the phone, Mom. I know you can't get hold of Trace, but do you have this other guy's number?"

She'd forgotten about Sven. "Yes, yes. Let me see—" She scurried through her room to find Trace's desk drawer and was hoping he'd have Sven's card. She saw Kelly Fielding's card and called it.

The line went to a disconnect message. Apparently, they'd changed numbers when Kelly had moved full-time to Portland. She looked at the card carefully to see if there was another number, and did find a cell. She dialed.

"Hello?" Kelly answered.

"Oh, Kelly, it's Gretchen, and I just got a call from Tony. He's in jail, for heaven's sake. He got arrested for picking up a police decoy for prostitution."

"Goddamn that guy. Boy, he's sure headed for the jaws of death, isn't he, Gretchen? Let me go find Sven. I think he's sleeping downstairs."

"I'm so sorry, Kelly, but I don't know who else to ask."

"Well, he's supposed to call us. I wonder what happened."

"Well, Tony was just being Tony, right?"

"Hang on a sec. Let me go get Sven."

Gretchen heard her feet tapping the stairs, then footsteps as she ran to the living room where the television was playing. Kelly woke Sven, who had probably fallen asleep on the couch.

She turned off the TV and, once Sven had collected himself, he grabbed the phone. "Gretchen, what's up?"

"Tony's down here in San Diego, and he got picked up for solicitation of a prostitute, a police decoy. He's asking for money to bail himself out, and I don't have it. And I'm not going to go down there. It's just not right. I'm not going to do it."

"I wonder why the hell he went down *there*?"

"I don't know, but, anyway, I'm not sure what to do. He said he's at the North Central Station. And he says he can't find the rest of his money."

"That asshole. After all the work we went through with all this stuff, and he's just blown his money again. I mean, how could he blow $25,000 in five days?"

"Because Tony is Tony, and he's extremely flawed."

"Can you get hold of Detective Mayfield? Maybe he can get some information and then call me back. Use this number." Sven gave Gretchen his direct cell.

"Okay, I'll try. If I don't reach him, then I'll text you his number and you can try. I just don't know who else to call. I mean, should I call Christy or what should I do? I don't want to bother Trace."

"No, don't call Trace. You have any reason to think Tony's in danger? I mean, maybe we should just let him sit there till morning."

"Well, he did say that Sam somehow got a message to him that he was after him or he was going to come get him or something like that, I don't know."

"Geez. So he sounded urgent, right?"

"Yes, he did. He was panicked. I've never heard him so frantic before."

"Okay, well, try to get ahold of Gus, and maybe he can do us a good one and get him isolated or put under special observation somewhere. At least until I can get down there and sort this out, but, geez, I feel like I've got a fourteen-year-old teenager who's driving without a license. I had no idea Tony was such a handful."

"Well, now you know what Trace has been going through. I'm just not sure why Tony keeps getting himself into these situations."

"Me neither, but if Tony wants to kill himself doing it I'm not going to stop him. It's just that now he's come closer to you and brought all this danger with him. That's not cool, Gretchen. You armed?"

"Of course I am."

"You lock all your windows and doors, and you get your guns out. Keep Angie with you at all times. Don't leave the house until I can get somebody over there to give you some protection. Okay?"

"Thanks, Sven. I really owe you."

"No, sweetheart, you don't owe me. Tony does. But, first, he owes an apology to you, your girls, to everybody. He's just maybe not redeemable. And I'm sorry to say that, but he's not worth all this effort we're having to go through just to keep him safe. I get him out of one mess and he jumps into another one."

"Thanks, Sven. I'm going to go load up, check the windows and doors, and try to go back to sleep."

"Well, keep your phone by you so we know you can reach us."

Gretchen and Angie ran around the house, making sure that every single window was closed and latched, that every door was bolted and dead bolted. She dug out two of Trace's guns, including his SIG Sauer, and loaded it, leaving an extra magazine on the nightstand just in case. She also got out his Smith & Wesson and did the same. Everything being checked and double-checked, she left one of the guns in the kitchen underneath her tea towels next to the stove. The other one she left upstairs in her bedroom. No matter which place she needed it, she'd have it on either floor.

Then she sat down on the couch with Angie by her side and gave Gus Mayfield a call.

"Gretchen? What's up, honey? Something wrong?"

"I'm sorry to bother you, but my ex, Tony, he's in jail down at Central North. He's gotten into some trouble with some gambling, and Trace and Sven have been trying to work it out. But he got busted for solicitation, and he's there, but he's scared that somebody's coming for him. He thinks somebody from Portland is after him, one of the criminals who lent him the money, who owns his gambling debts."

"Well, Trace is overseas, right?"

"Yes, everybody's over there. And I don't know when they'll come back. But you know their friend Sven was working with Tony to help get his debt paid off, and they were almost there. I mean, Tony has money coming in a week or so. They arranged it with this guy who Tony got into for a lot of money. They arranged it and all Tony had to do was just keep his nose clean until the house closed, until the guy could get paid off. I don't know why, but he came down to San Diego, and now he's in jail, and he's worried about some guy coming to get him. Sven asked me to tell you this to see if there's some kind of way he could be isolated someplace away from the rest of the population so nobody could mess with him?"

"Wow, let me see what I can do, but, boy, it's the wrong time of day for that. Let me call the station and see what they got on him, and I'll see if I know anybody there still. Most of my friends have retired now, so I don't have the clout I used to have, but I'll try."

"You don't have to call me back, Gus. Just give Sven a call. Here's his number." She gave him both Sven's cell and also Kelly's.

"I'll do what I can, and then I'll call Sven back. You go get some sleep. And, Gretchen?"

"Yes?"

"You got some protection?"

"Yes, sir, I do. And I'll use it if I have to. I got Angie here."

"Good girl, but be careful. I'll see if I can send someone over to help. I know a couple guys who sort of moonlight for the department. I'll see if one of them is available."

"Thank you so much."

Gretchen made sure all the lights were off, and she and Angie waited upstairs, in the dark, sitting in the big, armed reading chair in the corner of their bedroom. They could see the full vista of the street below, and so far there was no traffic, no foot traffic either. They were going to have to be vigilant.

Angie finally fell asleep in Gretchen's bed, and, though her daughter was able to nod off, occasionally snoring, Gretchen was racked with fear. Her mind was going a million miles a minute. She was imagining all the things that could go wrong. When she thought things were put to bed, all of a sudden everything blew up again.

She began to realize that this was what it was like to have Tony as part of her life. And she'd bent over backwards to try to accommodate him for years when they were married, and, now that she was on a different path and safely tucked in the arms of Trace, Tony still wouldn't leave her alone, couldn't stay out of their lives. And he was going to threaten everything she held dear.

Even if she could reach Trace, she didn't want to interrupt him in the middle of an important mission or distract his focus. That wasn't right. And Tony had no right to bring that on either of them.

Hopefully, Gus could arrange for some protection.

Around 5:00 a.m., she saw a car drive up to the front, park, and turn its lights out. No one got out of the car, so she figured perhaps Gus had sent someone and was protecting the house. Oddly enough, after she saw the car, she relaxed and soon fell asleep.

Gretchen awoke, hearing the sound of breaking glass. It came from downstairs in the kitchen. Angie had been startled, as well, and was clinging to her.

"Mom! Mom, what is that? I'm scared."

"Shh, please be quiet. I don't know what's going on." She got up and put her finger to her lips, pointing to the door to show Angie to lock it behind her. In her nightgown and her bare feet, she quietly moved out onto the landing and then carefully walked down the stairs looking for whoever was there. The car in the front was gone, and, as she looked through several of the windows, she didn't see anyone wandering around the outside.

Suddenly, an arm snaked around her to grip her neck and shoulders. A dirty hand covered her mouth, and the cool metal barrel of a gun pressed to her temple.

"You be quiet, little lady. Everything will work out. We're going to go for a little ride."

Gretchen hoped that Angie would stay put. But no sooner did she have that thought when she heard her daughter's voice from the top of the stairs, "Mom? Mom, is that you? Are you okay?"

She closed her eyes and waited for the next horrible thing to happen. Her thoughts raced, wondering what she should do. An image of something she'd learned in her self-defense classes popped up. Since both arms were up, one around her shoulder and mouth and the other to her temple, his belly was exposed. It was a risk, since he had the gun aimed at her head and could accidentally go off, but she was out of choices. She pushed the barrel of the gun away from her face with an open palm uppercut, then elbowed him as hard as she could right in the lower gut, which sent him reeling back, and the gun went off as he dropped it.

Angie screamed.

The morning light was beginning to come in through the windows, and Gretchen saw where the gun skittered across the granite floor to a corner in the kitchen. She scrambled to get it. He recovered himself and limped toward her as she turned around, aimed the gun at him, and told him to stop.

The man was small, but with his very fleshy belly, ruddy skin, and his angry demeanor, she was frightened to death. But she had to protect Angie. Aiming the barrel of the gun at his face, she said, "I know how to shoot this. You back up! You back up, and you go outside. I've got the police coming right now."

"That doesn't bother me at all. You and your daughter will be long dead by then." He still walked slowly toward her, step by step. "No need to make a scene out of this, Missy. You don't want to die. You don't want your daughter to die. All I'm looking for is a little bit of money."

"I don't have any money. I never have any money, thanks to my ex."

"Oh, we're going to take care of Tony too. Believe me, he's been a very bad boy. You know this though, right?"

As he stepped forward once more, she aimed and shot the floor right between his feet. This caused him to jump.

"Okay, I get your point. But you don't want things to end this way, do you? If you cooperate just a little bit with me, I promise you'll be safe. We'll even leave Angie here. She'll be safe and sound here, and your friends can protect her. I just need you to come with me to give a little extra insurance."

"Do you think I'm stupid? Do you really think I would do that?"

"Well, if you want to sacrifice Tony, if you want to tell that little girl up there that you made it so that her father will never come home, well, I guess that's your decision, right?"

Gretchen aimed carefully, her hands shaking. When he lunged at her again, she pulled the trigger, and the man fell to the floor, his head hitting the granite with a thud. Blood oozed out from his chest as he struggled briefly with his arms and then went limp.

CHAPTER 15

W ORD CAME DOWN to the group on Gran Canaria that a shipload of new merchandise, meaning children but mostly young girls, was arriving at two o'clock in the afternoon. It was bold of them to offboard in the middle of the day, but there was transportation being arranged, from cars and buses to airplanes, for parts unknown. Part of their cargo had already been sold or committed and was going to be departing shortly after arrival.

State gave Kyle the go-ahead to conduct a raid and try to secure the merchandise, with the help of the rest of Team 3. It was not thought that the perpetrators would be expecting a raid, especially from a SEAL team.

The project escalated to "urgent"—or "red"—when it was discovered that a missionary worker and his family from Africa were among the group arriving by boat. The doctor had maintained a mission in Nigeria for one of the large church organizations in Holland, although he was an American. Somehow, the protection detail that had been arranged for him—and had been working for many years—failed. With all the recent changes in the governments in Nigeria and other countries nearby, it was somewhat tricky for these groups now who were not doing anything but humanitarian work, first aid, clinics, and of course Bible training in schools to operate. One by one, many of them were leaving. Some had been raided with loss of life.

Carter Solvang, from California, and his wife and four daughters were the perfect targets for a militia group and got swept up in the raid on their school. Over half of the cargo arriving was from this one school and the surrounding countryside.

Dr. Solvang was a U.S. citizen, as were all of his children, although two of them were born in Africa but maintained their U.S. status. Dr. Solvang's wife was Dutch but was a green card resident of the U.S. Except for fundraising tours, the Solvangs hardly ever returned to the U.S.

Kyle woke the team up early, and they began their preparations. The boys from Tenerife and the other outer islanders were brought in quickly by private jet and soon all twenty-five of them assembled at the Mother House on Gran Canaria where they were triple and quadruple bunked.

Kyle showed the picture of the missionary and his family. "He's, of course, going to stand out because he's white, and we don't know what his condition will be or the condition of any of his family, but they will be our first priority, as well as any women and children who are with them. State Department would like us to save them all, but we're not given exact numbers, so we'll have to play it by ear."

Trace had a question. "You got this information from State. But do you trust Guerrero with this as well? Might he have one or two Civil Guard who can assist us?"

Kyle shook his head. "I've been told not to reveal it to anyone. We could use the extra manpower, of course, but we're not going to bring in naval forces for any ready-action command at this particular point. The USS Bulkeley is trolling these waters as we speak, only for backup support, should it be needed. The guided missile destroyer is about fifty miles offshore in Las Palmas, away from the main shipping lanes."

Kyle continued, "Twenty-five of us should be able to get at least the missionary and his family out and several others. We'll have to figure out a drop-off point and time, and we'll be calling in to the Navy to have them provide that transport plane as soon as we know how many and when. Currently, we understand another support vessel is also due to arrive shortly, with other capabilities. They're all on standby and are going to head closer in our direction so they can provide quick aid if we need it. We also don't want to start a war with the presence of these ships."

Kyle paced a step before turning back to his men. "The cargo ship's registry is Mauritanian, and we do have relations with this country. It is believed that the cargo traversed the country, partially protected by local militia. But, before you jump to conclusions, you need to remember that this is a country that has not had a terrorist attack since 2011 and has cooperated with the United States for anti-terrorism and anti-slavery events. They also recently had a peaceful presidential election and a peaceful presidential transition after their current president was convicted of corruption. They are staging for a new election coming up soon. And the other thing you need to take into account is this Muslim country still allows slavery, those who own slaves can continue to own slaves and the children of those slaves are also considered the property of the owners."

Kyle said the word "owners" in finger air quotes.

The reaction among the men was swift, whispering various forms of disapproval.

"We believe they are not in favor of supporting terrorist groups who raid villages and capture. It's the institution itself of slavery, not the raiding and capturing, as they're trying to balance between peace and the stability of being a leader in the African continent. The U.S. is trying to help them with this transition, but there are dangerous hotspots. They're not going to want to intercede or do anything at all that will distance them from the rest of their African neighbors, who are increasingly becoming more and more militant and threatening.

"However, we are trying to negotiate a peaceful takeover of the ship and return of the slaves as best we can. We also have learned that Mauritania is aware of the missionary and his family, and, although they will not defend them, they will help see to it that they have found their way into our hands. At this point, though, they do not know it will be a SEAL force meeting them at the dock.

"Here's the rough part, gents. We are forced to work with a UN representative, which is the weakest link in this program. Not sure if we can trust the gentleman, but we have to work through him and his staff, our State Department says. On Gran Canaria, while treated almost like a separate country, they still are part of Spain and, thus, are part of NATO. It would be an embarrassment if a NATO ally were to harbor criminals operating in an already agreed-upon prohibited criminal behavior. But that doesn't mean that some of the Guardia Civil isn't corrupt and been paid off handsomely."

It was decided that a first wave of SEALs would attend to the surveillance of the port, confirm when the ship would arrive, and which pier it would dock at. Trace was part of that group, and, as soon as they received their instructions, he left with the rest of the team of ten to communicate back to Kyle at the Mother House.

They rode in cargo vans, which lacked windows and were somewhat of a hindrance as far as getting their bearings. There was a rear window which showed little of the pier and the dock works beside. They parked the van and left their gear inside, again posing as American tourists, even bringing along fishing poles that had been provided in the van to complete the ruse.

They split up into two groups on the pretense of looking to book a fishing boat, and, luckily, since most Grand Canarians also spoke English as well as Spanish, Portuguese, and some Arabic, they were able to inquire about the potential for a fishing charter. They didn't have to mention that they were a group of ten but looked for boats that were larger, perhaps in the vicinity of where a much larger ship like a cargo ship could be docked.

The intel they received confirmed a two o'clock docking of a large, repurposed cruise ship from Mauritania, the Margarita Malaga.

When the team returned to the Mother House, they had an unexpected visitor. Guerrero showed up with three of his men. Kyle was immediately alarmed and stopped them at the front porch.

"We come bringing you information about a ship arriving today. Many in the militia, the guard, have been tasked with helping transfer human beings to other transports quickly to avoid detection. We believe it is human smuggling cargo mainly but also drugs and gold."

Kyle was hesitant to invite him inside. The group stood outside the front door, with Trace and Armando at Kyle's side.

"Wait here." Kyle asked Armando to stay at the front door on the outside, while he placed his call to the Head Shed. "I'm going to call for guidance, see what we can do next. It looks like our cover is blown anyway."

He got on his sat phone and relayed the information. He was given permission to bring the group in, carefully watch them, and not let them leave or send communications elsewhere. They were asked to check their listening devices and what weapons they carried.

Kyle went outside with Trace and spoke to Guerrero.

"Okay, I've been given the green light, but you are not to use your cell phones. In fact, we're going to confiscate them." Guerrero turned and gave instructions to his men who, one by one, gave them their cell phones.

"We're also going to have you searched, and I want to see what weapons you carry. I'm not going to confiscate the weapons, but I just need to know what kind of firepower we have. And, Guerrero, are you a hundred percent solid with all these people? I mean, I'm putting the lives of my men in your hands, so, if there is an ambush afoot here, if you don't know of something but something comes up, I expect you to let me know in time to save my men. This is way out of our normal protocol."

"I understand, sir. Lupe here is from my family, the cousin of my sister, and I have several others who I know from work experience. I have been paired with in the past. There's only one I don't know personally, but Lupe has recommended him and stands by him 100%. These men all, as well as myself, hope that we see the day someday when our government can function as a noncorrupt entity, free from Spain's influence and interference, and not make its money off of the piracy and trade that is out there."

"Okay. Well, we'll conduct the search and then we'll be on our way. You're to stay with our group at all times."

The men were brought into the house where several of the SEALs did a thorough search, examining their weapons and their extra rounds. The men had duty bags that most SEALs had as well, with extra equipment, long guns, and some small explosive devices, which impressed Kyle.

They were offered food and coffee, and, within thirty minutes, Kyle received the call that they were a go and to start heading down toward the pier.

Guerrero led the way, in his official civil guard vehicle. Trace sat in the Jeep beside him. In the seats behind them were two SEALs. Guerrero's other three men rode in two different vans with the rest of the group. It was a warm day already, the noontime beginning a hot streak that would last well until eight o'clock that evening. A brisk, hot wind floated down from the mountains and competed with the ocean breezes but gave little relief from the heat.

It was a workday, so people lined the streets in donkey-driven carts or go-karts—little lawnmowers with vans on them, as Fredo called them. People walked with bushels on their heads and rode e-bicycles, carrying bushels under their arms, or packed on platforms in the back. Frequently, they'd see a goat led by a child, but most of the animals that were headed for the marketplace downtown were chickens or ducks or pigs kept in cages.

"You people raise pigs here? With the high population of Muslims—" Trace started.

"Oh no, we are Muslim minority. But pigs are very well received here. Goats as well. But people with money will buy pigs. Better meat, easier to raise. Chickens, you know chickens get eaten all over the world. I don't much care for them," Guerrero added.

"How's your mother doing?" Trace asked.

"Thank you, she's in pain. She was due to have her surgery last Tuesday, but it was bumped for some particular reason. Here, people have things scheduled, but then it's set aside for a more high priority patient. Usually, it means a politician," Guerrero said without batting an eye. He kept his vision on the dusty road ahead.

"Is it chronic?"

"No, señor. She fell. She's been dealing with a fractured hip now for nearly eight days. Very painful."

"So what will the repercussions be for you with this action today?"

"Well, I think we will claim that you commandeered us. Perhaps it depends on what happens. But we are here as advisors, as guides to make sure there is as little bloodshed as possible. I think that is a worthy goal. You already had the information about the ship, it seems, so I didn't really give you anything new, but I will tell you that some of my brethren—no one in this group—will be on the other side of the fence, and I must be careful."

He looked at the SEALs in the back seat who sat stoically and listened to everything he and Trace were saying.

"So what have the other men been told?" asked Trace.

"They have been told to not intervene, to not do anything unless something has happened that risks your life or you're being taken captive. Then we have to act, but we aren't going to do anything but support. We hope that support is worth something to Uncle Sam. We would like you to get your cargo and then leave the Canary Islands as soon as possible. That is the safest for all of us."

That was good enough for Trace. At last, they reached the docks. Several of the fishing trawlers they'd seen earlier had left, leaving a wide space large enough for a cruise ship to dock, if necessary. They were dropped off at a lot near that space where a small cantina and several other little vendor shops and a liquor store were located. Music was everywhere around the port, and Trace noted a line of workers waiting to unload cargo, all with iron wristbands, indicating ownership. There were also several independent loaders and hand trucks standing idle.

Guerrero parked his vehicle in a lot under the trees, and the other two vans arrived next to him. Kyle grouped the men in teams, splitting in three different directions from the shadows, each taking up positions, armed with only handguns. Armando and a newbie named Armie stayed back at the vehicles. They were armed to the teeth with their long guns and scopes, and he was going to be in constant communication with Kyle in case something was needed.

Armando quickly found a local cantina and climbed up the back of it, holding onto the cistern, laying himself flat on the roof next to Armie, the other SEAL. They prepared their scopes and readied themselves for whatever was required. They could see through the branches of the trees, but the trees hid them from full view of the docks.

A horn blared in the distance, indicating a ship was approaching. And around the rocky pier, a large transport ship filled with containers slowly made its way into the harbor and docked broadsides at the pier. It was tied up for easy offloading. A hatch was opened, and a gangway was provided from the land side. Several officers, probably the harbormaster as well, came out to greet the ship captain and other officers who appeared on the gangway. They all cordially shook hands.

One of the officers signaled to a group of taxis and truck drivers to advance, and they did so, temporarily obscuring the entry. Kyle and the team moved in between the crowds beginning to arrive. Guerrero stood close by him. Trace stood behind them and whispered to Kyle, "How do we get the missionaries out first?"

"I'm going to have Guerrero request it. State sent me a printout that I can use. We'll see if it works."

Guerrero and Kyle made their way closer to the gate as passengers started unloading from the ship. Several private, paying customers came off first with luggage and helpers. They got into black Suburbans and took off. Over his INVISIO, Armando was tasked with getting pictures of all these VIPs exiting the ship. It hurt Trace to see these guys walk away to freedom without any repercussions, but that wasn't the prize they were looking for.

Finally, a group of young girls were let off, roped together through chains on their wrists. They were young, maybe ten, twelve years old, scared, and every single one of them barefoot. The crowd began to notice and whistle, some making sounds of objection. The girls were pulled off to the side and asked to sit on barrels and canvas bags that were stored, ready to be loaded.

Another group exited and joined the young girls, and then finally the missionary and his wife and children followed behind. Dr. Solvang appeared to be in relatively good shape, although he was sporting an injury to his eye or had incurred some kind of abuse about the face, but he walked normally, and he was allowed to hold the hand of his wife, who was also connected by chain to the children. They were herded to the right, next to the young Black girls, just as a large black bus arrived close by, presumably to take them to another location. Kyle dragged Guerrero forward and spoke to what he assumed to be the captain of the ship.

Trace stood nearby within voice range.

"Excuse me, sir. I have an official request from the State Department of the United States to release these prisoners." He handed the paperwork to the captain. Guerrero stood motionless, noncommittal, beside Kyle.

The captain glanced over it, frowned, and handed it to the representative from their harbor patrol.

Kyle got a quick response. "This has no jurisdiction here. This is not valid. These individuals are being transported of their free will to another location. They were evacuated from a war zone," the man said. His steely eyes bore into Kyle, and Trace was sure he got the same dose in return from his LPO.

"Then I shall have to inform the United States Navy, which is nearby, as you know, that you are being uncooperative. As a matter of fact, we are tasked with releasing all of these children and this missionary. We understand these were individuals taken not by choice, but by force, by violent force."

Kyle was good at this, Trace saw, and he had the attention of the captain and had earned the ire of the local official.

"As a NATO ally, you must honor the wishes of one of your own. The United States is a good friend. And we are good friends with the Mauritanians as well. It is our desire to continue to be so."

The ship captain nodded his head and revealed a tight smile.

"I am going to have to check with my superiors," said the harbormaster.

Kyle nodded and put the phone up to his ear, loudly declaring, "I'm going to check with mine. Perhaps you would like to speak to the captain of the Bulkeley, the guided missile destroyer? It's not more than twenty miles off your shore. Let me arrange this."

The official walked away with his ear to the phone, disappearing into the crowd.

The captain used this time to plead his case.

"I know nothing of this. I am paid to bring cargo in, and these passengers were bought and paid for."

Kyle assumed a stronger position, inhaled, and stood taller. "Were they purchased as people or was their passage purchased? I'm sure my Navy captain would like to know. We were told they were prisoners, involuntarily removed from their mission in Nigeria and transported across Mauritania to this ship. Perhaps my State Department needs to notify the embassy in Mauritania that your ship is carrying contraband, specifically United States citizens, beyond their will."

All of a sudden several vans with troops appeared, all with the Civil Guard insignia. Guerrero disappeared into the crowd, and Trace lost track of where he was. He was concerned that they'd walked right into a trap.

In the distance, Trace could see a helicopter was arriving. Kyle was still on the phone with the Navy when the harbor representative arrived. Noting the presence of the Civil Guard, the guard created a barrier between the public that was now growing in size and becoming increasingly curious and the offloaded passengers and cargo. Men sent to pick up material and deliver them into the city were objecting that they were being kept from doing their job. Lorry drivers and other workmen objected to the traffic jam created in the square next to the pier.

The public, including several local shopkeepers, started arguing with each other, and Trace could see that the groups that had been assembled were not homogeneous and were beginning to war amongst themselves such that it may begin a small riot. The whole area was destabilized.

Over his INVISIO, Trace heard the message from Kyle, which got delivered to all the SEALs. "We have a bird arriving. No one move. Just stay together and keep track of each other. Guard your sidearms, and don't get arrested."

The sound of the helicopter blades increased, and Trace could see there were three helicopters, not one, arriving over the small mountain range that traversed the island. One landed just outside the crowd and the other two off toward the parking lot, fifty feet away.

Captain Ronald Higby from the U.S. destroyer, a thirty-year man whom Trace recognized from naval newsletters throughout the years, walked up with his two aides, dressed in whites, and pierced the crowd, headed straight for the captain of the transport ship. They shook hands. There was some discussion that Trace couldn't understand, but he found that Captain Higby did most of the talking, and the transport ship captain did most of the nodding. He turned to the steady line of cargo workers and stopped, halting the offloading of anything further. A large moan rose from the crowd as people became agitated. Of note was the fact that the helicopters did not shut down but continued while awaiting instructions.

Higby was blocked from seeing the missionary, but, very gently and firmly, his two aides removed the three gentlemen who were blocking access. Soon Captain Higby was shaking hands with the doctor and his wife. He motioned for them and whispered something to the doctor.

Then he gathered together the group of young girls, and they headed toward the helicopters. On his way past Kyle, he saluted. Kyle returned the salute.

The transport captain was nonplussed. The representative of the harbor had disappeared temporarily but soon ran to the gangway and tried to stop the movement of the missionaries.

Trace prevented him from getting closer to Kyle.

"You hold on a second there. I think we do have jurisdiction here, and, unless you want a hundred sailors pouring into this port engaging in some kind of protection detail against your men here, unless you want that or you want a bunch of SEALs conducting an operation which will not end well for you, I suggest you just sit back and cooperate. This wasn't anything you knew about. This was something we learned through our intelligence. You need to cooperate or Uncle Sam will be all over your butt."

The gentleman from the harbor looked Trace up and down and sneered, spat, nearly hitting his shoes. Trace stepped into him and grabbed his arm, putting a handcuff on it.

"Maybe you would like to be taken as well? We can certainly do that. You like to explain your existence to the crew of a naval destroyer?" He didn't put the handcuff on the other arm as Kyle stopped him and pushed Trace aside.

"You can see my men are rather touchy about the subject of hurting innocent women and children. I'm sure you will have future cargoes that will make up for this loss, but we are taking these people back to where they can return to their domicile. They have been kidnapped, and, unless you want to be named as an accessory, you need to back off and let it happen."

The harbormaster was no doubt seeing his profits evaporate. The lucrative day was turning dangerous for him and too risky. His men were scattered and not organized, and he was delving into areas he wasn't sure he'd be hailed for.

"And just a reminder," Kyle continued, "we're not even talking about all this cargo coming off here, but, if you like, we can start an inspection process. I have enough guys to do it."

Kyle's jaw was set. The ship captain had been clearly moved and was ignoring the harbormaster. He shook hands with Captain Higby again, and they saluted one another. Higby again saluted Kyle and headed for the helicopter where Dr. Solvang and his family had already loaded. The others were loaded onto the other two choppers.

Everyone watched in silence as they took off and headed northeast toward the waiting destroyer. Trace was relieved that, so far, there had been no violence, but that didn't mean somebody wouldn't be coming for them later on.

Carefully, the team receded from the dock, leaving the harbormaster and the captain to themselves. The Civil Guard took no action and allowed them to just walk through their line of defense, over to their vans. Noticing Guerrero's Jeep was missing, Kyle and the rest of the group loaded in the two vans and took off for the home base.

Once inside his vehicle, he turned around and addressed the team. "I am hoping Guerrero is arranging something for us, some kind of protection, which I didn't ask him for. But he's gone, and I don't think he wants to be publicly involved any longer. I'm okay with that. I just want to get the hell out of this country. I'm going to wait for orders when we get back, and—if everything's okay—we're going to boogie out of here and head over to the airport."

"What did you tell the captain and the harbormaster?" asked Fredo.

"I told him we had received word that criminals had been involved in the hijacking and killing of villagers in Nigeria and that the Afrika Korps was asking for the names of people complicit. I promised them that if they allowed the safe passage of the prisoners their names would not be turned into the international forces. Whether or not they would actually do something is sort of a moot issue at this point, but, when you involve the United Nations and other countries and somebody else looking over your shoulder, all of a sudden a local dispute becomes something that can be quashed from a distance. They made the right move. I don't know how long, but—for right now—they were spared. But we got the members."

Kyle received word that no further action was required and they should pack up and head for the airport immediately where a transport plane had been given permission to land. Kyle told the group after his phone call, "Well, it won't be a comfortable ride, but at least it'll get you home."

Trace wanted to call Gretchen to let her know the good news, but he decided to wait until he was on the plane to do so. He hoped that everything at home was completely settled. He couldn't wait to get there.

CHAPTER 16

G RETCHEN SPENT THE rest of the early morning accompanied by a
team of police, forensics experts, the coroner, Gus Mayfield, and
several of his friends from the force.

She sat on the couch in the living room and answered questions *ad
nauseam*. Angie stayed by her side, but Gretchen wanted her there
mostly because she knew that the police would separate her from her
mother and ask her other questions. Not that they had anything to hide.
She just wanted everything to get uncomplicated real quick. She was
heading to collapse. She needed a shower. She needed to get some rest.
But she needed Trace most of all.

Gus Mayfield was true to his word. He and several of his former colleagues arrived at the house even before the 911 crew arrived. They
stayed away from the body of the intruder but counseled her on how to
handle the onslaught of police and personnel who were about to descend
upon her.

But she was still inconsolable. She felt like the ground had been
pulled out from under her. Now possibly even Tony's life was in danger,
although Gus told her otherwise.

"It's all over the station, Gretchen. Nobody's going to touch Tony.
He's been put in an individual holding cell, and, unless somebody has
some kind of access that I don't know about, he should be untouched
until he can get properly arraigned and released. I don't know all the
story of what's going on, but you certainly had justification to shoot this
man in your house, and this is his gun, not yours. You do have a right to
defend yourself, under certain circumstances, and this meets those

criteria. It's pretty evident he came to do damage."

"If they know where I live, then there'll be others looking as well. Does this mean I have to move or go into hiding somewhere?"

"I don't have an answer for that, sweetheart. I'd like to say no, but I don't know. I'm not sure where this guy was in the pecking order of things. But the detective took his wallet and identification. We've run some checks, and this guy, Sam, has a long rap sheet. I don't think you're going to have any trouble yourself, but I can't speak to some of these jerks who Tony's got himself involved with."

"Where is Sven? Has anybody called him?"

"I think you should be the one. Why don't you do it now before more police arrive?"

So Gretchen called, but it went to voicemail. Then she called Kelly's cell phone—reaching her—and gave the updates. Sven was on a plane, headed to San Diego, she was told.

"Gretchen, I'm so sorry about this. He'll be able to tell you what further steps you're going to need to take. When does Trace get back?" asked Kelly.

"I have no idea. I can't get ahold of him either. You know, when he's on these ops, sometimes I don't talk to him for days. Just, of all the time for this to happen, of course it'd have to happen when he's gone."

"Well, as in all ops, the unexpected is what is expected. And Tony made all this happen. He is really a loose cannon. Something has to be done about it. Maybe for his own good, he should go back to jail."

"Well, he's certainly afraid of that."

"As he should be."

Around eight in the morning, after some of the personnel had started to recede, Gretchen was greeted with the face of Sven Tolar, who rushed to her side and gave her a hug.

"I am so sorry you had to go through this. I had no idea Sam knew where you were. How do you think this happened?"

"One of the detectives said a neighbor's security camera caught Tony hanging around the outside of the house. He must have parked around the block and walked up. They found shoe prints like he was wandering around, a different size from the Sam guy's. Maybe he was trying to talk to me? But he changed his mind. I guess somebody followed him here, so that's how they found out where I lived. It was Tony again."

"Of course it was. And then he went off to go get drunk and find a hooker. What an asshole. What a liability to society."

Gretchen looked down at Angie, who was sleeping on the couch fitfully.

"I just was trying to protect her, even from all these things being said about her father. I don't know how she's going to take all of this, but it's more than I can handle right now. I just want to make sure that we're safe and that we can sleep."

"You can. If they're done with you, you go upstairs and shower and go to bed. I'll be downstairs. I've got some calls to make, some things to arrange, and I will see you when you get up. Don't worry about anything."

"Is it just you? I mean, what if they send a whole army over here after me? Will they have a whole gang that shows up at the house? Am I supposed to worry about that now?"

"I doubt it, but I have the cops on speed dial. Gus here has his crew who will stand watch until I get my people in place, at least temporarily."

Gretchen did feel somewhat relieved.

"You remember, we have the sale of the house and they're gonna get their money back. The problem now is who do we give the money to? And if we give the money to this person over here, what is this person over there going to say? Is he going to demand more money? Do you see what I mean? So I have to determine who gets paid off and why and where."

"I understand. So you'll have to go back to Portland or Eugene, is that correct?"

"I'm thinking they will reach me somehow. I mean, they do have my numbers, so we'll see. And if their connections are as good as they say, they're going to know Tony's in jail and he's untouchable. Not that it would make any difference."

"Well, they do need Tony to sign the papers to sell the house. If they kill him, how does that happen? And that ties the money up even further."

"I didn't think of that, Gretchen. Well, that may be Tony's protection for right now. And maybe we can impose on the police the bigger picture—the issue of your safety and the sale of the house and that he's needed elsewhere. Maybe we can get him an escort or they'll release him to me. I don't know. But we'll work out something. You just go take a shower and go to bed. Let me take your cell phone in case Trace calls, because I'd like to speak to him, and I don't want him to wake you up."

Gretchen handed Sven her phone, lifted Angie up, and helped her go upstairs to the bedroom. She laid her on the bed and went in to take a shower.

It felt good to have the warm water sluice down her body. She was so tired and so anxious from all of this. What she needed was a vacation away from all this crap, all this pressure and the worry. Trace was in harm's way and so was she, without him here. And that was the worst part, she thought. She could handle him being in places that he was trained to be in, with the team trained to protect him, but here at home? There was nothing set up and no one here truly to protect her. The police were so easily compromised she wasn't sure who to trust, and she really wanted to trust them. Trust somebody. She trusted Sven, but then he wasn't law enforcement. He had no official capacity.

She dried off and looked at herself in the mirror. "God, you've aged ten years, Gretchen. He's going to come home to a wild hag who mumbles and drools." She watched herself crying in the mirror.

When will this stop? she thought.

She climbed into bed and sunk into the nice, warm, lavender-scented sheets and pillow. This had been her sanctuary. This had been the place she had hoped to welcome Trace back to, help bring him back to San Diego life, to their life and their hopes and dreams and plans for the future. This had been a happy bed, a place of memorable worshiping of each other's bodies. Now she was reduced to soaking up the energy of past experiences here, begging for help, asking for God's protection, and begging also for that little kernel, that little flame of encouragement that would let her know that all would be well.

That someday, somehow they would be done with all of this.

CHAPTER 17

TRACE LANDED IN Norfolk, exhausted and sore, with a splitting headache he traced to not drinking enough water.

He checked his phone and discovered a message from Gretchen.

"Oh, Trace, things have really unraveled here. And I hope by the time you get this message that it's all cleared up, but Tony called me, and he's in trouble again. Apparently, he came down to San Diego and then got arrested. He's worried about them catching him in jail and doing something to him. I don't know what's going on. But I'm getting really exhausted and tired of all this. I just wish you were here to help counsel me. He asked me to put up money for his bail since he thought he'd be killed in jail, and I refused. I hope I did the right thing. It's actually the only thing I could do without you being here. So when you are some-place where you can talk to me, please give me a call."

Now that he was on the ground, he placed that call to Gretchen immediately. It was late morning on the East Coast, which meant even earlier on the West Coast, about 9:00 a.m.

"Hey, Trace, I'm glad to hear your voice," said Sven.

"Sven? Why are you answering Gretchen's phone?"

"Because she's upstairs trying to get some shuteye. We had quite a bit of activity last night. Apparently, Tony came down to San Diego and hung around here, got himself into trouble again, got arrested, and he's at the San Diego Central North Jail. And please hold onto your seat a bit and wait until I'm finished with the whole thing, because you're going to react. Sam showed up at the house."

"At Gretchen's house?"

"Yes, at your house, Gretchen's house, where you live with Gretchen and Angie."

"What the fuck! What's happened, Sven, and how did all this come undone? I thought you had a handle on this?"

"I understand how you feel, Trace, and I would feel the same way, but hear me out, please, before you go reacting. First of all, I didn't know Tony came down to San Diego. He was supposed to lay low and hang on to his money and wait for the house to close, and then I was going to accompany him, and we were going to deliver the cash. It would all be over. All he had to do was wait a few days, maybe a week. Everything was on track."

"That son of a bitch!"

"Hold on there, Trace. There's more. A lot more. All the conditions of the escrow were met, and we were just waiting for the funds to come through to close it. However, Tony being Tony, I guess he got a little homesick or something. He came down to San Diego. I really think he was going to try to get reconnected with Gretchen, but he never got that far. He got drunk, and he kind of wasn't thinking, and he hooked up with a San Diego decoy for prostitution, got himself in jail. And then of course getting bailed out was a problem for him because he can't remember where the rest of the money is. And he didn't want to call me, so he called Gretchen."

"Goddamnit, Sven. You didn't hear it from me, but I think the first thing I need to do is get rid of that son of a bitch. I mean permanently, don't you think?"

"You didn't mean that, Trace. That's not the right way. You know that. So here's what's happened. When Sam showed up at the house, your well-trained wife, and thank God for that, shot him with his own gun."

"Shot him? I mean, is he dead?"

"Oh, quite dead, yes."

"In front of Angie?"

"Yes, unfortunately. She was up the stairs, but she heard it all. Angie's tough, and I think she'll be traumatized for a bit, but she knew her mother was protecting them. The guy was a jerk apparently, according to what Gretchen told me, and I think the police have got the right angle on it. Gus Mayfield was called in, and I think he's helping to grease some skids here. The problem I'm having, Trace, is I got to find out who gets the money now that Sam's out of the picture. And that is a big problem, because if we give it to the wrong person and someone else shows up with his hand out, we've got a shit storm going on. Plus, we'll be out of money, and we didn't make any headway. So that's what I've got to try to figure out. And I'm in the middle of making some calls and trying to see what I can do. You're going to need some help around the house, some guards to protect her and Angie and possibly the other two girls too. I'm sorry to say it, but it's true, Trace. You can't do it all."

"Yeah, but I can't afford all this protection, Sven."

"Consider it a loan against our friendship. Trace, I really want you to think twice about what you're doing on the Teams, and I love you to death for being a warrior and a patriot for your country, but I think you could do a lot more if you were out of the Teams. If you could handle some of the scourge that now is coming into this country. You know, we used to be the place where nothing happened. But ever since 9/11, all of a sudden the barriers are cracked open, and we got all these idiots running around doing stuff, causing chaos. And the response to all of that is going to be a more heavy-handed government intrusion into everybody's lives. It's to all of our benefit if we can help quell this chaos and this mood of destruction. It's really sad and painful to watch, being a citizen of another country."

"I've thought a lot about it, Sven. I think I'm nearly there. I think Tyler is as well."

"Well, you just get yourself back to San Diego, and don't worry about anything else for right now. I took her phone so she could get some rest, and she really needs it. I know she wants to see you, so the best thing you can do is get here and get with her. That's the only thing that will console her. And Angie needs you too. I'm arranging the protection for Rebecca and Clover, and I've already talked to her husband about it, and he's all for the protection. I haven't been able to get hold of Rebecca yet, but I'm close. So just get home, Trace, and try not to worry."

"Fat chance of that, with all this news. Sven, I wish I'd never left."

"Hence what I was saying, Trace. You belong on our team here. You don't belong clear across the world. You're no longer a Boy Scout. You're a protector, you're someone who needs to protect his own, and we live in an increasingly hostile and volatile environment here at home, unlike ever has happened before. Never did I ever expect to see your country dissolve into this chaos. And local authorities are way outmatched, outgunned, outfought, outfinanced. It's just not a conclusion that's going to have a happy ending. You got to be here to protect what you love. You got me?"

"Loud and clear, Sven."

It took several hours before Trace could arrange his transport back, but he finally took a commercial flight nonstop to San Diego. He checked in with Kyle before he left.

"I'm sorry, Kyle. We got chaos at home, and this thing with Tony is just blown way out of control. I don't know how long I'm going to be involved in it, but I'm sorry I won't be available much for debriefing, but I'll do what I can."

After Trace told Kyle all of the particulars, especially Gretchen's sure shot on Sam, Kyle was most understanding.

"Well, you get it sorted out, and then we'll talk. I knew this was going to happen someday, Trace. Nothing is forever, is it?"

Trace felt tears form in his eyes. It made him mad, but he continued on anyway. "Nothing is forever, but we do our best to try to prolong death. That's sometimes, I think, the only thing I know how to do in life."

"Now give yourself some credit, Trace. You're far more than a killing machine or a death-defying machine. You're a lover, and you're a husband. A good husband and a father to girls who deserve and need you. Without you doing what you're doing, they'd be left in a puddle of shit. And you're helping to clear that up. There's no way the Navy or anything I could offer would entice you enough to pull your focus off of that. That's your prime directive. I don't blame you one bit. But don't sign any papers or do anything stupid as far as telling someone you're going to quit. You talk to me first, and then we'll work out some kind of an agenda, and maybe there's still a place for you somehow. But first things first, you take care of your wife and kids, and you see if you can help Sven get this fire put out."

"Thanks, Kyle. You know I learned how to deal with all of this under your guidance. If I hadn't seen some of the crap we've been through on these missions, if I hadn't seen how you held up with all these bad guys, how you ran our team, how you respected us, I would never have the cojones to do what I'm doing now. You trained me for this."

Kyle sighed. "Yeah, I'm sorry about that. I guess I wish I didn't do such a good job. But you go do yours. And we'll talk. I'll be praying for you."

When Trace landed in San Diego, he gave a call to Sven to let him know he was on his way. He picked up his Hummer and drove straight home after texting Kyle to let him know that he was back.

He parked in the driveway behind two remaining police vehicles. He didn't care that he blocked their access. Running to the front door, he dashed into the living room and found Sven sitting at their dining room table making calls and notes on a lined pad Gretchen had given him.

"Where is she?"

"They're upstairs questioning her. She's okay, Trace. Let them do their job," said Sven, standing to come over and greet Trace properly.

"Fuck that. I want to see her."

Trace dashed past Sven up the steps, taking two or three at a time, and crashed through the closed door to their bedroom.

"Trace!" Gretchen screamed as she ran to him. They collided in the middle of the room. She was shaking, sobbing with tears. Angie timidly stood by the side and Trace included her in their embrace. He got down on his knees. "Thank God my girls are okay. Did anybody hurt you, Gretchen? Are you okay, Angie?"

"No. Now that you're back, we're fine. Scary. It's going to take a while, Trace. But we're just trying to figure out what to do now. Do you think we have to leave?"

"No fucking way. This is our house. This is where we make our stand."

Trace heard someone clear their throat behind him, and he stood up and turned to face two uniformed San Diego police.

"I'm supposed to take pictures of the girls, make sure they're not injured."

Trace looked at Gretchen, who nodded her agreement.

"Get it over with," he sighed.

One by one, each of the women went with the female officers to the rest room to have their nude bodies photographed. Angie was allowed to wear her underwear.

"Thanks for your cooperation, ladies. Now, Trace, I'm going to give you my card. They'll have to come downtown and answer questions, make statements."

"They're not under suspicion, are they?"

"Not supposed to comment, but no, sir. Not as far as I can see, but you didn't hear it from me, understood?"

"Thank you. We'll cooperate."

"You might also want to get a good attorney, just in case. I doubt it will be needed. Again thanks for your patience, and thanks for your service, Mr. Bennett. I wish we had more like you here on the force."

"That's not my gig."

"Well, you take good care of each other, and we'll be in touch." The two officers left.

When they were alone, Gretchen whispered, "I don't think they're after me, Trace. I'm worried about this Organization. Has Sven found out anything yet?"

"I don't know. I ran past him, and I suppose he's got something for me, but that's not nearly as important as seeing you guys. I am so grateful that you're okay. I am never going to leave you guys alone like this again. Never. We're going to stay all together. And we're going to fight this thing. I don't care what it takes."

"Does that mean the Teams?"

Trace cut her off. "No decisions. Everyone knows I'm thinking about it. No decisions yet. Let's get this job done, and then we go on to the next one. Okay?"

"Absolutely, sweetheart."

"How much rest have you had?"

"I don't think I could go back to bed. Maybe I'll turn in early tonight, but there's just too much going on. Every little sound, every little thing that goes on, even a distant siren, I'm up. I'm alert. I can't function, Trace. I think the only thing I can do is just let time take care of me. And now that you're here, it'll be much better. Dear, go downstairs with Sven and let me get dressed. Angie and I will come down and join you. Maybe we'll make some lunch or something."

"You don't have to do anything, Gretchen. We can make something. Don't worry about it."

He noted that Gretchen's cheeks did begin to flush a bit now that he was in the room, and he hoped that Angie's glum expression turned around. But he was going to give them time, plenty of time to heal and get used to the new reality of their lives.

Because of what Tony had done, everything had changed. Now, instead of being an old fuddy grandfather enjoying his first grandchild, he was going to have to be looking over his shoulders all the time. And for this he knew he was going to need help. He decided to face the music and ask Sven what the score was. He halfway didn't want to know it, but it had to be done.

Sven hung up the phone and looked up.

"So, Sven, what do you have for me?"

"So far it's good, Trace. I got hold of someone who's agreed to take the funds, and I think I trust him, but we'll know further before it is time to release them. My guys did some inquiring up in Eugene, and turns out, this guy, Sam, was really the right-hand man of another fellow, an Albanian fellow who was always in the shadows. I think he's going to be easier to work with than Sam was."

"Well, that is progress then. When's the meet?"

"Well, first, we have to get Tony out of jail so he can sign the papers. My understanding is that they are just waiting for him. Escrow is ready to close."

"Thank God."

CHAPTER 18

G RETCHEN WAS GOING to give Angie some time to herself. She found her listening to music while she read one of her favorite books.

"What would you like to do today, sweetie?"

"I just want to have a normal family. I want to feel safe. I don't want to worry so much."

Gretchen sat on the edge of the bed, noting her pale complexion and dark bags under her eyes. Angie's room was done in pale pinks and greens, with posters, letters, pictures from friends, and lots of family pictures, especially ones with her sisters in them, hanging on the walls. It was a happy room, but the child living inside it was not. Gretchen reached for her hand.

"I am going to work very hard to make sure you have this, Angie. It's been a lot for all of us. Now that Trace is back, I hope some of the stability we felt before will come back. He is so much a part of that for us now, more than before. And with Tony—"

"I don't ever want to see him again, Mom. He's a complete loser. I'm embarrassed to have him as a father. Don't make me, okay?"

"I won't."

Gretchen felt the same way, but he was her children's father, and, in the event Angie changed her mind someday or Tony had a miraculous transformation, which wasn't likely, she would have to keep the connection quietly open. She knew it was going to be Angie's decision and wasn't hers to make. But she'd honor her request for now.

"I was thinking we could go down to the beach today? Gather shells? Trace needs a beach day too."

"Sure, whatever. Or we could just stay here. Are Clover and Rebecca coming over soon?"

"Would you like that?"

"Yes."

"Okay, let me see what I can do." She watched Angie put her earbuds in and open her book again. Leaning forward, she kissed her on the forehead. "I'm making some food downstairs. Should I bring you something?"

"I'm good," she said loudly, due to the music in her ears.

She patted her daughter's thigh and closed the door behind her. Worry traveled down the stairs with her. Entering her master kitchen, she began to make some fresh coffee.

Sven and Trace were still sitting at the table.

"Anyone want coffee?" she asked.

"Let me make it," Trace said as he started to get up.

"No, you talk. I'll join you when I get the coffee made. Both of you?"

"Not for me. I would love a beer if you have one, Gretchen," said Sven.

"Coming right up. I'm going to put out some fruit and cheeses. Anyone want some eggs or a sandwich?"

"Nah, just beer for me. Too late for breakfast," Sven scowled.

Trace shrugged. "Whatever you bring I will gratefully partake of, sweetie," he said at last and sat back down.

She put together a platter of fruit with some mangos and papayas she'd bought at the farmers market, added some grapes and unsalted crackers, with sliced cheeses made with peppercorns and herbs. She set it on the table with napkins in front of the two men, who began devouring it, just as she had expected they would.

The teapot squealed.

Bringing in the two steaming mugs, each filled with tons of cream, she sat beside Trace at the table. "What's the plan, Stan?" she asked.

"Sven was just telling me about the meeting he was setting up. How's everything upstairs?"

"Angie is still a bit quiet. She's reading, listening to music. She did ask if we were going to have the girls come over. Do you think we should make it a family day? Sven, should we have a talk with them about what the new normal is going to be? Or what it would be for now?"

Gretchen knew he wouldn't like being put on the spot, but she was advocating for her girls.

"Not a bad idea. We don't have to worry about forgetting something when we instruct the girls. There are going to be changes, you know that. At least temporarily."

Gretchen leaned in. "Please explain all this to me. I've been in a fog."

"Understood." Sven swung his computer around so Gretchen could see the faces of several men. "These are members of the Berisha crime family, an Albanian group which has been here for many years. They have family units located all over the U.S. and Canada, as well as Europe. They are a criminal enterprise. They partner with various other groups, some political, some just crime-related. They pick and choose to whom they partner, depending on their needs.

"In this case, they own a business that brings in girls from the Middle East and Africa, through their contacts there. They partner with another group in Seattle for gaming and sports betting and work with various casino groups, including some Native American tribes. It's a conglomerate. They can move easily around the globe, have amassed enormous assets and clout, pay off local officials, and try to eliminate people who stand in their way. Let me repeat what I've said earlier. They are extremely dangerous."

"So it's not about the politics or the power. It's about the Benjamins," said Trace.

"Exactly. They don't want to be in power, play that game. And if one of their partners starts to cross the line, they will either walk away or eliminate the competition. But they've learned how to work with other groups, not against them, and that makes them very effective."

"How the hell are we supposed to fight them?" asked Trace. "Seems impossible to me."

"In a word, carefully. Getting themselves in the paper or having their wings clipped is not good for business. We can't take them out, but we can be a bee in their underpants and cause them some pain."

"And they'd back away?" Gretchen asked.

"Theoretically," Sven said with a long face. "I wish I could tell you that it will be easy or quick. But, unfortunately, this is not the case."

Gretchen felt the ache in her eyes as her tears started to swell and then spill over onto her cheeks. Trace put his arm around her. She was glad he hadn't tried to sugarcoat it or said something about not worrying about it. It was her primary concern. Her family had gotten into the clutches of a dangerous flesh-eating entity. And she'd just killed one of their henchmen.

"So what does that mean for me? For Tony?"

"I don't have all that yet. They mainly want the money. That's the goal. The rest is collateral, complication to them."

"So we have to become their complication," said Trace.

"Yes, partially. I think we have a hidden ace. You, as a Navy SEAL and with the SEAL community behind you, you could cause some disruption to their little program. And some public attention since the public, at least for now, is with you guys. You are the good guys. We use that, leverage it to the highest so that they find it in their best interests to behave."

"How do we do that?" Gretchen wanted to know.

"There's a story there to be told. A good story. One of their members came after the wife of a Navy SEAL and her fourteen-year-old daughter. Huge public sentiment against this kind of thing. After all, you did nothing to harm them; it was your stupid ex. They perhaps don't have a code of ethics, but I doubt they'd want the public scrutiny."

"So we go public with it. Have Gretchen interviewed," said Trace.

"Exactly. Your police colleagues don't want that, I'm sure. But I doubt they have the resources nor the manpower to do a thorough investigation either. It's a hot potato for them. Perhaps this gives them, too, a way out. No one does time for the crime, but everyone walks away whole as they can be and leaves each other alone."

"Until Tony crosses the line again," swore Trace.

"Or someone else. If we go picking off their people, the Bone Frog group now becomes a target. I'd like them to be oblivious to our existence. I doubt they know anything about us. But they do know the SEALs. And that might be enough."

Everyone was silent for a few minutes. Gretchen, oddly enough, suddenly felt somewhat hopeful for the future.

Then Sven's cell rang.

"Tony, nice to hear from you. Is it all arranged?"

Sven put the phone on speaker and placed it next to their fruit platter.

"They said someone made my bail. But I want to know, who is going to pay for that asshat coming over to my ex-wife's house and scaring the shit out of her? They've got to pay. I've been telling everyone down here that it will be my mission in life."

Sven shook his head, held his hands up to Trace and Gretchen.

"Then it will be a very short life, Tony. If you have the burden of the money debt off your shoulders, can you live a straight and narrow life? Can you behave?"

"Behave? How about how they've behaved? That can't go unpunished. That has to be atoned for first, Goddamnit!"

Trace covered his face with his hands.

"So are you ready to be picked up?" Sven asked.

"In a few minutes. I'm filing charges against that asshole."

"But he's dead, Tony. Sam's dead."

"I'm gonna sue the bar and grill. Sam's assets. I'm gonna take it all, man. I'll get my money back if it's the last thing I do!"

"Tony, I'll come get you, and we'll have to talk. Don't do anything until I get there. Let me get you back to Portland, so we can complete the money transfer. I understand you have papers to sign."

"Sweet! I'll be rolling in dough then!"

"Tony, you do understand that money's committed now. It was supposed to go toward your children's education, Tony. It's not really your dough to roll in. It belongs to your girls, in reality. So don't get too cocky about it. Don't gamble away their lives as well as your own."

"That's a valid point. I'll certainly take it under consideration. So when are you coming down here?"

"I'll be down there within the hour. Don't sign or fill out anything, and I mean anything. I'll bring an attorney with me just to make sure everything is as it should be. But sounds like they got the bail money. Let me ask you this. If we can get the charges dropped, will you stop this ridiculous notion of going after the bar and grill?"

"I'll consider it."

"It might be your only option."

"No, sir. I met a lot of guys in here who know these guys, and they even said they'd help me get even!"

"Right after they report you to get a lesser sentence. You're way over your head, Tony. The sooner you figure that out, the less dangerous it will be for the family."

"By the way, can you arrange a meeting with Gretchen and the girls? I'd like to see them and apologize."

"Not my call. I'll see you soon. And remember, try to keep your mouth shut and don't sign anything. Agreed?"

After a pause, Tony hesitated and agreed.

"You see how it goes?" Sven said. "He's not capable of doing anything wise. Just not in his nature. He's so flawed I don't think anything could save him."

"You're right. And he's getting worse," added Gretchen. How could she ever have fallen for him in the first place?

"Problem is, it shades on everyone else in the family. We have to do something about that," said Trace.

"And that's what we're going to do. It might take a little time, but I think there is a path. We just have to put all the pieces together. I doubt they do the kind of in-depth research we do. But, on the surface, if they look into you and the SEALs and how Gretchen is so tightly woven in that community, I'd think they'd stop there and end their vendetta against you all."

"Until Tony kicks the hornet's nest again," sighed Trace.

Gretchen was still hopeful but cautious. "He's like a drunk driver who gets into accidents. Everyone else gets killed, and he survives, somehow. The further down he spirals, the more dangerous he gets too. Wish someone would just get rid of him."

"You never said that, hon," whispered Trace.

"I didn't hear it either," answered Sven. "No talk like that, Gretchen."

She was thinking to herself that she got rid of one bad guy and discovered within herself she wasn't remorseful. Maybe she could get rid of another. Someone had to stop Tony or he would destroy them all.

She had to protect her girls.

CHAPTER 19

T RACE'S EMOTIONS WERE cresting all over him, adding confusion to his reunion with Gretchen and the girls. She'd invited everyone to come over, and, after Sven left, they began playing Monopoly, Angie at last coming to life as she began fleecing everyone with her ruthless play and lucky rolls of the dice.

There were accusations of cheating, arguments about the rules, and passing Go mishaps with the bank, which was Gretchen, leading to more accusations of cheating and fraud. In the end, it was all good fun. Even Jack got in the groove, playing his own game piece and, at times, conflicting with his new bride.

Clover was blushing more, happier than Trace had ever seen her now that she was carrying the new little one. He was struck with how precious his family was now, how it was growing, stemming from his love of this wonderful angel who had come into his life and saved him in every way possible. How was it that his love for them could fuel his desire to kill? But that was happening. He wanted to protect the precious loved ones he was gloriously compelled to safeguard.

Jack was watching him. Sometimes it made him nervous. But he'd never raised a son, and he took advantage of feeling that wonderful connection passed down through the ages: how a man brings a boy into manhood, makes him more of a man so he could train his own boys. The true circle of life. Perfect as perfect could be.

And still there was much to be worked out. Sven and his crew would be working overtime in the coming days so that, when the transfer came, all the counter plays would be covered, just like in a game of chess.

Certain pieces would be protected, others sacrificed. Making the final decisive move was important and strategic.

And Tony was always going to be the wild card that could flush all their plans, the devil who changed all the plays at the first engagement, just like in battle. Wishing it wasn't so was a waste of time. Best to face it straight on and prepare, overprepare even.

He'd seen Gretchen come into this psyche as the hours went by, saw the warrior woman strength she'd always had but never trained. She was strong, perhaps even stronger than he was. It was awesome to see.

Kyle had once told him that he thought Christy was stronger than he was, that he'd known it the first time he met her. Trace could say the same.

"It's the hardest job you'll ever have, having a strong woman like that. Well, that and having children. Both are hard, but you'll love it even more."

Kyle was right. All good things were work. They were a practice. There was no cause, no mission that could be completed as planned—it was always a dance, looking for the opportunities and making the most of it. The worst thing to do was to become unconscious or to stop feeling.

And that's how Trace could justify being a killing machine. It was worth it. He wasn't dead inside. He was alive and honorable. He would always maintain that SEAL ethos. He was just that ordinary man who did extraordinary things. He did things others couldn't do, not because he was better, just because he could.

If there was a way he could stay as a SEAL and still work with Sven and his team, he wished he could. That would have to come later but soon. Kyle deserved to have an answer, and Sven was investing so much into his future, he felt he owed him as well. It was a hard, yet dangerous, problem to have.

At least he had a choice. And, whatever choice he made, it would be perfect.

He got a text that Sven and Tony were safely on their way to Portland. He would call with updates tomorrow. Sven was exhausted, but he needed to get Tony up to his compound to keep an eye on him.

Trace commented with a thumbs-up and a praying hands emoji.

"Thanks, brother," he texted and signed off.

Gretchen's phone rang. She got up to take the call in the kitchen. When her turn came up on the game board, everyone started calling to her.

"Just a minute, please," she answered from the kitchen. Trace could hear something in her voice.

He checked in on her. Her back was to him, and she was wiping tears from her eyes.

"What's up, Gretchen. Are you okay?"

She turned around, and he could see the tears, along with a happy, crazy smile. "What an amazing few days we've had, huh?"

"Yes. It's normal. You're on overload." He took her into his arms, even though the room called to her again. "Just a minute," he shouted back, with Gretchen clutched to his chest.

She sobbed, then stopped. He felt her spine stiffen as he released her to examine her face again.

"That was the doctor's office calling. Remember, they asked me to go get checked out for the police report?"

"Yes, something wrong?"

"No, not really." She placed her palms at the sides of his face. "Trace, sweetheart, I'm carrying your baby. We're going to have a baby, Trace."

Did you enjoy Second Time Love? I hope you will continue on with the story of Trace and Gretchen as they work on their new challenges while solving the problems of the past—still very much in love and with that love growing every day. Stay tuned for a Christmas novella coming out toward the end of the year, "Christmas Miracle."

It will be posted here when it comes out.

authorsharonhamilton.com/seal-brotherhood-legacy

You'll have answers to some of your questions and a continuation of new issues and problems that arise as this family copes with their collective hopes and dreams. You'll see Trace continue to protect his loved ones and the other innocents of the world he's tasked with saving as Gretchen becomes the warrior partner he's always needed in his life.

Lots of twists and turns ahead, so stay tuned!

ABOUT THE AUTHOR

 NYT and USA/Today Bestselling Author Sharon Hamilton's SEAL Brotherhood series have earned her author rankings of #1 in Romantic Suspense, Military Romance and Contemporary Romance. Her other *Brotherhood* stand-alone series are: Bad Boys of SEAL Team 3, Band of Bachelors, True Blue SEALs, Nashville SEALs, Bone Frog Brotherhood, Sunset SEALs, Bone Frog Bachelor Series and SEAL Brotherhood Legacy Series. She is a contributing author to the very popular Shadow SEALs multi-author series.

Her SEALs and former SEALs have invested in two wineries, a lavender farm and a brewery in Sonoma County, which have become part of the new stories. They also have expanded to include Veteran-benefit projects on the Florida Gulf Coast, as well as projects in Africa and the Maldives. One of the SEAL wives has even launched her own women's fiction series. But old characters, as well as children of these SEAL heroes keep returning to all the newer books.

Sharon also writes sexy paranormals in two series: Golden Vampires of Tuscany and The Guardians. In addition, S. Hamil has penned a new genre: Free To Love: Free As A Bird, the 5-book series about a hero Android who just might be the man to save the world from the flames of chaos, perhaps at the risk of his own safety.

A lifelong organic vegetable and flower gardener, Sharon and her husband lived for fifty years in the Wine Country of Northern California, where many of her stories take place. Recently, they have moved to the beautiful Gulf Coast of Florida, with stories of shipwrecks, the white sugar-sand beaches of Sunset, Treasure Island and Indian Rocks Beaches.

She loves hearing from fans through her website:
authorsharonhamilton.com

Find out more about Sharon, her upcoming releases, appearances and news when you sign up for Sharon's newsletter.

Facebook:
facebook.com/SharonHamiltonAuthor

Twitter:
twitter.com/sharonlhamilton

Pinterest:
pinterest.com/AuthorSharonH

Amazon:
amazon.com/Sharon-Hamilton/e/B004FQQMAC

BookBub:
bookbub.com/authors/sharon-hamilton

Youtube:
youtube.com/channel/UCDInkxXFpXp_4Vnq08ZxMBQ

Soundcloud:
soundcloud.com/sharon-hamilton-1

Sharon Hamilton's Rockin' Romance Readers:
facebook.com/groups/sealteamromance

Sharon Hamilton's Goodreads Group:
goodreads.com/group/show/199125-sharon-hamilton-readers-group

Visit Sharon's Online Store:
sharon-hamilton-author.myshopify.com

Life is one fool thing after another.
Love is two fool things after each other.

REVIEWS

PRAISE FOR THE
SEAL BROTHERHOOD SERIES

"Fans of Navy SEAL romance, I found a new author to feed your addiction. Finely written and loaded delicious with moments, Sharon Hamilton's storytelling satisfies like a thick bar of chocolate." —Marliss Melton, bestselling author of the *Team Twelve* Navy SEALs series

"Sharon Hamilton does an EXCELLENT job of fitting all the characters into a brotherhood of SEALS that may not be real but sure makes you feel that you have entered the circle and security of their world. The stories intertwine with each book before...and each book after and THAT is what makes Sharon Hamilton's SEAL Brotherhood Series so very interesting. You won't want to put down ANY of her books and they will keep you reading into the night when you should be sleeping. Start with this book...and you will not want to stop until you've read the whole series and then...you will be waiting for Sharon to write the next one." (5 Star Review)

"Kyle and Christy explode all over the pages in this first book, *[Accidental SEAL]*, in a whole new series of SEALs. If the twist and turns don't get your heart jumping, then maybe the suspense will. This is a must read for those that are looking for love and adventure with a little sloppy love thrown in for good measure." (5 Star Review)

PRAISE FOR THE
BAD BOYS OF SEAL TEAM 3 SERIES

"I love reading this series! Once you start these books, you can hardly put them down. The mix of romance and suspense keeps you turning the pages one right after another! Can't wait until the next book!" (5 Star Review)

"I love all of Sharon's Seal books, but *[SEAL's Code]* may just be her best to date. Danny and Luci's journey is filled with a wonderful insight into the Native American life. It is a love story that will fill you with warmth and contentment. You will enjoy Danny's journey to become a SEAL and his reasons for it. Good job Sharon!" (5 Star Review)

PRAISE FOR THE
BAND OF BACHELORS SERIES

"*[Lucas]* was the first book in the Band of Bachelors series and it was a phenomenal start. I loved how we got to see the other SEALs we all love and we got a look at Lucas and Marcy. They had an instant attraction, and their love was very intense. This book had it all, suspense, steamy romance, humor, everything you want in a riveting, outstanding read. I can't wait to read the next book in this series." (5 Star Review)

PRAISE FOR THE
TRUE BLUE SEALS SERIES

"Keep the tissues box nearby as you read *True Blue SEALs: Zak* by Sharon Hamilton. I imagine more than I wish to that the circumstances surrounding Zak and Amy are all too real for returning military personnel and their families. Ms. Hamilton has put us right in the middle of struggles and successes that these two high school sweethearts endure. I have read several of Sharon Hamilton's military romances but will say this is the most emotionally intense of the ones that I have read. This is a well-written, realistic story with authentic characters that will have you rooting for them and proud of those who serve to keep us safe. This is an author who writes amazing stories that you love and cry with the characters. Fans of Jessica Scott and Marliss Melton will want to add Sharon Hamilton to their list of realistic military romance writers." (5 Star Review)

PRAISE FOR THE
GOLDEN VAMPIRES OF TUSCANY SERIES

"Well to say the least I was thoroughly surprised. I have read many Vampire books, from Ann Rice to Kym Grosso and a few other Authors, so yes I do like Vampires, not the super scary ones from the old days, but the new ones are far more interesting, far more human than one can remember. I found Honeymoon Bite a totally engrossing book, I was not able to put it down, page after page I found delight, love, understanding, well that is until the bad bad Vamp started being really bad. But seeing someone love another person so much that they would do anything to protect them, well that had me going, then well there was more and for a while I thought it was the end of a beautiful love story that spanned not only time but, spanned Italy and California. Won't divulge how it ended, but I did shed a few tears after screaming but Sharon Hamilton did not let me down, she took me on amazing trip that I loved, look forward to reading another Vampire book of hers."

"An excellent paranormal romance that was exciting, romantic, entertaining and very satisfying to read. It had me anticipating what would happen next many times over, so much so I could not put it down and even finished it up in a day. The vampires in this book were different from your average vampire, but I enjoy different variations and changes to the same old stuff. It made for a more unpredictable read and more adventurous to explore! Vampire lovers, any paranormal readers and even those who love the romance genre will enjoy Honeymoon Bite."

"This is the first non-Seal book of this author's I have read and I loved it. There is a cast-like hierarchy in this vampire community with humans at the very bottom and Golden vampires at the top. Lionel is a dark vampire who are servants of the Goldens. Phoebe is a Golden who has not decided if she will remain human or accept the turning to become a vampire. Either way she and Lionel can never be together since it is forbidden.

I enjoyed this story and I am looking forward to the next installment."

"A hauntingly romantic read. Old love lost and new love found. Family, heart, intrigue and vampires. Grabbed my attention and couldn't put down. Would definitely recommend."

"Dear FATHER IN HEAVEN,

If I may respectfully say so sometimes you are a strange God. Though you love all mankind,

It seems you have special predilections too.

You seem to love those men who can stand up alone who face impossible odds, who challenge every bully and every tyrant ~

Those men who know the heat and loneliness of Calvary. Possibly you cherish men of this stamp because you recognize the mark of your only son in them.

Since this unique group of men known as the SEALs know Calvary and suffering, teach them now the mystery of the resurrection ~ that they are indestructible, that they will live forever because of their deep faith in you.

And when they do come to heaven, may I respectfully warn you, Dear Father, they also know how to celebrate. So please be ready for them when they insert under your pearly gates.

Bless them, their devoted Families and their Country on this glorious occasion.

We ask this through the merits of your Son, Christ Jesus the Lord, Amen."

By Reverend E.J. McMalhon S.J. LCDR, CHC, USN
Awards Ceremony SEAL Team One
1975 At NAB, Coronado

www.ingramcontent.com/pod-product-compliance
Lightning Source LLC
Chambersburg PA
CBHW051053030726
47504CB00006B/1602